BERNHARD HENNEN

TRANSLATED BY EDWIN MILES

amazoncrossing

Text copyright © 2004 Bernhard Hennen and James A. Sullivan
Translation copyright © 2015 Edwin Miles
All rights reserved.

Previously published as *Die Elfen* by Heyne Verlag in Germany in 2004. Translated from German by Edwin Miles. First published in English by AmazonCrossing in 2015.

Published by AmazonCrossing, Seattle

www.apub.com

Amazon, the Amazon logo, and AmazonCrossing are trademarks of Amazon.com, Inc., or its affiliates.

ISBN-13: 9781477827512
ISBN-10: 147782751X

Cover design and illustration: Franz Vohwinkel

Library of Congress Control Number: 2014917988

Printed in the United States of America

DEDICATED TO MELIKE, PASCAL AND XINYI, MY ALBENSTARS

—BERNHARD HENNEN

IN MEMORY OF JIM SULLIVAN

—JAMES A. SULLIVAN

Through the forest in the moonlight,
Late I saw the elves a-passing.
Heard their hunting horns resounding
Heard their bells a-kling, a-ringing.

Ponies white and wearing golden
Branching antlers, fleet as wind.
Like wild swans through the glades a-gliding
Came the band upon the wing.

Smiled the Fairy queen upon me,
Smiled and nodded, passed on by.
Does it mean a new love coming?
Does it mean that I must die?

("New Love" by Heinrich Heine, 1797–1856)

CONTENTS

THE MANBOAR

In the center of the snow-covered clearing lay the carcass of a bull elk. The torn flesh still steamed. Mandred and the three men with him knew what that meant: they had disturbed the hunter at his work. The carcass was covered in bloody streaks, the elk's heavy skull split wide open.

Mandred knew of no animal that hunted only to eat the brain of its prey. He heard a muffled noise and wheeled around. Snow cascaded from the branches of a tall fir tree at the edge of the clearing. The air swirled with tiny ice crystals. Wary, Mandred peered into the undergrowth. The forest was silent again. Far above the treetops, the green faerylight danced across the sky.

It was no night to be out in the woods.

"Just the weight of the snow breaking a branch," said blond Gudleif, brushing the stuff from his heavy cloak. "Stop scowling like a rabid dog. You'll see. All we're following is a pack of wolves."

Disquiet had crept into the hearts of the men. Each of them thought of the old man's words, how he had warned them of the death-dealing creature from the mountains. Was it anything more than feverish ramblings? Mandred was jarl of Firnstayn, the small village that lay by the fjord beyond the forest. It was his duty to ward off any threat to the village. The old man had spoken with such conviction, and Mandred knew he should have dug deeper. But still . . .

It was in winters like this one—winters that came early, that were far too cold, and in which the green faerylight danced in the sky—that the Albenfolk came to the world of men. Mandred knew that, and his companions knew it.

Asmund had slipped an arrow onto his bowstring and was squinting uneasily. Lean and red haired, he was a man of few words. He'd come to Firnstayn two years earlier. Word went around that he'd been a notorious cattle thief in the south and that King Horsa Starkshield had put a price on his head. This did not concern Mandred. Asmund was a good hunter who brought his share of meat to the village. That counted for more than any rumors.

Mandred had known Gudleif and Ragnar since before they could walk. Both were fishermen. Gudleif was stocky and strong as a bear. Perpetually in a good mood, he had many friends, although most who knew him found him rather simple. Ragnar was short and dark haired, in contrast to the mainly tall, blond inhabitants of the Fjordlands. Sometimes he was mocked for it, and in whispers, he was called a kobold child. Foolish nonsense, of course. Ragnar was a man with his heart in the right place, a man to be relied on unreservedly.

Mandred's thoughts turned wistfully to Freya, his wife. No doubt she was sitting at the fireplace, listening into the night. He had taken a signal horn with him. One blast meant danger, but if he sounded the horn twice, those in the village knew there was nothing out there to fear and that the hunters were on their way home.

Asmund had lowered his bow and placed one finger to his lips in warning. He raised his head like a hound sniffing out a scent. Now Mandred could smell it, too. A strange odor drifted over the clearing, a stink that reminded the men of rotten eggs.

"Maybe a troll after all," Gudleif whispered. "They say they come down from the mountains when the winter's hard. A troll could kill an elk with its fist."

Asmund looked darkly at Gudleif and signaled to him to be silent. The wood of the trees creaked in the cold air. A feeling crept over Mandred: they were being watched. Something was there. Something very close.

Without warning, the branches of a hazel thicket parted, and two white creatures sped across the clearing with a loud thrumming of wings. Mandred instinctively raised his spear, then let out a sigh of relief. Two ptarmigan. No more.

But what had startled them? Ragnar aimed his bow and arrow at the thicket. The jarl lowered his weapon. He felt his stomach tighten. Was the monster lurking there in the bushes? They waited, poised, silent.

An eternity seemed to pass, but nothing moved. The four men formed a wide semicircle around the thicket. The air crackled with apprehension. Cold sweat trickled down Mandred's back and gathered around his beltline. It was a long way back to the village. If he sweated through his clothes and they no longer protected him from the cold, the men would have to find somewhere to set up camp and start a fire.

Stout Gudleif kneeled and spiked the shaft of his spear into the ground, then dug into the fresh snow with his hands and formed a snowball. The snow crunched softly as he pressed it. Gudleif looked to Mandred, and the jarl nodded. The snowball flew in a wide arc into the bush. Nothing moved.

Mandred breathed easier. Their fear had brought the night's shadows to life. They themselves had scared up the ptarmigan.

Gudleif grinned with relief. "There's nothing there. Whatever it was that killed the elk is far away by now."

"A fine hunting party we make," Ragnar teased. "We'll be running from a rabbit fart next."

Gudleif rose to his feet and plucked his spear out of the snow. "I'll skewer this shadow," he said with a laugh, jabbing the point of his spear into the bushes.

Suddenly, he was jolted forward. Mandred saw a large clawed hand wrapped around the shaft of the spear. Gudleif let out a shrill cry that abruptly transformed into a throaty gurgling noise. The stocky man staggered back, both hands pressed to his neck. Blood gushed between his fingers and poured over his wolfskin doublet.

Out of the bush stepped a beast. A huge creature, half man, half boar. The weight of its massive boar head caused it to stoop forward, but it still towered above the men. The body of the beast was that of a colossus. Heavy, knotted bands of muscle stretched across its shoulders and down its arms to hands that ended in dark claws. Below the knees, its legs were unnaturally thin and covered with gray-black bristles. Where feet should have been were cloven hooves.

The manboar let out a deep, guttural grunt. Tusks like daggers jutted from its jaws. Its eyes, on Mandred, seemed ready to devour him.

Asmund swung his bow up. The arrow flew from the string. It struck the beast on the side of its head, leaving a thin, red graze. Mandred's grip on his spear tightened.

Gudleif's legs gave way. He swayed for a heartbeat, then tipped to one side. His hands, which had been clamped to his neck, let go. Blood still poured from his throat, and his stocky legs twitched helplessly.

A blind fury took hold of Mandred. He charged forward and rammed his spear into the manboar's breast. Like spearing a rock, the blade glanced off and left no visible mark. One clawed hand shot out and splintered the shaft of the spear.

Ragnar attacked the monster from the side to distract it from Mandred, but his spear, too, did nothing.

Mandred dropped onto the snow and drew an axe from his belt. It was a good weapon with a narrow, sharp blade, and the jarl swung it at the manboar's fetlock with all the power he could summon. The monster grunted at the strike, then it lowered its immense head and rammed the warrior. One tusk caught Mandred on the inside of his thigh, shredding the muscle and crushing the silver-clad signal horn that had been hanging from his belt. With a jerk, the manboar pulled its head back, flinging Mandred into the hazel thicket.

Half-numb with pain, Mandred pressed one hand to the wound while tearing a strip of cloth from his cloak with the other hand. He quickly stuffed the wool into the gaping wound, then removed his belt and wound it around his leg as a makeshift tourniquet.

Piercing screams rang from the clearing. Mandred broke a branch from the hazel bush and slid it under the belt. He twisted it, tightening the leather band until it wrapped his thigh as firmly as a hoop around a barrel. The pain nearly knocked him unconscious.

The screams from the clearing stopped. Cautiously, Mandred parted the branches of the thicket. His comrades lay scattered in the snow, lifeless. The manboar stood over Ragnar, leaning down and ramming its tusks into his breast again and again. Mandred's axe lay close to the monster. Everything in him pushed him to attack the beast, armed or not. There was no honor in slinking away from combat. But fighting a pointless battle was stupid. He was the jarl, and the welfare of the entire village rested on his shoulders. He had to warn the ones who were still alive.

A direct retreat to Firnstayn was impossible. His tracks would lead the beast straight to the village. He had to find another way.

Inch by inch, Mandred crept backward out of the bushes. Every time a branch cracked, his heart stopped. The beast showed no interest in him, though. It crouched in the clearing, enjoying its grim meal.

When he had crawled free of the bush, Mandred dared to raise himself halfway to his feet. Searing pain shot through his leg, and he instinctively put a hand to the wool stuffed in the wound. A crust of ice was already forming on his leg, and he did not know how long he would survive the cold.

The jarl hobbled the short distance back to the edge of the woods. He gazed up at the sheer cliff, its dark summit looming high above the fjord. There was an ancient stone circle up there, and close by was a stack of wood for a signal fire. If he could get one lit, the village would be warned. But the wood for his fire was two miles from where he stood.

Mandred kept to the edge of the forest, but his progress in the fresh powder was slow. The sight of the snow-covered field, climbing steadily around to the back of the cliff, did not put his mind at ease. There was no cover there, and the trail he would leave through the snow would be impossible to miss.

Exhausted, he leaned against the trunk of an aging linden tree and gathered his strength. If only he'd given the old man's warnings some credence. They'd found him one morning in front of the palisade that shielded the village. The cold had nearly frozen the life out of the old man's bones. In his feverish daze, he spoke of a boar that walked upright, of a monster that had come down from the mountains far to the north to spread death and decay among the villages of the Fjordlands. A man-eater. If the old man had talked of trolls coming from the depths of the mountains or of malevolent kobolds that dyed their wool caps in the blood of those they'd murdered or of the elfhunt with its white wolves, Mandred would have believed him. But a boar that went on two legs and devoured men? No one had ever heard of such a beast. They paid no heed to the old man's words, deriding them as fever dreams.

Then came midwinter's night. The stranger had called Mandred to his deathbed. He had been unable to find peace until Mandred swore an oath to look for the trail of the beast and warn the other villages on the fjord. Mandred still could not bring himself to believe the old man's words, but an oath sworn at the side of a dying man was not one to be broken lightly. And so Mandred, a man of honor, set out into the woods.

If only they had been more careful.

Mandred exhaled heavily, then hobbled out onto the wide field of snow. His left leg was completely numb. And while the cold had drawn the pain out of his wound, the freeze that had settled in its place made it harder for him to move. Again and again, he faltered. Half crawling, half walking, he struggled on. There was still no sign, no sound from the manboar. Had it finished its grisly meal?

Finally, he reached a broad swath of scree. There had been a rock fall there the previous autumn, but now the treacherous surface lay hidden under a thick blanket of snow. Mandred's breath came unevenly. Heavy clouds of white vapor formed in front of his mouth and settled onto his beard as hoarfrost. *Damn this cold.*

The jarl's thoughts turned back to the summer just gone. He had come here with Freya several times. They had lain in the grass and looked up to starry skies. He had boasted to her of his hunting adventures and of how he had joined King Horsa Starkshield on his campaign along the coasts of Fargon. Freya had listened patiently and chaffed him whenever he overembellished his heroic deeds. Her tongue could be as sharp as a blade. But she kissed like . . . *No, don't think about that.* He swallowed hard. He would be a father soon. But he would never see his son. Would it even be a son?

Mandred leaned against an outcrop of rock to catch his breath. He'd come halfway, and he cast his eyes back to the edge of the forest. The darkness of the woods had barely allowed the green faerylight to penetrate, but there on the mountainside, everything was as plain to see as on a cloudless night under a full moon.

He had always loved nights like these, even though the ethereal light frightened most who lived in the Northlands. It looked like enormous webs of cloth woven from sparkling starlight being drawn across the sky.

Some said the elves hid themselves in this light when they rode out to hunt on frost-clear nights. Mandred smiled. Such musings would have delighted Freya. She loved to sit by the fire on winter evenings and listen to stories. Stories of the trolls from the far-off mountains. Stories of the elves whose hearts were as cold as winter stars.

Something moved at the edge of the woods, jolting Mandred from his thoughts. The manboar. So the beast had come in pursuit after all. And that was good. With every step Mandred took up the cliff, he lured the monster away from the village. He just had to hold on. It could rip open his chest and eat his heart if it wanted, if only he could kindle the signal fire first.

Mandred pushed himself away from the rocky outcrop and immediately stumbled. His feet—they were still there, but he could no longer feel them at all. He should not have stopped. Was he going soft in the head? Even a child knew that stopping to rest in this kind of cold could spell death.

Mandred looked down desperately at his feet. Frozen, with all feeling gone, they would not warn him if loose stones slipped underfoot. They had become traitors to him, had defected to the enemy that was trying to stop him from lighting the signal fire.

The jarl laughed out loud, but it was a mirthless laugh. His feet had defected? Utter nonsense. He was slowly going crazy. His feet were simply dead flesh, as the man himself would be soon enough. In anger, he kicked at the rock outcrop. Nothing. As if his feet were not even there. But he could still walk. It was just a matter of will, and of being very careful where he stepped.

He looked back fearfully. The manboar had moved out onto the snowfield. It seemed to be in no hurry. Did it know this was the only way to the cliff top? There was no way for Mandred to escape, but he had never intended to get away with his life anyway. If he could just light the fire, then nothing else would matter.

A noise caused him to start. The beast emitted a deep growl. Mandred had the feeling that the manboar was looking him straight in the eye. At this distance, of course, that was impossible, but still . . . something brushed his heart like a chilly draft.

The jarl hurried. He had to hold on to his lead. To light the fire, he would need time. His breath was whistling. When he exhaled, there was a light, tinkling noise, like icicles jangling against one another high in the tops of the fir trees, only more delicate. The kiss of the ice faery. A faery tale, one told to children, occurred to him in that moment. In the story, the ice faery was invisible and went wandering through the Fjordlands on nights when it was so cold that even the starlight froze. If she came close to you, your steaming breath disappeared, and a gentle tinkling lay in the air instead. If she came so near that her lips brushed your face, then her kiss was the kiss of death. Was that why the manboar came no closer?

Again, Mandred looked back. The beast seemed to have no trouble moving through the heavy snow. It should have caught up with him by now. Why was it playing cat and mouse with him?

Mandred slipped. His head banged hard against a rock, but he felt no pain. He ran his mitts across his forehead. Dark blood dripped from the leather. He grew dizzy. That should never have been allowed to happen. He looked back frantically. The manboar had stopped. It stood with its head tipped far back, gazing up at him.

Mandred could no longer get to his feet. What kind of fool was he, looking back and moving forward?

With all his strength, he tried to get to his feet. But his half-frozen legs refused to function as they should. He could have used a large rock now, something to pull himself up with, but around him, there was nothing. He began to crawl. What an indignity. He, Mandred Torgridson, the most renowned warrior along the entire fjord, was crawling from his enemy on his hands and knees. He had bested seven men in single combat in King Horsa's campaign. For each defeated foe, he had proudly woven another braid in his hair. And now he was reduced to crawling away.

This was another kind of fight, he admonished himself. This monster was not something you could beat with weapons. He had seen for himself how Asmund's arrow had bounced off and how his own axe had left no mark. This was a fight with different rules. Victory did not lie in slaying the beast, but in kindling a fire on the cliff top.

In desperation, Mandred crawled forward on his elbows. The strength was now ebbing from his arms as well as his legs. The summit was close, though. Mandred looked up to the standing stones. They were crowned with pale caps of snow, standing out against the green shimmer in the sky. Just behind the stones, he knew, the wood for the signal fire was stacked.

With his eyes squeezed shut, he crawled on. The only thing in his thoughts was his wife. He had to rescue her. His strength could not fail him now. On. On!

He opened his eyes to a squint. The snow was gone. He was lying on bare rock. In front of him rose one of the pillars of the stone circle. He pulled himself up the pillar until, swaying, he was on his feet again. His legs would not carry him much farther.

The summit had been leveled and was as smooth as the bottom of a wooden bowl. Out of habit, he had moved around the outside of the circle. No one stepped between the standing stones. It was not a question of courage. Once, in summer, Mandred had spent an entire afternoon watching the summit. Not a single bird flew over the circle.

A narrow path wound along the edge of the cliff, making it possible to get around the eerie stones, but on his numb legs, he was no longer sure-footed enough to risk it. The choice had been made for him: he had to go between them.

As if expecting to be struck down without warning, Mandred ducked his head as he stepped into the circle. Ten steps, and he would make it to the other side. It was such a ridiculously short distance . . .

Anxiously, he looked around. No snow lay here, none at all on the bedrock. Inside the circle, it seemed, winter held no sway. Strange patterns of curved lines were etched into the rock under him.

The Hartungscliff dropped almost straight down to the fjord below. Seen from the village beneath, it looked as if someone had set a stony crown atop the cliff. The granite blocks loomed three times the height of a man, enclosing the rock plateau in a wide circle. It was said they had been standing there long before humans came to the Fjordlands. The stones were inscribed with patterns of intertwined lines, a web etched with such mastery that no human could match it. Looking at it too long made one feel drunk, as if from overindulgence in spicy winter mead.

Years before, a wandering skald had come to Firnstayn and asserted that the standing stones were ancient elven warriors cursed by their own ancestors, the Alben. He said they had been damned to an endless, lonely vigil, until the land itself, one far-off day, cried out to them for help and broke the enchantment. Mandred, back then, had laughed at the skald. Every child knew that elves were delicate creatures and no taller than humans. The stones were far too massive to be elves.

When Mandred had passed across the circle, an icy wind hit him from the front. He had all but done it. Nothing would stop him from . . . the woodpile? He had to be able to see it from here. It was on a rock ledge, stacked at the edge of the cliff, protected from the wind. Mandred dropped to his knees and crept forward. There was nothing.

From where he kneeled, the cliff fell away vertically almost six hundred feet. Had there been a rock fall? Had the ledge broken away? Mandred had the feeling that his gods were mocking him. He had used every ounce of his strength to get this far, and now . . .

Desperately, he looked out over the fjord. Far below, on the other side of the frozen strait, his village huddled in the snow. Firnstayn: four longhouses and a handful of huts, all ringed by a laughably weak palisade. The wooden wall, built from the trunks of fir trees, was meant to keep wolves at bay and to be an obstacle to plunderers. The palisade would never stop the manboar.

Cautiously, the jarl edged a fraction closer to the lip of the abyss and peered down at the fjord. The faerylight in the sky conjured green shadows in the snowy landscape. Firnstayn had gone into hibernation. Neither man nor animal could be seen along the paths. White smoke rose from the chimneys below the ridgepoles and was shredded by the gusts of wind and blasted across the fjord. Freya would be there, sitting by the fire, listening for the signal horn to tell her they were on their way back from the hunt.

But the horn had been destroyed. From his position, they would have heard its blast all the way down to the village. How cruel, this game the gods were playing with him and his family. Were they watching him now? Were they laughing at him?

Something clicked softly, and Mandred, weary, turned to face it. The manboar was standing on the other side of the stone circle and began to move slowly around the outside of the ring. So even that creature dared not step between the standing stones?

Mandred crawled away from the edge of the cliff. His life was over, he knew that much, but if he had the choice, then he would prefer the cold to kill him than to end as food for that beast.

The clicking of hooves grew faster. One more heave, and Mandred had done it. He lay within the enchanted ring of stones.

Leaden fatigue crept into his limbs. With every breath, the icy frost sliced into his throat. Utterly exhausted, he leaned against one of the stones. Gusting wind tore at his frost-stiffened clothes. The belt around his upper leg had loosened, and blood now seeped through the scraps of wool.

Quietly, he prayed to his gods. To Firn, the god of winter; to Norgrimm, the god of war; to Naida the Cloud Rider, ruler of the twenty-three winds; and to Luth, the weaver, who wove the threads of human fate into a precious tapestry for the walls of the Golden Hall, where the gods feasted with the bravest of the dead warriors.

Mandred's eyes closed. He would sleep the long sleep. He had forfeited his place in the Hall of Heroes. He should have died with his companions. He was a coward. Gudleif, Ragnar, and Asmund, none of them had run. The fact that the wood had fallen from the cliff was punishment for his fear of having to face the gods.

"You are right, Mandred Torgridson. The gods no longer protect the craven," rang a voice inside his head.

Was that Death? Mandred wondered. *Is Death just a voice?*

"More than a voice. Look at me."

The jarl could barely raise his eyelids. Warm breath hit him in the face. He was looking into huge eyes, as blue as the sky on a late-summer day when the moon and the sun shared the heavens between them. It was the manboar's eyes. The beast was beside him, just outside the stone circle, squatting low. Slaver dripped from its blood-crusted mouth. On one long tusk, fibrous scraps of flesh still hung.

"The gods no longer protect the craven," came the strange voice in Mandred's head again. *"Now the others can come for you."*

The manboar rose to its full height. Its jowls twitched. It seemed almost to smile. Then it turned away. It moved back around the stone circle and was soon out of sight.

Mandred tilted his head back. The ghostly faerylight was still dancing across the sky. *The others?* Darkness was already engulfing him. Had his eyelids fallen closed without his realizing it? Sleep . . . just for a little while. The darkness beckoned. It promised peace.

THE COURTING

Noroelle sat in the shade of the two linden trees and let the melody of Farodin's flute and Nuramon's voice caress her. It felt almost as if her two suitors were renewing her senses with their gentle airs. Wistfully, she watched the play of light and shadow in the canopy of leaves far above. Then she looked over to the spring bubbling up just beyond the shade in which she lay. Sunlight glittered on the stream that ran from the spring. Noroelle leaned forward and let her hand glide through the babbling water and felt the tingle of the magic that dwelled in it.

Her eyes followed the water to where it spilled into the little lake. The sunlight filtered through the water to the bed of the lake and made the gemstones sparkle that Noroelle had once embedded there so carefully. The stones soaked up the magic of the spring, and what was not bound by them flowed out into the brook and was washed away. Out there, the fields thrived on the magic of the water. And at night, the little riverbank sprites came out of their flowers and swarmed in the starlight to rhapsodize about the beauty of Albenmark.

The fields had dressed themselves in the blossoms of spring. A breeze carried the complicated scent of grasses and flowers to Noroelle. Beneath the trees, it mixed with the sweet odor of the linden blooms. Leaves rustled overhead and joined with the birdsong and the babbling spring water to form a backdrop to Farodin's and Nuramon's music.

While Farodin created a tapestry of sounds from all the resonances of that place, Nuramon lifted his voice above them, weaving words that made Noroelle feel like one of the Alben herself. She looked over fondly at Nuramon, who was sitting on a flat stone by the water, then back at Farodin, who sat with his back against the trunk of the larger of the two linden trees.

Farodin's face was that of an elven prince from the old songs, with a countenance whose fine elegance was praised as the glory of the Alben. His linden-green eyes were like jewels, and his snow-blond hair formed a pale frame around his face. He wore the traditional costume of the minnesinger—the tunic, breeches, cloak, and scarf—all of it fashioned from the finest faery silk. Only his shoes were of gelgerok leather. Noroelle looked at his fingers, the way they danced over the flute. She could have watched him play like that the whole day long.

While Farodin looked like the ideal of an elven man, no one would claim the same for Nuramon. The women at court openly derided his looks, only to gush about his unconventional handsomeness in private. Nuramon had pale-brown eyes and somewhat darker hair that tumbled in waves to his shoulders. In his sand-colored attire, he did not fit with the traditional image of a minnesinger, but he was no less handsome for that. In place of the silk of the faeries, he had chosen cloth woven from wool, far less precious, but so strong and soft that Noroelle, seeing his tunic and his forest-hued cloak, would have first chosen Nuramon's breast as the place to lay her head. Even his low-heeled boots, made from earth-colored and unusually supple gelgerok leather, awoke in Noroelle an urge to simply touch them. Nuramon's face was as mutable as his voice, which had mastered all forms of song and gave to every emotion a fitting sound. But while his voice embraced every shade of sentiment, his brown eyes only spoke of longing and melancholy.

Farodin and Nuramon were different, but each in his own way was splendid. And each in his own way was perfect, as the light of day is as attractive as the darkness of night. They were summer and winter, spring and fall. Noroelle had no wish to forgo any of that, and comparing the appearance of the two men brought her no closer to deciding on one or the other.

At court, some had advised her to look no further than her suitor's lineage when making her choice. But was Farodin a better elf because his great-grandmother had been a true Alben woman? And was it Nuramon's fault that his roots were in a clan that had branched from the Alben line many generations earlier? Noroelle did not want to make her decision dependent on her lovers' ancestry, but on the men themselves.

Farodin knew how one was supposed to court a highborn woman. He knew every rule and custom and always acted in such a measured and honorable way that one was compelled to admire him in every way. Noroelle was enchanted by the way he seemed to know what was deep inside her, to be able to reach down deep to what was innermost, always finding the right words, as if her thoughts and feelings were his to read. But this was also his flaw. Farodin knew all the songs and the old stories. He always knew which sweet words to use, because he'd heard them all before. But which words were truly his, and which belonged to the old poets? Was this tune his, or was it something he'd heard somewhere else? It made Noroelle smile, because this seeming flaw in Farodin, she knew, reflected more on her. Wasn't this beautiful place exactly the way the old singers had painted it? The sun, the linden trees, the shade, the spring, the magic? And didn't those same singers of old compose their songs in harmony with this beautiful place? Could she then think worse of Farodin for doing exactly what was called for here, now? No, she could not. Farodin was perfect in every way, and any woman in the faery realm would be happy to have him woo her.

But still she wondered who Farodin really was. He evaded her, as the Spring of Lyn evaded the eyes of the elves with its radiant light. She wished that he would lower his own mask, even just briefly, to let her see the wellspring underneath. She had often tried to get him to do just that, but he had not understood her overtures in that direction, and until now, she had not managed to see into his deepest self. Sometimes she feared that something dark might be lurking there, something that Farodin wanted to keep hidden at all costs. From time to time, he went away on long journeys, but never spoke about where he went or why. And when he returned, despite his clear joy at seeing her again, he seemed to Noroelle to be more closed than before he had left.

By contrast, with Nuramon, Noroelle knew exactly who she was dealing with. She had been told often enough that Nuramon was not the right one for her, that he was not worthy of her. Not only did he come from a large clan, but he also came from a bloodline marked by disgrace. For Nuramon carried in him the soul of an elf that, through all of the lives he'd been born into, had not found the purpose of his existence and had therefore never entered the moonlight. For the ones for whom this path was blocked, it meant being born within the clan over and over again until one's destiny was fulfilled. Nuramon, one of these unfortunates, was not able to remember his previous lives.

No other elf had been reborn as often as Nuramon. He had been through the cycles of life, death, and rebirth for millennia. And with his soul, he had also inherited his name. The queen had recognized in Nuramon the soul of his own grandfather and had given him his grandfather's name. The seemingly never-ending search for his destiny was the subject of high-handed derision even within Nuramon's own extended family. At least for now, no family member need worry about their newborn. But if Nuramon were to die, his soul would cast a shadow over his clan. No one knew in whom the next Nuramon would be born.

No, on balance, Nuramon could not look back at his ancestry and expect to be admired for it. On the contrary, everyone said that Nuramon would go the same way he always had. He would search for his destiny, die during the search, and be reborn again. But this view was abhorrent to Noroelle. She saw instead a virtuous man sitting before her, and as Nuramon sang another song to her beauty, Noroelle sensed that every word he spoke had its source in his deep love for her. What the cradle had denied him, he had earned for himself. There was only one thing he did not dare to do: to come too close to her. He had never once touched her. He had never found the courage to take her hand as Farodin did, let alone to kiss it. Whenever she tried to send him some harmless token of her affection, he would gently refuse it with sweet, intoxicating words.

Whichever way she looked, this way or that, at her two suitors, at that moment, she could not make up her mind. If Farodin opened up his innermost self to her, she would choose him. If Nuramon reached out to her and took her hand, then she would favor him. The decision was not entirely hers to make.

It had been just twenty years since their courtship began. It might be another twenty before they could expect her to decide. And if she herself was unable to choose, then the one who had shown the greatest loyalty would win her favor. And if, in that, they were also equal, then their courting might go on forever—a thought that brought a smile to Noroelle's lips.

Farodin began a new piece and played in such a heartfelt way that Noroelle closed her eyes. She knew the song. She had heard it one day at court. But with every note Farodin played, he surpassed what she had heard back then.

Set against Farodin's melody, Nuramon's voice paled slightly, until Farodin again began a new song.

"O Albenchild, see there a face," Nuramon sang now.

Noroelle opened her eyes, surprised at the sudden change that had come over his voice.

"Upon the waters shining bright," Nuramon sang as he looked at the water.

Noroelle's eyes could not follow his gaze, however, so spellbound was she by his voice.

"Fair Noroelle, go out, make haste, from the shade into the light," he sang.

Noroelle stood and did what he said. She moved a few steps away from the spring and kneeled at the shore of the lake to look into the water, but there was nothing there.

Nuramon went on. "A crystal tarn, your eyes so blue."

And Noroelle now saw blue eyes. They were her own, and Nuramon was comparing them to a mountain lake.

"Night hair adrift the zephyr's grace."

She saw her hair lightly brushing her neck and had to smile.

"Your mouth a faery smile true. O Albenchild, see there a face."

She observed herself closely and listened as Nuramon sang of her beauty in the various languages of the Albenkin. In the language of the faeries, everything sounded beautiful, but he could manage to flatter her even in the kobold tongue.

As she listened to him, she no longer saw herself, but another woman, more beautiful than she had ever felt herself to be, as noble as the queen and with a grace like that of the Alben themselves. And even though she did not see herself in this light, she knew that Nuramon's words were sung from his heart.

When her suitors fell silent, she turned away uncertainly from the water and looked to Nuramon, then to Farodin. "Why have you stopped?" she asked.

Farodin looked up to the canopy of leaves. "The birds are restless. They seem unwilling to sing anymore."

Noroelle turned to Nuramon. "Was that really my face I saw in the water? Or was it your magic?"

Nuramon smiled. "I cast no magic. All I did was sing. But it flatters me that you could not tell the difference."

Farodin suddenly stood, and Nuramon also rose to his feet. They gazed into the distance, out across the lake and the fields. The deep tone of a signal horn sounded over the land.

Now Noroelle, too, stood up. "The queen? What has happened?" she asked.

In a few paces, Farodin was beside Noroelle. He laid one hand upon her shoulder. "No need for concern, Noroelle."

Nuramon was there, too, and he whispered in her ear, "No doubt it's nothing that a host of elves can't take care of."

Noroelle sighed. "It was probably too nice to last the whole day," she said. A moment later, the birds rose into the air and flew off toward the queen's palace, which lay on a hill beyond the fields and the woods. "Last time, the queen commissioned you for the elfhunt," Noroelle said after the birds had disappeared from view. "I worry about you, Farodin."

"Haven't I always come back? And didn't Nuramon sweeten your days while I was gone?" he responded.

Noroelle released herself from Farodin's hand and turned to the two of them. "And if you both have to go this time?"

"No one will entrust me with such a duty," Nuramon argued. "That's how it has always been, and will always be."

Farodin was silent, but Noroelle said, "The appreciation that others refuse you, Nuramon . . . I will give to you. But go now. Fetch your horses and ride ahead. I'll follow and see you this evening at court."

Farodin kissed Noroelle's hand and said good-bye. Nuramon's own farewell consisted of a loving smile. Then he went to Felbion, his white horse. Farodin already sat astride his bay. Noroelle waved once more to both of them.

The elf watched as her two lovers rode across the field, away from the faery blossoms, galloping toward the forest and the castle beyond. She drank a little water from the spring, then set off after them. She walked barefoot across the field. She wanted to visit the faun oak. Beneath its branches, she could think more clearly than anywhere else. The oak, for its part, communed with her and, in earlier years, had taught her a great deal of magic.

As she walked, she thought of Farodin and Nuramon.

AWAKENING

Warmer than I expected, thought Mandred when he awoke. He could hear the twittering of birds somewhere close by, and it became clear to him that he had not entered into the Hall of Heroes. There were no birds there . . . and the air should be filled with the scent of honey from heavy mead and the smell of sappy spruce wood burning in the fireplace.

He had only to open his eyes to know where he was. But Mandred put it off. He was lying on something soft. Nothing hurt. His hands and feet felt somewhat tingly, but it was not uncomfortable. He did not want to know where he was. He wanted no more than to lie there and enjoy the moment, enjoy how wonderfully well he felt. *So this is what it feels like to be dead*, he thought.

"I know you're awake," said a voice, sounding as if it had difficulty forming the words.

Mandred opened his eyes. He was lying on the ground beneath a tree, its branches curving over him like a vault. Beside him, a stranger kneeled and prodded at his body with strong hands. The branches hung down to just above the stranger's head, but his face remained obscured in the play of light and shadow.

Mandred narrowed his eyes to be able to see more clearly. Something wasn't right there. The shadows seemed to swirl around the stranger's face, as if deliberately concealing it.

"Where am I?"

"In safety," the stranger replied curtly.

Mandred tried to sit up but quickly realized that his hands and legs were tied to the ground. All he could raise was his head.

"What are you doing with me? Why am I bound?"

From inside the swirling shadows, for a moment, two eyes blazed brightly. They were the color of pale amber, the kind of amber one occasionally found farther west, on the shores of the fjord after heavy storms.

"Once Atta Aikhjarto has healed you, you may go. I personally do not place so much stock in your company that I would tie you down to keep you here. He was the one who insisted on treating your wounds," the stranger said, then let out an odd clucking sound. "Your language ties my tongue in knots. It is devoid of any . . . beauty."

Mandred looked around. Apart from the stranger, so weirdly surrounded by gloom, there was nobody. From the low-hanging branches of the mighty tree, leaves fell as on a windless autumn day and drifted unevenly to the ground.

Mandred looked up at the canopy overhead. He was lying beneath an oak tree. Its leaves emanated a strong, spring green. It smelled of good, black earth, but also of rot, of decomposing flesh.

A golden ray of light stabbed down through the tangle of leaves and touched his left hand. Now he saw what was holding him: it was the roots of the oak itself. Around his wrist wound finger-thick knotted roots, and his fingers were covered with a fine, white mesh of rootlets from which the odor of decay was coming.

Mandred reared up, straining against his bonds, but all resistance was useless. Bands of iron could not have held him more securely than those roots.

"What is happening to me?"

"Atta Aikhjarto offered to heal you. You were on the brink of death when you stepped through the gate. He ordered me to bring you here." The stranger swept his hand to indicate the spreading branches. "He is paying dearly to draw the poison of the frost out of your body and give your flesh back its rose-petal hue."

"By Luth, what is this place?"

The stranger let out a bleating sound that vaguely reminded Mandred of a laugh. "You are where your gods have no jurisdiction. You must have angered them, because they normally protect you humans from passing through the gates."

"The gates?"

"The stone circle. We heard you praying to your gods." The stranger again let out his bleating laugh. "You are in Albenmark, Mandred, among the Albenkin. That is a rather long way from your gods."

This news startled Mandred. One who stepped through the gates to the world beyond was cursed. He had heard enough stories of men and women taken to the world of the Albenkin, and none of them came to a good end. But still . . . if one were stout of heart, it was occasionally possible to get them to render one a service. Did they know about the manboar?

"Why is Atta Aik . . . Atta Ajek . . . Why is the oak helping me?"

The stranger remained silent for a while. Mandred found himself wishing he could see the man's face and decided it must have been some sorcery that kept it so doggedly hidden from view.

"Atta Aikhjarto must think you are of some importance, warrior. They say the roots of certain old trees run so deep they reach even your world. Whatever it is that Atta Aikhjarto knows about you, it must mean so much that he is willing to sacrifice a large part of his power for you. He is drawing out your poison and giving you his own lifeblood in return." The stranger pointed to the fallen leaves. "He is suffering for you, human. And from now on, you will have the strength of an oak in your blood. You will never again be like the others of your kind, and you will—"

"Enough." A sharp voice cut off the stranger's words. The branches of the tree parted, and a figure, half human, half horse, approached the spot where Mandred lay.

Mandred stared in open disbelief at the new arrival. He had never heard of such a creature before: the muscular torso of a man growing from the body of a horse. The manhorse's face was framed by a black beard, twisted into ringlets. The hair on his head was cut short, and a circlet of gold crowned his head. Slung around his shoulders was a quiver full of arrows, and in his left hand, he carried a small hunting bow. He would have been the living image of a majestic warrior, were it not for the red-brown body of the horse.

The manhorse gave a short bow in Mandred's direction. "They call me Aigilaos. The queen of Albenmark wishes to see you, and I have been given the honor of escorting you to the royal court." He spoke with a deep, melodious voice, but accentuated the words strangely.

Mandred sensed the iron grip of the roots slackening before finally freeing him completely. The jarl could not take his eyes from the manhorse. The strange creature reminded him of the manboar. It, too, had been half human, half animal. He wondered what the queen of this manhorse would be like.

Mandred touched his upper leg. The deep wound had closed without leaving a scar. He stretched his legs uncertainly. No unpleasant prickle or itch. No pain at all. They seemed completely healed, as if the frostbite had never settled in them.

He stood up cautiously, still not trusting the strength of his legs. Through the soles of his boots, he felt the soft floor of the forest. That was magic. Powerful magic. Far beyond the powers of the witches in the Fjordlands. His legs and feet had been dead, but now the feeling had come back to them.

Mandred stepped up to the massive trunk of the oak. Five men with arms outstretched could not have reached around it. It must have been centuries old. Mandred kneeled in reverence at the trunk of the oak and touched his forehead to the fissured bark. "I thank you, tree. For my life, I am in your debt," he said and then cleared his throat, hesitant. Was this how one should thank a tree? A tree with magic powers? A tree that the faceless stranger held in such esteem, as if it were a king?

"I . . . I will return, and I will hold a feast in your honor," said Mandred. "A feast the way we do them in the Fjordlands. I . . ." He spread his arms wide. It was miserable to thank one's savior with no more than a promise. There should be something more substantial.

Mandred tore a strip of cloth from his breeches and knotted it around one of the lower branches. "If there is ever anything I can do for you, send a messenger to me with this strip of cloth. I swear by the blood that is soaked in its fibers that from this day forth, my axe will stand between you and all your enemies."

A rustling in the tree caused Mandred to look up. A red-brown acorn fell from the crown of the tree, glanced off his shoulder, and landed in the withering fallen leaves.

"Take it," said the stranger softly. "Atta Aikhjarto does not give gifts lightly or often. He has accepted your oath. Look after the acorn well. It may be a great treasure."

"A treasure with thousands of brethren growing on Atta Aikhjarto's branches every year," sneered the manhorse. "Treasures that stuff the bellies of swarms of mice and squirrels. You have been given a valuable gift indeed, human. Now come. You don't want to keep our queen waiting, do you?"

Mandred eyed the manhorse suspiciously, then bent and picked up the acorn. Aigilaos made him uneasy. "I'm afraid I may not be able to keep up with you."

Aigilaos grinned broadly. White teeth blazed behind the heavy beard. "You won't have to, human. Swing onto my back and hold the leather band on my quiver. Hold tight. I am no less powerful than a warhorse in your world, and I bet my tail I would beat any steed you have ever come across in a race. My tread is so light that barely a blade of grass bends beneath my hooves. I am Aigilaos, the fastest of the centaurs, famed for—"

"An even faster tongue," jeered the stranger. "They say centaurs' tongues are apt to get carried away. Sometimes they're fast enough to outstrip reality."

"And when they talk about *you*, Xern, it's to say you're such a curmudgeon that only the trees can put up with you," Aigilaos shot back with a laugh. "And only because they can't run away."

The leaves of the great oak rustled, although Mandred felt no movement in the air. Wilted leaves fell thick as spring snow.

The centaur glanced up at the mighty branches overhead. The smile had vanished from his face. "I have no grievance with you, Atta Aikhjarto."

A horn sounded in the distance. The manhorse seemed suddenly relieved. "The horns of Albenmark call. I must take you to the queen's court, human."

Xern nodded to Mandred. For a moment, the magic obscuring his face vanished to reveal a narrow, handsome visage . . . if one overlooked the massive antlers growing out of his thick head of hair. The sight took Mandred's breath away, and he recoiled, stunned at the sight. Was everyone here part animal?

Suddenly, everything that had happened came together for Mandred in a single clear picture. The manboar had come from here. It had spared Mandred deliberately during the hunt. It was no coincidence that he was the only one not slaughtered by the beast's lethal tusks. And the pursuit . . . was that perhaps part of some insidious plan? Was he meant to be driven into the stone circle? Maybe he was just the beast's quarry and had done exactly what it wanted. He had stepped into the stone circle after all.

The manhorse pawed restlessly at the ground. "Come, Mandred."

Mandred took hold of the quiver strap and pulled himself onto the manhorse's back. He would face whatever fate awaited him. He was no coward. May their queen have a thousand horns blown, he would not kneel before her. No, he would appear before her on his feet, standing proud, and demand blood money to atone for the blight her manboar had brought to the Fjordlands.

With his powerful arms, Aigilaos parted the protective curtain of branches and stepped out onto a stony field. Mandred looked around in astonishment. Here it was spring, and the sky looked to him to be much wider than it did at home in the Fjordlands. But if it were spring, how could a ripe acorn fall from a tree?

The manhorse broke into a gallop. Mandred's hands held tight to the leather strap of the quiver. Aigilaos had not lied. He raced like the wind across the field and past a massive ruined tower. A hill rose behind the tower, at its summit, a circle of stones.

Mandred had never been a good rider. His legs began to cramp from gripping the manhorse's flanks so hard. Aigilaos laughed. He was playing with him. But Mandred would not ask him to slow his pace, he silently vowed.

They passed through a bright birch grove. The air was filled with golden seeds. All of the trees were straight and fine, their trunks glistening like ivory. On none of them did the bark hang down in scraps and tatters as on the trees he knew from the Fjordlands. Tendrils of wild roses spread across scattered boulders of gray stone. It seemed almost as if, there in the grove, a strange, wild order prevailed. But who would waste their time tending to a patch of forest that yielded nothing? Certainly not a creature like Aigilaos.

The path climbed steadily and was soon little more than a narrow game trail. The birches gave way to beech trees, their canopy of leaves so thick that barely a gleam of light made it through. The tall, slender trunks looked to Mandred like gray pillars. It was eerily silent, which only made the muffled hoofbeats on the heavy bed of fallen leaves louder. Now and then, high in the crowns of the trees, Mandred noted strange nests resembling large sacks made of white linen. In some of the nests, lights glowed. Mandred sensed that he was being observed. Something was up there, and it followed them with curious eyes.

Aigilaos was still galloping at breakneck speed. They rode through the silent forest for an hour, perhaps even longer, until they finally came to a broad path. The manhorse wasn't even sweating.

The forest began to open up. Overgrown with moss, wide bands of gray stone cut through the dark earth. Aigilaos began to slow down. He looked around, alert.

Between the trees, half hidden, Mandred made out another stone circle. The standing stones were covered with ivy. A massive fallen tree lay across the circle. The place looked to have been abandoned long ago.

Mandred felt the fine hairs on the back of his neck stand on end. The air was a little cooler here. He had the oppressive feeling that something was lurking there, just beyond his field of vision, something that even the manhorse found sinister. Why had this stone circle been abandoned? What had happened here?

The path they were following led upward to a cliff top that afforded a breathtaking view of the land around. Directly in front of them lay a deep gorge that looked as if Naida the Cloud Rider had split the rocky earth with a tremendous bolt of lightning. A narrow trail hewed from the stone led down to a bridge that spanned the chasm below in a bold arch.

On the far side of the gorge, the land climbed again in gently rolling hills that, far in the distance, transformed into gray mountains. A multitude of small streams foamed into the abyss over the distant rim of the cliffs.

"The Shalyn Falah," said Aigilaos reverently. "The white bridge. They say it was carved from the finger bone of Dalagira, the giantess. Anyone crossing the bridge enters into the heartland of Albenmark. It has been a very long time since a human has seen this place."

The manhorse began the descent into the gorge. The ground underfoot was smooth rock, wet with spray, and Aigilaos moved cautiously, cursing as he went in a language Mandred did not understand.

When they came to a broad rock ledge, Aigilaos told Mandred to dismount. In front of them lay the bridge. It was only two steps wide and sloped away from the center line so that the spray did not gather in puddles but ran off. There was nothing to hold on to.

"Truly a wondrous construction," murmured Aigilaos testily. "Except it never crossed the builders' minds that creatures with metal-shod hooves might also like to use it. It is better for you to go across on your own two feet, Mandred. You are expected on the other side. I will take another route. Most likely it will be evening before I reach the palace, but the queen expects you at dusk." His face twisted into a smile. "I hope you don't suffer from vertigo, warrior."

Mandred felt slightly queasy as he looked at the bridge, as smooth as glass. But he would never show this manhorse his fear. "Vertigo is not in my nature. I'm a warrior from the Fjordlands. I can climb like a goat."

"You're as hairy as one, at least." Aigilaos grinned insolently. "See you at the queen's court." He turned away and clattered rapidly back up the steep path to the rim of the gorge.

Mandred looked at the bridge. In the tales of faeryland, the mortal heroes usually had to pass some kind of test. Was this his? Or had the manhorse led him astray?

Idle thoughts not worth thinking. His mind made up, Mandred stepped onto the bridge. It surprised him to find that the soles of his winter boots gave him a good grip. He carefully set one foot before the other. Fine spray from the river below beaded on his face. The wind tugged at his beard with invisible fingers. And soon, Mandred stood high above the abyss. The spray swept over the bridge in clouds that grew heavier with each step he took. *So this is what being a bird must feel like, flying between heaven and earth . . .*

Mandred's eyes roamed curiously over the stony surface. Nowhere could he see a joint. It seemed the bridge had been carved from a single stone. Or was the bridge truly fashioned from the finger bone of a giantess as Aigilaos had claimed? It was as smooth as polished ivory. Mandred banished the thought from his head. A giantess so huge would bury every inch of the Fjordlands if she fell. The story was no more than a fable, he decided.

The farther he went, the more his bravado grew. Finally, he stepped close to the edge of the bridge and looked down into the rift. The depths exuded a strange attraction. They aroused in Mandred an urge to simply jump, to give himself over to the freedom of the fall. The longer he looked down, the stronger the desire to give in to the urge became.

"Mandred?" A tall, slim figure stepped toward him from the mists. He was dressed head to foot in white, and his left hand rested on the pommel of the sword at his waist.

Mandred's right hand sprang instinctively to the place where his axe normally rested in his belt. It was only when his fingers went wanting that he realized he was unarmed.

The newcomer had not missed the movement of Mandred's hand. "I am not your enemy, human." He swept the hair from his face with a casual movement. "My name is Ollowain. I am the keeper of the Shalyn Falah. My queen has charged me with leading you on the last part of your journey to her palace."

Mandred appraised the man. His movements were as nimble as a cat's. He did not look particularly strong, but an aura of self-confidence surrounded him, as if he were the hero of many battles. His face was thin and pale. Pointed ears showed through light blond hair, stringy from the spray. His eyes did not betray his thoughts. Ollowain's face was a mask.

Mandred thought of the stories that were told on long winter nights. There could be no doubt; he was looking at an elf. And the elf knew Mandred's name. "Why does everyone in this place know who I am?" he asked, suspicious.

"News travels fast in Albenmark, human. Nothing that happens in her land escapes the eyes and ears of our queen. She sends her subjects messages that fly on the wind. Come now. We have a long ride ahead of us, and I will not allow you to keep my queen waiting. Follow me." The elf turned on his heel and stepped down into the narrow ravine that lay on the far side of the bridge.

Stunned, Mandred stood on the spot and watched the elf go. What was that about? *This is no way to treat a guest*, he thought angrily. What galled him even more was that Ollowain obviously did not doubt for a moment that he would come trotting along behind. In a temper, he followed the elf into the ravine. The reddish rock walls were seamed with strata of blue-gray and black, but the beauty of the canyon was lost on Mandred. He could not stop thinking that he was following the elf like a dog would its master.

If a Fjordlander had treated him like this, he would have struck him down without hesitation. In his homeland, no one would have dared treat him with such disrespect. Was he doing something wrong? Maybe the fault was his? The elf, no doubt, was open to a compliment. Every warrior is happy to speak about his weapons. "You carry an impressive sword, Ollowain."

The elf did not respond.

"I favor the axe in battle myself," Mandred said, trying again.

Silence.

Mandred balled his fists, then opened them again. *Self-important halfwit*. He was keeper of a bridge and errand boy for his queen. What difference did that make? For a true warrior, he was far too slender. "Among my people, only weaker men carry swords. The queen of the battle is the axe. It takes courage, strength, and skill to fight with it. Few warriors can count all three virtues in equal measure."

Still, the elf showed no reaction.

What was Mandred supposed to say to upset his composure?

Eventually, the steep rock faces fell away, and they came to a high white wall. It was built in a broad semicircle, as if retreating from the front of the narrow pass. Mandred knew the significance of the form: it made the wall longer. More archers could take up position in case an enemy was ever insane enough to try to attack the heartland of Albenmark through the pass.

At the center of the rampart rose a slim tower. A large, bronze-studded door opened as they approached.

"If that tower stood at the end of the bridge or, even better, higher up on the path on the other side of the gorge, the heartland would be easier to defend. A handful of men could hold off an army," said Mandred offhand.

"No blood may be spilt on the Shalyn Falah, human. Do you actually think you're smarter than the architects of my people?" Ollowain said without taking the trouble to turn as he spoke.

"If we're talking about architects who forget the rails when they build a bridge, then frankly, I have no great respect," Mandred replied sharply.

The elf stopped in his tracks. "Are you truly so simpleminded, or are you merely relying on the fact that you stand under the queen's protection, human? Didn't your wet nurse ever tell you what elves do to humans who show so little respect?"

Mandred licked his lips nervously. Baiting an elf . . . Was he completely out of his mind? He should have kept his mouth shut. But if he didn't respond now, he would lose face, unless . . . He smiled. There was another way.

"It says something about your courage, elf, to taunt an unarmed man."

Ollowain spun around, his cape swirling wide. His sword came to a stop with the hilt foremost, barely a finger's breadth from Mandred's chest. "You think you would be a danger to me with a weapon in your hand, human? Do your best."

Mandred grinned mischievously. "I don't fight unarmed men."

"They say the easiest way to recognize a coward is by the speed of his tongue," Ollowain shot back. "I hope you don't piss in your breeches."

Mandred's hand shot forward. He grabbed hold of Ollowain's sword and jumped back. That did it. He wouldn't really hurt this pompous fool, but a swat with the flat of the sword ought to show him he'd taken issue with the wrong man. A quick look to the battlements that topped the rampart showed that no one was watching. That was good. Ollowain himself certainly wouldn't go spreading the word that he'd taken a thrashing.

Mandred eyed his adversary. He was splendidly dressed, definitely, but he was no hero or wizard. Who would you appoint as keeper of a bridge, especially a bridge that no one in his right mind would ever cross? A snot nose. A nobody. He'd teach the peacock some respect, even if he was an elf.

He slashed the blade in the air a couple of times to loosen up his muscles. The sword was unusually light, completely different from a human sword, and sharp on both edges. He would have to be careful if he didn't want to injure Ollowain by accident.

"Are you going to attack me now? Or do you need a second sword?" asked the elf, bored.

Mandred stormed at him. He raised the sword high as if he wanted to split Ollowain's skull, but at the last second, he changed the direction of the strike to deliver a backhanded blow to the elf's right shoulder. The stroke caught nothing but air.

Ollowain had dodged by enough that Mandred missed him by inches. The white-robed warrior smiled arrogantly.

Mandred moved back again. The elf might have the stature of a young lad, but he knew how to fight. Mandred would try his best trick on him: a feint that had already cost three of his enemies their lives.

He moved forward again, his left fist raised as if to clout Ollowain in the face. As he did so, his right hand started a sword stroke from the wrist, taking aim at his adversary's knee. The first his enemies knew of this stroke, executed with such a slight motion, was when the blade struck home.

A punch knocked Mandred's hand aside. A kick hit the tip of the sword, causing it to miss its target. Then the elf rammed a knee between Mandred's legs.

Stars danced in front of Mandred's eyes. The pain . . . he could barely breathe. A blow to the chest knocked him off balance. A second sent him sprawling. He blinked, trying to see clearly again. The elf was so fast that his movements were blurry, almost ghostlike.

Mandred, helpless, lashed out around him to keep his rival at a distance. Something hit his right hand. His fingers went numb with pain.

His blade was now guided by no more than his instincts as a fighter. He felt powerless, while Ollowain seemed to be everywhere at once.

Mandred's sword swung in a sweeping arc. Then with a jolt, the sword was ripped out of his hand. A puff of air brushed his right cheek. The fight was over.

Ollowain had stepped back a few paces. His sword was back in its sheath as if nothing had happened. Slowly, Mandred began to see more clearly. It had been a long time since anyone had beaten him so soundly. The tricky elf had avoided hitting him in the face. No one at court would notice what had happened.

"You must have been very scared, elf," Mandred gasped, "to turn to magic to beat me."

"Is it magic if your eyes are too slow to follow my hand?"

"No human can move that fast without magic," Mandred persisted.

The specter of a smile played across Ollowain's lips. "Very true, Mandred. No human." He pointed to the gateway that opened into the tower, which now stood wide open. Two horses were waiting there, already saddled. "Would you do me the honor of following me?"

Every bone in Mandred's body hurt. He moved stiffly toward the gate. The elf stayed close to his side. "I don't need anybody to hold me up," Mandred grumbled.

"If you did, you'd cut a miserable figure at court," said the elf with a friendly glance that took the edge off his barb.

The horses waited patiently beneath the arch of the gate. No stable hands were to be seen, no one who had brought the horses here for them. A vaulted gateway ran like a tunnel through the stonework of the mighty tower. The gateway was empty, as were the merlons that topped the wall. Again, Mandred sensed that he was being watched.

Did the elves want to hide the strength of the garrison guarding the gate to the heartland? Was he considered an enemy? A spy perhaps? But if that were the case, would the oak have healed him?

A white horse and a gray were waiting for them. Ollowain stepped up to the white stallion and playfully patted its nostrils. Mandred had the impression that the gray was looking at him expectantly. Though he didn't know much about horses, he could see that these beasts were lightly built. They had slim fetlocks and didn't look very strong at all. Then he remembered that he'd been fooled by Ollowain's appearance, too. The horses probably had more endurance and were stronger than any other horse he'd ever ridden, Aigilaos excepted. Mandred smiled at his recollection of the blowhard manhorse.

Groaning, he pulled himself into the saddle. When he was halfway upright, Ollowain signaled to him to follow. The unshod hooves of the horses resounded dully from the walls of the tunnel.

Ollowain struck out along a path that took them over gently rising green hills. It was a long ride to the palace of the elven queen, past dark woods and over countless small bridges. Now and then, off in the distance, Mandred saw houses with boldly sweeping domed rooftops. Carefully set into the landscape, they looked to Mandred like gemstones mounted in an uncommonly precious setting.

What he rode through with Ollowain was a land of spring, and he remembered the faery stories that told of an elven world of perpetual spring. Again, Mandred wondered how long he might have slept beneath the oak tree. It could not have been more than two or three days since he had passed through the stone circle. Perhaps no more than a single day.

Mandred focused on organizing his thoughts; he did not want to find himself standing before the queen like a fool. He had managed to convince himself that the manboar had come from here, from the elven world. He thought of Xern and Aigilaos. Here, it seemed quite normal for humans and animals to be merged into one being—just like the manboar.

When the princes of the Fjordlands met to determine justice, it was Mandred's job to represent Firnstayn. He knew what had to be done to stifle a blood feud before it started. If a man from one clan was killed by a man from another, then the murderer's family had to pay the victim's family blood money. If this was paid, then there was no longer any foundation for revenge. The manboar came from here. The queen of the elves was responsible for the beast, and Mandred had lost three companions to it. Firnstayn was so small that the loss of three strong men threatened its very existence. He would demand a high recompense for the loss. Luth alone knew how many men from other villages the creature had slain. The Albenkin had wrought the damage, so they had to pay for it. That was only fair.

The elves had no reason to fear a blood feud with Mandred's village, but still he owed it to his dead friends to raise his voice at the court of the queen and call for justice. Did the queen of Albenmark already suspect as much? Was she aware of the debt she owed? Was that why she was having him brought to her palace with such haste?

It was late in the afternoon when they caught their first glimpse of it. Still far in the distance, the palace perched high atop a steep hillside beyond a broad swath of woods and meadowland. The sight of it made Mandred's breath catch. The palace seemed to grow directly from the rock it sat atop. The rooftops of its highest towers looked as if they pierced the sky. The walls were radiant white, while the rooftops shone with a blue-green shade that reminded Mandred of the color of old bronze. No royal seat of a prince of the Northlands could compare in even the slightest detail to the towers of this castle. King Horsa's golden hall itself appeared insignificant against such splendor. The woman who ruled this land . . . how powerful she must be. And how rich. So rich she could probably have all the longhouses of his village shingled with gold with a snap of her fingers. He should keep that in mind when he named the price she had to pay for his dead companions.

Mandred was secretly surprised at how slowly they seemed to approach the castle. Although the horses flew like the wind through the countryside, the palace on the horizon hardly seemed to grow any larger.

They passed a tree that looked as old as the mountains. Its trunk was as thick as a tower, and curious objects could be seen in its immense spreading crown. It looked as if the living wood had woven its own branches into round huts, and rope bridges stretched through the crown of the tree, connecting the huts. Mandred saw figures half-hidden among the branches. Were they elves like Ollowain? Or some other strange residents of this land?

Without warning, as if at some inaudible command, a flock of birds rose abruptly from the tree. Their feathers shimmered in all the colors of the rainbow. They flew low over Mandred's head, described a wide arc in the sky, then circled above the two riders. There must have been thousands, and the air was filled with the beating of wings. The play of colors in the birds' feathers was so brilliant that Mandred could not take his eyes off them until, gradually, the flock dispersed.

Ollowain had been silent for the entire ride. He seemed to be deep in thought and unimpressed by the wonders of the heartland. Mandred, though, could not drink in enough of what he was seeing.

They came to a shallow lake, the bed of which sparkled with gem-stones. *What kind of beings are these that they would throw such treasures into the water without a second thought?* But even as he thought this, he remembered that he himself had made offerings to his gods. On a silent night beneath a full moon, at the holy spring buried deep in the mountains, he had offered up the axe of the first man he had beaten in battle as a gift to Norgrimm, the god of war. And Freya and the other women honored Luth by braiding artfully woven bands of cloth into the branches of the linden tree in the village. The elves were obviously rich, so perhaps it wasn't out of proportion for them to offer their gods precious stones. And yet the wealth of the elves angered Mandred. He did not know how he had come here, but this kingdom could not be so far from his Fjordlands. Here they had more than they could ever need, but among his folk, in winter, there was always hardship. A tiny fraction of these treasures could banish that hunger forever. Whatever he asked as blood money for his dead companions would be a meaningless sum for the elves.

He wanted something else. Not gold or gemstones. He wanted revenge. The beast, the manboar, he wanted to see it dead at his feet.

Mandred observed Ollowain. A fighter of his caliber would be able to defeat the monster with ease. He was certain of that.

He sighed. Everything seemed easier here.

Together, the riders entered an open forest of beech. The lilt of flutes drifted on the air. From somewhere in the treetops rang a voice so clear that one's spirit was uplifted just by the listening. Mandred understood nothing of the song, but his anger vanished. What remained was sadness for the friends he had lost.

"Who is that singing?" he asked Ollowain.

The white-robed warrior glanced up to the treetops. "A girl of the forest folk. Strange creatures. Their lives are closely tied to the trees. If they don't want to be seen, then no one can find them—except perhaps others of their kind. They are renowned for their song and their skill with the bow. They move among the branches like shadows. Beware their forests if you ever find yourself in a feud with them, human."

Mandred looked up to the trees uneasily. Occasionally, he believed he could make out a shadow up there, and he was glad when they were out of the forest again. Still, the melody of the flutes followed them for some time.

The sun was already grazing the distant mountains by the time they reached the broad valley above which the queen's palace towered. An encampment of tents had been erected alongside a small stream. Silk banners fluttered in the wind, and the tents themselves seemed to vie with one another to be the most extravagant, the most magnificent. On the hills stood houses flanked on all sides by porticos. Some of these houses were connected to one another by long patios, overgrown with roses and ivy. The structures on the hills all around were so diverse that Mandred could scarcely look away. He was struck by the fact that there was no defensive wall encircling the elven settlement and that not a single watchtower could be seen on the surrounding hills. It was as if those who dwelled here were absolutely secure in the belief that this valley would never be attacked. Even the queen's palace, as impressive as its sky-high towers were, was hardly built with defense in mind. It was meant more to please the eye of a peaceful observer than to deter a ravening army.

Mandred and Ollowain followed a broad avenue, shaded by trees on both sides, that led to the gate. Oil lamps had been lit along the sides of the avenue, bathing it in a golden glow.

The tunnel that served as a gate here was shorter than the one at the fortification in the pass behind the Shalyn Falah. Elven soldiers in ankle-length chain mail tunics stood leaning on their shields. Their eyes followed Mandred—alert, but discreet. In the expansive courtyard, various high officials were gathered, and they looked at him, unflinching, as he passed. Beneath their gaze, Mandred felt dirty and insignificant. They were all attired in expensively embroidered garments that caught the light from the oil lamps. Their clothes were adorned with beads and stones for which Mandred didn't even have names. He, though, was dressed in rags. A pair of torn, bloody breeches. A worn-out fur jerkin. He must have looked like a beggar to them. He raised his chin defiantly. He would clothe himself in pride.

Ollowain swung out of the saddle. Mandred noted a fine tear in the warrior's cloak. Had he actually struck him during their duel after all? Ollowain would not needlessly or heedlessly put on something torn.

Mandred, too, dismounted. A goat-legged servant hurried over and took the gray's reins. Astonished, Mandred stared at the bizarre stable hand. The servant stank like an old billy goat. Another half-animal, half-man thing. They even let them into this grand palace.

A tall elf stepped forward from a group of dignitaries in the courtyard. He wore a long, dark cloak hemmed with silver braid embroidered with an intricate pattern of interwoven leaves and flowers. Lustrous white hair cascaded to his shoulders, and a crown of delicate, silvery leaves encircled his temples. His face was pale, almost colorless, and his lips no more than a thin line. His eyes burned a cold, light blue. Ollowain bowed briefly to the newcomer. The difference between the two of them could hardly have been greater. They looked to Mandred like light and shadow.

"It is my privilege to greet you, Master Alvias. As Queen Emerelle wished, I have escorted the human safely to the palace." Ollowain's voice left no doubt that his queen's wishes were his command.

Each looked to be taking the other's measure with his eyes, and Mandred had the impression that they were talking silently with one another. Finally, Master Alvias made a sign to Mandred to follow.

They climbed a wide stairway that led to a portico, and as they rose, Mandred felt a sense of dread engulf him, as if he were trapped in a nightmare. Everything around Mandred had an air of oppressive beauty and was steeped in a strange magic. It was a place of such consummate perfection that it frightened the jarl.

They passed through two expansive halls, either one large enough to have contained his entire village. In galleries hung enormous banners decorated with eagles and dragons, but also with animals the likes of which Mandred had never seen. Though he could feel no draft, the banners rippled as if touched by a light breeze. The walls themselves were even stranger. Looking closely, he could see that they were made of white stone, like the bridge of Shalyn Falah and the fortification beyond the pass. The stones of the walls, radiating a pale white light, must have been enchanted. From any more than a few paces away, one lost the impression of being surrounded by stone. It was like moving inside a hall of pure light.

Whenever they approached a portal, the doors swung wide as if moved by an unseen hand. In the middle of the second hall, there was a spring that spilled from the mouth of a stone monster and poured into a small, round pond. The beast was surrounded by armed warriors, also made of stone. Unsettled at the sight, Mandred felt his heart beat harder. If he needed final proof of the magical powers of the elf queen, this was it. She turned anyone incurring her displeasure into a petrified ornament for her castle.

Another high door swung open before them, and they entered another hall, the walls of which were hidden behind a shimmering, silvery curtain of water. This hall had no ceiling overhead, the sky instead arching high above them, glowing dusk red. Soft music hung in the air. Mandred could not think which instrument might be able to pour forth such delightful sounds. The music swept away the dread that had been growing in his heart since he had entered the first courtyard. Yet this was still no place for humankind, and he knew that he was not meant to be here.

Some three dozen elves were waiting in this hall, and all eyes suddenly turned to look at him. It was the first time that Mandred had seen elven women. They were tall and slim, their hips more boyishly narrow than those of human women, and their breasts were small and firm. Among humans, Mandred would have found no pleasure in the sight of such childlike bodies, but the elves were different. Their faces had a beauty that made one forget everything else. Was it the curve of their lips, their ageless faces, or their eyes, the depths of which beckoned with the promise of mysterious pleasures? Some wore flowing dresses of a cloth so fine it seemed to have been woven from moonlight. Rather than concealing the merits of their slim bodies, the dresses they wore emphasized them all the more. Mandred's eyes settled on one of the women, even more tantalizingly dressed than the others. Her breasts shimmered rose-colored through the cloth, and alluring shadows lay between her thighs. It was a dress no human woman would have dared to wear.

Opposite the door they had come through, seven steps led to the elven throne. The throne was a plain chair made of dark wood, inlaid with black and white stones depicting two snakes twisted inextricably together. Beside the throne rose a low column with a flat silver bowl on top. In front of the royal seat stood a young elven woman, somewhat shorter than the other women in the hall. Dark blond hair fell in waves over her naked, milk-white shoulders. Her lips were the color of forest berries, and her eyes were the same light brown shade as the fur of a fawn. She wore a blue dress threaded with silver.

It was before this woman that Master Alvias bowed. "Emerelle, my queen, this is Mandred, the mortal who entered your realm unbidden."

The queen looked intently at Mandred. It was impossible for him to read her thoughts from her face, which remained unmoving, as if carved from stone. An eternity seemed to pass. The music had faded, and now everything was still and silent, save for the rush of water.

"What do you seek, Mandred the Mortal?" the queen's clear voice finally rang.

Mandred's mouth was dry. He had spent many hours on the ride here thinking of what he would say when he faced the elven queen, but as he stood before her now, his mind was suddenly empty. All that remained was concern for his loved ones and fury for the death of his companions. "I demand blood money for the murders committed by one of your subjects, Queen. That is the law of the Fjordlands," he said.

The water's hiss grew louder. Mandred heard scandalized murmurings behind him.

"Which of my subjects is supposed to have committed such deeds?" asked Emerelle, her voice calm.

"I don't know its name. It is a monster, half human, half boar. I have seen many similar beings on my way to your castle."

A deep crease appeared between the queen's brows. "I know of no being as you have described, Mandred."

Mandred sensed the blood rush to his cheeks. *Such an impudent lie.* "A half man, half horse was your messenger, and in the courtyard, a mangoat led the horses away. From where else should a manboar come, Queen, if not from your realm? I demand—"

The water plunged down the walls in a loud roar.

"You dare call our queen a liar?" shouted Alvias, indignant. A host of elves surrounded Mandred.

He closed his hands into fists. "I know what I have seen."

"Observe the rights of hospitality." The queen had barely raised her voice, but all present obeyed her. "I invited the human to this hall. Anyone who raises his hand against him raises it against my honor. And you, Mandred, rein in your tongue. I say to you, such a being, as you have described it, does not exist in Albenmark. Let us hear your account of what this manboar did. I know very well that you humans avoid the standing stones. What was it that brought you here?"

Mandred told her about the futile hunt and the power of the manboar. When he had finished, the crease between Emerelle's brows had only deepened. "I am sorry for the death of your companions, Mandred. May they be received with joy in the halls of your gods."

Mandred looked at the queen in amazement. He waited for her to continue, to make him some kind of offer, but none came. *That can't be the end of it*, he thought, but the silence only grew deeper. Mandred thought of Freya. Every hour he lost here put her in greater danger, and there was no telling if the manboar had already attacked Firnstayn.

Awkwardly, Mandred lowered his eyes. What was his pride worth if it was paid for with the blood of those dearest to him? "Queen Emerelle, I . . . ask for help in the hunt for this monster. I . . . I beg forgiveness if I have offended you. I am just a simple man. Battling with words is not what I am good at. I wear my heart for all to see."

"You came into my palace, Mandred, and insulted me before my royal court. Now you ask me to consider endangering my hunters for your cause? You wear your heart for all to see, indeed, human." Emerelle's hand moved in a circle over the silver bowl, and she glanced fleetingly into the water. "What do you offer me for my assistance? Is not blood settled with blood among your people?"

Her response surprised Mandred. The princes of the Fjordlands would have stated their demands openly, not haggled like shopkeepers. He kneeled before her. "Free my land from the manboar, and I will be at your command. I will belong to you."

Emerelle smiled softly. "Mandred, in truth, you are not a man I would wish to have around me every day." She fell silent and looked again into the silver bowl. "I ask for what your wife, Freya, carries beneath her heart. Your firstborn child, Mandred the Mortal. The friendship of the elves is not won with a few cheap words. I will come for the child one year from today."

Mandred felt as if he had been struck by lightning. "My child?" He looked pleadingly at the other elves but found no sympathy on their faces. What was it the faery tales said? The hearts of elves are as cold as winter stars.

"Take a dagger and stab me in the heart, Queen. Take my life, here and now. That price I will pay without a blink, if you help my people."

"Fine words, Mandred," the queen replied coolly. "But what would be gained by spilling your blood on the steps of my throne?"

"What do you gain with a child?" protested Mandred in despair.

"This child will cement a bond between elves and humans," she replied, as calm as ever. "The child will grow up among my people and will have the best teachers. When your child is old enough, it can decide for itself whether to stay with us forever or to return to its human brothers. If the child wants to return, we will send rich gifts with it, and I am certain it will find a place among the leaders of your folk. But the most valuable gift it will take to the human world is the friendship of the elves."

Mandred felt as if this graceful woman were squeezing his heart in a hand of iron. How could he promise his unborn child to the elves? But then . . . if he refused, was it possible his child would never be born at all? How long would it be before the manboar invaded the little settlement at the fjord? Had it perhaps been and gone already?

Despondent, Mandred asked, "Is Freya . . . is my wife still alive?"

The queen's hand glided over the silver bowl. "Something conceals the creature you call the manboar from me, but it seems to be waiting close to the stone circle, even now. It has not yet attacked your village." She looked him in the eye. "What is your decision, Mandred?"

I will have more children with Freya, he thought to himself. *Perhaps she is carrying a girl there under her heart, and the loss will not weigh so heavily.* He was the jarl of his village. He was responsible for everyone who lived there. What was one life against many?

"You will have what you ask, Queen." Mandred's voice was little more than a whisper. His lips did not want to form the words, yet he forced himself to answer. "If your hunters kill the manboar, my child will belong to you."

Emerelle nodded toward an elf dressed in light green, indicating that he should step forward. "Farodin of the Askalel clan, you have proved yourself often and well. Your wisdom and your experience should help make the hunt successful. I name you to the elfhunt."

Mandred felt a shudder run down his spine. The elfhunt. How many stories had he heard about this secretive fellowship? No prey ever escaped these sinister hunters, it was said. Whatever they hunted was as good as dead. Their hounds were wolves as big as ponies, and liquid fire flowed in the veins of their mounts. They rode across the night sky and concealed themselves in the faerylight before swooping on their quarry like eagles. Only the most noble and brave could ride with the elfhunt. All who set out were both warrior and wizard, so powerful that dragons feared them and trolls hid away in their castles. *This is the fate to befall the manboar*, thought Mandred, rejoicing inwardly. They would slaughter the beast in bloody revenge for his dead friends.

The queen named others, but those she named seemed to be absent from the throne room. Finally, she pointed to one figure, clad in brown, who seemed startled at the mention of his name. "Nuramon of the Weldaron clan, your day has come."

A murmur ran through the gathered elves.

A woman stepped forward from a group. She seemed particularly distressed. "Queen, you do not seriously want to put him in such danger. You know his destiny."

"That is the reason I have called on him," she answered evenly.

Mandred stole a glance at the brown-haired elf. He seemed anxious and looked like anything but an experienced hunter.

"The elfhunt will ride out early on the morrow to kill the monster that we have heard about. And you, Mandred the Mortal, will lead it. You know the beast, and you know the land it is ravaging," the queen said, leveling her gaze on Mandred.

The murmuring in the room fell silent in a heartbeat. Again, Mandred felt all eyes on him. At first, he could not believe what Emerelle had just said. He—in the eyes of those present, the lowest of them all—*he* had been chosen to lead the elfhunt. He wished at that moment that Freya were at his side.

AN EVENING
AT COURT

Nuramon stood in the center of his chamber. The room's walls and ceiling were richly adorned with frescoes. Seven. The queen had named seven to the elfhunt, and there were seven chambers. The rooms had been built for the companions of the elfhunt to equip themselves and rest. Here their relatives could come to honor them. And here Nuramon stood, utterly alone.

Honey-colored barinstones were set into the ceiling and walls, emitting a warm light. A long recess was cut deep into the wall all along one side. Inside lay various weapons and items of kit, jewelry and treasures each possessing a magic Nuramon could sense. All of it, at one time or another, had been worn by his predecessors. It was tradition for those returning from the elfhunt to leave something for the next to ride out.

As one of the chosen, Nuramon had the right to claim these items for himself. At least, that's how Farodin had explained it. But Nuramon had no desire to own any of them—he did not want to take away their shine. For equipment, then, he was left with what he himself possessed, and that was not much. Custom required that his relatives visit him here to lend their support and provide him with whatever he might need. But Nuramon knew that would not happen. No relative sat on the stone bench opposite the recess, and no gift lay there.

Hadn't the queen bestowed upon him a great honor, naming him to the elfhunt? Had he not earned the right to have his clan come to him, as was customary, to show their joy at his being chosen? Instead, everyone had reacted with surprise. They mocked him openly and did not even afford him the courtesy of keeping their voices down while they did. He was an outcast, and he knew that not even the queen could change that.

What was there in the world apart from Noroelle? What else kept him here? His parents had gone into the moonlight long ago. He had no brothers or sisters, and just as many friends. There was only Noroelle.

She was the only one who seemed unconcerned by his birthright. And if she had heard of the queen's choice, she would have shared her happiness with him. She would have come to visit him in this chamber.

Nuramon had heard stories of the last elfhunt. The companions had kept a troll prince away from the Kelpenwall. Their families had furnished weapons and precious objects of every kind from which the hunters could choose. And any elf whose offering was accepted by the hunters was filled with pride.

At that very moment, no doubt, in the other chambers, his companions were being presented with the equipment they would need. Even the human, he knew, would have someone attending to him. Nuramon wondered if any elf had ever before envied a human.

The sound of steps before the door shook him out of his melancholy thoughts. He turned, hoping suddenly to see a cousin, an uncle, or one of his aunts, someone from his clan. But before the door opened, Nuramon heard a female voice speak his name. Then the door swung wide, and a woman wearing the gray robe of a enchantress stepped into the room.

"Emerelle," he exclaimed in surprise. His queen looked utterly changed. Less like a queen, more like a wandering sorceress of great power. Her pale-brown eyes sparkled in the glow of the barinstones, and she was smiling. "*You* have come to visit me?" he asked.

She closed the door. "And it would appear I'm the only one." She stepped toward him with such elegance and power that Nuramon could have believed he was gazing at an elf from the old days, from the tales of the heroes. The queen, of course, had lived through those times. She was not the child of elves, but born directly from the Alben race, and had seen them before they abandoned the world. Somewhere in this palace, Emerelle kept hidden the Albenstone, her legacy from the Alben, a treasure she would one day use to go after them. But why had she come here dressed like an enchantress?

As if reading his thoughts, she answered. "It is tradition that the queen pay a visit to each member of the elfhunt. And as I heard voices at every room except yours, I thought I would start here." She stopped in front of him and looked at him expectantly.

He breathed in the fragrance of fresh spring flowers, the scent of the queen, and it calmed him. "Forgive me," he said quietly. "I am not familiar with all the traditions." He lowered his eyes.

"Haven't you ever dreamed of being part of the elfhunt?" she asked. "Every child dreams of it and knows the customs. They know every step of the way in this night."

Nuramon sighed and looked into her eyes. "A child who finds no acceptance dreams of smaller things."

He thought of the time after his mother and father had entered the moonlight. He was still little more than a child, but nobody came to take him in. His relatives spurned him, so he returned to the tree house of his parents. He had been lonely there. The only Albenkin willing to tolerate his presence were those who cared nothing for the curse that seemed to hang over him. And they had been few.

"I know how hard it is," said the queen, drawing Nuramon out of his recollections with her words. "But my decision will serve as a sign to the others. They are still surprised, but soon they will look at you through different eyes."

"I wish I could believe that," he said, avoiding Emerelle's gaze.

"Look at me, Nuramon," she commanded. "You may not forget that I am *your* queen, too. I cannot make the others love you, but I will treat you as I treat them. You feel lonely, and you are asking yourself if you still belong among the elves at all, but the others will see your true nature soon enough." She lowered her eyes. "You have grown above the suffering of your youth. It seems Noroelle has awakened powers in you that none suspected. Now the moment has come. I am giving you the recognition you deserve, equal to what is in you."

"And I will use the opportunity, Emerelle."

The queen turned and looked at the door behind her. "No one is coming, but as the hunters of the elfhunt have always been provided for, I would like to take it on myself to outfit you. I will have what I can offer brought to your chamber later."

"But—"

"No, not a word. It is not your place. Look up there," she said and pointed to the image of an elf fighting a dragon. "That is Gaomee. She defeated the dragon Duanoc, which had found its way into our realm through the Halgaris Gate."

Gaomee. Duanoc. Halgaris. Names from the sagas, names that stood for great deeds, reminiscent of heroic times.

At one time, many dragons came to Albenmark, but only a few found their place in this world and forged an alliance with the elves. Duanoc was far from accepting such a pact, or so the old tales said, at least. Young Gaomee slew Duanoc. A shudder ran down Nuramon's spine.

The queen continued. "Gaomee had no family left. I chose her, which also caused no few eyebrows to rise. I saw in her something that I once saw in myself." Emerelle closed her eyes, drawing Nuramon completely under her spell.

He had never before seen the queen's closed eyelids. She would look like this when she slept, dreaming of things that only an elf of extraordinary power could comprehend.

"I see Gaomee so clearly in my memory . . . she stood here in front of me, the tears rolling down her cheeks," said Emerelle. "She had nothing of what she would need to ride with the others against Duanoc, so I outfitted her. I will not allow one among the hunters to be poorly equipped, especially when the hunt will take them into the human realm."

"Then I will accept your offer," said Nuramon, transfixed by the fresco of Gaomee overhead. The queen had opened up a path for him, a path he never would have believed was his to follow. He had long ago resigned himself to a life lived apart from his fellow elves.

"I know this is new for you," said the queen gently. "But this is a turning point for your soul. Never before has one with the name Nuramon been part of the elfhunt. You are the first. The elfhunt brings with it distinction among the elves, without exception. So when you return, there are many here who will have to think again about how they ought to treat you."

A smile crept over Nuramon's face.

"Why do you smile? Let me share your thoughts," Emerelle commanded.

"I am reminded of the fear on the faces of my relatives when you named me to the elfhunt. Now I am more than just a disgrace. I am a danger. They fear that if I die, a child will be born who carries my soul.

They would have done better to come here and equip me as best they could, in the hope that I survive. Their aversion to me seems greater than their fear of my death . . ."

Emerelle looked at him benevolently. "Don't judge them too harshly. They have to come to terms with how things are now, and this is new for them. Few of us who live through the centuries can quickly adapt to the new. No one could suspect that I would call on you. Not even you expected it."

"That is true."

"And are you clear on how things will proceed from here?"

Nuramon was confused for a moment. Was she talking about his life or about this conversation?

Before he could say anything, Emerelle went on. "No elfhunt is without its dangers for those who ride out. For this reason, the queen gives each of the companions her counsel to take with them on their journey."

Nuramon was ashamed of his ignorance. "I will accept it, whatever it may be."

"It pleases me that you have such trust in me," she said and laid one hand on his shoulder. "You are different from the others, Nuramon. When you look out on the world, you see something different from what most elves see. You see the beauty in what others shrink from. You see what is worthy where others pass by in disgust. And you speak of harmony in places others cannot bear to be. Because you are how you are, I give to you the counsel I once heard spoken by the Oracle of Telmareen. 'Choose your kinfolk for yourself. Pay no heed to your reputation. Everything you are is within you.'"

It was as if a spell had been cast on Nuramon. That he should hear the words of the Oracle of Telmareen from the queen herself. For a long moment, he savored the feeling that she conjured up in him. Then, unbidden, a question occurred to him. He hesitated, but finally he gathered the courage to put the question to her. "You said that you heard this counsel. To whom did the oracle speak? Whom did it so counsel?"

Emerelle smiled. "Follow your *queen's* counsel," she said, and kissed him on the forehead. "The oracle was speaking to me." With those words, she turned away and went to the door.

Nuramon, speechless, watched as she left.

Before closing the door behind her, and without turning back, she said, "I saw Noroelle in the orchard."

When Emerelle was gone, Nuramon sank onto the stone bench and pondered. The oracle had once given the same advice to the queen? Had she called on him for the elfhunt because she saw herself reflected in him? Nuramon was suddenly aware of just how much he had deluded himself about the queen. He had always seen her as aloof, as a woman whose splendor one could only admire as one might admire a distant star. But never, never would he have ever considered that he and she might have something in common.

Emerelle was both a role model and an ideal to the elves and the other Albenkin who stood under her protection. How could he have excepted himself from their number? Not only had she opened up a path for him that she herself had once traveled, but she had also spoken about Gaomee. On the elfhunt, he would look to Gaomee as his guide, but higher still hovered the counsel of the queen.

He called her words to mind once more and thought of Noroelle. He left the chamber and saw Mandred at the end of the corridor amid a group of elves. The human was thanking them in a loud voice. Nuramon smiled. He would not want to trade places now with Mandred or any of the companions, not for anything this palace had to offer.

Making his way along the corridor, he noted that there were no women there with Mandred. It didn't surprise him. Word of the impropriety with which he had stared at the women at court had apparently spread. He was glad that Noroelle had not been exposed to the human's staring in the Royal Hall. How could anyone be so indiscreet?

Just then, in a ringing voice, Mandred said, "Come, my friends. Cast some spell to make me fit inside this armor, and I will be happy to take it . . . Stop! Keep those swords and other toys away from me. I am Mandred. Don't you have a decent axe?"

Nuramon shook his head. Raw voice, raw temper. But of a kind that one could not so easily forget.

On his way to the orchard, Nuramon wondered how Noroelle would take the news of his being named to the elfhunt. Would her fear for him outweigh her joy? The queen had mixed praise for Noroelle with her words. And it was true; his beloved had changed him. She had given him self-confidence, and he had thrived on her affection.

It was not long before he reached the orchard, which was laid out atop a broad spur of rock only accessible from the palace. It was night, and he looked up to the moon. That was the goal of life, to one day enter the moonlight. Through all these years, the moon had been his confidant. His ancestors—those who had previously borne his soul and worn his name—may have felt the same companionship with the moon. The sheen of its light touched him like the hint of a cool breeze, and it lent the warm spring night a little freshness. Nuramon moved beneath the trees.

He stopped beneath a birch and looked around. It was a long time since he had been in this garden. It was said that every tree here possessed a soul and a spirit, and anyone with an open ear could hear them whispering. Nuramon listened, but heard nothing. Were his senses still too inadequate?

Now was the time to find Noroelle. This was an orchard, so he would most likely spy her beneath a fruit tree, he thought. He looked for the fruit that the trees here bore year round. He saw apples and pears, cherries and mirabelles, apricots, peaches, lemons, oranges, plums and . . . mulberries. Noroelle loved mulberries.

At the very edge of the garden stood two mulberry trees, but Noroelle was not there. Nuramon leaned against the wall and looked out over the land. By night, the tent encampment in front of the palace looked like a display of colored lanterns. "Where are you, Noroelle?" said Nuramon softly.

Immediately he heard a whispering in the treetops. "She is not here. She was not here."

Astonished, he turned around, but saw only the two mulberry trees.

"It is us." The words came from the branches of the larger of the trees.

"Go to the faery pine. It is a wise tree," added the smaller. "But before you go, take with you some of our fruit."

Surprised at the offer, Nuramon asked, "It is said, isn't it, that mulberry trees with a soul are known for their concern for their fruit?"

The larger tree's leaves rustled. "That is true. We are not like our soulless cousins, but you are on your way to Noroelle."

The smaller tree rustled. "It would be an honor for us if she tasted our fruit."

Two mulberries fell directly into Nuramon's hands. The berry from the smaller tree was a deep red. That from the larger was white.

"My heartfelt thanks to both of you," said Nuramon, touched at the gift, and he went on his way. He seemed to remember seeing a pine tree close to the birch.

When he reached the faery pine, it came back to him: as a child, he had played there in winter with the faeries from the riverbanks. The tree was neither tall nor broad and, in fact, rather plain. But it was surrounded by an aura that would admit no cold, the result of a kind of magic that Nuramon also knew. The pine possessed healing powers. He could sense them clearly.

Its branches moved in the breeze. "Who are you to disturb me?" the branches murmured.

A rustling then came from all sides. A moment ago, everything had been silent; now came the sound of whispering.

"Who is it?" the trees seemed to be asking.

"An elfling," came the answer.

The faery pine then said, "Silence! Let him answer."

"I am just a simple elf," said Nuramon. "And I am looking for my beloved."

"What is your name, elfling?"

"Nuramon."

"Nuramon." The word chimed from the branches overhead. The other trees, too, began murmuring his name. "I've heard about you."

"About me?"

"You live in a house in a tree, an oak named Alaen Aikhwitan. Your house is made of the wood that once contained the soul of the mighty Ceren. Do you know Alaen Aikhwitan? And have you heard of Ceren?"

"Ceren is not familiar to me, but I know Alaen Aikhwitan," said Nuramon. "I feel his presence when I am home. His magic keeps the house cool in summer and warm in winter. My mother learned the art of healing from him, and I learned how to heal from her. But the tree has never opened himself to me."

"He has to become accustomed to you first. You're still young. His messengers have told me about you . . . about your loneliness." A hundred questions came to Nuramon's mind, but now the pine asked, "Who is your beloved?"

"Her name is Noroelle."

A cheerful whisper rustled in the treetops all around, and Noroelle's name was spoken several times. The voices of the trees mixed with the rustling of their leaves in such a fashion that Nuramon could not make out what they were saying about her.

The faery pine could understand it, though. "She is not here. She has not been here tonight."

"But the queen said she was here in this garden."

"The queen says what needs to be said. Noroelle is not here, but she is not far away. Go to the terrace, where the linden and olive stand side by side."

Nuramon would have gladly stayed and found out about Ceren, but just then, it was more important to find Noroelle. He thanked the tree and wended his way toward the terrace.

He saw the linden tree and the olive tree soon enough. They stood before the stone wall that rose to the terrace above. As he drew closer, he spied a narrow stairway.

Noroelle stood at the stone parapet that edged the terrace. She was wearing a white robe and looked like a ghost descended from the moonlight.

She had not seen him yet. He stopped beneath the linden tree. The faery pine was right; the queen had said what had to be said. She had arranged this encounter carefully. Noroelle up there. He below. The circumstances cried out for a poem, spoken from the shadow of the linden tree, up into the moonlight.

Noroelle was saying something. Was she speaking with the moon? Was she simply talking into the night? Nuramon suddenly felt out of place. He was eavesdropping, and Noroelle had no idea he was there. She turned to one side. She was not speaking to the moon, nor to the night. She was speaking to an elf. A blink of an eye later, Nuramon saw to whom she had turned. It was Farodin.

Nuramon wanted nothing more than to leave, and he staggered from the shadow of the linden tree into the shadow of the olive. Leaning against the trunk, he listened halfheartedly to the words spoken over-head. Farodin had found a new voice, and it seemed to please Noroelle. For the first time, Farodin was speaking of his love for her, speaking from the depths of his heart.

Then it was over.

Up through the branches, Nuramon saw how Noroelle yielded to Farodin's charm in the moonlight. He had never seen her so happy. Farodin sealed his farewell with a kiss and left. Noroelle remained behind and looked out into the night, a smile on her lips. And because Nuramon loved her, he, too, had to smile. It was not important that Farodin had evidently won her for himself. His beloved was smiling, and her smile moved him.

Nuramon observed Noroelle for some time, and he saw the way her smile faded and faded until, eventually, it was replaced by a face of sadness. With the disappearance of her smile, his own vanished, too, and when she softly spoke his name into the night, he held his breath. Farodin made her smile, but the thought of Nuramon brought only concern. When he saw a tear run down her cheek, he could not contain himself any longer. He drew a quiet breath and whispered, "O hear me, fairest Albenchild."

Noroelle started in surprise.

"Heed this voice inside the tree."

She looked down, and their eyes met. And she began to smile again.

"Like a faery from my dream, come on the evening wind to me."

Noroelle wiped away her tears, took a deep breath, and said quietly, "But how can an elf be like a faery?"

"Well," he began, then went on quickly. "Your dress like silver birch bark glows. And I am blinded and beguiled." He moved from the shadow of the olive tree back to the linden. "With love! The linden surely knows. O hear me, fairest Albenchild."

"I hear you, tree spirit, but I must admit I have never heard a tree speak in rhymes."

Nuramon answered in a whisper. "It was no less difficult for me to speak in the voice of an elf to please my faery."

"It seems to me I just heard an olive tree speaking."

"Our roots are linked. We are one spirit clad in two kinds of bark. Love and life unite in us," he replied.

"Aren't there enough birch trees down there? Why is it that you yearn for me?"

"As you see, I stand here at the edge of the garden, my gaze turned up to you. The queen of this place told me that I should be of service to lovers when they come to speak to their loved one up above."

"I know this garden, and I know that you and all the trees are only supposed to listen and not to speak. Could it be that you have broken your silence for my sake?"

"Everyone must break their silence sometime. Eternity is deep and wide."

"Do you love me, then?"

"Oh, yes."

He saw her touch a branch. "You are a wonderful tree. And your leaves are so fine." She pulled the branch toward her and kissed a leaf. "Is that good, my tree?"

"It is like magic. And for that, I would like to give you something."

"Perhaps an olive?"

"No, no. Everyone who stands up there helps themselves to an olive, and I have nothing against that. I do not want to give you what anyone can have from me. For my beloved, it must be something special. No effort is too much. You know how jealously the mulberry trees yonder hoard their fruit?"

"Yes. Which is why it's smarter to look for trees without a soul. Trees with souls have to be cajoled to give up even a single one of their fruit."

"That is just what I have done. I . . . I felt a breeze go by, and it blew all the way to the mulberry trees at the other end of the garden. On the breeze, I asked each one to let me have a piece of their fruit. At first, they refused. What was *I* supposed to do with their berries? But when they discovered that their berries were destined for you, suddenly they grew generous."

"But how did you manage to get the mulberries here to you? You stand here, but as you point out, the others are quite some distance away."

"Ah, well, the berries were passed from tree to tree, and finally laid upon the grass. All day long, I stretched my roots to reach this gift for my beloved."

"So do you have the berries now?"

"Oh, yes. And I would like to give them to you."

"But how? Should I come down to you? Or will you lay them on a leaf and hand them up to me with a branch?"

"We trees have great magical powers. Look." Nuramon threw the red berry so that it landed on the parapet right in front of Noroelle. Then he threw the white berry, and Noroelle deftly caught it. "Did they both arrive?" he asked.

"One lies in my hand, the other in front of me," she said. "They are so lovely and fresh."

Nuramon looked on as she ate the berries, watching her lips, mesmerized.

After she had eaten the fruit, she said, "Those were the sweetest berries I have ever tasted. But what should become of us now, my tree spirit?"

"Do you not want to come down here to me and put down roots in the earth?"

"*You* could as easily uproot yourself and come up the steps to me," she replied.

"Hear me, beloved. Hear what I propose. A young man sleeps and dreams here in my shade. Would he, perhaps, be acceptable to you instead?"

"I would say . . . yes. Bind yourself to him and come to me. The spirit behind your voice, in this body, that is what I wish for this night. Come to me, Nuramon."

He hesitated. But was today not a day of marvels? He had been named to the elfhunt. The queen had revealed her own prophecy to him. The trees had spoken with him.

Nuramon summoned up his courage, stepped out of the shadows of the linden, and climbed the steps to the terrace, where Noroelle was waiting. At first, he wanted to keep his distance, as he always had, and not even try to touch her, but standing there, she was more alluring than she had ever been before, the night wind sweeping at her dress and her long hair. A soft smile rested on her lips.

"I heard what the queen did. You can't imagine how happy it makes me," she said gently, her head tilted to one side.

"And you cannot hide your happiness from me," responded Nuramon.

"I always told you that someone would recognize you for who you truly are, one day. I knew it. Oh, Nuramon," she said and opened her hands to him, wanting to reach out, but hesitating.

Nuramon overcame his reticence and finally took her hands in his.

Noroelle looked down, as if to reassure herself that his hands were actually touching hers. She held her breath.

He kissed her tenderly on the cheek, and she sighed. When his lips gradually moved closer to her mouth, she began to tremble. Their lips touched, and Nuramon felt her return his kiss and all the tension flow from her body.

She clasped him in her arms and whispered in his ear, "That was just the right moment, Nuramon. But still so surprising."

They looked at each other for a long time, and Nuramon had the feeling that what was between them had never been any different than it was at that moment.

After some time, Noroelle asked, "Tell me what happened this evening."

Nuramon told her everything, not forgetting the queen's veiled compliment to her. Noroelle seemed particularly moved when he spoke about the connection to Gaomee and the oracle's prophecy. Nuramon finished by saying, "I feel the change in me. The queen has kindled a fire that now has to burn. I'm the same as I was before, but I can finally act."

"Is that why you can touch me only now?"

"I was scared before. And when I'm scared, I do foolish things. I was scared you might turn your back on me. I was scared you might choose me. I was torn."

"You and Farodin, you're both very odd. Today, at the lake, it looked like you would never try to get closer to me and as if Farodin would never vouchsafe me even a hint of what is deep inside him. Tonight, though, you have both been transformed."

"Except that Farodin was faster than me."

"That isn't fair, Nuramon . . . only because he found the way to me first? Should I chastise you because the queen was alone with you in your chamber? No. A night for me is just one moment, and because you both came to me tonight, you came in the same moment. You see time as scarce merchandise, Nuramon."

"Is that so surprising? If my fate is to go the way of my predecessors, then every moment left to me is precious."

"You will not go down that path. You will live a long life and go into the moonlight."

Nuramon looked up to the moon above. "It is so mystifying that something I love as much as the moon has not taken my soul into it in all this time." He fell silent and thought of all the stories he had heard about the moon. His grandmother had told him about how things looked in the human realm.

"Did you know that in Mandred's world, the moon changes its shape?" Nuramon asked.

"No, I have never heard that."

"It's true," he said. "And it is much smaller than our moon. As the days pass, it loses part of itself. It transforms night by night into a sickle, until it disappears completely. Then it gradually grows to its full size again."

"That sounds like magic. I don't know very much about the Other World. I learned some of their languages from my parents, but really, I know nothing about the world of humans. Which magic might work there? Can elves go into the moonlight in the human world? What happens if they die there?"

"Those are questions that only the wise can answer."

"But what do you think, Nuramon?"

"I think the magic that works there must be related to our own, and that an elf can go into the moonlight of the humans. It's just that the moon is farther away, so it is a much longer journey. And if an elf dies in the human world, then it is no different than if an elf dies here. Death does not separate the realms." He looked at her and saw a shadow of concern in her expression. "You are afraid for us, for our lives."

"The elfhunt almost never ventures into the human world. Can you remember if an elf has ever died there and been reborn here?"

"It is said that one of my incarnations perished outside our world, yet here I am."

Noroelle laughed, stroked his cheek, and then looked at him as if spellbound. "Your face is unique."

"And yours is—"

She put a finger to his lips. "No, you have spoken such words to me for years. Now these words are for you. Be silent, fairest Albenchild." She took her finger from his lips, and he was silent.

Gently, she stroked his hair. "You always thought the women here would only ever make fun of you. And they do. It's true. They taunt you for your name, for your fate . . . they do it because you have always been taunted. But your looks have not been lost on them. You would not believe the things they say in low voices behind their hands, the whispers I've heard."

Nuramon went to say something, but Noroelle again laid her finger to his lips. "No. You have to hold your tongue now, like the two trees down there." She took her hand away. "You are far more than what these women secretly see in you. The oracle was right. 'Everything you are is within you.' And everything that is within you . . . is what I love, Nuramon," she said, and kissed him.

When she moved her lips away from his again and looked at him, he cautiously began to speak. "Everything has changed. I can barely believe that I'm here with you. What's happened?" He looked around, as if he might find the answer there on the terrace or in the depths of the night.

"Nothing that you or I or Farodin could have contrived. This was something only the queen could make possible. The world is at your feet now."

"It's not the *world* I want."

She nodded. "When you both return, I will decide. You have done everything you could. Now it's up to me . . . I must admit, I'd hoped you both could spend many more years courting me, but that was probably a dream. I have to choose one or the other. What a loss, whichever of you I have to turn away. But what good fortune for another woman."

They looked at each other, not saying a word. Nuramon knew how much her rejection would hurt him. For him, there was no other, not one for whom he could feel such love. He kissed her hands once again, stroked her cheek, and said, "Let's try, for now, not to think about it. It is something to face when Farodin and I return."

She nodded.

"Will you be there tomorrow, or do we say good-bye now?"

"I will be there," she said quietly.

"Then I look forward to tomorrow. What color dress will you wear?"

"Green. Obilee made it," Noroelle said and absently swept a strand of hair from her face. Nuramon liked the unconscious gesture. She grasped the strand between her ring finger and little finger when she swept it back.

"Then it has to be beautiful," he said.

"I'm very curious about what the queen is having brought to you. Whatever it is, it will be more precious than anything that anyone else could have given you."

"Given? I will accept it for the elfhunt, but when we come back, I will return it."

Noroelle laughed. "No, Nuramon. The queen is generous. She won't take it back."

He kissed her on the forehead. "I have to go now, Noroelle."

"Maybe one of your relatives will still find it in their heart to visit you in your chamber."

"I will believe it if it happens." He took her hands in his and said, "But who knows?" He looked up at the stars. "Everything seems possible tonight." Then he let go her hands. "Good night, Noroelle."

She kissed him farewell.

When Nuramon was at the door to the banquet hall, he looked back at her one more time. She was simply perfect, her flawlessness clearer to him now more than ever before.

When he reached the corridor where those named to the elfhunt had their chambers, he realized that all of the doors were now closed. All the expected visitors were already there. No one seemed to be waiting for new arrivals. From the confusion of voices, it was clear that many had come.

In front of his own door, Nuramon stopped and listened. There was no sound from inside. He hoped so dearly that one of his own relatives had found the courage to visit him and was inside the room, waiting.

Nuramon opened the door and looked in. A figure stood inside, motionless, beside his bed, his back to Nuramon. Nuramon's joy lasted no more than a heartbeat, though. In his absence, someone had brought in an armor stand, and in the dim light cast by the barinstones, Nuramon—hoping beyond hope—had mistaken it for an elf.

Crestfallen and again alone, he closed the door behind him. He crossed to the armor stand and looked at the queen's gifts: a cloak, a suit of armor, and a short sword.

Nuramon lifted the wine-red cloak from the stand and weighed it in his hand. It was heavy, made of wool and linen, a work of superb craftsmanship and woven with magical threads that would keep any gust of wind or drop of water at bay. It would protect him from both heat and cold.

Noroelle also possessed such a cloak. She had brought it with her from Alvemer. The queen, no doubt, had not given him this one thoughtlessly. A gift from Alvemer was a piece of Noroelle's hometown. If he had to ride through winter in the human world, then he would ride warm.

He folded the cloak and laid it on the stone bench. He looked the armor over with curiosity. It was dragon mail, the armor of a dragon slayer. Armor like this was renowned for being tough yet supple, and it required extreme skill to make such an outfit. The armor had been assembled from many pieces of dragon skin, and it protected the upper body and arms. Whoever had put this piece together was clearly a master of his trade. He had sliced each fragment of dragon skin into a multitude of thin layers, then worked them and reassembled them as he had seen fit. Drop-shaped pieces had been stitched between the individual layers. Probably trimmed dragon scales, Nuramon thought, but what they really were remained the armorer's secret. The leather gave off an agreeable odor. The stink of dragon had been eliminated during the tanning of the skin and replaced by the milder scent of the forest.

The only place that dragon mail was still made was in Olvedes, the only place where the fire-spitting monsters were still a danger. The armorers of Olvedes were renowned throughout Albenmark and were known to leave their mark on the pieces they made. Nuramon released the baldric and lifted the armor from the stand. He searched the inside for the sign of the armorer who had made this masterpiece. He found it hidden on the breastplate: an image of the sun and a name underneath in small letters. Xeldaric.

Nuramon was moved. Xeldaric was one of the greatest armorers who had ever lived. He had gone into the moonlight in the Royal Hall after handing over his life's work to the queen: a complete suit of Alben armor. Nuramon was still a child when he heard about it.

To wear a suit of armor made by the hands of Xeldaric was a great honor. And even if one did not go to the trouble of searching for the sign of the armorer, it was easy to see that the armor was a truly breathtaking gift. At first glance, it might have lacked the uniformity of plate armor, but every piece of it was where it was supposed to be and told the history of the dragonhunt. The green skin of the dragons of Olvedes had been worked in alongside the brown leather of the forest dragons of Galvelun and the red sun dragons of Ischemon. Together, the fragments formed a mosaic in the colors of the forest, each flowing into the other.

Nuramon returned the armor to the stand. He took up the sword belt that he had laid on the bed. On it was a sword in a plain leather sheath. The cradle-shaped pommel and cross guard were gold and elaborately worked, and the grip was finished in strips of mother-of-pearl and copper. Nuramon slid the weapon from its sheath, and his breath caught. The blade was made of starshine, a metal only found on the highest summits. The sword was as much a masterwork as was the armor. Intertwined runes were engraved in the center of the broad cross guard. It was only on second glance that Nuramon realized what was written there: Gaomee. He was holding Gaomee's sword in his hands. The weapon with which Gaomee had defeated Duanoc. And now it was his to wield.

THE CALL
OF THE QUEEN

Farodin had farewelled his visitors early. He wanted to be alone to gather his thoughts, but this was proving difficult. From next door rang the sounds of drinking and merrymaking. The human was mad. No one in their right mind got drunk the night before the elfhunt. And that braying laugh could only mean that Aigilaos had joined him in his folly.

He lay on the hard bed, familiar to him from other nights like this one. A quiet pleasure stole over him as he recalled the events of the evening. He had finally dared to open himself to Noroelle. Finally dared—in his *own* clumsy words—to speak directly of his love for her. And those few sentences, spoken from his heart, gave him what a thousand songs could not. He was certain that he had won Noroelle for himself this evening.

A gentle knock on the door roused him from his thoughts. A kobold carrying a large signal lamp entered. "Please pardon my interruption of your rest the night before the hunt, my lord. The queen wishes to see you. Please follow me."

Surprised, the elf threw his robe around his shoulders. What could have happened?

The kobold peered left and right along the corridor cautiously. His nostrils flared like a hound picking up a scent. "All clear, my lord," he said in a conspiratorial whisper. He hurried down the corridor in long bounds and opened a door hidden behind a tapestry that depicted a stag hunt, then led Farodin up a narrow stairway normally used only by kobolds and gnomes. Beneath a landing, he opened a second hidden door that concealed a tiled passageway. Now and then, the kobold turned back and smiled at Farodin. He was obviously enjoying the role Emerelle had assigned him.

They came to a spiral staircase hidden inside a massive column. Farodin could hear soft strains of music seeping through the walls.

He thought uneasily of the last time Emerelle had given him a secret assignment. Then, too, he had killed for his queen. Seven hundred years earlier, during the troll wars, something inside Farodin had been destroyed. Only the queen knew about it, and she had taken advantage of that knowledge. He kept this dark part of his soul hidden away. At court, one only ever saw the gracious and rather superficial minnesinger, but when he met Noroelle for the first time, a seed of hope sprang to life inside him, that he might again be the elf he had once been. She alone had wrought that miracle.

The kobold stopped short at the end of the spiral stairway, in front of a gray wooden door. "I may escort you no farther, my lord." He handed the lantern to Farodin. "You know the way. I will wait here."

Farodin felt a slight draft on his face as he stepped through the door. The melody of an old, familiar song drifted on the air. It was a song his mother had often sung to him when he was still a child, a song about the exodus of the Alben.

The passage opened at the back of a statue of a dryad. With an effort, Farodin edged through a narrow gap between the statue and the stonework of the wall, coming out on a small balcony high above the hall of the falling water. He glanced up to see the roof of a tower, twisted like the shell of a sea snail.

"I am happy you answered my call so quickly, Farodin." It was a voice he knew well. The elven warrior turned. Behind him, Emerelle had emerged onto the balcony. She wore a plain white nightgown and had wrapped a thin shawl around her shoulders.

"I am deeply concerned, Farodin," Emerelle went on. "An aura of disaster surrounds the mortal. There is something about him that evades my magic, and I am frightened at how he managed to reach Albenmark at all. He is the first human ever, the first we did not summon. No other has ever made it through the gate to Albenmark alone."

"Perhaps it was just a coincidence," Farodin said. "A caprice of the magic."

Emerelle nodded slowly. "That is possible. But there may be more behind it. There is something else beyond the stone circle . . . something hiding itself from me. And Mandred is connected to it. Be on your guard, Farodin, when you ride into the Other World. Mandred's story cannot be true. I have spent many hours conferring with the elders. None of them has ever heard of a manboar."

Emerelle paused, and when she continued, the concern was gone from her words. She sounded cool and accustomed to giving orders. "If the human is a liar, Farodin, kill him. As you killed the princes of Arkadien and all the other enemies of Albenmark for me."

NIGHT IN THE PALACE

Mandred was leaning against the centaur's flank. The red stuff the centaur had brought with him—wine, he came to learn—was strong. Mandred had heard of it before, but all they drank in Firnstayn was mead and beer.

He raised the heavy gold cup unsteadily. "To our friendship, Aigil . . . Ailalaos? Your name is unpronounceable."

"You think mine's bad. You should hear the names of the one-eyed trolls up on the Klippenburg," the centaur slurred. "The trolls of Dailos are crazy . . . They tear out one of their own eyes to honor their greatest hero."

Mandred was impressed. That was loyalty. No chance of anything like that among the elves. They were all so . . . the warrior couldn't think of a suitable word. Cold, decorous, arrogant? They certainly had no idea how to celebrate. Then again, they had brought the goblets with them and offered him this little banquet hall to spend the night in. Just as he was getting into the swing of things with Aigilaos, the elves, one after the other, had said good night and left. *Soft. Every last one of them.*

"A man who can't drink is not a man," declared Mandred.

"That's the truth," the centaur agreed, his voice raw.

Mandred tottered back a step and clinked goblets with Aigilaos again. These gold cups weren't really suitable for a proper toast. The elves certainly made pretty things, but they were not exactly robust. His goblet already had a sizable dent in the side. With mead horns, that was unthinkable. For a moment, Mandred was worried he might be in trouble for the damage. Then he remembered that the elves had been generous with their gifts. If they took him to task about the chalice, he would simply return one of the gifts as compensation.

The warrior looked at the things they had given him, set out in a row on a stone bench beside the door. A chain mail tunic beyond anything even the princes of the Fjordlands possessed. A gold-clad helmet with flexible cheek plates and an attached chain-mesh braid that hung far down the back of his neck. A richly embroidered leather quiver filled with light javelins. A boar spear, its long blade giving off a bluish shimmer. A magnificent saddle with silver fittings, and the queen had promised him a horse from her own stable in the morning, one that was willing to carry a human, was how she had put it. Mandred snorted in annoyance. As if a horse would cause him any trouble. If the beast acted up, he'd simply wallop it on the head; that had always worked. No one liked a smack on the head, not even a bloody-minded horse.

"You look down, my friend," Aigilaos said and threw one arm around Mandred's shoulders. "We'll run the beast to ground soon enough. You'll see. Tomorrow night we'll stick its head on a pike in the middle of the village."

"Better kill the dragon before you carve up its hide," came a familiar voice.

Mandred turned. In the door stood Ollowain, dressed in flawless white. With a long stride, he stepped over a pile of dung marring the colorful mosaic of the floor. "I see you've succeeded in giving the hunters' chambers the ambience of a stable," he said, a thin smile on his lips. "In all the centuries of the elfhunt, no one else has ever managed that."

Mandred planted himself in the elf's path. "Unless I'm mistaken, the hunt has never been led by a human before either."

Ollowain nodded deliberately. "Even the mighty make mistakes." He reached down and loosened the sword belt around his hips. He wrapped the silver-studded belt carefully around the sheath, then handed the weapon to Mandred. "I should not have hit you."

Mandred looked at the slim sword in astonishment, but did not take it. "Why not?" In the same circumstances, he would not have acted any differently than Ollowain. What was dishonorable about beating up someone dumb enough to pick a fight with a better fighter?

"It was inappropriate. You are a guest of the queen," the elf said. He pointed to the slice in his cape. "You missed me by a hair's breadth. You—a human. That made me angry . . . but be that as it may, I should not have hit you. You are skillful . . . for a human."

Mandred reached for the sword. It was the weapon he had fought Ollowain with, a sword fit for a king. "Actually, I'm not very good with a sword," Mandred replied, grinning. "You should have given me an axe."

Ollowain's eyebrows twitched momentarily, but his face otherwise remained an expressionless mask. He reached under his cape and came up with a red finger-thick braid. "This belongs to you, mortal." His eyes were sparkling.

It took Mandred a moment to realize what Ollowain was holding out to him. Shocked, he lifted his hand to his hair and found the stumpy remains of one of his braids just above his temple. Anger flared inside him.

"You . . . you've mutilated me, you treacherous bastard! You . . . monster! Elf spawn!" Mandred tried to draw the sword, but the belt was wound around the cross guard and sheath, and he was not able to unsheathe it even an inch. In a temper, he flung the weapon aside and raised his fists. "I'll pound that pretty nose of yours to porridge!"

The elf dodged Mandred's fist with a quick bob.

"We'll give him a thrashing to remember," Aigilaos growled and reared onto his hind legs.

Ollowain dived under Aigilaos's whirling hooves and came to his feet again in a single fluid movement, then punched the centaur on his flank.

Aigilaos let out a furious cry. His hooves lost their grip on the mosaic floor, and he started to slip and skidded through a puddle of spilled wine.

Mandred tried to jump out of the way of the tumbling centaur, but his friend, in a desperate bid to hold on to him, threw his arms out wide, and both of them hit the floor. The fall knocked the wind out of Mandred. For a moment, he lay there, gasping for breath. Half crushed under the centaur, he was having trouble even moving.

Ollowain grabbed hold of Mandred's arm and pulled him out from under Aigilaos when the centaur tried—in vain—to get back on his feet.

"Take small breaths," the elf ordered.

Mandred panted like a dog. He felt dizzy, but slowly, slowly the air returned to his lungs.

"How can anyone be so egotistical as to drink himself blind the night before a dangerous hunt?" Ollowain shook his head. "Every time I see you, you manage to make me lose my self-control, Mortal Mandred. If your own well-being means nothing to you, think about the well-being of the men and women who will ride with you. Tomorrow, you're the leader. You are responsible for them. I'll send some kobolds to muck out this stable, take the wine, and leave a few buckets of water behind. And I hope you're halfway back to your senses by morning."

"Milksop," Aigilaos slurred. "Someone like you could never understand a real man."

The elf smiled. "Indeed, I have never tried to imagine what a horse might be thinking."

Mandred held his tongue. He would have liked nothing more than to knock Ollowain down, but he knew he would never be able to beat the elf. Worse still, deep down, he knew Ollowain was right. It was stupid of him to get drunk. The wine, so sweet, so easy to swallow, had seduced him. It had numbed his fear, the fear that Freya no longer lived, the fear of having to face the manboar again.

VALEDICTION

The Royal Hall was seldom as busy as it was that morning. Noroelle stood close to one of the walls, where the water streamed down in a whisper. At her side was Obilee, her ward and confidante, a delicate girl of just fifteen. Her timidity showed in the way she stood, but her expression reflected her curiosity. Like Noroelle, she came from Alvemer, and to the older elf, she was the younger sister Noroelle had always wished for. Obilee, with her blond hair and green eyes, had little in common with Noroelle when it came to looks, but they knew each other as well as any siblings. Like Noroelle, she had left her homeland when she was still young. Noroelle had come here with her parents, whereas Obilee had been put into Noroelle's care by her grandmother.

"Look, Noroelle," Obilee whispered. "Everyone is looking at you. They want to know what favors you will give to your suitors to take with them. Watch out. They'll pick up every gesture and every word." She moved her lips closer to Noroelle's ear. "This is the hour when new customs are born."

Noroelle looked around quickly. Feeling so many eyes on her made her anxious. She was often at the royal court but had not yet grown used to it. Speaking low, she replied, "You're mistaken. It's the dress they are looking at. You have really outdone yourself this time. Anyone would think you had faery hands."

"Perhaps it's a little of both," said Obilee, smiling. Then she looked past Noroelle, and her smile gave way to astonishment.

Noroelle followed her companion's gaze and saw Master Alvias approaching her. He nodded pleasantly. "Noroelle, the queen would like to see you at her throne."

The elf noticed the many curious glances that Alvias's approach attracted, but she hid her uncertainty. "I will follow you, Alvias," she said, then turned to Obilee. "Come along."

"But she just wants—"

"Come with me, Obilee." Noroelle took the young elf by the hand. "Listen carefully. We will be standing before the queen in a moment, and she will ask me who you are."

"But the queen knows who I am, doesn't she? She knows who everyone is here."

"But you have never been introduced to her. Once I've spoken your name, you will be a part of court society."

"But what do *I* have to say?"

"Not a word. Unless the queen asks you something, of course."

Alvias said nothing. There was neither a smile nor distrust to be read on his face. Noroelle and Obilee followed the master to the queen's throne. Those they passed met Noroelle with words and gestures of respect. When they came to the throne, Master Alvias stepped to one side, and Noroelle and Obilee bowed their heads.

"I greet you, Noroelle," Emerelle said and looked to Obilee before asking, "Whom do we have here?"

Noroelle turned slightly and gestured elegantly at the young elf. "This is Obilee, the daughter of Halvaric and Orone from Alvemer."

Emerelle smiled at the young elf. "Then you come from the clan of the great Danee. You are her great-granddaughter. Everyone here will be watching the path you follow. With Noroelle, you are in good hands." She turned back to Noroelle and said, "It has not escaped me that there is a bond between you and two companions of the elfhunt."

"There is," Noroelle replied.

"You enjoy the affections of both Farodin and Nuramon."

"That is true."

"An elfhunt in which the queen and her warriors' beloved do not see eye to eye is doomed to fail from the start. So I ask you, will you, as the beloved of Farodin and Nuramon, release them for the elfhunt?"

Noroelle's mind went back to the fear that had accompanied her dreams the night before, where she had seen Farodin and Nuramon suffering. Despite her pride in both of them, she would have preferred them not to have to be part of the elfhunt. But she understood that the queen's question was a gesture, no more. Noroelle was not free to reject Emerelle's wish. If the queen called on the assistance of the men Noroelle loved, then she could not refuse. She sighed softly and noticed that silence had settled over the hall. The only sound was the low drone of the water.

"I will surrender them for the elfhunt," said Noroelle finally. "Whatever task *you* charge them with, they will do for *me*."

Emerelle stood and approached Noroelle. She said, "So are the queen and her warriors' lady united." She took Noroelle and Obilee by the hand and led them back up the steps to stand beside her throne. She took her seat again.

Noroelle had stood there often, but as usual, she felt out of place. She saw admiration in many eyes, but a trace of mockery in some as well. Neither the one nor the other pleased her. With a curt motion, the queen gestured to Noroelle to lean down to her. "Trust me," she whispered in Noroelle's ear. "I have sent many on the hunt. And Farodin and Nuramon will also come back."

"I thank you, Emerelle, and I trust you," Noroelle said.

Now Master Alvias stepped up to the queen. "Emerelle, they are waiting at the door."

The queen nodded to Alvias, who turned, spread his arms wide, and called in a resounding voice, "The elfhunt is waiting at the door." He pointed to the far side of the enormous hall. "Once loosed, they will pursue their quarry until they have completed their task or failed. Once we open this door, there is no turning back for the hunters." The elves crowding the hall parted to form a broad aisle, along which Alvias strode. "As is customary, you must advise your queen," he said, directing his words at several elves close by, clearly representing all present. "Consider the circumstances. There is a fearsome beast in the human realm. Close to our borders. Should our queen keep the door closed and accept that something is roaming the lands beyond, something that could one day be a danger to us as well? Or should she open it and give us the chance to free the people of the Fjordlands from the beast? Both paths could lead to fortune or ruin. If we keep the door closed, the beast might one day find a way through it to us. If we open it, elven blood may be spilled in the service of mortals. The choice is yours."

Alvias gestured toward Emerelle, his hand open. "Advise the queen on how she should proceed," he said and returned to Emerelle, bowing before her.

The eyes of all present turned from the door to the queen and back again. Soon, the first voices rose exhorting Emerelle to open the door, but others spoke against it. Noroelle saw that those against included Nuramon's relatives. She had expected nothing else. The fear in their eyes was obvious, but it was not fear for Nuramon. It was the fear of his death and its consequences.

The queen asked among her subjects, selecting this one or that to explain their choice, listening patiently. This time, she consulted with more of them than usual. When she asked Elemon, one of Nuramon's uncles, why he wanted to see the door remain closed, he replied, "Because to open it could lead to hardship, as Alvias said."

"Hardship?" the queen said and looked intently at him. "You're right. That may happen."

Now Pelveric from Olvedes stepped forward. Among the soldiers, his words carried considerable weight. "Emerelle, think of the elven blood that might be spilled. Why should we help the humans? Why should their problems concern us? When was the last time they helped us?"

"It was a long time ago" was all Emerelle said. Finally, she turned to Noroelle and whispered, "I want to hear *your* counsel."

Noroelle hesitated. She could advise the queen to keep the door closed. Like so many others, she could speak of elven blood and the thanklessness of the humans, but she knew that such words only showed her apprehension about the lives of the men she loved. Here, now, it was about much more. Quietly, she said, "My heart fears for Farodin and Nuramon, but the right thing to do is to open the door."

Then the queen rose majestically to her feet. The murmur of the waters flowing down the walls swelled gradually. Emerelle gazed across the hall to the entrance at the far side. She seemed not to notice the glittering mist as it filled the air, rose to the open sky above, and transformed into a broad rainbow in the sunlight. All at once, the walls behind the water began to glow. There was a hiss, and a breeze wafted through the hall. The wings of the door swung wide to reveal the band of hunters. The water settled again, but the mist and the rainbow remained.

The hunters paused momentarily beneath the arched doorway before entering. At their head was Mandred, the human, who looked up with awe at the rainbow, then turned his eyes to the queen. Behind him

came Farodin and Nuramon, and behind them Brandan, the tracker;
Vanna, the sorceress; Aigilaos, the archer; and Lijema, the wolfmother.
It was an unusual sight, a human among the companions of the elfhunt,
though he looked more like the elves than did the centaur, Aigilaos. The
elves, however, had grown accustomed over the years to the possibility
that centaurs could be part of the elfhunt. But a human? That Mandred
marched at the head of the company made the spectacle even stranger.
Until today, every elfhunt had been led by an elf.

Nuramon and Farodin resembled the heroes of the old sagas. Farodin,
as usual, looked flawless, and Nuramon—for the first time—also looked
the ideal of an elven warrior. And not only in Noroelle's eyes. She saw
the esteem in the eyes of those standing there. It made her happy. Even
if their recognition turned out to be short-lived, no one could take this
moment away from him.

The small troop approached the queen. When they came to the
steps leading to the throne, the elves went down on one knee. Even the
centaur made an effort to bow as deeply as he could. Only Mandred
remained upright, and seemed surprised at the obeisance displayed
by his companions. He was about to follow their lead when the queen
spoke to him in his language.

"No, Mandred. In the Other World you are the jarl of your com-
munity—a prince among men. You do not need to kneel before the
elven queen."

Mandred looked at her in surprise, but said nothing.

"The others, arise," said the queen. These words, too, Emerelle
spoke in the language of the Fjordlands. Some of those present were
obviously not familiar with the language and watched the proceedings
with resentment.

The language of the Fjordlands. Noroelle's parents had taught her
many of the languages of humans, but Noroelle herself had never left
Albenmark. The wild human lands were a place she had only ever seen
in her imagination.

The queen turned back to Mandred. "You have been twice honored
at my hand. You are the first human ever to take part in the elfhunt, and
I have made you its leader. I cannot expect you to behave like an elf. My
choosing you has offended many among the Albenkin, but the power

of Atta Aikhjarto lives in you. I trust your senses. None of us knows your homeland as you know it. You will be a good leader for your companions, but in everything you do, remember what you promised me."

"I will keep my word, Queen."

Noroelle had heard of the pact the human had made with the queen. She looked keenly at Mandred and was surprised at his appearance. Having arrived at court late the evening before, she had had no opportunity to see him until now. And she had not ventured into the wing of the palace where the companions had been billeted the night before. She had heard the various rumors that surrounded Mandred, though, and seeing him now, she concluded that not all could be fairly ascribed to him. True, he was as broad as a bear, and at first glance—with all that hair, red as sunset, cascading wildly over his shoulders—he looked threatening. He had twisted several thin braids into his hair and, like many of the centaurs, was also bearded. His face was coarse but honest. He looked unusually pale to her, and dark rings surrounded his eyes. Perhaps, in all the excitement, he hadn't been able to sleep? He must have been very proud at being honored by the queen in this way. Now he bore a great responsibility. Noroelle shuddered at the thought of the price he had to pay for the queen's help. If she were ever to have a child, she would never give it up. She looked at the two men she loved . . . the question was not whether she would have a child, but rather, with whom.

As if he had heard her thoughts, Mandred briefly looked at her and smiled. Obilee grasped her by the hand. The girl was shaking. Noroelle kept calm and looked into the human's blue eyes. What she saw there was not the lecherous gaze she had been told about at court. As coarse as he looked, there was great depth of feeling in his eyes. One could feel safe in his presence, and she knew she could entrust the men she loved to his care. She looked to Nuramon and Farodin. Ever since they had declared their love to her twenty years earlier, one or the other of them had always been close by. Now she would be alone, and she did not know for how long.

"You know what has to be done," said the queen. "You are equipped and rested. Are you ready?"

The elven warriors answered one by one, each with the words "I am ready."

"Farodin and Nuramon, approach." The two elves did as Emerelle commanded. "I am your queen, and you stand under my protection. But you also serve another, your lady. I cannot speak for her. She has decided." She led Noroelle down the steps to Farodin and Nuramon. Obilee trailed behind. "Here she is."

Noroelle took them both by the hand and said, "If you serve me, you serve the queen."

"Then we will always serve the queen," declared Farodin.

"May our deeds please you both," said Nuramon.

She kissed their hands.

Noroelle knew that the moment of departure had arrived, but it had come too soon for her liking. She did not want to say farewell to the men she loved here, in front of everyone. "Your lady has one more wish. She would like to accompany you as far as the Aikhjarto gate."

Farodin exchanged a glance with Nuramon. "We are obliged to do what our lady requests."

The queen smiled and took Noroelle and Obilee by the hand. "Here, Mandred, are two more who will be in your charge as far as the gate. Treat them well."

"I will," the jarl said.

The queen looked up, as if she could see something in the gleam of the sun that was hidden from more common eyes. "The day is still young, Mandred. Go and save your village."

Mandred took his place at the head of the elfhunt, with Noroelle and Obilee in the middle. The assembled Albenkin wished them luck as they made their way back down the aisle. Noroelle turned for a moment to look at the queen and saw her standing in front of her throne, a look of apprehension on her face as she watched the small company depart. Was she afraid that something might befall them? If that were so, then until that moment, Emerelle had kept her fears well hidden.

Obilee pulled Noroelle out of her thoughts. "I wish I were part of the elfhunt," she said.

"Right now, it looks like you are."

"You know what I mean."

"Of course. But didn't you hear what the queen said? And haven't I myself told you often enough that you look like Danee? One day, you too will be as revered as she is, as both a great sorceress and master of the sword."

The company strode through the hall and out into the open courtyard beyond, which was crowded with Albenkin. Even the kobolds and gnomes had come to watch the departure of the elfhunt. An elfhunt led by a human was something special. This was a day that would be talked about for years to come.

The companions' horses stood ready, their equipment already stowed. Only the centaur, Aigilaos, still took a number of bags and bound them to his back, cursing in a low voice about his stiff neck. The previous night had obviously not been particularly comfortable for him.

While Master Alvias arranged two more horses, Noroelle watched Farodin and Nuramon. They suddenly looked so uncertain. Very soon, both of them would be separated from her. What words would they find for her in this situation? What words could console their beloved?

"Is the elfhunt ready?" called Mandred, as court ceremony required. His companions nodded, and the human called, "Then ride."

And the elfhunt set off. At its head rode the human, behind him, Noroelle. To her left rode Nuramon, to her right, Farodin. Behind her came Obilee, and around her trotted Brandan, Vanna, and Aigilaos. Lijema brought up the rear. Loud cries of farewell accompanied them to the gate, and the kobolds cried loudest of all.

Once through the gate, Noroelle could scarcely believe what she saw before her. Across the broad meadow were gathered more Albenkin than had ever assembled before. All of them were there to see the elfhunt ride out. High above the meadow, the wings of the riverbank sprites glittered in the sunlight. The faeries were well-known for their curiosity. Close to the road they traveled along stood elves from both the heartland and from the farthest corners of the kingdom. Some of them had not managed to reach the royal court the day before, but they did not want to miss the departure of the elfhunt this morning. From here and there, shouts of greeting rang out. On the hills that edged the forest, too, elves stood in front of the houses of the emissaries, waving as the small band rode past.

All of a sudden, Noroelle saw a little faery flying close to Mandred's head. The human swatted at it like he would a bothersome insect, but missed. The faery shrieked and flew to Noroelle. Mandred looked around. He had heard the shriek but evidently was unable to see what made it.

Gradually, Mandred increased their speed. He seemed to have acquired a liking for riding an elven horse. She hoped he would not fall. It was said that he was far from skillful when he rode on Aigilaos's back.

When they had left the Albenkin and their well-wishing behind, and with the wide meadowlands ahead of them, Lijema galloped past on the right and, a moment later, was riding beside Mandred. Mandred looked at her in surprise. But Lijema took her wooden flute from her belt and blew into it. She blew hard, that was clear, but no sound could be heard from the flute.

Moments later, Obilee cried, "There! Look there!" She pointed off to the right. Something white broke from the forest's shadows and approached rapidly.

"There they are," Aigilaos called.

"There are seven!" said Nuramon.

"Seven?" Farodin spoke now. "Incredible."

Mandred turned in his saddle. "Seven what?"

Noroelle knew, as any of the Albenkin would. The white wolves of the elfhunt. Until the moment they joined the hunt, no one could say how many there would be. The more wolves that appeared, the more important the occasion . . . at least, that's what people said.

"Those are our wolves," Lijema shouted to Mandred.

"Wolves? Those are *big* wolves."

Noroelle smiled. The wolves were the size of ponies, their pelts heavy and white.

"Are they dangerous?" she heard Mandred ask. But over the sound of hoofbeats, Lijema did not hear what he said. "Are they dangerous?" he repeated, more loudly.

Lijema smiled. "Of course."

When the wolves caught up with the riders, four of them took positions at the head of the band. One ran at the left and one at the right, while the seventh wolf loped at Lijema's side.

The riders soon reached the edge of the forest and reined in their horses to look back one last time at the queen's palace.

Farodin and Nuramon were captivated by the sight, and even Mandred seemed affected. Nuramon's face, in particular, betrayed his secret fears. And although Farodin tried to keep his feelings hidden, Noroelle saw through his mask of composure.

The wolves were impatient and surrounded Mandred's horse. The human seemed unsure how to deal with the creatures and kept a wary eye on them at every moment. *He must have had bad experiences with wolves*, thought Noroelle. Maybe wolves in his world were a danger to life and limb, like the wolves in Galvelun were for the Albenkin. When Mandred saw Noroelle watching him, he leaned down in the saddle and stroked the largest of the wolves on the fur of its neck, as if to prove his courage. It pleased the beast.

"Shall we ride?" the human asked. The wolf growled and looked up at him.

Lijema laughed. "It does not speak the language of the Fjordlands, but it likes you." Speaking in Elvish, Lijema explained to the wolves why Mandred could not understand them, then she translated the human's question. The wolf tilted its head and grew suddenly restless. The restlessness spread to the other wolves, and they began to trot around, one or two running ahead then returning to Mandred. They wanted to be on the move.

"Do they understand what you say?"

"Every word," said Lijema. "Believe me when I say they are smarter than some of the elves."

"And them? How do they speak?" Mandred asked.

Lijema stroked the fur of the largest of the wolves. "They have their own language. I speak it, too."

Noroelle smiled. This human wore his heart on his sleeve. The way he watched the large wolf, the way he raised his eyebrows and chewed at his lip, there was only one thing he could be thinking: a wolf like that would be the perfect creature to take in search of game.

"They must make great hunting companions," said Mandred, and Noroelle had to make an effort to stop herself from laughing aloud.

"No doubt," Lijema replied.

"Are they as loyal as dogs?"

Lijema laughed cheerfully. "No, you can't compare them to dogs. They are much smarter. Say again what you just said."

"In Fjordlandish?"

"Yes."

"Shall we ride?"

Once again, the animals suddenly grew restive, wanting to be on the move.

"Well, then . . . let's ride," Mandred cried, and the elfhunt set off again.

The silence between Noroelle and her two suitors persisted. The seven wolves stirred Noroelle's concern for the men she loved. The animals had a sense of the gravity of the danger awaiting the hunters. They themselves decided how big the pack would be that joined the elfhunt. When Gaomee had ridden against the dragon Duanoc, eight wolves accompanied her. What kind of beast could it be, lurking there beyond the stone circle? She trusted in the skills of Nuramon and Farodin, but even great heroes died in battle. What if the worst came to pass? What if Nuramon was wrong? What if an elven soul that died in the human world could not be reborn in Albenmark?

They passed the faun oak and Noroelle's lake. Only yesterday, she had sat here listening to Farodin and Nuramon. Noroelle wondered whether such a day would ever come again.

When they reached the fortified tower at the Shalyn Falah, they halted briefly while Aigilaos departed. With his horseshoes, he could not cross the white bridge. The centaur cursed the ancient structure, then muttered that he would see them at the gate and cantered off.

Noroelle watched the centaur leave and thought of the stories that were told about him. No doubt he envied the elven steeds with their unshod hooves and elven dexterity, able to cross the bridge without a second thought.

"Why did he have his feet shod at all if it prevents him from crossing the bridge?" Mandred asked.

"They say the kobolds at court told him he would be able to gallop faster with horseshoes," Lijema answered. "He believes he's faster now but has to accept the detour whenever he comes this way."

Mandred laughed. "Sounds just like Aigilaos."

They moved on. At the tower of Shalyn Falah, Ollowain was waiting for them. Mandred greeted him coolly, which drew an amused smile from Ollowain. They passed the tower quickly. Noroelle wondered what had occurred between Ollowain and Mandred.

They reached the far side of the Shalyn Falah and followed the wide path on the other side, riding past the remains of the stone circle at Welruun. The trolls had destroyed it a long time ago. Noroelle had not been there to witness it, but the trees and the forest spirits remembered it well. In earlier times, the gate of Welruun led to one of the prince-doms of the trolls. Noroelle could clearly feel the power of the seven Albenpaths that crossed there to form a major Albenstar. The trolls had found a way to seal the gate, and no elf knew what magic they had used to do so.

The forest grew denser and denser. Noroelle remembered how, when she was younger, she had come here often. She loved these woods.

The troop followed the path downhill, trotting between the birch trees until they reached the large clearing, within which stood the rise with the stone circle. At the foot of the rise, they stopped and waited for Aigilaos. Mandred dismounted and, saying nothing, moved away from the others. He wanted to pay a visit to Atta Aikhjarto.

Noroelle had heard that the oak had saved Mandred's life. She wondered what Atta Aikhjarto had seen in Mandred. The faun oak had once confided in her that old Atta Aikhjarto could see into the future. What did the old oak know that would make it curtail its own powers to save the life of a human?

Noroelle allowed Farodin to assist her from her horse. Nuramon came a moment too late and instead helped Obilee dismount. The young elf was so taken by Nuramon's gesture that her cheeks turned red. He led her to Noroelle.

They sat together in the grass, but it was still too early for words. The others also soon fell silent, and even the wolves were unusually hushed.

Only when Aigilaos appeared did the companions start speaking again. "Was I gone too long?" he asked, out of breath. His flanks were bathed in sweat.

"No, Aigilaos. No need for concern," said Noroelle.

The centaur was exhausted and had to rest. Again, silence settled over the band.

Now the only one missing was Mandred, and then the elfhunt could finally depart. More than an hour passed before the human returned. Noroelle would have given a great deal to know what Mandred had found out from Atta Aikhjarto, but the human simply asked, "All set?"

The companions nodded. Noroelle felt rather guilty, for she knew she was responsible for the silence that had infected the others. Now she wanted to make up for that. "Come, I will go as far as the stone circle with you."

On the way up the rise, Noroelle felt the power of the Albenstar like a breeze against her skin. This place had lost none of its magic. Leaning against a stone and gazing into the circle, in the center of which a wall of mist swelled and surged, was Xern. Without turning around to them, he asked, "Who goes there?" But he asked in Fjordlandish, fully aware that it was Mandred approaching.

The human stepped forward and said, "The elfhunt."

Xern turned to face them. "Then this gate is open to you. Mandred, you entered this world with little more than a spark of life left in you. And you leave it with the power of Atta Aikhjarto. May that protect you and your companions." He gestured with his open hand toward the wall of mist.

Farodin and Nuramon looked expectantly at Noroelle. Finally, she broke her long silence. "Keep in mind that you are doing this for me. And keep in mind that I love you *both*. Watch over each other. That is my wish."

"I would lay down my life for Farodin," Nuramon declared.

And Farodin said, "Nuramon's suffering will be mine. What befalls him will befall me."

"By the Alben, I don't want either of you to sacrifice himself to save the other. Take care not only of each other, but of yourselves as well. I don't want fate to take my decision away from me, with pain. Come back, both of you."

"I will do everything in my power to make sure we *both* return," said Farodin.

"And I *promise* you, we will return," said Nuramon.

Farodin seemed surprised. His companion was making a vow that he could not guarantee. Who knew what would happen out there? But his promise was precisely what Noroelle wanted to hear.

Noroelle gave Obilee a sign and turned back to her two lovers. "I want to give you something to remember me by during the hunt."

Obilee produced two small bags.

Noroelle took them from her and gave one to Farodin, the other to Nuramon. "Open them," she said.

The two elves did as bidden and looked at what lay inside the bags. While Nuramon just smiled, Farodin exclaimed in surprise, "Mulberries."

"There is magic in them," she explained. "They will give you strength and fill your stomach more than you might suspect. Think of me when you eat them."

Farodin and Nuramon exchanged a glance, then Nuramon said, "We will. And not only when we eat them."

Noroelle embraced Farodin first and kissed him good-bye. He wanted to say something, but she laid two fingers on his lips. "No. No sweet parting words, no declarations of love. I know what you feel. I see it in your face. Don't try to put that on your tongue, for a word will make me cry. And I am still smiling." So Farodin remained silent, and stroked her hair.

Then Noroelle released Farodin and threw her arms around Nuramon. She kissed him as well. He took her face in his hands and looked at her for a long time, as if trying to engrave her image and every detail in his mind. Then he gave her a final smile and let her go.

The companions mounted their horses. Only Aigilaos was already looking ahead at the surging wall of mist. Mandred called out, "Follow me, my companions," and the elfhunt stepped into the stone circle.

Farodin and Nuramon rode last of all, behind the wolves. They looked back at Noroelle one final time. Then they, too, vanished into the mist.

Xern turned from the stone circle and slowly walked away. Obilee took Noroelle's hand. As the mist dissolved, Noroelle's fear grew. She felt as if she had just seen Farodin and Nuramon for the very last time.

THE HUMAN WORLD

As the fog surrounding them cleared, they were met by the icy breath of the human world. Nuramon uttered a few warming words to drive the cold out of his clothes. He looked around curiously. They were standing in a stone circle atop a high cliff. Far below them lay a village.

Mandred had walked his horse to the edge of the drop. It looked almost as if he wanted to ride the mare over the rim. The village across the fjord seemed to hold a strong attraction for him. It had to be the village he had spoken about at court.

"I've found the tracks," called Brandan. "Very fresh, as if the manboar has just been here."

The top of the cliff was exposed to the wind, and there was nothing to eat so high up. But what would have kept the beast here so long? Had it been waiting? Nuramon smiled. Nonsense.

"Mandred," said Farodin, his voice sharp.

The human started at the elf's voice. Then he pulled at the reins and steered his mare away from the edge of the cliff. "Sorry . . . I just had to see how things looked down there. It looks like the manboar hasn't attacked Firnstayn yet."

He took his place at the head of the band and led them down the cliff. The wolf pack ran ahead of them, fanning out. They had picked up the manboar's scent as well.

Although the tracks obviously led away from the village, it seemed to Nuramon that the human was growing more and more uneasy with every step. "Something the matter, Mandred?" he asked.

"The horses," said the warrior through clenched teeth. "They're bewitched, aren't they?"

Nuramon did not understand what he meant. "Why would anyone bewitch a horse?"

"They don't sink into the snow. That's impossible. The snow here's at least knee-deep."

Nuramon noticed Farodin and Brandan grinning. What did they know? "Why should horses sink into the snow?"

"Because that's what they do," Mandred said and reined in his mare. "If the horses aren't bewitched, then the snow's bewitched." He swung out of the saddle and instantly sank to his knees.

Brandan laughed.

"I don't find that funny," said Aigilaos, speaking up. He trotted to Mandred's side, gouging a deep track in the snow as he moved. "These long-ears think we're a riot. I've never figured out how they manage to stay on top of the snow. But it's no enchantment, and it makes no difference if the horses are shod or not."

Nuramon expected the human to be insulted, but instead his eyes suddenly lit up. "Do you think the queen would give me this horse when we get back?"

"If you prove yourself, she might, mortal," said Farodin.

"Do you think I could breed one of my stallions with this mare?"

Aigilaos let out a braying laugh.

The idea struck Nuramon as bizarre. What did the human have in mind?

"This is no place to stand around cracking jokes," warned Vanna. "It's going to snow soon. We have to keep moving, or we'll lose the trail."

Mandred mounted his horse once again. The band moved off in silence, following the tracks in the snow.

Nuramon gazed out over the land. He had imagined the human world differently. The snow here was packed and rough, and the lines of hills were formed so irregularly that he found it difficult to commit the landscape to memory. How were they supposed to find the manboar in this chaos? He saw a thousand things that were different in Albenmark.

All the new impressions made Nuramon tired. He rubbed his eyes. This world seemed vast and incomprehensible. When he saw a tree, he was so drawn into the details of it that he was barely able to see the tree as a whole. And it was difficult to gauge distances. Things looked closer than they really were. To him, this world felt constricted. Now Nuramon understood why the queen had named Mandred to lead them. His knowledge of this world would prove invaluable.

The companions followed the manboar's trail the entire day. They rode fast when the tracks crossed open land, then more carefully when they passed through the woods or crossed rocky ground. They were prepared at any moment to catch up with their quarry. At least, that was Nuramon's impression.

Brandan, in the last few hours, had emphasized several times that the tracks of the manboar seemed strange. They were simply too fresh. It was almost as if the snow refused to fall into the boar's tracks. This made Nuramon uneasy, and Lijema also looked worried. The others gave the impression that they heeded Brandan's warning, but not one seemed to doubt that they would finish the task they'd been given. The elfhunt was under way, and the wolves in particular, so happy to race ahead, gave Nuramon the feeling that nothing and nobody could stop them, not even in this strange world.

In the afternoon, it stopped snowing. They followed the trail into a dense forest. The manboar could have been lurking anywhere in there. Finally, Mandred decreed that they should make camp before it grew too late. Brandan memorized the location of the tracks, then they followed Mandred. Farodin's expression grew unusually ill-tempered, and Nuramon did not know why.

They moved out to the edge of the forest and pitched their camp. Aigilaos was hungry and wanted to go hunting. He had seen other tracks in the snow, and he and Brandan went off together.

Nuramon and Farodin unsaddled the horses. Vanna, the sorceress, kindled a small fire in the center of camp, but she seemed distracted. There was something playing on her mind. Lijema and Mandred saw to the wolves. The wolfmother answered all of Mandred's questions. The big animals were calm, which Nuramon took as a good sign.

Farodin set down one of the saddles, then paused and turned to Nuramon. "Is this how you imagined the elfhunt would be?"

"Honestly? No."

"Everything looks brighter from the outside. But we track down our prey, kill it, and return to our queen. That's what it comes down to."

"You've been here before, haven't you? In the human world?"

"Yes, many times," said Farodin. "I remember the last time. Our task was to find a traitor and take him back to the queen. It was like now. Almost the moment we came through the gate, we picked up the trail. A few hours later, we were already on our way back, but that was not a real elfhunt."

"And does the Other World seem as strange to you as it does to me?"

"You mean this . . . tightness?"

"Yes, exactly that."

"It is the air. The queen explained it to me once. The air is different here, not as clear as in Albenmark."

Nuramon thought about that.

"Everything is different here," Farodin went on. "If you search for the beauty and clarity of Albenmark, you'll search in vain. Things don't fit together in this world." He pointed to an oak tree. "That tree does not match this one." He slapped the trunk of the oak beside him. "In our realm, the things around you might be different, but everything exists in harmony with everything else. It is no wonder that humans find our lands so beautiful."

Nuramon said nothing. He felt an attraction to the Other World. There was so much to discover here, and if one only knew the secrets of this place, then maybe one could find harmony here as well. "Nothing here seems incongruous to Mandred," he said softly, looking briefly across at the human.

"His senses are not as finely tuned as ours."

Nuramon nodded. Farodin was right. Nevertheless, perhaps there was an order to everything here, but it took senses even sharper than an elf's to see it.

When the work was done, Nuramon sat at the edge of the forest and let his eyes roam out across the countryside. Farodin joined him and held out his little bag of mulberries to him.

Nuramon was surprised. "Are you sure?"

His companion nodded.

He accepted Farodin's offer, and they ate a few mulberries in silence.

As dusk settled, Lijema wondered aloud what was keeping Brandan and Aigilaos.

Nuramon stood. "I'll find them."

"Should I come along?" asked Farodin.

"No," Nuramon said and looked to where the sorceress crouched. "Better ask Vanna if everything is all right," he said in a whisper. "She's been quiet the whole time. There is something on her mind."

Farodin smiled and stood up to go and join Vanna, and Nuramon left the camp, following the tracks left by Aigilaos and Brandan.

The tracks were easy to follow. The prints from Brandan's boots were certainly hard to make out, but Aigilaos had plowed a deep furrow through the snow. Nuramon looked down at his feet a number of times, thinking about how Mandred had sunk in the snow. Perhaps it was an enchantment after all that let him walk on top of the snow. He tried to leave clear tracks. And he *could*, but it took a lot of concentration, and he had to put his feet down as clumsily as he was able. If he didn't, they refused to sink in the snow.

After a while, the tracks changed. Nuramon saw that his companions had picked up the trail of a deer. Then they had split up, Aigilaos moving to the left, Brandan to the right. The deer's tracks led straight ahead. Nuramon followed Aigilaos's tracks because they were easier to see.

Suddenly, he heard a sound. He stopped and listened, but there was nothing more than the wind drifting through the forest. Then he heard a low hiss. It may have been just a little crusted snow, blown from a tree close by. But the hissing sound came again, and then again. Sometimes longer, sometimes shorter. *Some animal that lives in this forest?* Nuramon wondered, knowing that it could just as easily be the manboar.

Nuramon cautiously moved his hand to the grip of his sword. He considered calling out for Aigilaos and Brandan, then decided not to. The moody centaur would fire an arrow at *him* if he spooked their prey with a thoughtless shout.

The sound seemed very close now, but Nuramon did not put too much trust in his senses. This world was confusing. His eyes had deceived him often enough today. It could just as easily happen with his ears.

Warily, he moved off Aigilaos's trail to follow the hissing sound. Soon, between the trees, he saw a clearing. The sound seemed to be coming from there.

From the edge of the glade, Nuramon peered ahead, trying to make out anything recognizable. Close to the center stood three oaks. An unpleasant smell reached him on the wind, making him pause for a moment. Something about the smell wasn't right. But what *was* right in this world for elven senses?

He stepped carefully into the glade and looked around. There was no one to be seen. But with every step, the hissing sound grew louder. Whatever it was, it had to be coming from behind the three oaks. Nuramon's hand tightened around the cool grip of his sword.

When Nuramon had almost reached the three oaks, he saw to his left a broad spoor leading from the forest. Aigilaos's tracks.

He hurried toward the three trees. The hissing came horribly loud and long now. He saw a broken band of gold lying in the snow. Quickly, he rounded the oaks and stopped dead in disbelief.

In front of him in the snow lay Aigilaos. The centaur's head was tipped far back, and he was making the hissing noise through his open mouth. His curled beard was matted with blood. At his throat, Nuramon saw four thin wounds. If not for those, he realized, the centaur's bellowing would have rung from one end of the forest to the other. Like this, he was barely able to make a sound. Something had literally cut out his voice. His screaming was no more than a deep breath blasted from his throat.

There was more pain in Aigilaos's face than Nuramon had ever seen in any other creature. His eyes stood wide open. Over and over, he tensed and tried to bellow, but all he could get out was that pitiful hiss.

All four of the centaur's legs were broken, one with the bone protruding through the skin. His long belly had been slit open. A pool of blood had formed in the snow and frozen, and a portion of his innards spilled out. One arm lay crushed beneath his body. The other was dislocated and, like his legs, broken. His sides were marked with long slashes, as if some marauding predator had set upon him.

Nuramon did not want to imagine the pain that Aigilaos must have felt. He had never seen a living thing as mutilated as the centaur.

"Farodin! Mandred!" shouted Nuramon, uncertain whether to fetch help or stay and try to do something for Aigilaos. He looked down at his own hands and saw them trembling. He had to do something. His companions at the camp were certain to have heard him.

"I'll help you, Aigilaos."

The centaur ceased his voiceless screaming. His face convulsed, and he looked up at Nuramon.

It was hopeless. The belly wound alone would kill the centaur. The slashes to his throat had also done severe damage. Was he supposed to lie to the centaur? "I will ease your pain." Nuramon laid his hands on Aigilaos's forehead and looked into his tearing eyes. That the centaur was still conscious was a miracle. "Just a moment longer," said Nuramon, then he focused on the magic he would need.

It began with a tingle in the tips of his fingers. Nuramon concentrated on his heartbeat and felt a cool tremor run down through his arms to his hands. Under his fingers, he felt Aigilaos's forehead grow warm. He could feel the centaur's racing pulse and how his own heartbeat grew faster to match his companion's. Then both heartbeats slowed again, and Aigilaos became calmer. So far, so good, even if the centaur was beyond rescue.

As Nuramon let go of Aigilaos's forehead, he saw the lines of the centaur's face slowly relax. And again, with all the blood staining the snow, it amazed him that Aigilaos was even conscious. He resolved to fight against his companion's death, as hopeless as the attempt might seem. He had no experience with centaurs. Maybe they could survive such wounds. Carefully, he laid his hands on Aigilaos's slashed throat.

Aigilaos felt no more pain and gazed steadily into Nuramon's eyes. Then he shook his head and glanced down at the elf's sword.

Nuramon was horrified. Aigilaos knew that the end had come. And now it was up to Nuramon to draw Gaomee's sword and make his death as swift as possible. The sword that Gaomee had once wielded so heroically to defeat Duanoc was now to be stained with the blood of a companion.

Nuramon hesitated, but in the centaur's eyes was a plea he could not ignore. It overcame him. He had to do it. Out of compassion, he had to. He drew the sword.

Aigilaos nodded.

"We will meet again, Aigilaos. In the next life." Nuramon raised the sword and brought it down. But the sword tip stopped just before it struck the centaur's chest. Aigilaos looked up in confusion. "I can't do it," said Nuramon in despair, shaking his head. The words of farewell he had said to the centaur rang inside him like an enormous bell. *We will meet again, Aigilaos. In the next life.* Who could say that the words were true? Nuramon did not know for certain that Aigilaos's soul would be able to find its way from this world back to Albenmark. To take his life here might rob him forever of the chance to be born again.

Nuramon threw his sword aside. He had come close to staining the weapon with the blood of a comrade. There was only one thing left for him to do. He had to use what magic he knew to try to save his companion's life.

Nuramon once again checked the wounds on Aigilaos's throat. Mandred had described the manboar as a coarse and primitive beast, but these cuts had been made so precisely that they seemed to have come from a knife. Was the manboar also capable of using weapons? Or had some other beast mauled Aigilaos like this? Another thing puzzled Nuramon: apart from the blood of his companion, there were no tracks to be seen leading away, not even the tracks of the deer that Aigilaos had been hunting. And there was no sign of Brandan either. Maybe he was lying somewhere out there in the forest, as mutilated as Aigilaos.

Nuramon suppressed the desire to call out for the rest of the party. Doing so might only attract the beast. He placed his hands carefully over the narrow wounds. The moment he thought of the magic, the tingling in his fingertips began again. This time, however, he did not feel the tremor in his arms that he had before. Instead, the tingling transformed into a pain that spread from his fingertips to his hands and into his joints. Pain for healing. That was the trade-off that was inherent to his magic. When the pain finally faded, Nuramon removed his hands from Aigilaos and looked at his throat. The wounds had closed.

Then he looked at the gaping slit in the centaur's belly, knowing that such an injury was beyond his power. He needed a spell that would bring an entire body back to life. Nuramon bent low over Aigilaos's torso. "Can you speak again?" he asked the centaur.

"Don't do it, Nuramon," Aigilaos begged, his voice husky. "Take the sword and bring this to an end."

Nuramon placed his hands on Aigilaos's temples. "It's only pain." He knew very well that the more serious the wound, the greater the pain he himself would have to endure. Still, he focused on the task and tried to calm his breathing.

"I wish you the luck of the Alben, my friend," said the centaur.

Nuramon did not reply. He let his magic flow through his hands into Aigilaos's body. He thought of those he had healed in the past. A great many trees and animals, but only rarely an elf.

A searing pain suddenly shot through his hands and up his arms. This was the price he paid for healing. This was what he had to withstand. Then the pain grew and turned into something appalling. Nuramon closed his eyes and fought it, but all of his attempts to dissipate it failed. It hit him like a lightning bolt inside his head. He knew he only had to let go to end it. But stopping meant that Aigilaos would be lost.

It wasn't just the number of injuries nor just the damage wrought by the belly wound. There was something else here, something that Nuramon couldn't contain. Was it poison? Or perhaps magic? Nuramon tried to relax his mind, but the pain was too great. He felt his hands begin to cramp and his body start to shake.

"Nuramon! Nuramon!" he heard a raw voice shout. "By the gods!"

"Silence. He is healing him," came the voice of an elf. "Oh, Nuramon."

The pain grew, and Nuramon clenched his teeth. There seemed to be no end to the agony. It rose and rose. He felt his own senses begin to fade.

For one moment, Nuramon thought of Noroelle. And the pain was suddenly gone.

All around was quiet.

Nuramon opened his eyes slowly and saw Farodin's face above him. "Say something, Nuramon."

"Aigilaos?" was all that escaped him.

Farodin looked aside, then back at Nuramon. He shook his head.

Beside him, Mandred cried out. "No. Wake up. Wake up! Don't go like this! Speak to me!"

But the centaur was silent.

Nuramon tried to stand. Slowly, his strength returned.

Farodin helped him to his feet. "You could have died," he whispered.

Nuramon stared down at Aigilaos. Mandred was bent over the centaur, weeping. Aigilaos's face was indeed calm, but his body was still a horrible sight.

"Have you forgotten what you promised Noroelle?"

"No, I have not," whispered Nuramon. "Which is why Aigilaos had to die."

Nuramon tried to turn and move away, but Farodin held him firmly. "You could not have saved him."

"But what if he could have been saved?"

Farodin said nothing.

Mandred stood and turned to face them. "Did he say anything?" The human was looking expectantly at Nuramon.

"He wished me luck." It was all the elf could say.

"You did everything you could. I know that," Mandred said, but the human's words did not console Nuramon.

He picked up the sword, looked at it, and thought of what Aigilaos had asked of him. He could not tell Mandred that.

"What happened? And where's Brandan?" Farodin asked.

"I don't know," said Nuramon slowly.

Mandred shook his head. "We can count ourselves lucky if he's still alive." He looked at Aigilaos and sighed heavily. "By the gods. No one should die like that." Then he looked around. "Damn it. It's already far too dark."

"Then we'd better find Brandan quickly," said Farodin.

They turned and looked at Aigilaos again and decided to come back for him later that night if they possibly could.

Nuramon led Farodin and Mandred back to Brandan's tracks. Night had fallen in the meantime. "I should have brought the barinstones from the camp," said Farodin. The elf's tracks were hard enough to follow in daylight. The darkness made it impossible. They were not expert trackers.

Suddenly, from some distance behind them rose a monstrous howling. All three turned, then Mandred shouted, "The camp! Come on!"

They set off running, and Nuramon realized that Mandred had great difficulty moving in the darkness. He was constantly running into low branches, but then he dropped back and ran behind Farodin. He cursed the whole time at the way he sank to his calves in the snow with every step while the elves ran lightly on top of it.

Finally, they reached the camp. It was empty.

The fire burned, and the horses were standing quietly, but Vanna, Lijema, and the wolves had disappeared. While Farodin kneeled beside his saddlebags, Nuramon circled the camp, searching for tracks. Mandred stood as if paralyzed. He probably thought that all was lost.

The forest was silent.

Nuramon found the tracks of the wolves and the elves. They led along the edge of the forest. There were no signs of battle or struggle. He told his companions of his discovery, and Farodin threw him and Mandred each a barinstone. They were clear and glowed with a white light.

A howling reached them from deep in the forest, and they set off again. They shouted out for Vanna and Lijema, but no answer came.

They found a blood trail and followed that. The wolves and apparently Vanna and Lijema, too, had followed the blood before them.

Soon they came across a dead wolf, its throat torn out. Apprehensive, they went on following the tracks, finding more drops of blood every few steps.

They could still hear the howling up ahead. Suddenly, among the trees in front of them, they could see the white wolves leaping. There was a shadow there, and the wolves were on it. A huge form. It lashed out wildly, and the baying of a wolf turned into stifled yelps of pain. Then they heard a woman screaming.

They reached a clearing. The light of the barinstones expelled the darkness. Nuramon saw the wolves pursuing a hulking, hunched form moving off quickly into the darkness.

In the light from his stone, Nuramon found Vanna, the sorceress, in the middle of the clearing.

"Come back! This is no time for revenge!" she screamed after the vanishing wolves. "Come back!" But they did not listen to her. The sorceress's legs gave way, and she buckled over something in the snow.

Mandred and Farodin were with her in an instant. Nuramon approached more slowly and looked around. Three wolves lay dead in the clearing. The leader of the pack was among the dead. Something had been rammed into its back. Nuramon noticed a sharp odor in the air. It was the same stink he had detected when he'd found Aigilaos. It was the reek of the beast.

When Nuramon reached his companions, he saw in the light of his barinstone that Vanna was kneeling beside Lijema. When the sorceress straightened up, he could see that the wolfmother's breast had been torn open. Something had punctured her chest and destroyed her lungs and heart. Her eyes still shone, but her face was frozen in a mask of astonishment.

Vanna pressed her forehead lovingly to the dead woman's.

"What happened?" asked Farodin.

Vanna said nothing.

Farodin took hold of the sorceress by the shoulders and shook her gently. "Vanna."

Her large eyes seemed to look right through him. She pointed off to one side. "Brandan is over there, behind that tree. The boar . . ." She broke off.

Nuramon ran. He needed to get to Brandan as fast as possible. In his mind's eye, he could still see Aigilaos.

An argument broke out between Mandred and Farodin. The human wanted to pursue the beast, but Farodin was not going to allow it. How could they fight about such a thing at a time like this? Brandan might still be alive.

Nuramon reached the edge of the clearing and found him. The tracker lay on his back. He was injured slightly on one side of his head and on one leg. He was unconscious, but his heart still beat, and he was breathing slowly. Nuramon laid his healing hands on Brandan's wounds. Again he felt the tingling come, followed by the pain. After a moment, the wounds scabbed over beneath his fingers. That would do for now. He would finish healing him later.

He picked Brandan up with an effort and made his way with heavy steps back to the others. Under the load he carried, his feet sank in the snow.

He heard Farodin talking patiently to Mandred, trying to persuade him. "The beast is toying with us. We can't let it provoke us into doing something thoughtless now. We can hunt it down tomorrow."

"As you think best," said Mandred with reluctance.

When they saw Nuramon approaching, the worry on their faces was clear. They ran to him.

"Is he . . . ?" Mandred began.

"He's alive, but we should get him back to camp."

It was a hard walk back. Mandred carried Brandan while Farodin and Nuramon took the body of Lijema between them. They left the dead wolves where they lay. Along the way, Mandred tried to wake Brandan, but the tracker rested deep in unconsciousness.

At the camp, Farodin took care of Lijema's corpse, wrapping the body in a cloak. Mandred and Vanna sat at the fire and listened to the sounds of the forest. Brandan's head lay in Nuramon's hands, absorbing his magic, while Nuramon watched Vanna and Mandred. Their faces and the way they were sitting said more than any words could. Two members of the elfhunt had been killed, and their wolves were either dead or gone.

Nuramon looked up to the moon. His grandmother had spoken the truth. Only half of it could be seen, and it looked far smaller than the moon in Albenmark. He thought back to the last time he had spoken with Noroelle. *What happens if you die in the human realm?* He could only hope that Lijema would be reborn. He did not know what happened to a centaur after death. There were some among the Albenkin who said that in death, centaurs went directly into the moonlight. He hoped the souls of their dead companions were not lost.

As the pain seeped out of Brandan's body and into Nuramon's hands, Nuramon closed his eyes and thought of Aigilaos. Farodin was right: the centaur had been beyond rescue, but he still wondered whether his thoughts of Noroelle and of the promise he had made her had contributed to Aigilaos's death. Maybe . . . maybe with a little more effort, he could have saved him.

The pain ebbed away, and Nuramon opened his eyes. Farodin, Mandred, and Vanna were standing around him. He let go of Brandan. "Don't worry. All is well."

But the worry they felt was only replaced by relief when, a few moments later, Brandan awoke.

He was exhausted, but he could tell them what had happened. "It was on me without warning. There was a terrible smell, and it was as if I were paralyzed. I could do nothing. Nothing."

He had been knocked unconscious by the manboar and used as bait. The last thing he remembered was the sound of breathing, but it was a horrible, guttural sound.

Nuramon told Brandan and Vanna what had happened to Aigilaos. He described the centaur's fate to the last detail, but kept to himself that Aigilaos had begged him to kill him. Brandan and Vanna listened in distress and horror.

Farodin shook his head. "Something about this manboar is not right. It is more than just a beast."

"Whatever it is, we can kill it if we don't let ourselves get split up again," said Mandred.

"We will take watches. The bastard won't catch us by surprise," Farodin replied.

Before they could decide who would take the first shift, two of the wolves slunk back into the camp. They were silent and came with their tails between their legs, but they were uninjured. Mandred was happy to see the animals back and stroked the head of one of them. Vanna welcomed the second. The wolves were exhausted, and they stank of the manboar.

"What is that?" asked Farodin, pointing to the muzzle of the wolf that Mandred soothed.

To Nuramon, it looked like blood.

The human looked more closely. "Frozen blood. But look how light it is."

Nuramon could make out a silvery shine but could not be certain that it wasn't just frost.

All of them moved closer and examined the blood.

"The boar can be injured," Mandred muttered. "Tomorrow we hunt it down and avenge our friends."

Farodin nodded. He had made up his mind, and Nuramon and Brandan had, too.

Only Vanna did not respond. She looked closely at the muzzle of her wolf, which was also bloody.

"What's the matter?" said Farodin.

The sorceress left the wolf and moved across to sit between Nuramon and Farodin. Her face was lined with concern, and she took a deep breath. "Listen closely to me. This is no normal elfhunt, and I say that not just because we have failed so miserably and two of our companions are dead."

"What do you mean?" said Mandred. "What do you know that we don't?"

"At first, it was just a vague notion. It seemed so absurd that I pushed it aside. I held my tongue. I felt a presence that was different from anything else I know. When we started following the manboar's trail, I picked up its smell, and the suspicion returned. But the smell alone was not proof enough. Only when I finally stood opposite the beast and saw the wolves fighting it, when I looked into its blue eyes and it used its magic to . . . to do what it did to Lijema, only then did I know what we are dealing with. But I still didn't want to believe it. Now that I see this blood, there can be no more doubt . . ." She fell silent.

"About what?" Mandred pushed.

"It might mean little to you, Mandred, but this creature you call a manboar is a Devanthar. One of the old demons."

Nuramon was stunned. Impossible. He saw the horror he felt on the faces of Farodin and Brandan as well. Nuramon knew little about the Devanthar, but they were said to be creatures of the shadows, dedicated to chaos and destruction. A long time ago, the Alben had battled the Devanthar and wiped out all of them. It was said that they could change their form and were powerful wizards. Probably the only one who really knew what the Devanthar were capable of was the queen. Nuramon could not believe that Emerelle had knowingly pitted them against such a creature. What Vanna was telling them could not be true.

Farodin looked at the sorceress, his face a mask. He said what Nuramon was thinking. "That's impossible. You know that."

"Yes. I thought so too. Even when I saw the creature right in front of me, I did not want to believe it. I persuaded myself that I was wrong. But this blood, with its strange silvery sheen, has opened my eyes. This beast *is* a Devanthar."

"Well, you are the sorceress. You know the old wisdom," said Farodin, but he sounded far from convinced.

"What do we do now?" asked Brandan softly.

Vanna avoided the others' eyes. "We are the elfhunt. We have to finish it. We will face a creature that was a worthy adversary for the Alben."

Mandred's face revealed how horrified he was. Only now did he seem to truly comprehend what Vanna was saying. So the Alben and their power were known even among humans . . . perhaps, for Mandred, the Alben were akin to gods.

"No elf has ever killed a Devanthar," said Farodin.

Nuramon exchanged a look with Farodin and thought once more of his promise to Noroelle. With resolve in his voice, he said, "Then we shall be the first."

THE WHISPERER
IN THE DARK

Farodin had withdrawn to the shadows at the edge of the clearing. Not much longer, and the last watch would be over. They had decided to break camp before dawn and try to pick up the Devanthar's trail. They would stay together. The creature could not be allowed to toy with them again, using one of them as bait.

The fire had burned down to a heap of glowing embers. The elf avoided looking directly into the light, knowing that doing so would mean impairing his night vision. He heard a soft snoring. Mandred had actually managed to fall asleep. Since the day before, when he realized that his village had not been ravaged by the beast, the human had changed. Despite the horrors they had faced, he remained calm. He was obviously still convinced that the elfhunt would kill the monster, even after Vanna revealed what it was they were hunting. There was something touching in the human's naïve trust in the elfhunt.

From the corner of his eye, Farodin noticed movement. Not twenty steps away, he made out a shadow among the trees. Farodin lifted the bow in his lap, then immediately lowered it again. The trunks of the trees and the thick undergrowth made a clear shot impossible. The creature was trying to provoke him, but he would not fall for it.

The elf took several arrows from his quiver and jabbed them into the snow in front of him. He could shoot faster that way, if necessary. Were the Devanthar to attempt an attack on the camp from the edge of the clearing, he would get off at least three shots. The demon was certainly not invulnerable. It was time for it to pay for what it had done.

Farodin blinked. Was that really the beast he could see there? Or was the night playing a trick on him? If one stared too long, one could see all kinds of things in a dark wood.

Pull yourself together, the elven warrior rebuked himself. A light breeze swept across the snowy landscape. Deep in the forest, a branch cracked under its load of snow. One of the wolves raised its head and looked into the forest where Farodin had seen the shadow. The wolf let out a puling whine and lowered its head flat onto the snow.

A biting stench hung in the air for the span of a single breath. Then all that remained was the smell of the cold.

"I'm waiting for you in the mountains, Farodin with the blood-stained hands."

The elf started up in alarm. The words . . . he had heard them inside himself.

"Show yourself." His voice was no more than a whisper. He did not want to wake the others yet.

"And again, I find one of you alone," the voice inside his head mocked. *"You seem very sure of yourself, Farodin. Would it not be smarter to wake your companions?"*

"Why should I do what you expect? Predictability is the truest ally of defeat. Why should we face you in a place you choose?"

"Things have to happen at the right place, at the right time. That is important. You yourself plan the place and time very carefully when you travel in Her Majesty's service."

"Which explains why I will not listen to you," said the elf.

"I could kill any of you with no more than a thought. You're nothing but a pale reflection of the Alben. I'd hoped for more when I sent the human to Albenmark."

Farodin let his eyes sweep the camp. He could still hear Mandred's low snore. Should he trust the words of a Devanthar? Had the queen been right in her suspicion?

"Do you really think the human could have passed through the gate on his own?"

"Why would you nearly kill your own messenger?"

"To make him all the more convincing. He did not know in whose service he acted, and because of that, your queen could detect no lie in his words."

"If it is our death you want, then do it here in the camp. Now. I'll wake the others."

"No. Ask Mandred about the Cave of Luth. I will wait for you there in the evening, three days from now."

Farodin thought about whether he might still stall the Devanthar and wake the others. Perhaps the wolves had injured it. Why did it not show itself if it felt so invincible? They should kill the beast here and now. He would accept no haggling.

"One of my thoughts alone has the power to kill, Farodin. Don't invite death."

"Then why are we still alive?" the elf asked with confidence.

"As we speak, Brandan's heart has stopped, Farodin with the blood-stained hands. Your doubt has killed him. If you are not in the mountains in three days, then all of you will die the same death. I thought you were a warrior. Consider well, do you want to die with a sword in your hand under the eyes of your enemy, or in your sleep like Brandan? You think yourself so gifted with a sword. Perhaps you will even kill me. I will be waiting."

Three steps away, a huge figure stepped out from between the trees. Farodin's hand flew to his sword. How had the Devanthar been able to creep so close without his noticing? There had been no sound, no shadow among the trees. Even the foul stench of the creature had grown no stronger.

The manboar nodded its head, as if in scornful greeting. Then it blurred again into the shadows.

Farodin charged. The crusted snow crunched beneath his boots. In two heartbeats, he was at the place where the demon had just been standing, but the Devanthar was long gone. There were no tracks in the snow, nothing to show that the beast had even been there. Had the shadowy figure been no more than a phantom? Was the demon trying to lure him away? Farodin glanced at their camp. His companions still lay by the fire, wrapped in their blankets. Everything was quiet.

In the old stories, it was said that a Devanthar could lie twice with one word. Farodin wished he could see what lay behind the demand to come to the cave.

It had grown colder. He slapped his hands against his thighs to drive the numbness from his fingers. Then he returned to the tree where he had leaned his bow.

He pulled the arrows out of the snow and checked them carefully. He had chosen war arrows for the manboar, with flat heads and barbs that curved inward. The points were only loosely attached to the shafts. Any attempt to pull such a projectile out of a wound resulted in the shaft pulling free and the head with its barbs remaining deep in the flesh. Farodin wished he had been able to shoot at least one of them at the manboar.

Again, he looked over at his companions. He had to be sure. "They can lie twice with one word," he repeated to himself in a whisper. If he went back to the camp now, he would be doing exactly what the demon expected of him. And they had been doing that ever since they had passed through Aikhjarto's gate.

Farodin picked up his bow and quiver and crossed to the fire. Fine ice crystals danced in the air. Never before had he experienced a winter as cold as this. What made humans settle in such an inhospitable place? He laid the weapon on his blanket. Then he kneeled next to Brandan. The tracker had turned onto his side. A smile was on his lips. What did he see in his dreams?

Farodin decided that he would not disturb Brandan's dream. He was already turning away when he noticed a tiny crystal of ice at the corner of Brandan's mouth. Farodin leaned forward in alarm and shook the hunter's shoulder.

Brandan did not stir. In his sleep, his smile had become his death mask.

OLD WOUNDS

May the firelight guide you through the dark."

Farodin held the flaming torch to the funeral pyre. The fire was slow in taking hold of the spruce branches. Thick white smoke rose skyward. It still carried the smell of the forest, the scent of pine needles and sap.

Farodin turned away. It had taken them hours to build the pyre. It had been impossible to move the dead centaur, so in the end, they had carried Brandan and Lijema to the clearing.

Mandred kneeled beside the fire. His lips moved silently. The human surprised Farodin. He seemed to have taken Aigilaos quickly into his heart like a brother.

The wind turned. Like a heavy veil, the smoke enveloped them. The first odors of burning flesh hung in the air.

Farodin fought down a feeling of nausea. "We have to get moving," he said. "The hour is already late."

Nuramon looked at him accusingly, as if he were completely heartless. Or did he suspect something? Vanna had been unable to say what had killed Brandan. Farodin had kept that part of his conversation with the Devanthar to himself. He did not want to rob them of their courage, he told himself. They could not be allowed to find out that the Devanthar could kill with a mere thought. Maybe it was just an illusion. Maybe Brandan had died from something else. It was enough if he were the only one to have to agonize over that question.

"Let's go." Mandred stood and knocked the snow from his breeches. "We will hunt this monster down, and we will slay it."

To Farodin's ears, the language of the Fjordlands sounded like a menacing hiss. The queen must have been mistaken. This human would never betray them. Like all of them, he was a dupe of the Devanthar, no more.

The elf pulled himself into the saddle. He felt tired. He had lost his confidence and, along with it, a good part of his strength. Or was that the guilt he felt? Would Brandan still be alive if he, Farodin, had not hesitated? He looked at the wolves. Only two of those wild hunters were still with them. They carried their tails in fear, tucked between their hind legs, and trotted close to the riders as they left the clearing.

Farodin eased his horse up next to the human as they rode. "What kind of place is that—the Cave of Luth?"

Mandred made a sign in the air with jerky movement of his hand. "A place of power," he whispered. "Luth, the weaver of fate, is said to have spent a long winter there. It was so cold that the walls of the cave turned white from his breath." The warrior stuck out his bearded chin. "It is a holy place. We will finish off the manboar there, for the gods will be on our side, if . . ." The human's eyes locked onto the polished shaft of the boar spear that lay crossways on the saddle in front of him.

"If what?"

"If they let us get that far," Mandred said. He pointed north. "The cave is high in the mountains. The passes will be snowed under. No one goes there in the middle of winter."

"But you've been there?" asked the elf suspiciously.

Mandred shook his head. "No. But the ironbeards will show us the way."

"Ironbeard? What is that?"

Mandred smiled fleetingly. "Not an enemy and not something to fear. At least, not for us. It's the trolls who avoid them. The priests took them up there. They're carved from the trunks of holy oaks. Images of the gods. Anyone traveling to the Cave of Luth must make sacrifice. You win the gods' favor that way . . . usually, anyway. The wooden statues have long beards, and you knock something iron into them. Nails or an old knife or the broken blade of an axe. In time, the wooden beards turn into ironbeards."

"You sacrifice nails to your gods?" said Farodin, dubious.

Mandred looked at him disapprovingly. "We don't swim in riches here in the Fjordlands. Iron is expensive. Chain mail, like the kind every guard in your queen's castle wears, is something only the princes and kings in my land possess. Our gods know that."

And the trolls fear iron, thought Farodin, but he did not voice the thought. Their weapons were always made of wood or stone. He thought of the battle at Welruun, where the trolls had destroyed the stone circle and the gate that led to the valley of their royal caves. They needed no iron or steel. Their sheer strength was enough to bash in a helmet with a bare fist. But they shied away from the touch of iron, so armor actually offered a certain protection from the brutes. Farodin remembered his battles against those colossal ogres with disgust. Whenever he thought of them, he sensed their rancid stink in his nose.

"You must sacrifice to the ironbeards." The human's voice jerked him out of his ruminations. "Even if you don't believe in them."

"But of course."

Farodin nodded indifferently. He should not have stirred up the memory. Aileen. The trolls had killed her just five steps from him. He remembered the way she looked when the monstrous stone axe cleaved her chain mail shirt as if it were silk. Seven hundred years would pass before he could love again. In all those centuries, he had not given up hope. Every member of Aileen's family had been killed in the troll wars, so it had taken a very long time for them to be reborn. And no one could have foretold into which family they would be reborn. Farodin had spent centuries learning a seeking spell, finally tracing her to Alvemer. She had come back as Noroelle, but he had never said a word to her about her past. He wanted her to fall in love with him again, and he wanted her love to be pure, not some sympathetic affection born out of an old sense of duty. Seven hundred years . . .

"You're worried about the trolls, aren't you?" Mandred said as he straightened up in the saddle. He stroked the shaft of the boar spear with his hand. "Don't be. They will respect this. And they fear my clan as well. They've never managed to kill any of my ancestors."

Grimly, Farodin replied, "Then your ancestors and I have something in common."

"What do you mean? Have you run into a troll at some point?" asked the human with some awe.

"Seven of them have not survived running into me." Farodin was not one to boast of his deeds. All the troll blood in the world could not extinguish the burning hatred he felt for them.

Mandred laughed. "Seven trolls? No one kills seven trolls."

"Believe what you like," Farodin snapped. He pulled at the reins, turned his stallion aside, and dropped back until Nuramon and Vanna overtook him. He wanted to be alone with his thoughts.

THE WAY
INTO THE ICE

Mandred pressed four rings of mail over a rusted nail in one of the ironbeards, the effigies of Firn. *Stuck-up pack of elves*, he thought. Of course, not one of them thought to sacrifice anything to the god of winter when they passed by one of the ironbeards, and now they were in trouble. The driving snow was coming down heavier, and they still had not found the cave.

"Coming, Mandred?"

Mandred glared at Farodin, climbing ahead. He was the worst of them. There was something sinister about that one. Mandred thought he was too quiet sometimes, as were men who had something to hide. But Mandred made sacrifice for him, too. "Forgive them, Firn," he whispered and made the sign of the protecting eye. "They come from a place where it's spring in the middle of winter. They don't know any better."

Mandred rose to his feet, only to have to support himself on the shaft of his boar spear a moment later. He had to catch his breath. Never before had he been so high in the mountains. They had left the tree line behind hours earlier, and all around there was nothing but rock and snow. When the sky was clear, they could see they were close to Splitbeard and Troll's Head, two peaks from which, even in the hottest summers, the snow never disappeared completely. They were so close to the gods that even a slight exertion left them short of breath. This place had not been created for humans.

Mandred reached for the reins of his mare. She seemed unaffected by the cold and, of course, did not need to trample a path through the deep snow. It made no difference how brittle the crust on the old snow was, she—like the two wolves and the elves—never broke through. They let him go ahead as pacesetter. Without him, they would no doubt have made twice the progress.

Mandred pressed ahead defiantly into the icy wind. The snow pricked his face like needles of bone. He squinted and did what he could to protect his eyes with his hand. He hoped the weather would not get any worse.

They were working their way up a long glacier, bordered on the left by steep walls of rock. High overhead, the winter storm howled among the crags. *Hopefully, that's just the storm howling up there*, thought Mandred uneasily. *They say there are trolls here in winter.*

He turned and looked back at the elves behind him. They seemed untroubled by the cold. They must have cast some spell to protect themselves, but he would not grumble, and god forbid that he should ask the elves for anything.

Darkness was quickly gaining on them. They would have to stop soon. The danger of slipping into a crevasse in the glacier was too great in this gloom. The damned weather. Mandred ran a hand over his forehead nervously. His eyebrows were crusted with snow. He had to convince them that it made no sense to keep searching now. Even if they didn't fall into a crevasse, they could easily walk right past the cave without seeing it.

Suddenly, he stopped. He smelled something foul, and it reminded him of the reek of the beast. He squinted into the flurrying snow. Nothing. Had he imagined it?

One of the wolves let out a long howl.

The beast was here. Very close. Mandred dropped the reins and wrapped his hands around the shaft of the boar spear. Just ahead, a shadow appeared through the snow.

"For Aigilaos!" he cried, charging.

Only at the last second did he realize what was standing there in the snow. Another ironbeard. But this one, unlike the others, was not facing higher up the glacier. It was turned to the wall of rock. Narrow stone steps carved into the rock led upward. They were far too narrow for the horses to climb.

"That's it," said Vanna as she came beside Mandred and pointed up the path. "Many Albenpaths cross somewhere up there. They form an Albenstar."

"An Albenstar?" Mandred asked.

"A place of power, a place where two or more Albenpaths cross."

Mandred was far from certain what she was talking about. Probably the paths once followed by the Alben. But what business did they have in Luth's cave? Had they come to pay homage to the god?

"I have felt the presence of the paths for hours," Vanna said. "If seven paths cross at this place, then we will find a gate there."

The warrior looked at the elf in surprise. "A gate? But there's neither house nor tower there. It's a cave."

Vanna smiled. "If you say so."

Farodin turned to the blanket that was strapped behind his saddle. He withdrew a second sword and slung the belt around his hips. Brandan's sword. Then he rolled the blanket out and threw it over the stallion's back.

"The horses will find a place out of the wind and wait for us for as long as they can stand the cold," said Vanna. She scratched the smaller of the two wolves between the ears and talked reassuringly to it. "You stay here and protect the horses from trolls." She winked at Mandred.

The others followed Farodin's lead and threw blankets over the horses. *They're probably not half as cold as me*, thought Mandred angrily. He patted his mare's nostrils. She looked at him with her dark eyes in a way that Mandred did not like. Did she know something about his fate? Horses shouldn't be able to look so sad.

"We'll slit the beast's belly and get out again as fast as we can. It's far too cold to dawdle here," said Mandred, spurring his own courage.

The mare pressed her soft muzzle into his hand and snorted gently.

"Ready to go?" asked Vanna quietly.

Instead of answering, Mandred headed for the rock wall. The weathered steps had been chiseled directly into the gray stone. Mandred made his way up with care. Ice crackled underfoot. He put his left hand against the stone to help keep his footing. The steps became narrower the higher he went until there was hardly enough room to set a single boot.

Mandred was gasping for air when he finally reached the top of the stone steps. In front of him opened a ravine, its walls so close that it was barely wide enough for two men side by side.

He cursed silently. The manboar had chosen this place carefully. Only one of them at a time could face him there. Far along the ravine, a reddish light flickered, making the overhanging snow on the rocks above look like frozen blood. Mandred made the sign of the protecting eye again. Then he moved ahead slowly. The thin air was heavy with smoke. Somewhere ahead, sappy spruce wood was burning. The smell would cover even the stink of the manboar. "Vile beast," Mandred muttered.

The manboar had surprised them at every turn. It seemed almost as if it could make itself invisible. All that truly betrayed its presence was its smell. Mandred moved forward cautiously. High above him, a huge block of stone was wedged between the walls, framing the path like a lintel over a door. Is that what Vanna meant when she talked about a gate?

Pebbles clattered down from one of the rock walls, and Mandred lifted his boar spear in alarm. Far above him, something was climbing along the inside of the ravine, but in the darkness, he could not make it out.

He moved faster now. The narrow ravine gradually widened and dropped into a small basin. A dark mouth opened in a rocky wall, not a hundred steps away. The Cave of Luth. The valley floor here was littered with large chunks of rock. A fire crackled next to the mouth of the cave.

"Come out and surrender," Mandred called as he lifted the boar spear in both hands over his head in challenge. "We're here." His voice rang from the rock walls all around.

"He will only show himself when we are where he wants us to be," said Farodin grimly. The elf twisted free the brooch that held his cloak closed and let the garment fall.

Mandred considered doing the same with his heavy fur coat. It might restrict his movement in a battle, but it was simply too cold to disrobe. And if necessary, he could take it off in an instant with one hand.

Farodin strode ahead. He dodged between the rocks scattered over the valley floor with catlike grace.

"Stay together," Mandred ordered. "We can defend ourselves better."

Vanna wore her fear openly. Her eyes were wide, and the spear in her hands shook.

Nuramon was the last to come into the basin. The remaining wolf walked close beside him. It had its ears back and held its head low.

"Is there anything else you can tell us about the Devanthar, sorceress?" said Mandred.

"No one knows much," said Vanna. "In the old stories, the descriptions are always different. Sometimes they were like dragons, sometimes like shadowy ghosts or huge snakes. It's said that they can change their form, but I'd never heard of a manboar before."

"That doesn't help much," Mandred muttered, clambering down into the basin.

Farodin waited for them at the fire, where a large pile of firewood was stacked—splintered tree trunks and branches of green spruce. The elf pushed one of the branches aside to reveal a log of dark wood. Mandred had to look twice to realize what it was.

"The Devanthar doesn't seem to think much of your gods."

Mandred dragged the carved image out from among the branches. It was one of the ironmen, this one an image of Luth himself. Many of the things sacrificed to it had been broken out of the wood, leaving deep notches. In disbelief, Mandred ran his fingers over the disfigured statue. "It will die," he murmured. "Die! No one scorns our gods and goes unpunished." He turned to Farodin. "Did you see it?"

The elf raised Brandan's sword and pointed to the cave. "I suspect it is waiting for us in there."

Mandred spread his arms wide and looked up to the night sky. "Gods of heaven and earth, give us the strength to be your avenging arm. Norgrimm, turner of battles, help me destroy my enemy." He turned to the cave. "And you, manboar, fear my wrath. I will feed your liver to the ravens and the dogs."

Mandred stalked toward the cave, making the sign of the protective eye one last time. The mouth in the wall opened into a tunnel that turned off sharply to the left and quickly opened into a cave bigger than the banquet hall of a king and stunningly beautiful.

In the middle of the cave was a large boulder. The cave floor in front of it was black with soot. *This must be where Luth sat at his fire,* thought Mandred reverently.

Shimmering ice gleamed on the walls. Behind the ice were uncountable lights, like small flames, that rose all the way to the roof of the cave where their light reflected in hundreds of icicles. It was as bright in the cave as a meadow on a summer's day.

Stone columns came down among the icicles hanging from the roof of the cave and melted into massive shafts rising from the floor. Mandred had never seen anything like it. It looked to him as if the rock here could grow as icicles grew from the roofs of the longhouses. This was truly a place of the gods.

Behind him came the three elves. They looked around, obviously as impressed as Mandred. "I sense only five," said Vanna.

Mandred followed her gaze. They were the only ones here. "Five what?"

"Five Albenpaths cross here. For one schooled in the magic, a way between the worlds opens here. One who starts his journey at such a place will not lose his way, but this gate is sealed. I doubt that we could open it."

Mystified, Mandred looked at the elf. He didn't understand a word she'd said. Elven mumbo jumbo.

"That is as it should be. You are not supposed to open it. Your journey ends here." The voice resounded in Mandred's head. The jarl swung around in alarm. The beast was standing in the cave entrance behind them. It looked even bigger than it had the night he first encountered it, and its massive frame was stooped.

The head of the Devanthar was the head of a wild boar, covered with black bristles. Only its blue eyes did not look like an animal's. They sparkled, mocking them. Tusks as long and lethal as daggers jutted from its jaws.

The beast's torso was that of a powerful man, but its arms were longer than any man's and hung almost to its knees. Its legs were an amalgam of human legs and the back legs of a boar, and they ended in large cloven hooves.

It spread its hands and talons extended from its fingertips. Mandred felt sick at the sight. The manboar *had* changed. When it had attacked him and his three companions that night in the clearing near Firnstayn, its claws had not been so long.

The wolf let out a long, low growl. It had its ears back and its tail tucked between its legs, but its teeth were bared.

The manboar tipped its head back and let out a spine-chilling bellow that started low and grew higher and louder until it became a shrill scream.

Vanna pressed her hands to her ears and fell to her knees. Was this some kind of magic? Mandred took a step toward the manboar, and a chunk of ice fell at his feet. He knew what was happening in an instant. Looking up, he saw hundreds of icicles break from the roof of the cave, a rain of crystal daggers.

Mandred threw his arms over his head. The cave filled with the noise of shattering ice. Something grazed his forehead, and an icicle as big as his arm hit the floor in front of him and exploded. He felt smaller pieces pelting his back, then something hit him hard on his head.

Vanna lay curled on the floor of the cave. An ice dagger had pierced her through the thigh. Her deer-leather trousers were soaked in blood. Nuramon had been hit on the head. He was leaning against one of the stone columns, dazed, rubbing his forehead. Only Farodin seemed unscathed.

"Enough games." The elf drew his swords and held one of them high. "Do you recognize this blade? The man who owned it is dead, but it will strike you. I will cut the life out of you with it."

Instead of answering, the manboar charged into the cave. Vanna tried to crawl out of its way, but the creature was on her in a heartbeat. A backhand blow sent her sprawling, and she did not move. Then the beast kicked a hoof down on her. Her skull cracked like a clay wine cask dropped on a stone.

With a piercing cry, Nuramon threw himself at the monster, his sword raised high. The Devanthar reacted with astonishing speed. Swinging to one side, it evaded Nuramon's stroke. One of its taloned hands tore the elf's cloak to tatters.

Mandred charged forward and tried to plunge his boar spear between the beast's ribs. One of the manboar's hands knocked the blade aside, almost tearing it from Mandred's grip, and Mandred lost his footing on the ice-covered floor.

The wolf had its teeth sunk into one of the beast's legs, and Farodin attacked in a whirlwind of strokes. The manboar did not try to evade his attack and lunged at Farodin instead. One taloned hand swung down.

Farodin threw himself back, but the Devanthar's claws left four deep gouges in his left cheek. The wolf tore at the manboar's leg. Mandred found himself wishing they hadn't left the other wolf with the horses. It would have been far more useful here.

The beast spun around and brought one fist down on the wolf's back. Mandred heard a loud crack. The animal yelped. Its hindquarters twisted to one side, twitching, but it kept its teeth sunk in the manboar's leg. Pale blood streamed between the black bristles. A kicked hoof shattered the wolf's fangs and jaw.

The manboar swung wildly. Nuramon had tried to attack it from behind. One clawed hand knocked the short sword from his grasp, and a second blow ripped through the dragon-skin breastplate.

"Don't think," Farodin shouted. "It can read every thought. Don't think about what you're doing. Just attack."

Mandred's boar spear cut into the beast, causing a deep wound beneath its ribcage. With a furious grunt, the creature whirled to face him.

Mandred raised the spear to ward off the blow aimed at his head. The shaft of the boar spear splintered under the force, and Mandred was thrown backward. But before the beast could go after him, Farodin was there. In a fierce display of swordsmanship, he drove the manboar back from Mandred, giving him the chance to get back on his feet.

The jarl looked at the destroyed weapon in his hands. The blade of the boar spear was as long as a short sword. He tossed the useless half aside. Blood ran down his arm. He had not even noticed that the beast had hit him.

Farodin and the manboar were circling each other in a deadly dance. They moved so fast that Mandred dared not lunge at the beast for fear of blocking Farodin.

The elf's breath was coming in short gasps. The thin air. Mandred could see Farodin slowing down. A lunge from the manboar tore the chain mail tunic over Farodin's left shoulder with a jingling sound. In the same moment, Brandan's sword came up. Blood sprayed, and one of the manboar's hands went spinning through the air. Farodin's stroke had severed it at the wrist.

The manboar grunted and retreated. Was that fear in its blue eyes?

Farodin stalked after it. The beast lowered its head and charged at him. Its tusks sank into Farodin's chest, and the two of them tumbled to the cave floor.

"Mandred . . ."

The point of Brandan's sword had gone clean through the creature's body and jutted from its back. And still the beast lived. In dismay, Mandred saw the monster pushing itself up.

"Nuramon . . ." Blood dripped from Farodin's lips. "Tell her . . ." His eyes clouded.

"Farodin!" Nuramon cried. In an instant, he was on the beast. He raised his sword with both hands and brought it down on the manboar's head. With a crunch, it glanced off the skull, but it left a deep, bloody furrow behind. The force of his own blow sent Nuramon tumbling backward, blank horror on his face.

Still half stooped, the beast turned on Nuramon. But then, without warning, it stopped.

My last chance, thought Mandred. He stepped up behind the man-boar. Without hesitating, he took hold of its tusk in his left hand and jerked the mighty head to one side. With his right hand, he drove the blade of the boar spear down through the monster's eye. The elven steel dug deep into the Devanthar's skull.

The manboar reared one last time. Mandred was hurled back against the stone where Luth once sat. Leaden pain thumped in his chest.

"The dogs will eat your liver," he coughed.

A DREAM

The dream came to Noroelle suddenly, untarnished and pure. In the beginning, her eyes gazed out over the springtime landscape around her house, and farther, out over the cliffs along the Alvemer coast. She saw an eerie winter landscape, craggy mountains, and dense forests filled with voices and cries. A centaur lay dead at the foot of an oak, more terribly mutilated than any creature she had ever seen. It was Aigilaos. Then she was looking at Lijema lying in the snow, not moving, her body torn open. Then Lijema transformed into Brandan, lying by a campfire, rigid in death as the howls of wolves in agony rang from the forest.

Her eye moved on and came to a cave of ice filled with the sounds of battle. She could not see who was fighting whom. She could only see the ones cut down. Vanna, the sorceress, and one of the wolves. The clamor of battle abruptly stopped, and Noroelle saw Farodin on the ground. A wound gaped in his chest, and his eyes were lifeless.

Noroelle screamed and screamed without drawing breath.

Without warning, she was once again standing beside the empty throne in the queen's hall. She looked around, but she was alone. The water was silent. The walls were dry. Daylight came from above and lit the hall. Noroelle looked down over her body. She was wearing a white nightdress.

A door opened slowly. Loose-robed elven women, their faces invisible to her behind veils, entered the hall, carrying two biers between them. Noroelle knew who they were bringing to her. In her misery, she turned away. The sight would be too much to bear.

The women came closer and closer until, finally, they came to a stop before the steps that led up to the throne. Noroelle, from the corner of her eye, watched the bearers, who did not move but stood there as still and silent as statues. She did not want to accept—and could not endure—the sight of the dead bodies of her two beloved. But her eyes disobeyed her will and turned to the corpses of Farodin and Nuramon. Their bodies looked unmarked, but all the life was gone.

Trembling, Noroelle looked around, as if there had to be someone close by, someone to stand by her in her hour of need. There was no one. Then she saw blood running down the walls and gushing from the fountains.

She ran. Out through the side door that was reserved for the queen, she ran from the hall. She ran as fast as she could and did not look where her feet carried her.

Then she was back beside her lake. She returned to the spring and was relieved to find not blood but water coming from it. Weary, she leaned against one of the linden trees and began to cry. Still inside her dream, she realized it was only a fantasy. She knew, too, how many times she had seen the truth in her visions, and because of that, she was afraid to wake.

After a while, she kneeled by the lake and looked at her image mirrored on the surface. Nothing remained of what Farodin and Nuramon had seen in her. Her tears dropped into the water, making her reflection blur.

"Noroelle," came a voice she knew and trusted.

She stood and turned around. Nuramon. "Is it really you?" He was dressed in trousers and a tunic made of simple linen. His feet were bare.

"It is really me," he said, and laughed.

Noroelle sat on the stone by the water and made a sign that he should come and sit with her.

He sat next to her and took her hand. "You've been crying."

"I had a terrible dream. But it's over now. You're here." She looked around. "It's strange. Everything is so clear, as if it weren't a dream at all."

"You have power over this dream world. I sense that. Anything you want to happen will happen. The pain has bestowed this power on you. It has awakened desires in you."

"This is not the first time I have seen you in my dreams, Nuramon. Do you remember the last time we met in my sleep?"

"No. And that's because I am not the Nuramon from your dreams. I am not an image that you have fashioned for yourself. I have come into your dream from outside."

"But why?"

"To apologize to you. I have not kept my promise. We will not return." He said it in such a quiet voice that she remained quite calm.

"Then what I saw before . . . it was the truth?"

He nodded. "The elfhunt failed. All of us are dead."

"But you are here."

"Yes. But I cannot stay long. I am no more than a ghost, and Death will take me away again soon enough. One day, I will be born again. Now you know what happened. And you have not had to hear it from someone else's lips." He stood. "I'm so sorry, Noroelle." Nuramon looked longingly at her.

She rose to her feet. "You said I have power over this dream."

He nodded.

"Then take my hand, Nuramon."

He did what she bade.

"Close your eyes."

Nuramon closed his eyes.

She thought of her chamber. She had often pictured the day she would lead Farodin or Nuramon to her bedroom. And because, in the waking world, it would never again be possible, she decided to make it happen in this one. She led him out onto the meadow, not far, and wished she were in her room.

Suddenly, her walls were around them. The plants transformed into ivy and crept up the walls, quickly covering the entire ceiling. The lake and the linden trees vanished. The ground underfoot turned to a stone floor, and furniture made of living wickerwork rose out of it. She had rarely sensed such power in her dreams. "Open your eyes, my love," she softly said.

Nuramon did so and looked around with a smile. "I had pictured it differently."

"It is only this big in my dream. And it should not surprise you that plants flourish here."

He laid his hands on her shoulders. "I wanted so much to be able to keep my promise."

"And I wish that fate had allowed me to decide for myself. Now all we have left is this dream." She waited for him to say or do something, but Nuramon hesitated. She would have responded to his slightest caress long ago, but he had avoided touching her all these years. It was up to him to decide. She would not take that away from him.

When he unfastened the straps of her nightdress between her shoulders, Noroelle sighed with relief. Finally, he had dared to take this step. He looked unwaveringly into her eyes. The terrors of the human world had changed him. They had made him more serious.

Her nightdress slid from her body and onto the floor.

Nuramon lowered his eyes.

She had not expected that. He was, of course, bound to be curious about the body he had so often praised in song, curious about how she really looked undressed. But hadn't he been too quick to look? Then she thought about what he had just said. He could not stay very long. They did not have much time. And nothing would be worse than being separated at the wrong moment.

He took her in his arms and whispered in her ear. "Forgive me. I am no longer the man you used to know. It is difficult for me to be here. I am no more than a shadow of who I once was."

Noroelle said nothing, as there was nothing she wanted to say. Neither could she bring herself to consider the price that Nuramon may have to pay for wresting these few precious moments away from Death. She moved a few steps back from him and waited.

Nuramon undressed. Something wasn't right . . . she looked him up and down. It wasn't his body . . . his body was perfect. She recalled what the women at court had said. Some of them had openly expressed their wish for a night of love with him. And now that Nuramon stood naked before her, she could understand more than ever what made those women forget about the curse on his soul. She had never thought that Nuramon might truly be like one of the legendary minnesingers, whose amorous adventures women gushed about. How could he have kept that body hidden?

When Noroelle again looked into his face, she realized what it was about her lover that wasn't right. Inscribed on his face was a mute pain. He had suffered a great deal.

Slowly, tenderly, he came to her. He reached out his hand and touched her, as if to reassure himself that she truly stood in front of him. Softly, he stroked her shoulder.

Noroelle ran her hands through Nuramon's wild hair, then moved her fingers down his neck to his chest. His skin was smooth and soft. She took him in her arms and kissed him, closing her eyes. She felt his warm fingertips slide down her back, leaving a cool shiver behind them.

Together, they sank onto the bed. It seemed different than in the waking world, the wooden meshwork slightly finer, the soft foliage denser. Nuramon ran his hand over the leaves. Had he never seen a bed like this? Or did its softness surprise him?

They stopped and looked at one other for a long moment. So this was the end of the long path they had followed. She had dreamed of this moment so many times. And even though this was only a dream, everything felt more urgent, more vivid than it ever had before.

Nuramon touched her hair, rubbed it gently between his fingers, kissed it. He stroked her cheeks with the palms of his hands, then moved them lower, to her throat, her breasts. He paused there, and Noroelle looked at him affectionately. He should see in her eyes that he could do with her whatever he dared.

Then she felt his hand slide quickly down between her breasts to her navel. A quiver ran through her. It was more than just trembling at his touch. There was a trace of magic in it, too, but she could not tell if it came from Nuramon's healing hands or her magical sense. Perhaps it was a little bit of both.

He slid his hands over her hips to her back, then he lifted them from her body, but kept them so close that Noroelle could still feel the warmth of his fingers.

She closed her eyes and let herself sink back on the bed. She felt him slowly moving over her, his hands caressing her breasts, her face. She could hardly believe how warm his body felt. It had to be some kind of spell to cause such heat.

When she felt his manhood graze her thigh, she wrapped her legs around him. A shudder, then another and another ran through her body.

When he pushed into her, her breath faltered. She had dreamed so often of nights of love with Farodin or Nuramon. She had felt desire and found fulfillment, but no dream had ever overflowed with sensual pleasure like this one. This time, all her magical senses were on fire. It must be like this in the waking world. And it would have been if . . .

Nuramon hesitated in his movements. She wondered what he was waiting for. She opened her eyes and saw his face above her. He seemed almost shy as he returned her gaze. Had she frightened him with the way her breathing stopped for a moment? Noroelle ran her fingers through his hair, then over his lips. Her smile should tell him everything.

Carefully, he began to move inside her.

And in the same moment, everything around her blurred. She could not tell if it was because of the dream or if her magic or his was heightening her sensitivities and disorienting her senses.

With every movement he made, new worlds seemed to open up to her. Lights and colors swirled around her. Then she saw his face. It came and went and seemed more lovely than ever before. And the smell of him, too. There were so many fragrances that connected them, and she seemed to sense them all: the linden flowers, the mulberries, the old oak where Nuramon had his house. It was as if some enchantment had sought out all of these scents in her memory and pulled them into the dream.

Nuramon's supple skin was equally arousing. He seemed to envelop her like a soft blanket and had warmed her own cool body deliciously. She felt him breathing evenly and deeply, and she took in his breath and savored its pleasant taste.

Then she heard herself. She heard herself whispering Nuramon's name. She said it louder and louder, so loud that she surprised herself, until she screamed, all her senses merging in ecstasy.

In the space of a heartbeat, Noroelle was awake. Everything she had felt a moment earlier paled, flying from her body with a final tremble. She dared not open her eyes to see what she could already feel. Nuramon was gone. She wanted to reach out and feel him there, but it was impossible. She wanted to say his name, but her lips didn't move. And now, when she tried to open her eyes after all, she discovered that her eyelids would not obey. She was trapped in her body, uncertain whether she had truly woken or was still dreaming.

Abruptly, she sensed the presence of another in her room. Was it Nuramon? Had he come back to her in the waking world?

Whoever it was in there with her, he came to her bed. She heard his cautious steps clearly. He stopped when he reached her and did not move until she could no longer tell if he was still there. After some time, she was certain she was alone again.

Then she heard footsteps outside her room. The door opened, and she heard Obilee's voice calling her name. Her confidante came closer, sat beside her on the bed, and touched her. "Noroelle."

Desperately, Noroelle tried to regain control over her body.

Obilee stood and closed the shutters. Then she returned to Noroelle and covered her with her blanket.

Noroelle's breath caught. She tossed and turned and, a moment later, was back in charge of her body. She opened her eyes and sat bolt upright.

Obilee jumped in fright.

"Nuramon!"

The young elf smiled.

"I had a dream, Obilee." Noroelle saw her nightdress lying beside her. And she knew that the window had been open. "Or more than a dream. He was here . . . he was here body and soul." She hesitated. "But if he was here, then . . ." Then the elfhunt had failed. Then everything was as Nuramon had told her in her dream. It was over. The men who loved her, the men she loved, were dead.

THE HEALING

Nuramon stood before the dead Devanthar as if numbed. The demon had done something before Mandred killed it. An aura of magic had surrounded it like a shadow. Now the beast lay there, motionless. The blade of Mandred's boar spear jutted from its eye. The human was on his knees on the cave floor, trying to catch his breath.

Nuramon gave himself a shake. Finally, he could think clearly again. He turned and saw the dead bodies of Vanna and the wolf. Farodin lay on his back, a gaping wound in his chest.

In an instant, Nuramon was beside him. "Farodin!" he shouted, but his companion had lost consciousness. His breathing was flat, and Nuramon could barely find a heartbeat. Despite the bloody furrows on his cheek, his face reminded Nuramon of a sleeping child's.

Nuramon had promised Noroelle that both of them would return to her. Now Farodin's life was fading before his eyes. The pale haze of his breath was like the dwindling of hope. The dead could not be healed.

Nuramon took his companion's hand. It was not yet completely cold. There was still a little warmth there. Once, Nuramon's mother had told him that there was a threshold beyond which nothing could be done but to watch as one of the Albenkin died. When he looked at the wound inflicted by the Devanthar, he knew that Farodin was beyond saving.

His friend had found the courage to take on the impossible, all to save them. Nuramon owed it to him to try everything, as he owed it to Noroelle. It was up to him to find the same courage that Farodin had found. If this was the end and there was nothing left to win, then at least he would die trying to save Farodin's life.

He closed his eyes and thought of Noroelle. In his mind, he saw her face . . . and began to cast the spell.

The pain was instant and pierced deep inside his head. It felt like every vein in his body had turned into a red-hot thread.

Nuramon heard himself scream. Something reached out and gripped his throat. He had to struggle for every breath. Would he have to suffocate to give Farodin back his breath? Then something took hold of his heart and crushed it without mercy. The pain was overwhelming. He wanted to release Farodin but could not feel what he was doing. It felt as if his body were gone. He thought of Noroelle, and when he did that, he knew he had to hold on to Farodin, whatever the cost. He had to suffer these agonies. He did not know if he was still alive nor if Farodin was any better. He had lost all sense of time. All he had left was the pain that was overwhelming every sense he had. And one thought: don't let go.

Suddenly, a jolt ran through him. The pain retreated to his hands, flowing out of him like a liquid. He was dizzy and could not trust what he felt. He heard a voice say his name. When he looked up, he saw a shadow speaking to him.

It was a long time before he recognized Mandred's voice. "Damn you. Say something!"

"Noroelle." His voice rang strangely in his ears, as if it came from far away.

"Come on! Don't drop off now! Stay awake!"

Nuramon realized he was crouching beside Farodin. He still had one hand on his companion's chest, and he held Farodin's hand with the other. Soon, he felt Farodin's heartbeat. His breathing returned. Pale vapor puffed into the icy air in front of his mouth.

Nuramon felt cold. His veins felt like they were made of ice. Was he dying, or was the life flowing back into him? He could not tell.

Finally, he looked into Mandred's face. The human, awestruck, was staring at him. "You are a great wizard. You saved him." Mandred placed his hand on Nuramon's shoulder.

Nuramon released Farodin and fell onto his back. Exhausted, he looked up to the cave roof and watched the magical flames flickering behind the ice. Slowly, slowly the turmoil inside him subsided.

Mandred looked around, alert. "Do you hear that?"

Nuramon listened and could make out a faint humming noise. "What is that?"

"I don't know." The human jerked the remains of the boar spear from the Devanthar's eye socket. The shaft was splintered down to a single arm's length. "But I'll find out."

Nuramon knew that it wasn't over yet, not completely. He had to check that Farodin was truly cured. Exhausted, he straightened up and examined his companion. Farodin was sleeping peacefully. The wound in his chest had closed completely. Nuramon could sense Farodin's strength returning with every breath he took. He'd done it. He had not broken his promise.

From the cave exit came a piercing shriek. Nuramon, in alarm, reached for his sword. When Mandred came running back, he lowered the weapon again.

The human looked agitated. "Something's rotten here."

Nuramon stood up. He felt light-headed. "What is it?"

"Come see for yourself."

He followed Mandred for a few paces, then turned and looked back at Farodin. He was reluctant to leave him in the presence of the dead Devanthar, but Mandred was clearly unnerved, and he finally hurried after him.

When he reached the cave mouth, Nuramon could scarcely believe what he saw: a thick wall of ice sealed off the exit of the tunnel and obscured any view beyond it. On the far side, though, a light slowly brightened and dimmed.

"What is that?" the elf asked.

"I have no idea," said the jarl. "I tried to smash a hole through it with the spear, but I can't even scratch it." The human raised his spear and rammed it at the ice with all the strength he could muster, but the point just slipped off with a shrieking noise. "Nothing." He looked hopefully at Nuramon. "Maybe you could use your hands and . . ."

"I'm a healer, Mandred. No more, no less."

"I know what I saw. You yanked Farodin back from certain death. Try it."

Nuramon nodded without enthusiasm. "But not yet. I need to rest." The elf could clearly feel the magic at work in the wall of ice. Was this the Devanthar's revenge? "Let's go back."

Mandred trudged reluctantly back into the cave. Nuramon followed. In his mind, he replayed the battle against the Devanthar. They had fought well. Each had done their respective races proud, humans and Albenkin alike. Something troubled him. It was strange that they had prevailed so easily. Or had their wrath so transformed them that their strength had been equal to that of the Alben?

When they were back at the scene of the battle, Nuramon examined the dead Devanthar. His scrutiny was not lost on Mandred. "We defeated that thing, and we'll break through that wall as well."

The human was wrong, but how could he think any differently? The Devanthar was an enemy of the Alben. If they wanted to properly gauge their victory, then they had to weigh what they had done against the deeds of the Alben and ask themselves how the Alben would adjudge their situation. And that was precisely what was bothering Nuramon. The Alben could only assume one thing . . .

"We'll freeze to death," said Mandred, dragging Nuramon out of his musing. The human was sitting beside Farodin with his boar spear. "You won't find any rest here, Nuramon. We have to try to break through the wall while you've still got any strength at all."

"Calm down, Mandred. I'll recover awhile here, just like Farodin. And we won't freeze."

The human still looked worried.

"That goes for humans as well," said the elf and sat down beside Mandred. He took Noroelle's little bag from his belt and opened it. "Here, take one." He held out the mulberries to Mandred.

The jarl hesitated. "That was a gift from the woman you love. Are you sure you want to share it with me?"

Nuramon nodded. There was magic in the berries. If they sustained an elf and left him feeling warm and good, then they would no doubt work true wonders on a human. "We fought side by side. Think of this berry as the first of Noroelle's gifts. When you come back with us, she will shower you with riches. She's very generous."

Each of them took a mulberry. Mandred looked over gloomily at the bodies of Vanna and the wolf. "Is there any reason to call this a glorious victory?"

Nuramon lowered his eyes. "We survived a battle against a Devanthar. Who else can make that claim?"

The human's face grew serious. "Me. I already fought it once. And I escaped once. Not because I was such a great fighter, but because the Devanthar wanted me to. And when I look at the cadaver lying there, I can hardly believe that we have done what only the Alben ever did."

Nuramon looked at the body of the Devanthar. "I know what you mean."

"The Alben. For you, they are the fathers and mothers of your people, but for us, they're like gods. Not our gods, but just as powerful. We speak about them in one breath. Gods and Alben."

"I understand that."

"Then tell me how it was possible for us to beat that monster."

Nuramon looked at the ground. "Maybe we didn't. Maybe it did with us what it had already done with you."

"But it's lying there. We killed it."

"And it might still be that it has achieved the ends it wanted to achieve. What if my powers are not enough to break through that wall? Then we die here."

"But it could have killed us earlier."

"You're right, Mandred. This has nothing to do with you . . . The beast could have killed you easily. It's about Vanna, Farodin, or me. One of us is meant to be held prisoner here."

"But you told me that the souls of the Albenkin return. If you die here, you'll be born again."

Nuramon gazed up at the roof overhead. "Look at these lights. This is a place of power, and it was not by accident that the Devanthar chose it for this battle. It may be that our souls never find a way out of here. It may be that they are trapped in here for eternity."

"But didn't Vanna talk about a gate?"

"Yes. She thought this place was rather like the stone circle close to your village, except that the gate here is sealed. She also said that we are not able to open it. Perhaps the manboar sealed it once and for all to make sure we stay inside."

Mandred nodded. "Then *I'm* to blame for bringing you here. If I hadn't come to your world—"

"No, Mandred. We cannot escape our fate."

"Oh, Luth, why did it have to happen here, in your cave? Why do you weave your threads into our shrouds?"

"Don't say that. Not even to gods I don't know." Nuramon looked at Farodin. "We have both done the impossible today. And it was not the first time for either of us. Who knows, maybe we'll still manage to get through that wall."

Mandred held out his hand. "Friends?"

Nuramon was taken aback. Never before had anyone openly offered him their friendship. He took Mandred's hand and also one hand of the sleeping Farodin. Both their hands felt cold in his, but he could give them warmth. He told Mandred, "Take his other hand."

The human looked at him in surprise. "An enchantment?"

"Yes."

They sat there, and Nuramon exchanged his warmth for their cold. And because new warmth was constantly radiating from inside him and less and less cold came from his two companions, the chill in Mandred's and Farodin's bodies was soon banished.

It was Mandred who broke the silence. "What do you think, Nuramon? Which of you did the Devanthar want?"

"I don't know. Maybe the Devanthar could see things that might one day have come to pass. Perhaps Vanna would have become one of the great sorceresses. And Farodin is a hero. Epic poems have already been written about him. Who knows what he might become?"

"Did he really kill seven trolls?"

Nuramon shrugged. "Some say more."

"More than seven?" Mandred looked at the sleeping elf with awe.

"He is not one to boast about his deeds. That same reserve means that he is often sent as an envoy representing the queen," Nuramon said. He had always envied Farodin for that, although he had never told him so. He had never understood why it seemed to make so little difference to Noroelle.

"What reason might the beast have had to kill you?" Mandred pressed.

"Who knows what drove it? But let us be silent now and breathe calmly. In the end, we'll still freeze to death."

"Fine. But first you have to promise me one thing."

"What would that be?"

"Don't ever say a word to anyone that I sat here and held your hand."

Nuramon nearly laughed out loud. Humans were the strangest creatures. "You have my word."

"And I promise that you will always be able to count on Mandred," said the human solemnly.

Something in Mandred's manner touched a chord in Nuramon. "Thank you, Mandred," he said. Other elves would not have placed much stock in the friendship of a human, but it meant a great deal to Nuramon. He thought for some time, then finally said, "From this day, you are an elf-friend, Mandred Aikhjarto."

THE CHILD

Noroelle closed her eyes. A year had passed since the night of the dream, the night she had spent with Nuramon in her sleep. And it had been more than a dream. A child had been growing inside her through four seasons. Today was the day she would give birth. She felt it as plainly as she felt the water she floated in or the touch of the water nymphs attending her.

She opened her eyes. It was night, the sky clear. In moonlight, the elves were born, and into the moonlight, they would one day return. She felt cool water wash her limbs. The magic of the spring flowed through her, reaching even the child she carried. It stirred inside her.

One of the three nymphs supported her head. Noroelle felt her chest rising and falling as she breathed. The second nymph sang a song from her distant home, the sea. The third remained by Noroelle's side in silence, prepared to read from Noroelle's eyes her slightest wish or need. All of them had come from Alvemer to help her at the birth. They were the familiars of the sorceress from the sea, whose name no elf knew. Their naked skin glittered as if covered with tiny diamonds. Noroelle's gaze swept across the water and to the meadows beyond, where the wings of countless riverbank sprites shimmered in the light of the moon.

On the shore stood Obilee, the queen, and several women from her court. Young Obilee beamed with happiness, but Emerelle's face was expressionless. The two faces were like a mirror of the year behind Noroelle.

Obilee had told her the old stories of men who had visited their lovers after death to father a child, but the queen had openly voiced her doubt and had been cool and detached.

Noroelle felt the child in her belly move. The queen's hostility was less important to her than the question of whether she could be a good mother to her child. She had already heard the stories that Obilee told her through the long nights. And she knew the part that her confidante always left out: that the child was born with the soul of the woman's lover. The thought troubled Noroelle, because it meant that Nuramon had fathered himself. He would be his own father, and she would be the mother of her own lover.

She had wondered if she could be a mother to Nuramon, and the idea frightened her. But now, lying here, she knew the answer. Yes, she could do it. She would remember the father as he was. And this child . . .

It was time. Her mother, once, had told her so much about giving birth. But nothing could prepare her for what she now felt. The child moved as if a powerful spell had been cast. Her body changed in that moment. Noroelle sensed it clearly, her body growing where the child wanted to go, constricting behind it. It was a change that kept on happening, and Noroelle felt her body take in the magic of the spring's waters as a kind of reciprocation, like the ebb and flood of the tide, to complete the transformation and prepare the path for the child to follow. She felt the child's urgency. It had been inside her long enough and now wanted to be born into the world.

Time itself seemed to stretch. The moonlight on the water, the nymph's song, the child, even the most trifling details—she would remember all of it as long as she lived. She breathed steadily, closed her eyes, and let things happen as they should.

Suddenly, she felt something leave her body, followed by a wave of new sensations. Her whole body shuddered, transforming a final time. Then she heard the newborn's cry. Spellbound, she opened her eyes.

The singing nymph was holding the child so that only its head was above the surface of the water. It was so small, so fragile. And screaming for all it was worth.

The nymph touched the umbilical cord and was taken by surprise when it simply fell away. Noroelle knew that for other Albenkin, a sharp knife was needed to cut the cord that connected mother and child.

"A boy," said the nymph quietly. "It is . . . a beautiful boy."

The other two nymphs pulled Noroelle back to the riverbank and gently lifted her out of the water. She sat there on the flat stone and looked at the little creature that the singer still held in the water.

Someone laid a hand on Noroelle's shoulder. She looked up and saw Obilee beside her. She grasped her friend's hand. Then she stood and looked down at herself. Unmarked. But she had heard so much about the births of other elves. That they took hours or even days of strain, and that the wonderful occasion was overshadowed by terrible pain. For Noroelle, there was no sign at all that she had just given birth. Only on the inside did she feel weak and empty. The child was missing from her body.

The women from court came to her and rubbed her dry with cloths as soft as petals. They helped her put on a white robe. Obilee handed her the cloth with which she would swaddle the child.

She looked out expectantly at the nymph holding her newborn son. Finally, the nymph swam to shore and lifted the child to Noroelle. His skin was completely smooth, and the water pearled and rolled off it.

Noroelle took the boy in her arms and wrapped him carefully in the cloth. She looked at the child curiously. He had her blue eyes, and now that he was with his mother, he stopped crying. The little hair he had on his head was as brown as Nuramon's, and she dried it gently with the cloth. But her mother had told her that her own hair had been brown at birth and had only darkened as she got older. The child obviously took after her. Only his ears were clearly different. A little long, certainly, but not pointed at all. That too might also change in time.

The queen came to Noroelle's side. "Show me the child. Let me see if it carries the soul of a known elf."

Noroelle held the boy up to the queen. "Here is my son."

Emerelle reached out with her hand to touch the child on the forehead. But she quickly drew back and stepped away. A look of dismay crossed her face. "This is not Nuramon's child. You were wrong, Noroelle. It is not even an elf-child."

The newborn started to cry again.

Noroelle recoiled fearfully from the queen and pressed her son to her breast. She tried to calm him.

"Look at its ears," said Emerelle.

The ears were certainly more rounded than for a normal elf, but they might take on the usual form, given time. What worried Noroelle more was that the queen could not see Nuramon in the child. "Are you certain that Nuramon's soul is not in my son?"

"The child takes after you, indeed. But it is not the child of an elven father."

Noroelle shook her head determinedly. The queen was wrong. "No. That is not true. It's not possible. It was Nuramon who came to me that night."

"It is as I say. Listen well." Emerelle pointed her finger at Noroelle. No one had ever gestured so threateningly at Noroelle before. "In three days, you will bring your child before my throne. I will decide its fate, and yours, then." With that, the queen turned away and left the shore, with her entourage following behind.

Noroelle wanted to turn to the nymphs, but they had vanished. She looked over the meadow beside the lake. The little riverbank sprites, too, were gone. Only Obilee was still with her.

Her friend wrapped a cloak around her shoulders. "Take no notice of what the others say about you. You have a son."

Noroelle thought about what the queen had said. "You should stay away from me . . ." She felt nauseous and dizzy.

Obilee held on to her. "Come. Let me lead you."

Together, they left.

It should have been the most wonderful day of her life. Now everything was destroyed. The queen scared her. What did she mean, she would decide the fate of the boy and Noroelle? It sounded like a verdict. Could Emerelle judge them without knowing what had happened that night, a year before? Who could have fathered this child if not Nuramon? Had some other among the Albenkin visited her, rendered her powerless, assaulted her as she slept? Noroelle looked into her child's eyes and did not want to think about that possibility. Even with his misshapen ears, he was a beautiful boy. The queen had to be mistaken.

For the first time in her life, Noroelle did not trust her queen. Emerelle was keeping something from her. She had seen it in Emerelle's eyes. For a second or even less, Noroelle had perceived fear there.

"Will Emerelle take your child away from you?" Obilee asked.

Noroelle, shocked, stopped short. "What?"

"She scared me. Do you think she's telling the truth?"

Noroelle stroked her son's cheek. "Look at him. Can you see anything bad in his eyes?"

Obilee smiled. "No. He's beautiful. He looks just like you."

"I will do whatever the queen bids. But I will not allow harm to come to this child."

Obilee nodded. "What is his name?"

"There is only one name I can give him." She kissed the boy softly. "Nuramon," she whispered.

THE ABANDONED VALLEY

Holding the child in her arms, Noroelle made her way through the forest. It was the first night of the boy's life, and a soft wind was blowing. Her son had his hand wrapped around her little finger. He made no sound, as if he sensed the presence of the elven soldiers close by, searching for them.

There. A young red-haired soldier was coming right toward them. He wore a long coat of mail. The wind tugged at his gray hooded cloak. The fighter stopped and looked in their direction. He had beautiful green eyes. Puzzled, he rumpled his brow. He might have sensed something, but Noroelle was certain he could not see through her blinding spell. Finally, he moved past them, only to turn around sharply after a few steps. He was now so close that he could almost have touched them if he had reached out. He did not see them, though, and instead shook his head, mumbled something, then marched away.

It was a simple matter for Noroelle to evade the soldiers. She passed straight through their ranks without being seen. They may have been good fighters and even good trackers, but they were not sorcerers. Deceiving them was easy.

When Noroelle came to the leader of the troop, she paused and looked at him. Like the others, he wore a gray hooded cloak that hid his face but allowed a glimpse of the shining armor he wore underneath.

"Are you sure you understood the queen right?" asked the redheaded soldier. "It's just that . . . I cannot believe it."

The troop leader stood impassively, apparently unimpressed. "If you had seen her wrath, you would not ask that question." The leader's voice sounded familiar to her.

"But why did she send us? Noroelle is a enchantress almost without peer. And we have no one with us who could find her here. Why didn't the queen send a sorcerer with us?"

"Probably because she did not count on Noroelle resisting her like this, not even knowing our orders."

"I don't know if this is an order I can carry out."

"You should have thought of that before you swore your allegiance to her."

"But to kill a child . . ."

Noroelle shied away from the soldiers. What she had just heard was beyond her comprehension. Had she built up a false impression of Emerelle all these years? She would have never dared believe that the queen would send soldiers to kill a helpless child. Capture was the worst that Noroelle had feared. What had happened to make Emerelle issue such orders? Or had the queen always been like this and Noroelle had simply never realized it?

The queen had not only issued the outrageous order to murder Noroelle's child, but she had also lost her trust in Noroelle. She could have waited for Noroelle to appear in the Royal Hall with her baby, as she had demanded, and Noroelle would have obeyed if the queen had not dispatched her soldiers to Noroelle's home.

But there was something Noroelle didn't understand. Why had she only sent swordsmen? The troop leader's answer was not enough. Because if Emerelle could not imagine Noroelle opposing her order, why had she sent her soldiers at all? There was more going on here, but whatever it was, Noroelle now knew what she had to do.

She would never hand over her baby to the queen and her bailiffs. She would take him to a safe place. And there was only one place that Emerelle could not easily detect the child: the human realm.

Noroelle left the forest and made her way slowly across the broad meadows. She thought of Farodin and Nuramon. Since the two of them had set off a year before to hunt a beast in the human world, her life had changed. One of the elfhunt's wolves had returned injured to the queen's court, a mute emissary of a terrible fate. A short time later, her lovers' horses also came home.

Back then, when the horses returned, Noroelle remembered her dream. Her lovers' bodies had never been found. Those who had gone out to search for them reported that Mandred's village had not been molested. If she had not dreamed this dream of Nuramon and given birth to her son, she would never have believed that he and Farodin were dead.

Noroelle spent the entire night walking, crossing the heartland, seen by nobody. When the morning sun rose over the mountains, she came to a remote valley. She carried her son close to her body in a wrap that wound behind her back and over her shoulders. He had not made a sound the whole time and had even slept a little. "Good child," she said softly and stroked his head. Then she sat down on the grass and lifted the boy to her breast. When he had had enough, she laid the boy down beside her and looked at him. It would be painful, but it was the only way to save her son.

Noroelle rose to her feet. The Other World. She would cross the border. It was true that she knew a lot about the Albenpaths that passed through the three worlds and connected them to each other, but she had never applied this knowledge. The established gates, like the one her lovers had passed through, were not for her. Emerelle would have posted guards at all of them, and it would be too easy to follow the path she had taken if she escaped through such a gate. In places of great power, like Atta Aikhjarto's stone circle, up to seven invisible paths came together, tying the three worlds together with bands of magic. If you stepped through such a powerful gate, you always came out the other side at the same place. But the fewer Albenpaths that crossed, the more unreliable the door to the Other World. If you tried to pass through such a smaller Albenstar, no one could say where in the human world you would end up. If anyone attempted such a crossing without great magical skill, they might find themselves a victim of time. Noroelle knew she had to protect herself from such a fate. One mistake, and stepping through a gate could mean stepping through hundreds of years.

She also had to be careful to choose a path that led to the human world. She had no desire to go to the Shattered World. That place was no more than the ruins of a world, the remains of the battlefield on which the Alben had fought their enemies, a desolate place now, between Albenmark and the Other World, made up only of barren islands surrounded by emptiness. Those islands, today, served as places of exile or as a kind of refuge for hermits and outsiders. She would never take her son to a prison like that, which was why she had come to this valley.

Noroelle felt the presence of an Albenstar with just two intersecting paths. She closed her eyes and concentrated on the power. Even if

Emerelle managed to track her this far, it would be impossible to pick up her tracks again in the Other World, Noroelle thought. She could go through this star a hundred times and come out in a hundred different places in the human world. The band between the worlds here was weak. The faun oak had explained to her that a band like this one broke free with every heartbeat and reconnected to another place. Noroelle saw this as a sign that the fabric between the human world and Albenmark had once been so severely shaken, long ago, that the two worlds had nearly broken apart completely.

Noroelle looked into the sun. It would give her the strength she needed. It would not be the magic of the water, the magic of her lake, but the magic of the light that helped her open the gate. She thought of the light that penetrated to the bed of her lake. Then she thought of the spell, and the transformation followed its course. There was no turning back.

The sun began to shrink. Noroelle looked around. Everything was changing. The colors grew murkier and everything looked coarse and blurred. Trees paled and were replaced by shadows of trees. Spring turned into winter, a meadow became a snow-covered field. The mountains gave way to rolling hills. Soon every similarity to the world she knew had disappeared.

So this was the Other World.

It was indeed very strange. Noroelle wondered what Nuramon thought of this realm the first time he saw it. No doubt he had been as astounded as she was now.

Noroelle's magic warmed her against the chill of winter. She could walk barefoot on the snow without feeling its chill. Without her warmth, though, her son would quickly freeze to death, so she went in search of humans.

She wandered aimlessly for a long time through the snowy wasteland and saw not a single animal. Winter here seemed to allow no room for life. But finally, she saw the footprints of a rabbit. The sight reassured her, and she continued on. For where there was life, there was also hope for her son.

She spent a long time looking for signs of humans until, finally, she saw a thin column of smoke rising beyond a line of hills. She followed the sign and found a house, as plain as any house could be. At least, it seemed that way to her. She had to acknowledge, though, that she had no experience whatsoever of human houses. This one was small and made of timber. Its beams were warped, its roof askew.

Slowly, Noroelle moved closer to the hut. With every step, she feared a human might suddenly open the door and step outside. She did not know if the magic that still made her invisible would work on human eyes. She had to be ready for anything.

When she reached the door, she listened and heard furniture being moved across wooden planks. A clear voice chirped a merry tune. The song itself was unfamiliar, but she liked the sound of it.

Noroelle kissed her son and whispered softly, "Nuramon . . . I hope I am doing what is right. This is the only chance. Live well, my son." She released the infant from the invisibility spell and set him down in front of the door. The child stayed quiet but did not take his large eyes off her.

Only when Noroelle turned and began to walk away did he begin to cry. Tears welled in her own eyes. But she had to go. This was for him, to keep him safe.

Noroelle hid behind a tree not far away. The child's crying was so heartbreaking that for a moment, she considered going to him, picking him up, and staying forever in this world with him. But the queen would find them. Noroelle knew that she would have to use her magic if she wanted to survive in the human world, and magic caused tremors in the Albenpaths. The queen's bailiffs would soon use these to locate her. But her son was still too little to use the power that Noroelle sensed in him. And because, in the human world, there were no mentors to teach him, his talent would probably remain dormant forever, and he himself would be safe from the queen's wrath.

From her hiding place, Noroelle saw the house door open and someone step out. It was a human woman. Curious but apprehensive, Noroelle watched the woman who would be a new mother for her baby, Nuramon. The woman wore heavy garments against the cold but looked as if she were wide of hip and shoulder even underneath her clothes. Noroelle thought of Mandred. It seemed that stoutness was a characteristic of humans.

The woman's eyes grew wide with amazement when she saw the baby. She looked around suspiciously, no doubt wondering who would lay a child at her door and then disappear without a trace. Hesitantly, she bent down above Noroelle's son. The woman's face looked hard. She had a lump of a nose and small eyes. But as she leaned over the child, she smiled, and Noroelle could see the warmth of her heart reflected on her face. The woman consoled the child in a language Noroelle did not know, but the words sounded so loving that the child grew calm again. The woman looked around one more time to see if anybody was near, then she took the boy into the house.

The instant the door closed behind the woman, Noroelle flitted back to eavesdrop. She wanted to be as sure as could be that she had not made a mistake with this woman, even though she knew she could not stay long enough to be truly certain.

Noroelle heard the woman speaking, and her voice was one of pure joy.

There was a man in there, too. He seemed less thrilled. Noroelle could hear that his voice was full of doubt. But after looking upon the child for a while, he seemed to change his mind. Even if the humans' words sounded coarse to her ears, she felt that her son would be safe here. Now all she had to do was make sure the queen never found him.

She retreated to the cover of the trees. Originally, she had planned to return to the same place she had entered the Other World, but now she decided against it. She wanted to make it as difficult as she could for the queen. She would travel for a day and a night as far as she could from this crooked hut, and only then, with the aid of her sun spell, would she make the return passage to Albenmark. There she would follow the Albenpaths to the heartland and surrender to the queen.

THE QUEEN'S VERDICT

The soldiers found Noroelle beside the faun oak. She surrendered herself to them without resistance but did not betray the whereabouts of the child.

The swordsmen led her to the queen's palace, their troop leader riding at the front. His name was Dijelon, a soldier so loyal that he was ready at any time to sacrifice himself for his queen. He had uncommonly broad shoulders for an elf, a characteristic not hidden by the blue cloak he wore nor by his long black hair. When the door to the Royal Hall opened in front of them, Dijelon paused in his stride.

Master Alvias was standing in front of him. The elderly elf did not so much as dignify Noroelle with a glance. "Follow me," he said to Dijelon. "The rest of you are to wait here."

Noroelle was not surprised at Alvias's reaction. She was obviously being treated as an enemy. She stopped beneath the arch of the doorway and gazed into the hall. Nearly all of the queen's court was present. They all wanted to be there to see the arrival of the fallen sorceress for themselves. Until the moment her child was born, Noroelle's standing at court had steadily grown. But now, in a stroke, all of that was gone. Only the trees had held themselves aloof from the queen's wrath. The faun oak had made her feel that everything had happened too fast for events to be seen in their true light.

Noroelle looked at the water that tumbled from the walls in foaming cascades. The queen clearly wanted to make sure that Noroelle knew the power waiting for her in the Royal Hall. The show of force was hardly necessary. Noroelle knew only too well that no one in Albenmark could stand up to the queen.

"We found her at the faun oak," said Dijelon. "She would not reveal the whereabouts of the child."

The water on the walls instantly ceased to fall, and a grim silence fell over the hall.

"Noroelle, the sorceress, returns." The queen's voice was quiet but filled the entire hall. "And she has no idea of the harm she has brought down on us. Give me one reason to let you set foot in my Royal Hall, Noroelle."

"To banish me from it again with your judgment," she responded.

"Then you accept that you have done something abhorrent?"

"Yes. I have opposed you. And no one who lives under your aegis should ever do that. But I am not only here to hear your verdict. I am also here to accuse."

A murmur ran through the crowded hall. No one in Albenmark had ever challenged the queen so openly in her own court. But Noroelle had no intention of holding her tongue about what Emerelle had wanted to do to her child. It surprised her that the queen had convened this meeting so publicly. Like this, everything would be brought to light.

"Then step before the throne of Albenmark, if you dare."

Noroelle hesitated for a moment, then stepped through the door and approached the queen's throne. This time, the eyes of those she passed were utterly impassive to her.

She bowed before the queen and looked briefly to one side. Beside Master Alvias stood Obilee. Her young friend was close to tears.

"Before I decide your fate, I will hear what you have to say," said the queen, her voice icy. "You said there was someone you wanted to accuse. Of whom do you speak?"

Clearly, of Emerelle. But Noroelle did not want to risk a direct attack on the queen in front of her entire court. "I accuse Dijelon," she said instead. "I accuse him of coming to my home three days ago to kill my son."

Noroelle saw the soldier stiffen. She knew that he had acted on the queen's orders, and she was curious how far his loyalty went.

The queen glanced momentarily at Dijelon then back at Noroelle, as if only to ascertain that the soldier was still present. "Did he succeed?"

"No."

"What do you think I should do in this case, Noroelle? Advise me."

"I am not looking for amends, and I have no interest in seeing Dijelon punished. I would like to know only one thing. What made him want to take the life of my son?"

"Oh, Noroelle. You know that Dijelon's fealty to his queen forbids him from answering. So I will answer for him. He was acting on my orders."

A murmur ran through the courtiers. "But am I correct in thinking this answer will not satisfy you? You are wondering how I, the queen of all assembled here, could order the death of one of her Albenkin."

"Yes, I am."

"Then what if it were not one of the Albenkin, but—"

"He is my son, the child of an elf. That makes him a descendant of the Alben."

The gathered elves were outraged at her interruption. The soldier Pelveric shouted, "How dare you," and others supported him.

Emerelle remained calm. She raised her hand, and silence returned. "Noroelle, if you are the water, then the father of the child is fire."

Noroelle realized what the queen was insinuating, and suddenly, she was afraid. "Tell me who the father of my child is. A human, is that it?" Noroelle asked. She thought of her son's rounded ears.

"No. There have been liaisons between humans and elves before today. No, Noroelle." She stood. "Hear my words. Nothing is as it once was. On the night that Noroelle's child was born, something was set in motion that we have to bring to an end, with all the power we possess. We have lived protected lives for so long, though we have had to battle trolls and dragons. I remember when the world that lies between ours and the humans' still flourished. I know the deadliest of all threats. Never will I forget what the departing Alben allowed me to see. I witnessed the downfall of the Shattered World. I saw the final battle against the enemies of our ancestors, against the Devanthar."

Noroelle went rigid. The name of the old enemy had never been spoken aloud in this hall.

"The beast Farodin and Nuramon went to hunt was a Devanthar," said Emerelle. "It became clear to me when the wolf returned from the elfhunt, because the stench of that evil still clung to the poor creature, the stench of an evil supposed to have been defeated long ago."

"Then a Devanthar killed Farodin and Nuramon?"

"I wish I could answer that. But one thing is certain. The Devanthar prevailed. It came to you that same night and conceived your child with you."

The queen's words left Noroelle feeling cold and numb. That was impossible. She had dreamed of Nuramon . . . and now the face in her dream was supposed to be that of a demon? She looked at those around her and saw the horror and revulsion on their faces. The soldiers behind her fell back. Even Obilee turned pale.

The queen continued. "When I saw the child, I was overcome by a dark suspicion of what its father was." She pointed to her magic bowl. "And when, in my doubt, I looked into my mirror, the Devanthar's deception was revealed to me. It penetrated our heartland, and we did not even notice it."

The crowd in the hall was growing increasingly agitated. An uncle of Nuramon called out, "What if this demon is still here?"

"A fair question, Elemon," said the queen, placating Nuramon's kin. "But I assure you, it was only here on that night. Then it escaped to the Other World."

"But it could return," Elemon protested.

"It was clear to the beast that if it remained in Albenmark, I would soon recognize its presence. Now that I know it exists, I will see it immediately if it tries to enter our world again. No, my Albenkin, the demon came here to sow its seed. That was its task, and it succeeded in it."

"Where did it come from?" asked Master Alvias, who otherwise rarely said a word. "It was said that the Alben destroyed the Devanthar, every last one."

"This one must have survived all the battles."

"What have you done to us?" Pelveric shouted at Noroelle. "How could you let such a demon seduce you?"

The queen gave voice to what Noroelle was thinking. "Her love was greater than her discretion."

"What can I do?" asked Noroelle, her voice low. "If you demand it, I will seek the Devanthar and fight it."

"No, Noroelle, that is not your job. Just tell me where the child is."

Noroelle looked at the floor. Deep inside, she felt that it was not right to betray the child. She had seen nothing demonic in him. Besides, not even she could find the way back to her son. "I don't know where he is. I took him to the Other World. I do not wish to say any more than that."

"But it is a demon child, the spawn of a Devanthar, the beast that very likely killed the men you love."

"I may have been deceived in my dream, but I have never seen anything more clearly than the innocence of that child. I will not allow anything to happen to him."

"Through which gate did you enter the Other World?"

"At a place where two Albenpaths meet." Noroelle knew that there were countless such places in Albenmark.

"Tell me where the Albenstar is."

"Only if you swear to me, by the Alben, that no harm will come to my child."

The queen remained silent for a long time and studied Noroelle. "I cannot afford such an oath. We have to kill the child. If we don't, a terrible misfortune could befall us. One day, he will learn to use his magic. It is far too dangerous to let him live. You are his mother, and you have to love your child, though it be the offspring of a demon. But consider the price Albenmark will have to pay for your love if you do not tell us where he is."

Noroelle hesitated. "If my son loses his life, will his soul be reborn?"

"I have no answer to that. The boy is neither Devanthar nor elf. Think of fire and water. It may be that his soul falls in between and is lost. It might also be that your son's soul, in death, divides into Albenchild and Devanthar. Only then would the Albenchild be reborn."

Noroelle was stricken. A Devanthar. She should have felt disgusted, but could not. She was unable to look at her son as a demon's child. She had conceived him in a moment of love. Could that make him evil? No. A mother knew her child's soul. And she had seen nothing bad in her boy. But there was no proof, nothing but her word that it was so. Everything else spoke against her. She knew that the queen's judgment might cost her her life, but she was calmed by the certainty that she would be reborn. So she said, "Because my child might only have this one life, it would be wrong of me to let him die."

"Sometimes, you have to send what you love the most to its doom," the queen replied.

"I may sacrifice my own life or my own soul. But I cannot decide the fate of another."

"Maybe you already have. Remember what you said? 'Whatever task you charge them with, they will do for me.' Were you not courted by

Farodin and Nuramon? It may be that the Devanthar has killed their souls, so perhaps it would not be the first time that you destroyed what you loved."

Noroelle grew angry. "You are Emerelle, the queen. I thank you for exposing my visitor that night as a deceiver. That gives me hope that Nuramon and Farodin still live. There is no certainty about their fates, but even if I sent them to their deaths, then I did so unwittingly, because I did not know the true danger they faced. How could I have known what even the queen did not know? If I were now to betray my son, then I would knowingly incur my guilt."

Emerelle seemed unimpressed. She merely asked, "That is your final word?"

"That *was* it."

"Did you spirit the child away alone? Or did you have help?" She turned and looked at Obilee, who was trembling with fear.

"No. All Obilee knew was that I intended to keep my son out of harm's way."

The queen turned to Dijelon. "Did Obilee hinder you or lie to you in any way?"

"No, she was too frightened to try," the soldier replied, then turned his cold, gray eyes on Noroelle.

The queen, too, turned back to Noroelle. "Then hear my judgment." She raised her arms, and the water suddenly began to flow again from the springs. "You, Noroelle, have brought upon yourself the gravest of guilt. Though a powerful sorceress, you were not able to tell the difference between your beloved and a Devanthar. As the demon child grew in you, you did not see its true nature. Your love for your son is so great that you would sacrifice all the races of Albenmark for him. Even faced with this truth, you put your child's life above the lives of everyone else. Though I might understand you as a woman, as the queen, I cannot accept your choice. You have betrayed Albenmark and force me now to punish you. You will not suffer death only to be reborn. You will be banished, but your exile will not be to the farthest reaches of Albenmark or to the Other World. Your punishment is eternal exile to an island in the Shattered World. The gate to that place will not lie in Albenmark, and no one will ever be able to find a way to you."

A cold fear wrapped around Noroelle's heart. It was the most dreadful punishment that could be handed to an Albenchild. She turned to the court but saw only abhorrence and anger on the faces of those gathered there. Then she thought of her son, and the memory of his blue eyes gave her the strength to follow the path that fate had given her to its end.

"You will live forever in that place. If you seek death, you will have no hope of rebirth," proclaimed Emerelle, her voice flat. "Not even your soul will be able to leave that place."

Noroelle knew what that meant. She would never go into the moonlight. In such a place, no Albenchild could ever find their destiny.

"Do you accept this judgment?" asked Emerelle.

"I do."

"One final wish is yours," said the queen.

Noroelle had many wishes, but could speak none of them. She wished that all of this had never happened. She wished Nuramon and Farodin were there, that they could rescue her and take her away with them to a place where no one would ever find them. All of it nothing but dreams.

She looked at Obilee, still so young. Her having been Noroelle's confidante would certainly hurt her. "I wish only one thing from you," Noroelle finally said. "Do not extend my shame to Obilee. She is innocent and on the verge of an extraordinary future. Accept her into your entourage. Let her speak here for Alvemer. Knowing that this wish will be fulfilled, I will go into eternity with my mind at peace."

Emerelle's face softened and her eyes shone. Her chilly aloofness vanished. "I will grant your wish. Use this day to say your farewells. I will come to your lake tonight, and we will leave together."

"Thank you, my queen."

"Now go."

"Without the soldiers?"

"Yes, Noroelle. Take Obilee and spend this final day as you like."

Obilee came to Noroelle and threw her arms around her. Then they walked side by side through the gathered elves. Noroelle knew that she would never again return to this hall. With every step, she said good-bye. Her gaze drifted through the sea of faces, the familiar and the unfamiliar. Even those who had scorned her when she entered now looked at her with compassion.

FAREWELL TO ALBENMARK

Noroelle chose three of the magical stones that had been lying on the bed of the lake all these years and returned to Obilee. The young elf sat at the shore and paddled her naked feet in the water. Noroelle laid the three stones on the flat rock beside Obilee. Then she dried herself and put on her green dress. It was the same dress she had worn when Farodin and Nuramon rode away.

It made Obilee smile to see her wearing the dress. She looked down at the three magical sparkling stones. "They're lovely."

Noroelle had chosen a diamond, an almandine, and an emerald. "The diamond is for you."

"For me? But you said I should keep them for—"

"Yes. But there are three, and this one is yours. Take it."

Noroelle had not had much time to teach Obilee the secrets of magic. The stone would serve her apprentice well. It was as if it were made for her.

Obilee held the crystal against the weak light of the fading day. "I will make a pendant of it and wear it on a chain. Or will that make it lose its magic?"

"No, it won't."

"Oh, Noroelle. I don't know if I can manage without you."

"You will. The faun oak will help. It will teach you what it once taught me. Ollowain will instruct you in how to wield a sword, for you are a descendant of the Danee." Noroelle had made all the necessary preparations. Her friend would be in good hands and would do well.

For herself, Noroelle had stowed a few things in a bag, all she would need and no more. For her family in Alvemer, she had found words that Obilee would pass on. "Remember everything I told you?" Noroelle asked.

"Yes. I will never forget your words. Nor your gestures or the tone of your voice. It will be as if you yourself are speaking."

"Wonderful, my Obilee," Noroelle said as she gazed out at the sun, low on the horizon. "The queen will come soon, and she will have her Albenstone with her."

"The stone? Really?"

"Yes. She needs her power to create a barrier. Or it would be easy for me to escape from wherever she sends me."

Obilee lowered her eyes. "I want to go with you, wherever you go."

"Use your head, Obilee. I have been exiled, and that means forever. Why should you throw your life away?"

"But then at least you would not be alone."

"True, but then I would cry for your sake, and not because of my loneliness." Noroelle took a step back. The despair on Obilee's face upset her. "The queen would never allow someone to go with me into exile."

"I could ask her."

"Obilee, please understand . . . knowing you are here will be my solace. I'm sure that when you think of me, there will be moments when you . . . lose hope. But all you have to do is imagine me with you, sharing in whatever it is."

"But if I stay here, the sadness will be like a black cloud smothering my life."

"Then you have to come here, to my lake. The best hours of my life were spent in this place. I awakened the magic of the spring and set the magical stones in the lake. I was happy here with Farodin and Nuramon. It was here that I got to know you, too."

"And this is where you had your child," said Obilee, looking out gloomily over the water.

"Also true. But I don't remember that with sadness, nor anger. I love my son, even if he is what the queen sees in him. I have to pay for that. But you . . . you can learn from my mistakes."

Noroelle suddenly heard steps in the grass. She turned around, and when she recognized the slight figure approaching them, she rose to her feet.

Emerelle was wearing a flowing blue dress decorated with gold and silver threads. Noroelle did not know the dress, and she had seen a lot of the queen's clothes. Old runic signs were woven into the silk. In her left hand, Emerelle carried an hourglass, but her right was closed in a fist.

Noroelle now realized which spell the queen was going to cast to make it impossible for anyone to find a way into her prison. Once Emerelle had taken her to that place, she would smash the hourglass on an Albenpath, scattering the grains of sand to the four winds. No one would ever be able to gather them all again and replace the glass. The barrier would stand forever.

Emerelle showed her what she had in her right hand. It was a rough stone with five grooves. A red gleam pulsed inside it. So this was the queen's Albenstone. Noroelle had often wished for a chance to see it, but she had never thought it might come under these circumstances.

Noroelle sensed power in the stone, though it was keeping its true power hidden. Anyone not knowing its secret would have taken it for no more than one of the magic stones in her lake, but in truth, the stone possessed power that Noroelle did not even dare to dream about. It was said that all of Albenmark drew its strength from this one stone. The queen could use it to open or close gates, to create Albenpaths or destroy them. She could use it to create an impenetrable barrier at the entrance to Noroelle's island of exile. The Albenstone would be the walls of her prison, and the sand from the hourglass the lock.

Noroelle turned to Obilee and embraced her. "You are the sister I never had." She heard her friend begin to cry, and she fought tears herself. The time for good-byes had come, and she kissed Obilee's forehead. "Farewell."

"Farewell, and think of me often."

"I will," said Noroelle, unable to hold back her tears. With trembling hands, she took her bag and stepped before the queen.

Emerelle looked at her for a long time. It was as if she were trying to read in Noroelle's eyes whether she had cast the right verdict. She looked so dignified that any doubt Noroelle had ever had about her queen evaporated. Then Emerelle turned and led the way for Noroelle to follow.

Noroelle turned back once more to Obilee. The young elf would certainly not have it easy, but she would find her destiny, Noroelle was sure of that. She thought of Farodin and Nuramon. She had told Obilee everything she needed to know in case her lovers returned, but the premonition that had struck her when the elfhunt rode out had not been wrong: she would never see the men she loved again.

She walked behind the queen but harbored no grudge against her. Emerelle was her queen, and nothing would change that. Over the course of the day, she had asked herself several times what she would have done if the queen's decision had not involved *her* son. She had to admit that she would have supported her. But because Noroelle was the boy's mother, she chose to accept eternal exile rather than allow her flesh and blood to come to harm. That was why she had to leave this world. An elf could not alter her fate, even though it would never lead her into the moonlight. Noroelle looked back. As long as her lake existed, the Albenkin would remember Noroelle, the sorceress.

THE SAGA OF MANDRED TORGRIDSON:

OF SVANLAIB AND WHAT HE FOUND IN THE VALLEY OF LUTH

Svanlaib was his name. He was the son of Hrafin from Tarbor, just twenty winters old, and as strong as a bear. He built the best ships on the fjord and hewed images of the weaver of fate for his neighbors. One day, old Hvaldred, the son of Heldred, came and told him of the ironbeards of Luth that stood high in the mountains beyond Firnstayn and pointed the way to the cave of the weaver of fate. And Hvaldred told him also that the ironbeards of Luth had been defiled, the cave desecrated, and that no one could make sacrifice to the fate weaver in that place.

On hearing this, Svanlaib grew angry and said, "I will travel to Firnstayn. I will go into the mountains and demand atonement for this act." He hewed a new image of the fate weaver from an oak trunk. And all who lived in Tarbor made sacrifice to Luth, and the weaver made of wood grew a beard of iron.

Svanlaib gathered his things and set off for Firnstayn. He carried the image of Luth on his back and climbed high into the snow and ice, where he saw the ironbeards and made sacrifice to them, as custom demanded. He followed the path the ironbeards showed him until he came to the Cave of Luth, but he found it sealed by Firn's breath. Seeing this, a great anger overcame him, and he took the ironbeard he had carved and hoisted it above his head. And Luth broke down the wintry wall where a hero's strength could leave no mark.

Svanlaib waited, for he dared not set foot inside the cave. Then he heard voices and footsteps drawing near. From inside stepped the son of Torgrid. Youthful was he, and his hair was red. At his side were two of the Albenfolk, elves from Albenmark.

Svanlaib asked who it might be coming from the cave. He did not know the son of Torgrid.

The man with the red hair spoke and said, "I am Mandred Aikhjarto, son of Torgrid and Ragnild."

On hearing this, Svanlaib opened his eyes wide with wonder. Many were the stories told of Mandred Torgridson and the manboar he had gone to hunt and of how both hunter and hunted had vanished. It was said that Mandred had thrown himself on the boar, that they had plunged together into a chasm in a glacier, and that he did it to save his village.

Svanlaib asked the mighty Mandred what had happened. Mandred brought his liberator news of the death of the man who was a boar. And Mandred thanked Svanlaib, for with the power of Luth, he had broken down the boar's ice wall. He said of the elves that they had helped him. Their names were Faredred and Nuredred. They were brothers and princes of the elves, at Mandred's service.

Now the son of Torgrid took the ironbeard that Svanlaib had carried and thrown, and he set it where the burned remains of the defiled ironbeard had stood. To honor Luth, Mandred laid the head of the boar at the foot of the graven figure.

But what occurred in the cave was not told to Svanlaib and only later revealed. In the cave, Mandred had spoken with Luth, and the elves stood as his witnesses. The weaver of fate had disclosed the son of Torgrid's destiny to him. And from that day on, time held no dominion over Mandred. But Luth had not told him the price he would have to pay. So did Mandred return to Firnstayn, with Svanlaib and the elven brothers.

FROM THE ACCOUNT OF SKALDEN HROLAUG
VOLUME TWO OF THE TEMPLE LIBRARY OF LUTH IN FIRNSTAYN,
PAGES 16 TO 18

THE PRICE
OF THE PROMISE

When Mandred looked up to the spring sky, it was such a clear blue that it brought tears to his eyes. Free again. At last. With no sense of day or night, it was hard to say how long they had been in the cave. It could not have been more than a few days. Still, there must have been some kind of magic at work, for how else could they have entered the cave in winter and emerged again in spring?

Mandred watched an eagle high over the glacier, soaring majestically in huge, slow circles.

Up here in the mountains, the winter never completely disappeared, but the sun still warmed their faces as they made their way through the crusty snow down to the fjord.

His companions were silent. In the morning, they had laid Vanna and the dead wolf to rest in a small cave not far from Luth's valley. They seemed lost in unvoiced thoughts. And Svanlaib . . . there was something odd about the boat builder. No doubt part of how he was behaving could be explained by the awe he must have felt for the elves. What mortal, after all, had been granted the chance to meet in the flesh the characters from the sagas of the skalds? But there was something else in the way Svanlaib was acting. Something furtive. Mandred could practically feel the young man's eyes boring into his back. Svanlaib had asked him a number of strange questions. Somehow, the boat builder seemed to know him.

Mandred grinned with satisfaction. And no wonder. After all, he had personally killed seven men in the king's name, and he had lured the invincible manboar high into the mountains and skewered it with his boar spear. He looked at the splintered shaft of the weapon he held in his right hand. A heavy, bloody bag hung from it just below the blade. The bag had been fashioned from a piece of the beast's skin. Inside it was the Devanthar's liver. *I will keep my promise*, Mandred thought grimly.

The descent from the mountains to the fjord took three days, and they were days in which every step took them deeper into spring. New light-green growth adorned the branches of the oak trees. The smell of the forest was intoxicating, though the nights were still bitterly cold. Svanlaib had pestered Farodin and Nuramon with countless questions about Albenmark. Mandred was glad to not be bothered by the boat builder's chatter, but he knew the young man's eyes were still on him. Whenever he thought Mandred wasn't paying any attention, Svanlaib stared at him. If he hadn't rescued them from the cave, Mandred thought several times, Svanlaib would have gotten to know Mandred's fists very personally by now.

When they finally left the forests behind and all that separated them from their first glimpse of Firnstayn was a high meadow, Mandred began to run. His heart was beating like a drum. When he reached the top of the ridge, he could look down at the fjord and his village. High above him lay the cliff with the stone circle. He would make a sacrifice to the gods up there. But first, he would take Freya in his arms.

And his son. He had dreamed about him in Luth's cave. He had grown into a young man and was dressed in a long shirt of chain mail. A swordsman; his name was known far and wide in the Fjordlands. Mandred smiled. The part with the sword must have been a slip. A real warrior fought with an axe. That was one thing he would have to teach him.

Mandred was amazed at how industrious the villagers had been. Three new longhouses had been added, the dock extended farther out into the fjord, and there were more than a dozen smaller huts. The palisade had been taken down and replaced by a much wider earthen wall.

It seemed a lot of new families had come to the village during winter. Maybe they'd been driven out of their homes by hunger. Mandred's hand gripped the boar spear more tightly. There would probably be some fighting. One was not born a jarl. It was a title that had to be earned, and there were bound to be plenty of hotheaded young men in the village who would be happy enough to challenge his rank. Mandred looked back to his companions, who had also crossed the high meadow now. If he went home with two elves at his side, some would perhaps reconsider picking a fight with him. Nuramon and Farodin would have to spend at least one night in his house. He wanted as many in the village as possible to see the two elves. Then, by the end of summer, the story of the hunt for the manboar would have spread even to the most distant valleys of the Fjordlands.

Nuramon looked up at the stone circle, and Mandred could see the yearning in his eyes. But Mandred said, "Be my guests for one night, my comrades. We will sit at my fire and drink to the memory of our dead friends." He hesitated briefly, then added, "You would be doing me a great service. I want every man and woman in the village to see you."

The two elves exchanged a look. It was Farodin who nodded. Together they began the descent to the village.

Ever since seeing Firnstayn again, an uneasiness had been growing in Mandred that simply would not settle. Had Emerelle already come? No, that was impossible. A year, she had said. He still had time. He would find a way to save his firstborn.

It was the village . . . something about it was not right. It had grown too quickly. They had stored a great deal to last them through the winter, but it would never have been enough to feed so many. And the rooftops of the new houses . . . the wood had darkened, and white trails of seagull droppings caked the ridges of the roofs. The wooden shingles looked as if they'd seen more than one winter come and go.

Mandred recalled the other dreams he'd had in Luth's cave. They had been grim, filled with the clashing of weapons. There had been trolls and powerful soldiers, and he had finally seen himself riding under a magnificent white banner flaunting a green oak tree as its crest. The men who followed him were strangely armed. They wore armor made entirely of iron plates, and their faces were hidden beneath heavy helmets. They looked to Mandred like a wall of steel. Even their horses were clad in steel. Mandred had worn the same armor as the men he led. He smiled and tried to suppress his somber mood. The armor was a good omen. If he could afford so much steel, it meant he would one day be very rich. The future held good things in store. And soon he would be holding Freya in his arms again.

When he reached the shore of the fjord, Mandred waved his arms and called out wildly at the top of his voice to draw the attention of those on the other side. "Hey-o, come over! There are three warriors and a pilgrim waiting here, and our throats are parched!"

At that point, the fjord was still more than a hundred paces across. Someone on the dock saw them and waved back. Then one of the round leather boats the fishermen used was made ready. Two men paddled it across the fjord but stopped at a safe distance from the shore. Mandred had seen neither of the men before.

"Who are you? And what business do you have in Firnstayn?" shouted the younger of the two suspiciously.

Mandred had already considered that the two elves might be frightening to his fellow villagers. Tall and well armed, they did not look like regular travelers. The fact that they were not human would not be noticed by anyone at first glance.

"I am Mandred Torgridson, and these are my companions, Nuramon, Farodin, and Svanlaib Hrafinson."

The reply from the boat rang across the water. "You bear a dead man's name, Mandred. I hope you are not here to poke fun. Firnstayn is not the place for such humor."

Mandred let out a guffaw. "The manboar did not kill Mandred. I slayed the beast." He thrust the boar spear high in the air so that the men in the boat could see the bag tied to it. "And this is my trophy! You two must be newcomers. Fetch Hrolf Blacktooth or old Olav. They know me well. Or bring Freya, my wife. She'll knock your heads in with a ladle if you keep me waiting any longer."

The men in the boat conferred quietly for a moment, then they paddled the leather boat to the shore. They stared at him, and their expressions were strange. "You really are Mandred Torgridson," said the elder of the pair, and there was reverence in his voice. "I recognize you, though you don't seem a day older than the last time I saw you."

Mandred looked the man up and down. He had never seen him before. "Who are you?"

"Erek Ragnarson."

Mandred frowned. He knew a child by that name. A cheeky scamp with red hair. He was the son of his friend Ragnar, who was killed by the manboar.

"Take us across," said Svanlaib. "Let's discuss these things over a jug of good mead. My throat's as dry as a dead dog's bone, and this is no place to receive tired travelers. You remember me at least, don't you? I was in the village not a few days ago."

The older fisherman nodded. Then he made a sign that they should come aboard. When Nuramon and Farodin climbed over the gunwale, Mandred saw that Erek secretly made the sign of the protecting eye. Had he noticed what they were?

The short trip across the fjord took place in silence. Erek continually glanced over his shoulder. Once, he seemed ready to say something, but then he shook his head and turned away again.

Dusk was coming on by the time they moored the boat. Smoke billowed from the roofs of the longhouses. Mandred smelled meat cooking and fresh bread, and his mouth watered. Good food again. Roast meat and mead instead of mulberries and spring water.

He walked along the dock, his step firm and long, but he felt as if a large seagull were flapping wildly in his belly. He hoped he could stop himself from shedding tears when Freya came.

At the end of the dock, a large dog blocked his path. It growled menacingly. Other dogs came running from the village, followed by men with spears.

Mandred unfastened the hide bag from his boar spear and tossed the dogs bloody chunks of flesh. "Here, mutts. I brought you something to eat." Then he looked up. He knew none of the men.

"Mandred Torgridson has returned," announced the older fisherman in a solemn voice. "It was a long hunt." With a gesture that showed his authority, he shooed a path between the armed villagers. "Make way for Jarl Mandred."

Good man, thought Mandred. He did not know him, but Erek seemed like a man he could trust to get things done.

More and more villagers gathered to gawk at the strangers. Mandred threw the rest of the liver to the dogs that ran around the villagers' legs and finally tossed them the piece of hide that had served as a bag.

He was a little surprised that Freya had not come. No doubt she had some urgent task to finish first. When she baked bread and cooked, nothing could drag her away from her stove.

His longhouse had survived the winter well, but someone had replaced the two carved horse heads on the gable with two boar heads.

Mandred opened the solid oak door, threw the heavy woolen curtain aside, and waved his companions inside. Smoky twilight filled the interior of the windowless hall. Coals glowed red in the long fire pit in the middle. A young woman was turning a spit with a goose impaled on it. She looked up in surprise.

"Mandred Torgridson has returned," Erek announced, pushing past Nuramon and Farodin at the entrance.

"For shame, Erek. Drunk before sundown," the woman chided him. "Take your drinking mates and get out. There's no place in my house for them."

Mandred looked around in astonishment. He could not see Freya anywhere. "Where is my wife?"

The fisherman lowered his head. "Bring us mead, Gunhild," he hissed in a tone that left no room for protest. "Then call the elders together. Send for lame Beorn and Gudrun and Snorri. And bring mead for everyone, damn it! Today is a day our grandchildren will talk about."

Mandred hurried past the wall with the sleeping compartments and threw back the last curtain. Freya was not there, either. Beside her bed, the cot he himself had carved at the start of winter hung from the ceiling. It was empty.

"Sit down, Jarl." The fisherman gently took him by the arm and led him to the fireplace. Mandred sat, straddling one of the benches. What was going on here? He felt his head spinning.

"Remember how you once gave little Erek Ragnarson an old knife and spent the afternoon with him, showing him how to dress a rabbit?" The fisherman's words came haltingly. His eyes were moist and shimmered in the firelight.

Gunhild set down a jug of mead on the bench between them and set a loaf of bread beside it. It smelled delicious. Mandred tore off a chunk of bread and stuffed it into his mouth. It was still warm. Then he took a long draft of mead.

"Do you remember?" Erek persisted.

Mandred nodded. "Yes. Why?"

"The boy . . . that . . . that was me, Jarl."

Mandred set down the jug.

"We all thought you were dead," said Erek, and the words came flooding out of him. "We found them . . . my father and the others. But not you . . . and not the monster. There are many stories about what happened that winter. Some believed you lured the manboar out onto the ice and sank into the depths of the fjord with it. Others thought you went into the mountains. They say that Luth was saddened and hung a curtain of ice over the mouth of his cave for you. Nothing could convince Freya that you were dead. She drove the men out of the village to search for you all through the following spring. She went with them herself until the child was born. A strong boy. He brought her peace. His name is Oleif."

Mandred breathed slowly and deeply. Time had passed, that much he knew. It was spring, although it should still have been winter. It had always been light in the cave. Only the light beyond the ice flared brightly before falling dark again, over and over. He forced himself to stay calm.

"Where is my wife? And my son . . ." Mandred looked up. The men with the spears had come into the hall and were staring at him. More and more strangers entered through the low oak doorway. Nuramon and Farodin avoided meeting his eye, and Svanlaib, too. What did they know that he did not?

Erek laid one hand on his shoulder. "Mandred, I am the boy you gave that knife to. You've been gone nearly thirty winters. Do you remember . . . when I was still very little, before I could even walk properly, one of Torklaif's dogs set upon me." Erek pushed up the left sleeve of his coarse shirt. His lower arm was furrowed with deep scars. "I'm that boy. And now tell me why you are not an old man, Mandred. You were more than twice as old as me, but I see no silver in your beard and no weariness in your eyes." He pointed to the longhouse door. "You are the same man who left this house nearly thirty years ago to fight the manboar. Was this the gift you paid for with your son?"

A cold fury gripped Mandred. "What was that? What about my son? Where is he?" He jumped to his feet, knocking the jug of mead from the bench. The onlookers recoiled from him. Farodin's right hand rested on the pommel of his sword. He was keeping a sharp eye on the spearmen.

"What happened to Freya and my son?" Mandred shouted, his voice breaking. "What is going on here? Is the whole village bewitched? Why are you all so different?"

"You're the one who's different, Mandred Torgridson," snapped an old woman. "Don't look at me like that. Before you chose Freya, you were happy enough to have me sit on your lap. It's me, Gudrun."

Mandred stared at the weathered face. "Gudrun?" She had once been as fair as a summer's day. Was it possible? Those eyes . . . yes, it was her.

"The winter after the monster came was even worse. The fjord was frozen solid, and one night, they came. At first, all we heard were their horns in the distance, then we saw the chains of light. Riders. Hundreds. They came across the fjord from the Hartungscliff, from the stone circle. They rode straight across the ice. No one who was there will ever forget that night. They were like spirits, but alive. The faerylight was like waves rolling across the sky, and the village was covered in green light. Their horses' hooves hardly even scraped the snow, but they were flesh and blood, the cold elf queen, Emergrid, and all her court. They were beautiful to look at. And terrifying, too, for their eyes mirrored the chill in their hearts. The most magnificent of their horses carried a delicate woman. She wore a dress that looked like it was made from butterflies' wings. She seemed untouched by the cold, though the night was bitter. A man in black and a soldier in a white cloak rode at her side. In her entourage came falconers and lutists, soldiers in shining armor, and women dressed as if for a summer feast. And wolves as big as highland ponies. They came to a stop in front of your longhouse, Mandred. In front of this hall."

In the fire pit, a piece of wood exploded, sending sparks flying to the soot-blackened roof, and Gudrun continued. "Your wife opened her hall to Queen Emergrid. Freya met them with mead and bread, according to the laws of hospitality, but the elf queen took nothing. She demanded what you promised her, Mandred. Your son. The price for this village to survive and for the beast to be taken from us."

Mandred buried his face in his hands. She came. How could he ever have promised her that? "What . . . what of Freya?" he stammered. "Is she . . . ?"

"When the elves took away her son, they took away her will to live. She wept. She begged for mercy for her child. She offered her own life instead, but Queen Emergrid took no pity on her. Freya ran barefoot through the snow, and she followed the elves all the way to the Hartungscliff. We found her there the next morning, in the center of the standing stones. She had ripped her dress to rags, and she cried and cried . . . We brought her back to the village, but Freya did not want to be under one roof with us anymore. She climbed to the top of your grandfather's burial mound and called on the gods and the darkest spirits of the night for revenge. After that, her own spirit grew more and more confused. We always saw her with a bundle of rags in her arms, holding it the way you might hold a baby. We took food to her, Jarl. We tried everything. On the first spring morning after the equinox, we found her dead on your grandfather's barrow. She died with a smile on her face. We buried her that same day in the barrow. A white stone marks her grave."

Mandred felt as if his heart must stop beating. His anger was gone. Tears flowed over his cheeks, and he felt no shame for it. He went to the door of the house. No one followed him.

His grandfather's burial mound lay a short way outside the new earth wall that now protected Firnstayn, close to the large white boulder on the shore of the fjord. This was the place his grandfather had landed and come ashore. He had founded the village and named it after the boulder, as white as midwinter snow. Firnstayn.

Mandred found the white gravestone on the side of the low burial mound. He dropped to his knees and stayed that way for a long time. His hands stroked the rough stone tenderly.

In the darkest hour of the night, Mandred thought he saw a shadow in a torn dress on the summit of the barrow.

"I'll bring him back, Freya," he whispered. "May it cost my life, I'll bring him back. I swear it by the oak tree that saved me. Let my vow be as strong as an oak." Mandred searched for Atta Aikhjarto's gift, and when he found the acorn, he pressed it into the black dirt of the grave. "I'll bring him back to you."

The moon appeared between the clouds. The shadow atop the burial mound had vanished.

RETURN TO ALBENMARK

It was winter in Albenmark, but despite the beauty of the snowy landscape, the winter chill was as hard on him here as in his own world. Here, too, Mandred had to work hard, slogging a path through the deep snow while his elven companions walked lightly beside him. Now, though, his strength failed him. At Freya's grave, he'd been ready to take on anything Albenmark could throw at him, but today, he was downcast and felt nothing but emptiness inside.

His son would be a stranger to him, and thinking about him offered little consolation. He *did* want to see him . . . but had little hope that they might be reunited. Oleif would have grown to manhood years ago, and it may well be that he called someone else his father. The fact that it was winter in Albenmark made Mandred's dejection complete. This was the land of elves and faeries. It was supposed to be a land of eternal spring. That, at least, was what it said in the faery stories. It had to be a bad omen, finding this world in the grip of winter. It didn't matter that Farodin and Nuramon had assured him a hundred times that the seasons here went through their cycles just as they did in the human world.

Atta Aikhjarto had not spoken to him at the gate when they crossed over. Did trees hibernate once they shed their leaves? No one had met them at the gate, although the queen apparently knew everything that went on in her dominions.

On the first day, they marched as far as the Welruun gate, and encountered no one on their journey. Mandred thought he knew why. Doom had followed them to Albenmark. From the beginning, an unlucky star had hung over the elfhunt, and the light from it had not yet died. They had lived through a story like something from the old heroic sagas . . . and those stories inevitably ended in tragedy.

On the morning of their second day in Albenmark, when Mandred awoke in their freezing campsite and made himself get up, he did so only because he didn't want anyone in the future to be able to say he had not followed his path to its end. He would take the elfhunt—the first ever to have been led by a human—home again. What was left of it, at least. He wanted to know what disaster would finally seal their fate.

No watchman challenged them at the Shalyn Falah, and even when they reached Emerelle's castle, no one was there to meet them. It was as if the elves had all died out. Their steps echoed eerily when they passed through the massive gates. Mandred sensed that they were being watched, but look as he might, all he saw were deserted battlements and empty window arches.

Farodin and Nuramon had hardly spoken a word on their journey. Even they seemed unsettled.

Why are they avoiding us? Mandred wondered in annoyance. They had certainly been away long enough, but they were returning victorious. They deserved a more fitting welcome than this. But who was he to understand how an elf thought? Whatever had happened here must have something to do with their ultimate doom . . . the final fateful stroke that brought every saga to an end.

Nuramon and Farodin were walking faster now. The rhythm of their steps reverberated from the transparent walls in a hollow staccato beat.

At the far end of the enormous hall waited a figure, all in black. Master Alvias. He bowed his head momentarily to Mandred but did not even acknowledge the presence of Farodin and Nuramon.

"Welcome, Mortal Mandred, jarl of Firnstayn," said Alvias. "The queen has foreseen your return at this hour. She would like to see you and your companions. This way."

As if opened by an invisible hand, the door to the Royal Hall swung wide, and it seemed to Mandred that every soul in Albenmark was gathered inside. A throng of elves and centaurs, fairies, kobolds, gnomes, all standing silently.

Mandred felt as if something large had gotten wedged in his throat. The silence of the enormous gathering was even more unnerving than the endless empty halls and courtyards had been. Not a cough to be heard, not a cleared throat, nothing. Mandred looked up to the ceiling. A white dome of ice had replaced the rainbow of spring. It reminded him of the Cave of Luth.

A passage opened through the crowd to the foot of the throne. The time that had passed had left no mark on the queen. Emerelle still looked like a young woman.

Master Alvias joined a troop of young soldiers who stood to the left at the foot of the throne, while Farodin and Nuramon kneeled before the queen.

A trace of a smile played on Emerelle's lips. "So, Mandred the Mortal, still you do not deign to bow before the queen of Albenmark."

Less than ever, thought Mandred.

Emerelle's hand moved to the bowl beside her throne. "As often as I looked into the water, I saw neither you nor your companions. What happened to you, Mandred, leader of the elfhunt? Did you find what you were hunting?"

Mandred cleared his throat. His mouth was as dry, as if he'd swallowed a wagonload of flour. "The beast is dead," he said. "Slain. Its head lies at Luth's foot, and I fed its liver to the dogs. It was slain at our hand, and by our wrath." Mandred noted a disparaging frown cross Alvias's face. Mandred didn't care. The old crow could think what he liked of him. Or better yet . . . Mandred smiled grimly. The high and mighty conceit of Alvias and the others would evaporate once they discovered what the elfhunt's quarry had *really* been.

"We rode out to hunt down a creature that was half man and half boar," Mandred said, then paused for a moment, as a skald might, to stoke his audience's intrigue. "But what we found was a creature that should not have existed since the days of the Alben. It was a creature known to Albenmark as a Devanthar."

Mandred observed the crowd from the corner of his eye. He might have counted on at least one fainting flower faery, but instead of a shocked murmur, all that followed was more silence, as if his news came as no surprise to the folk of Albenmark.

The silence nonplussed him. His voice halting a little, he reported what had befallen them during the hunt, the terrors they had faced and the companions who had been lost. He described their trek up the glacier, spoke of the desecrated ironbeards in a voice filled with wrath, and praised Farodin's heroic courage and Nuramon's skill as a healer. He told the story of the Devanthar's trap and of how many years the demon had stolen from him, and as he did, his voice nearly failed him. When he came to his return to Firnstayn, he glanced for a moment to his companions, who were still kneeling beside him. "With the two companions who still remained from the elfhunt, I went—" Farodin shook his head, the slightest of gestures, and Mandred fell silent.

"What was it you were going to say, Mandred?" asked the queen.

"I . . ." Mandred did not feel that he should conceal what had happened. Still, he hesitated for a moment. "I wanted to say that we returned to Firnstayn to spend one night among my people." His final words fell in a tone of ice.

The queen betrayed no special reaction. "I thank you for your report, Mandred," she said, her voice formal. "The three of you have accomplished great deeds. What do you think the Devanthar intended? What do you think was behind the things it did?"

Mandred gestured toward his companions. "We have spent many hours on that question. We believe it wanted to create a prison for the elven souls in the Cave of Luth. What we don't know is whose soul it wanted. In the end, the beast failed. We killed it, and we escaped."

The queen looked at the three men before her in silence. Was she waiting for something? Had he skipped over some silly elven tripe that was supposed to bring his report to an end? For a heartbeat, it seemed to Mandred that the queen's gaze was focused on Nuramon.

"I thank you and your companions. The elfhunt achieved what it set out to do. You have completed your task well." She paused briefly, and now her eyes came to rest on him. "Because you were in your village, you know that I went there to claim what I was due. Now I would like to introduce you to Alfadas, your son." The queen gestured toward one of the soldiers standing beside Alvias.

Mandred's heart jumped. The man looked like an elf. His ears were hidden beneath blond hair that fell to his shoulders. Only when Mandred looked closer did he notice the fine differences. This Alfadas—as Emerelle, in her superior way, had named his Oleif—wore an ankle-length mail shirt and a flowing cape. He was almost a head taller than Mandred. His height hid the fact that he was somewhat broader and more powerful of build than the other elves. But as strange as he might look, his warm brown eyes left no doubt. He had Freya's eyes. And it was with Freya's smile that his son greeted him. But why the devil did he not wear a beard? His chin was as smooth as a woman's . . . or an elf's.

Alfadas stepped down from the platform on which the throne stood. "Father, I never stopped hoping." He laid one hand solemnly over his heart and bowed his head.

"You do not bow to your father," said Mandred sternly, and threw his arms around the soldier. "My son!" By the gods. His boy smelled like a rose. "My son," he said again, but more quietly now, and released him from his embrace. "Alfadas?" The name felt wrong on his tongue. Mandred looked him up and down. He looked like one of the heroes of old. "You're . . . tall," he noted, simply to say something, but also to gain some control over the feelings that threatened to overwhelm him. His son, the child that only days earlier he thought had just been born. And here he was, a man.

What had the Devanthar and Emerelle done? They had snatched his son away from him in a way he could never have imagined. A few days earlier, he'd been looking forward to holding his newborn in his arms, and now a man stood before him in the prime of life. Oleif could have been his brother. They had denied him so much. All the hours he would have spent teaching Oleif what made a man of honor. Carefree summer evenings spent fishing together along the fjord. The first campaign of war, when his youngster would become a man. Long forays hunting in the winter.

Despite everything, he knew that he could count himself lucky. How would it have been to face a man older than himself and to have to call him son?

He looked Oleif up and down one more time. A fine-looking man, he was. "I'm happy I'm still older than you, boy." Mandred smiled mischievously. "There might still be one or two things I can teach you. I'm afraid these elves have no idea how to fight with an axe and . . ."

His son smiled broadly . . . like an elf.

"Alfadas is to follow you now," Emerelle ceremoniously declared. "I have taught him what there was to be learned here. Now it is up to you to lead him into the human world and teach him as you see fit."

Mandred could not be certain whether Emerelle's words carried a touch of irony. "I will do that," he said, his voice strong enough so that everyone present in that enormous hall could hear it.

Beside Mandred, Farodin suddenly stood up, his mail shirt ringing softly. "My queen, I beg a question."

Emerelle nodded agreeably.

"Where is our beloved? We have done what she wished."

To Mandred, it felt as if the air in the Royal Hall suddenly grew cooler.

"Remember the terrace overlooking the orchard?" asked Emerelle in a formal tone.

"Yes, Majesty." Farodin made no more pretense of hiding his desire to see Noroelle again. Nuramon, too, was on his feet now, unbidden.

"You must go there."

"By your leave, Majesty," said Nuramon.

The queen granted them a curt nod.

His companions strode back through the Royal Hall to the high door. Mandred watched them go, glad that they, at least, had a loved one they could return to, even if he had never understood how two men were able to love the same woman without bashing in each other's heads.

When Farodin and Nuramon had departed, the queen spoke to Mandred in a solemn voice. "Mandred, I declare the hunt for the manboar complete. The beast caused some measure of ill, but in the end, the form that it had taken was defeated. You and your companions shall spend one final night in the hunters' chambers. You should refresh your body and soul, remember those who did not return, and say farewell to one another."

Emerelle stood up and went to Oleif. She took his hands in hers.

"You were almost a son to me, Alfadas Mandredson. Never forget that."

For Mandred, the words of the queen were like hot coals falling in tinder. Oleif already had a mother. And she would no doubt still be alive today if Emerelle had not demanded their son as the price of the elfhunt. Only with great effort did he manage to hold his temper in check. Despite his anger, he saw that saying good-bye to Oleif was truly painful for Emerelle. Not even the cold-hearted queen of the Albenkin was completely devoid of feeling. Mandred understood how foolish it was to put all the blame on her. It was true that she was the one who had demanded his child as the price for sending the elfhunt, but he had accepted it. And he had done so without even asking Freya, though she was still carrying the child beneath her heart. The manboar had been beaten, but his decision had cost Freya—the woman he had wanted to save most of all—her life. What must she have felt when the elves had stood before her, simultaneously beautiful and merciless, and demanded from her the one dear thing she still had in her life? Had she accepted the trade, or had she put up a fight? What had taken place that night? He had to know.

"Queen . . . what did my wife say to you when you had the child collected?"

A deep crease formed on Emerelle's forehead. "I did not have Alfadas collected. I rode to Firnstayn with my entire court. I did not go like a thief under cover of night and snow. I visited your village like a royal court should, to honor you and your son. But I alone went to your wife." She looked at Alfadas. "Your mother was very afraid. She held you at her breast, protecting you . . . I told her about the elfhunt. I will never forget her words, Mandred. She said, 'Two lives for a village. This is the jarl's decision, and I accept it.'" Emerelle stepped back from Oleif and looked into Mandred's eyes candidly. The woman, so small this close, stood a mere hand's breadth from him.

"Was that all?" asked Mandred. He knew how fractious Freya could be. That was another thing he had loved about her.

"Some knowledge, mortal, brings only pain. You did what had to be done. Let this rest, Mandred . . . ask no more."

"What were her words?" he persisted.

"Do you really want to know? Then so be it. 'But I curse my husband for what he has done. I curse him for tearing out his family before it has even had time to put down roots. May he never again find a house he can call a home. Let him wander without rest. As restless as my own soul, from which he has taken everything that might have kept it warm.'"

A lump as hard as rock had lodged in Mandred's throat. He swallowed, but the sensation would not go away. He felt like he was strangling.

"I tried to console her," Emerelle went on. "I tried to tell her about her son's future, but she did not want to hear it. She sent me away from her doorstep. She only cried when the door was closed again. Know this, Mandred. This has nothing to do with taking pleasure in being cruel to mortals. It was your son's destiny to grow up in Albenmark. The day will come when the elves will need the help of humankind. And it will be the dynasty that grows from the seed of your son that will remain true to Albenmark as a world burns. Now it is up to you, Mandred. Take your son back to the Fjordlands. Give him everything that a son can only get from his father. Help him find his place among the humans."

"Is his fate as bitter as mine, Queen?"

"Some things I see plainly, Mandred. Others are vague, and many I cannot see at all. I have already revealed too much about your futures." Emerelle made an expansive gesture that took in her entire court. "No one should know their fate too clearly. No life can flourish in the shadow of the future."

NOROELLE'S WORDS

Farodin and Nuramon walked out to the terrace in silence, each deep in his own thoughts. After all they had been through in the past few days, they were eager to see Noroelle again and to hear for whom she had decided. Farodin looked back on all the years he had courted her, while Nuramon looked forward to the moment he could say to Noroelle that he had kept his promise.

When they stepped through the gate and out into the night, they were surprised to find someone else standing on the terrace. A blond elf woman in a pale-gray dress was waiting there, her back turned to them. Her head was tilted back. She seemed to be looking up at the moon.

They approached with hesitation. The elf half turned her head and seemed to be listening. Then she sighed and turned around.

Nuramon recognized her in an instant. "Obilee."

Farodin was at once bewildered and alarmed. He and Nuramon knew, of course, that almost thirty years had passed here in Albenmark as surely as they had passed in the human world, but it was only on seeing Obilee that he truly understood what that meant.

"Obilee," said Nuramon a second time and looked the elf up and down. She was smiling, but her smile could not mask the melancholy in her eyes. "You've turned into a beautiful woman, just as Noroelle said you would."

Farodin was looking at the very image of the great Danee standing before him. When she was younger, there had only been the vaguest of similarities, but now she was barely distinguishable from her grand-mother. He had seen Danee for the first time at court. He had been a child at the time, but he still remembered very clearly the awe he felt when her eyes briefly met his. "Now I see it, too. You wear some part of Danee's aura, as Noroelle always said you did."

Obilee nodded. "It seems Noroelle was right."

Farodin looked down to the orchard. "Is she down below?"

The young elf avoided his eye. "No, she isn't in the orchard." When she looked at him again, there were tears in her eyes. "She isn't here anymore."

Farodin and Nuramon exchanged an uneasy look. Farodin thought of the thirty lost years. Could Noroelle have believed anything other than that they were dead? Had she left the queen's court and retreated into some lonely existence?

Nuramon thought of the silence that had hung over the Royal Hall. Everyone in there had known something. What could have happened to make Obilee so mournful? Not death, for after death came rebirth. It had to be something more painful, and the very thought made Nuramon afraid.

"Noroelle knew it," said Obilee. "She knew you'd return one day."

Farodin and Nuramon said nothing.

"Years have passed, yet you are wearing the same things you wore the day you rode out . . . ," said Obilee.

"Obilee? What has happened?" asked Farodin directly.

"The worst, Farodin. The very worst."

Nuramon began to shake. He thought of all they had been through. He had done everything he could to keep his promise.

Obilee had not the courage to go on, and Farodin asked, "Has Noroelle turned away from us? Has she returned to Alvemer? Is she disappointed?"

Obilee took a step back and took a deep breath. "No . . . hear my words. They are the words Noroelle spoke the night she went away." Obilee raised her eyes to the sky. "'I knew you would return. And now you are there and hearing the fate that has befallen me.'" She spoke the words as if she were Noroelle. In its melody, her voice captured every nuance and emotion. "'Do not think poorly of me when you find out what I have done and where my fate has taken me. Not long after you left Albenmark, I had a dream. In it, you came to visit me, Nuramon, and we made love. A year later, I gave birth to a son. I thought the boy was your child, Nuramon, but I was wrong. It wasn't you who came to me in the night. It was the Devanthar you had gone to hunt in the Other World.'"

Nuramon and Farodin caught their breath. The mere thought that the Devanthar had been able to get close to Noroelle was intolerable.

Farodin thought of the battle in the cave. The demon had made it too easy for them. Now he knew why. Had it all been a sham? Had the Devanthar only ever been searching for a way to get to Noroelle?

Nuramon shook his head in disbelief. The beast had taken on his form to seduce Noroelle. It had exploited her love. She had dreamed of him, and the Devanthar had used that to get close to her and . . .

Obilee took hold of Nuramon's hand, drawing him out of his painful musing. "'Nuramon, don't be hard on yourself. The demon wore your face, and I allowed myself to be seduced by your countenance, your body. But don't think for a moment that I feel any contempt or disgust because of that. I love you even more than I did before. Condemn the Devanthar, not yourself. It turned what we feel for each other against us. Only when we stand up for what we are and what we feel, only then can what it did fade away. Its deed will pale to insignificance. Do not blame yourself.'" Obilee looked at him as if she were waiting for some kind of reaction. There was a pleading in her eyes that he could not resist. He sighed heavily and nodded.

Now Obilee took Farodin's hand. "And you, Farodin, do not believe that I had already made my choice. I had not settled secretly on Nuramon. That is not why the demon came to me.'"

"But where are you, Noroelle?" Farodin asked, as though the woman he loved could actually hear his words. He was perplexed.

Obilee smiled and tilted her head to one side, as Noroelle herself had so often done. But her eyes could not hide her sadness. "'I knew that you would ask this question, Farodin. The single spark you entrusted to me that night, that one glimpse into your innermost soul was enough for me to know you as I had always wished I could. I can read what is inside you as surely as I can read Nuramon's face. So where am I? It will hurt you to hear it, for I am in a place where no one will ever be able to reach me. The queen has banished me from Albenmark for all eternity. There are barriers between us that you are not able to break down. All I have left is the memory, the memory of the night before you rode out, when both of you left me with so much. You, Farodin, revealed to me the radiance of your true being. And you, Nuramon, touched me for the first time.'"

Obilee stopped speaking for a moment. She seemed hesitant, but after a little while, she continued. "'You should also know why I was banished. The child I bore had round ears, and the queen recognized it as a demon child. She saw in it the child of the Devanthar. I was ordered to appear at court with my son three nights after the birth. But the queen sent Dijelon and his soldiers that same night to kill the child. I took him to the Other World, to a place that the queen would have great difficulty finding. And when I stood before Emerelle, I refused to reveal where he had found refuge. Forgive me if you can, for I saw nothing evil in the eyes of the child. Now you know what taints me, but it does not have to taint you as well. Forgive me for acting so foolishly.'" Obilee began to cry, for Noroelle, too, back then, had been unable to hold back her tears. "'Please remember those lovely years we spent together. There was nothing about either of you that was bad or wrong, and nothing happened that we have to regret. Whatever may come, don't forget me . . . please don't forget me.'" Obilee could hold back her own emotions no longer.

"Those were Noroelle's own words," she said, her voice tear choked, and she pressed her face into Nuramon's shoulder. Nuramon looked at Farodin and saw his face expressionless as a mask. No tears, no stir of emotion, not the slightest sign of sadness. Nuramon himself could hardly comprehend what Obilee had said. It was too much to cope with all at once.

But what Farodin saw in Nuramon's eyes and on his face was everything he himself was feeling inside. All the tears, all the agony. It seemed to him as if his feelings had divorced themselves from his body. He stood there, unable to understand why he could not weep as well.

It was a long time before Obilee had herself back under control. "Forgive me. I did not think it would be so painful. I've carried those words inside me all these years . . . words that Noroelle spoke to a child and that you are now hearing from a woman." Obilee turned away and walked over to the edge of the terrace. She picked up something from the railing and returned to them. "I have a final gift from Noroelle to give to you." She opened her hands and showed them an almandine and an emerald. "These are stones from her lake. They are meant to remind you of her."

Farodin took the emerald and thought of the lake. Noroelle had once told him that the magic of the spring would cause the stones to grow.

Nuramon touched the almandine where it lay in Obilee's hand. He hesitated, stroking the smooth surface of the red-brown stone with his fingertips. He sensed magic . . . Noroelle's magic.

"I can feel her, too," said Obilee. "She gave me such a gift as well." She wore a diamond on a chain around her neck.

Nuramon took the almandine in his hand and felt its soft magic. That was all that remained to him of Noroelle: the warmth and the breath of magic of this gift.

Obilee withdrew from them. "I have to go now," she said. "Forgive me. I need to be alone."

Farodin and Nuramon watched her as she left the terrace.

"She carried that pain inside her for thirty years," said Nuramon. "If these few days felt like an eternity to us, then she has lived through thousands of eternities."

"So this is how it ends," said Farodin. He could not believe it. Everything in his life had been built around Noroelle. There were many things he could have imagined happening, that he might die, that Noroelle would choose Nuramon, but he had never thought that something like this could . . .

"How it ends?" Nuramon seemed unprepared to accept that. No, this was not the end. It was the beginning, the beginning of an impossible journey. Some say that one should not tempt fate too often, but he would do everything in his power to find Noroelle and set her free. "I will speak to the queen," he said.

"She won't listen to you."

"We'll see," Nuramon said as he turned to leave.

"Wait!"

"Why? What do I have to lose? And you should ask yourself how far *you* are willing to go for her." With those words, Nuramon disappeared into the palace.

"To the end of all the worlds," whispered Farodin to himself, and thought of Aileen.

THREE FACES

The door to the Royal Hall stood open. Nuramon could see the queen at the far end, beside her bowl of water. He was about to enter the hall when Master Alvias suddenly blocked his path. "Where are you going, Nuramon?"

"I want to speak to the queen about Noroelle, to ask for clemency," Nuramon replied.

"One should not set foot in this hall in anger."

"Are you afraid that I might raise my hand against Emerelle?"

Master Alvias looked down at him. "No."

"Then let me pass."

Alvias half turned and looked to the queen, who nodded. "She will receive you," he said reluctantly. "But keep a tight rein on your emotions." So saying, Master Alvias stepped aside.

While Nuramon strode quickly through the hall, he heard the door being closed behind him. The queen moved down and stood before the steps that rose to her throne. Her face was an image of calm and good. For Nuramon, Emerelle had never before looked more like the mother of all the Albenkin.

Nuramon felt his anger ebb. The queen stood silently and looked at him as she had on the night she had visited him in his room and boosted his courage. He thought of the counsel of the oracle that she had shared with him and which had meant so much to him.

"I know what you are thinking, Nuramon," said the queen. "I appreciate that you have not yet learned to hide your feelings."

"And until now, I have always thought highly of your sense of justice. You know that Noroelle is not capable of doing anything evil or reprehensible."

"Did Obilee tell you what happened?"

"Yes."

"Forget for a moment that Noroelle is your beloved, then tell me that she is free of blame."

"She is what I love most. How am I supposed to forget that?"

"Then you cannot understand why I had to do it."

"I am not here to understand. I am here to plead for mercy."

"The queen has never revoked a verdict."

"Then banish me to wherever Noroelle is. At least grant *me* this mercy."

"No, Nuramon. That I will not do. I cannot banish one who is innocent."

And what was Noroelle? Wasn't she herself more victim than culprit? She had been deceived, and for that had to atone. Wasn't it up to Emerelle to put all her powers to work to punish the true perpetrator? "Where is the Devanthar?" Nuramon asked, changing his tactics.

"It fled into the human world. No one can say in what form it has disguised itself. Only one thing is certain. It is the last of its kind. And it is plotting against us, planning our downfall. The core of that creature is revenge."

"Would Noroelle's guilt be less if we track down and destroy the demon?"

"The Devanthar has played its game. Now it is waiting to see what comes of it."

Nuramon felt his despair rising. "But what can we do? There must be something we can do."

"There is something . . . but the question is whether you are prepared to do it."

"Whatever you ask. I will promise anything to ensure Noroelle goes free."

"A bold vow, Nuramon." The queen hesitated. "I will take you at your word. Choose your companions and find Noroelle's child. Keep in mind that he is a man now. Many have already searched for him, all without success. You are not the first to ride out in search of him. But perhaps you will enjoy more luck . . . You have the incentive you will need to find the demon's child."

"Noroelle feared for the life of her son. Will we also have to?"

Emerelle looked at Nuramon and said nothing for a long time. "Noroelle had the choice. She chose eternal condemnation because she shielded the child of a Devanthar."

"How can I bring myself to do what she was not able to?"

"Are your promises always so short-lived?" Emerelle asked in reply. "If I am to free Noroelle, then you and your companions must kill her child."

"How can you torment me like this?" replied Nuramon quietly.

"Think of the guilt that can be ascribed to you and your companions. You failed in your quest, and because of that, the beast was able to find a way to Noroelle. It took your form, abused Noroelle, and created this child. And Noroelle could not give up the child because she could not stop herself from thinking that you were the boy's father and that he carried your soul. She even gave him your name. You would be doing it not only for Noroelle, but also for yourself and for the sake of your companions."

Nuramon wavered. He could not close his eyes to the truth of what she said. He was certain that he could never murder a child. But Noroelle's son had long since grown to be a man. No doubt his true nature had already revealed itself. "I will find Noroelle's son and kill him."

"Then I will select companions for you among our best soldiers. What about Farodin? He will certainly accompany you."

"No. I will accept the help of your soldiers, but I will not ask Farodin to join me. When Noroelle returns, she will hate me for killing her child, and justifiably. There will be no blood on Farodin's hands. She will find the love she deserves in his arms."

"Very well. That is your decision. But you will certainly have nothing against accepting horses from my stable. Choose any you want, to suit you and those who ride with you."

"I will do that, my queen."

Emerelle stepped close to him. She gazed at him now with a look of deep sympathy. A calming fragrance surrounded her. "All of us have to follow our fate, wherever it may lead. But it is up to us to decide how we tread that path. Trust in the words of advice I gave you that night. They are no less valid today. Whatever they may say about you in the future, no one can ever say you betrayed the one you love. Now go and rest in your chamber. The elfhunt has returned. You should take the time you need to recuperate. You can decide for yourself when you want to go out again. This time, you will not ride as an elfhunt, but only in the service of the queen."

Nuramon thought of the armor Emerelle had given him. "I would like to return the armor, the cloak, and the sword."

"I see that the dragon scale and the cloak have served you well. Leave them in your chamber, as is the custom. The sword should remain yours. It is a gift." Emerelle stood on the tips of her toes and kissed him on the forehead. "Now go, and have faith in your queen."

Nuramon did as she said. He looked back at her one more time before he left the Royal Hall. She was smiling pleasantly. When he was outside again and standing before the others, he could not comprehend the turn their conversation had taken. Emerelle had received him like a caring mother, judged him like a hard-hearted queen, then sent him on his way like a good friend.

THREE GRAINS
OF SAND

Farodin leaned his forehead against the wall. A sliver of light fell through into the secret passage that led onto the balcony in front of the queen's chamber. He was not supposed to be here.

He was wearing an inconspicuous gray doublet, close-fitting gray trousers, and a gray hooded cloak. On his hands he wore thin leather gloves, around his waist a broad belt, and on his arms bracers with sheaths for daggers. He hoped he would not have to use the weapons. Far below, deep in the labyrinth of hidden stairways and passages, he heard the laughter of the kobolds, an entire generation of which had grown up since the day that Noroelle had been judged guilty.

Farodin balled his hands into fists in his helpless rage. The pain was still too fresh. He had served the queen so many times as her covert executioner, and never had he doubted her higher understanding of what was right and just. He had never even considered the possibility that her secret death sentences might be nothing more than caprice. Now her judgment had destroyed his own life, though he still stood and breathed.

No one knew Noroelle the way he knew her. No one knew that she had once been Aileen, his Aileen, who had lost her life in a battle against the trolls. He had searched for her for centuries, and now that he had found her, she had been torn away from him again. But this time, he could not hope for Aileen's rebirth. Were Noroelle to die in exile, there would be no way back. Her soul would be trapped in that place forever.

Tears of fury streamed down Farodin's cheeks. Noroelle had been deceived by a Devanthar, a creature known to be a master of deception. And the demon had fed on her love.

Why had the beast taken Nuramon's form? Farodin tried in vain to hold down his growing suspicion. Had the Devanthar perhaps known something? Would Noroelle have chosen Nuramon when the elfhunt returned? Had her words to Obilee been no more than a way to console him, spoken lightly in the certainty that she would never see either of them again?

And she must have succumbed very quickly to the charms of the false Nuramon. They had courted her for so many years, and in all that time, she had been unable to reach a decision. And then suddenly—in a single night—she did? That, too, must have been part of the enchantment cast by the Devanthar . . . at least, that's what Farodin tried to tell himself.

Noroelle was innocent. She was pure of heart . . . she *remained* pure of heart. She lived. That was why he would find her, Farodin swore. It made no difference how long the search might take. The queen had had no right to inflict on Noroelle the most severe of all punishments. He would never accept her verdict. Farodin looked at the shard of light at the top of the stairs. He really was not supposed to be here . . . but what difference did it make? Emerelle had exploited him to dispense her form of justice whenever the usual laws had fallen short. Now he would dispense his own justice.

Determined, Farodin squeezed through the narrow gap. He crept to the railing of the balcony and looked over it cautiously into the depths. A dome of ice below hid the Royal Hall from him, but he knew that Emerelle was holding court down there.

He stepped across to the wide double door of the queen's chamber and found it unlocked. A sign of her hubris? Was she relying on a taboo being more secure than any lock?

Farodin swept away the shallow footprints he had left in the fresh snow and cautiously pushed the door open. In all the centuries that he had served as Emerelle's assassin, he had never once set foot inside her chambers. The modesty of the furnishings surprised him. The few pieces in the room were of a plain elegance. The embers of the fire in the fireplace bathed the bedroom in a red twilight. It was a warm and cozy place.

Farodin looked around in confusion. He knew there had to be a dressing chamber where she kept her splendid garments. Noroelle had once spoken of it. There was where he should start his search. He had to find the dress that Emerelle had worn when she led Noroelle into exile. But where could the entrance to the royal dressing chamber be hidden? Besides the double door to the balcony and another door that must have led to the stairway, he saw no other. He ran his hands over the walls, looked behind tapestries, and finally found himself standing before a large mirror. It was framed in ebony with inlaid mother-of-pearl. Farodin's fingers glided over the stylized leaves and flowers. One rose was surrounded by a visible gap. Carefully, the elf pressed the pearly bloom. A soft click sounded, and the mirror slid aside. Farodin, startled, took a step back. Behind the mirror was a room filled with glowing figures. Headless figures. The elf exhaled and laughed at himself. No more than dresses worn by wicker dummies so that they held their form. Beneath the wicker forms stood scented candles that made the dummies glow like oversized paper lanterns.

The room was as magnificent as the queen's bedroom was plain. Farodin was dazzled by the multitude of scents. Peach, musk, and mint were the main aromas. Emerelle dressed herself not only in her royal robes, but also in royal fragrances.

The room followed the curve of the outer wall of the tower. From the door, one could not see the entire room. Farodin stepped over the threshold, and the mirror door closed behind him with a light scrape. The elf was still dazed by the sights and smells of the room. Along the walls, velvet cushions were set on narrow ledges, resplendent with the queen's jewels. Pearls and precious stones in all the colors of the rainbow sparkled in the warm light. It must have been a delight for Noroelle to wander among all the magnificent dresses and jewels.

The room had no windows, which seemed strange to Farodin.

"Noroelle," Farodin whispered. She had loved the queen's dressing chamber. All the dresses, hunting outfits of velvet and suede, evening dresses elaborately embroidered, transparent silken garments as delicate as a breath that Emerelle would certainly never wear in the presence of her court. Sumptuous brocade formed around whalebone and wire, corsets stiff with ceremony, and court formalities unchanged in centuries. Endless shelves were filled with shoes on racks. Tight-fitting dancing shoes, shoes of cloth, boots with heavy leather tops. One wide ledge was piled high with gloves.

Farodin kneeled and retrieved a ring from his leather bag. Three small dark-red garnets were set in it. It was Aileen's ring. It had been of immeasurable help to him in his search for her, a kind of anchor set firmly in the chasm of the past, and it helped Farodin to concentrate on the woman he loved. The emerald, Noroelle's parting gift to him, would be a second anchor. He whispered the familiar words of power and wove the seeking spell. It was the only spell he had mastered, and it had proved its worth in the centuries he had spent searching for Aileen.

Among all these garments, there had to be the one that Emerelle had worn when she banished Noroelle. Finding it would be the first step to finding Noroelle. Farodin had a plan of his own, but one so desperate, he would not speak to a soul about it.

The power of the magic flowed through the elf. He felt the precious emerald in his hand. Then he slowly stood up. Eyes closed, Farodin felt his way through the room, led by nothing more than a vague feeling. Longing and memory began to compress. For the space of a heartbeat, it was as if he could see through Noroelle's eyes. He was looking into the queen's visage. In the lines of her face, he saw resolve, and restrained sadness. The image blurred. Farodin opened his eyes. He was standing in front of one of the dummies; it wore a robe of blue silk. Worked into the robe were threads of silver and gold that formed interwoven patterns of runes. The light from the candle made the wickerwork frame look like bones beneath the dress.

A shudder ran down Farodin's spine. So this was what Emerelle had worn when she sent his beloved into exile. His fingers glided across the delicate material. Tears came to his eyes. For a long time, he simply stood there and struggled to control his emotions.

The runes on the robe were permeated with magical power. He sensed a prickling sensation on his skin when his fingers touched them. And there was more . . . he relived Noroelle's feelings at the moment of her banishment. Something of what she had gone through had been trapped by the runes, but there was no fear. She had resigned herself to her fate. She was at peace with herself and with the queen when she went.

Farodin closed his eyes. His entire body began to tremble. The power of the runes had pervaded him as well. He saw an hourglass smashed on a stone and felt how the magical equilibrium convulsed. The way to Noroelle was sealed. She had been carried away. Untraceable . . .

The elf's knees failed him. In his desperation, in sheer defiance, he cast the seeking spell a second time. He already knew what had taken place. Knowing it was one thing, but experiencing it through the magic of the runes was something entirely different.

"Come on," he whispered. "Come to me." He held out his hand and thought of the hourglass. A wind whipped at him, trying to tear him away. He stood surrounded by swirling sands, as if caught in the vortex of the hourglass.

Shaken, Farodin opened his eyes. It was only a vision, an illusion born out of his own yearning. And yet . . . it seemed darker, suddenly, inside the chamber. As if something were in the air that did not belong there, something that was slowly smothering the light of the candles.

Three tiny, glowing points rose from the surface of the cold blue silk and hovered over Farodin's hand. Three grains of sand from the hourglass that Emerelle had smashed, caught in the folds of her robe.

The spell and the storm of emotions had drained Farodin. But the three points of light, slowly fading, planted a seed of new hope in his heart. He would find Noroelle again, even if it meant another seven hundred years of searching. He pushed the emerald deep into his pocket, but he wanted to hold the particles of sand in his hand. They were the key. If he could recover every grain of sand from the smashed hourglass, then he could break the queen's enchantment. It was the one and only path that led to the woman he loved.

NIGHT DEPARTURE

It was deep in the night, and the palace had long fallen silent. From outside came the low whisper of the wind. Nuramon stood at the unshuttered window and looked out into the bright night. It had stopped snowing. The light of the moon reflected from the snow, enveloping everything in a silvery sheen. Morning would come soon, and the silver would turn to gold. Nuramon could not imagine a better time for him to go.

Everything he would need was packed. All his preparations were made. He wanted to leave that same night. The armor and cloak that he had returned to their stand caught his eye. They had served him well in the human world, but now, Nuramon wore the clothes Noroelle had last seen him in—plain garments of soft leather. They gave him no protection in battle, but he doubted he would need that. He was not going into the Other World to face a beast, but to kill a man who was most likely unarmed. There was no honor in such a task, and he would hate himself forever for seeing it through.

He looked at his sword. The queen had given him Gaomee's sword as a gift. She obviously wanted him to carry out his task with that blade. Ever since he had first held the sword in his hand, a curse seemed to cling to it. But he would not give it up because of that. Who would want to hold this weapon once his ill-fated fingers had touched it?

There was a knock at the door.

"Come in," said Nuramon, hoping it was someone sent by the queen, a companion whom he could swear to silence. A vain hope . . .

Mandred and Farodin entered. Their faces showed their despondency.

"I'm glad to see you're still awake," said Farodin. He seemed agitated.

Nuramon tried not to let anything show. He wanted to keep the queen's ignoble commission hidden from his two comrades. "I can't sleep," he said. It was the truth. He had not closed his eyes at all that night.

Farodin gestured toward Mandred. "Mandred told me that you spoke privately with the queen. So she granted you an audience after all."

"She did."

"I also tried to see her, but ever since you were in with her, she has refused to meet anyone. Strange rumors are circulating," said Farodin.

"What kind of rumors?" Nuramon asked, making an effort to keep his own disquiet in check.

"Some say the queen placated you and that you accepted her verdict. Others claim she gave you permission to search for Noroelle."

"Emerelle gave me no such permission, but I have accepted her verdict."

A look of skepticism crossed Farodin's face. "Something I would not have expected of you."

Finally, a sign of emotion from Farodin. Maybe it was for the best to stoke his contempt. Then Farodin could face Noroelle with a clear conscience.

Mandred was looking warily from one to the other. The human seemed to realize that Farodin had misunderstood Nuramon's words.

"How can you doubt Noroelle like that?" Farodin continued in a deeply disappointed tone. "Did you ever love her?"

Though his companion's words were unjustified, they still hurt. "I love her more than ever, which is why it hurts so much to know that there is nothing more that we can do. We cannot force the queen to release Noroelle," Nuramon said, all the while finding it hard to hold back the truth.

Now it seemed that Farodin's suspicions had been kindled as well. He looked at Nuramon as if he could read his innermost thoughts.

"The lad's lying," said Mandred, his voice dry.

"And he's a bad liar," Farodin added.

Mandred looked at the bags lying on the stone bench. "One might almost suspect he wanted to go off and find the woman he loves without us."

"What did the queen say?" Farodin pressed. "Did you plead for banishment for yourself? Can you go to Noroelle?"

Nuramon slumped onto the bench beside his bags. "No. I tried everything, but the queen would accept nothing. She would not banish me. Even if we tracked down and destroyed the Devanthar once and for all, it would not change anything."

"So you've decided to go off alone to look for her."

Nuramon looked up at Farodin for a long time. It was impossible to keep his true plan a secret from him. "I wish it were that simple. I wish I could just take my things and set off and try to find a way to help Noroelle." He paused. "If I asked you to let me go and not ask any questions, would you?"

"I owe you a debt. You brought me back from the brink of death . . . but I wager that fate has bound us to each other. And don't forget that Noroelle has not yet made her choice. Our destiny is to search for her together."

"A few hours ago, those words could have come from me," Nuramon said. But the meeting with Emerelle had changed everything.

"What did the queen say to you?" asked Farodin again. "Whatever task you have accepted from her, I will not think less of you. Tell me."

"Very well," said Nuramon, standing up. "She said that there is one possible way to rescue Noroelle. And I promised to do whatever she demanded."

"That was a mistake." Farodin smiled sympathetically. "Won't you ever learn that?"

"You know me, Farodin. And you know how easy it is to make me act rashly. Emerelle knows it, too."

Mandred spoke up again. "So what is she asking you to do?"

Nuramon avoided meeting the human's eye. Of the three of them, he had paid the highest price.

"What does she want of you?" Farodin persisted.

Again, Nuramon hesitated, reluctant to answer. As soon as his companions knew the truth, all happiness would vanish from his life.

"Say it, Nuramon."

"Are you sure you want to hear it, Farodin? Sometimes not knowing the truth is better. If I tell you now, nothing for you will be the same as it was before. If I say nothing, you could be happy . . . I beg of you. Let me go, ask no more, and don't follow me. Please."

"No, Nuramon. Whatever the burden, we have to carry it together."

Nuramon sighed. "As you want . . ." A thousand thoughts raced through his mind. What if he lacked the strength to carry out the deed? Had he secretly wanted to share the blame with Farodin? Was that why he was giving in? Or was it arrogant to want to make this decision alone? Did Farodin have a right to find out what the queen was demanding of him? "I am going in search of Noroelle's son. To kill him," said Nuramon quietly.

Farodin and Mandred stood looking at him as if they were still waiting for him to speak.

"Let me go alone. Farodin, listen to me. Wait here until Noroelle returns." Nuramon knew what would happen next. There was no turning back.

Farodin shook his head. He spoke as if numb. "No. No, I can't do that. You expect me to sit here and wait for Noroelle? What am I then to say to her when she returns? That I let you depart knowing full well you went to kill her son? Now that I know it, I have two choices, and only two. Either I stop you, or I go with you . . . and if I stop you, it won't help Noroelle. So I have to share your fate. To save her."

Mandred shook his head, stunned and bewildered. "Oh, Luth, what kind of net have you woven for these elves?" he murmured.

"It looks as if your gods are not kind to us," Nuramon said. "But we ourselves are to blame in the end. The queen reminded me of our failure in the cave." He explained Emerelle's reproach to his companions.

"So we're at fault for not being Alben now?" said Mandred, suddenly furious.

"If that is so, then it's a fault we were born with, and our entire being is marked by it," replied Farodin. He paused for a long moment. "It looks like the only paths ahead of us are murky," he finally said. "Let us ride."

Nuramon turned to the human. "Our paths separate here, Mandred. You have found your son. Take time for him and be the father that fate has so far stolen from him. You are not damned as we are. Follow your path, and let us go our own dim way."

The human pulled a sullen face. "More of your daft elven drivel. If the queen said *we* had to beat the beast, then I'm as much a failure as you. From now on, our paths are inseparable."

"But your son," said Farodin.

"He will come with us. I have to see for myself if he's good for anything. Don't take this the wrong way, but I can't make myself believe that it's good for a young man to grow up around elven royalty. The perfumes here clog a man's lungs. The soft beds, the fine food . . . I'll bet he's never even learned to gut a deer or that you have to hang meat for a few days to make it tender. Don't even try to keep me from taking him along. From this moment on, where you go, Mandred goes."

Nuramon exchanged a look with Farodin. They knew from experience how pigheaded Mandred could be and that it would be all but impossible to make him change his mind. Farodin gave the faintest of nods.

"Mandred Aikhjarto," said Nuramon loudly. "You're as steadfast as old Atta himself. If that is your wish . . . then we are honored to have you at our side."

"When do we leave?" Mandred asked, hungry for action.

Before Nuramon could answer, Farodin said, "Now. Before anyone notices something they should not."

Mandred laughed heartily. "Then let's get to it. I'll pack my stuff," he said and left Nuramon's room.

"The human is so loud we'll be lucky to get away unnoticed," said Farodin.

"How old is Mandred? How long does a human live?" asked Nuramon.

"I don't know exactly. A hundred years?"

"He's prepared to sacrifice a good part of his short life to help us. Do you think he knows how long our search for Noroelle's child could take?"

Farodin shrugged. "Hard to say. But I do know that he means what he says. Don't forget the power of Atta Aikhjarto. When it saved him, the old oak changed him. He is not like other humans, not anymore."

Nuramon nodded.

"Could this get any worse?" asked Farodin abruptly.

"If we do what the queen asks, we will free Noroelle. But she will hate us forever, and we will have to live with that. So no. How could it get worse?"

"I'll get my things" was all Farodin said. Quietly, he left the room.

Nuramon stood at the window and looked up to the moon. Noroelle's hatred, he thought sadly. It could, in fact, be worse. It could be that she falls into despair and loses whatever hope she has left, because the men she loves have killed her son. Fate—or Luth, as Mandred called it—was leading them along a painful path indeed. There must come a time when happiness would return.

It wasn't long before Farodin came back. They waited in silence for the human and soon heard voices in the passage outside.

"It's revenge. Blood for blood," said Mandred.

"Revenge changes nothing. My mother is dead. What does Noroelle's son have to do with that?"

"He's also the son of the Devanthar. The guilt for the blood his father spilled has passed to him."

"That is utter nonsense," protested Alfadas.

"That's what the elves have taught you. In my world, a son takes his father's word. And you will do just that."

"Or what?"

Nuramon and Farodin looked at each other. Suddenly, there was a deathly silence outside.

"What are they doing?" Nuramon asked quietly.

Farodin shrugged.

The door flew open. Mandred's face was bright red. "I've brought my son along. He's honored to be joining us."

Farodin and Nuramon reached for their packs. "Then let's go," said Nuramon.

Alfadas was waiting outside the door. He avoided Nuramon's eye, as if ashamed of his father.

Quietly, they made their way down to the stables.

A light still burned down there, in spite of the late hour. A bow-legged stable hand opened the door as if he had been waiting for them. He was not alone. Four elves in long gray cloaks were standing by the horses. They were equipped as if for war, all wearing light mail tunics, all well armed. Their leader turned around to face them, a thin smile on his lips. He looked at Mandred.

"Ollowain," the mortal groaned.

"Welcome, Mandred," the warrior replied before turning to Nuramon. "I see you have already chosen fellow hunters for yourself. That will boost our fighting strength."

Alfadas was surprised. "Master."

Mandred winced as if a horse had kicked him between the legs. Nuramon knew what Mandred thought of Ollowain. Another cruel twist of fate that this particular warrior had schooled his son.

Nuramon stepped forward. "Were you chosen by the queen?" he asked Ollowain.

"Yes," Ollowain replied. "She said we should wait here and be ready to ride. She knew you would not lose any time."

"And did she tell you what our assignment was?"

Ollowain's smile vanished. "Yes. To kill the demon child. I cannot know what is going on inside you, but I can imagine how bitter this path must be. Noroelle was always good to me. We must see in the child not Noroelle's son but the son of the Devanthar. It is the only way we can carry out our mission."

"We will do our best," said Farodin.

Ollowain introduced the elves waiting with him. "My sentinels, the best guardians of the Shalyn Falah. Yilvina, a whirlwind in battle with two short swords." He gestured toward a diminutive elf on his left. Her hair was short and blond, and she returned Nuramon's look with an impish smile.

Next he introduced Nomja, a tall warrior woman. She must have been very young, with something childlike still in the lines of her face. She leaned on her bow as an experienced fighter might, but the pose looked rehearsed.

"And this is Gelvuun," he said, gesturing to the warrior who wore a long sword buckled in a sheath on his back. Gelvuun returned Nuramon's gaze without expression, but this came as no surprise. Nuramon had heard of him before. He had a reputation as surly and morose, a hard case. It was said there were trolls more sociable than Gelvuun. But no one would dare tell him that to his face.

Ollowain went to his horse and took the long-handled axe hanging from the saddle horn. In a single, flowing movement, he turned and flung it toward Mandred.

Nuramon's heart missed a beat. Then he saw with relief that Mandred caught the axe in midflight. The mortal ran his hand over the double-bladed weapon almost tenderly and admired the intertwined elven knot work decorating it.

"Nice workmanship." Mandred turned to his son. "This is what a man's weapon looks like." He wanted to return it, but Ollowain shook his head.

"A gift, Mandred," said Ollowain. "In the human world, one must be ready for trouble at any time. I'll be interested to see if you fight any better with an axe than you do with a sword."

Mandred whirled the axe playfully in the air a few times. "A well-balanced piece." Suddenly, he stopped spinning it and raised the axe head to his ear. "Hear that?" he whispered. "It's calling for blood."

Nuramon felt his belly tense. Had Ollowain perhaps gifted the mortal a cursed weapon? Nuramon had heard grim stories of swords that had to spill blood whenever they were drawn. They were weapons of wrath, forged in the worst days of the first troll war.

An oppressive silence had settled over the group. Apart from Mandred, it seemed no one else could hear the call of the axe, but that might mean nothing.

Finally, Alfadas went to one of the stalls farther back in the stable and saddled his horse. His action broke the spell of silence.

Nuramon turned to the stable hand. "Did the queen have horses prepared for us?"

The goat-legged stable hand pointed off to the right. "Standing right there." Nuramon could hardly believe what he saw. It was his horse.

"Felbion," he shouted and strode across to the stallion.

Farodin, too, was surprised to see his brown again. And even Mandred said, "By the gods. There's mine, too."

They led the horses to Ollowain. "How is that possible?" asked Nuramon. "We had to leave them in the Other World."

"We found them at the stone circle above the fjord. They were waiting there for you," Ollowain explained. He looked to the stable hand. "Ejedin has looked after them well. Haven't you?"

"Course I have," replied the faun. "The queen herself was even here, and more than once, to see to the horses."

Nuramon took the appearance of their old mounts as a good sign for their mission. Even Farodin's mood seemed to lift.

Nuramon had noticed that Farodin seemed extremely cool toward Ollowain. It was not a matter of distaste, though, as with Mandred. Perhaps it was that Farodin no longer trusted Emerelle as he once had and was therefore suspicious of Ollowain as her servant.

A silvery dawn was breaking as the small troop led their horses out into the courtyard. All was quiet in the palace. The only ones who would see them ride out were the guards at the gate. The contrast with their last departure could not have been greater. Then, they had left as heroes, in broad daylight. Now, they crept away like assassins.

THE SAGA OF ALFADAS MANDREDSON:

THE FIRST JOURNEY

*I*n that same winter, and side by side, Mandred and Alfadas left the
dominions of the Albenfolk. The father wanted to be sure that his son
was worthy to succeed him. And so they left, and with them went the
elven princes Faredred and Nuredred, and together they sought adventure
wherever it may lie. They shied from no fight, and anyone who stood in
their path rued it before the first blow fell. Alfadas followed his father to
places where no Fjordlander had ever set foot before. But Torgrid's son
was prone to fretting for the well-being of his own boy. He taught Alfadas
how to fight with the axe, but seldom allowed him to put his skills to the
test. And if ever the danger seemed too great, Mandred set his son to
watch the horses or the camp.

A year passed, then Alfadas said to Mandred, "Father, how can I
ever learn to be like you when you shelter me from every peril? If you
live in fear that something might befall me, then I will never become jarl
of Firnstayn."

Thereupon, Mandred saw that until then, he had deprived his own
flesh and blood of any prospect of glory. He asked the elven princes for
counsel, and they told him that he should set his son a test. That very night,
Mandred slipped away and climbed a steep and dangerous mountain.
Reaching the summit, he rammed his axe into the ice there and returned
to the valley without it.

Next morning, he spoke to Alfadas and said, "Climb that mountain
and bring back what I hid up there."

Alfadas set off along the path that Mandred had showed him. Hardly
had the boy turned out of sight when a great fear came over Mandred,
for the ascent was full of hazards. But Alfadas strived up and up and
discovered a cave close to the summit. Inside, he found a sword buried
in the ice. He took the sword and climbed on to the summit to enjoy the

view, and there, he found the axe of his father. He left it where it was and returned to the others in the valley. They were more than a little surprised to see the unknown blade. Mandred, though, grew angry. "Son, that is not the weapon I hid up there."

Alfadas replied, "But Father, the only weapon hidden up there was this sword. Your axe was jutting clearly from the ice on the summit. Had I an eagle's eye, I could see it from here. That is how much it was hidden. You gave me the wrong goal, but you showed me the right path."

Mandred had to climb the mountain once more to retrieve his axe, and he came down again grumbling. When Faredred and Nuredred explained to the son of Torgrid that in Alfadas's sword, they recognized a blade from Albenmark, Mandred's wrath dissipated, and he was proud of his son. For this sword was worthy of a king.

Alfadas decided that in the future, this sword would be his weapon, because Luth had given it to him. He said to his father, "The axe is the weapon of the father, the sword that of the son. So will neither father nor son ever have to measure himself against the other."

They continued their journey, but Mandred still doubted his son. Shortly, they passed through a mountain range. It was said that a troll lived there in a cave. At night, they heard the sound of hammering and thought the troll was trying to frighten them. Faredred and Nuredred determined to climb down and kill the monster, but Mandred held them back. To his son, he said, "Go and find the troll. I will judge you on your actions."

Alfadas went down to the cave of the troll and found him inside, standing at an anvil. The troll spied him and raised his hammer. Alfadas lifted his sword and threatened the troll with it, saying as he did, "Part of me sees an enemy and says, strike him down. Another part sees the smith at his work. Decide which one you would rather be."

The troll chose the former and attacked, but Alfadas eluded the blows of the hammer and let the troll taste the steel of his blade. Then the troll yielded and said, "My name is Glekrel. If you spare my life, I will give you a gift fit for a king."

Alfadas did not trust the troll, but when the monster fetched a suit of elven armor and presented it to him, Alfadas was overjoyed and threw off his own armor to try on the new. Before he was outfitted again, the troll *attacked. The young warrior was enraged at this treachery and hacked off one leg of the troll. He took the elven armor as his own and went on his way. This very armor is even today in the king's possession as a reminder of those early days. Even the trolls know the story, for Glekrel survived and told them what Mandred's son had done to him.*

The next morning, Alfadas returned to his companions. And when Mandred saw his returning son, he was once again proud to be his father, for Alfadas now truly looked like a king.

Then the companions passed through the regions of the south and came across a wide sea and mighty kingdoms. They performed great deeds, and their names even today remain on the lips of those who live there. Once, they fought back a hundred warriors from Angnos to rescue a village that reminded them of Firnstayn in its early years. Another day, they rid the Fortress of Rileis of its ghosts. In many a duel, Alfadas proved himself a skilled swordsman, able to stand beside Faredred and Nuredred. In this way, two more years passed, until Mandred and Alfadas, out of friendship with the elven princes, followed them to the town of Aniscans, where the princes went to search for a changeling.

FROM THE ACCOUNT OF KETIL THE SKALD
VOLUME TWO OF THE TEMPLE LIBRARY OF LUTH IN FIRNSTAYN, PAGE
42

THE HEALER
OF ANISCANS

Three years had passed since they left Albenmark, and still not a day went by that Nuramon did not discover something new in the human world. The languages, in particular, fascinated him, and he learned a great many of them. At the same time, it surprised him how difficult it was for Mandred to learn them. Alfadas, whom Mandred persisted in calling Oleif despite his son's reluctance to accept the name, also found new languages difficult. Growing up among elves seemed in this case to be of little benefit. Strange, these humans.

The search for Noroelle's son had so far been fruitless. They had crossed the broad forests of Drusna; had passed through the kingdom of Angnos, ravaged by war; had spent moons searching among the far-flung Aegilien Islands; and had lately visited the kingdom of Fargon. It was a green and fertile land, a land that wanted the people to come and conquer it, as Mandred never tired of saying. In recent years, many refugees fleeing the war in Angnos had gone there, and they took their beliefs with them. Some of the few inhabitants who had lived there for generations encountered the newcomers with curiosity, but others saw them only as a danger.

The companions had followed many trails. Their only hope was that the son of an elf and a Devanthar possessed magical powers. If he made use of such a gift, he would surely attract attention. People would talk about him. Based on this, they had tracked down every story they heard of magic or miracles to its source. They had been disappointed every time.

While their search demonstrated the endurance of the elves and Alfadas, as the years passed, Mandred grew more and more impatient. Many times, he drank himself into a stupor, as if wanting to forget that a human lifetime might be too short to search for a demon's child.

It came as a surprise to Nuramon that Alfadas, unlike his father, but very like an elf, maintained his calm throughout. He even put up with Mandred's lessons with a patience that bordered on self-sacrifice. Alfadas seemed to have inherited little from his father, except perhaps for his pigheadedness. For even after three years, Alfadas refused to recognize the axe as what Mandred called the queen of weapons, which visibly pleased Ollowain.

A new spring was in the air as they came down from the mountains to the town of Aniscans, chasing a clue. Nomja, Yilvina, and Alfadas had become good friends and were at times wont to forget the seriousness of their mission. Gelvuun remained a loner, rarely opening his mouth. Farodin had once told Nuramon that the trolls had knocked out all of Gelvuun's teeth and that was why he never said a word. Nuramon still did not know if Farodin had been joking.

Of them all, it was Ollowain who never lost sight of the duty laid upon them. He constantly pushed them to spend no more time than necessary in one place and to move on the moment a trail had petered out.

Farodin, by contrast, took every opportunity to get away from the group. He was always the one who volunteered to scout the trail ahead. Sometimes Nuramon got the impression that Farodin was not searching for the child but was secretly keeping watch for something else. Perhaps he was even trying to hinder their journey to avoid the need to kill Noroelle's son.

Mandred rode at Nuramon's side. Together, they led their small troop down through the hills to Aniscans. The human, whose friendship Nuramon had accepted in the ice cave, often entertained the others with the things he said and did and, for a short time, made the elves forget the reason behind their journey. And though the fun was often followed by the realization that finding what they were seeking would mark the start of a lifetime of suffering, Nuramon was glad of Mandred's talent for lightening the mood.

"Hey, remember the time we ran into that gang of bandits?" asked Mandred with a grin. The human perceived time differently than the elves did. A year, and he was already reminiscing. It was strange, as the feeling that they had been through a lot over a long period of time had also passed over to Nuramon.

"Which bandits do you mean?" replied Nuramon. They had encountered several, and most had just as quickly turned tail and fled.

"The first ones," said Mandred. "The ones who really put up a fight."

"I remember." How could he forget the raiders from Angnos? He and the other elves had been wearing their hoods up, and at first glance, it was not at all clear that they were Albenkin. For the bandits, that discovery was a rude awakening, but they had stupidly shown no inclination to give up the fight. They thought they had the upper hand based on sheer numbers. They quickly learned a painful lesson in the difference between quantity and quality.

"Now *that* was a fight." Mandred looked around. "I'd love to run into a few cutpurses lurking in these woods."

Nuramon said nothing. Mandred's wish could only mean one thing. Alfadas would have to steel himself for another practice session that evening. Mandred just could not stop himself from trying to interest his son in the axe as a weapon. But Alfadas had shown his father often enough that he was more than a match for him with the sword. The times that Mandred was defeated by his son, Nuramon could never be sure of the older warrior's feelings. Was he proud or offended? And there were times when Nuramon wondered whether Mandred surreptitiously held back in their battle practice, for fear of injuring Alfadas.

They crested a hill and had a clear view over the river valley below. Nuramon pointed to the city on the western shore. "Aniscans. We can finally put the wilderness behind us."

"And we can finally get to a tavern and drink something decent. My stomach's starting to think that someone's cut my head off," quipped Mandred. "Reckon we can find mead down there?"

One could almost believe that Mandred had forgotten his grief over Freya, but Nuramon saw through the outward appearance to a man who was trying to dull his pain with drink.

Slowly, they rode down the slope on the other side of the hill. At the bottom, they found a road that led straight on to the town. A bridge crossed the river in seven low arches. The river was swollen with snowmelt that had brought with it a great quantity of wood from the mountains. Men with long poles stood on the bridge, prodding at drifting tree trunks and branches to prevent them from catching sideways against the pilings.

Most of the buildings in Aniscans were built of quarried stone and were light brown in color. They were high, massive constructions built close together. The only decorative touch was the shingles on their rooftops, which were a radiant red. All around, on the outskirts of the town, were vineyards. Mandred would definitely find somewhere to slake his thirst, thought Nuramon bitterly.

"A land of fools," the human suddenly exclaimed. "Look. A rich town like that, and they don't even bother to build a wall. Firnstayn has better defenses than this place by far."

"They didn't count on you coming to visit, Father," said Alfadas with a laugh, and the rest of the troop joined in. Even Gelvuun grinned.

Mandred turned red. "Flippancy is the mother of many a misfortune," he said, his voice humorless.

Ollowain laughed merrily. "It looks as if the spring sun has melted the crust of ice over the barbarian king. And wonder of wonders, there's a philosopher underneath."

"I don't know what kind of insult *flossofer* is supposed to be, but this barbarian king is about to stuff his axe down your throat."

Ollowain crossed his arms over his chest and pretended to shake. "But suddenly the winter returns to freeze the prettiest flowers of spring."

"Now you're calling me a flower?" Mandred growled.

"Just an allegory, my friend."

The human creased his brow. Then he nodded. "I accept your apology, Ollowain."

Nuramon had to bite his lip to keep from laughing out loud. He was glad when Alfadas, a moment later, began to sing, a welcome interruption to the unhappy little clash. The lad had an exceptional voice . . . for a human.

They followed the road by the river, passing stables and small farmsteads. Cows grazed in the meadows beside the road. The landscape here seemed strangely disordered. In all his time in the human realm, Nuramon had never managed to get used to the otherness of the world, but he had learned to see the beauty in its strangeness.

The buildings of the town were huddled around the base and up the sides of a hill, on top of which rose a temple. Its walls were surrounded by scaffolding, and the hammering of stonemasons could be heard far beyond the river. The construction was not decorative in the least and had walls as thick as those of a fortress tower, but Nuramon found a certain charm in its coarse plainness. To anyone approaching from far away, it seemed to cry out that there was nothing here to distract the faithful, for no work of art can compare with the beauty of true belief.

Nuramon thought of the old mendicant they'd encountered a few days earlier in the mountains. His eyes fervid, the man had told them about Aniscans and the priest whose name was apparently a household one all along the river valley: Guillaume, who spoke of the god Tjured with such zeal that the power of his words passed over to those who came to listen to him. It was said that the lame could walk again if they came and heard him and he touched their limbs with his hands. His magic seemed able to drive out any suffering, vanquish any poison.

How many times had they followed such rumors in the past three years? But every time, they had found nothing. They were looking for a man around thirty years old who could work miracles. This short description matched Guillaume just as it had matched a dozen other men, not one of whom had possessed any sort of actual magical power. People were far too simpleminded. They were only too ready to be taken in by any charlatan who showed them some trick or sleight of hand.

The mendicant had claimed that in his childhood, where the town of Aniscans now stood, there had been no more than a small stone circle where the people came for the summer and winter solstices to make sacrifices to the gods.

Nuramon looked up. The stone circle had most likely stood on the small hill where the stonemasons were working on the temple.

The hooves of their horses clattered over the cobblestones of the bridge. Some of the workers turned to watch them pass. They wore plain aprons and broad-brimmed hats of woven straw. Humbly, they bowed their heads. Warriors were held in high regard in this kingdom, it seemed.

Nuramon looked across to the houses and public buildings. Their walls were made of rough-hewn stone and appeared heavy and solid.

Measured against what the humans normally managed to build, they were not badly constructed at all. Most of the walls were straight, and few of the rooftops sagged under the burden of their shingles.

Before leaving the bridge, Mandred and Alfadas positioned themselves at the head of the band. Anyone seeing the two of them would assume that princes from the wild north had come visiting, bringing a mysterious retinue in tow. The inhabitants of the town turned and watched them ride by with astonishment, but soon went back to their daily routine.

Strangers were clearly nothing new in this town.

There existed, though, an unrest that had nothing to do with them. The closer Nuramon and the others came to the temple, the more palpable it became. There was something going on in Aniscans. The entire town seemed to be on its feet, the townsfolk pushing through the narrow alleys and up the hill. Soon, he and his companions were unable to go any farther on horseback. They were forced to dismount and take their steeds into the courtyard of a tavern where Nomja, the archer, stayed with them. Then they rejoined the throng streaming toward the temple. Around them, the atmosphere reminded Nuramon of a kobold wedding, everyone mingling and mixing and in high spirits.

Nuramon picked up scraps of conversation from those around them. The people were talking about the miracle healer and his spectacular powers, about how he had brought a drowned child back to life the day before and about how more and more strangers were coming to town to see Guillaume. An older man spoke with pride of how the king had invited Guillaume to his court to take up residence there, but the priest had apparently turned down the offer to leave the town.

Finally, the small troop reached the public square in front of the temple. In all the jostling of the crowd, it was hard to estimate how many had gathered, but there must have been hundreds. Wedged in among the sweating, milling humans, Nuramon felt increasingly unwell. All around him was the reek of sweat, unwashed clothes, rancid fat, and onions. From the corner of his eye, he saw Farodin holding a perfumed handkerchief over his nose. Nuramon wished that he could find some sort of relief like that. Humans and cleanliness were two things that simply did not go together. It was something he'd learned indirectly from Mandred a long time ago. In the past three years, Nuramon had grown somewhat less sensitive to the multitude of smells that assaulted his nose in the human world, especially in the towns. But here in the crowd, the stench was truly overwhelming.

Suddenly, somewhere ahead, a voice rose above the sounds of the crowd. Nuramon craned his neck to see but could not make out the speaker among the tumult. He seemed to be standing close to the tall oak tree spreading its branches across the center of the square.

The voice was melodious, sonorous, and the speaker well versed in the art of rhetoric. No syllable passed his lips heedlessly. Every word was carefully accented, spoken like the philosophers of Lyn, who practiced debating for centuries to take their vocal abilities to the limits. In doing so, the true art lay not in being able to rely on the strength of one's arguments, but in performing the words in such a way that the spirit surrendered unconditionally to the voice. What the man up ahead was doing was something like casting a spell.

The people pressing around them took no further notice of Nuramon and his striking companions. They were too captivated by the voice.

Farodin pushed his way to Nuramon's side. "Hear that voice?"

"Magnificent, isn't it?" Nuramon replied.

"That's what worries me. Perhaps we have found what we've been looking for."

Nuramon said nothing. He was terrified of what would have to be done if that was really Noroelle's son speaking.

"Ollowain," said Farodin. "Take Yilvina and Gelvuun. Go around to the left. Mandred and Alfadas, take the middle. Nuramon and I will circle right. For now, all we do is observe him. In this crowd, we can do nothing else."

The companions separated. Nuramon went ahead of Farodin. They pushed their way carefully through the throng of people who stood there mesmerized. The voice of the priest overpowered the murmurings of the crowd.

"Accept the power of Tjured," he said in all gentleness. "It is a gift I bring to you from him."

A moment later, someone cried, "Look, look! He is healed! The wound has closed!" The crowd shouted in jubilation.

An old woman threw her arms around Nuramon's neck and kissed him on the cheek. "A miracle," she exulted. "Another miracle he's done. He is the blessing of our town." Nuramon looked at the old woman with incomprehension. It must truly have been a miracle for her to kiss a stranger.

Now the preacher raised himself above the crowd. He helped a visibly relieved man to his feet. "That is the power of Tjured, our god."

At the sight of the healer, Nuramon stopped in his tracks. He sensed that Farodin, beside him, also came to a halt.

The priest climbed onto a well beside the oak and spoke to the gathering, but Nuramon barely heard a word he said. He was entranced by the man's bearing and gestures. Guillaume had black hair that fell to his shoulders. Like all the priests of Tjured, he wore a cowl of deep indigo. His face was oval, his nose thin, his chin smooth, and his mouth curved. If Noroelle had a twin brother, he would look like this priest.

This man was her son.

Nuramon saw Guillaume turn to a man with stringy gray hair whose hand seemed to be stiff. He took the man's hand and spoke a prayer.

Nuramon fell back in fright. It felt as if something had reached deep inside him, as if a powerful hand had grabbed at his soul. It was an eerie feeling that lasted only the blink of an eye. Dazed, the elf staggered back and ran into a young woman.

"Are you ill?" she asked in concern. "You're pale."

Nuramon shook his head and pushed forward to the edge of the crowd, now pressed into a tight knot around the well.

The man who had come to Guillaume raised his hand. He balled his fingers into a fist, then stretched them again. "He's healed me!" he cried, his voice breaking. "I'm healed!" The gray-haired man threw himself on the ground at the priest's feet and kissed the hem of his cowl.

Guillaume seemed embarrassed. He took the old man by the shoulders and raised him up.

He can work magic like his mother, thought Nuramon. The queen had been mistaken. Noroelle's son was no demon child. He was the opposite. He was a healer.

Suddenly, someone in the crowd shouted, "Guillaume! Guillaume! Someone here has fainted!"

"He's dead!" screamed a woman in a shrill voice.

"Bring him to me," the healer commanded, his voice calm but firm.

Two burly men in leather aprons carried a gaunt figure to the well, a man in a gray cloak. Guillaume threw back the man's hood. Before the healer lay Gelvuun.

Nuramon looked to Farodin, confusion in his eyes. Farodin made a sign to him to wait. Then he whispered, "I hope Mandred doesn't do anything stupid."

A murmur went through the people at the front of the crowd. Guillaume had swept Gelvuun's hair back, revealing the points of his ears. Gelvuun, normally so dour, looked as peaceful as a sleeping child.

Guillaume bent over him. The priest looked shaken. Whether it was because of the sight of an elf or something else, Nuramon was not able to say. Then Guillaume looked around, and Nuramon felt the eyes of Noroelle's son sweep over him. An ice-cold chill ran down his spine. The healer's eyes were a radiant blue.

The priest rose and said, "This man does not stand under Tjured's protection. He is one of the Albenfolk and not a human. And he is beyond help. He came here too late, and I cannot see what the nature of his illness was. It seems his heart simply stopped beating, but it is said that the Albenfolk are destined to live a life after life. Pray for his soul. I will inter his body with honor, though he never prayed to Tjured. The mercy of our god is boundless. He will take pity on this elf as well."

Again, Guillaume's gaze brushed Nuramon. There was something paralyzing in those magnificent blue eyes.

"Come, Nuramon," whispered Farodin. "We have to go."

His companion took hold of his arm and pulled him through the crush of spectators. Nuramon could not shake that face and those eyes from his memory. It was Noroelle's face, Noroelle's eyes, now part of the man at the front of the crowd.

Suddenly, he was being shaken.

"Snap out of it," said Farodin, his voice harsh.

Nuramon looked around in surprise. They had left the square and were again in one of the narrow alleys. He had not noticed at all how far they had gone. "That was Noroelle's face," he said.

"I know," said Farodin. "Come on."

They found Nomja and the horses. Mandred and Alfadas entered the tavern courtyard a few moments later. They were supporting Yilvina between them. The young elf was pale and seemed barely able to stand upright on her own.

Mandred was beside himself. "Did you see that? Damn! What happened?"

Farodin looked around. "Where is Ollowain?"

Alfadas gestured toward the entrance to the yard. "There."

The master swordsman's face was etched with fear. "Come. We are no longer safe here." He looked back to the street. "Let us put some distance between us and the demon child. Ride. Mount up, and let's get out of this place."

"What happened to Gelvuun?" asked Nomja.

Nuramon said nothing. He was thinking of the strange power he had felt, that clawing deep inside him. He thought of the blue eyes, of how much Guillaume, with every gesture and movement, reminded him of Noroelle. Now Gelvuun was dead, and Yilvina looked as wretched as if she had only just sidestepped oblivion.

"What happened?" Ollowain asked, and turned to the pale elf.

Yilvina was struggling for breath. "He had pushed forward . . . he was almost at the front of the crowd. As soon as the priest took the old man's hand . . ." She looked up to heaven. Tears rimmed her eyes. "I don't know how I can describe it. It was like a talon reaching into my chest to tear my heart to pieces." She began to sob. "It was . . . I could sense Death . . . eternal death, with no hope of rebirth or the way into the moonlight. If I had not stopped a few steps behind . . ." She could not go on.

"He saw you? And he attacked immediately?" asked Nomja.

Ollowain hesitated. "I'm not sure . . . I don't think it was an attack. It happened at the same moment that he healed the old man. I could sense his power . . . Yilvina is right. I felt Death's presence myself."

Mandred turned to Nuramon. "How did he do that?"

The mortal overestimated Nuramon's abilities. Because, that one time, Nuramon had transcended himself and healed Farodin, Mandred had developed the habit of asking him for his opinion on anything that carried the slightest whiff of magic. "I have no idea, Mandred."

"I can tell you," said Ollowain. "It's the demon child's magic. It is evil to the core. It can kill us where we stand. A simple spell that heals a human can destroy us. Now I see the danger that the queen sees in Noroelle's son. We have to kill him."

"We will not," said Nuramon, and there was resolve in his voice. "We will take him to the queen."

"The false healer at that well can kill us all with a spell," said Ollowain. "Can't you see that?"

"I see it."

"Then how do you expect to make him leave this town?"

"I won't make him do anything. He will come with us voluntarily. He did not know what his healing hands did to our companion. He is not the demon child the queen expected him to be."

"Do you plan to take a stand against the queen? She sent us out to kill him."

"No, Ollowain. The queen sent *me* out to kill him. I alone have to justify my actions to the queen."

"I don't know if I can let you do that," said Ollowain slowly. "Why, Nuramon? Why have you changed your mind?"

"Because I have a sense that killing Guillaume would be a fatal mistake. No good can come of it. We have to bring him before the queen. Then she can see him face-to-face and make her own judgment. Let me go and speak to him. If I am not back by noon tomorrow, you can kill him."

Ollowain shook his head. "You really want to deliver a demon child to Emerelle's court? A man whose magic kills elves? Go. Talk to him. We won't see you alive again. You've got until tomorrow, at dusk. Then I'll go after him my way. Until then, we camp outside the town."

Nuramon looked for support on the faces of the others, but none spoke against Ollowain, not even Mandred. On a sign from Ollowain, they mounted up. Alfadas took the reins of Gelvuun's and Nuramon's horses.

Farodin was the last of their small band to leave the tavern yard. He leaned down from the saddle to Nuramon. "Are you sure you want to take the risk? What if what happened to Gelvuun happens to you?"

Nuramon smiled. "Then I'll see you in the next life."

WITH GUILLAUME

Throughout the afternoon, Nuramon observed Guillaume. He listened to his sermon and watched as he buried Gelvuun's body. Finally, he followed Noroelle's son through the city, but as he did so, he had the uneasy feeling that he himself was being followed. He looked back often but saw no one acting out of the ordinary, just the inhabitants of Aniscans going about their daily business. He tried to shake off the feeling and turned his attention back to Guillaume, following him until he reached the hill leading up to the temple and disappeared into a narrow building. Built of coarse, quarried stone, it was like most of the other buildings in town. If this was Guillaume's home, then it was clear humility was important to him.

Nuramon stopped where he was for a while and observed the house from the alley opposite. He waited for Guillaume to open the shutters and let in the day's last gleam. But the shutters remained closed, and as night came down over Aniscans, Nuramon saw warm candlelight between the slats.

Nuramon gathered his courage and stepped up to the healer's door. Now all that was left to do was knock, but he could not bring himself to do it. He was afraid, though not that he might suffer the same fate as Gelvuun. He was afraid of making a serious mistake. Nuramon did not know Guillaume, nor did he know how he would take being told the truth. Then he thought of Noroelle. This was his only hope of saving Guillaume from death and rescuing Noroelle. And that would only happen if the queen realized that killing Guillaume would be a mistake.

He knocked.

All remained still inside the house, and Nuramon wondered whether he should knock a second time. Just as he was raising his hand again, he heard steps. His heart beat faster. In a moment, the door would open and Noroelle's face would be looking back at him. He threw back the hood of his cape; he wanted Guillaume to know immediately with whom he was dealing.

A bolt clacked, and the door opened. Nuramon had not been wrong. It was Guillaume, though the young priest seemed not in the least surprised to find a stranger at his doorstep. Unable to utter even a single word, Nuramon stared into the face of Noroelle's son. He wondered how Guillaume's expression would change when he discovered the truth about his origin.

"Come in, Albenchild," said the priest amicably. He smiled. Then he led the way into the house. He had clearly been expecting this visit.

Guillaume's house was plainly furnished. The room that Nuramon entered took up the entire first floor. Almost everything the priest needed was here, from the stone stove to a prayer shrine. Only a bed was missing. A stairway opposite the front door led upward. Most likely the bedroom was on the second floor, Nuramon thought.

"You have come because of your companion," said Guillaume, and he sat down at the small table in the center of the room. An oil lamp on the table cast a low light. Next to it was a wooden plate with scraps of meat on it. Guillaume gestured to a second chair at the end of the table, inviting Nuramon to sit.

Nuramon accepted the invitation in silence.

The priest pushed the plate aside. "I'm afraid your companion has already been laid to rest in the cemetery. I hope that will not interfere with his rebirth."

"Among my people, it is said that the soul separates from the body at the moment of death," Nuramon explained. "If a soul path exists between your world and Albenmark, then Gelvuun has already followed it and now waits to be born again."

"Then his soul was already gone when I buried his body."

"Yes, but that is not why I have come. I am here because of you."

His words did not seem to surprise Guillaume. "Because I killed him."

Nuramon started. "How do you know that?"

Guillaume lowered his eyes. "I knew it as soon as I examined him. He had marks on his neck like he'd been strangled . . . marks that seemed like only my fingers would fit them." He paused and looked at Nuramon. "It is not easy to read the faces of elves. I see no anger in yours. Still, you must be here to demand retribution."

"I have not come for that either."

Guillaume gazed at him curiously.

"I only want to know what you see in your own future."

"I am a seeker, a servant of Tjured. I believe this world to be full of hidden gifts, but that few are able to find them. I know the power of the gods is gathered in certain places, and I can sense those places. I can follow the invisible rivers that join them." He was talking about the Albenpaths, Nuramon knew, and he thought of them as the paths of his gods. "I use this knowledge to heal people and to preach peace. I want the hate in this world to disappear. But after today, it seems the price may be too high. What kind of gift is it that heals humans and kills the Albenfolk?"

"I can give you an answer to that question, but think hard about whether you want to hear it."

"You know something of the power from which I create my miracles?"

"I know its origin."

"Then you are cleverer than every wise man and every priest I have ever met. Please tell me."

"Should I really do that? If you listen to me, then you will also find out why I and my companions have come to this town, why I am here, and why I risk being so close to you."

"Do you know my parents? My true parents?"

"Yes. I know them both."

"Then speak."

"You are the son of an elf named Noroelle, who once accepted the most terrible of all punishments to save your life," Nuramon said, so beginning the story of Guillaume's past. He spoke of Noroelle, of his and Farodin's love for her, of the manboar and the elfhunt, of Guillaume's rescue and Noroelle's exile. As he spoke, he observed Guillaume's expression and saw that the young man's open face grew more and more earnest. Crease by crease, the similarity to Noroelle vanished. He finished by saying, "Now you know who your parents are and why you possess a power that heals humans, but kills elves."

Guillaume stared at the table. Then, without warning, he began to weep. The sight of Guillaume's tears hurt Nuramon, too, not only because Guillaume once again looked so like Noroelle, but also because he had brought him to this. It took all his self-control not to break out in tears himself.

After a long silence, Guillaume finally spoke. "And like a fool, I thought my power was a gift from Tjured."

"Where your ability came from makes no difference. You have done good for humans, as your mother always did for the Albenkin. Until the night she . . ." He didn't want to say it again.

"Tell me more about my mother," Guillaume asked in a low voice.

Nuramon took his time. Until late in the night, he told Guillaume about the twenty years he had spent never far from Noroelle. His words brought back to him all the memories of what he had been through with the woman he loved. When he reached the end of his retelling, his mood shifted. Now that all was said, it was clear to him that all was lost and that Noroelle would probably never return. Guillaume, too, seemed deeply upset to have learned of his mother's sacrifice.

"You have cleared up the mystery of my parentage," said Guillaume. "And you have explained to me where my powers come from. But you have not told me why you are here."

Nuramon sighed heavily. It was time. "I asked my queen what I could do to rescue Noroelle. And she told me to ride out, find you, and kill you."

Guillaume accepted this news calmly. "You could have done that long ago. Why have you let me go on living?"

"For the same reason your mother brought you to this world back then. Because I sense nothing of the Devanthar in your soul."

"But my healing powers killed your companion. That can only be the birthright of my father. And who knows what else is sleeping inside me?"

"Would you have accepted the death of Gelvuun to heal that man's hand?"

"Never."

"Then at least your spirit is free of the Devanthar's terrible power, even if the essence of the beast is in your magic."

"But isn't that the tragedy? In my innocence, I am guilty. My mother was banished because of me. Your companion died because of me. I could do nothing to prevent either one. It is as if my guilt lies in the simple fact that I exist."

"And that is also why killing you would be wrong. I want to complete my mission a different way. Not as the queen envisioned, though I will probably make her my enemy."

"You would let me escape?"

"I would, but my companions would find you again quickly enough." Nuramon thought of Ollowain. "You must understand why I am here. If I were not, then you would already be dead. I have come to make you an offer, one that might save your life and free Noroelle. It is a faint hope, though, and no more."

"Speak."

"I want to take you to the queen and keep you safe on the way to Albenmark. When you speak to Emerelle at court, you may be able to convince her of your true nature, as you did with Noroelle and also with me. That is all I can offer you."

"Then I will accept it," Guillaume replied without hesitation. "For my mother's sake."

Without showing it, Nuramon admired Guillaume. He wondered whether he himself would have consented so readily, for there was no certainty at all that the queen would be merciful, and Emerelle might well stand firm in her decision to kill him. Despite all that had happened, Nuramon still had so much trust in the queen that he doubted she would close herself to his plea.

"When do we leave?"

"We should be out of town by midday. We don't need to rush."

"Then tell me something about Albenmark."

Nuramon told Guillaume about the heartland of Albenmark, but also something of Alvemer, Noroelle's homeland. As the cock began to crow, Nuramon came to an end and suggested they leave with the dawn after all, to get away unnoticed.

Guillaume agreed and quickly packed what he would need. Then he thanked Nuramon for telling him the truth. "I will never forget what you have done for me."

Nuramon was satisfied. He had achieved what he wanted, even though it meant he had rebelled against the queen in doing so. Ollowain would complain, certainly, but they would take Noroelle's son to Emerelle. It was a compromise Ollowain would have to swallow. Nuramon would stay vigilant, though, and keep one eye on Ollowain.

Guillaume prepared himself a porridge of millet, hazelnuts, and raisins. He asked Nuramon if he would also like something to eat, but Nuramon thanked him and declined. Guillaume was just starting to eat when some kind of commotion started in the town outside. Nuramon listened. He thought he heard screams. At the sound of hoofbeats, he jumped to his feet and his hand went to his sword.

"What's going on?" asked Guillaume.

"Get your things," Nuramon said. In the alleys, battle sounds mixed with cries of agony. The town was under attack.

Guillaume quickly stood and grabbed his bundle.

The noise of battle drew nearer. Suddenly, someone pounded against the door, and Nuramon, horrified, saw it swing open. A figure stormed in, and Nuramon drew his sword against the intruder. He was stunned to see who came barging in.

THE DISASTER

Farodin slammed the door and slid home the wooden bolt. "Put your sword away, or you'll kill the only ally you have in this town." He looked around quickly. "Is there another exit?"

Guillaume stared at Farodin as if he were a ghost. "What's going on out there?" Guillaume asked.

"Armed men. They occupied every road leading out of town, then stormed the temple. They don't seem to like priests like you very much." Farodin stepped over to the window that opened onto the temple square and cracked open the shutter. "Look."

The soldiers outside were well equipped. Nearly all were wearing chain mail and helmets with black horsetail plumes. Half were armed with axes or swords, and their round red shields flaunted a white bull's head. The rest carried crossbows. And though they dragged the priests out of the half-finished temple with no regard for their well-being, it was clear that they were more than simple bandits. They were disciplined, and their archers secured the square while the axe men hounded the priests across to the oak tree.

A blond giant barked an order, and one of the priests, a corpulent, older man, was separated from the others. A rope was tied around his ankles and the other end thrown over a strong fork in the tree. The priest was jerked off his feet. He tried desperately to push his robes up to cover his privates.

"Father Ribauld," Guillaume whispered in shock. "What are they doing?"

"I heard them saying your name, Guillaume." Farodin looked the young priest up and down. He was certainly no fighter. "You have mortal enemies in two worlds . . . what have you done to make these men come looking for you?"

Pensive, the priest swept his hair from his eyes. It was a small gesture, yet it filled Farodin with pain. Aileen and Noroelle had swept their hair aside in just the same way when they were deep in thought.

Guillaume was surprisingly thin and delicate. In his face, Farodin saw Noroelle as if in a distant mirror. She lived on in him.

Farodin had followed Nuramon because he feared his friend might help Guillaume try to escape. In the three years they had been on the road, Farodin had come to terms with himself and accepted the queen's order. The day before, in the temple square, he had been prepared to kill Guillaume. But now . . . he had to turn away. The man's resemblance to Noroelle was too much for him. If he turned his sword against Guillaume, it would be like turning it against Noroelle.

Ollowain had given him a warning when he left the camp to secretly follow Nuramon. His words still rang clearly in his ears: "Don't forget that he is the child of a Devanthar, a master deceiver. He abuses Noroelle's face as a mask, but evil is hiding behind it. A Devanthar is nothing less than hatred of the Alben incarnate, and of us, their children. Whatever good may have survived in him will have been poisoned by the legacy of his father long ago. You saw what happened to Gelvuun. We can't take him prisoner. In reality, we would be *his* prisoners. Even if we were to lay him in irons, a single word of power could kill us all. And imagine the damage a creature like that could do in Albenmark. How are we supposed to fight him? We have to carry out Emerelle's orders. Today at midday in the temple square, I saw the queen's wisdom with my own eyes."

"They are here because of something I did *not* do," said Guillaume in answer to Farodin's question.

"What?" Guillaume's words dragged Farodin out of his thoughts.

The soldiers in the square started beating Ribauld with long canes. The man swung back and forth helplessly. His screams rang out across the square and must have been heard even in the far corners of the town. No one came to the priest's aid.

"You see on their shields? The bull's head?" Guillaume asked. "Those are King Cabezan's men, his personal guard. Cabezan sent for me once already. They say his arms and legs are rotting on his living body and that he's dying slowly and painfully. He ordered me to heal him, but I won't do it. If I save his life, hundreds will die. Cabezan is the cruelest of tyrants. He had his own children murdered because he feared they were after his throne. He's insane, he's possessed somehow . . . anyone wishing an audience must appear before him naked. He's afraid of weapons that might be hidden under their robes otherwise. Any man who wants to be part of his guard has to beat a newborn to death with his bare fists, in front of Cabezan. The only men he tolerates in his presence are those with no conscience. He rules over Fargon, and evil rules with him. I will not heal him. I *must* not. When he dies, a curse will finally be lifted from this land."

The cries of the priest still rang out across the square.

"I must not . . ." Tears stood in his eyes. "Father Ribauld is like a true father to me. I grew up in a poor farming family. When my parents—my foster parents—died, he took me in. He is . . ."

One of the younger priests, dragged from the temple with the others, was pointing an outstretched arm toward Guillaume's house.

"Is there another way out?" Farodin asked again. Two soldiers were already marching across the temple square toward them.

Guillaume shook his head. He picked up a long bread knife from the table and slipped it into the sleeve of his cowl. "I'll go. Then at least they will not kill you as well, but King Cabezan will never see me alive."

Nuramon stepped into his path. "Don't do it. Come with us."

"You think it is smarter to follow you to a queen who sent you to kill me?" There was no challenge in Guillaume's words, only a deep sadness. "I know you wish me no evil, but if I go out there now, maybe I can save your lives and the lives of my brethren. And if you are able to tell the queen of my death, then perhaps she will have mercy on my mother." He pushed back the bolt and stepped out onto the temple square.

Farodin could not believe that Nuramon did not try to stop Guillaume. He ran to the door, but he was too late. Guillaume was already in the hands of the soldiers.

"Knights of the king," he proclaimed. "Leave my brethren in peace. You have found me."

The blond captain signaled to his men to lower their crossbows. He stepped over to Ribauld and grabbed the old man by the hair, twisting his head far back.

"So you're the wonder healer," the captain shouted. He pulled a knife from his belt and calmly stabbed Ribauld in the throat. "Then show us what you can do."

Farodin held his breath. Guillaume was still standing too close to the house. If he used his healing powers, he would kill both of the elves.

The old priest hung from the tree like a slaughtered cow on a butcher's hook. He swung back and forth on the rope, clutching at his throat.

Farodin threw open the shutters, and they cracked against the wall. He gripped the sill with both hands and vaulted through the window, landing nimbly in front of the house. "Keep your hands off my prize, mortal." His voice was like ice.

The blond captain shifted one hand to the pommel of his sword. "You've made your entrance. Now leave."

"You reach for your weapon? Shall we duel?" Farodin smiled. "I am the queen of Albenmark's best fighter. Do you really want me as your enemy? I came here to fetch Guillaume, the priest. As you can see, I was in his house. I found him before you did, and I will not let you snatch away *my* prize. At midday yesterday, he killed an elf. And he will answer for that."

"The queen of Albenmark's best soldier," the captain mocked. "And I'm Umgrid, king of Trollheim." The men around him laughed.

Farodin swept back his hair, revealing his pointed ears. "So you are Umgrid?" The elf tilted his head. "You're certainly ugly enough for a troll." He turned in a half circle and looked at the rooftops of the buildings enclosing the square.

"Anyone not a troll had better leave now. This square is surrounded by elves, and we will not let Guillaume be taken from us."

Some of the soldiers exchanged nervous glances and raised their shields.

"Words! Nothing but words!" shouted the captain, but his voice betrayed his unease.

"You should ask our permission before you let any of these cutthroats go," said Nuramon now. He had his sword drawn and was standing in Guillaume's doorway.

"Shoot them down!" The captain snatched a crossbow from one of his archers and took aim at Farodin.

The elf dived forward. He braced against the rough cobblestones with his hands and rolled over his left shoulder, the leap carrying him almost as far as the well. The crossbow bolt grazed his cheek, leaving a bloody streak.

Farodin kept moving, jumping around, not giving the crossbowmen a stationary target. He landed at the feet of an axe man, who hit him with his shield. The blow knocked Farodin off balance, and he staggered back, bumping against the edge of the well. He dodged to one side, and an axe swinging at his head missed by a whisker.

Farodin knocked the human's shield aside with a kick. He drew his sword and, in a backhand swing, slit the soldier's belly open. The elf snatched the axe from the dying man's hand. Soldiers were closing in on all sides. Nuramon, in the doorway, was holding off two more. The situation was hopeless. They were outnumbered at least ten to one.

Farodin sprang from the edge of the well and slung the axe at a crossbowman who was taking aim at him. The axe found its target with a grim crunch.

The elf dodged another axe, parried a sword, and stabbed one of his attackers in the shoulder over the top of the man's shield. The soldiers had him encircled now, but they kept their distance.

"So who else among you wants to die?" Farodin challenged them.

During the fight, the giant captain had donned a helmet and buckled a shield to his arm. "He is ours," he bellowed, raising a twin-bladed axe and charging Farodin.

They came at Farodin then from all sides. He crouched low to avoid the first furious wave. He swept his sword in a low circle. Like a hot knife through wax, it sliced through the legs of any who came too close.

Something grazed Farodin's left arm. Warm blood soaked his shirt. Lethal and calm, he fended off an axe blow aimed at his chest, his sword shattering the wooden shaft. The humans moved clumsily, he saw. It was something he had observed often in Mandred. They were courageous and strong, but compared with an elf who had spent centuries mastering the sword, they were like children brandishing sticks. Still, the outcome of this battle was hard to doubt; there were simply too many of them.

Farodin moved through the ranks of his enemies like a dancer. He ducked under thrusting swords and used his own to parry, returning blow for blow.

Until he came face-to-face with the blond giant.

"I'll wear your ears on a string around my neck," hissed the man. He attacked furiously with a mighty swing at Farodin's sword arm, but changed direction in the middle of the swing.

The feint made no difference. Farodin danced clear of the sword, then kicked the bottom edge of the giant's shield. With an ugly crunch, the iron-clad top edge of the shield slammed into the giant's chin. His teeth went through his bottom lip, and he spat blood.

Farodin spun and kicked the captain's shield again, knocking it aside. He swung his sword and hit the giant in the face with the flat of the blade.

The captain staggered back. Farodin caught him, pulled the helmet off his head, and set his sword at the man's throat. "Enough! Stop now, or your leader dies!" the elf cried in a loud voice.

The soldiers fell back. An unnatural silence settled over the square, broken only by the groans of the wounded.

Nuramon moved away from Guillaume's house. His leather helmet was smeared with blood.

"We're pulling back to the temple!" Farodin shouted to him.

"You'll never get out of Aniscans alive," growled the captain. His tone was threatening and loud enough for his men to hear. "The bridge is guarded. Every road is sealed. We came prepared for the healer to cause trouble. Surrender, and I promise you a quick death."

"We are elves," replied Farodin calmly. "Do you really think you could stop us?" He waved to Nuramon, and his companion retreated inside the portal of the temple together with two priests.

Guillaume was as pale as a corpse. During the battle, he had simply stood and watched. He was so clearly incapable of hurting anyone.

"You are bleeding, elf," said the blond soldier. "You're flesh and blood, like me. And you can die like me. Before the sun goes down, I'll drink wine from your skull."

"For a man with a sword at his throat, you seem remarkably confident about the future," Farodin said as he retreated slowly, backing toward the high temple gate.

The crossbowmen around them reloaded.

Farodin thought of Mandred and the rest of their troop. He had left them behind at their camp in the vineyard. Would they come? They must have seen the attack on the temple.

He threw his prisoner to the ground and jumped through the temple gate. Crossbow bolts whizzed past. Nuramon slammed the heavy oak door and swung the crossbeam into place. Farodin looked at Nuramon's blood-soaked tunic with concern. "How bad is it?"

The elf looked down. "More human blood than mine, I'd say."

Inside the temple, it was dark and cool. Massive wooden columns rose to the ceiling, which was supported by heavy beams. The temple was a single high room. There was no furniture and no platform on which a speaker might stand. The only decoration was a menhir, half as high again as a man, with intertwined lettering engraved into its surface. The temple walls had been whitewashed and were separated by two galleries that ringed the walls at different heights. Above the galleries, high windows set in the walls let in a feeble shimmer of morning light. Oil lamps burned in niches along the walls, and pale smoke rose from copper incense pans that had been laid in a ring around the menhir.

The entire construction reminded Farodin more of a fortress tower than a temple. What sort of god was Tjured? Judging by the behavior of his followers, he was certainly no warrior. The two priests went down on their knees before the menhir in the middle of the circular hall. They prayed humbly to their god and thanked him for their liberation.

"Guillaume?" called Nuramon, who was still standing close to the double doors at the entrance. "Where are you?"

Guillaume appeared from behind one of the columns. He seemed uncommonly calm, almost enraptured. "You should have let them take me. After that bloodbath, they won't rest until we're all dead."

"Could it be you have a death wish?" asked Farodin, an angry edge to his voice.

"Didn't someone send you to kill me, too? What sense is there in fighting for the right to be my executioner?"

Farodin gestured dismissively. "Anyone who broods on death in a battle can count on losing his life. You'd do better to make yourself useful. Get us to the back entrance. Maybe we can slip out that way unseen."

Guillaume spread his hands in a gesture of helplessness. "This is a temple, not a fortress. There are no back entrances, no hidden tunnels, no secret doors."

Farodin looked around in disbelief. Beside the entrance, a spiral staircase climbed to the two galleries. High up, just below the beams supporting the ceiling, curved high stained glass windows with images of priests, recognizable by the deep blue cowls obviously favored by the Tjured sect. Perplexed, the elf gazed at the windows. One of the glazed images showed a priest being pushed into a large pot on a fire. In another, a priest was having his arms and legs hacked off, and a third showed a blue-cowled monk being burned on a pyre by wild men wearing animal skins. Almost all of the windows showed similarly murderous scenes. Now Farodin understood why Guillaume was so calm. To die horribly was clearly the ultimate fulfillment for a Tjured priest.

A thunderclap snapped Farodin out of his thoughts. Fine dust filtered through cracks in the temple portal. A second thunderclap followed. The heavy doors creaked on their hinges. Farodin cursed under his breath. It seemed the king's guard had found something they could use as a battering ram.

"Stop praying and do something useful," the elf snarled at the two priests kneeling at the menhir. "Get the oil lamps out of the niches. Nuramon, look around and see if you can find a torch. Then everyone get up to the highest gallery. I'm going to get us out of this cage."

One of the thick oak planks creaked and split. The door would not hold much longer.

Farodin drove the priests mercilessly. As they climbed the spiral staircase, they had to bundle their robes to avoid stumbling, like a woman would have to gather her skirts. From the second gallery, they could reach the temple windows, which were set in deep recesses because of the thickness of the walls. When he stretched, Farodin could just reach the bottom edge of the recess. He pulled himself up and into the recess and found himself standing before the image of a priest whose smashed limbs were threaded through the spokes of a wheel. The faces of his torturers looked like masks, and the artist had given no thought at all as to how the colors of the glass could harmonize with the morning light. It was an inferior work, the kind of thing that one with even a little aptitude might improve upon with a year or two of halfway ambitious diligence. Shoddy work like this could not bear comparison to the windows in Emerelle's palace, which were assembled from thousands of glass fragments. Albenmark's most talented artists had spent decades working on them, and their masterpieces created a consummate play of light and glass at any hour.

Farodin drew his sword and smashed the agonized face of the glass priest. The panes shattered, and with a few swift strokes of the sword, Farodin cleared away the lead framework so that he could observe the men attacking them in the temple square below.

Down in the gallery, Farodin heard the priests lamenting, Guillaume's voice the clearest among them. "By Tjured, he has destroyed an image of the holy Romuald. We are lost."

Farodin took a step back inside the alcove so that he was out of sight of the square. From where he stood, he could see that the tower was encircled by wooden scaffolding. Just a small step below the window was a narrow platform for the stonemasons who worked on the facade. From there, one could move farther along the scaffolding. Farodin looked at the construction skeptically; everything about it looked rickety.

At one side of the tower was a boarding house for pilgrims. Statues of saints were set in alcoves along its facade. It was certainly more decorative than the tower where the faithful prayed to Tjured. With a little pluck, it would be possible to jump from the scaffolding down to its roof. From there, they could make their way across other rooftops and escape the king's troops.

Farodin climbed back down from the window. The priests were waiting for him, their faces stony. Nuramon shrugged helplessly. "I can't understand them."

"What is so hard to understand?" asked a young, red-haired priest. "You have destroyed an image of Saint Romuald. Romuald was an ill-humored man who only found his way to Tjured late in life. Then heathens in the forests of Drusna murdered him. He cursed all who raised a hand against him, and within a year, his killers were dead. The heathens were so impressed that they turned to Tjured by the thousands. It is said that Romuald's curse continues to the present day. Anyone who damages an image of him should prepare for the worst. Romuald is still bad tempered, even as a saint."

Farodin could not believe what he was hearing. How could anyone believe such rubbish? "You've done nothing," said Farodin. "Romuald's curse is on me and me alone. You don't need to worry, we—" With a crash, the temple doors split open.

"Nuramon, go ahead. Lead the priests. We have to climb over the framework outside to the roof of the building next door. One at a time. We'll be less conspicuous that way. And we shouldn't put too much weight on the scaffolding."

The shouts of the soldiers reached them from the hall below.

"Pour the lamp oil over the scaffolding when you escape," Farodin added.

"Why me?" Nuramon asked. "You know the way—"

"And I'm better with a sword."

Nuramon looked at him, offended.

"Just go! I'll hold them off."

Heavy steps were climbing the spiral stairs. Farodin took some of the lamps and threw them down the stairs. Then he ripped one sleeve from his shirt and soaked it with oil. He ignited the cloth on the flame of a lamp. The oil was poor quality and difficult to get burning. When it did catch, it gave off thick black smoke. The elf threw the torn sleeve down the stairs and watched as the flames licked at the spilled oil from the lamps he'd thrown. The flames quickly burned the cloth to ash . . . and went out.

Farodin stared down the stairs in disbelief. Could they have used oil any cheaper? The first soldier rounded the curve of the steps. He raised his shield in alarm, suddenly wavering when faced with Farodin. The men coming behind him shoved him forward.

Farodin stretched and loosened his muscles. He would show the humans a good fight.

From the corner of his eye, he saw a group of archers lining up on him from the hall below. Their aim was poor, though. Crossbow bolts thudded into the wooden panels of the gallery, and one shattered a large window.

Spurred on by the angry shouts of his fellow soldiers, the man with the shield took a big step up the stairs, and slipped on the oil. He fell back heavily onto the steps, taking several of his comrades down with him.

"Come on," Guillaume called from the window alcove. "The others are already on the roof."

The elf slid his sword back into its sheath. Guillaume took his arm and pulled him up to the alcove. The priest was astonishingly strong for a man so thin. He had helped Farodin up with one hand. Was this strength also part of his father's legacy?

A crossbow bolt crunched into the arched roof of the alcove above their heads. From the square in front of the temple, the voice of the soldiers' commander could be heard. Their escape route had been spotted.

"You go first," said Farodin.

Guillaume hesitated.

"What are you waiting for?"

"I . . . I'm afraid . . . of heights. When I look down, it's like I'm paralyzed. I . . . just can't. Leave me behind."

Farodin grabbed Guillaume's arm roughly. "Then we go together." He dragged him to the edge of the alcove, and they both jumped onto the wooden platform below the window. The scaffolding shuddered under their impact. His heart pounding, Farodin pressed back against the stone wall.

A dull thud, and the framework shuddered again. Somewhere below, a wooden strut gave way and clattered into the depths. Below, near the entrance to the temple, a group of soldiers were holding a heavy beam between them and slamming it against one of the main supports. The idiots seemed oblivious to the risk of sixty feet of scaffolding crashing onto their heads.

Something below splintered. A jolt ran through the framework. One of the stonemasons' platforms tilted and fell, breaking several stays on the way down.

Farodin felt his belly clench painfully. A few heartbeats more, and the entire construction might collapse.

"Watch out," shouted Guillaume.

The elf spun around. The soldier who had slipped on the oil moments earlier jumped onto the platform just behind Farodin and Guillaume. A splintering sound accompanied the heavy man's landing on the boards. His axe sliced forward in a glittering arc.

Farodin dropped low, ducking the blow. He swung one leg, trying to hook his foot behind his adversary's ankle. Suddenly, the entire platform gave way. The elf reflexively grabbed hold of a wooden stanchion even as the soldier, arms wheeling, tumbled into the depths. For a moment, the heavy wooden platform seemed to regain a precarious balance, but it was angled down steeply.

Farodin's heart was thumping hard. They had to get off the scaffolding. As if to underline the thought, a crossbow bolt slammed into wood a hand's width from his head.

Guillaume had managed to rescue himself along a narrow board connected to a ladder that led down to the next level. Guillaume crouched on the board with his arms wrapped around his knees and pressed himself back against the tower wall. Nuramon and the two Tjured priests were lying low on the roof of the pilgrims' house to stay out of sight of the crossbowmen in the square. Farodin could see the captain of the guard dividing his men into small squads and sending them out to surround the building. The escape had failed.

Again, the battering ram crashed into the scaffolding below. A squealing, creaking sound ran through the fragile construction. The platform next to Farodin tilted. The elf looked down apprehensively. If it fell, the platform would slice through a dozen cross-struts like an enormous blade.

Farodin swung hand over hand along a beam to where Guillaume crouched. The priest had his eyes closed and was praying softly.

"We have to get away from here," Farodin shouted. "This whole thing is going to fall any second."

"I can't," Guillaume groaned. "I can't move another inch. I . . ." He swallowed hard. "My fear is stronger than me."

"You're afraid of falling? Move, or we both die." Another shudder ran through the scaffolding, reinforcing Farodin's words. The tilting platform next to them rocked back and forth. Suddenly, a sharp report rang out. The final splinter still holding the platform snapped, and it plunged earthward.

Farodin grabbed hold of the priest and pushed him forward. Like a giant cleaver, the falling platform chopped through poles and struts. One large section of scaffolding came free from the rest and tilted slowly toward the oak tree on the temple square.

With the unsuspected strength of panic, Farodin lifted the priest and carried him in his arms like a huge child. Guillaume clung to him in mortal fear. Farodin could hardly see where he was treading.

The whole structure seemed to be in motion. The planks they were moving along were shaking more and more. Farodin saw the pegs that held the scaffolding to the wall pull free. They were too late. They wouldn't make it down the ladder to the platform below, from where it was just a short jump to the roof of the pilgrims' house. They would have to risk a leap from higher up.

Farodin ran as he had never run before. Struts and splintered timbers rained down around them. The framework swayed like a drunkard. The elf knew that carrying Guillaume, he was too heavy to make such a jump. The priest clutched at Farodin like a drowning man pulling his rescuer under with him in fear.

Without warning, the plank Farodin was running along gave way. Two more steps and they would have reached the jump-off point. As he fell, Farodin reached for the heavy rope slung around a beam that was tilting into the depths.

Something heavy hit Farodin in the back as hard as a troll's fist. He felt several ribs break. The rope had swung him toward the pilgrims' house and now began to swing back.

Half-conscious, Farodin let go. Guillaume let out a shriek as they fell, and they hit the roof hard. Slate shingles smashed under the impact. Farodin was spun around. With nothing to hang on to, he rolled down the slope of the roof. His hands scrabbled helplessly at the smooth shingles, then he slipped over the edge of the roof. With his left hand, he managed to grab hold of a protruding beam. His body swung down and slammed into the wall of the house.

"There's one," someone below him shouted.

Farodin had his other hand on the beam now. He held on, but he did not have enough strength to pull himself up again. Crossbow bolts cracked into the wall beside him.

With a ear-splitting shriek, the scaffolding surrounding the temple collapsed. Dust billowed over the square.

Something hit Farodin's right thigh, and the elf cried out in pain. A bolt had passed through his leg and impaled itself, blood-smeared, in the wall.

Slowly, Farodin's fingers were losing their grip on the end of the beam. His will was broken. He could fight no more.

"Take my hand."

Farodin looked up into frightened sky-blue eyes. Guillaume had crawled to the edge of the roof and was reaching down to him.

"I can't . . . ," said Farodin.

"Tjured, cast out my fear," the priest murmured. Sweat covered his face as he pushed himself a little farther down and grasped Farodin's wrist. With a heave that nearly dislocated his shoulder, Farodin was back on the roof.

Farodin was more gasping than breathing, and his body felt cold. The wound in his thigh was bleeding heavily.

Guillaume, who had held on with one foot hooked through broken shingles and into the rafters below, half rose. He looked at Farodin's wound with concern. "I'll bind your leg. Or you'll—"

A spark of life still flared in Farodin. In fear, he crawled away from Guillaume. "Don't touch me. You—don't try . . ."

Guillaume smiled tiredly. "Bind. I said nothing of healing. But I want—" Then he coughed. Blood ran from his lips. The priest raised one hand and dabbed at his mouth. He stared at the blood on his fingers. A darker patch spread rapidly across his cowl. A crossbow bolt had hit him just under the ribs and passed through his body.

Guillaume tipped sideways like a felled tree. Farodin tried to catch him, but it happened too fast. The priest tumbled over the edge of the roof. Farodin could only listen as Noroelle's son struck the cobblestones of the temple square.

THE SEALED WINDOW

The roar of the collapsing scaffolding could be heard as far away as the vineyard. Mandred squinted against the bright morning light. The foreign soldiers were hanging something from the oak tree on the temple square, but it was too far for Mandred to be able to make out exactly what was happening.

"We have to go into the town," said Mandred insistently.

"No," said Ollowain for the third time. "Do we know what's going on in there? Nuramon and Farodin have probably found a place to hide and are waiting for those murderers to disappear."

"*Probably* isn't good enough," Mandred said as he swung into his saddle. "Seems to me that *friend* means something different to elves than it does to humans. I for one am not going to sit around here doing nothing any longer. What's wrong with you?" He looked to Oleif and the two warrior women. He expected little from the elven women. They were too closely tied to Ollowain, but his son . . . They had been riding now, father and son, for three years. Had he failed to teach him even the slightest sense of honor in all that time? Of course, Mandred knew that by himself, he could do nothing, that even the five of them could hardly expect to prevail against such overwhelming numbers. But simply sitting there, waiting and hoping that their friends would escape? That was not the way a man ought to behave.

Oleif gave Ollowain a questioning look. His son seemed surprised at Ollowain's lack of action.

"You all saw nearly a hundred men ride across the bridge at dawn," said Ollowain.

Mandred stroked the shaft of the axe dangling from the horn of his saddle. "Then it promises to be an exciting fight. The way I see it, we're evenly matched." He pulled the reins and turned his horse onto the narrow path that led from the vineyard down to the valley.

When he reached the road that led into the town, he heard hoofbeats behind him. He didn't turn, but pride filled his heart. For once, Oleif had chosen not to act like an elf.

They rode side by side without speaking. Their silence said more than words could.

Five soldiers had been posted to guard the bridge. Mandred saw one of them draw back his crossbow. A brawny fellow with a shaven head blocked his path, the tip of a spear aimed at Mandred's breast.

"In the name of the king, turn back. This bridge is closed," the soldier called out.

Mandred smiled broadly and bowed. As he did so, his right hand slid into the leather loop on the handle of his axe. "Urgent business brings me to Aniscans. Clear the way, my friend."

"Make tracks, or I'll slit your belly and hang you from the nearest tree with your own guts." The guard jabbed his spear within an inch of Mandred's throat.

Mandred's axe came up and splintered the shaft of the guard's weapon. A backhand swing split the man's skull.

The jarl leaned low over his horse's neck to offer the crossbowman as small a target as possible. Oleif jumped from his saddle and charged the surprised guards. He avoided their spears and swung his long sword in lethal sweeps. Neither shields nor mail could withstand the elven steel. In seconds, all five soldiers were on the ground.

The bridge was clear. It looked as if they had not been seen from the far shore. Mandred swung from his saddle and kneeled next to the crossbowman. The soldier was no longer conscious; a kick from Oleif's horse had turned his face to a bloody pulp. Mandred pulled a knife from his belt and cut the man's throat. Then he searched the dead men. He found a thin leather moneybag containing a few copper pieces and a silver ring, dark with patina.

"Father, you can't."

Mandred glanced up at his son then turned to the man with the shaved head who had threatened to hang him by his entrails. "Something bothering you?" asked Mandred, patting at the heavy man's clothing in search of hidden coins.

"You're robbing the dead. That's . . . offensive. It's immoral."

Mandred turned the guard onto his side. He had large, fleshy ears and wore a single earring set with a pretty pearl. The jarl jerked the ring from the man's ear. "Immoral?" He held the pearl against the light. It was the size of a pea and gleamed with a pink sheen. "Stealing from the living might be immoral, but it does these men no harm if I relieve them of their valuables. If I didn't do it, their own comrades would."

"Don't talk about comrades. Right now, it seems to mean nothing to you that your so-called friends might be fighting for their lives. Ollowain was right."

Mandred went to the next corpse. "Would you keep one eye on the other shore while you preach, Son? You and Guillaume would get on like a house on fire. And what exactly was Ollowain right about?"

"He said you were like an animal, acting only on instinct. Neither good nor evil . . . just primitive."

One of the dead spearmen wore a silver ring set with a large turquoise. Mandred tugged at the ring, but it was tight on the man's finger. "You keep the far shore in sight" was all he said. Mandred spat on the dead man's hand and rubbed spittle on the finger to make the ring slide off more easily, but it didn't help. Irritated, he drew his dagger.

"Don't do it, Father," Oleif said.

Mandred set the tip of the dagger at the base of the finger and whacked the handle with the flat of his hand. With a gristly crunch, the steel sliced through the thin bone. The jarl picked up the finger, slipped off the ring and put it in his leather bag with the rest of the loot.

"You're *worse* than an animal," shouted Oleif.

Mandred rose to his feet. "I don't care what you think about me or animals, but never again say that my friends don't matter to me."

"Ah, I understand. In pure unselfishness, we bide our time here while they fight. You don't want to spoil their fun."

Mandred swung up onto the saddle. "You really don't understand what we're doing here, do you?"

"Oh, I do. I do. That's very clear to me. You've been filling your purse . . . I guess so you can drink yourself blind in the next town and go whoring. Maybe that's why Freya cursed you."

Without warning, Mandred slapped Oleif hard on the side of his head. "Don't *ever* mention your mother's name and whores in the same breath again."

The young warrior swayed in the saddle, dazed by the force of the surprise blow. Red streaks marked his cheek.

"Now shut up and listen to me. You might learn something," Mandred said, speaking in a low voice that accentuated his words. He had to stay in control. More than anything, he would have liked to give this big-mouthed son of his a decent hiding. What had the elves done to him?

"Most human soldiers are afraid of battle. They talk big, but when it comes down to it, their guts are filled with fear," he said to his son. "My own fear is that there might be crossbowmen in the buildings over there, waiting to shoot us down the moment we cross the bridge. If they are posted there, then they'll wait until we get so close they can't miss. I dismounted, and I've been filling my purse to give them a little more time to sit with their fear. Because they fear us just as much as we fear them. They're afraid of missing us, and afraid we'll get inside those buildings before they can reload. The longer they can see us and the longer they have to wait, the more likely one of them is to get rattled and fire off a bolt. Then at least we'll know what's waiting for us."

For a few heartbeats, a tense silence stood between father and son. All there was to hear was the sound of trees and branches in the river, scraping past the sturdy pylons of the bridge.

Oleif looked to the houses across the river. "You're right," he said. "If we ride blindly into a trap, then we will be useless to Nuramon and Farodin. Nothing is moving over there. Do you think we can cross the bridge safely?"

Mandred shook his head. "War and safety make poor bedfellows. Besides, whoever's waiting for us on the other side, they're not the usual breed of soldier. Your run-of-the-mill soldier would have tried a shot by now. Instead of greenhorns, we might be facing some crafty old bastards, veterans who've been through plenty of battles. They'll know this game, and they'll be happy to wait."

Mandred leaned low over the neck of his mare and dug in his spurs. "See you on the far shore."

They rode across the long bridge at a flat gallop.

Mandred eyed the buildings suspiciously, but no hail of arrows greeted them as they rode off the bridge. The five soldiers they had left behind were apparently the only guards posted on this side of the town.

Mandred and Oleif reined in their horses. Before them lay a broad, meandering road that led first to the market and then continued to the temple square and the hill. Aniscans appeared to be deserted. Nobody moved in the alleyways. Slowly, they rode on. Frightened eyes followed them from behind half-closed shutters. From the hill ahead came sounds of screaming and shouting, and they could hear the clear ring of sword on sword.

"If I were in charge, I'd let us ride into the town then close off all the exits," Oleif declared.

Mandred nodded. "Looks like the elves taught you more than pretty words or how to warble a song. Let's dismount. We'll be more mobile on foot."

They left the main road and moved into the labyrinth of narrow lanes and alleys, leading their horses by the reins. Mandred looked around uneasily. The entire town was a single enormous trap. They could only hope that no one had observed the carnage they'd left at the bridge.

The two men crossed a narrow square of compacted clay. A large building with walled-up windows loomed over one side of the square. With its high gateway leading into a rear courtyard, it looked almost like a castle.

"We'll leave the horses there," said Mandred, and he led his mare through the gate.

Many windows opened onto the courtyard on the inside. The building seemed strange to Mandred. For a moment, he saw a young woman with a half-open bodice at one of the windows. Then she disappeared. No one stepped out through the only door that led into the building, and no one called down to them from the windows. Mandred was happy enough for it to stay that way.

Opposite the gate stood an open shed with a long workbench. Wooden shoes were stacked on the bench, and beside them, neatly organized, lay an array of wood-carving tools: planes, chisels, and knives with oddly crooked blades. Here, too, there was no one to be seen.

Mandred slung the reins through one of the iron rings set into the wall. Then he gazed up at the windows that looked out on the courtyard. "I know you're watching us. If these horses are not here when I return, then I'll come up there and cut your throats." He reached into the leather purse on his belt and withdrew a single coin, which he held high in the air. "But if I find the horses watered and fed, then I'll leave this silver piece."

Without waiting for an answer, Mandred shouldered his axe and went back out through the gate.

"Do you have a plan?" Oleif asked.

"Of course," Mandred replied. "Don't worry. All we need to do is follow the sounds of battle."

His son's brow creased. "Is there another plan?"

Mandred waved off the question in annoyance. "Too many plans give you headaches, and you end up doing nothing at all. A good leader doesn't just talk. He acts."

Mandred broke into a jog. He stayed close to the walls to give a shooter a more difficult target. The clang of swords was very close now.

Suddenly, a soldier came staggering out through the door of a house. Strapped to his arm, he carried a large round shield with a white bull's head. In the doorway behind him, Nuramon appeared. The elf had one hand pressed to his left hip. Dark blood welled out between his fingers.

A punch from Mandred sent the surprised soldier to the ground before he could raise his shield.

"It's good to see you, mortals," Nuramon croaked. He lowered his sword and leaned against the door frame, exhausted.

The two men followed the elf back into the semidarkness inside the house. They crossed a devastated kitchen, stepping over two bodies that blocked the entrance to the dining room. Here, too, all the shutters were closed, the light from outside only falling in narrow stripes. Farodin lay on the long dining table that dominated the room. A young priest with flaming red hair was leaning over him.

"You must not move, my lord," the young man was saying to Farodin, his voice almost pleading. "The wounds will open up again. And you have lost a lot of blood."

Farodin pushed the Tjured priest aside. "I can lie around when we're clear of this town and in safety."

"But you'll . . . ," the priest began again, upset.

Nuramon calmed the young man. "I'll take care of his injuries later."

Farodin sat upright and turned to the humans. "You took long enough. Where's Ollowain?"

Mandred avoided the elf's eyes.

Farodin snorted contemptuously. "I thought as much." In a few words, he told Mandred and Oleif about the attack on the temple and their escape.

"What about Guillaume?" asked Oleif when Farodin was finished.

The elf pointed to the closed shutters. "Out there in the square."

Mandred and his son crossed the room and looked out carefully through a narrow gap. The king's soldiers were everywhere. They had piled wood from the collapsed scaffolding all around the holy oak. From one of the branches, head down, hung two naked and defiled bodies. One a stout older man, the other . . . Guillaume. Their bodies had been flayed with canes. Crossbow bolts and the broken shafts of spears jutted from their torsos.

Mandred turned away in disgust. "Why are they doing that? You said they were supposed to present him to their king."

"Guillaume was no longer presentable after he fell off the roof," said Farodin, his voice cold. Then he pressed his mouth shut until it was no more than a thin, bloodless line.

"The crossbow bolt that hit him was meant for Farodin," said Nuramon in a flat tone. "I—"

"Guillaume wanted to die," Farodin interrupted him angrily. "You know that. He wanted to go out and give himself to those murderers."

"To save us," replied Nuramon. "I'm not accusing you of anything. Between Emerelle and Cabezan, Guillaume saw no room to live anymore. All he had left was the choice of how he wanted to die. When the soldiers picked up his body, they flew into a rage. They desecrated his body and hung him from the tree."

"And now they're going to come for us," said Oleif, who was still standing by the window.

Mandred glanced outside and let out a curse. The man he'd knocked unconscious in front of the building had come to. He ran onto the square, shouting and pointing at the house where they were hiding. "All this talk about goddamned morals. I should have just slit the bastard's throat."

Farodin reached for his sword, which lay beside him on the table. "They would have come for us in any case." He turned to the priest who had treated his wounds. "Thank you, mortal. Go and find your fellow priest and hide. We won't be able to protect you much longer." He tried to stand, but his wounded leg would barely carry him.

Mandred thrust his shoulder under Farodin's arm, supporting him. "I need no help," Farodin muttered.

Mandred let him go. The elf stood on his own feet. Swaying, but still, he stood. "It makes no sense to fight here. Let's try to get to the horses. If they haven't replaced the guard at the bridge, we might still be able to escape." He waved Oleif over to him. "Help Nuramon. He's less prickly."

"Don't go out through the door," the red-haired priest suddenly said. "I . . . want to thank you, too. My brother Segestus . . . I don't need to look for him. He is long gone. There is another way out. Follow me."

Mandred looked to Farodin. "We've got nothing to lose," said the elf. "Bolt the doors. That will hold them off a little while. What kind of route was it that Segestus took?"

Without answering, the priest lit a lamp and led them from the kitchen into a pantry. The room was fully stocked with amphorae in every conceivable size and form. From the ceiling hung hams and smoked sausages.

The priest led the way. Mandred hung back a little and stuffed two large sausages inside his tunic. They were setting off down an unknown path, trying to escape, and Luth only knew when they would get a chance to eat something decent. He would have liked to have taken an amphora of wine as well. The god Tjured must certainly be of some importance if his priests were able to keep up such a well-stocked larder. *Strange*, thought Mandred. He had heard of Tjured for the first time only two weeks earlier, but that could no doubt be explained by his ignorance.

The young priest led them to a low arch. Beyond that was a stairway that led deeper, and from there, they found their way into a room that contained huge barrels. Mandred's eyes widened. He had never in his life imagined having to look *up* to barrels. They stood in rows along the walls on both sides, and ahead of them, the cellar disappeared into darkness. There was an entire lake of wine stored down there.

"Naida's tits, priest, what do you do with all this wine? Bathe in it?" asked Mandred.

"Aniscans is a town of vintners. The temple often receives gifts of wine. We trade in it." He paused, looked back, and silently counted off the barrels they had passed on his fingers. Then he waved them onward and finally led them between two high barrels. Hidden in the darkness was an opening into a low tunnel.

"Some say there is a second town hidden beneath Aniscans. They mean the great storage vaults of the winemakers. Many of these chambers are connected by tunnels like this. If you know your way around down here, you can go from one end of town to the other on a rainy day without getting your feet wet. But you can get hopelessly lost as well . . ."

"Well, at least you wouldn't die of thirst," said the jarl.

The priest looked at Mandred in discomfort. Then he ducked and disappeared into the tunnel.

Mandred pulled his head low between his shoulders but still banged the roof of the tunnel several times. The weak light from the lantern was almost completely blocked by those ahead of him, and he found himself feeling his way along in the gloom. The air down here was stuffy, and an acidic odor hung in the air. Soon, he had the feeling that they'd been on the move for hours. He counted his steps to distract himself. At three hundred thirty, they reached a second vault filled with barrels.

The priest led them through it to a stairway, and they climbed up through a hatch that opened into a sunlit courtyard. "Where do you need to go now?"

Mandred blinked in the light and took a deep breath of fresh air.

"Our horses are tied up in a courtyard. It's a big place next to a small square, and all the windows facing the square are walled up," Oleif explained. "Can you tell us how to get back there?"

The priest reddened. "A house with walled-up windows?" He cleared his throat in embarrassment.

"Something wrong?" asked Mandred. "I was wondering why they'd turned a house into a fortress."

Again, the priest cleared his throat. "It's . . . because of the tavern on the other side of the square. The publican built a special bar up on the second floor. Anyone who wanted to drink there had to pay a copper more for a jug of wine."

"And?"

The priest writhed in embarrassment. "From the bar, one had a good view into the windows across the square."

Mandred was slowly losing his patience. "And what was over there to see?"

"It is a house . . . where lonely men go. From the bar, one could see what went on in the rooms. And that was why the owner walled up the windows."

Nuramon laughed out loud and, a second later, pressed his hand to the wound on his hip. "A brothel. You left the horses at a brothel, Mandred?"

"In the *courtyard* of a brothel," said Oleif, who had also turned red. "In the *courtyard*."

"I bet it's the only brothel in town," added Farodin. "And you found it without even trying."

Mandred could not understand what was so funny about the situation. "I didn't know anything about it. There's the workshop of a respectable tradesman in the courtyard. That's all I saw."

"Of course," replied Farodin with a grin. "Of course."

Mandred looked at the two elves in amazement. The battle and Guillaume's terrible death . . . it must all have been too much for them. They'd cracked. It was the only way he could explain this strange outburst of mirth.

"You know your way around here, priest. Show us the shortest way to this . . . brothel," Mandred said.

The young man led them along narrow alleys and through hidden yards. Occasionally, they heard the shouts of King Cabezan's soldiers close by, but they were not seen. Mandred was starting to feel that they should already have reached the brothel when the priest abruptly stopped and signaled to the others to be quiet.

"What's the matter?" hissed Mandred, and he pushed his way to the front. Cautiously, he looked out onto the square. They had reached their goal, but there were seven soldiers standing in front of the tavern opposite the brothel. A scrawny tavern girl was serving them tankards of beer and wooden plates piled high with cheese and bread.

"Doesn't Luth love twisting the strings of fate into knots?" Mandred sighed. He turned to his companions. "I'll distract the soldiers. You get to the horses. What about you, priest? Do you want to escape with us?"

The young man considered for a moment, then shook his head. "I have friends here. They will keep me hidden until the scum are gone again."

"Then you shouldn't be seen anywhere near us," Mandred said. "Thank you for getting us this far. You should go and find those friends now."

"What are you planning, Father?" Oleif asked. "You don't intend to take on seven men alone, do you?"

Mandred stroked the rune-covered blade of his axe. "There are two of us. You just make sure you get Nuramon and Farodin to the horses as quick as you can. If you can at least make it to the edge of town, you might get some help from Ollowain if you run into trouble."

"What about you?" asked Nuramon. "We can't just ride off and leave you behind."

Mandred waved his hand dismissively. "Don't worry about me. I'll get out of here one way or another. Not even the manboar was able to finish me off."

"But you shouldn't . . ."

Mandred was through listening to his friends' objections. The soldiers searching for them might appear at any moment. The time for words had passed. He gripped his axe more firmly and strolled out into the square.

"Hey, lads," he hailed. "Am I glad there's something in this town to drink besides grape juice."

The soldiers looked up in surprise. "What's your business here?" asked a soldier with stringy hair and a stubbled chin.

"I'm a pilgrim, on my way to the Temple of Tjured," said Mandred. "They say there's a healer there, a real miracle worker." He stretched. "This gout is turning my fingers to claws."

"The priest Guillaume, you mean. Poor bastard died this morning trying to heal himself." The soldier gave a spiteful grin. "We're just having a little wake."

Mandred had nearly reached them. "Then I'll drink to his memory. The man—"

"There's blood on his axe!" one of the soldiers shouted.

Mandred charged, knocking down the man in front with a swing of his axe and ramming his shoulder into a second man's chest, causing him to fall. A sword blade grated noisily over the mail shirt he was wearing but did not penetrate it. Mandred wheeled around, blocked one attack with his axe, and hammered his fist into a soldier's face. A thrown hatchet breezed past him. The jarl pulled his head down and charged again. No armor was able to withstand the deadly double-sided blade of his axe. Like a reaper in the wheat, he cut the soldiers down. Suddenly, he heard a shout of warning. He turned around.

From one of the side alleys, more soldiers with their bull-headed shields suddenly came storming into the square. Oleif stood directly in their path while Farodin and Nuramon hobbled to the brothel courtyard to try to escape.

Mandred broke away from the soldiers still standing and ran to his son's aid. Oleif moved with the grace of a dancer. As a fighting style, it looked effeminate, Mandred thought, but he had to admit that none of the soldiers were able to break through the lethal whirl of Oleif's long sword.

Fighting side by side, father and son were slowly forced back to the entrance of the courtyard. When they were in the archway and could no longer be attacked from either side or behind, the king's soldiers pulled back.

Mandred and Oleif pulled the heavy gates closed and dropped the solid crossbeam into place. Gasping for breath, the jarl sank to the ground. With his left hand, he toyed with one of the braids in his hair. "I forgot to count," he murmured wearily.

His son grinned lopsidedly. "I'd say at least three. Plus the two on the bridge makes five. If you keep commemorating the men you kill like that, you'll soon be needing new hair."

Mandred shook his head. "Thinner braids will do it." Grunting, he hauled himself to his feet.

Nuramon and Farodin were at the horses. The elves would be useless if it came down to fighting their way out of the town.

A bald, scar-faced man appeared in the doorway that opened into the courtyard. Mandred had rarely seen a man so ugly. His face looked as if it had been trampled by a herd of cattle. "The horses have been watered and fed, warrior," the man called to Mandred. "Now I would thank you to get out of my place."

"Is there another exit?" Mandred asked.

"No doubt there is, but none I would show you. You go back out through that gate, same way you came in. There's no shelter here for anyone running from the king's guard."

Oleif took a threatening step toward the doorway where the man stood, but Mandred grasped his arm and pulled him back. "He's right. I'd do the same in his shoes." The jarl tilted his head back and looked up to the windows. Two young women were watching what was going on down in the courtyard with curiosity.

"Is this place really a brothel?" Mandred asked.

"Aye," answered the scar-faced man. "But if you ask me, you boys don't have time to dally with any girls, warrior."

Mandred untied his purse from his belt and weighed it in his hand. Then he tossed it to the man. "There's a chance your house here will suffer some damage in the next few hours. But we might be able to spare it that . . . will you open the gate for me when I ask you to?"

"If it means I never see any of you again, you can count on me."

"Then wait by the gate." Mandred turned to his son, and a grin spread across his face. "You were right. I really do leave all my money in brothels."

"I'm sorry—"

"Forget it. Help me." They went across to the shed, and Mandred swept all the wooden shoes from the bench. The bench top was oak, three inches thick. Mandred stroked a hand over the speckled wood. "The rules of a siege are simple, my boy. There are the ones inside the walls. They sit around and wait for something to happen, then fight back as well as they can. And there are the ones outside the walls. They always have the advantage, because they decide what happens and when. I think it's time we turned those rules on their head."

Oleif looked at him but did not understand what he meant.

Mandred stuffed several of the carpenter's chisels and knives in his belt. "I don't think I've ever told you that you've turned out pretty well . . . even if it was Ollowain who taught you."

"Do you think we're going to die here?"

"No true warrior should die in his bed." There was so much he still had to say to his son, but time was not on their side. Suddenly, his mouth felt like dust. "I . . . I wish we'd been able to spend one summer together in Firnstayn. It's only a simple village. But in its way, it's lovelier than anything I ever saw in Albenmark." He swallowed. "I bet no one ever taught you fly-fishing when you were with the elves. In late summer, the fjord is full of salmon . . . Enough chatter. Let's not give the men out there any more time to regroup. Now they're spread out through the town searching for us, and we might still get through." He hauled at the workbench. "Damn, that's heavy." He glanced back at the two elves.

"They'll be no use to us in a fight. And with two riders in the saddle, the horses are too slow," he said, then hesitated. "I'll stay here . . . I'll slap my mare's rump the moment we get through the gate. Once she takes off, Nuramon will have his hands full just trying to stay in the saddle. He won't be able to try any heroic nonsense. Maybe he'll make it out of town that way."

Oleif drew a deep breath. Then he nodded. "I'm staying with you. May the gods stand by them in their search for Noroelle. Their lives have a goal . . . but I don't even know which world I'm meant to be part of."

Mandred threw his arms around his son. "I'm proud to have ridden at your side . . . Alfadas," he said, his voice half choked. It was the first time he had called him by his elven name. For a few heartbeats, overcome by emotion, neither man moved. Then they walked together back to the horses.

Nuramon, downcast, looked up as they approached. "Do you have any idea how we can get out of here?"

"Of course." Mandred hoped that his grin didn't look completely put on. "We give them a good clobbering, smash some skulls, and ride away at our leisure. But I fear that riding two to a saddle would be a little cramped."

Farodin chuckled quietly. "Delightfully straightforward. A true Mandred plan."

"Isn't it?" The jarl went to Nuramon and helped him into the saddle. "Stay on the horses, or you'll just be in the way."

When the two elves were mounted, Mandred and Alfadas returned to the workshop. Between them, they heaved the massive bench and carried it in front of them like a huge shield.

"I have one last thing to ask of you, my son," said Mandred.

Alfadas's face was contorted with the effort of holding the heavy bench aloft. "What?"

"If we get out of this alive, then stop using that toilet water. That's for women and elves, and it keeps Norgrimm far from your side. Best not to go into battle without the goodwill of the god of war." Mandred jutted his chin toward the gate. "Open it, scar face."

The owner of the brothel jerked the crossbeam free and shoved open the two heavy gates.

"For Freya!" Mandred bellowed at the top of his lungs as they charged.

Crossbow bolts rattled against the bench like hail. Pressed close to the wood, the two men stormed blindly out onto the square until they ran into a group of soldiers. The heavy bench sent five men sprawling.

Mandred quickly looked around. What he saw shook him to his bones. At the windows all around them stood crossbowmen, reloading as fast as they were able. The alleys leading onto the little square were barricaded and manned. And the troop of soldiers they had rammed were on their feet again and pulling back quickly, clearing the firing line.

Suddenly, Mandred heard hoofbeats. A snow-white stallion leaped over one of the barricades. The woman riding it reined hard, wheeled the horse around, and aimed her bow. In a single smooth motion, she released one arrow and reached into her quiver for the next. With a scream, a bowman tumbled from a window of the tavern opposite.

Hoofbeats rang from another alley, and Ollowain flew over a barricade, cutting down a spearman as he came. He was leading Nuramon's horse by the reins. "Come on, mortal. Mount up. You might have taught me something about honor, but that doesn't mean I'll wait for you forever."

Mandred grabbed hold of the saddle horn and pulled himself onto the horse's back. He saw Yilvina at a third barricade. She had dismounted and, with her twin short swords, was hacking into the soldiers like a berserker.

Suddenly, the air was filled with crossbow bolts. The horses whinnied shrilly. Something hit Mandred in the back, and he slumped forward.

Nomja was still firing arrows when a bolt hit her stallion in the head. Blood sprayed over the beast's white hide, and it buckled as if struck by lightning. Nomja leaped nimbly from the saddle, evading the trampling hooves of the other horses. She raised her bow defiantly and fired back.

"To Yilvina," Ollowain shouted. "She has cleared a path for us."

Mandred steered his horse to Nomja's side and reached a hand down to her. "Come on!"

"One more," she shouted, and the arrow was already flying from the string. She turned to Mandred and a sudden jolt went through her. Mandred grabbed hold of her as she was about to fall and pulled her onto the horse. Despite her size, she felt almost as light as a child.

Mandred wheeled his horse around and spurred it forward. With a mighty leap, they cleared the barricade and rode down the alley at breakneck speed. Very soon, they were at the bridge. No more soldiers challenged them. It seemed that every last man had been at the small square by the brothel.

Only when he was on the bridge did Mandred dare look back. His son, Farodin, Nuramon, Ollowain, and Yilvina, they had all made it. Their band had taken a beating, to be sure. None had gotten away unscathed, but they were free.

A feeling of indescribable happiness came over Mandred. He had been so certain that he was about to die. He lifted his axe in triumph and swung it high overhead. "Victory! By Norgrimm! We got away! We escaped! Victory!"

He slipped one arm around Nomja, still lying across his saddle, to help her sit upright. Her head lolled to one side.

"Nomja?"

The elf's green eyes were open wide, staring sightlessly at the sky. Only now did Mandred see the hole the size of a hazelnut in her temple.

THE HOLY SCRIPTURES OF TJURED:

BOOK SEVEN:
THE DEATH OF THE PROPHET

*A*nd it came to pass that on that very day an angel appeared to King Cabezan in his dream. The angel had wings of silver and carried a silver sword. But of all the angel's radiance, most radiant of all were its eyes, which were of a pale blue. And it said unto Cabezan, "Send out your soldiers, for an affliction has befallen Aniscans. The prophet Guillaume fears for his life, for the children of Alb have been sent to kill him for no reason but that one of them came too late to Guillaume's healing hands."

Thereupon, Cabezan ordered his best soldiers to mount their horses, and he sent them to Aniscans, and their captain was named Elgiot.

At that time, no wall surrounded Aniscans, and the children of Alb were able to enter the city undetected. They were seven in all, six elves and a troll, and they sought Guillaume in the temple. But Guillaume was not there, and they found only the other priests of Tjured. The children of Alb took the priests to the giant oak tree in front of the temple and killed them there.

Then the prophet heard what was happening in the city, and he left his house. And behold! He surrendered himself to the children of Alb. He stood before them and bowed. He spoke to them, saying, "Do with me what you will. Tjured will judge you on your acts." When Guillaume said this, the elves beat him to the ground, and the troll hung him from the great oak. But the prophet still lived, and he prayed to Tjured, whereupon a she-elf took her bow and fired arrows at him.

While this was happening, King Cabezan's soldiers rode into the city, and they fought the children of Alb for the life of the prophet. But the she-elf fired flaming arrows at the oak until it caught fire and burned utterly. The soldiers of Cabezan avenged her deed and slayed her. For

Guillaume's sake, they let the other elves and the troll escape, for they hoped in their hearts that the prophet still lived.

The tree was blackened from its trunk to its leaves before they could pour enough water on it to extinguish the flames. When they cut the prophet down from the tree, he, too, was blackened and lifeless. But behold! Water dripped from the tree onto his face and washed away the soot. Guillaume's white face appeared from beneath. The soldiers washed the body of the prophet, and they saw that his only wounds were from the iron arrowheads in his body, and that the flames had not harmed him. Guillaume opened his eyes and took the leader Elgiot by the hand and said to him, "They have chosen their path. May Tjured grant them the mercy they deserve." The prophet died beneath the blackened tree. Thus did the children of Alb bring a curse down upon them. So it is said.

FROM THE SCHOFFENBURG EDITION
VOLUME FIVE, FOLIO FORTY-THREE R.

THE JARL OF FIRNSTAYN

The companions rode north, high into the mountains above of Aniscans. They buried Nomja beneath a silver fir at the edge of a glacier lake. Her weapons they hung from the branches of the tree.

A gloom settled over both elves and humans. Nuramon did what he could, but even with his powers, it was two weeks before they had all recovered from their injuries. The damage done to their souls would take longer to heal. None of them had suspected that the death of the dour, taciturn Gelvuun might leave such a gap in their number, let alone the loss of Nomja, whom they all had liked.

When there was no longer any excuse to delay their departure further, they agreed to travel together to Firnstayn and from there return to Albenmark through the Albenstar at the stone circle above the fjord.

The journey to Firnstayn took them nearly three moons. They went out of their way to avoid villages and towns, to draw as little attention as possible. Twice, far off, they saw troops on horseback under King Cabezan's banner. From traders whose caravan they joined for a day, they learned of the terrible incident in Aniscans. The town, it was said, had been attacked by demons who had murdered the benevolent healer Guillaume and desecrated the Temple of Tjured.

None of the companions spoke out. None tried to redress the wrong by telling the truth. Not even later, on board a huge grain ship taking them across the Neri Sea to Gonthabu, the royal city of the Fjordlands; in that week at sea, they heard ever more lurid versions of the story.

It was the height of summer when they finally reached Firnstayn. Alfadas was surprised at how small the settlement nestled on the shore of the fjord was. From the way his father spoke of it, he had imagined something much more remarkable. Nine longhouses and no more than three dozen small huts were ringed by a wooden palisade atop an earthen wall.

At the entrance to the settlement squatted a bulky, wooden watchtower. They had barely reached the crest of the hill above the village when a blast from a signal horn sounded. And as they approached the gate, a troop of archers lined up along the palisade.

"Hey-o! Have the people of Firnstayn forgotten the laws of hospitality?" Mandred yelled angrily. "Before your gate stands the Jarl Mandred Torgridson, and he demands his right to enter."

"You who call yourself Mandred," replied a stout, young warrior, "the clan whose name you have usurped has been erased. I am the elected jarl of Firnstayn, and you and your companions are not welcome here."

Alfadas glanced at his father, expecting him to break into one of his outbursts of temper at any moment, but Mandred remained surprisingly sedate. "Well spoken, Jarl. I would have said the same in your place." His father removed a silver armband he had cheated a trader out of in a game of dice. "I offer this for a barrel of mead and invite you to drink with me and my son."

The young jarl eyed Alfadas. Then he shook his head. "You are overplaying your hand, storyteller. How can a man have a son who is nearly as old as himself?"

"If you want to hear that story, then drink with me at my cost," Mandred called back with a laugh.

"Open the gate, Kalf." An old man pushed his way forward to the spiked top of the wall and waved to them. "Do you believe us now? Look. He's even brought the elves back with him." The old man quickly made a protective sign in the air. "Don't make a fool of yourself by refusing to let elves enter the village, Kalf. You know the old stories."

"I greet you, Erek Ragnarson," Mandred called. "Good to see that you and that leaky relic you call a boat aren't yet at the bottom of the fjord. Will you sail out with us? I want to teach my son to fish before I move on."

"Open the gate," Erek ordered, his voice firm. No one opposed him.

Mandred and the elves stayed in Firnstayn for three weeks, three weeks in which Alfadas learned to see the world of humans through different eyes. He enjoyed the rough respect with which he was treated and the way the young women looked at him. Life was simple. The most important thing you had to remember was to watch out for bad-tempered pigs roaming the muddy village paths. There was no luxury. The coarse wool that the women spun scratched the skin. The houses were drafty, and the smoke stung your eyes when you sat till late in the longhouses and drank and told stories. Alfadas listened in disbelief when Kalf spoke of scouting parties of trolls being seen in the forests across the fjord the previous winter. That was why they had reinforced the palisade surrounding the village. Even the elves took the news seriously.

After twenty days in the village, the elves, especially Ollowain and Farodin, began to push for them to ride up to the Albenstar.

Kalf was the only one to feel relieved when, on the morning of the twenty-first day, Erek Ragnarson ferried the small band across to the far side of the fjord. But Alfadas went with a heavy heart, for he left Asla, Erek's granddaughter, standing on the shore. In her quiet way, she had captured him body and soul. There wasn't an elven woman of Emerelle's court who was not more beautiful than Asla, but in Asla burned a passion that the elves, who counted their lives in centuries, barely knew. She was not one to hide her feelings behind pretty words, and there were tears in her eyes as Alfadas crossed the water.

Again and again, Alfadas looked back as they rode up the path to the standing stones. When he could hardly see her any longer, the girl in the blue dress, with her blond hair blowing in the wind, still stood by the waterline.

"You should acknowledge Kalf as jarl," said Mandred abruptly. "He is a good man."

Alfadas was surprised at his father's words. "*You* are the jarl of Firnstayn," he replied, upset.

Mandred looked sharply at him. "More than thirty years ago, I was. I don't belong to this world anymore. It would not be fair to Kalf and all the others born after me if I returned to Firnstayn. And not fair to you either, my lad. Your time has come."

Alfadas didn't know what to say to that. They had dropped back a little behind the elves, and the others could not hear what they were saying.

"Every year, come the midwinter gathering, the village elects the jarl for the year ahead. I don't think anyone would make you jarl this winter. You have to prove yourself first—in battle and also in day-to-day matters. I see all the signs of a fine leader in you, my son. And I know you will find your feet if you stay here."

Mandred reined in his mare and looked down to the village. His voice was hoarse as he went on. "She's still standing there and watching. Look . . . but don't think too long. You won't find a woman like her in Albenmark. She's proud, and she won't take any guff from you, and no doubt she'll make your life a misery more than once. But she loves you, and she will grow old with you. No elf can give you that. One day, the only thing keeping an elf-wife at your side will be sympathy or habit."

"If I were to stay, then it would be because of that news about the trolls," Alfadas replied earnestly.

His father suppressed a smile. "Of course. And I have to say, if I were a troll, I'd think twice if I knew there was a man in the village who'd been schooled in swordsmanship by Ollowain and who'd learned every dirty trick that *I* know in the last three years . . . And just in case you don't like the life here, come up to the stone circle on a night when the moon is full and call Xern's name. I'm sure you'll be heard."

"I'll stay one winter, for now," Alfadas decided. And he was surprised at how relieved his decision made him feel.

"Fine . . . because of the trolls," Mandred said, and he glanced almost casually back down to the far shore of the fjord. "She's a stubborn lass. She's still waiting for you."

"Won't you stay, too? Firnstayn could use your axe."

"No one is waiting there for me anymore. I couldn't stand living in the shadow of the oak over Freya's grave. The Devanthar took away the woman I loved. I'm going to help Farodin and Nuramon find their way to the one *they* love. And I'm going to finish my feud with the Devanthar. My past is ashes, and my future is blood. I feel better knowing you won't be riding beside me. Maybe . . ." He hesitated. "When the Devanthar is dead, maybe I can live in Firnstayn in peace." He smiled. "I mean, if Jarl Alfadas Mandredson doesn't mind letting a stubborn old man into the village."

The shadow of a cloud edged over the rim of the cliff above. The birds and crickets fell silent, and Alfadas had the feeling that he would never see his father again.

SILVERNIGHT

They rode in silence through the night forest. A mild autumn wind plucked the last of the leaves from the branches. Mandred had never before sensed the magic of Albenmark as keenly as he did at that moment. The moon hung low in the sky and was bigger, far bigger, than in the human world. It shimmered red against the darkness. "There's blood on the face of the moon," he'd heard the elves whispering, and he understood that it was a warning that something bad lay ahead.

The light was the strangest of all. It was not unlike the faerylight he'd seen sometimes over Firnstayn on clear winter nights, but this light was silver. And it wasn't spread across the heavens, but hung among the trees all around, like veils made from a cloth woven of moonlight. Occasionally, bright sparks danced among the branches, like stars come down from the night sky.

This time, their path had not led them to Emerelle's palace, and they had not crossed the Shalyn Falah, the white bridge. Nuramon had explained to Mandred that, on the last night of the fall, the elves celebrated Silvernight. They gathered in a clearing in the middle of the Old Wood. It was from that clearing that the Alben had abandoned the world. On that one night, Emerelle was able to cast a spell that allowed the elves to hear the voices of their ancestors—the elves who had gone into the moonlight.

The companions had already been riding through the woods for hours, and by Mandred's reckoning, it must have been close to midnight when they heard the first soft strains of music. At first, it was no more than a breath, a barely perceptible change in the sounds of the forest. The *whoo-whoo* of owls and the rustling of mice in the dry leaves faded more and more as the music of a flute sounded in the distance. Mandred thought he saw a goat-legged creature playing a shepherd's pipe among the shadows of the trees and dancing to his own tune.

Then other sounds mixed with the music of the flute, sounds the mortal could not ascribe to any instrument he knew.

The elves seemed restless, almost like the children in the Fjordlands waiting for the sweets they were given during the apple festival.

Between the silhouettes of the trees, Mandred could now see the glow of a red light. A huge lantern—no, it was a tent with a light burning inside. The forest opened up, and Mandred was spellbound by the sight that met his eyes. They had reached an enormous clearing, in the middle of which a large hill sloped up to a pinnacle of rock, like a stone needle jutting from the summit. Seen from below, it looked as high as the moon. Fifty men with outstretched arms would not have been enough to encircle the base. Thousands of lights danced around the rugged stone to the sound of the music.

Surrounding the hill stood dozens of menhirs, like little brothers of the needle of stone. Among the menhirs, all around them, the elves were dancing a high-spirited farandole. The rest of the clearing was a field of tents, lighting the night like giant paper lanterns. There were so many; it was clear that far more had come to the festival than only the elves of Emerelle's court.

The rhythm of the music suddenly changed, and Mandred saw a single figure break from the ranks of the elves' dance. Swathed in glistening light, the figure floated to the tip of the stone needle, and with arms spread wide, it seemed to greet the moon.

As if in answer to the greeting, flowing light spilled from the stone needle, quickly enveloping the entire hill and pouring out over the clearing. It came as far as Mandred and his companions, and the jarl held his breath in apprehension. He had seen a similar light once before, when he had dived into the clear waters of the fjord one summer afternoon. He could clearly remember how he had looked up to the sun from underwater and how the water had altered the sun's rays.

Still, he dared not breathe. A feeling of dizziness overcame him. The light seemed to flow through him and to carry him along with it.

Mandred heard voices.

"No, he seems well enough."

Blinking, Mandred looked around. He was lying in the long grass. "What happened?"

"You fell off your horse," Nuramon replied. "But it doesn't look like you've hurt yourself."

"Where is the light?" Mandred tried to sit up. He was lying beside a red tent. The wonderful light that had come streaming from the rock had disappeared.

Nuramon helped him to his feet.

"You are the first mortal ever to attend the Silvernight," said Ollowain, his voice stern. "I hope you appreciate the privilege."

"Sword master?" Two elves in shimmering armor approached. "The queen wishes to see you, alone."

Farodin and Nuramon looked at one another in surprise.

"Have we fallen from grace?" asked Mandred drily.

"It is not our place to interpret the orders of the queen." Without another word, the elven guards left with Ollowain.

"Has he been invited or taken away?" asked Yilvina in bewilderment.

"Do you think Emerelle knows how late he came to help us in Aniscans?" Mandred asked.

"I believe she wants to hear what he has to say before she talks to us," replied Farodin. This time, the look he shared with Nuramon was one of concern.

The moon was low on the horizon by the time the two guards returned. Mandred and the others had been left with their doubts for more than an hour while the rest of the Albenkin in the camp carried on a merry festival. Now they followed the two soldiers to the queen's saffron-colored tent. *It's bigger than a longhouse*, thought Mandred with envy.

When Mandred tried to follow his companions inside, the guards crossed their spears, preventing him from entering. "Forgive us, mortal," one of the elves said. "Tonight you are not permitted to see the queen. Just being present at this festival is an honor never given to any other human."

Mandred was about to deliver a sharp rebuke when he heard the queen's voice very clearly from inside and saw her shadow cast on the wall of the tent. She seemed much bigger than she had in the Royal Hall, but that must have been a trick of the light. "I am pleased to see you back safe and well," she said.

"My queen, your wish has been fulfilled. Noroelle's son is dead," said Nuramon.

"You know very well what my wish was, and equally well that it has not been fulfilled. Guillaume did not die at your hand, nor at the hand of any of your companions. Do not tell me that my wish has been fulfilled." The queen's voice was as cold as the moonlight. Mandred had never heard her speak like this before. "You cannot begin to appreciate how much you have disappointed me, nor how great is the damage that will grow from your actions. This was never simply about Guillaume having to die. It was also about *how* he died. Do not dare to ask me about Noroelle. Your success might have redeemed Noroelle's guilt, but as things are, nothing has changed."

Mandred could hardly believe what he was hearing. What did Emerelle want? Guillaume was dead, wasn't he? Farodin and Nuramon did not deserve to be treated like this. More than anything at that moment, Mandred wanted to knock the two guards aside so that he could go into the tent and teach their queen a lesson in fairness.

"Majesty," replied Nuramon, and Mandred heard defiance in his voice. "All I regret is that I was not able to prevent Guillaume's death. Noroelle's son was not what you saw him to be. And if he bore any guilt at all, then it was no more than the guilt of being born."

"You saw what his magic was capable of, and you wanted to bring him here. Whatever you say or think, he was the son of a Devanthar. Even in death, he is still the beast's tool. You had an entire night in which to carry out my order unseen. In that night, you changed the destiny of Albenmark. Out there in the Other World, something is happening . . . in the water. I cannot see what it is. The Devanthar . . . it is using the way Noroelle's son died to its own ends. It has not given up on taking its revenge on us. From this moment on, we have to be on our guard. No one shall leave Albenmark. And none shall return. I have appointed Ollowain as my chief gatekeeper, for he has proved himself my most trustworthy warrior. Now you have my permission to leave."

Mandred was perplexed by what he had heard. What was the queen afraid of? No human ruler was as powerful as she was, and yet she was sealing the gates to Albenmark as if her land was some kind of castle waiting to be besieged.

ALAEN AIKHWITAN

At Nuramon's side, Mandred rode into an expanse of woodland. Somewhere in there was the elf's home. Farodin had gone to his family, but he planned to join them that evening to talk over what they might still be able to do now that the queen had stationed guards at every door between the worlds. Nuramon seemed downcast, and Mandred could sympathize. The queen, after all, had destroyed any hope he may have had of ever seeing Noroelle again.

To Mandred, the forest seemed an uncanny place. He could not orient himself in it. The trees confused his senses. The deeper they penetrated into the woods, the harder it became for him to gauge which direction they were riding in. Perhaps it lay in the path that Nuramon had chosen. Mandred watched his companion, and it seemed to him that Nuramon was letting his horse choose which way to go. The horse, for its part, moved through the trees with such familiarity that it barely had to change direction at all. The animal clearly knew how to get to Nuramon's house.

There were no obstacles to overcome, and the path they were following was level. Perhaps that was what was confusing Mandred. From a distance, the woods had looked as if a tree-covered hill rose at its center. If that was true, they should have been on its lower slopes long ago. But all around them, nothing rose any higher than an anthill. His confusion might also have had its roots in the huge variety of life in the undergrowth around him, all the birds, all the wild game that did not shy away from watching them in the distance, as if wanting to witness Nuramon's homecoming.

The farther they pressed into the woods, the bigger and more ancient the trees became. The sheer variety in the elven forest continually surprised Mandred. Oak trees grew side by side with poplar, birch with fir, beech with willow. They all grew in harmony, as if each tree were striving to fit in with those around it. It made him think of Aikhjarto.

"How many of these trees are like old Atta Aikhjarto?" he asked the elves.

Nuramon looked at him as if he'd counted on just about anything except that question.

"Are the trees Albenkin, too?" Mandred added, surprising Nuramon a second time.

"Oh, yes," the elf replied. "The ones with souls are, of course. But there are not many of them left in this forest. The times when the great Alaen Aikhwitan held council are over."

"Alaen Aikhwitan? Is that a brother of Atta Aikhjarto?"

"You could say that. The oaks are the oldest. Some say they were the first Albenkin. You will see Aikhwitan soon." Nuramon smiled, but Mandred could not tell if the smile was mischievous or friendly. He still found it difficult to read emotions on the faces of the elves.

They rode past bigger and bigger trees, and Mandred wondered how big Alaen Aikhwitan might be. How far might its powers reach? "Did all of these trees have souls?"

"Yes. Together they formed a large conclave. But that was a very long time ago. Now the only one left from those days is Alaen Aikhwitan. The other souled trees are much younger."

Mandred looked around reverently. If the trees here had once formed a kind of council, then the forest now was like an empty town hall where the only one left was the mayor. How lonely it must be for Aikhwitan.

The branches of the trees overhead were tightly interwoven, like a fine cloth. Hidden away somewhere beyond the wooden roof was the sun, and only occasionally did a spear of light reach the ground. The trunks were like columns built by giants. The solemn mood of the place seemed to banish Nuramon's gloom. He seemed more at ease here.

They rode around a huge trunk. Mandred turned in the saddle and looked back. It was a fir tree. In his world, not even oaks had trunks like that.

"Something wrong?" asked Nuramon with a smile.

"Pretty big, your . . ." Mandred broke off halfway through his sentence. They had reached the edge of a clearing, in the middle of which stood an enormous oak. It still had leaves, as if this titan knew no other seasons than spring and summer. The oak was so big that its shadow stretched away from them to the edge of the forest on the far side of the clearing.

Mandred's breath caught. The trunk of the oak was like a cliff. It didn't look like a tree; it looked like something that trees would grow on. A wooden stairway wound upward, spiraling around the trunk in broad sweeps. And high up, close to the crown of branches, Mandred could make out a single window. His eyes widened. The window must have been very large, even though it looked tiny next to the trunk. "You don't live up there . . . ?" asked Mandred.

"I do. This is Alaen Aikhwitan, and up there is my house," Nuramon replied casually.

"In this gigantic tree?"

"Yes."

"But you said it has a soul." The idea of living on something that could think seemed strange to Mandred. You would feel like a flea on a dog.

"It is a very hospitable tree, Mandred. My family has lived here for generations."

Nuramon suddenly lowered his eyes. No doubt he was thinking of the stigma that hung over him and his kin. Mandred could not understand that. To be reborn. Humans dreamed of just that, but for Nuramon, it seemed to be some kind of curse. Some among the Albenkin waited millennia for their liberation. *Millennia* . . . an easy word to say, but Mandred realized that he couldn't understand what that must really mean. A life so long was beyond a human's imagination. The elves used the time they had to take whatever they did to the point of perfection. If they were reborn, did they remember their previous life? Mandred thought of the festival two nights earlier. Is that what it looked like when an elf went into the moonlight? It had been beautiful but overwhelming at the same time. Unearthly. What he had seen on that hill was not something human eyes were meant to see.

They dismounted and led the horses toward the oak. With every step, the tree seemed to Mandred to become more menacing. "Which is more powerful, Aikhjarto or Aikhwitan?" he finally asked.

Nuramon shook his head. "You humans. Power matters so much to you. But I guess you want to know where your Aikhjarto fits in the framework of this world. All I can tell you is this. Aikhjarto's power lies in the gate between the worlds, in his wisdom, and in his generosity." He pointed ahead. "The power of Aikhwitan lies in his size, his knowledge, and his hospitality."

Mandred was not satisfied with that answer. These elves were always beating around the bush. Was Nuramon trying to say that it wasn't possible to compare one with the other? Or were they equals? Useless elven claptrap. Why couldn't they give a man a straight answer?

The elf spoke again. "You don't need to worry, Mandred. Look how calmly the leaves are blowing in the wind, see how they reflect the light. Look at the bark. The cracks in his trunk are so wide and deep that when I was a child, I was able to put my hands completely inside them. I found footholds as well, and I climbed from down here all the way up to the house. It may seem threatening to you just because it is so big, but old Aikhwitan has a good soul."

Mandred looked more closely at the tree. He looked at the leaves that Nuramon had spoken of, and the muted light. And it was true: up there, things really did look tranquil.

They reached the base of the stairway, which was made of pale wood, and unsaddled the horses. Mandred wondered where the stables for the horses were. Even the queen had stables inside her palace. Nuramon made no move to take the horses anywhere. He removed their harnesses and laid them with the saddles by the trunk of the oak. "They won't run off," he said. "Let's go up."

Nuramon's horse was loyal to him, but Mandred's mare had certainly not forgiven him for the incivilities of recent months. It would be a real pity to lose her, and he followed the elf only with reluctance.

When they had rounded the massive trunk once, Mandred looked up. They were still a long way from the house. What did Nuramon do if he came home drunk? Sleep among the roots? On the other hand, he had never seen his friend drunk. In contrast to Aigilaos, the elves had no idea how to drink or carouse. Mandred wondered why they bothered celebrating at all.

Mandred rattled the handrail to see how stable it was. Good carpentry. Something solid to hold on to if you had a sore head.

Nuramon strode ahead with a spring in his step. "Come on. You have to see this."

Mandred followed, out of breath. *Stupid to live in a tree like this*, he thought. Sensible people only had to take one step across a threshold to call themselves home. The elves could keep all their climbing around.

Soon, they had climbed high enough to look out over the tops of all the other trees of the forest. Nuramon pointed to a snowy peak on the horizon. "The Iolid Mountains. The children of the Darkalben used to live there."

Mandred didn't like the sound of that name. Darkalben. And their children. Nuramon must be talking about the legendary dark elves. In Mandred's world, terrible stories were told about the dark elves. It was said that they dragged humans into crevices in the rocks to feed on their flesh. They could not be seen at night because their skin was the color of darkness. Mandred wanted nothing to do with creatures like that, and it surprised him that Nuramon could talk about them so easily.

They climbed the rest of the way in silence and stopped at the entrance to the house. From here, they could look out over the land all around and see as far as the queen's palace. The Shalyn Falah and Aikhjarto's gate must lie somewhere beyond the palace. Everything else he could see was unknown territory. No human had ever explored any of the lands that stretched before them, that was certain. Ever since leaving Firnstayn, Mandred had been thinking about what he was supposed to do as a castaway in the elven world. What could he possibly do that the elves couldn't already do far, far better?

He thought of Aigilaos. If only he still lived. Roaming the woods with him, hunting and drinking, telling tall tales of imagined heroics and shocking the fine she-elves at court with crude compliments . . . that would have been the life. Mandred smiled to himself at the thought. He missed the centaur. He would have been a great companion to the manhorse. Mandred was determined to see his blood feud with the Devanthar through to its end. He did not know where to even begin to search, and he also did not know how he was supposed to get out of Albenmark now that Emerelle had stationed guards at all of the gates. But he would find a way. He owed it to Aigilaos . . . and to Freya.

Nuramon pushed open the circular door. It was neither closed nor bolted; the elves clearly had no fear of thieves. The elf hesitated before entering. "The Other World confused my sense of time," he said. "It feels like centuries have passed, not years."

"It isn't the time. It's the fate," replied his companion.

Nuramon started. "What did you say?"

"They're not my words," replied Mandred, abashed. "I once heard them from a priest of Luth. He said, 'Time may seem to be long when the fate takes many turns.'"

"The words of a clever man, and it is a sign of wisdom to remember them."

Mandred was pleased. Finally, a little recognition for something besides brawn and brawling.

"Come in. You are welcome in my house." The elf swept his arm wide in a gesture of hospitality.

Mandred stepped inside, into the heart of the tree.

The first thing he noticed was the special scent of Nuramon's home. It smelled of fresh nuts and leaves. Both the inside walls and the door were made of the same wood as the stairs they had just climbed. The light from the window, dimmed by the foliage overhead, spread evenly; there were shadows in places, but no corners that were completely dark. Mandred saw reddish-brown barinstones set in the walls. They reminded him of the elfhunters' chambers in the queen's castle and of how they had glowed at night. What a treasure a single one of those stones would be in the human world.

A cool breeze swept in from the door, and a few oak leaves were strewn on the floor, but they were not dry or wilted. They were alive, as if they were still part of the tree. Mandred looked around and wondered why, with all the openings in the walls, the place did not feel even draftier.

The furniture inside was somewhat plain, which matched the character of the room. There was nothing excessive inside, and that by itself made the place attractive. Nothing seemed fragile or delicate, but as robust as the oak around them.

A wooden stairway wound up to the floors above, which could not be seen from outside because of the heavy foliage. The floor they were standing on was built in such a way that the trunk of the oak had been partly hollowed out. Mandred wondered why Alaen Aikhwitan had acquiesced to that. What heroic deeds had Nuramon's ancestors done to deserve this honor? The curved ceiling blended into the walls so exquisitely that it was as if Aikhwitan's wood flowed into the paler wood of the walls and floor. "Which tree does this light wood come from?" asked Mandred.

Nuramon set his pack down on a bench. "It is the wood of Ceren."

"Is that a kind of tree?"

"My mother said it was a birch tree. On the night before the elf-hunt, I found out that its name was Ceren. Among the trees, Ceren is legendary."

"Ah. And will Aikhwitan accept me being here? I'm sure no human has ever set foot in your house before."

Nuramon smiled. "You've made it this far. Do you feel at all uncomfortable now?"

Mandred did not. He felt safe. Protected somehow. He looked around again. "And no one else lives here? Your house doesn't look like no one's lived here for thirty years."

Nuramon looked blankly at Mandred. "What do you mean?"

"I see no dust or dirt. Only these leaves on the floor. But they don't look out of place either somehow."

"It is just as I left it."

These elves led a simple life. It was probably the tree itself that kept the place clean, and Nuramon had never even thought about it.

While Nuramon went upstairs with the few items he had, Mandred poked through the adjoining rooms. Although he had never been here before, the house felt familiar. Maybe it was because he knew Nuramon, and his home matched him.

In the center of the tree house was a large room with a long dining table. *What a waste*, Mandred thought. The table was far too large for one person. Then Mandred remembered that Nuramon had spoken of his family. Perhaps, sometime in the past, his entire clan had lived here. A table that big could seat twelve with ease. It had to be dispiriting to live alone in a house like that with his memories. Mandred was well aware that exactly that was the reason he no longer wanted to live in Firnstayn. Being there alone with his memories of Freya . . . it was not for him. As much as he loved Alfadas, he could not be happy in the village again.

Mandred was tired and sat down at a window in a neighboring room, where a heavy cushion offered a wonderful place to rest. From the window, he could see as far as the distant range of mountains. They seemed less threatening now than they had a moment earlier, when Nuramon spoke of the Darkalben and their children. Didn't he say they had once lived over there? And what became of the children of the Darkalben? Mandred thought about that, and as he did, he fell into a peaceful sleep.

He dreamed of a man's voice on the wind, and it whispered to him, "It is time to break my silence. Tell me what happened to you."

Mandred told the voice in his dream about the manboar and his own failure in the ice and snow, about his rescue by Aikhjarto, the elfhunt, his son, and the search for Noroelle's child.

When Mandred finished, he waited for another whisper to come on the wind, but the voice was silent, and the wind died away.

Mandred awoke with a jolt. He sat up and looked outside. It was dark. The wind softly jostled the branches and leaves.

Mandred yawned and stretched. He had the feeling he had only been asleep for a short time, but he must have slept some hours, for it was night. He looked around. The barinstones gave off a warm light. Then he noticed a smell. Meat. He leaped to his feet and went into the room next door, to the dining table. On it lay raw vegetables. Freshly harvested, he could see. Through the open door to the kitchen, he could see Nuramon. He was standing at the stone oven and pushing something into it. Not only did Alaen Aikhwitan tolerate Nuramon living inside him, he allowed him to light a fire. It seemed not to make the slightest difference to the oak.

The elf turned in Mandred's direction and came to join him in the other room. "Finally awake, I see. I did not realize how exhausted you were. I've been out hunting in the forest in the meantime." The elf picked up the vegetables from the table.

Mandred was ashamed of himself. He had lazed around and slept and missed the hunt. "That spot by the window is too cozy. You can't keep your eyes open."

Nuramon laughed. "My mother often sat by that window and talked with Aikhwitan."

The jarl turned and looked uneasily into the other room. It frightened him to think that a spirit had been inside him as he slept. "I felt as if I heard a voice," he said, then told Nuramon about what had happened.

Nuramon dropped the knife he'd been peeling the vegetables with. He looked surprised, but also a little hurt. "I spend my entire life here, and Aikhwitan never says so much as a word to me. But along comes a human, out of the blue, and he's already chatting with him." He shook his head. "Forgive me. Of course he would speak to you. Aikhjarto saved you, after all. He must have sensed that."

Mandred felt queasy. He had not asked for the goodwill of a tree and had not wanted to hurt Nuramon's feelings. Trees. Who would have thought they could be so fickle? In his world, they said nothing. And that was a good thing. He took Nuramon by the arm. "Come on. Maybe he'll speak to you, too."

They went to the window and listened, but there was nothing to be heard in the rustling of the leaves. The whispers did not return, and Mandred was left wondering whether he had really heard the voice or if it had just been a dream.

"I can sense his presence everywhere, but that's all," said Nuramon. The elf was making an effort to play down his disappointment, but he couldn't do it. "Let's finish the food."

Back in the kitchen, Mandred saw the source of the wonderful smell. Several pieces of meat were simmering nicely. He was amazed at how quickly Nuramon had prepared the meat. There were no leftover innards in the kitchen, no blood or skin to be seen. It was impossible for him to guess what kind of animal the meat came from. It was as pale as poultry. The sight of it made Mandred's mouth water. "What is that?" he finally asked Nuramon.

"Gelgerok," answered the elf.

Mandred was curious. During the long search for Noroelle's son, the elves had often talked about gelgeroks and had described them in detail, but Mandred could still not really imagine what such a beast looked like. "Is the carcass somewhere around here? Can I see it?"

"I'm sorry, Mandred. I shot it, and I left the parts I didn't need for Gilomern."

"Gilomern? Who's that?"

"He lives in the forests. He is a hunter, but he's happy to take what others leave behind."

"Is he also an elf?"

"Yes."

"A friend?"

"No. Gilomern doesn't care much for friendship. But it is common practice for us to leave him his share. No doubt he has already fetched the gelgerok. Don't worry. Sooner or later, you'll see one of them."

Nuramon set about slicing the vegetables. "Mandred, would you take care of the gravy for the meat? I've cut the herbs, and spices are there. It's best to pour off the meat juices from the pan and then mix everything how you like it."

The trust the elf had in him. Here he was, Mandred Torgridson, the jarl of Firnstayn, conqueror of the manboar, and he was being asked to cook. If the people of the Fjordlands knew that, they wouldn't be telling stories about Mandred the jarl, they'd be warbling a drinking song about Mandred the cook. What was it Nuramon had said so many times during the search for Guillaume? "You'll make a human of me yet." If Mandred wasn't careful, Nuramon and Farodin would make an elf out of him, and he'd end up actually enjoying cooking.

Tentatively, he set about the task Nuramon had given him, and in no time, he was surprised at how good the gravy tasted. As he made it, he watched to make sure the meat didn't burn and even took the bread out of the oven. When Nuramon tried the gravy and pronounced it delicious, Mandred could not hide his pride. Of course it was delicious.

While he and Nuramon were setting out the food on the table, Farodin arrived. He was carrying baggage and laid it on one of the many empty chairs. "Looks like I arrived just in time." He seemed to have come in a good mood and with a big appetite.

"Finally, something decent to eat again," said Mandred. What they had set out here was nothing like the small portions the elves in the palace had meted out to him. Nuramon had come up with vegetables and meat in abundance, and Mandred could hardly wait to sit and eat.

As they ate, Mandred kept one eye on Farodin. What would the elf say about his gravy? So far, they had not mentioned it, but he would change that. Mandred turned to Nuramon. "This meat's excellent, really. Even the vegetables taste amazing." He looked at Farodin. "Am I right?"

Farodin nodded politely and said to Nuramon, "Noroelle always spoke highly of your talents as a cook. And I learned to appreciate them, too, on our travels. This is superb. The gravy especially."

Mandred exchanged a wink with Nuramon, then he leaned back and asked, "Can you keep a secret?"

"Naturally," answered Farodin, pushing a small chunk of meat into his mouth.

"I made the gravy," Mandred said with relish.

Farodin hesitated, then went on chewing slowly. When he had swallowed, he smiled conspiratorially. "You're pulling my leg."

"Not for a moment," said Nuramon.

"Well then, Mandred. My compliments to you," said Farodin, and there was genuine appreciation in his voice.

Mandred was proud. If you could surprise an elf, you could find out what they truly thought. "But you have to promise me never to tell a soul that Mandred Torgridson stood before a stove," the jarl said.

"I'll promise you that if you promise me you'll never mention to anyone that I couldn't tell the difference between a human's cooking and an elf's," Farodin replied.

It was a fair trade. Mandred could live with it.

Soon, they had finished their meal, and Mandred saw it as an honor that they had left most of the meat to him. That was hospitality.

They went into a large adjoining room with a floor made of small stone slabs. In the center of the room, a mosaic of gemstones had been fashioned. It showed an elf defending himself from a troll. This seemed to be where Nuramon's family once held councils of war.

Farodin positioned himself beside the broad window that offered the sweeping outlook over the land. Far in the distance, the lights of Emerelle's palace glittered. Mandred stood at the mosaic while Nuramon leaned against the wall close by the door and stared at it. Restlessness had taken hold of Mandred. If it had been up to him, he would already be on his way.

The cheerful mood during their meal was gone. Farodin turned his back to them. One didn't have to be a priest of Luth to know what was on the elves' minds. Although no longer allowed to leave Albenmark, they still desperately sought some means to rescue the woman they loved. Their long silence only underscored how hard all of this was for them.

Nuramon looked at Mandred. "I've been wanting to ask you something for days, Mandred. Please excuse me for being so direct. But why didn't you stay back there in Firnstayn?"

"Because it is my son's place now," he replied without hesitating. "Sometimes fathers have to leave their sons their inheritance early. If I had not been trapped in the ice cave, I would be an old man now. My time in Firnstayn has passed. It was a question of fairness, and it was right for me to leave, to give Alfadas the chance to become jarl if he can prove himself in the eyes of the people."

"You're a fighter, Mandred. Is it enough for you to be the father of a jarl? Is that all you still want to achieve?" Nuramon asked.

Mandred looked at the elf in surprise. Was Nuramon trying to insult him? Of course that was not enough. "I'm going to hunt down the manboar—I mean, the Devanthar. It robbed me of the life I was supposed to live, and I'll kill it for that. Because of what it did, I lost my wife . . ." He bit his lip as his emotions threatened to overwhelm him. "And I would like to help the two of you. Nothing and nobody can give me Freya again. But you . . . you can still get your beloved back."

"Such confidence from the mouth of a human," said Farodin cynically. "The queen has guards at every crossing. Even you can't get back to your own world." The elf did not turn to face them as he spoke.

"Farodin's right," said Nuramon. "The queen may keep the gates closed for hundreds of years. It is possible that you will never see your homeland again."

"I've said my good-byes to my homeland. Don't give yourselves a headache for my sake. Think about how we can rescue Noroelle."

Nuramon lowered his eyes. "At least we know we can expect no help from the queen. She will never change her mind."

"What exactly did the queen do with Noroelle?" Mandred asked. "I've never really understood what happened to her. Explain it to me. Then I might be of more use to you."

Farodin snorted contemptuously.

Nuramon, though, was still friendly. "The queen took her to the Other World and, from there, exiled her to the Shattered World."

"And what is this Shattered World?" Mandred had heard the elves talk about that place often enough in the years they had spent searching for Guillaume, but he had never managed to get a clear picture of what it was. "How can a world break? I mean . . . a world is not a clay pot."

"The Shattered World is an ancient battlefield," said Farodin. "It is the place where the Alben fought the Devanthar and destroyed them. In the course of the war, the world was torn apart. There are only a few gates that lead there, from here or from the human world. It lies between our world and yours. Think of it as a few islands adrift in an ocean of nothing. It is of no consequence anymore, so we call your world the Other World as if the Shattered World no longer existed at all. The path to Noroelle leads us first to your world, Mandred. When we get there, we have to search for the gate to that island in the middle of nothing where Noroelle is a prisoner. Once we've found the gate, we will have to break through the queen's magic. And I'm afraid that, against the queen's will, we will never be able to free Noroelle from her captivity. It is hopeless."

Nuramon took several steps in Farodin's direction. His companion's words seemed to anger him. "Nothing is hopeless. Just because we don't see a way does not mean there isn't one. The question is how far we'll go to reach our goal."

Farodin turned around and looked at Nuramon. His expression was icy. "You know how far I would go."

"Would you still do it if it meant never being able to return to your family because you had brought eternal disgrace onto yourself? Or if it meant being exiled if the queen ever saw you again? Or if Noroelle herself would turn from you because of the things you'd done? Would you accept all that to save her?"

An oddly cryptic smile flashed over Farodin's face, although Mandred had found no humor in Nuramon's words. "Without a moment's hesitation."

"Then we speak no more about the queen's proscriptions, but about what we have to do."

"I will go with you, wherever the road may lead," said Mandred. "I have a debt to repay. At least one." If he had never come to the elven world, then Noroelle would still be with Farodin and Nuramon today. The manboar had used him as bait to lure the elfhunt to the human world. He had never understood why that mattered to the Devanthar. Did it simply want to kill a few elves and show Emerelle that a Devanthar had survived the war with the Alben? Or did it have some deeper plan? And why had it sired Guillaume? Unlike Emerelle, Mandred could not see what danger might still arise from the dead demon child. It made no difference what the final goal of the Devanthar might be. One thing was certain: it was Mandred who had given the fiend a way into the world of the elves, and he had to do his part to make up for the damage done. But his other debt weighed far more heavily on him. With his promise to Emerelle, he had killed Freya. And this promise, too, only came about because of the manboar. His wife had cursed him rightly.

"Whatever path you tread, Mandred Torgridson will tread it at your side."

"But how are we supposed to get to the Other World?" asked Farodin.

The jarl balled his fists. To him, it was obvious who they had to fight first. "If you're ready to defy your queen, then we should go out and fight for a way to the Other World."

Farodin dismissed the suggestion with an elegant gesture. "No, Mandred. If the queen has something guarded, then it is secure. The gates are not open to us."

"If the door's closed, then we bash our heads through the wall."

Farodin grinned. "With these walls, not even *your* skull would make a dent, mortal."

"Wait." Nuramon's eyes lit up. "*Through* the wall. A good thought. A brilliant thought . . . through the wall with our heads."

Mandred had no idea what had gotten the elf so excited. Farodin was actually right. These gates were not gates as a human would understand them. And there were no walls either.

Nuramon laughed. "We're blind. We need a human to open our eyes to our own world."

"What are you talking about?" asked Farodin.

"It's obvious. We will take the same path to the Other World that Noroelle took. We'll ignore the guarded gates and create our own."

"Nuramon, you're overestimating your abilities," snapped Farodin. "That is the most foolish thing I've ever heard you say, by far. We don't possess Noroelle's skill with magic."

But there Mandred thought differently. "Nuramon is a great magician," he protested vehemently. "You of all elves should know that. You were no more than a piece of raw meat in the ice cave . . . and Nuramon saved you from certain death. If that wasn't the power of sorcery, then I don't know what you call magic at all."

"Just because a horse wears horseshoes, it's a far cry from being a blacksmith."

"What do horses have to do with this?" Mandred shouted.

"Let me explain it so a human can understand . . . Alfadas is an outstanding fighter, no question. Ollowain turned him into a master of the sword. But how good is he with an axe, Mandred?"

The jarl understood. "Mediocre at best," he said through gritted teeth.

"And the same is true of Nuramon. I am deeply in his debt for healing me, not only in the ice cave but also when we escaped from Aniscans. I don't want to call his skills into question in any way, but opening a gate is simply a different thing. Penetrating the border between two worlds . . . you are talking about potent magic."

"I watched while Nuramon fought for you at the border between life and death, and he brought you back to life. Show me a boundary more insurmountable than that."

The elves looked at each other in surprise. It was clear that they had never looked at it from that vantage point.

Nuramon seemed slightly embarrassed. Finally, he broke the silence. "What did your parents tell you about the Albenpaths when you were a child?" he asked Farodin.

The elf hesitated before answering. "They told me that they run through our world and connect it with other worlds."

"Like the Albenstars," Mandred said, surprising the elves once again.

"How do you know that?" asked Farodin.

"Vanna told me about them when we were on our way to the Cave of Luth," Mandred replied. "I've never forgotten it. But what's so special about the paths?"

"It is said that the Alben traveled along these paths," said Farodin. "At the gates that we also call major Albenstars, seven such paths intersect."

"And now think about what Mandred said in his brilliant simplicity," said Nuramon.

Mandred wasn't sure whether to take the elf's words as praise or insult.

Farodin looked at him. "If the major Albenstars are the doors, then what are the walls? That is the question."

Mandred didn't know where the elves were going with this. He had the feeling that Farodin expected an answer from him. Nuramon, too, was looking at him. "The Albenpaths that lead to the gates?"

"Not exactly," said Farodin.

Nuramon gave him the answer. "The minor Albenstars. The ones that do not produce a stable gate. It is possible to use magic to open a gate at such a star and cross over to the Other World."

Farodin seemed troubled. "You asked me what my parents told me about the Albenpaths. Let me tell you what they also told me about the Albenstars. They said that anyone attempting a passage by force or by ignorance could end up a victim of time and space and be lost forever. Noroelle is a great sorceress. She knew what she was doing. Compared with her, we are children. You may be an extraordinary healer, but that kind of magic is as foreign to you as it is to me."

"So you want to give up?" said Nuramon.

"No. I couldn't do that. This search is my life, more than you suspect." Farodin took out a small silver bottle and a cloth. He spread the cloth on the table, then carefully opened the bottle and emptied the contents onto the cloth. "You can see here how great our chances are."

A tiny mound of sand lay on the silken cloth.

"That isn't . . . ," Nuramon began, then stopped.

Farodin nodded. "After we found out Noroelle's fate, I crept secretly into the queen's dressing chamber and found there three grains of sand. It is said that if all the grains of sand are recovered, then the spell of the hourglass can be broken. As we were searching for Guillaume, I was able to find another fifty-three."

"That's why you went off alone so often," said Nuramon accusingly.

"Yes. All told, I now have fifty-six grains. There are probably no more in Albenmark. The rest are certainly in the Other World. They were carried away in all directions by the wind. I think it was part of the spell that the grains of sand were strewn as far and wide as possible."

Mandred could hardly believe what he was hearing. He had been collecting grains of sand? How could fifty-six grains of sand help them? Just collecting grains of sand at all, it was insane. How could he even tell the difference between those few grains and ordinary bits of grit?

Nuramon gazed at the tiny pile on the cloth. "A small hope indeed. But perhaps there are other ways."

"This is the only one I see."

"Then let's start with it," said Mandred.

Both the elves agreed.

The problem of the closed gates remained. Farodin thought there had to be a safer route than attempting to bypass the gates and risking the passage through one of the minor Albenstars with their limited skills.

Nuramon, however, insisted that they could do it. "We don't have to try to cross where two Albenpaths meet. That would be foolishness, of course. But shouldn't it be possible where three or four paths meet?"

"But where do we learn how—" Farodin broke off, startled.

Nuramon peered around the room as if he had caught sight of someone.

Mandred, though, could see no one. He looked around warily. What had shocked the elves like that? As if he had spoken aloud, a low voice answered in Fjordlandish. "Hear me."

Whoever was speaking was there in the room with them. That much was certain, even though Mandred could not see the speaker. "Listen to what the old oak knows," the voice continued. A gentle breeze swept across the room.

Farodin immediately threw himself across the table in alarm and covered the grains of sand with the silken cloth.

"Alaen Aikhwitan," Nuramon called.

Mandred recalled his dream from hours earlier.

"Yes, that is me." The tree no longer whispered, but spoke in a deep male voice, deeper than any human voice. "You are Nuramon. I've known your soul for quite some time. And you, Mandred . . . you carry my brother's mark. Of you, Farodin, I have only heard. You would be surprised what the trees say about you."

Mandred was silent and apprehensive. The voice of the oak filled him entirely. Farodin did not dare to say anything, although perhaps for another reason. Only Nuramon was able to break the spell of the voice. "Are you revealing yourself to us to help us? Will you teach us the magic we need?"

Alaen Aikhwitan rumbled as if he were about to chastise Nuramon. "Albenkin have sought me and my counsel for a very long time. And I will guide you, too. But teach you I will not. You, Nuramon . . . you I have already taught all I can, through your mother. And I owe nothing to you, Mandred, or Farodin." The voice grew softer again. "What you are seeking can only be taught by one tree. Go. Go where the elven sorceress was trained. Go. You will be taught there, too. Don't linger! Go . . ." The voice faded and disappeared.

"The faun oak!" cried Nuramon.

AT THE
FAUN OAK

It had started to snow by the time they rode past the lake where they had sat with Noroelle so many times. Farodin pulled his cloak closer around his shoulders, but there were no clothes that could warm the chill in his heart. He had no great hope of ever attaining the power he would need to open a gate to the Other World. Maybe Mandred was right. Maybe they should risk attacking the elves who guarded one of the gates and force their way back into the human world.

In the distance, beyond the forest, rose Emerelle's palace. Did she know that they were here? It was said that she knew everything that happened in Albenmark. But wasn't it possible that she had spread that rumor herself? She certainly had not known about the Devanthar entering their world. Or had she? Had she let it happen to deflect some other—far worse—fate for her people? Farodin sighed deeply. His breath formed a white cloud in front of his mouth. Not even a trace of a breeze ruffled the wide meadow. The snow was falling more heavily now, and the palace blurred in the distance.

Who knew what Emerelle was thinking? Farodin had murdered in her name. He could not say how often, but not for a moment had he doubted that whatever he did for her he did to prevent something worse from happening to his people. Had he made a mistake, thinking like that? The queen suffered from the curse of being able to foretell the future, but what lay ahead could change, and certainty was never possible.

Only once had Emerelle talked about this with him. She had compared the future to a tree. It started with the trunk, she said, which then divided into two and sprouted branches, which went on dividing. Afterward, Farodin had gone into the garden and sat down beneath a tree. He tried, from below, to follow the path of a single branch with all of its offshoots. It was impossible. One would have to cut the tree down to be able to say anything accurate about it. That's what it was like with the future.

"Shitty weather," grumbled Mandred, riding beside him. "Humans say it's always spring in your world. Some spring this is."

"That is what happens when know-it-alls talk about places they've never been," Nuramon joked. He tugged on Felbion's reins and pointed some distance ahead. "There she is."

Gloomy and bare of leaves, a massive tree loomed before them. It was not as big as Alaen Aikhwitan, but still huge. The riders dismounted and covered the last stretch on foot.

Farodin could clearly see a large split in the oak's trunk. The bark had peeled back, and the wood beneath was rotten. Around the base of the tree lay dry branches, the faun oak's sacrifice to the storms of autumn. The oak looked decrepit, almost as if she were dying.

Farodin was horrified. Never before had he seen a living tree rot in Albenmark. It just didn't happen.

Nuramon, too, seemed disturbed at the sight.

They stood uncertainly before the mighty trunk and looked up to the crown above. There was no voice to be heard. Farodin observed his companions from the corner of his eye but saw no sign that the faun oak might be speaking to one of them.

"My feet are nearly frozen off." Again, it was Mandred who broke the silence.

"We're supposed to talk to her," said Nuramon hesitantly. "But how?"

"Alaen Aikhwitan spoke to you for the first time—what—the day before yesterday, right?" Mandred said and stamped his feet, trying to kick out the cold.

"Yes," said Nuramon. "What about it?"

"You lived in your oak tree for many years. I'm just thinking we might have to wait here a very long time before the faun oak speaks to us. Do you think we could light a fire while we wait?"

"Fire?" The voice rang out inside Farodin so suddenly that he stepped back in surprise. "It would take a human to introduce himself to a tree by lighting a fire beside it."

"I have to apologize for our friend," Nuramon said quickly. "He can be a little impulsive."

"Do not let him light a fire. I can still feel him thinking about it. And he wanted to take my dead branches for it. Doesn't he have any manners at all?" The tree spoke in a shrill woman's voice.

Mandred moved off a short distance. He said nothing, but wrapped his arms around his chest as if to show that he was still freezing.

Farodin began to doubt if bringing the human along had been a good idea.

"We are here because of Noroelle," Nuramon said softly.

"Noroelle." The faun oak's voice softened until it sounded almost wistful. "Ah, Noroelle . . . she would never even have considered lighting a fire here. It seems long ago that I last saw her."

"We want to find her."

"A good idea," the oak agreed. It sounded sleepy, and its branches creaked a little.

"We need your help to do that," said Farodin, joining the conversation.

"How am I supposed to do that?" The voice of the tree sounded thin and drawn now. "It's not like I can leave here and join you on . . ."

"Your oak is falling asleep," Mandred scoffed. "If I hadn't mentioned fire, it would never have woken up."

"Fire?" The old tree sighed. "Get this insolent human away from me, or I'll have him sprout roots where he stands. Let him find out for himself what trees have against fire."

Mandred didn't need a second warning. He retreated to where the horses were standing.

"Now he's thinking about an axe," grumbled the tree. "I really ought to . . ."

"Spare him," said Farodin. "Even if he doesn't know how to behave, he would give his life to rescue Noroelle."

"I know . . ." Again, the voice sounded thin. "I sense that Atta Aikhjarto holds him in high regard. Atta Aikhjarto never makes mistakes . . . I think . . ."

"Please don't fall asleep," said Farodin. "You are our only hope."

"Children, it is winter. My juices aren't flowing anymore. It is time to rest. Come back in spring. Elves have time . . . like trees . . ."

"Faun oak?" asked Nuramon. "Can you teach us one of the spells you taught Noroelle? Teach us how to open a gate at one of the minor Albenstars."

He received no answer.

"It's asleep," said Farodin in resignation. "I'm afraid we will have to wait until spring. If it will help us at all . . ."

They stood there awhile longer, but the oak did not respond to any of their questions. Finally, they returned to the horses. Farodin was about to mount up when he caught a fleeting movement in the undergrowth behind the oak. The elf pulled himself into the saddle. "Don't let anything on," he said quietly. "Someone's been eavesdropping."

"One of the queen's spies?" asked Nuramon.

"I don't know. I'll ride into the woods and drive out whoever it is."

"What if he's on our side?"

"Then why hide?" asked Mandred.

"My sentiment exactly." Farodin jerked the reins around and dashed toward the bushes, leaning low over the mane of his horse. Without hesitation, Mandred followed.

Before they could even reach the edge of the woods, a goat-footed figure stepped out. It raised its hands as if to show it was unarmed.

"Ejedin?" Farodin recognized the queen's stable hand.

"What are you doing here?" Mandred growled. He was having trouble controlling his mare and finally gave her a thump on the head.

"What am I doing here?" White teeth flashed in the faun's black thicket of a beard. "My great-grandfather planted an acorn here, an acorn that he brought with him from his home in Dailos. Ever since then, the fauns and sileni that serve at court have tended the faun oak. She passes on messages for us to our far homeland and has been of great service to us in other ways. So the question is not of what I am doing here, but rather of what *you* are doing here."

"Don't get fresh, you little—" hissed Mandred.

"Or what, Mister Master Horseman? You'll whack me like your horse?" He raised his fists. "Come down here and show me what you've got."

Mandred was already climbing out of his saddle when Farodin steered his stallion between them and held Mandred back.

"You think the queen will reward you handsomely?" the elf asked casually.

The faun licked his long tongue over his lips. "I don't think there's anything I can tell her that she doesn't know already. But maybe *we* can do a little business?"

Farodin eyed Ejedin suspiciously. The fauns had a reputation for being devious but were also famous for the relationship they nurtured with the souled trees. "What kind of business are we talking about?" Farodin asked.

Nuramon had joined them in the meantime and listened in silence.

"I think I might be able to get the faun oak to talk to you for maybe an hour or two each day," said the faun.

"And what's your price?"

"Bring Noroelle back."

Farodin could not believe what he'd heard. This had to be some faunish trickery. "Why should you even care about that, Ejedin? And don't try to tell me our unhappy story has touched your delicate heart."

The stable hand broke out in a ringing laugh. "Do I look like one of those soppy riverbank sprites? This is about the faun oak. Since Noroelle left, it's been in a terrible state, sleeping through spring and even summer." He pointed to the deep gash in the trunk. "Look how sick she is. Borers got in and nested under her bark early last year."

"How can that be?" Nuramon asked. "Borers only feed on dead wood."

"And on trees that have given up on life," replied the faun.

"Maybe I can strengthen the decaying wood again," said Nuramon cautiously. "I've never tried to heal a tree, but perhaps it is possible."

"Don't get my hopes up," the faun replied harshly. "Come tomorrow at the same time, and I'll wake the oak for you. And don't bring that human again. He upsets her, and that doesn't do her any good at all."

THE FIRST LESSON

Nuramon removed his hands from the faun oak's wound. He hadn't been able to do much. The wood beneath the bark was certainly a little stronger, but the oak's true suffering lay in her sadness at the loss of Noroelle. Nuramon got the impression that his beloved had been like a daughter to the oak.

The faun leaned close to the tree and placed one cheek against the bark. "Hear me, faun oak," he whispered, but what he said after that was too quiet for Nuramon to catch. Moments later, Ejedin moved back from the tree and stood behind Nuramon and Farodin, watching.

"Did she hear you?" asked Farodin.

But Ejedin said nothing. He only stood and stared at the oak. He nodded, and it was clear that the faun oak was speaking to him. After some time, he said, "She is ready to hear what you have to say."

Nuramon exchanged a look with Farodin, who silently prompted him to speak. He said, "Hear me, faun oak."

The tree said nothing.

"We beg you. Teach us. Do not wait until spring. Every day is vital. And though your lessons might take many months, it may matter in the end that we start now."

"Those are fine words," the oak replied. Her voice spoke directly to Nuramon's spirit. "Are you a sage, to say such a thing?"

"Far from it," Nuramon answered. "It was Alaen Aikhwitan who told us to come to you. And he said we should not tarry, as if it is a matter of urgency."

"Alaen Aikhwitan's counsel mattered long before my time. I felt his presence through your hands, Nuramon . . . When you were here yesterday, I was sleepy. It was a bad time. Now Ejedin and your healing hands have woken me, but I cannot say when I will tire again. So hear what I can do for you," the voice of the oak said, gaining strength. "I can teach you the magic that will allow you to use the paths the way the Alben once did. In you, Nuramon, I see the student of Alaen Aikhwitan and the favorite of Ceren. My magic will not seem strange to you. But you, Farodin, must put down new roots and grow beyond what you now are, for your magic does not come from any tree. You must want to be more than you once were, and more than you are now. Something unfamiliar is required of each of us. We must sow our seeds in frozen ground to be able to harvest in spring."

"Are we able to learn what you want to teach us by spring?" asked Farodin doubtfully.

The faun oak was silent for some time before answering. "What you have not learned by then will never be of any use to you. Pay attention and keep a clear head."

The faun stepped forward. "Will you drive out the borers?"

"They are warm in me. They are resting and suspect nothing. To send them out in this cold would be cruel. I will decide about them in spring."

Nuramon knew what the tree meant. The oak would decide in spring if Farodin's and his own skills were sufficient to save Noroelle—and therefore to save the oak herself.

"Well, my two elven apprentices. I see that you have many questions. What I will now tell you I once told Noroelle." The oak took her time before speaking again. It seemed almost as if she were trying to put Nuramon's and Farodin's patience to the test. "We know of five worlds. Their roots are what we call Albenpaths. They pass through each of the worlds and connect them to each other. The power that flows in them is what makes sorcery and the natural magic of our realms possible." The oak was speaking faster now, and her voice sounded like the voice of a young woman fresh from resting. "The Alben, a long time ago, traveled along these paths from one place to another and from one world to another. The Albenstars are junctions where the paths cross, join, and separate again. The magic is most powerful in these places. The more paths, the more powerful the magic." The oak then added, "I once told this to Noroelle."

Nuramon stared at the trunk of the faun oak. He imagined his beloved as a young elf, sitting by the trunk in springtime and listening to those words, words that took many things only known from old stories and turned them into certainties.

The faun oak started to speak again. "I can teach you the magic you need to open a gate to the Other World, but listen well. The magic does more than create a way from one world to another. If you go searching for Noroelle in the Other World, then remember well the paths and stars you follow. Maybe one day, you will be able to travel the paths between the Albenstars of one world, as the Alben did. I will explain to you the dangers and give you a feeling for the magic. You will never master it as completely as Noroelle did. She is so powerful that she does not have to step through a gate. She can simply stand and watch the world change around her. That way is not open to you. You will be able to open a small gate, and you will be able to close it again, but beware sealed gates and magical barriers. If you force your way through one like that, you may become a victim of time. If you pass through minor Albenstars or fail miserably with the spell, you will only be a victim of space. Are you ready to follow Noroelle's trail and walk the paths of the Alben to find her again?"

Nuramon did not have to think long, though it was Farodin who answered first. "We are."

"Teach us. In Noroelle's name," said Nuramon.

The faun oak laughed, and it sounded almost like the bright laughter of the riverbank sprites. "Then be my students."

So this was the start of their search for Noroelle. Nuramon hoped only that the queen would not grow suspicious. They would visit the faun oak often between then and springtime, and Emerelle could see what was happening in her realm. But was it really any surprise that they should go to the faun oak, as mournful for Noroelle as the tree was? However much Nuramon wanted the teachings of the oak, he feared the gaze of the queen just as much. And the oak was right: they were on the trail of Noroelle.

In spring, they would find out how far down it they had gone.

OAK DRAM

Spring had settled over the land, and the faun oak was dressed in fresh, crisp green. "I have taught you everything you are able to learn from me," said the oak, its words settling in Farodin's thoughts. Despite all the hours of practice, he had never gotten used to the feeling of something alien inside him.

The significance of the oak's words was not lost on him. As much as he had perfected his seeking spell over the centuries, his achievements in other kinds of magic were meager. It was true that he had learned how to open a gate at an Albenstar and also how to move along the hidden paths, but Nuramon far outstripped him in skill.

Now the time had come to depart. Nuramon and Ejedin stood at his side; the faun had accompanied them to the oak whenever he could.

"Be careful, and remember what I have told you," warned the tree. "Never open a gate needlessly, and break through sealed gates and barriers only when you are certain that something lies beyond. If you make an error with the magic, you will be thrown out of the fabric of time the moment you step through a gate. The fewer the paths that connect at a star, the more difficult it is to cast the spell. And where the mortal is concerned, consider well whether you want to expose him to the danger. Not even I can say how the magic of the Albenstars will affect him. For you, this is about Noroelle, but is he really prepared to take the same risk? Sometimes, it is better to leave a friend behind for his own well-being."

"Anything but that," groaned Ejedin. "If he spends another day at court, I'm going back to Dailos."

"What's he done?" asked Farodin in surprise. Mandred had stayed away through the winter because the faun oak could not tolerate his presence. The jarl had traveled around Albenmark a lot in that time, and neither Farodin nor Nuramon had found much time to look after him.

"Why don't you ask what he hasn't done? Since he got to know the two centaurs, he's been driving me crazy. Just the day before yesterday, his friends came into the stables in the middle of the night, blind drunk, and tried to do unspeakable things with the mares. And Mandred just stood there and egged them on."

The two elves looked at each other with concern. "What happened next?"

"A huge brawl with the palace guard. Mandred spent a night in the dungeons, and the two centaurs were banned from the heartland. And yesterday, I had to stand there and watch him harness his mare to a wagon loaded with amphorae of Alvemerian wine. A mare from the queen's stables is no draft horse. Can you imagine that?"

"Do you know where he was heading?"

"I think he wanted to get out of the heartland," said the faun and sniffed contemptuously. "He'll be back when the wine runs out."

The faun oak spoke again. "The humans are a peculiar race. But back to the two of you—before you go, I would like to see the stones that Noroelle left for you. I have sensed their presence since the day I took you as my students."

Farodin plucked the emerald from the leather purse tied to his belt. He saw Nuramon take a chain from around his neck; an almandine pendant hung from it. They held the stones out toward the tree.

"Guard these treasures well. They may be of use to you in the future. I can't teach you what might help you to unravel their magic, but remember that the power of Noroelle dwells in them. That power might serve you well one day . . . now go, my pupils. Spring is here, and I want to make my decision. The borers must leave my bark. This very night, when the fauns and sileni dance around me and perhaps even the riverbank sprites are singing, I will send them away. But the two of you should not seek my guidance any longer." And with those words, the faun oak wrapped itself in silence.

Farodin and Nuramon said good-bye to Ejedin and set off to find Mandred. From what Ejedin had told them, they had some idea of where he would be.

They crossed the Shalyn Falah, and by early evening, they had reached the stone circle not far from where Atta Aikhjarto stood. They had already seen the wagon from some distance away and found Mandred's mare grazing contentedly close to the destroyed watchtower.

A group of young soldiers was also camped there, and Nuramon and Farodin observed them carefully.

They dismounted and walked in the direction of Atta Aikhjarto. A smell of wine and damp clay hung over the meadow. Farodin continually looked back. He imagined he could feel the eyes of the soldiers on them.

"Do you see that?" asked Nuramon. The roots of the oak coiled through the grass like snakes of wood. A dark-red puddle had formed in a hollow in the clay soil.

Farodin kneeled, dipped a finger in the liquid, and sniffed at it. "Wine. The tree would have to be completely drunk to do something like that."

A broad grin spread across Nuramon's face. "Only a human could think of watering a tree with wine. I wonder what Atta Aikhjarto has to say about it?"

Farodin did not expect to hear a word from the mighty souled oak. The only noise disturbing the peaceful spring evening was a ragged snoring. After all these years with the mortal at their side, it was a sound Farodin knew only too well.

The elves picked their way among the shards of amphora and puddles of wine covering the slippery earth. The branches of the oak were hanging unusually low and formed an arbor around the trunk. Farodin went to push the branches aside but stopped halfway through the gesture. The veins on the delicate pale-green leaves stood out darkly.

Nuramon, who had noticed Farodin's surprise, pulled one of the branches close and held a leaf against the light of the setting sun. "The wine looks as if it's gone all the way to the leaves."

Had Mandred finally achieved his goal? Many times he had spoken of wanting to drink with Atta Aikhjarto to properly commemorate how the old oak had saved his life. Was it possible to get an oak tree drunk? Farodin looked up at the leaves in despair.

"Do you feel that?" Nuramon looked around in astonishment.

Farodin heard a whispering in the leaves as if a light breeze were blowing. But nothing else.

"The tree. Atta Aikhjarto is singing. I feel it inside me." Nuramon stood where he was and lifted one hand to his heart. "It is . . . extraordinary! I've never heard anything like it."

Farodin pushed the branches aside. He could hear nothing of the sort. The only sound in his ears was Mandred, snoring. The human was lying with his back propped against the trunk. His beard was soiled with vomit. Around him lay even more clay shards. It seemed he'd smashed every amphora after he'd emptied them. Wanton destruction.

Nuramon kneeled beside Mandred and shook him gently by the shoulder. Their companion gurgled in his sleep, babbled something unintelligible, but did not wake up.

"Maybe it's better if we leave him behind," said Farodin. "For him and for us."

"You're not serious," replied Nuramon sharply. "Are you blind? He is doing these things out of desperation. He doesn't know how to cope in this world. We *have* to take him with us. Albenmark is no place for him."

"Yeeerrrss, I'm coming . . . ," Mandred slurred. The human stirred and tried to sit upright but immediately collapsed again. "I'm coming." He belched. "Bring me a horse."

"All of you are coming." It was a woman's voice. The branches parted, and a female warrior in a long mail tunic stepped into the arbor. She had two short swords buckled at her hips. Yilvina.

"Don't try to flee," the young elf said firmly, and her right hand moved to the grip of one of her swords. "You're surrounded. I command the guard at this gate. I have been ordered to escort you to the queen. She is hunting in the Old Wood and wishes you to accompany her."

Farodin tensed. "And you would draw your sword against us, with whom you rode for three years?"

Yilvina returned his gaze steadily. "Don't make me. The queen's command is clear. And I was warned that you would attempt to escape through the gate."

Farodin reached for his sword belt. "So I am supposed to lay down my sword."

"No, you mule. I'm not here to drag you off to the dungeon. I'm here to escort you to the queen. Do you think I'm enjoying this?"

Nuramon laid a hand gently on Farodin's arm. "Enough. We'll comply."

THE ALBENSTAR

The water sprayed high, raining over their heads as they dashed at full gallop through the stream. Felbion charged up the embankment on the other side. Nuramon ducked under a low branch and turned to look back. Mandred had to do all he could just to stay in the saddle. The human was clinging to his mare's mane and looked unnaturally pale. His riding technique had certainly improved in the years they had ridden in search of Guillaume, but he was no match at all for his elven friends.

Nuramon slowed his steed to a leisurely trot. Yilvina had kept up with him effortlessly. She laid her hunting spear across the saddle in front of her. Farodin rode close behind her and nodded to Nuramon. The moment had come. For five days, they had ridden with the queen's hunting party, and they had been watched without respite the whole time. Some hours earlier, they had flushed out a large stag and pursued it wildly through the dense forest, leaving the rest of the hunters behind. The others were after more noble game; early that morning, the centaur Phillimachos, the queen's tracker, had seen the tracks of a large gelgerok. Only a few of the riders had gone after the stag, and as it became more and more difficult to follow their quarry through the heavy undergrowth, those who had ridden with Nuramon, Farodin, and the human had been left behind. All except Yilvina, who made no effort to conceal the fact that she was there to guard them. How were they supposed to shake her off? They would have been far more likely to lose Mandred if they tried to leave Yilvina behind on another wild ride.

They reached a clearing where blackberry bushes and birch saplings grew. On the north side rose a moss-covered cliff with a spring at its foot. The stag was nowhere to be seen.

Yilvina looked defiantly at Nuramon. "A good spot to rest, I think." She jammed her spear into the sandy ground and swung out of the saddle. "Don't let the mortal do it," she said, then headed toward the spring without waiting for an answer.

"What am I not supposed to do?" asked Mandred in surprise. Then a lewd grin spread across his face. "What's anyone supposed to do with such a scrawny woman?"

"She knew. She knew the whole time," said Nuramon as the elf woman walked away from them. She had given no indication at all—not a single word, not a single hidden sign—that she was on their side. But regardless of what she thought was right, Yilvina had pledged loyalty to the queen.

"I'll do it," said Farodin as he dismounted. He pulled the spear from the ground and followed Yilvina to the spring.

Mandred's jaw dropped. "By the gods, what are you doing? You can't—"

Nuramon grabbed hold of the reins of Mandred's horse before he could say it. "Let him go. Farodin knows what he's doing. So does Yilvina."

"She saved our lives in Aniscans. He can't just . . ."

Farodin crouched beside Yilvina. They seemed to exchange a few words.

Then Farodin stood up and raised the spear. Yilvina kneeled beside the spring, her head lifted proudly. Nuramon flinched as the spear came down. Farodin swung it like a club and delivered a hard blow to the side of Yilvina's head. She collapsed forward and did not stir.

Mandred shook his head. "You elves are crazy. How can you just bash our companion like that?"

It mystified Nuramon that the human found this all so hard to understand. "In her own way, she made it clear to us that she accepted our escape," he explained. "She left her spear impaled in the ground to show that she would not raise it against us. But her honor and her vow of loyalty to the queen made it impossible for her to simply let us run away."

"Couldn't she just have said that she lost us?" asked Mandred.

Nuramon sighed. "She was assigned to guard us. *Losing* us would be a disgrace for her."

"The other riders who were with us when we started chasing the stag all got left behind," said the jarl.

"Guarding us was not *their* responsibility. For them, the chase was simply too much," said Nuramon.

Farodin had returned while they were speaking and mounted up. "Let's ride." He looked toward the edge of the clearing. "And hope we have no unseen guards shadowing us."

Nuramon looked into the forest in apprehension. It took little skill to hide in the shadows of the trees. He followed Farodin, but he had an uneasy feeling. Mandred rode close by his side.

"So why shouldn't *I* have whacked her?" Mandred asked. "Wouldn't that have been better? In fifty years, probably less, I'll be worm food anyway. What Farodin did will probably follow him for centuries."

"I think she was scared you'd be a little too enthusiastic and smash her skull in."

"I can bash someone very gently, too," said Mandred.

"Well, I'm afraid you have something of a reputation." Nuramon was tiring of the topic, but there was clearly no hope of getting the mortal to drop the subject.

"So what will happen if the queen sends someone to my world to find us?" Mandred asked. "That Phillimachos seems to be a top-notch tracker."

"To avoid anyone following us, we'll use an Albenstar where only three paths cross. Anyone opening a gate in the same place after us will come out somewhere else in your world."

Mandred frowned. "Sorry . . . the faun oak couldn't stand me, so I don't have much of a grasp of your magic."

Nuramon explained what he could about the minor Albenstars. Their connection between the worlds was so unstable that if you used them to cross from one world to another, it was not possible to come out in the same place twice. Because, by nature, such stars were rather fleeting, there were no fixed gates as there were with the major Albenstars. Finally, he told Mandred about the hazards of using the Albenstars.

The mortal listened attentively, then seemed to sink deep into his own thoughts. Nuramon would not think less of him if he chose to stay behind. Not wanting to influence his decision, Nuramon drove his horse forward until he caught up with Farodin. "I have a question, Farodin."

"Let's hear it."

"How did you find the grains of sand?"

"I used a kind of magic, a spell I last cast more than fifty years ago. The spell lets me find anything at all, as long as I know what I'm searching for."

"Couldn't you use it to find Noroelle?"

"No. She is in the Shattered World, but I may be able to find the gate we need to reach her." He hesitated. After a moment, he added, "But to do that, I have to know what it is I'm looking for. I've been able to sense the grains of sand every time, provided I get close enough to them."

Nuramon struggled with the idea of chasing down grains of sand. "There has to be another way to free Noroelle."

"Maybe. But until we have found another way, this is all we have. We should find out first if we are able to open a gate between the worlds at all. I still have my doubts."

"We can do it. I'm certain."

"Unless the queen has sent someone to follow our tracks," said Farodin.

Nuramon looked back, but saw no one.

"Just now, back at the clearing, there was someone hiding in the bushes," Farodin continued.

"Why didn't you say something?" asked Nuramon indignantly.

"It wouldn't have changed anything."

Nuramon did not at all like the way Farodin kept what he knew to himself and made arbitrary decisions that affected all of them. "Whom do you think it was?"

The elf shrugged. "Someone who prefers to avoid open confrontation. I'm hoping we can surprise whoever it is when we open the gate . . . if we manage it. And it would be smarter not to look back all the time. We should make whoever it is feel safe."

They rode on until they finally reached the edge of the forest and open grassland lay before them, then they let the horses have their head. They galloped toward the hill country between them and Yaldemee. The horses enjoyed the chance to charge across open land. Farodin's chestnut led the way while Felbion and Mandred's mare, which he still had not named, rode neck and neck.

Mandred sat low in the saddle, leaning far forward over the mane of his steed. He drove her on with wild whoops. He seemed to be enjoying the race, and Nuramon fell back a little to give the mortal the small victory of not coming up last.

They reached the hills without seeing any trace of a pursuer. Perhaps they had been successful in shaking off whoever it was. To be safe, they decided to take a detour and rode for some time along a shallow river to wash away their tracks. Farodin openly doubted that they would be able to fool Phillimachos with tricks like that.

Late in the afternoon, they reached the small valley that the faun oak had told them about, hidden among the hills.

They dismounted. The moment Nuramon's feet touched the ground, he sensed the power of an Albenpath.

Slowly, they led the horses forward. There was no more than an ash tree and a few bushes in the valley. The grass-covered hills rose steeply on both sides. With every step, Nuramon felt the surging of the Albenpath. It was like crossing a frozen river on ice so thin that he could feel the water sliding underneath.

At the end of the valley, Nuramon stopped. Close to the ground, he sensed a vortex. The power of the Albenpaths streamed in from three sides, merged, and flowed apart again along three paths. They had reached their goal.

Nuramon scanned the land around him. There was nothing to show that an Albenstar existed here. No stone marking the location, no clearing.

Farodin, wary, searched the area for any traces of other Albenkin, but there was no sign that anybody else had visited this place recently. The faun oak had advised them well. They could open a gate to the Other World here without being disturbed.

In the past few days, Nuramon had done his best to buoy his companions and, in particular, to allay Farodin's fears. But now he felt the first pangs of doubt himself. He had learned a lot in the winter, and the faun oak had told him that he possessed great talent, but nothing could erase the fact that he had never before opened a gate.

"We are here. I can feel the Albenstar," Nuramon told his friends, but he spoke more to Mandred than to Farodin.

"Do you think the horses will go through the gate, too?" asked Mandred, looking suspiciously at the grass as if there had to be some kind of sign that they were standing at an Albenstar. "I've gotten used to not wearing my feet down to the bone."

"We'll just have to see," Farodin answered.

"Take a last look around. Breathe in the air," said Nuramon. "This may be the last time we see Albenmark." Anyone breaking the queen's laws as often as they had could not count on ever setting foot there again.

"I'm sure it's the last time," Mandred declared.

Farodin said nothing, but Nuramon, deep down, felt that he would see Albenmark again one day, even if he had no right to.

Nuramon began to weave the spell. Still standing, eyes closed, he concentrated on the streams of the Albenpaths that came together in the star. Then he raised his head to feel the sun shining on his face. The magic was a spell of light and warmth, and he felt both of these now on his skin. Magic and heat had often been allies in his healing and were not strangers to him. He opened himself to the power of the sun and let it flow through him and on to the Albenstar. The magic tore a wound in the vortex, and for a moment, Nuramon felt as if he would be sucked into the Albenstar. He fought against it with all his strength, but the power was too strong. Suddenly, something gripped him by the shoulders, and he threw open his eyes. He could hardly see. It was as if the power of the sun that he had absorbed now radiated from his own eyes. He was aware of two shadows close to him. Farodin and Mandred, he thought.

Nuramon closed his eyes again and tried hard to hold on to the magic that was threatening to escape his control. He kneeled, laid his hands on the warm earth, and allowed the sun's power to flow down through his arms, as if the Albenstar were someone injured whose wounds Nuramon had been called upon to heal. This was no healing spell, though, and the wound he had opened was not supposed to close, not yet. What he had thought of as a wound in the Albenstar had to be part of the magic. Maybe the wound itself would become the gate. He felt the power flowing out through his fingertips and expected the pain that had always come when he performed his magic. But it didn't come, and because of that, Nuramon stayed on guard. If it came suddenly, he did not want to be caught unawares and be overwhelmed.

Something began to pulse, a force in one of the paths that set it apart from the others. It was like the difference between water from a stream and water from the sea. This had to be the path that would take them to the Other World. Then, without warning, the pain came. Searing heat poured down through Nuramon's hands to his fingertips. He fought desperately to withstand it, but the pain grew and grew and soon became unbearable. Nuramon threw himself back from the Albenstar and opened his eyes. The light that had taken away his sight was gone, and he saw his companions standing at his side. Beside them rose a broad column of light that made Nuramon think of a gash in the world.

"You've done it," cried Farodin.

Nuramon rose to his feet and cautiously stepped closer. He had caused an injury to the Albenstar, and released the power of the sun into it.

While Mandred stood gaping, as if nailed to the ground, Farodin circled the pillar of light. Nuramon could feel how the column was drawing power from the vortex. He was terrified; if he had made a mistake, they might all die. "Do you think this really is the gate we wanted to create?" he asked.

"I'm not connected to the fabric of your magic, but from outside, everything looks just as the faun oak described it," said Farodin. "What choice do we have? I'm willing to risk it."

Mandred tugged at the reins of his mare. "Let me go first."

"Out of the question," said Farodin. "It's too dangerous. It's for our sake that you are even here, so let me go ahead. If I burst into flames, then feel free to tell Nuramon what I think of him." He forced a smile.

"We're going to my world, and no one but Mandred Torgridson will be the first to set foot there." And with that, he simply strode ahead and suddenly disappeared into the light.

Farodin shook his head. "He's such a pigheaded . . ." He fetched his horse, then asked, "Who's next, you or me?"

"I opened the gate. I want to close it again," replied Nuramon.

Farodin lowered his eyes. "Considering our rivalry for Noroelle, I'd like . . ." He broke off. "Let's forget it and hold to what Noroelle said before the elfhunt." Without another word, he followed Mandred into the light.

"To me, Felbion," Nuramon called, and the horse came. "Go ahead. I'll follow." The horse didn't balk, but stepped into the light and disappeared.

The magic that would close the gate within a few moments was something like a turn of a hand inside Nuramon's spirit, a gesture he completed with his will. It was no more than a healing spell for the wound he had caused the Albenstar. When it came to that kind of magic, he knew what he was doing. The moment he thought it, it would be irreversible.

Nuramon was about to step into the light when he became aware of a figure standing on the hill at the entrance to the valley. It was a woman. She raised a hand and waved timidly.

Obilee. There was anxiety on her face. Even at this distance, he could see that. She may even have been crying. He waved back. There was no time to do any more. The column of light was already shrinking. He wondered why Obilee had not revealed herself to them sooner. Then he went into the cool of the light.

A heartbeat later, scorching heat was beating down on him. Was this the last thing he would ever feel? Had his sorcery failed? One step, and the light of the gate vanished. Overhead, a merciless sun beat down.

He was relieved to see that his companions were there, but when he looked around, his relief evaporated. On every side was sand, as far as he could see. It was the Other World, certainly. He could never confuse this sky with the sky over Albenmark, for the air here, even on the clearest day, still looked murky.

A desert. Of all the places they could have come out, they were in the middle of a desert. Fate was toying with them again. Mandred's Luth had woven another of his nets, sending them into this wasteland. Nothing could show more clearly just how little hope they had of ever finding Noroelle again.

Mandred sat in the shadow of his horse, breathing heavily. Farodin simply kneeled in the sand in disbelief, picked up a handful of the stuff, and let it trickle between his fingers.

IN THE LAND
OF FIRE

I will let nothing show, thought Mandred. *One step after another.* They had been traversing the wasteland for two days. Nuramon told them they were following one of three paths, but Mandred could see no sign of it. At least they were no longer in the dunes. In front of them stretched an endless plain, where white rocks jutted through the sand like the bones of giants.

He could not stand the looks of concern the others kept giving him. "I'm fine," he snarled at Farodin. Damned elves. The heat seemed to make no difference to them. They were not even sweating.

Mandred ran his tongue over his parched lips. His mouth was dry, and his lips felt as rough as hemp rope, the skin split and scabbed. His face was badly burned from the relentless sun, and it hurt.

He looked for his shadow. Too long. Midday was still a long way off, and the heat was already unbearable.

Mandred chided himself, *Don't show any sign of weakness.* How could the elves put up with the heat? Nuramon did seem a little tired, and he wasn't half as tough as Farodin, but he was still holding up well. Mandred thought back to the days when they were hunting the man-boar. Nuramon had worked some sort of magic that had wafted warm air under his clothes. In the middle of the coldest winter ever, the elf had not frozen. Could they also cool the air under their clothes? Was that their secret? It had to be something like that.

He'd stopped sweating himself, too, Mandred thought tiredly. Not because he had grown accustomed to the heat, but because he was as dried out as an old chunk of cheese. He dabbed at his lips with his tongue again and realized it was swollen.

Mandred grasped the saddle horn. Even his horse seemed not particularly affected by the heat. He had shared the last of his water with her that morning, and she had looked at him with her large dark eyes as if she felt sympathy for him. Horses that felt sympathy for humans . . . this heat was driving him crazy.

It was so eerily quiet in the desert that you could hear the wind rolling the grains of sand.

Step by step. Ever onward. The horse was pulling him along. It felt good to rest, to let the mare support him a little. The two elves led their horses by the reins, but he let his horse lead him. He was too weak to do anything else.

The breeze freshened. Mandred let out a rough, husky noise. Two days earlier, it would have been a laugh. A fresh breeze? Just wind. Wind as hot as the blast of air that would hit you when a baker opened his oven. What an ignoble way for a warrior to die. He could have cried, but he was too dry for tears. He was as arid as an old apple. What a godforsaken way to go.

He raised his head. The sun stabbed at his face, its rays like daggers. Mandred turned slightly to the side. His eyes scanned the horizon. Nothing. No end to the desert. Just bleached stones and yellow sand.

It started again. The air congealed. It became thicker and somehow streaky, almost like something set in aspic. Then it shuddered and melted away. Would he also melt away in the end? Or would he get so dried out that he suddenly burst into flames? Maybe he would simply keel over and stop living.

Mandred snatched the leather canteen from his belt, pulled off the cap, and lifted the rim to his lips. Nothing. He knew he'd drained the last drop from it long before, but a single drop would do. Just a reminder of water. In desperation, he twisted the leather, but all he wrung out of it was hot air. He coughed and let it fall again.

He looked ahead distrustfully at Farodin, walking ahead of him. His canteen was bigger. He still had water and just didn't want to share it.

I will not beg, Mandred rebuked himself. Whatever an elf could stand, he could, too. He was much bigger and stronger than those two bastards. It wasn't possible that they could bear up to these agonies better than he could. Their canteens had to be bigger. Or maybe they had enchanted canteens that never ran dry. Or . . . yes, that was it. It wasn't magic, no. They had stolen his water, at night, while he slept. It was the only explanation, the only way they could keep on going, step by step across this accursed sand. But they would not cheat him, not Mandred Torgridson. He touched the axe at his belt. He would keep his eye on them. When they were least expecting it, he would strike. Stealing his water. Scum, the pair of them. And after all they'd been through together.

His right hand slipped from the saddle horn. He staggered a few steps, then his knees gave out. Nuramon was at his side instantly. His skin looked reddish, and he had dark rings around his eyes . . . but his lips were not cracked. He had enough to drink. *His* water. Mandred's left hand cramped around the shaft of the axe, but he couldn't pull it from his belt. Nuramon leaned closer. His hands were pleasantly cool. When he stroked Mandred's face, the burning in his skin stopped.

Close above him, Mandred saw the elf's throat. A throat full of deliciously wet blood. All he had to do was bite. He still had the strength to tear open a throat with his teeth, didn't he? He let out a rapturous sigh at the vision of all that blood soaking his marred face.

"Nuramon?" For the first time ever, Mandred heard fear in Farodin's voice. "What is that?"

Farodin had stopped walking and was pointing to the southern horizon. A thin brown line had appeared between the sky and the desert beneath. It grew with every heartbeat.

For Mandred, the air felt like it had curdled into a tough, suffocating mass. His throat burned with every breath he took.

"A storm?" asked Nuramon, uncertain. "Could it be a storm?"

A gust whipped sand into Mandred's face. He blinked to clear his eyes. Nuramon and Farodin grabbed him under the arms and dragged him behind a knee-high shelf of rock. Nuramon's stallion nickered anxiously; his ears were back as he stared at the brown mass rolling down on them.

The elves managed to get the horses onto their knees behind the rock shelf. Mandred groaned aloud when he saw Farodin douse a cloth with the last of his water and wrap it around his horse's nostrils. In her fear, Mandred's mare was making strange growling noises. Suddenly, the sky disappeared. Flurries of swirling sand instantly reduced the world to something just a few steps across.

Nuramon pressed a damp cloth to Mandred's nose and mouth. He sucked greedily at the moist material. He had narrowed his eyes to slits, but the sand still found a way in.

Farodin had chosen their refuge well. In the lee of the flat rock, left and right of them, they could see the fine sand like an endless veil flying past. Earth and sky seemed to have merged into one. From above, sand and dust peppered them, but the wind drove most of it over them and away.

Despite the cloth covering his mouth, Mandred felt sand seeping between his teeth and into his nose. The stuff was in his clothes, and it scoured his weather-beaten skin. The cloth was soon completely clogged, and Mandred again felt as if he were suffocating. Every breath was an agony, even though the storm at least protected him from the worst of the heat.

He squeezed his burning eyes closed. All sense of time passing was lost to him. The storm was burying them alive. His legs were already half engulfed in sand, and he had no strength left to fight free.

Mandred felt utterly desiccated. He thought he could feel his thickening blood slowing in his veins. So this was what it was like to die.

ELVEN PATHS

Look at this." Farodin waved his companion over. Nuramon hesitated. He was leading Felbion by the reins, and they had tied Mandred across the horse's saddle. The human was in a deep coma. His heart still beat, but slowly, and his body was far too warm. A day at most, Nuramon had said in the morning. Since then, eight hours had passed. They had to find water, or Mandred would die. The elves could not survive the heat too much longer either. Nuramon's cheeks were sunken, and fine creases had formed in rings around his inflamed eyes. It was clear that his struggle to save Mandred's life had driven him to the limits of his own endurance.

"Come on," Farodin called. "It's beautiful and horrible at the same time. Like looking into the water in Emerelle's bowl."

Nuramon went ahead to Farodin. Now that he stood so close to his companion, Farodin said he could almost physically feel Nuramon's exhaustion.

"You have to rest," Farodin said.

Nuramon shook his head without emotion. "He needs me. The only thing keeping him from dying is my healing power. We have to find water. I . . . I'm afraid I won't be able to hold out much longer. Are we still following the elven path?"

"Yes." It had fallen to Farodin now to lead them along the invisible path. They had cast lots for which of the three Albenpaths to follow. And since it had fallen to Nuramon to keep Mandred alive, it was up to Farodin to keep them on the right track. It had to lead somewhere, even if only to another Albenstar.

"What did you want to show me?" Nuramon asked.

Farodin pointed some distance ahead, to a flat patch of rock that was almost completely buried beneath the sand. "There in the shadow. You can see the direction from my tracks. Do you see it?"

Nuramon blinked against the bright light. Then he smiled. "A cat. It's sleeping." He started to walk toward it happily.

Farodin followed behind, more slowly.

Curled up close to the rocks lay a cat, its head lying on its paws. Its fur was a yellow ochre and matted with sand, like the braids in Mandred's hair. It was emaciated, the body haggard and the fur disheveled. It looked asleep.

"See where her head sticks up slightly above the rock?" asked Farodin. Nuramon stopped.

You had to be very close to the cat to be able to see the back of its head. It was bare. More than bare. The fine, blowing sand had worn down the fur and the skin beneath and had polished the bone of the cat's skull, making it gleam white.

"She looks so peaceful," said Nuramon gently. "She laid down in the shadow of the rocks, fell asleep exhausted, and died of thirst in her sleep."

Farodin nodded. "That's what must have happened. The dry heat preserved her body, and the rocks protected her from the flying sand. She may have been here for weeks. Maybe even years. Impossible to say."

"And you think it's like looking into Emerelle's bowl? Is that our future?" Nuramon asked.

"If we don't find water soon. And I don't hold out much hope of that. Since we came through the Albenstar, we have not seen a single animal. Not even tracks. Nothing living walks this desert."

"The cat did," Nuramon replied, with surprising vehemence.

"Yes, she did. But coming here was a mistake, and she died for it. Do you think Mandred will live to see the next sunrise?"

"If we find water . . ."

"Maybe we should slaughter one of the horses and give him the blood to drink."

"I think it would be better if one of us took the two strongest horses and rode ahead, switching the horses when they get tired. You or I, we could cover a lot more ground and look for water."

"Which of us do you have in mind?"

Nuramon looked up. "Is that so hard to guess? My healing power is keeping Mandred cool and alive. You can't do that. I'll stay behind. The horses will last until at least this evening. If you find water anywhere, let the horses drink, then fill the canteens and come back in the cool of the night."

"And if I don't find water by sundown?"

Nuramon looked at him without expression. "Then you have another day to save at least your own life." Farodin returned his gaze as if sizing him up. "A day on horseback will preserve your own strength. I'm sure you'll get through another day that way. It makes no sense to then come back to us."

"A solid plan," Farodin said and nodded appreciatively. "Thought through with a cool head. It's just that it would take a braver man than me to see it through."

"A braver man?"

"Do you think I could stand before Noroelle and tell her I abandoned my two companions in the desert so that I could find her?"

"So you still believe you can find Noroelle like that?"

"Why not?" asked Farodin harshly.

"How many grains of sand have you discovered since we came back to the human world?"

Farodin lifted his head defiantly. "None. But I have not been looking. I was . . . the heat. I've been using what little magic I have to cool myself a little."

"Which would hardly have used up all your strength." Nuramon gestured broadly to the expanse of horizon. "This here is what has robbed you of your strength and your courage. This view. I don't believe that we are here by coincidence. Fate wanted us to understand how senseless our search is. There has to be another way."

"Then how? I can't listen to you going on about some other way anymore. What is that other way supposed to look like?"

"How do you think you can find all the lost grains of sand?"

"My magic carries them to me. I just have to be close enough."

"And how close is that? A hundred paces? A mile? Ten miles? How long will it take to search the Other World? How will you ever know for certain that you have found all of them?"

"The more I find, the stronger my seeking spell becomes."

Nuramon swept his arm over the desert again. "Look around you. I don't even know a number to use to talk about how many grains of sand are out there. It is utterly futile . . . and because you obviously have the strength to attempt the futile, then you are the right one to look for water here. If one of us can do it, it's you. Use your magic to find the next waterhole."

Enough was enough. "Do you think I am that stupid?" Farodin asked. "Finding something as tiny as a particular grain of sand in a desert is one thing. Finding a waterhole is far, far simpler. Do you seriously think I haven't already used my powers to search for water? Why do you think I showed you the dead cat? That is our future. There is no water within at least a day's ride of us. Only the water inside us. Our blood . . . It's as simple as that. I tried the first time just before I saw the cat. There's nothing."

Nuramon gazed east. His face was strained. He seemed not to be listening to Farodin at all.

"Has the sun burned the last trace of civility out of you? Say something. Did you even hear what I said?" Farodin demanded.

Nuramon pointed ahead into the empty desert. "There. There's something there."

A gust of wind puffed a thin wave of sand toward them. Like a breaker against a rocky shore, it collapsed onto the few rocks protruding from the sand. Not far behind it, a second thin wave of sand followed.

"There it is again," shouted Nuramon, excited.

"What?"

"We're standing here on the Albenpath. It runs through the desert as straight as an arrow. Imagine it going straight on from here. A little over a mile, I'd say . . . See how the flurries of sand blow over it. There's something there."

Farodin looked where Nuramon pointed. But there was nothing to see. No rocks, no dunes. Just sand. He looked doubtfully at his companion. Had he lost his mind? Had the hopelessness of their situation driven him mad?

"It happened again. Damn it . . . look!"

"We should try to find a little shade," said Farodin, trying to sound soothing.

"Another wave of sand is coming. Will you please look."

"You . . ." Farodin could not believe what he saw. The sand wave split. For a second or less. Then the gap closed again. It was as if the flying sand had glided over and around a rock that had momentarily blocked its path. Except that there were no rocks there.

Farodin's hand automatically fell to the grip of his sword. "What is that?"

"I have no idea."

"Some kind of invisible creature?" Who would benefit from being invisible? A hunter. Someone waiting for prey to wander past. Had he been secretly watching them, waiting for them right now on the path they were planning to follow? Farodin drew his sword. It felt unusually heavy in his hand. The sun had drained the power from his arms.

It made no difference what was out there. They had to face it. Every moment they hesitated only cost them more of the little strength they still had. "I'm going to take a look. Watch what happens."

"Wouldn't it be better—"

"No." And without letting himself get caught in more discussion, Farodin swung onto his saddle. He held the sword angled across his chest.

He reached the place in a few moments. Once again, the desert had deceived him, making something look much farther away than it actually was. He found a ring of dark basalt stones set into the sand. They looked like large cobblestones. Not a single grain of sand lay on the flat stones. Was it a magic circle? Farodin had never seen anything quite like it before.

He walked his horse around the stones. The blowing sand divided around the circle as if it were running into a glass wall. Some distance from the circle, half buried, Farodin noted a low, inelegant pyramid made of quarry stones. A human skull perched on top of it. Farodin looked around and noticed a number of other low stone mounds close by. On one of them lay several human skulls. What kind of place was this? Alert, he looked around, but apart from the stone ring and the mounds, there was no sign that either humans or elves had ever lived here.

Finally, Farodin dismounted. The ground there was steeped in magic. Albenpaths came from every direction and merged inside the ring. Carefully, the elf stretched one hand toward the invisible barrier. He felt a light tingling in his skin. He stepped into the ring. Nothing held him back. Apparently, the aversion spell on the circle only kept the sand at bay. But why the skulls? The coarse mounds did not match the elegant plainness of the ring itself. Had they been built later? Were they meant as a warning?

The area bound by the basalt ring measured a good twenty paces from one side to the other. The stones that formed it were a single pace across, if that. Inside the ring, the ground was sandy, no different from the desert all around.

Farodin closed his eyes and tried to turn his mind entirely to the magic of the Albenpaths. There were six paths that met inside the ring. Opening a gate here would be easy. And wherever it spat them out again, it had to be better than this desert.

He waved to Nuramon, who brought the two horses and Mandred. "An Albenstar," Nuramon cried in relief. "Salvation. Open the gate."

"You can do it better."

Nuramon shook his head angrily. "I'm too exhausted. It is all I can do to keep the last spark inside Mandred burning. You have learned the magic, too. Do it."

Farodin cleared his throat. He was about to say something, but checked himself. He almost wished there had really been some kind of invisible monster lurking there. The way of the sword, that was his way. The ways of magic were still foreign to him, despite all the hours he had spent learning from the faun oak.

He laid his sword on the sand and sat with his legs crossed and eyes closed. Then he tried to free himself from every thought, every fear. He had to empty his spirit and fuse it to the magic. Slowly, before his inner eye, an image of paths of light formed, paths that crossed in the darkness. And where they crossed, they also distorted. Their lines warped and twisted into a vortex. Every Albenstar was unique, with a distinctive pattern of these interweaving lines at its heart that differentiated it from every other star. Experienced sorcerers used the patterns to orient themselves as they traveled the Albenpaths.

Farodin imagined himself reaching into the middle of the paths of light with his hands. Like a gardener untangling tendrils of flowers, he pulled them apart in his mind until he had created a hole that grew larger and larger and finally transformed into a gate. It emanated a dark attraction from within. It did not lead to Albenmark.

Unsettled, he opened his eyes. He was looking at the naked, gleaming skull atop the pyramid of stones. What was it trying to warn them of?

"You've done it," Nuramon said, but there was doubt in his voice that belied his words.

Farodin turned around. A gate had opened behind him, but it looked completely different from the one that Nuramon had created. Bands of light in the colors of a rainbow streamed around a dark mouth that seemed to open into nothingness. A line of white light, straight as a ray of sunlight, cut through the dark, but it was not able to brighten the blackness that surrounded it.

"I'll go first," said Farodin. "I—"

"I think this gate leads to the Shattered World," Nuramon said. He gazed at it with a look of frank unease. "That's why it looks different. It looks just as the faun oak said it would."

Farodin ran his tongue nervously over his lips. He reached for his sword and slid it into its scabbard. With the palm of one hand, he patted sand from the folds of his breeches, realizing even as he did so that he was doing it simply to delay making a decision. Then he stood up. "The gate is wide enough. We can go through together if we lead the horses."

As they stood at the threshold of the gate, Nuramon said softly, "I'm sorry. It was not the right moment to argue with you about the grains of sand."

"Then let's have the argument some other time."

Nuramon did not reply. Instead, he tugged at the reins of his horse and stepped forward.

Farodin had the feeling that the gate actually sucked him in. With a jolt, he was inside the darkness. He heard a horse whinny but could not see it. The line of light had disappeared. He felt like he was falling, falling for an eternity. Then he felt soft earth beneath his feet. The darkness dissolved, and blinking, Farodin looked around. Icy fear took hold of his heart. The spell had failed. They were still standing inside the black ring of basalt, and the desert stretched away to the horizon on every side.

"Maybe I should try—"

"Our shadows," Nuramon cried. "Look. Our shadows have disappeared." He looked up to the sky. "The sun is gone. Wherever we are, it is not the world of humans."

A high-pitched cry sounded in the sky above. Overhead, a falcon circled. It seemed to be observing them. After a while, it turned and flew away.

Farodin looked up to the sky, a radiant blue that paled slightly as it neared the horizon. No clouds, no sun. The elf closed his eyes and thought of water. The more he focused his thoughts on water, the drier his mouth felt. Then he could sense it. It was like being momentarily dunked into a fresh mountain spring.

"That way." He pointed to a large dune on the horizon. "Before sundown . . ." He stopped and looked up to the sky again. "Before it gets dark, we'll find water over there."

Nuramon said nothing. He simply followed Farodin. Every step drained a little more of the energy they still had. They were so exhausted that they could no longer walk on top of the soft sand. Instead, like humans, they sank to the ankle with every step they took.

The dune they were walking toward seemed just as far off as when they started. Or was Farodin just imagining that? Did time stretch endlessly when there was no sun overhead to measure the passing hours? Had half an hour or half a day passed when the blue of the sky, finally, began to fade?

When they eventually reached the dune, they were on the verge of collapse. "How is Mandred?"

"Unwell," Nuramon replied. He continued to set one foot in front of the other without stopping or looking up.

Farodin's silence demanded more than any question.

"He'll die before dawn." Nuramon still did not look up. "Even if we find water, I don't know if I can save him."

Water, thought Farodin. Water. He could feel it. It wasn't far. He slogged onward. The dune was worse than the plain had been. With every step, they sank into the deep sand, but also slipped back a little, as if the dune was trying to fend them off, to prevent them from reaching its crest. A light wind drove the fine grains into their faces, burning their eyes.

When they finally reached the ridge, they were too drained to take any pleasure in what lay before them. It was a lake, its water a deep blue, fringed by thousands of palm trees. Strange halls stood close to the shore.

Only two low dunes still separated them from the oasis. They half trudged, half slipped down the back of the large dune they had just climbed. Their horses neighed high-spiritedly. Now it was the horses leading the elves, pulling them along as they held on to the reins. The beasts had scented the water.

Without warning, something slammed into the sand beside Farodin. He reflexively ducked to one side. A black-feathered arrow had just missed him, but he could not see the shooter anywhere. And the falcon was back, circling over their heads again.

Then the air was filled with a whirring sound, and a cloud of arrows came flying over the low dune ahead. They stabbed into the sand just a few steps in front of them, forming an almost perfectly straight line, like a border they were not allowed to cross.

When Farodin looked up again, riders had appeared above them on the crest of the dune. There were three dozen, at least. They were mounted on animals the elf had never seen before. With their long legs and strangely formed heads on top of curving necks, the beasts were so extremely ugly that it took his breath away. They had white fur and a large hump growing on their backs.

The riders wore long white cloaks. Their faces were veiled. Some carried sabers, others were armed with long spears with hand guards, from which colorful tassels dangled. But most striking of all were the leather shields they carried. They were shaped like a pair of giant spread butterfly wings and were just as brightly colored. The riders looked down at the two strangers and said nothing.

Finally, one of the riders separated from the troop. He skillfully steered the beast he rode down the dune and stopped behind the line of arrows.

"Envoys sent by Emerelle are not welcome here." It was a woman's voice, muffled by the speaker's veil. She spoke Elvish.

Farodin and Nuramon looked at one another, dumbfounded. "Who is that?" asked Nuramon in a whisper.

The rider had obviously overheard his words, because she said, "We call ourselves the Free of Valemas. In this part of the Shattered World, Emerelle's word carries no weight. You may spend one night here, outside the oasis. Tomorrow, we will take you back to the gate."

"I am Farodin of Albenmark, of the Askalel clan," Farodin replied angrily. "One of my companions is closer to death than life. I don't know what grudge you carry against Emerelle, but I know one thing. If you don't help us, then you are sacrificing the life of my friend to your wrath. And I swear I will avenge him in blood if he dies because of your neglect."

The veiled rider looked up to the other warriors behind her. It was impossible for Farodin to see which of them might be the leader. They were almost identically attired. Neither did their weapons betray anything about their ranks. Finally, one of them raised an arm high in the air and let out a shrill whistle. The rider was wearing the heavily padded glove of a falconer. High overhead, the falcon responded with a shriek of its own. Then the bird folded its wings and dived, landing moments later on the outstretched hand.

As if this were a signal for peace, the woman nodded to them. "Come. But remember, you are not welcome here. I am Giliath of the Free, and if you want to start a fight with anyone, Farodin, then I hereby accept your challenge."

THE FREE

The white-cloaked warriors gave them water. Then they surrounded the three companions and led them into the oasis. In the shadows of the palm trees, vegetable beds had been laid out and a kind of grain unfamiliar to Farodin had been planted. A network of narrow channels traversed the palm grove, and as they approached the lake, Farodin saw wooden bucket wheels.

Scattered among the trees stood small cob houses, their walls painted with complex geometric patterns. Looking at the houses, Farodin could see with how much care they had been built and were now maintained. There were no beams or windowsills that had not been painstakingly carved and decorated. But it was nothing compared with the magnificence that Valemas in Albenmark—although abandoned—still possessed. Its inhabitants had left many centuries earlier, and no one knew where they had gone. The people here had to be their descendants. Farodin looked around, taking in everything he could. He had been in old Valemas just once. Every house there was like a palace, and even the streets had been decorated with mosaics. It was said that the inhabitants of Valemas, in their pride, had once revolted against the queen. They would not tolerate anyone ruling over them. After countless disputes, they had finally turned their backs on Albenmark.

As things now appeared, the descendants of the people of Valemas had neither forgotten their resentment of the queen nor lost an ounce of their pride. The only difference was that they no longer lived in palaces. Along the lakeshore stood seven arching halls unlike any others Farodin had seen. They had been built from the curved trunks of palms, bent until they looked like the ribs of ships, and then anchored into the earth at both ends. Between the trunks stretched mats of elaborately woven reeds that formed the walls and ceilings of the halls.

When they reached the open square between these reed halls, Giliath made a sign for them to stop and dismount. Curious locals came from all directions: women draped in colorful robes and men who wore skirts. They stood silently and gazed at the new arrivals in mute hostility. Not even the children laughed.

Mandred was lifted from his horse and carried away. Farodin wanted to follow, but Giliath blocked his path. "You can trust us. We know what the desert does to careless travelers. If he can still be saved, he will be."

"Why do you treat us with such contempt?" asked Nuramon.

"Because we don't like Emerelle's bootlickers," Giliath replied. "Everyone in Albenmark defers to her. She smothers anything and anyone who is different. If you live there, you live in her shadow. She's a tyrant who presumes the right to decide for herself what is right. And what is not. We know very well how you all try to ingratiate yourselves with her. You're no more than the dust under her feet, you—"

"That's enough, Giliath," interrupted a sonorous male voice. A tall warrior stepped forward from the troop that had escorted them. On his hand, he carried the falcon; over its head he had slipped a colorful cap. He nodded his head in a brief greeting. "My name is Valiskar. I command the soldiers in our little society, and I am responsible for you as long as you remain our guests." He looked fiercely at Farodin. "I remember your clan. The descendants of Askalel were always very close to the queen's court, unless I'm mistaken?"

"I am not—"

Valiskar interrupted him. "Whatever you have to say you can say to the council. Know that in Valemas, decisions are not made by one person. Now follow me."

He led them into the largest of the seven halls. Inside, almost a hundred elves had gathered. Some stood in small groups, conversing, but most of them were sitting on carpets along the side walls.

At the end of the hall, in front of a blue banner emblazoned with the horse of Valemas, sat a silver-haired elf. He had his hands folded in his lap and seemed to be deep in thought. As Farodin and Nuramon moved through the hall, silence settled over the large room and the remaining elves moved back to the walls. The closer they came to the silver-haired elf, the more clearly Farodin sensed the aura of power that surrounded him.

He only raised his head when they were standing directly in front of him. The irises of his eyes shimmered like amber. "Welcome to

Valemas." With a gesture, he indicated to them to sit before him on a carpet. Hardly had they sat when two young elves hurried over with a jug of water, clay cups, and a bowl of dried dates.

"I am Malawayn, the oldest among the people of this oasis. You must excuse our modest fare, but the days when we lived in excess are long gone. Now tell us why you have undertaken the long journey from Albenmark to Valemas."

In turns, the two companions told the story of their travels and adventures. The longer they talked, the clearer it became to Farodin that the hostility they were met with at first was disappearing. Obviously, anyone who rebelled against Emerelle could count on unconditional hospitality in Valemas.

When they finally finished, Malawayn nodded. "The queen decides, and explains nothing. So has it always been. In my view, she has done the two of you and Noroelle a terrible injustice." He looked at those assembled in the hall. "I believe I speak for all of us when I offer you our assistance in your search."

There was no sound to be heard inside the large hall, no murmur of assent, and hardly anyone gave even the slightest nod or other gesture to confirm Malawayn's words. Yet the difference from the mood when they arrived could not have been greater. Indeed, Farodin could still sense bitterness, melancholy, and anger, but he also felt that they had been accepted into the hearts of the gathered elves. Like them, he, too, was a victim of Emerelle.

"How can you sit there in peace with these strangers?" At the end of the hall, a young woman stood up. Farodin recognized her from her voice. It was Giliath, the veiled warrior woman who had spoken with them at the foot of the dune. It seemed she had joined the gathering late. She had exchanged her equipment and white robes for a simple wrap skirt and a short silken blouse. Now one could see her long dark-brown hair tied back in a braid. She was so fit and her body so well trained that one could more suspect than actually see that she had breasts. She was not pretty. Her chin was too angular, her nose too big, but she had full, sensual lips, and her green eyes glittered with passion when she pointed angrily at Farodin. "That one, not an hour ago, threatened blood revenge against our people if we did not bend to his will. We retreated to this place to escape Emerelle. We wanted our freedom, and now you tolerate an elf from her entourage who treats us with the same condescension as his queen? I insist on my right to teach him better manners with the sword."

"Is it true that you threatened our people with blood revenge?" Malawayn asked, his voice cool.

"It was not like she said," Farodin began, but the old man cut him off with a gesture.

"I asked you a simple question. I expect no excuses, just a clear answer."

"Yes, it's true. But you should—"

"Are you now trying to tell me what I should and should not do?"

"It was not like it sounds," said Nuramon, trying to appease the old man. "We—"

"And you think you have to explain to me how the things I hear are to be understood?" Malawayn seemed more disappointed than angry. "I should have known better. Anyone coming from Emerelle's court brings their arrogance with them. According to our laws, Giliath has every right to challenge you, Farodin."

Farodin could not believe what he was hearing. How could anyone be so stubborn? The friendly mood all around them had vanished. No one there had any interest in hearing what they had to say. "I apologize for my words. I do not want to fight with anyone."

"Are you so smug to think you are invincible, or is your tongue driven by fear?" Giliath asked. She stood before him with her legs apart and her hands on her hips.

"If the insult is too serious, then only blood can atone for the words spoken," declared Malawayn. "You will dance to the blade song. Your duel will end when the first blood flows. If you are injured, then your blood will pay for your words. If Giliath loses, then you have earned a place among us, and we will accept what you have told us, for we are a free people."

Farodin drew his dagger. Before anyone could restrain him, he cut the back of his own left hand. "Women and men of Valemas." He raised his hand high so that they could all see the blood running down his arm. "I have spilled my own blood to make amends for my words. May this settle the dispute."

The assembly stared at him in icy silence.

"You should really stop trying to inflict your will on us, Farodin," Malawayn said. "Though your journey through the desert may have weakened you, you will bow to our customs, and you will fight." He stood and clapped his hands. "Bring the drums. In the blade dance, every stroke follows the rhythm of the drumbeat. We start with a slow rhythm to give you time to accustom yourself to it. The fight and the beat of the drum will both increase their tempo quickly. Traditionally, each dancer wields two swords. Do you require a second?"

Farodin shook his head. Sword and dagger were enough. He stood and began to stretch, to loosen his aching muscles.

Nuramon came up beside him. "I don't know what's gotten into them. This is absolutely insane."

"I'm beginning to understand why Emerelle never offered them the chance to return to Albenmark," Farodin replied in a low voice. "But don't say anything else about it. We don't want to give them any grounds for another blade dance."

Nuramon reached for Farodin's hand. A pleasant warmth spread through Farodin, and when Nuramon released him, the cut was gone. "Don't kill her." Nuramon smiled, trying to cheer his friend.

Farodin looked at his opponent. Valiskar had trusted her to be able to cope with two warriors alone when he sent her down the dune to meet them. He would have to be on his guard. "Let's hope she doesn't chop me to pieces. Something tells me she'd rather stick her sword through my heart than let the duel end with a little nick. 'When the first blood flows.' That can mean many things."

Farodin unbuckled his baldric so that it wouldn't hinder him in the fight. Then he took a small ring from the leather bag in which he kept the silver bottle and Noroelle's stone. The ring was the only thing that remained to him of Aileen, apart from memories. Three small dark-red garnets were set in it; the cut of the stones captured the light from the oil lamps on the walls. He ran one thumb over the stones as if testing them. They would ruin the lining of any glove. It had been a long time since he had last worn that ring.

"Ready?" called Giliath. She had chosen two short swords and stood waiting in the center of the hall.

In the meantime, two drums had been brought to the entrance of the hall. They were as big as the huge wine barrels they had seen during their escape through the vaults of Aniscans and had been set up with the skins vertical. An intertwined pattern of knots was painted on the pale skin. Two women stood beside them, drumsticks crossed across their chests, waiting for a signal that the blade dance should begin.

The spectators in the hall had moved all the way back to the walls, leaving a fighting area perhaps twenty paces long and five across.

Farodin took up his position.

"Each beat of the drum stands for one step or one stroke," Giliath explained. "The perfect sword fighter moves with the lightness of a dancer. Even if you lose, you will save face if you have fought with grace."

Farodin nodded, though he fundamentally disagreed with her. He had never fought to impress anyone with his skill. He fought to win.

Giliath signaled to the drummers. "Begin."

The first drumbeat sounded. Giliath took a step to one side and raised her swords. Farodin followed her movement with a turn.

With the next drumbeat, she aimed a slow, sweeping stroke at his head. Farodin parried with his dagger. *Any child could fend off such a stroke*, thought Farodin in annoyance. This blade dance was simply foolish.

The natural cadence of the drums was very deep, and Farodin could feel it in his belly. The drums were struck in turn, so each beat resonated for a long time.

Slowly, the tempo increased. Even though Giliath started with strange, exaggerated movements, she was, without doubt, an experienced fighter. Farodin followed the rhythm but did not copy Giliath's style just to pander to their audience. He parried her strokes with economical movements and stayed on the defensive, studying his adversary's movements.

The faster the drums beat, the more Giliath's movements flowed. Stroke followed stroke. She drove him away, then jumped back, danced around him playfully, then darted forward again. Drumbeats and the ring of steel on steel merged into a melody that now began to take hold of Farodin. Unconsciously, he moved to the rhythm and began to enjoy the fight.

Suddenly, Giliath crouched and took Farodin by surprise by dodging one of his strokes instead of parrying. Quick as a snake, her blade shot forward. Farodin tried to dodge, but the blade sliced through his breeches. The drums fell silent.

Giliath stood back. "You weren't bad for one of the queen's bootlickers."

Farodin touched the leg of his breeches. He felt no pain, but that meant nothing when one fought with very sharp blades. Carefully, he separated the cloth. His thigh was uninjured. She must have missed him by a hair's breadth.

Giliath's brow creased. "Lucky," she shouted to the crowd.

Farodin gave her a disdainful smile. "If you say so." He could see her arrogance crumble. She would try to land a second blow quickly, and perhaps, in her impetuousness, she would drop her guard.

"Then we continue," Giliath said, and she raised her swords, taking up a peculiar stance. The sword in her left hand stretched before her as if for an attack. She raised the sword in her right hand over her head, angled forward, the tip directed straight at Farodin's heart. She reminded Farodin of a scorpion with its sting raised in threat.

This time, the drums rapidly increased in tempo. Giliath came at him forcefully and pressed him back hard, but she made no move to attack with the sword in her right hand. The whole time, she kept it raised over her head, ready to strike the moment the opportunity came.

Farodin was amazed at her speed and that she had him on the defensive again. Her attacks came so fast that he barely found an opening for a riposte. He had to end this game, or she would.

Her blade jabbed forward, a strike aiming at Farodin's hip. He was just able to catch the strike in time, then faked a slight stumble, leaving his chest undefended.

This is what Giliath had been waiting for. Like the sting of the scorpion, her second blade lashed forward. Farodin turned inside her attack and brought up his dagger. Steel met steel with a clang. They were standing so close that he could feel Giliath's breath on his cheek.

Their blades were crossed at the level of their heads. Giliath broke the impasse and stepped back. Farodin stroked her cheek lightly with his hand as she did so and also stepped back.

"The fight is over," he announced in a loud voice, and everyone in the hall could see that he had won. A thin line of blood trickled from a cut on Giliath's cheek and down her neck.

She laid one sword on the ground and touched her face in disbelief. She looked at the blood on her fingers, perplexed. But instead of protesting, she stood and lowered her head to Farodin. "I bow my head humbly before the victor and apologize for my words," she said in a toneless voice, clearly still shaken by the unexpected end to their fight.

Angry voices rose on all sides. Many were not prepared to accept the outcome of the fight, and loud were the accusations of treachery leveled at the queen's courtier.

Nuramon ran to Farodin and embraced him in congratulation. "How did you do that?" he whispered.

"The ring," Farodin replied. He released himself from Nuramon's embrace and raised his hand so that the small treasure with the sharp-edged stones could be seen by all. The deep red gems looked like drops of blood set in gold.

"I challenge you to the blade dance!" A young warrior was standing in front of Farodin. "The way you won the fight was dishonorable. It offends me and my people."

Farodin let out a long sigh. He was about to say something in reply when Malawayn's voice rose above the din. "My brothers, the matter is settled. Until the first blood flows, that is the law. It doesn't say anywhere that the blood must flow because of a sword. Let us accept the outcome, though it was born more from cunning than skill."

Despite Malawayn's intervention, the clamor settled only slowly. Many of the younger elves left the hall in fury.

With a gesture, silver-haired Malawayn invited Farodin and Nuramon to sit at his side. He poured them each a mug of his wine and offered them fruit from the heavy silver plates set before him on the carpet. Little by little, it grew quieter in the hall.

When they had eaten together, Malawayn asked them to tell him about Albenmark. It was Nuramon who responded, and he made every effort to put what had just happened out of the minds of those around them. Farodin envied his ability to bring a story to life so vividly that anyone listening could practically see Albenmark before their eyes.

In return, the companions heard a great deal about life in the desert. The elves of Valemas had turned a muddy waterhole into a blooming oasis. It had taken them a long time to find this place, for like their ancestors, they loved the desert country. And they joked that it was the heat of the desert that made them so hot-blooded.

They also talked about how they often rode into the world of humans. The mortals there called them the Girat, which, in their language, meant something like *ghosts*, and they treated the elves of Valemas with the utmost respect.

"Whenever they meet us, they insist on presenting us with gifts," Malawayn said with a smile. "I think they see us as some kind of bandits to be paid off."

"And you let them go on believing that?" Farodin regretted the words as soon as they were out of his mouth.

"We have no choice. We lack so much here that we gladly accept any gift. We don't relinquish our honor by doing so. We take nothing by force, although we easily could." He lowered his head and gazed into the winding pattern of the carpet. "What I miss the most are the stars in the sky over Albenmark."

"What if you make peace with the queen?" asked Nuramon.

Malawayn looked at him in surprise. "We elves of Valemas may have lost much, but we have not lost our pride. We will only return to Albenmark if Emerelle asks us to, and if she will guarantee our freedom there."

Then you will never return to Albenmark, thought Farodin to himself.

AT THE EDGE
OF THE OASIS

As a child, Nuramon's thoughts had often turned to the desert and the fabled old city of Valemas. He had envisioned how it might look there but had never actually visited. This oasis was far different from what he had imagined the city of legend to be like. For one thing, there was no sun here, neither the sun of Albenmark nor that of the human world. But the sorcerers of this society had woven a canopy of light and pitched it like a tent over their settlement and the surrounding desert. They had even taken day and night into consideration; the light faded through an unusually long dusk and returned some hours later in a brief dawn.

The bond with the desert was plain to see and feel, despite all the water. Even the soft wind that blew here tasted like the desert.

Nuramon was following a path that he had been told led to the edge of the settlement. Valiskar had showed him the way. Apparently, the border of their domain lay at the end of the path. The other regions of the Shattered World were generally perceived as islands in an ocean of nothingness. It was this ocean that Nuramon wanted to see for himself. He had left his companions behind with the horses at the spring, and they were resting there in one of the cob houses. Despite the efforts of the healers of Valemas, Mandred was taking a long time to regain his old vigor. In his feverish sleep, he called out the name of Atta Aikhjarto repeatedly. Farodin had stayed with him; despite the hospitality they had been shown in recent days, he still mistrusted the inhabitants of the oasis.

But Nuramon was far too curious to linger there. He even began to walk faster, wanting to reach the edge of the oasis as quickly as he could.

Suddenly, the path he was on came to an end at a statue of Yulivee, the woman who had founded the oasis. Her image was to be found in many places in Valemas. The elves of the desert revered her almost as much as Mandred revered his gods. She had been a beautiful woman.

Her sandstone likeness wore a self-assured smile, and two polished stones of malachite had been set in the eyes. Nuramon had seen a sculptor setting gemstones in the eyes of a statue at the queen's court. First, the stones were set in the carved eye sockets, then the stone eyelids were placed over them and fused to the stone of the statue with a magic spell. Like that, the eyelids overlaid the malachite, and it looked as if the eyes were real and might blink at any moment. The figure gestured invitingly toward a stone at its side.

Nuramon accepted the invitation and sat down. The view the seat afforded him was surprising. He was at the edge of the oasis, that was clear. In front of him, however, lay not the sea of nothingness—as he had silently expected—but the desert. Perhaps one had to go out there, farther and farther, to reach the true boundary of this region. Nuramon suddenly realized that something wasn't right. The breeze was cool on the back of his neck, and at the same time, he saw fine sand swirling up and being blown toward him. But it never reached him. It disappeared, as if it had never existed. Was it possible that the desert that opened in front of him was no more than an illusion? An image of the real desert that began on the other side of the oasis and led to the stone ring? That would be a powerful spell indeed.

Nuramon stood and took a step toward the desert. Immediately, he could sense the power of the magic. A barrier like a wall of the finest glass separated the settlement from the phantasm out there. Cautiously, Nuramon raised his hands and felt for the unseen wall.

There was a crackling beneath his fingers. Hastily, he pulled his hand back. The desert blurred before his eyes, and the horizon darkened, the darkness spreading over the land with uncanny speed. It pressed toward him, swallowing first the dunes and then, step by step, the sand and rocks of the plain. But just before it reached him, the darkness lightened and grayed in the glow of Valemas. The town's radiance reached far. An abyss opened at Nuramon's feet, a pit of blue-gray fog that was slowly seething. That had to be the ocean on which the islands of the Shattered World floated. The darkness above it was the sky of this desolate world.

Somewhere out there was Noroelle. And maybe she, like he, was looking out into this vast emptiness at that moment. No doubt, like the sorcerers of this place, she had shaped her world to suit herself.

Nuramon could only hope that she was not in some place of perpetual mourning. If he had any chance to overcome this fog, he would take it and go however far was needed. Perhaps there was a way to reach Noroelle directly, a path that circumvented the queen's barriers.

Nuramon returned to the stone beside the statue and sat down again. And as he watched the image of the desert return, he thought about the idea that had just occurred to him. Was there perhaps some kind of boat that could sail on that fog like a normal ship could sail the seas?

A voice jolted him out of his ruminations. "You saw it?"

Nuramon's hand flew automatically to the grip of his sword as he spun around. Beside the statue of Yulivee stood a man in loose pale-green and white robes.

"Whoa! Not so fast, stranger," he shouted.

Then Nuramon noticed that the man had no feet. His robes simply fluttered in the air. They billowed much more than the gentle breeze there would move them. The figure's green hair swirled around his head as if ruffled strand by strand by unseen fingers.

"Never seen a spirit before, I'll wager," said the man.

Nuramon could not take his eyes off this apparition. "Spirits I've seen, but none like you." The figure seemed almost elf-like. Pointed ears protruded through his hair, but they seemed somehow meatier than elven ears. His hands were exceptionally large and misshapen; he could have wrapped Nuramon's head in just one of them. But the spirit's head was elongated and his chin pointed, and the broad grin he wore could not change that.

"My name is Nuramon. What is yours?"

"Names. Phooey," said the spirit, waving dismissively. "Life would be so much easier if we didn't have names to deal with. Names are just an obligation. Someone knows your name, and next thing you know, he's calling it out and telling you, 'Do this. Do that.'" He raised his eyebrows, and his pale-green eyes glittered. "I'm one of a kind here. In Valemas, there's only one djinn. And that's me. Even when I'm sometimes here, sometimes there . . ." He pointed to a spot next to Nuramon, disappeared in a chilly draft, and reappeared at the place he'd pointed to. "And even then, I'm still the same one." The spirit bowed to him. "Quick, what's your favorite color?"

Nuramon hesitated, then said, "Blue." He was thinking of Noroelle's eyes.

The spirit whirled around, and when he stopped and grinned at Nuramon again, he had blue hair and blue eyes and wore blue and white robes. "And I'm still the same one and the only one in these parts, even if you see me in blue. So who needs a name? Just call me *djinn*."

Nuramon looked at this being in amazement. A real, live djinn, floating in front of him. He had heard of them. It was said that all trace of them had been lost, but that some had hidden themselves away in Albenmark's few deserts. Others even claimed the djinns had never existed.

"Well, djinn . . . perhaps you can help me."

The spirit's face turned serious. "Finally. Finally someone who can appreciate my infinite wisdom."

Nuramon had to smile. "Well, you're very modest."

The djinn bowed. "Absolutely. I would never say a word about myself that was not true." He came close to Nuramon and whispered, "You should know that once"—he looked left and right—"once I lived in another place. It was an oasis of knowledge in the ubiquitous desert of ignorance."

"Hmm. And what knowledge did they safeguard there?"

The djinn adopted a look of incomprehension. "Everything, obviously. The knowledge that *was*, the knowledge that *is*, and the knowledge that is *yet to come*."

This merry spirit must have thought him an idiot. Even Emerelle could only vaguely see the future. Still . . . if this djinn was not just some mirage conjured up by his overwrought mind, and if his words contained a grain of truth, then he might be able to help them in their search for Noroelle. "Where is that place?" he asked the spirit.

"You should picture it as an enormous library. And you will find it inside the fire opal in the crown of the maharaja of Berseiniji."

"A library? In a stone?"

"Yes."

"That's hard to believe."

"Would you rather believe the fire opal is an Albenstar that moves around?"

Nuramon did not answer that. The djinn was right: an Albenstar that was not tied to one place seemed more unbelievable than a stone in which spirits gathered all the worlds' knowledge.

The djinn went on speaking. "The fire opal was our gift to Maharaja Galsif. We owed him a debt of gratitude, so we entrusted him with the opal and became his mentors. And we were good mentors." He disappeared again and reappeared on Nuramon's left. "Galsif was a clever man and guarded our knowledge with great wisdom. And in his wisdom, he did not tell his son about our presence. His son was a tyrant and a fool and not worthy of our knowledge. We spirits went in and out of the opal without anyone noticing. There can be no place safer than the crown of a mighty ruler."

Nuramon thought for a moment. It all sounded extremely fanciful. "In that *library*, could I discover how I might travel through this world from one island to another?"

"You could, if the library were still there, but it disappeared a long time ago. After Galsif, many generations of rulers came and went before Maharaja Elebal overthrew the neighboring kingdom and pushed east. In the end, he fought in the forests of Drusna, where he and his entire cohort disappeared. Once he was gone, his kingdom disappeared, and the crown, which was lost with Elebal in Drusna, has been missing ever since. Before it vanished, I could sense the opal from anywhere I happened to be in the human world and find my way to it. But ever since, I have not been able to detect it when I go wandering in the world of the mortals. Perhaps the crown and the fire opal have been destroyed. Or perhaps they have not and instead are surrounded and safeguarded by magic. It could be that they turn up again, someday. But until that day, you will have to make do without the knowledge contained in the library. I can still answer your question, however, because my knowledge is wide, but you will not like my answer."

The djinn floated to the edge of the oasis, and from one moment to the next, the darkness returned. "You've already seen it. Look at that stuff. Who but the Alben could stroll across that gray fog? It would be fatal to go out there. What is out there fundamentally has nothing to do with what is in here. It is more like the background to the Shattered World, what's left behind when a world disappears. The individual islands lie unimaginably distant from one another. Of course, there are Albenpaths and also Albenstars here in the oasis. But we can only really use the one path that leads to the human world. All the rest lead into the darkness and end somewhere between the islands. If you were to take one of those paths, you would be lost forever. And trying to move outside the Albenpaths will also get you nowhere. I can fly. I've even been out there, but I came back quickly, before I lost sight of Valemas's light. Even if you could fly, you would not get far without food or water. Believe me, Nuramon, even *I* would be doomed out there. For every being there is feeds on something, and out there is *nothing*. There is no way through the emptiness from one island to another."

So that was that for Nuramon's idea. If it wasn't even possible for a spirit to travel through the Shattered World, then getting around the queen's barrier like that was out of the question. They would have to tackle it from within the human world.

"I can see that this troubles you, but life is too long to fill with misery. Look at me. I've found a new home here and live quite a cheery life among these elves."

"Forgive me, djinn, but that is no solution for me. I have to break through a barrier surrounding an Albenstar to reach a particular place in the Shattered World. I don't even know where this Albenstar is, only that it is somewhere in the Other World."

"But you will find it, won't you?"

"I will search for it in the elven way, and one day, I will find it. But what then? How am I supposed to overcome a magical barrier set up to protect the Albenstar?"

"I can't tell you how to get rid of an obstacle like that, but I can tell you that it's been done often enough. Great power is needed to defeat great power, every time."

"Then my companions and I are lost."

"I know what's bothering you. The queen of Albenmark is the one who put up this barrier."

"How do you know that?"

"Because her power is matchless. So for you and your companions, it all looks rather bleak." The djinn floated around Nuramon. "Gracious me. An elf who wants to break his own queen's enchantment. Who ever heard of such a thing? Around here, they say you're all so nice and obedient in Albenmark."

"I implore you, don't say a word to anyone about my plans."

"I will keep your secret as secret as my own name. And because I admire Albenkin who have a bit of spunk, I'll even help you. You should know that breaking down barriers around Albenstars has a history. Even though the fire opal is missing and my own knowledge of spells of banishment is unfortunately rather limited, I can point you toward a place where all the knowledge of the worlds has been collected for millennia. The gate to reach it lies in Iskendria. Of course, this library is but a pale shadow of the library of the djinns, but why hold all the knowledge of the worlds in your hands when all you need is a pinch of it?"

Iskendria. The name had a ring to it that Nuramon liked. "Where is this Iskendria?" he asked.

"Follow the Albenpath that leads north from the stone circle. Go until you reach the sea." The djinn whirled and pointed off to the side. "Then head to the west and follow the coast. You can't miss Iskendria." The spirit folded his arms.

"Thank you, djinn."

"Oh, gratitude means a lot to us. I spent many years in the human world. How many wishes did I fulfill there, and how seldom did anyone say thank you?"

"Can I do anything to help you?"

"You can sit with me on this stone and tell me your story. Trust me, in this oasis, your secrets are safe. No one here is going to trot off to Albenmark and tell the queen."

Nuramon nodded and sat down beside the djinn on the stone. Then he began to talk. Each time he told it, the story grew longer, for he was pouring out his heart.

The djinn listened patiently, wearing an expression that did not fit with his merry temperament. When Nuramon finished, the djinn began to weep. "That is probably the saddest story I have ever heard, elf." The djinn sprang up from the rock, wiped his eyes, and grinned broadly, his teeth flashing. "But it isn't over yet. You can cry, or you can laugh." The djinn's face changed so that one half was happy and the other half miserable. "You've got to choose. You have to ask yourself, is there any hope, or isn't there?" He slapped the happy cheek, and the grin and the smile lines spread all the way across his face. "A bit of optimism, elf. Go to Iskendria. You will find a way, I'm sure. And if there really is no hope, then you'll still have plenty of time left for despair."

Nuramon nodded. The djinn was right, of course, even if his cheerfulness was not in Nuramon's character. He didn't know if he should be angry with the spirit for tossing his sad story aside so lightly, but the smile on the face of this odd being was enough, and he could not resist smiling himself.

When Nuramon stood up, the djinn was again floating beside the statue. "Go to Iskendria with an optimistic heart. Yulivee went there many times, and she was very wise. It was she who created the gate through which the elves of old Valemas left Albenmark. She created the stone ring out there, and the elves here owe her their thanks for the light spell, for the barrier, and for the mirage of the desert on the other side. Yulivee always said that travel was the best teacher. And she was a good student. May what she learned out there in the human world and in the Shattered World be yours to learn, too." So saying, the djinn dissolved and disappeared. On the breeze rang the words "Farewell, Nuramon."

Nuramon stepped up to the statue of Yulivee and looked into her shimmering eyes. He did not know whether he could take what the djinn had told him seriously or if there really was a town called Iskendria back in the human world. One look at Yulivee's face was enough. He would tell his companions about the town, and he would convince them that Iskendria was where they had to go.

TALES OF THE TEARAGI:

THE COMPANIONS OF VALESHAR

*T*he great desert wanderer Valeshar knew our forefathers. We have encountered him on only a few occasions, and we do not know how he is able to survive in the depths of the desert, but it is said that he and the desert are one. One day, we happened to meet Valeshar's companions. The night before, we had heard the ghouls howling in the dunes, and so we were fearful of the day. At midday, as we crossed the endless plain of Felech, we saw a rider in the distance. We thought the ghouls had sent a demon to fetch us. But then we saw Valeshar's robes, red as fire.

We immediately pitched our camp, to be able to offer a fitting reception to the great lord of the desert. But behold! From Valeshar's shadow appeared three more riders on horseback. Two of them were Girat and very pale, and they were armed as for battle. But the third was a Girat of the fire. He had long, flaming hair that burned in the wind, and his skin was as red as the heart of a blaze. His weapon was a great axe with a blade that shone in the sunlight. The three Girat were mounted on splendid, untiring horses.

We received Valeshar according to our custom, and he was a good guest, as always. He drank and ate with us in peace and seemed pleased with our offerings. Valeshar introduced his companions to us. The two pale Girat were Farashid and Neremesh, but the Girat of the fire was called Mendere.

Farashid had hair as light as the sun and eyes of jade. Neremesh's hair was the color of the windy mountains, and his eyes were the brown of the desert in the south. Mendere was a giant with a wild, flaming beard. His blue eyes were like oases in the desert. The Girat of the fire did not have his master's manners. He ate without cease and drank water as if it had no end, to our great astonishment. Neremesh explained to us that Mendere had to extinguish the flames that danced in his belly. Then we understood that Mendere's actions were of benefit to us all, for he did not want our tents to catch fire.

After we had eaten, Valeshar bade us lead his companions to the sea. We were afraid of the Girat of the fire, but out of respect for Valeshar, we agreed to take the three with us. The Girat did not speak our language, and we knew none that they commanded. So it was that we had few words to share. We admired Mendere's self-sacrifice in drinking so much water for our sakes, and he did not shy from the wine when it came to quenching the flames in his belly. When he asked for raki, we were afraid that Mendere would only cause the fire inside him to burn all the brighter. But who opposes the word of a friend of Valeshar? So the Girat drank raki. At first, nothing happened. But in the night, we heard such groaning and moaning that we fled the camp, believing the ghouls were upon us. When we dared to return, we discovered Mendere tossing and turning on the ground, battling the flames the raki had fueled inside him.

The closer we came to the sea, the redder grew Mendere's skin. It was only the hands of Neremesh that could drive the fire from Mendere's arms and face. Since that day, we have held to a rule: never offer a Girat of the fire raki.

After long travels, we came to the sea, and the three Girat departed with the few words of our language that they had learned. They rode in the direction of Iskendria and left us behind. But we were curious. What could they want in Iskendria? No doubt they were traveling on their master's business. The people of the desert had long known that the inhabitants of Iskendria were so foolish as to deny Valeshar his tribute. Now, though, doom was riding toward them in the form of his companions.

FROM *TALES OF THE DESERT PEOPLE*, COLLECTED BY GOLISCH REESA
VOLUME THREE: THE TEARAGI, PAGE 143 FF

IN ISKENDRIA

The journey through the desert had been a torment for Farodin. Sometimes it felt as if the dunes were mocking him. Uncountable were the grains of sand, and they threw in his face the impossibility of the task he had set himself. He could only hope that, in time, his magic would grow more powerful. Farodin wanted to stay true to the path he had embarked upon. His doggedness had led him to Noroelle after almost seven hundred years, and he would find her this time, too. He was determined to recover enough of the sand from the destroyed hourglass to reverse Emerelle's enchantment, even if it took centuries.

Farodin looked to the high city walls on the horizon. Iskendria. Was it wise to come here? They would have to pass through another Albenstar, and the magic was dangerous. What if they leaped in time now? They probably wouldn't even notice. But for Noroelle, it would mean many more years of loneliness. If they found some clue in the library, if they discovered how to break Emerelle's banishment spell and to find the Albenstar through which Noroelle had passed into the Shattered World, then their search would end quickly. But Farodin had his doubts. Was it conceivable that Emerelle did not know about the library? Hardly. So she must assume that whatever knowledge it contained would not help them. Was it possible that she was mistaken? He had been pondering this throughout their journey. It was a waste of time to think about it any longer. The only answer they would find was in the library itself.

A faint smell of decay hung in the air. Farodin looked up. They had almost reached the city.

The last mile of the road into Iskendria was lined with graves. One of those tasteless things that only humans could come up with, thought the elf. Who wanted to be greeted by memorials to the dead when they visited a city? Crypts and pretentious mausoleums stood side by side, crowding the road. Farther back, the grave sites became plainer, until they were marked by no more than a simple stone that showed where someone had buried a corpse in the sand.

In the pompous marble and alabaster burial houses, the local under-takers had quite obviously not covered the bodies with earth. Farodin wished they had put as much effort into fashioning sarcophagi that actually sealed as they had into decorating the mausoleums with statues of the dead. Most of the statues were of men and women who looked very young. It was no surprise to Farodin that people didn't get old in a city that greeted visitors with the stench of the dead. If one were to believe the statues, there were only two kinds of people who made up the rich of the city: those who gazed sagaciously and looked as if they took themselves very seriously indeed, and those who treated life as a party. The sculptures of the latter sort showed them stretched out casually atop their sarcophagi, toasting passing travelers with raised goblets of wine.

The newer graves and statues were painted in garish colors. Farodin found it hard to comprehend how humans could delude themselves into thinking they looked good with kohl-rimmed eyes while wearing an orange dress and a purple wrap over the top. In contrast, the desert sand had long since eroded the color from the older statues and monuments, and they were much easier on the eyes of an observer.

The morbid impression that Iskendria made on travelers was some-what redeemed by the women who stood beside the road. They received visitors to the city with warm smiles and friendly gestures. Unlike the desert dwellers, they did not protect themselves from the sun with bulky robes and veils. On the contrary, they showed as much skin as possible, if one overlooked the layers of powder and makeup they wore. Some had even given up on clothes completely and had painted their bodies with mystifying patterns of spirals and curves.

Mandred, clearly familiar with this form of welcome, waved to the women. He was in an excellent mood. Grinning broadly, he turned his head this way and that, not wanting to miss a single glimpse of these women.

The road was paved with huge stone slabs and led straight as an arrow toward the walls of Iskendria. A short way ahead of them, a caravan made its way along. It consisted of those ugly animals the humans called camels, and a small group of traders who were chatter-ing excitedly. Suddenly, one of the traders broke away from the group and spoke to a woman with unnaturally red hair. She sat with her legs spread wide upon the pedestal of a marble carouser. After some brief haggling, he pressed something into her hand, and they disappeared together behind a half-collapsed mausoleum.

"I wonder what a ride round here costs?" Mandred murmured, watching the two vanish.

"Why do you want to ride? Haven't the last—" Nuramon stopped. "You don't mean . . . are those . . . what did you call them? Whores? I thought you found them in large buildings, like in Aniscans."

Mandred laughed heartily. "Oh, there were plenty of whores in the streets of Aniscans, too. You just don't have the eye for them. Or maybe it comes down to love. Noroelle is certainly something different from these whores." He grinned. "Though some of them really are very pretty. But when love already keeps you warm, then there's no need to look for pleasure anywhere else."

It angered Farodin to hear their human companion mention Noroelle and these painted females in the same breath. It was . . . no, he could not find a fitting image for the absurdity of comparing Noroelle and these women. He thought of dozens of metaphors for Noroelle's beauty, metaphors from a song he used to sing to her, and not one of them would be appropriate for the prettiest of these humans. Now *he* was doing it. He was thinking of his beloved and these women at the same time. He looked at Mandred testily. Riding with this barbarian so long had left its mark.

Mandred had obviously misunderstood his look. He stroked the moneybag at his belt. "Those camel drivers could have been a bit more generous," he said. "Twenty silver pieces. How long is that supposed to last? When I think what they gave Valiskar . . . they're on to a good thing, those brothers of yours at the oasis."

"Those are no brothers," said Nuramon. "They're—"

Mandred waved it off. "I know, I know. They really made an impression on me. They're very simpathekish spirits."

"Do you mean *sympathetic*?" asked Farodin.

"Elven blah-dee-blah. You know what I mean," Mandred replied. "They've really got something going. Those ragheads with their camels, all they have to do is see the elves of Valemas and they're hell-bent on giving them gifts. It's fantastic . . . sympachetic. No banging heads, no threats, no curses. They just come out and accept the gifts. And the camel drivers are happy about it. They must be some tough guys, the Free of Valemas."

Farodin's thoughts turned to Giliath. He would have liked to have spoken to her again, to find out whether she really would have killed him. She had come close. After the fight, she had withdrawn, and though they had stayed five more days in the oasis, he had not seen her again.

"Hey, lass." Mandred slapped a dark-haired girl on the thigh. "You understand me even if you don't speak my language."

She flashed a voluptuous smile in reply.

"I'll come back and find you as soon as we've found a billet in the city."

She pointed at the money pouch on his belt and glanced enigmatically toward a broken crypt.

"She likes me," proclaimed Mandred proudly.

"At least, she likes what's hanging on your belt."

Mandred laughed. "Then she'll like what's hanging underneath it, too. By the gods. I've missed the curves of a girl in my arms."

Mandred's words stung Farodin. The human was so refreshingly simple. It must have had something to do with the short lives they led.

A large double gate rose ahead of them at the end of the street. It was flanked by two massive, semicircular towers. The walls themselves must have been at least fifteen paces high, and the towers nearly double that. Farodin had never before seen a human city surrounded by such massive fortifications. Iskendria, it was said, was many hundreds of years old. Two major trading routes and an important river converged inside the walls of the port city.

At the gate stood guards with breastplates of reinforced linen. They wore bronze helmets decorated with black horsetails. Travelers leaving the city exited through the gate on the left. No one bothered them, but anyone trying to enter the city had to pay a toll to the guards.

"Did you see that?" said Mandred indignantly. "These sharks charge a piece of silver for the honor of visiting their city."

"I'll pay for you," said Farodin evenly. "But keep your head. I don't want any trouble here." He kept a wary eye on Mandred.

As the guard at the gate stepped up to them, Farodin pressed three pieces of silver into his hand. The man had scars from the pox and bad breath. He asked something that Farodin did not understand, and the elf shrugged helplessly.

The guard seemed unsettled. He pointed to Mandred and repeated his question. Farodin offered another silver piece to the man. The guard took it, smiled, and waved them through.

"Sharks," hissed Mandred again.

A busy street opened before them on the other side of the gate and ran straight as a string ahead of them into the city. The caravan they had followed along the coast road to Iskendria disappeared through an arched gateway into a walled courtyard. Farodin saw more than a hundred camels standing inside. Apparently, the courtyard was a meeting point for merchants from far away. It was no place for Farodin or his companions. They would just stand out among the traders, and that was to be avoided at all costs. They continued along the street.

Most of the buildings were built of brown mud bricks. Only occasionally did they exceed two floors. They were open to the street and, at ground level, housed handicraft stores, food stalls, and bars.

In front of one of the bars, children sat plucking robins. The birds were still alive. Without gutting them, they tossed the small birds into seething oil. It turned Farodin's stomach to watch. It made no difference how big the cities they built might be, humans were savages.

The three companions were the slowest of those moving along the broad main street. Everyone here seemed to know where he or she was going, and everyone was in a hurry to get there. Sweating laborers pushing barrows piled high with bricks, water sellers lugging huge amphorae strapped to their backs, messenger boys with oversized leather satchels, women taking baskets of vegetables to market. Among all these people, Farodin felt out of place. His ears were hidden beneath a headband, so he did not stand out, but being incognito made no difference to how he felt. Rarely had he ever felt so foreign in the human world.

Farodin observed an old woman wearing a sea-green wrap dress following two servants who were carrying baskets of goods. The old woman was haggling with a boy holding a long pole hung with more than twenty birdcages. Finally, one of the servants paid the youngster a few copper coins. The boy then opened one of the cages and retrieved a white dove from inside. With care, he handed the bird to the old woman. With a laugh, she threw the dove into the air. The bird flew in a circle, seemingly confused at its newly gained freedom, then flew east in the direction of the salt lakes.

Farodin was at first impressed by this noble gesture, but then he wondered whether the boy had caught the birds just so that rich women could have the pleasure of releasing them again.

The farther they followed the street, the higher the buildings on either side became. Now most of the walls were plastered white over the mud bricks. Some of the walls were painted with murals depicting ships at sea or storks wading through clumps of reeds.

Farodin found the confusion of smells pressing in from all sides dizzying. The scents of herbs and spices mingled with the stink of the city. All around were the odors of unwashed humans, donkeys and camels, excrement. The noise was beyond description. Street traders shouted their wares at the tops of their voices, while the water sellers and the young girls selling fragrant flatbread and gold-brown pretzels from baskets chanted in an endless singsong drone.

Farodin was soon wishing he were back in the loneliness of the desert. His head was throbbing. The heat, the noise, and the stench were more than he could bear. And if all that were not enough, he felt the Albenpath that had led them parallel to the coast road and all the way here to the city growing weaker and weaker. Farodin was certain that they had not left the path. It felt to him as if the path were sinking deeper beneath the stones of the street with every step.

Nuramon, too, seemed uneasy. They exchanged a glance for a moment. "We have passed two minor Albenstars," he whispered excitedly. "This city is like a spider's web. So many paths cross here, but they lie underground. That is unusual. I don't know if I will be able to get to their power and open a gate."

"Maybe there are tunnels," Farodin suggested. "There has to be some way to get to the stars. Every major Albenstar is protected by magic to stop it from sinking beneath snow or sand."

"What if they decided to forgo that magic here?" Nuramon said. "Perhaps to better hide the gate from the humans? Just look at the crowd. What other possibilities are there here than to hide the gate deep beneath the earth?"

"Did your djinn actually say when he visited this library?" Farodin asked.

"No."

"It may have been centuries ago. Maybe there's no longer any gate that leads there from here."

Nuramon did not reply. What could he have said? He had put all the hope he had left into the library. And now that they were here, they would search until they found a gate.

Mandred seemed to have picked up nothing of his companions' low spirits. He seemed captivated by all the strange impressions and leered openly at every halfway attractive woman. Sometimes, Farodin almost envied his companion. His life was short, and he took that in stride surprisingly easily. Nothing seemed to darken his mood for very long. He was always able to find something to be interested in, even if no more than chasing the fleeting joys of a night of boozing or love. Perhaps he even lived a better life?

They must have gone a mile when the street they had been following intersected with an incomparably grander boulevard flanked by rows of high columns. Uncertain where they ought to go, they turned onto this magnificent thoroughfare. The hustle and bustle here was even more extreme than before. On the right and left, beyond the columns, were arcades of shops. These, too, opened wide doors directly onto the street and touted expensive wares. Cloth from every land in the world and prettily decorated vases and containers. Curious passersby watched goldsmiths fashioning delicate jewelry from the finest of wires.

Every third column had a ledge five paces above street level, and on each ledge stood a larger-than-life-sized statue. In garishly painted robes, they gazed nobly down onto the people walking below. Some were draped with gilded chains and trinkets. Farodin wondered whether they were meant to depict gods or, perhaps more likely, particularly successful merchants.

From a short distance ahead of them came a heartrending whimpering. A moment later, they came to a square where market stalls of colorful cloth had been set up. Each stall was home to dozens of amphorae.

"A wine market," Mandred crowed. "Those are all amphorae of wine." A skinny trader with a red nose waved to him and smiled, holding up a clay cup. "He wants me to taste it."

Nuramon pointed up to a pole that jutted high above the wine stalls. A young woman was impaled on top of it. Her clothes had been torn from her body, and she was covered in bloody streaks. She whimpered softly. As Farodin gazed up at her, she shivered, and he saw how the weight of her own body drove the point of the pole deeper into her flesh.

"Do you really want to drink here?" Nuramon asked.

Mandred turned away in disgust. "Why are they doing that? What did that girl do? A city as lovely as this . . . and then that. Is she a child-murderer?"

"Ah. And that would naturally justify torturing her to death so barbarically. How could I have missed that?" Farodin replied, sharper than was called for. What could Mandred do about the cruelty of the rulers of Iskendria?

In silence, they pushed on through the crowds along the boulevard until the milling throng around them suddenly, as one, grew uneasy. From not far away came the beating of a drum and the bright clang of cymbals. The people around them pushed back all the way to the columns. The cries of the merchants and the drone of conversation among the crowd fell silent. The street was quickly empty but for the three companions, who were left standing out there.

"Hey, Northman!" A burly blond man stepped from the line of humans. "Get out of the way!" He was speaking the language of Fargon. "The queen of the day is coming!"

A procession turned from a broad side street into the columned boulevard. Young girls in radiant white dresses hurried ahead, strewing rose petals over the cobbles.

The three companions darted out of their way. The blond man pushed over to them. His face was covered in stubble, and his sky-blue eyes sparkled. "Foreigners, am I right? I bet you just got here. You need a guide. At least for the first few days, till you find your feet and get to know the laws of Iskendria."

The flower-strewing maidens were followed by a troop of soldiers with breastplates of bronze and helmets on which black plumes of feathers waggled. They carried large round shields painted with the grim face of a bearded man. Strangely, they carried their spears the wrong way around, with the tips pointing at the street. Black capes embroidered in gold along the edges hung from their shoulders. Farodin had never seen soldiers so splendidly outfitted in the human world. Silent and solemn, they strode across the rose petals.

"The temple guard," explained their self-appointed guide. "Pretty to look at, but a nasty bunch. Don't get on the wrong side of 'em. Anyone picking a fight with the temple will find themselves in the horse market before they know it."

"What's so bad about your horse market?" asked Mandred.

"They lock you in an iron cage, haul you up a mast, and let you starve to death. If you're lucky. If you've offended Balbar, the god of this city, then they'll smash your arms and legs with iron bars and chain you to the heretic's stone in the marketplace. You'll lie there until your wounds get infected and you rot while you're alive. At night, the stray dogs will come and feed on you."

Revolted, Farodin turned back to the procession while Mandred listened eagerly to the stranger's stories. The next group to pass consisted of dark-skinned men in red frocks. Large drums were buckled around their hips. They beat a slow marching step and set the tempo for the rest of the parade.

An enormous open litter came next, carried by at least forty slaves. On it was a golden throne flanked by two priests with shaven heads. On the throne itself slumped a young girl. Her face was painted with lurid makeup. She looked down at the crowd apathetically.

"Isn't she pretty?" asked the blond with a cynical edge. "In an hour, she'll be facing Balbar in person." He lowered his voice to a whisper. "They've fed her wine and opium. Just enough so she doesn't fall asleep during the procession and is still awake when she goes to meet Balbar. You should see that. You'll understand Iskendria better if you do."

Behind the litter followed a group of black-robed women. They were wearing masks depicting hideous visages, faces frozen in screams of misery, pain, and sadness.

"She's really going to meet a god face-to-face? And we could watch?" Mandred asked with interest.

"Wager your ass on it, Northlander. By the way, the name's Zimon of Malvena. No pressure, but believe me, you'd be well advised to have a guide here."

Nuramon pressed a silver coin into his hand. "Tell us everything we need to know about the city."

The procession had passed by, and all around them, the general hubbub was starting up again. "Let's go to the temple square." Zimon waved them out onto the street, and they followed in the wake of the procession. "So what brings you to Iskendria, gentlemen? Looking for someone who can use the service of your swords? Paymasters like that are easily found in the caravanserais. I'd be happy to take you there."

"No," Mandred replied companionably. "We want to go to the library."

Farodin flinched inwardly. In moments like this, he could kill Mandred. What did it matter to a shady hustler like this what they were doing here?

"The library?" Zimon eyed Mandred in amazement. "You stump me, Northman. That's close to the harbor. They say all the world's knowledge is stored there. It is more than three hundred years old and holds thousands of scrolls. There is no question on this earth that you won't find an answer to in there."

Farodin and Nuramon looked at each other. A human library where you could find the answer to any question. That was as likely as a horse that laid eggs. Still, it was remarkable that such a library existed in Iskendria, of all places. Was it perhaps a pale mirror of what lay hidden beyond the Albenstar in the Shattered World?

They came to a broad square, in the center of which stood a statue ten paces high. Its sculptor had carved the figure of a man with a square-trimmed beard, sitting on a throne. The arms of the figure were bent at a strange angle and rested on his lap. The hands were open as if expecting gifts to be laid in them, and there was, in fact, a wooden ramp that led up to the hands. The statue's mouth was open wide as if it were trying to scream. Pale smoke billowed out of it.

Behind this enormous idol rose a temple, its soaring columns painted crimson and crowned with gold-studded capitals. The temple gable bore a gaudily painted high relief of Balbar wading through the ocean, his huge fists battering galleys into the waves.

On the steps of the temple, the priests had assembled. They were intoning a hymn with gloomy solemnity. Farodin did not understand a word of it, but their singing sent a shudder down his spine.

The litter had been set down at the foot of the statue. The drummers increased the tempo of their rhythm.

Thousands of people stood in the square and joined in the monotonous song of the priests. Farodin, from the corner of his eye, noted that Nuramon had grown very pale. Even Mandred was silent; all his sociability had vanished.

The two shaven-headed priests who had earlier been standing on the litter now led the young girl up the wooden ramp. She moved like a sleepwalker.

All three stepped onto the open palms of the idol. The priests forced the girl to her knees. They laid chains across her shoulders and hooked them into eyelets of iron set into the hands of the god. The floral wreath that had decorated her hair fell off. She crouched impassively, trapped by her intoxication and mute submissiveness. A female priest with long, loose hair came up to her, holding a golden pitcher. She anointed the girl's forehead, then emptied the contents of the pitcher over the girl's robe.

With the other two priests, she stepped back from the hands of the idol and onto the wooden ramp. As she did so, the tempo of the drums increased again. The clanging cymbals were shrill and painful to listen to. The monotonous chanting grew louder.

Suddenly, the arms of the statue jerked upward. The hands of the god clapped into the wide-open mouth, and the girl disappeared inside. The singing and the drums instantly fell silent. A muffled screaming could be heard. Then the arms came down again. Held fast by the heavy chains, the young girl still squatted on the god's open palms. Her hair and the robes she wore blazed fiercely. She writhed in her bonds, and her screams filled Farodin's ears.

Mandred stared wide-eyed at the burning girl, while Nuramon turned away, wanting to leave the square. But their self-appointed guide blocked his path. "Don't do it," he hissed.

Several of the faithful around them were already looking suspiciously in their direction.

"If you leave, you will offend Balbar. I already told you what the priests here do to blasphemers. Look at the ground if you can't stand the sight, but don't leave now. Say a prayer to Tjured, Arkassa, or whoever you believe in."

The girl's screams grew fainter. Finally, she slumped forward, dying. The priests began their bleak song again. Slowly, the crowd dispersed.

Farodin felt sick. What kind of god was it whose believers paid homage with such indescribable cruelty?

"Now we can go," said Zimon flatly. "No one's forced to take part in the sacrificial ceremonies. It's easy enough to avoid this barbarity. I've been living here two years, and I still don't understand the two faces of Iskendria. It's a city of art and culture. I'm a sculptor myself. Nowhere else is my work as appreciated as it is here. The rich are obsessed with having statues of themselves. And there are wonderful festivals. In the library, learned scholars from all around the world argue about the fine points of philosophy. But here in the temple square, a child gets burned to death every single day. You simply can't believe that they're the same people."

"Every day?" said Mandred in disbelief. "Why do they do that? It's . . ." He raised his hands helplessly. "It's . . ."

"Seventy years ago, King Dandalus from the Aegilien Islands came here and laid siege to Iskendria. His fleet brought a huge army to the city walls. They built catapults and towers on wheels. He had even brought miners with him. Their job was to dig tunnels under the walls. The siege lasted two moons. Potheinos, the king of the city, knew Iskendria was doomed. He promised that he'd sacrifice his own son to Balbar for the god's help in lifting the siege. Immediately, a plague broke out among Dandalus's soldiers. He was forced to give up the siege and retreat to his camp. Potheinos sacrificed his son. And he promised Balbar a child every day if the god destroyed his enemy. Two days later, the Aegilien fleet sank in a terrible storm. Our coast is a desert. With no more food or water, Dandalus had to abandon the siege completely. Without ships, he was forced to move west along the coast. Only one man in a hundred of those who'd left the Aegilien Islands ever went home again. No record of what became of King Dandalus is to be found anywhere. The Balbar priesthood claims their god went in person and fetched Dandalus and ate him. Since that time, no one has tried to conquer Iskendria again. But the city bleeds for what it has won, for Balbar eats its children. The royal family is gone. Today, the city is ruled by Balbar's priests and the merchants. Iskendria is a very generous city. It has accepted legions of outsiders inside its walls, but woe betide any who break the laws of Iskendria. They know only one kind of punishment here. Mutilation, to death."

Farodin wanted to get back out of this city of child-murderers immediately. He even caught himself imagining throwing the shaven-headed priests down the statue's fiery gullet.

"We will take your advice to heart," said Nuramon gravely. "Can you tell us of a good guesthouse?"

Zimon grinned. "The brother-in-law of a friend of mine has a place at the harbor. He even has a stable for the horses. I'd be happy to take you there."

THE SECRET LIBRARY

Water," gasped the man in the iron cage. He was the last one still alive. Seven large cages hung at the east end of the horse market. One of the many death sentences of Iskendria was to lock the condemned in these cages and let them die of thirst in public.

Mandred felt for his flask.

"Don't think about it for a second," hissed Farodin, nodding toward the temple guardsmen standing in the shadows of the colonnade. It was too dark to say how many there were. "He may be hanging there for good reason."

The condemned man had one arm stretched out of the cage and was waving desperately in their direction. Mandred was glad it was dark, because it meant he could not see the man very well. His memory turned to the march through the desert, how he had damn near died of thirst himself. Spontaneously, he untied the flask and tossed it up to the prisoner.

A shout rang out from the end of the square. Mandred did not understand a word. In the two weeks they'd been in the city, he'd learned no more than the most necessary words, the ones you needed to survive there: *water, bread, yes, no,* and *let's make love.*

Two guards stepped out from between the columns.

Farodin and Nuramon took off at a run. Mandred took a final look at the prisoner, who drank greedily in deep swallows. It was one thing to lop the head off a criminal, but hanging them up like that for days under Iskendria's murderous sun, to finally die in agony . . . that was just low. No one deserved to die like that.

Mandred hurried after the elves. Farodin and Nuramon moved soundlessly and had disappeared down a dark alley some distance ahead of him. The jarl felt good. He'd done the right thing.

Behind him, a horn sounded. Close by, a second horn replied. And then a third blared in the direction they were running. Mandred cursed. The guards were encircling them. Someone behind him barked an order.

Before Mandred turned down the alley after the elves, he heard the sound of soldiers' hobnailed sandals not far away.

"This way." Farodin stepped out of the shadows of a doorway and pulled him into a narrow hallway inside a building. It reeked of fish and damp washing. Somewhere overhead, a couple was arguing loudly. A child began to cry.

The hallway made a sharp turn to the left and ended at a courtyard. Nuramon was standing there beside a well, and he waved to them. "Here it is."

Mandred had been completely unable to keep his bearings in Iskendria. The night before, after an unsuccessful search, they had climbed out of a well somewhere in the city. They had been scouring the city's catacombs night after night for two weeks, trying to find an Albenstar that would transport them safely to the library the djinn had spoken of.

In that time, Mandred had begun to suspect that his two companions hadn't truly mastered the gate spell. They had tried to explain the problem to him. Apparently, to open a gate, one had to be standing right on top of a star. But here, the stars lay buried beneath the rubble of centuries. The Albenkin still seemed to make use of the legendary library, though, which meant that somewhere in that labyrinth of tunnels, sepulchers, and drains, there had to be a hidden entry point to an Albenstar. It was this hidden access that they had spent every night searching for.

Iskendria had been established at an extraordinary location. It was not just the meeting point of roads and waterways. More than thirty Albenpaths also crisscrossed the city, though they did not follow the crooked alleys, running instead through walls and rocks.

Nuramon had slung a rope attached to a grappling hook down the inside of the well and was already climbing down. Farodin followed him. The elves were talented climbers. Mandred, though, hated hanging on ropes just as he hated crawling around underground like a rat.

A shout rang out at the courtyard entrance. Guards. Mandred took hold of the rope and lowered himself into the dark shaft. The raw hemp rope burned his hands. As he felt for the opening in the well wall with his feet, faces appeared at the edge of the well overhead.

Angry, Mandred looked up. He wanted to throw a curse or an insult back up at their pursuers, those butchers from the temple. Running away like this chafed at him. But his command of the language was too minimal, and he had nothing to say. Nothing, except . . . he grinned broadly and leaned far out into the well shaft so that they could see him. "Let's make love!" he bellowed up at them. He stretched his balled fist in the guards' direction and laughed spitefully. One of the soldiers hurled his spear down the well. Mandred hastily ducked it and retreated into the tunnel. The two elves, meanwhile, had lit three lanterns.

"What has gotten into you?" Farodin snapped at him.

"It was just something to say . . ."

"I'm talking about what happened at the horse market. Are you so sick of living? We had an agreement. You do nothing that might attract attention, remember?"

"You wouldn't understand."

"Damn right," said Farodin in an icy tone. "I can't understand. What you did was pointless. Do you think you saved the life of the man in the cage? No. His agony will just last an extra day or two, that's all. I simply don't understand you."

Mandred did not reply. What was he supposed to say? The two elves could never understand it. How were they supposed to? What he'd done was idiotic; he was well aware of that. When it came down to it, it helped nobody. And yet he would do it again.

Gritting his teeth, he followed the elves. They clambered over piles of rubble, waded through flooded tunnels, and felt their way through subterranean halls, their ceilings propped up with pillars, their walls painted with hideous demons. Again and again, they stumbled across images of Balbar, flames spewing from his maw.

It was mostly Nuramon who took the lead down there. Apparently, he was the more talented when it came to following the Albenpaths. For Mandred, though, paths that could not be seen were just eerie. No doubt there were other secret markings down there that showed which way to go. But the moment you tried to follow the Albenpaths, again and again you ended up facing a wall or a collapsed tunnel. Like now. They found themselves in a narrow chamber with walls of dark-red sandstone. On the wall opposite was a round entrance stone, an entry to a burial vault, that reminded Mandred of a millstone. Two wavy lines had been chiseled across the center of the stone.

"It goes on that way," said Nuramon with certainty, pointing at the stone. The two elves turned and looked at Mandred.

Of course. If it takes brute force to solve a problem, then I'm good enough for them, thought Mandred peevishly. He put down his lantern and stepped up to the entrance stone. It was set into grooves in the floor and ceiling to prevent it from falling.

Mandred pushed with all his strength and was surprised at how easily the stone could be rolled aside. An intense odor of dust, spices, and incense hit them.

Mandred exhaled deeply. He knew the smell. It was the smell of the sepulchers beneath the city . . . down where some form of magic stopped the bodies of the dead from rotting and they dehydrated instead. Graves like this frightened Mandred. When the dead did not rot as they ought, then perhaps they also did other things that the dead should not.

Without hesitation, the two elves entered the chamber. They held their lanterns high, lighting up the tomb. It was three paces wide, perhaps five deep. Long recesses had been carved into the walls, and the dead lay inside them as if on stone beds.

Mandred's stomach tightened as he looked around. The faces of the dead were brown and sunken, their lips pulled far back so that it looked as if they were grinning. Mandred glanced back toward the stone at the entrance. He would not have been surprised to see it roll back into place, as if pushed by some ghostly hand, and for the dead to rise the moment they were sealed inside. He eyed the corpses furtively. No doubt about it, they were grinning at him with malice. From the look of things, they had every reason to be in a bad mood. Someone else had been in this crypt before Mandred and his companions. The shrouds of the dead were in tatters. One of them had even had a hand torn off. Grave robbers.

This seemed not to concern the elves in the slightest. They shone their lanterns into the recesses and searched for secret doors, even though they most likely had hit another dead end.

Mandred uttered a silent prayer to Luth. One of the dead moved its head. The jarl hadn't actually seen it move, but he was certain the corpse had been facing the door moments before and not looking at him.

Cautiously, he backed away a short distance. The wall opposite the door seemed the safest place. There were no grave recesses there, and the stones seemed weathered. Something had been scratched into one of them, a circle with two wavy lines. "Shouldn't we get out of here?"

"Soon," Nuramon replied, bending over the dead man that was staring at Mandred. Did his companion really notice nothing?

"Careful." Mandred pulled him back.

Nuramon pulled free of Mandred's grasp. "The dead can't hurt anybody. Control your fear," he said. He spoke to Mandred as he would to a child, then he leaned into the recess again, even taking hold of the body to push it aside a little. "There's something here."

Mandred felt as if his heart were about to jump from his chest. The things they were doing. You never tamper with the dead.

"There's less dust here, and a hidden lever . . . ," Nuramon said.

A soft creaking sounded from the entrance to the sepulcher. Mandred leaped for the entrance, just a few paces away, but he was already too late. The round stone had rolled back in front of the entrance. In blind panic, he dropped the lantern; the glass shattered on the stone floor. The warrior had his axe in his hand. He knew that the dead would rise up at any moment. Slowly, looking left and right protectively, he moved backward. The elves did nothing. In their arrogance, they must have thought him crazy, though they were obviously keeping well clear of his axe. Did they not comprehend the danger they were in?

Mandred retreated farther. Only when he again stood with his back to the blank wall would he feel halfway certain that nothing could take him by surprise.

Nuramon cautiously raised one hand. "Mandred . . ."

The jarl took another step back. Around him, everything blurred, like a reflection in water when a stone is tossed in. The light from the elves' lanterns dimmed. Something under Mandred's feet cracked and broke. The room seemed to grow larger. Where was the wall? Why hadn't he bumped against it yet? The elves were staring like cows.

Mandred glanced at the floor. Bones, he saw. And gold. Armbands, rings, pressed metal ornaments of the kind sewn onto festive clothing. But there had been no bones and no gold a moment earlier. What was going on here?

Suddenly, the floor began to shake. Something was coming toward him. Mandred turned and saw Balbar, the god of the city. He was a giant, as tall as two men, maybe taller. The square-cut beard, the face a mask of rage—there could be no doubt, it was truly the god of the city. A god made entirely of stone.

Mandred raised his axe. Nothing around him made sense anymore. He was standing in a high-ceilinged tunnel now, dimly lit by barinstones.

Balbar's right hand shot out. Mandred was hauled into the air. He thrashed with his hands and feet, as helpless as a child. Balbar's left hand closed around Mandred's neck and his right held Mandred's feet. The god of Iskendria bent him like a willow branch. The jarl screamed. It felt like his muscles were being torn from his bones. He fought Balbar's stony grip with all his strength. The stone colossus seemed set to snap his spine like a twig and overcame all of Mandred's resistance effortlessly.

"Liuvar!" yelled Farodin.

The god instantly froze.

Farodin shouted something else that Mandred did not understand, and the god set Mandred down on the floor. Groaning, he crawled off to the nearest wall. All around lay shattered bones. The other intruders had been less lucky than he.

"A gallabaal. Practically none of the Albenkin have ever seen one. A stone guard. Great magic is needed to create such a being."

Mandred rubbed at his aching back. He for one would have been happy never to have laid eyes on the thing. "Naida's tits, how did you stop it?"

"That was no skill. It was enough to say the elven word for *peace*. Are you all right?" Farodin asked.

Stupid question, thought Mandred. With a deep sigh, he pushed himself to his feet. He felt as if a herd of horses had stampeded over the top of him. "Never felt better." He eyed the stone giant doubtfully. "And that thing is out of action?"

"It will wake again when the next stranger enters."

Mandred spat on the statue's feet. "You miserable hunk of rock. Count yourself lucky you took me by surprise." The jarl slapped the flat of his axe on the palm of his hand. "I would have chopped you into cobblestones."

With a jerk, the giant returned to life.

"Liuvar!" Farodin shouted again. "Liuvar."

Then Nuramon appeared. "Masterful sorcery. A perfect illusion. You have to actually touch the wall at the back of the tomb to notice it at all, it looks so real. It's like what the elves of Valemas did to hide the border to nothingness. Really—" Nuramon stopped in his tracks when he saw the stone guard. He looked it over appreciatively. "A gallabaal. I'd always thought such stone guards were just fanciful." Without giving it another glance, he pointed down the hallway. "Down there we'll find a major Albenstar. I sense its power."

Their path led them along a high tunnel with a dull light glowing at the far end. It was unmistakable that these rooms had not been fashioned by human hands. The masonry here was seamless. The only decoration on the walls was a floral pattern, its colors as bright as if the artist had only just completed his work.

Finally, they entered a wide, perfectly round domed hall. Dimly glowing barinstones had been cemented into the walls, bathing the room in an even light that allowed no shadows. The floor was a mosaic, a black circle on a white field, and in the center of the circle were two golden, snaking lines, like the ones he'd noticed earlier. Mandred smiled quietly to himself, but did not crow about his triumph. There had been signs pointing the way here after all. He had not been mistaken. And he knew that the two elves, just then, also realized that he had understood the nature of this labyrinth better than they had.

"Six paths cross here," said Nuramon matter-of-factly. "It is almost a major Albenstar. I'm certain this will lead us to the library." The elf stepped into the middle of the circle, between the wavy lines. He kneeled and touched the floor with the palm of his hand. Focusing, he closed his eyes and became motionless.

It seemed an eternity to Mandred before the elf looked up again. His forehead was beaded with sweat. "There are two special lines of force," he said. "I don't know which of them I have to use to open the gate. I don't understand it. This gate is somehow . . . different. The sixth line . . . it feels somehow younger. As if someone has drawn a new line of force."

"Then it has to be the older one that opens the gate," Farodin said calmly. "What's so hard about that?"

"It's . . ." Nuramon ran his tongue over his lips. "There's something there that the faun oak did not tell us about. The new line seems to be affecting the older structure of the Albenstar. The patterns are distorted . . . or maybe it would be better to say that they have been shifted into a different harmony."

Mandred understood nothing of what they were saying. *They should just do something*, he thought.

Now both elves were crouching in the circle and pressing their hands to the floor. It looked like they were feeling the pulse of something invisible. Or did the world itself perhaps have a pulse? Mandred shook his head. What a nonsensical thought. How could rock and earth have a pulse? Now he was starting to think like these crazy elves. Maybe it would be enough to whack a hole in the floor with his axe, and they could climb down into the Shattered World.

Radiant as polished gold, a gate opened. It looked like a flat disk of light. It stood in the center of the circle and stretched from the floor to just beneath the cupola of the ceiling. Mandred took a few steps to one side. From there, the disk looked as thin as a hair.

"Let's go," said Farodin. His voice was strained. But before Mandred could ask him what was worrying him, the elf had disappeared into the golden light.

"Something wrong?" Mandred turned to Nuramon.

"It's the new line of force. It supports the gate spell, but it also changes it, and we can't tell whether it is simply strengthening it or somehow manipulating it. Maybe you should stay here. Honestly, we are not sure at all that this gate leads to the library."

Mandred thought of the temple guards and the punishment Iskendria meted out to those who broke its laws. He would rather disappear into an unknown world with perhaps no chance of coming back than be chained up in the horse market for the stray dogs to eat, his arms and legs smashed.

"It goes against my grain to abandon my friends," he said solemnly. It sounded better than talking about the dogs.

Nuramon seemed abashed. "Sometimes I feel as if we are not worthy to ride with you," he said quietly. Then he reached out his hand to Mandred, as he once had years before, in the ice cave.

The jarl was not easy with the idea of holding hands with another man, but he knew it meant a great deal to Nuramon. Together, they stepped through the gate.

Mandred felt an icy draft against his cheeks. The gate opened above an abyss. He instinctively stepped back and gripped Nuramon's hand tighter. Beside them, Farodin floated in nothingness.

"Glass," the elf said calmly. "We're standing on a thick sheet of glass."

Mandred let go of Nuramon's hand. He bit his lip, annoyed at himself. Of course. He could feel that he was standing on something, but there was nothing beneath his feet to actually see. How was it possible to produce glass so ingeniously that it stayed invisible, yet could carry the weight of a human and two elves?

They were standing above a wide circular shaft that faded into a somber light in the distance beneath them. Mandred guessed it was at least a hundred paces deep. There was something fearsome about looking down into the immense pit, so much so that he was close to grasping Nuramon's hand again. What kind of madman would dream up something like this? To stand over a chasm as if you were floating.

This place reminded Mandred of the inside of an enormous circular tower, except that the mad builder had forgotten to put in any floors. Around the inner wall, a ramp spiraled gently down into the depths. Down below, it looked as if the walls drew closer together. Mandred was ashamed of his fear of this abyss. On stiff legs, he fixed his gaze on the wall and marched across the glass plate. *Just don't look down*, he thought the whole time, hoping that his companions hadn't noticed anything. He let out a sigh of relief when he reached the ramp and there was something beneath his feet he could not see through. He leaned against the wall and looked up to the domed ceiling that stretched above their heads. It showed a black circle cut by two wavy lines. This time, Mandred felt no triumph.

In silence, he and his companions made their way down the ramp. It was unnervingly narrow, and Mandred stayed close to the wall. There wasn't even a railing to hang on to. Did the Albenkin have no fear of heights at all? No fear of the unsettling wish to simply let oneself tumble into the chasm, as if summoned from below by a voice whose temptations you could scarcely resist?

Trying not to think about the abyss, Mandred looked at the pictures that decorated the wall on his left. They showed figures girdled by gleaming light, striding through forests or crossing wind-tossed waters in slim boats. The pictures told a story without words, and looking at them calmed Mandred's churning thoughts. But then the harmony of the images was broken. Other figures appeared, creatures that looked like humans but for the animal heads atop their shoulders.

Suddenly, the two elves stopped short. The unknown artist had painted the manboar. It had been defeated by one of the figures of light, its foot on the beast's neck. The monster was painted as truly as if the scene had occurred before the artist's own eyes. Even the blue of its eyes was accurate. But the figure of light had no face. The section of plaster where the face had been was broken away. Until then, Mandred had seen no damage anywhere to the murals on the wall. Time had passed by these works of art without leaving its mark.

The jarl felt the fine hairs on his neck rise. Something was not right here. Why had they encountered no one? If this was the library, why were there no books? And why did the only damage visible on any of the paintings erase the face of the warrior who had once defeated the manboar? Could it really just be a coincidence?

Farodin's right hand rested on the pommel of his sword. He looked ahead down the spiraling ramp.

"There's a portal down there," said the elf quietly. "We would do well to be as silent as possible." He looked at Mandred. "Who knows what's waiting for us here."

"So are we in the library you've been looking for?"

Farodin shrugged and went ahead. "Wherever we are, we're no longer in your world, mortal."

As quietly as he could, Mandred followed the elves. It took quite a long time for them to reach the portal.

The murals now depicted bloody battles between the figures of light and the men and women with animal heads. The manboar's likeness did not appear again. Whatever its fate, it played no role in the later battles.

The portal at the end of the spiral path was more than four paces high. Beyond it lay a long, narrow corridor, its walls clad in polished granite. It had to be at least twenty paces up to the ceiling. Strange rungs had been attached up there, as if one were supposed to swing along beneath the ceiling. Large barinstones glowed between these rungs at regular distances. The walls themselves were completely covered with columns of tiny characters. Who could read something like that? Mandred tilted his head back. And how could anyone read what was written higher up?

Some distance ahead, a seat upholstered in leather hung from four iron chains. The way it was hanging reminded Mandred of the cradle he had built so long ago. It had hung from the center beam of the long-house on four strong ropes. The jarl felt a knot in his throat. The past was the past. It was foolish to dwell on such things.

They had gone some twenty steps down the corridor when, on the left, another high corridor with inscribed walls branched off. The main corridor disappeared in the distance. At regular intervals, more seats were suspended from the ceiling.

The elves decided to continue straight ahead. It made no difference to Mandred which way they went, as long as it didn't lead them over another abyss.

They had passed by three more side corridors when Farodin raised his hand in warning. The elf drew his sword and pressed against the wall. A short distance ahead was another junction. Mandred lifted his axe to his chest. Then he heard it. Hoofbeats. Instantly, he thought of the painting of the manboar. The beast had cloven hooves.

Mandred felt his fingers growing moist. He waited for the taunting voice of the manboar to appear in his thoughts. Instead, he heard the clink of chains. The hoofbeats fell silent. Something squeaked softly. Then a voice mumbled something and let out a deep sigh.

Mandred could not bear the tension any longer. With a wild battle cry, he stormed around the corner—and cannoned into a centaur suspended from the ceiling. The centaur screamed in surprise and lashed out wildly with its hooves. One hit Mandred in the chest and knocked him off his feet. In the meantime, his companions had appeared and now looked on in stunned silence. Then Nuramon broke out in a loud laugh. Even Farodin smiled.

In front of them hung a white centaur wearing two harnesses that were fastened with chains to the ceiling. With the aid of a crank handle and a block and tackle, he could raise and lower himself in front of the wall.

"Your behavior betrays a poor upbringing, gentlemen," the centaur said, speaking the Dailish tongue. Mandred had no difficulty understanding him, although the words sounded strangely stilted. "In the circles I move in, it is customary to apologize when someone, in his impetuosity, has rammed his head into another's"—the centaur cleared his throat in embarrassment—"hindquarters. But as you are clearly not conversant with simplest rules of such etiquette, and despite your sudden appearance, I will take the lead and introduce myself. My name is Chiron of Alkardien, erstwhile tutor to the King of Tanthalia."

Mandred scrambled to his feet. The two elves, meanwhile, had recovered and introduced themselves in return.

The centaur turned the squeaky crank attached to the block and tackle and lowered himself to the floor. He skillfully extricated himself from the two heavy belts. Mandred had never seen a centaur like this one before. A thin band of red silk around Chiron's head held back his long white hair. His face was lined with deep folds, and a magnificent white beard billowed against his chest. His skin was uncommonly pale. But most unusual of all were his eyes, which were the color of freshly spilled blood.

"Sorry," Mandred finally managed to say.

The centaur wore a quiver over his shoulder; it contained a number of scrolls. In a holder on his leather belt were three styluses and an inkwell. He was obviously unarmed and therefore seemed quite harmless. *On the other hand, he has those red eyes*, thought Mandred. *You should never carelessly put your trust in creatures with red eyes.*

He introduced himself. "Mandred Torgridson, Jarl of Firnstayn."

The centaur tilted his head and looked from one to the other. "You're new here, am I right? And my guess is that you did not come here with the assistance of Sem-la."

Mandred looked to his companions. They seemed to understand as little of what the centaur was talking about as he did.

Chiron let out a sigh that sounded to Mandred more like a snort. "All right. Then I will first take you to Master Gengalos. He is the keeper of knowledge responsible for this section of the library." He turned. "If you would care to follow me . . ." He gave a little cough. "And would one or the other of the honored elves perhaps explain to the human that it is impolite to stare at the hindquarters of a centaur?"

What a stuck-up windbag, thought Mandred. He was about to give the centaur an appropriate response when a warning glance from Farodin made him hold his tongue. Mandred followed the others, keeping his distance. One more remark from Chiron and he'd stuff the handle of his axe up the centaur's ass.

Chiron led them out of the labyrinth of granite walls and into a spacious room. Thousands of round clay tablets lay on wooden shelves set in close-spaced rows. Mandred briefly looked at a few of them and shook his head. The tablets looked like chickens had scratched their way across them. Who could read this stuff? Just looking at them gave Mandred a headache.

"Tell your human he should put those tablets back at once," the centaur snapped at the two elves.

Defiantly, Mandred picked up another one.

"Take the tablets away from the idiot," Chiron cursed. "Those are dream rings from sunken Tildanas. They record the memories of whoever takes them in his hand and looks at them, and every recorded memory is forever erased from the mind. Let this childish fool look at them for a while, and he won't even remember who he is anymore."

"Is story time nearly over?" Mandred asked. "Maybe you can scare children with your tall tales, Redeye, but not me."

The centaur's tail twitched in affront. "If the human knows better . . ." Without turning back to Mandred again, he walked on.

"Better put those back," said Nuramon. "What if he's right? What if you could no longer remember Alfadas or Freya?"

"That nag doesn't scare me," replied Mandred indignantly. Then he put the tablets back onto their shelf. The scrawls on them seemed more dense now. Mandred swallowed. Could that broomtail have been telling the truth? He would not let anything show. "Anyway, why should I look at them if I can't even read what's on them?" he said, but the tone of his voice did not sound nearly as relaxed as he wanted it to. "Don't get me wrong, Nuramon, but I don't believe a word that red-eyed mare says."

"Of course not," said Nuramon, stifling a smile.

Mandred and Nuramon hurried to catch up with Chiron and Farodin. The centaur was talking enthusiastically about the library. It seemed that all of the knowledge of the Albenkin was gathered there. "We even have two scribes who work in the library at the harbor in Iskendria. As a rule, what humans write isn't worth the parchment it's written on, but for the sake of completeness, we collect those writings as well. Having said that, they compose only a tiny fraction of our collection."

Mandred hated the preening braggart. "Do you have the seventeen songs of Luth?" he asked loudly.

"If they are of any importance, then someone will certainly have made the effort to write them down. Master Gengalos will know that. Personally, I am interested in perfect forms of the epic, not verses recited by slurring bards in smelly chambers."

Chiron had led them to a second ramp that led downward in wide spirals. Mandred imagined himself pushing the priggish centaur into the depths. Whatever the half horse said, if they didn't have the seventeen songs of Luth, then this whole place wasn't worth the dirt it was dug from. Every child in the Fjordlands knew those songs.

Meanwhile, Chiron continued with his account of the library. Apparently, there were more than a hundred visitors in attendance at that moment, although in their long march so far, Mandred had seen no one apart from the centaur.

The centaur led them on through corridors and halls, and after a while, even Mandred began to feel intimidated by the sheer quantity of knowledge stored there. He could not begin to imagine what the writers could fill so many scrolls, books, clay tablets, and inscribed walls with. Was it all the same stuff, just in different words? Were these books like the women who met at the stream to wash clothes and chattered over and over about the same trivialities without ever getting bored? If everything in this library were really important and worth knowing, then any normal human would despair. Ten lifetimes would not be enough to read everything recorded there. Maybe not even a hundred. It was as if people could never truly comprehend the world because its sheer variety was past all understanding. There was something liberating about that thought. Seen like that, it made no difference if you'd read one book or a hundred or a thousand—or none at all, like Mandred. You would not understand the world any better.

Gradually, they began to pass through sections of the library where they also saw visitors. Kobolds, individual elves, a faun. Mandred noticed a strange creature with the body of a bull and the torso of a human, with wings that grew from its flanks. Then he saw a female elf talking excitedly to a unicorn, and a moment later, he spied a gnome climbing a shelf, a basket full of books on his back. The other visitors paid no attention to them as they passed. Two elves, a human, and a centaur . . . a party like that seemed less than spectacular here.

Finally, Chiron led them into a hall with colorfully painted ribbed vaults. The hall contained a large number of lecterns, but there was only one reader in attendance, a slender figure wearing a sand-colored cowl. The hood was pulled low over the face, and the book before the figure had purple pages with writing in gold ink. Oddly, beside the lectern stood a number of small baskets of withered leaves. A strange odor hung in the air, something at once oppressive and familiar. It smelled like dust and parchment. Mandred could even discern the smell of the leaves. But there was something else . . . more a slight trace than a fact.

Chiron quietly cleared his throat. "Master Gengalos? Please excuse me if I am disturbing you, but three visitors entered the library through the gate above the Alben gallery. They strayed into the granite corridors. And that one tried to kill me with an axe." The centaur looked disparagingly at Mandred. "I thought it wise to bring them to you, Master, before they did any real damage."

The figure in the cowl raised his head, but the hood still fell low over his face, which lay in shadow. Mandred, for a moment, was tempted to throw back the master's hood with a deft movement. He was used to seeing whom he spoke to.

"You have done well, Chiron. I thank you." Gengalos's voice sounded warm and friendly, a dramatic contrast to the remoteness he otherwise emanated. "I will now relieve you of the burden of care for these newcomers."

Chiron briefly bowed his head, then retreated.

"We would like—" began Farodin, but Gengalos cut him off with an abrupt gesture.

"There is no 'we would like' here," responded the hooded figure. "Anyone entering the library must first serve the library. Only then can you receive any of its knowledge in return."

"Our apologies." Nuramon had adopted a diplomatic tone, and he bowed before the keeper of knowledge. "We are—"

"Who you are does not interest me," said Gengalos with a dismissive gesture. "Whoever comes here submits to the laws of the library. Do so, or leave." He paused for a moment as if to underscore his harsh response. "If you would like to stay, then you will first render your services to the library." He pointed to the baskets that stood beside his lectern. "These are poems written by flower faeries on oak leaves and birch bark. Even after centuries, we have found no satisfactory way to preserve the leaves, so the poems have to be transcribed. But it needs to be kept in mind that the text and the veins in the leaves form a single harmonious whole, and this needs to be maintained in the transcription if the poems' deeper levels of significance are not to be lost."

Mandred recalled the boisterous little faery creatures he had seen in Albenmark. He could not imagine how those little chatterboxes could write anything worth preserving.

Gengalos turned in his direction. "Appearances are deceiving, Mandred Torgridson. Few are as able as they when it comes to putting fragile feelings into words."

The jarl swallowed. "You . . . can see into my head?"

"I need to know what brings our visitors to the library. Knowledge is a valuable thing, Mandred Torgridson. One cannot hand it over to just anyone."

"What is our task?" asked Farodin.

"You and Nuramon will take one of these baskets and transcribe the poems onto parchment. When I am satisfied with your work, then I will help you in your search. This library holds the answer to practically any question that can be asked, if you know where to look."

"What about me?" Mandred asked, abashed. "With what can I earn the right to be here?"

"You will relate the story of your life to a scribe. Every detail. I have the impression that yours is a story worthy of being put down in writing."

The jarl looked at the floor, feeling slightly foolish. "That's . . . someone is supposed to write down my life?" He had a bad feeling about that, almost as if someone wanted to snatch something away from him.

"Would you not like to grasp at least the tail end of immortality, Mandred Torgridson? Your story will be read when you yourself have long turned to dust. You have no need to hide your light under a bushel. Who has ever heard of two elves like Farodin and Nuramon choosing a human like yourself as their companion?"

Mandred nodded hesitantly. He still had the feeling that he would be parting with something valuable if he told his life story. But was that just superstitious fear? He should not stand in the way of his companions. They had taken so much onto their shoulders to make it this far. "Fair trade," he said. "I agree."

"Splendid, mortal. I thank you for your bequest to the library." Gengalos's words gave Mandred a pleasant feeling. Like brandy warming him on a winter night from the inside. "I will show you your quarters. The library is as big as a small city. A city of learning, built of books. There are three kitchens that operate day and night, and two large refectories. We even have thermal baths in one of our more remote wings." He turned again to Mandred. "And we have a very well-stocked wine cellar. A number of the keepers of knowledge, myself included, put little store in asceticism. How can the spirit soar freely if we keep our bodies in chains? This way, all who study here are well catered for."

ON YULIVEE'S TRAIL

Nuramon was still finding it hard to believe that the djinn in Valemas had actually been telling the truth. Though his desire to find Noroelle meant he would readily follow up the clue, he had secretly doubted the spirit's word. But it seemed he had done well to tell his companions about Iskendria.

They had been in the library for nine days, and he and Farodin had spent five of those transcribing the poems of the flower faeries. Since then, they had been searching for any records they could find concerning the magical barriers. It was exciting rummaging through the vast store of learning in those halls. And even for Mandred, the days they spent there were far from dull. He spent his time exploring the library and enjoying the sumptuous meals provided for them in their quarters. The wine cellar quickly became his favorite place. Of all the knowledge gathered there, Mandred was interested only in the Aegilien and Angnosian sagas. To Nuramon's surprise, he had a centaur read the stories to him in Dailish. Compared with Elvish, Dailish was easy to learn, but Mandred had picked it up in the course of a single winter from the two centaurs at Emerelle's court—quite an achievement for a human. The jarl enjoyed the sagas of Eras the Pandrid and Nessos the Telaid so much that Nuramon had jokingly named him Mandred the Torgrid and said that he foresaw a prodigious future for the Mandridian family line.

Farodin had shut himself away in a study room. The keepers of knowledge had assigned a young elf named Elelalem, whom everybody called, simply, Ele, as his assistant. Farodin sent the poor fellow hunting through the entire library for texts. Because Ele spoke all of the languages needed in the library, he often served as Farodin's translator as well. Farodin wanted to learn more about the gate spell, but he was also searching for any accounts of magical barriers and wanted to find out more about the grains of sand.

Nuramon still did not believe that the grains of sand could be the solution. It was true that Farodin had collected a few dozen grains, but there had to be other possibilities. Instead of sticking to their familiar paths here in this house of learning, Nuramon kept watch for fresh chances. He had just come from the horses, which he had fetched from the stable at their guesthouse and now kept with an elven woman who lived unrecognized among the humans. In the city, she was known as the widow of a well-to-do trader and one of Iskendria's richest women. To avoid being recognized as an elf by the humans, she kept her ears and face hidden behind a veil and revealed herself only among other Albenkin. Her name was Sem-la. Nuramon wondered how, over the years, she managed to hide the fact that she did not age. The veil might work for the course of a single human lifetime, but what then? Did a niece appear from some distant city to inherit all her wealth?

From Sem-la's estate, a wide corridor ran underground to a gate from where one could enter the living areas of the library. Nuramon had never before heard of elves and humans living in such close proximity. Sem-la had told him that she had contacts all over the world and that she carried on her trading activities with humans and with other Albenkin and their settlements. Then Nuramon realized for the first time that both the human world and the Shattered World, too, were not places of exile where the Albenkin went to live free from Emerelle's rule. They lived well here, even if it meant that the meals Sem-la served were human meals and not to be compared with the food in Albenmark. But anyone coming here was used to the human world.

Nuramon climbed a long stairway and finally reached the place that Gengalos had told him about. It was a narrow hall, and very high. Left and right loomed shelves packed with heavy tomes. Nuramon was surprised at that, for in Albenmark, knowledge was seldom entrusted to books. Your parents taught you what you needed to know, and the wise ones gave instruction in what was truly important. If you had a question, then you went to someone who could answer it. Nuramon silently wondered how many thousands of animals had lost their skins to provide all of the parchment in these volumes.

An old gnome stepped out of an alcove. "Don't suffer from vertigo, do you?" he croaked.

"Not at all," said Nuramon.

"Good. That saves *me* the climb. I'm not the youngest these days." The old man pressed his hands to his back. "A lifetime spent in these halls. Oh, it is not without its pains, but look how magnificent this place is."

Narrow wooden planks had been attached to the shelves and served as catwalks. High above, Nuramon could make out a figure in a white robe that seemed to be floating beside the shelves. Between the shelves, a number of large recesses opened into the walls; these were places where one could withdraw to read. Carefully positioned barinstones lent a fiery glow to the entire hall.

"What brings you here?" the old gnome inquired.

"Gengalos sent me. Somewhere here there is supposed to be a book about Yulivee," Nuramon replied.

"Ah, Master Gengalos. He has sent you to the right place. We have not only chronicles here *about* Yulivee, we also have a collection of the writings of Yulivee herself. They were a number of separate tales originally, but we bound them together to form one volume. Perhaps that would be of interest?"

Nuramon could hardly believe his luck. "No doubt. Where can I find it?"

"Go down this way to rack twenty-three, then climb up to the one hundred fifty-fourth shelf. You will find Yulivee's tales up there." The gnome stepped over to the wall of shelves. "Use the ladders to get there. You can move freely along the catwalks, and there are boards you can pull out if you want to sit and read."

Nuramon only nodded. The shelf he was looking for was probably fifty paces above where he stood. That was not a height to worry him at all. He looked up once again to the figure he had seen up there a moment earlier.

"Master Reilif," said the gnome by way of explanation.

"One of the keepers of knowledge?" asked Nuramon in a low voice.

"Yes. He often comes here and never misses the opportunity to climb up there himself. You should know that I am duty-bound to fetch any book an inquisitive visitor might wish for."

Nuramon smiled at the gnome. "But it is like you said. I don't suffer from vertigo, so you don't need to trouble yourself."

"My thanks, elf. And I'm glad it's *you* who has come here. They say there's a human at large in the library. He broke through the barriers. An uncouth type, they say, who does nothing but drink, eat, and make a mess."

"His name is Mandred. He's one of my companions."

The gnome immediately reddened.

"What is your name?" asked Nuramon, taking off his weapon belt as the oldster watched him anxiously. The gnome was obviously afraid that Nuramon was about to draw his sword.

"Builax," came his unsteady reply.

"Don't worry. I know my companions very well. So far your assessment has been quite accurate. My name is Nuramon, and I would like to give you my sword for safekeeping." He handed the weapon to Builax. The fear on the gnome's face vanished as fast as it had appeared. He placed the sword in a small nook alongside his writing implements and other belongings, then he led Nuramon along the wall of books. They stopped in front of the twenty-third rack.

"The book you are looking for is the eighth one along."

Nuramon set about the ascent via the ladders and rungs. When he reached the one hundred fifty-fourth shelf, he felt suddenly restless. This is where the book of Yulivee's writings was supposed to be—the key to reaching Noroelle. Carefully, he stepped onto the catwalk. It offered his feet a good grip and was wide enough to walk along. Nuramon let his hands glide across the backs of the books on the shelf. He pulled out the eighth book in the row. It was bound in pale-brown leather and, in its plainness, barely differed from the books left and right of it. Neither on the cover itself nor on the spine were any characters or adornment of any kind. When he opened it, he saw that the pages were also free of ornament or decoration. Even the title had not been particularly emphasized. It filled just four lines, and the text began directly beneath it. Nuramon smiled. This book was obviously deemed to be of little value. Whoever assembled it had forgone anything that might make it stand out. But for Nuramon, it was a treasure beyond price. Reverently, he read the title: *The Stories of Yulivee, Who Abandoned Albenmark, Wandered through the World of Humans, and Founded the Town of Valemas Anew in the Shattered World, Related in Her Own Words in the Presence of the Keepers of Knowledge and Recorded Here by Fjeel the Swift.*

Nuramon was holding the narrative of an elf who had left Albenmark of her own free will with those who followed her. Like Nuramon, she had been searching. And she, too, had had to decipher the magic of the Albenstars before she reached her final destination. Nuramon hoped deeply that, with Yulivee's book, he was following a trail more promising than Farodin's sandy path.

THE ACCOUNT
OF YULIVEE:

THE QUESTIONS OF THE KEEPERS
OF KNOWLEDGE

You have asked me where I learned my magic, and I will answer you. Know that in Albenmark, I was already a powerful sorceress. I had mastered the magic of light, of life, and of appearances. And all of these were to benefit me in the new oasis of Valemas. In the Shattered World, we found a desert land like our homeland. There I created an expanse of sky, a lake, an illusion of distance, and much more besides.

When I left Albenmark, I led my companions through a stable gate. At that time, I knew little of the paths and the stars of the Alben. But travel is the best teacher, and I was an attentive student. As foreign as the human world may be, there are many of the Albenkin there, in hidden corners—recluses, holders of old learning. We encountered other communities that had abandoned Albenmark. We talked with them, exchanged experiences. We taught them what we knew, and they taught us in return.

But from no one did I learn as much as from the oracle Dareen. She is the only oracle to have left Albenmark for the world of humans. She does not live in the Shattered World. Those who step through her gates in the human world do not leave that world; they emerge instead in a distant place, where they may listen to the wisdom of Dareen. She showed me the way and opened my spirit for me. I saw the Albenstar in the desert that would become the gate to the new Valemas. My destination stood before my eyes, and from that moment on, I searched for the way there. Dareen changed my life with a few words and images. A world opened up for me, the existence of which I had never even suspected.

You ask me where Dareen is hiding, but I can tell you no more than I already have, for I am bound by an oath.

FROM VOLUME 23/154/8, SHEET 424.A,
IN THE NARROW HALL IN THE HIDDEN LIBRARY OF ISKENDRIA

DIFFERENT PATHS

This was it. This was what Nuramon had been searching for. He had read Yulivee's tales with pleasure, but only when he reached the questions put to her by the keepers of knowledge did he find something that pointed to a direct route. Yulivee had encountered the oracle Dareen, and through the oracle, she had seen the place she was searching for. And the same could happen for them if they could find the way to reach Dareen. If the oracle received them, then they would be close to finding Noroelle.

Nuramon let out a small cry of delight. Then he heard steps and creaking on the rungs of the ladder that led past the alcove to which he had withdrawn to read.

It was Master Reilif who approached. The keeper of knowledge stepped off the ladder and joined Nuramon in the alcove. His face was half covered by a hood, and only his fingertips protruded from the sleeves of his black cape. As slim as he was, he could have been an elf. With small steps, he moved closer.

"Please excuse my outburst of joy, Master Reilif," said Nuramon. "I did not mean to upset the harmony of the library."

"There can be only one penalty for what you have done," the keeper of knowledge replied in a voice that betrayed not the slightest trace of emotion. He sat opposite Nuramon and pushed his hood back a little, revealing gray eyes that seemed to bore into Nuramon. "You must tell me what made you cry out like that."

"Gladly, Master. And perhaps you can help me," Nuramon said, willingly telling the keeper of knowledge all he had read of Yulivee's story. He finished his account saying, "But what made me so happy was finding what I have been searching for."

"And that would be?" asked Reilif patiently.

"I discovered that Yulivee had been to the oracle Dareen. Now I want to find this oracle. I have many questions . . . questions to which I am unlikely to find an answer here."

"Then you have recognized that these halls house dead knowledge. Knowledge can only be brought to life when someone takes it into themselves. Here you have heard about Dareen. Now you have to find your way to her," said Reilif.

"Yulivee did not say where the oracle was to be found."

"But I can tell you. I am a keeper of knowledge. I have read a great many books in these halls, Yulivee's among them."

Nuramon wondered why Reilif had listened to him so patiently if he already knew Yulivee's story.

"Back then, we were all curious," Reilif said. "We all wanted to know where this oracle had hidden herself away, but Yulivee did not want to tell us. She hinted at certain things that led us to suspect that the oracle must be in Angnos. We were not able to say with certainty, however. All the envoys we sent to find her returned empty-handed."

"Angnos," said Nuramon quietly. It was a kingdom he and his companions already knew. The search for Guillaume had led them there. It was an untamed land, full of adventure. "Thank you, Master Reilif."

The keeper of knowledge stood. "You will find the oracle. I am certain. Remember these words that Yulivee once spoke. 'You came to us. Your voice rang. You showed us the stars. They sparkled. We could see them.' That is what she said when we asked her whether she might be able to reveal to us something more about Dareen. Solve the puzzle of those words, if you can." With that, Reilif left the alcove and climbed back up to his shelf.

Nuramon wondered how old the keeper of knowledge was. From what he had said, Nuramon could tell that he had encountered Yulivee personally. In the books, it said that she had come to the library 1,832 years ago.

Nuramon stroked the leather binding of the book thoughtfully and finally slid it back into its place on the shelf. He glanced at Reilif one last time, but the master sat again before his bookshelf, immersed in what he was reading. Nuramon climbed back down the ladder. He turned to take a final look at the narrow hall. Of all the rooms he had seen in the library, he liked this one the most. Perhaps he would return here one day. Noroelle would certainly love this place.

Nuramon went in search of Farodin. He found him in his study room. Young Ele was in the middle of reading something aloud in Dailish. Mandred was sitting in one corner of the small room, listening to Ele read. The text was about the Aegilien Islands and the elves who sailed to sea from there. Nuramon leaned against the wall and listened to the young elf's words.

"'No end to the siege was in sight. They were not able to break through the invisible wall. The twelve sorcerers surrounded the island aboard twelve ships, and then the inhabitants of Zeolas grew afraid, for they knew that twelve powerful sorcerers could destroy the might of their magical wall, even when the splinters of the mirror had not been collected. The sorcerers raised their hands, spoke their incantations, and with a mighty roar, the enemy's wall burst asunder. In this way did Zeolas fall.'" Ele paused. "That's all that's written here."

"Thank you, Ele," said Farodin. "We will read the other texts later." Then he turned to Nuramon. "We have discovered a great deal. There are many indications that we won't need all of the grains of sand to break Emerelle's spell."

"Fate is smiling on us," Mandred added, but he showed no sign of moving from his obviously comfortable spot in the corner.

Nuramon waited until the young elf had left the room. Then he pushed himself from the wall and moved toward Farodin. "I have good news, too, something that might take us farther."

Mandred stood up. "Tell us," he said.

Nuramon related what he had stumbled across in Yulivee's book. As he repeated Master Reilif's words, he noticed that Farodin was only half listening to him. He seemed more interested in exchanging looks with Mandred, who paced restlessly back and forth. Even the mention of the oracle seemed to hardly interest the pair. When Nuramon had finished, the room fell silent.

Finally, Farodin said, "Mandred and I have found out a lot. We are holding on to the hope that we don't need all of the grains of sand to break Emerelle's spell. Once we have found enough of the grains, they will lead us to the location of Noroelle's gate. And I have discovered texts that will help me perfect my seeking spell. Why should we bother with Yulivee? She and Valemas are behind us. We have come a long way since then, and now you tell us we're supposed to turn again and try another way?"

Farodin's reaction did not take Nuramon completely by surprise. When he saw his companions' unenthusiastic looks, it was clear to him what was coming. Farodin was used to giving the orders and tolerated no answering back. "In other words," Nuramon said, "you don't like the path that I have laid out."

"I see no path," replied Farodin.

"My way has been good enough for you this far."

"What do you mean, *your* way? Until now, I have not taken a single step that I was not convinced was the right one to take. And that will continue."

"My path could be a shortcut. I will put it plainly. Your grains of sand are not the solution to this puzzle. We have to take a different road if we want to rescue Noroelle. Have you forgotten the desert? This is a world of sand. Have you been to the sea and put your head in the water? Have you seen what makes up the bottom of the ocean? I would try to find this oracle ten times over rather than wander aimlessly through the world, picking up an occasional grain of sand."

"I know," said Farodin. "Following a path to its end was never one of your strong points."

Nuramon was stunned. He understood Farodin's allusion well enough, but what could he possibly do about the fate of his own incarnations? He hadn't asked to carry their soul. He knew little about them, but one thing was certain: all had died young and none had ever seen the moonlight. In his wildest imaginings, he never would have expected Farodin to attack his feelings like this instead of convincing him with his arguments. "Have you always thought that of me and just kept it to yourself?"

"I think of you as someone who is taking a very long journey to reach the moonlight."

"What does the moonlight have to do with our search?" said Mandred now, entering the fray.

Farodin raised his hands in conciliation. "You are right, Mandred. This is not what we should be discussing here. But as far as the oracle is concerned, I am not prepared to give up a certainty for a maybe. Has it even occurred to you that this oracle very likely went into the moonlight long ago? How long has it been since Yulivee was there?"

Nuramon said nothing.

"Your silence says it all. You admit there are no answers to my questions. I say we stay on the path we have already begun to follow. Sooner or later, we will reach our goal."

"For me, a chance at sooner is better than the certainty of later. The oracle has knowledge that will help us."

"Assuming you find your oracle and get answers to your questions. What can she offer us that we can't find in these halls?"

"Look around, Farodin. For all my respect for this place, I also see that it only preserves the learnings of the past, the knowledge of those who can no longer tell it to us in their own voice. What we need is knowledge of the present and the future. We should take Yulivee as our model."

Farodin folded his arms across his chest. "Could it be that you have lost interest in Noroelle? Are you more interested in following Yulivee's footsteps now?"

Nuramon balled his hands into fists. "How blind are you? You of all people should know how foolish your accusation is. Although . . . now that I think about it, just this kind of blindness is in your nature. You only see what you want to. Isn't it obvious to you that I could have brought our courtship of Noroelle to an end years earlier?"

"*Could have* . . . two words that fill the mouths of failures," Farodin replied coolly.

"Don't you think you failed in your love of Noroelle? You put on the appearance of the perfect minnesinger, but you never understood what Noroelle was really waiting for. She wanted you to speak your love in your own words, not through songs that were written for someone else. And she wanted me to touch her with my hands, and not only my words. Why do you think it took me so long?"

Farodin's mouth twitched at one corner.

"I watched you, Farodin. And I wondered what it was about you that didn't tally. What do you keep hidden deep inside? What is it that you don't want to reveal even to the woman you think you love? Is there nothing behind all your borrowed words but an empty heart? What kind of love is it that can't be called by its own name?"

Farodin's hand slipped to the pommel of his sword. "You're standing at a threshold neither of us wants to overstep."

"Farodin, we crossed our thresholds long ago. Do you really think I would follow a man incapable of love?"

Mandred grabbed hold of Farodin by the shoulder and pulled him back. The mortal obviously thought that blood would flow any moment. "That's enough, Nuramon," he said sharply.

"It seems we've run out of things in common," said Farodin, his expression stony.

"Long ago. We've just refused to face the fact until now." Nuramon turned to face Mandred. "And you? What is your path?"

The jarl hesitated.

Nuramon thought back to the Cave of Luth, where he had sealed his friendship with Mandred. Back then, the two had been bound by many things.

"I'm sorry, Nuramon. I know how deeply I am in your debt. Yet . . . I'm not very good at putting my thoughts and feelings into pretty words. But Farodin is right. I think it is better to follow the trail of the sand. It may be a long journey, but it *will* lead us to where we want to go. I'm sorry . . . I . . ." Mandred's voice failed him.

So he was alone again. "I don't need your pity. You're the ones I feel sorry for. Go your own miserable way and look for your grains of sand. I will follow my own path."

"Don't be a fool, Nuramon," said Mandred. He gestured placatingly. "We're one boat. I'm the hull. Farodin is the helm. You're the sail that catches the wind."

"You haven't understood it yet, have you, mortal? I don't need anyone anymore to decide which way I go. The storm has torn your sail away. Now see how far you can paddle with your hands." With that, Nuramon turned and left the room.

THE LOG OF
THE GALLEY *PURPURWIND*

*T*hirty-fourth day of the voyage: We heaved to in the lee of the islands
of Iskendria and waited for Sem-la's barges. The oarsmen had some
time to recuperate. As agreed, we took on board a crate of desert glass,
a marble statue, and ten bales of fine cloth from Iskendria. But no one
told us that we were to expect passengers: an elf from Albenmark named
Farodin and a human, clearly from the Northlands, by the name of
Mandred. Sem-la paid the cost of their passage. It is clear that neither
possesses gold of his own, but they are otherwise well equipped. Their
horses alone, beasts from Albenmark, are worth a king's ransom.

Thirty-fifth day of the voyage: Slow headway north-northwest. Windless
and burning sun. The oarsmen tire quickly. The human we took on board
is surprisingly well educated. He knows a lot about the sea, and he can
row for three men. He has great strength in his arms. He would be a boon
for the Purpurwind, the more so because he speaks Dailish and could be
of use in trading with the centaurs of Gygnox. Perhaps we should try to
put in at Gygnox this trip. The human talks constantly about old sagas
he heard in Iskendria and about the Fjordlands in the North. If he knew
the seas that we have sailed.

Thirty-sixth to thirty-eighth days of the voyage: Calm seas. Crew
content. Curiosity about the human.

Thirty-ninth day of the voyage: The crew is confident. South wind,
mild weather. We are making good headway, faster than expected, and
the oarsmen can preserve their strength. Afternoon: A spectacle ahead
of us. We crossed the heading of a ship of mortals, an Aegilien galley.
An enormous sea serpent appeared. The humans did what all newlings
do: they turned tail and fled. As expected, the sea serpent chased them
and smashed their ship as if it were no more than a little fishing boat.
We took the few survivors on board.

An hour later, the sea serpent appeared again, breaching not twenty
paces to starboard. The humans we had rescued fell into a panic, and

many jumped overboard. The fools don't know that one need only steer toward a sea serpent to unnerve it. The beasts attack only those who fear them. Mandred, alone among the humans, showed no fear. He took a harpoon and hurried to the bow. He actually shouted at us to attack the serpent. When the creature eventually dived and swam off, the human was disappointed. He cursed it as it went. We all laughed, for he cursed in Dailish. He sounded almost like a centaur . . .

Forty-fifth day of the voyage: Entering shallow waters. Steered with caution through the sandbanks off the human city of Jilgas. We put the survivors of the sea serpent's attack ashore here. Before sundown, we set anchor off Gygnox. Perhaps the human can still be persuaded . . .

Fifty-first day of the voyage: Good business with the centaurs of Gygnox, thanks to Mandred. All the human lacks is the body of a centaur. He drank with them and sang crude songs. After that, they were ready to trade with us. Of note: although there is a gate to Albenmark close by Gygnox, Mandred and Farodin don't want to use it. Are they perhaps exiles?

Fifty-third day of the voyage: Weighed anchor. Calm sea, oarsmen drunk. Human on the drum. The elf from Albenmark seems unwell. He finds us somewhat too rough and ready for elves, most likely. What a little time in the human world will do to an elf. Evening: Farodin surprised I keep a log, not understanding that anyone who trades in Iskendria quickly learns the value of writing. The elf from Albenmark has asked us to change course. He speaks of something he has to collect from the bottom of the sea. It is no great detour for us, and I am curious besides, and so agree.

Fifty-fifth day of the voyage: We reach Farodin's destination after a stretch of hard rowing. Crew tired and restless, don't understand change of course. As for Farodin, the water is too deep. He is courageous, but he can't make it to the sea floor. I offer to go instead, for I have a spell of water and air, but Farodin tells me I would not be able to find what he seeks. So we dive together, and from time to time, I give him air. On the sea floor, a strange thing: he digs into the sand and gestures to me to return to the surface. On board again, he opens his hand: just sand. He searches in it for something: a single grain. Admittedly, some magic seems to cling to it . . .

Fifty-seventh day of the voyage: A storm, out of nowhere. We have to battle to get through. Finally, though, no injuries, only minor repairs, no cargo lost. A good storm . . .

Sixty-seventh day of the voyage: Coast of the city of Tilgis, in the east of Angnos. Time to bid farewell. The human and the elf from Albenmark were good reinforcements for us. I tried again to persuade them to stay, but they were not to be swayed. What a loss. I would have liked to present Farodin especially to my prince. My only consolation is the good trade I made with him. Four barinstones for four hundred Angnosian dinars . . .

Seventy-eighth day of the voyage: We reach the straits of Quilas and sail through the gate. Evening: Arrival in Reilimee. Cargo unloaded. End of the voyage. Seventy-eight days, that is a good time.

RECORDED BY THE ELF ARANAE, CAPTAIN OF THE *PURPURWIND*, IN HER LOG, IN THE YEAR 1287 AFTER THE FOUNDING OF REILIMEE

THE LOST HOMELAND

Mandred was as excited as a young man heading to the midsummer feast to dance with his girl, and then some. He let his mare feel his heels, urging her up the gently sloping hillside. It must have been three years or so since the last time he had been in Firnstayn. All his traveling had upset his sense of time, and he could not say exactly how long ago he had said good-bye to Alfadas. Had his son been elected jarl?

It was a golden fall, as it had been when Mandred left Firnstayn. The best season for fly-fishing.

With a snort, the mare reached the crest of the ridge. From here, one had a broad view over the fjord. It was still more than a mile to Firnstayn. Mandred shaded his eyes with his hand and squinted into the low sun. Below him lay a large town encircled by a solid stone wall with stout towers. Landing stages reached out into the fjord, and some twenty sizable ships were tied up there. The shore was lined with storehouses, and on the hill where Erek's longhouse had once stood was a stone castle fit for a prince.

Had he taken a wrong turn in the mountains?

Confused, Mandred turned and looked toward the cliff where the stone circle stood. That was the Hartungscliff, and below it, his village had to lie. It was no use deceiving himself.

Mandred felt as if an invisible hand were pressing on his throat. He swallowed hard. Now Farodin had reached the top of the hill as well. The elf reined in his chestnut and gazed down at the fjord in silence.

"We . . . we must have been gone quite a while," said Mandred, his voice faltering. He closed his eyes and thought of the time with Alfadas, the few years he had with his son. As if it were yesterday, he remembered them rowing out onto the fjord in Erek's boat and how Alfadas, in high spirits, had shoved him overboard, into the water. He thought of the twenty-pound salmon he had caught, bigger than any fish his son ever hooked. They had gotten drunk together, sat on the shore, baked the salmon over a fire, and eaten it with stale bread.

How old would Alfadas be now? How long did it take to turn a small village into a large town? Twenty years? Forty?

They had come here from the west, riding through the wilderness of mountains, and had not seen another human being for weeks. No one to sit with at a fire and to tell them the latest news or old stories. With that, he might have been prepared. Mandred chewed at his bottom lip and tried desperately to master the emotions that threatened to overwhelm him. The elves had told him about the danger of traveling through the gates. After his experience in the ice cave, he should have known.

But back then, they had been sent through time by the Devanthar's evil spell. Farodin and Nuramon had learned how to control the gates. How could this have happened?

Driven by his own disquiet, he spurred his mare down the hill. He had to get to Alfadas. What would his son look like now? Did he have children of his own? Maybe even grandchildren?

They passed through the heavily fortified city gate, and the guards did not stop them. It must have been market day. The streets were full of people, and all around, stalls had been set up against the buildings. A wonderful smell of apples hung in the air. Mandred dismounted and led his mare by the reins. He peered at the faces of all who came toward him, looking for familiar lines.

Even the clothes the people wore had changed in the time he'd been away. Almost everyone he saw was dressed in fine cloth. A holiday mood prevailed. Firnstayn had grown rich, but Mandred could not orient himself. No house he knew still stood.

Finally, he could no longer take the uncertainty. He stopped a gray-haired man who wore a white shirt colorfully embroidered at the shoulders. A heavy neckband with silver horseheads at the ends showed him to be a man of some importance.

"Where do I find Jarl Alfadas?" asked Mandred excitedly. "What's happened to this place?"

The old man's brow creased. He narrowed his blue eyes a little, obviously trying to work out what kind of rogue was firing questions at him. "Jarl Alfadas? I know no jarl by that name."

"Who's in charge of this town?"

"You're not from these parts, are you, warrior? Have you never heard of King Njauldred Bladebreaker?"

"King?" Mandred nearly choked. "A king rules in Firnstayn?"

"Now you're poking fun," the old man grumbled angrily. He turned to walk on, but Mandred held him back by the sleeve.

"Look at me. Have you seen me before?" Mandred waggled his head, causing his thin braids to whip his face. "I am Mandred Torgridson, and I am here to find my son, Alfadas."

Around them, people had come to a stop. Several men rested their hands on their swords, ready to intervene if the foreigner continued harassing the old man, who had suddenly turned deathly pale. He could not have looked more frightened if he'd been face-to-face with a ghost. "Mandred Torgridson," he repeated, his voice flat.

The name was taken up by the crowd standing around and, like a wildfire, was passed though the press of people. Soon, the name was on everyone's lips.

"Then you must be here for the wounded elf woman," the old man finally forced himself to say. "She lies in the king's longhouse. He brought in healers and witches from near and far . . ."

"I'm here for Alfadas, my—"

Farodin laid a calming hand on his shoulder. "Which elf do you mean?"

"Hunters found her in the Larn Pass. She was more dead than alive. They brought her here to the royal halls because no one knew how to help her." The old man closed his eyes. Suddenly, he reached out with one hand and touched Farodin's cheek. "You are . . . I mean, my lord, you . . . you are also . . ."

"Where can we find the king's hall?" Farodin asked politely but firmly.

The old man led them personally through the town. Somewhere in the crowd, someone shouted, "Jarl Mandred has returned!" At that, the crowd grew, and the jostling on all sides increased. Some just stood and stared as they passed. Others tried to touch Mandred, as if to convince themselves that he was no ghost.

Eventually, they reached the hill on top of which stood the royal hall. A broad flight of steps flanked by statues of lions climbed to the seat of power. Only when the two newcomers began to climb the steps did the crowd stop behind them.

Mandred felt himself torn. It annoyed him that the old man had told him nothing about Alfadas. On the other hand, he was proud. He was famous. Everybody in the town seemed to know his name. No doubt there was a heroic song about his battle with the manboar.

They had climbed almost as high as the banquet hall when Mandred turned and looked back out over the square. Every face below seemed turned up to him. All commerce on the street had come to a standstill.

The jarl drew his axe from his belt and raised his arm to the sky. "Hail the people of Firnstayn! Here speaks Mandred Torgridson, come home to visit his heir!"

Jubilant cries rose in response. Mandred reveled in the shouting and rejoicing. When he finally turned away again, a stout figure was waiting for him at the top of the steps, a warrior with a wild red beard streaked with bands of gray. An escort of well-armed young men surrounded him.

"So you claim to be Mandred," said the old warrior in challenge. "Why should we believe you?"

The jarl still had his axe in his hand. He felt inclined to drum a little respect into the man, but then he smiled. The old man's mulishness, that had to be in his blood. No doubt.

"Mandred Torgridson is easy to recognize, because he travels in the company of an elf," said Farodin now. He swept his long blond hair back, giving the men above a better view of his pointed ears.

The king creased his brow. He suddenly grew serious—alarmed, even—as though he had just received some terrible news.

Mandred stood as if made of stone. If the old man up there was his grandson, then Alfadas had to be long dead.

"Are you Faredred or Nuredred?" asked the king respectfully.

"Farodin," replied the elf.

Mandred felt his knees begin to shake. He stiffened, trying to hold himself still, but he had lost his self-control. "Alfadas," he said softly. "Alfadas."

The king came down the steps and threw his arms around Mandred. And again, jubilant cries rose from the square.

"Are you all right?" asked Njauldred quietly.

Mandred nodded. "What about Alfadas?"

The king pushed one arm under Mandred's armpit and around his back, supporting him. To everyone else, it probably looked like a gesture of friendship. "We'll talk in my hall. Not here."

Slowly, they ascended the final few steps. The doors of the royal hall stood wide open. Inside, flaming torches cast a bright light that reflected from the gold-clad columns. Captured banners hung from the high ceiling. At the opposite end of the hall, a throne of dark wood stood on a pedestal.

Mandred was amazed at the splendor of the place. Not even Horsa Starkshield's golden hall was as impressive as this. One of the walls was decorated with shields the size of doors and with stone axes that looked far too heavy to have been made for human hands.

From behind one of the columns stepped a young, red-haired woman. She wore a long dress of deerskin decorated all over with small bones, feathers, and stone amulets. "Sire, she will not live beyond sundown. There is nothing we can do."

"Then bring a stretcher. We will carry her up to the stone circle. Mandred and his companion Faredred have come for her," replied the king.

"She is not strong enough even for that. On a stretcher, wrapped in warm blankets, she would not survive the journey to the top of the cliff. It is a miracle she has lived this long."

"Take me to her," Farodin ordered. "Immediately."

The king nodded to the woman in the deerskin dress. She took Farodin by the hand and led him away.

Mandred leaned against one of the columns. The sight of the hall had managed to make him forget his weakness for a moment. "Alfadas?" he pleaded, staring at the gray strands in the king's beard.

Njauldred clapped his hands and opened his arms in a sweeping gesture that took in his entire retinue. "Bring mead and two horns. Then leave me alone with my ancestor."

Ancestor. Something in Mandred recoiled.

The young warriors withdrew. A maid brought the drinking horns and left a large jug of mead for them. The horns were beautiful, bound with wide hoops of gold.

"How long has Alfadas been dead?" Mandred asked in a toneless voice.

"Drink" was all Njauldred said. "Drink, and I will answer all your questions."

Mandred raised the horn to his lips. The mead was sweet and spicy. Delicious. When Mandred filled a second horn, Njauldred told him, without hesitation, that he was the eleventh king of the Fjordlands in Alfadas's line. He laid one hand consolingly on Mandred's shoulder and began to talk. "Not long after you left Firnstayn, Alfadas was elected jarl, and in a few years, he rose to become a prince. He was the king's confidant and led his troops in times of war. After some years, an elf came to Firnstayn just after the midsummer feast to ask Alfadas for help. An army of trolls had invaded Albenmark, and things looked very bad for the elves. Alfadas consulted with the king and the princes of the Fjordlands and assembled the greatest army the North had ever seen. They traveled through gates that the elves opened for them and fought side by side with centaurs, kobolds, and elves. The war dragged on for many years, and when the trolls were finally driven out of Albenmark, they began to attack towns and villages in the Fjordlands. They captured Gonthabu and murdered the king and his entire family. A short time later, Alfadas caught up with the raiders at the Göndir Fjord and made them pay dearly. Still on the battlefield, the other princes named Alfadas to be their new king. With their elven allies, they drove the trolls far back to the north. Alfadas named Firnstayn as the new capital because it stands close to a gate to Albenmark and is already so far in the north that it is not far from the trolls' border. Since those times, there has been an alliance between the elves of Albenmark and the humans of the Fjordlands."

"What became of my son?" Mandred asked.

"He died a hero's death. Alfadas was caught in an ambush and murdered by trolls, who took away his body. Alfadas's elven friend Ollwyn went and brought him back and took bloody revenge for Alfadas's murder. Your son was buried in Firnstayn. His final resting place is at his mother's side, beneath Mandred's Oak," the king said softly.

Bitterness and pride fought inside Mandred. How he would have loved to share a few carefree weeks with Alfadas once again, as they had back when they first came to Firnstayn together. He raised his drinking horn to the ceiling. "May you find a place of honor beside Luth at the table of the gods," he said. His voice was heavy with emotion. Then he tipped out a little of the mead as an offering to Luth and drained the horn.

"He will certainly have his seat at the table of honor," said the king. He had stood up and now pointed at one of the columns decorated with gold. Hammered into the metal were broad bands of figures, warriors on horseback. Njauldred indicated one of the riders, who had driven his lance into the body of a giant. "See that? That is your son at the moment he killed Gornbor, the troll prince." The king then gestured along the length of the hall. "You will find Alfadas's likeness on almost every one of these columns. His deeds of valor are without number. Often he rode out with the elf Ollwyn. They hunted the scouts that the trolls sent out. He is our pride, but also our curse, for no one since has been able to match his heroism."

"Are you still fighting the trolls?" Mandred asked.

"No. There has been peace between us for a long time. Sometimes, if a boat is driven far north in a storm, the fishermen catch sight of one of the large troll ships in the fog. Hunters in winter sometimes find their tracks in the snow, but the battles are over." The king looked gravely at Mandred. "Why did you come here, Mandred Torgridson?"

"To see Alfadas, my son, one more time, and embrace him."

The face of the king grew stony. "You know full well that no human lives through the centuries. Tell me the true reason you are here."

The king's tone startled Mandred. He sounded almost hostile. "When you travel with elves, time passes differently. I believed that only three or four years had passed since I last saw Alfadas. Look at me. I'm still a young man, Njauldred. But I'm the father of Alfadas."

The king stroked his beard thoughtfully. "I see that your pain at the news of Alfadas's death is real, so I will choose to believe you. Even so, your arrival in Firnstayn troubles me."

Mandred was surprised and slightly irritated. "I am not after your throne, Njauldred."

"I would let you have it if you wanted it," replied the king peevishly. "I'm talking about your saga. And Alfadas himself said it many times."

"Said what?"

"That you would return to your people in their hour of greatest need. But we do not live in need, Mandred. So I am wondering, what is coming? First, we find an elf woman, seriously injured, the first elf anyone in the entire kingdom has seen in more than thirty years. And now you. With an elven companion so graceful and distant as if he were an emissary of Death. I am deeply troubled, Mandred. Will there be a new troll war?"

The jarl shook his head. "I doubt it. I have no feud with the trolls. I've never even seen one."

Njauldred pointed at the picture of Alfadas and Gornbor. "They're terrible creatures. One of them is as strong as ten men, they say. Be glad if you never cross one's path. No man alone can defeat a troll. Except for Alfadas."

"What about this elf woman? Where did she come from?"

The king shrugged. "No one knows. She is seriously injured. She looks as if a bear attacked her. When she was found, she was nearly frozen to death. She has a high fever, and she speaks in her sleep, but we can't understand her language. I hope your companion is a mighty sorcerer. The only thing that can save her now is powerful magic. My daughter Ragna is a skilled healer. She cooled the elf woman's fever and stopped her pain, but her wounds have not healed, and it has been weeks now. She has been getting weaker and weaker. Ragna is afraid that she will die tonight. Now your companion is there."

Mandred wished it were Nuramon sitting at the elf woman's bedside now. He would have pulled her back even from the gods' Golden Hall. But Farodin . . . the blond elf was a fighter, not a healer. "Can you take me to her?"

"Of course." The king looked at him with large eyes. "Are you a healer, too?"

"No." Mandred smiled. The king probably thought that anyone living through the centuries must be capable of anything.

They left the hall and entered a side wing. Mandred admired the artfully knotted tapestries that decorated the otherwise bare stone walls. Njauldred led him up a narrow stairway to a corridor with several doors. A shallow brazier kept the cold of the stone walls at bay. Before the last door stood a soldier with the young woman in the deerskin dress whom Mandred had seen earlier in the banquet hall.

Ragna spread her arms in helplessness. "He won't let anyone in. At the start, we could hear their voices. It has been quiet for a long time now."

"And there was a light," said the soldier, awed. "Why don't you tell them about that, Ragna? A silver light came from under the door. And there was a strange smell. Like flowers."

"And there's been no sound from inside since?" asked the king.

"Nothing," the guard confirmed.

Mandred stepped up to the door.

"You'd better not," said Ragna. "He made it very clear that he would not tolerate anyone else in the room with him. In the skalds' sagas, the elves are more polite."

The jarl grasped the doorknob. "He will accept me," he said, though he was not at all certain. "But none of you should try to follow."

Mandred stepped into the room and immediately closed the door behind him. He found himself standing in a small attic room. A large part of the room was filled by a bed. A colorful tapestry had been stretched across the beams of the sloping ceiling. It showed hunters in pursuit of wild boars. The room smelled like flowers.

A heavy woolen blanket and several sheepskins lay on the bed. A shallow depression showed in the mattress. Farodin was kneeling before the bed, his face buried in his hands. But Mandred could see no elf woman, and there was nowhere in the small chamber where she would be able to hide.

"Farodin?"

Slowly, the elf raised his head. "She has gone into the moonlight. It was her destiny to pass on the news."

"You mean she's dead?"

"No. It's not the same thing." Farodin straightened and stood up. His face betrayed no expression. "She is where all Albenkin go one day.

She's passed on her burden to me." He drew his sword and tested the edge with his thumb.

Mandred had never seen his companion in a mood like this. He did not dare to speak. A single drop of blood trickled down the blade of the sword.

"Trolls," Farodin said, breaking the long silence. "Trolls. There was a war with them, but it ended many years ago. At the end of the war, they captured a large sailing ship. Almost three hundred elves were on board, and they were carried away as prisoners. Some still live. Yilvina is one of them."

"Yilvina? Our Yilvina?" Mandred thought of the young, blond elf woman. With her two short swords, she had always seemed invincible in battle. How could she have been taken prisoner?

"Yilvina and half a dozen others, yes. They are still alive, after more than two hundred years in captivity. Prince Orgrim, the leader of the troll army, simply held on to them, although peace had been restored long before." Farodin pointed to the empty bed. "Shalawyn escaped. They hunted her like a wild animal. She was trying to get back to Albenmark to report to Emerelle."

"Are we supposed to take her message to Albenmark in her place?" Mandred did not like the idea of meeting the queen again.

Farodin wiped the blood off his sword with the blanket, then slid the blade back into its sheath. "It would be pointless to even try. Emerelle would send an emissary to the troll king's court to inquire about the prisoners. The emissary would take Prince Orgrim to task, and Orgrim would deny outright that he still held any elves prisoner. The one witness to it has gone into the moonlight. And if Emerelle were to press the point and insist that Orgrim was lying, it might be enough to trigger a new war with the trolls. The queen won't take that risk. Everything will stay as it is."

"So Shalawyn escaped for nothing," Mandred said.

"No, mortal. The trolls must pay for what they do to their prisoners. She told me everything."

Mandred took a step back. Something in Farodin's gaze put him on his guard. "What . . . what do they do?"

"Don't ask. There is only one thing you need to know. Prince Orgrim will bleed for it. I will find a way to reach him, and he will regret what he has done."

AT THE
ORACLE'S GATE

Nuramon walked ahead of Felbion along an Albenpath. He did not hurry. He could sense how the power of the path was being drawn by an Albenstar. A hope filled him, hope that he might finally reach the oracle Dareen.

Again and again, he had chased down false leads. The humans of Angnos were unable to tell the difference between magic and deception, and what they called an oracle was no more than a fraud. He had heard nothing from any of them that he could not have said himself. Since those disappointing encounters, Nuramon had focused his search on an old oracle, one who had been silent for a long time or who refused all visitors.

The route from Iskendria to Angnos and the journey through the kingdom had been arduous. He had detoured around towns and villages and only spoken to lone travelers and occasional hermits. No one recognized him as an elf. He wore a hood that covered his ears and part of his face. His voice remained the voice of an elf, but how many humans had ever heard an elf speak? No doubt they thought of him as a secretive wanderer from some faraway land, which, in a manner of speaking, he was.

As he traveled, he memorized the network of Albenpaths and soon knew so many of them in Angnos that he had taken the risk of jumping from one Albenstar to another without leaving the human world. He was amazed at how easily it came to him. The magic was the same. All he needed to do was choose a path that didn't leave this world, and still, he had been unsuccessful. .

Recently, he had passed through a region whose paths were new to him. He had not seen a human for days but had seen signs of Albenkin, changes that could only have been made by elven hands. In many places, the way the plants grew reminded him of Albenmark, and the unusual fertility of the area led him to suspect that a magical spring lay close by, similar to Noroelle's spring. All of these signs came together in the sparse, rugged land, the stony soil of which was otherwise nearly barren.

When he thought of the desert, he wondered whether he was somehow doing this world an injustice. The ocean of sand had shown him that even in the human world, there were landscapes of great beauty.

The Albenpath, the power of which he now felt beneath his feet, climbed steadily, heading directly for a mountain ahead. But the path did not seem to lead to the summit, and it could be that it led straight through the rocks.

When Nuramon had ascended as far as he could and stood directly before the wall of rock where the Albenpath vanished, he thought of the possibility that the oracle he was seeking might live inside the mountain itself. He left the path and set off to walk around the mountain, with Felbion at his side. As he walked, he kept a lookout for a cave or a hidden entrance leading into the rocks. He crossed two more Albenpaths, both of which disappeared into the mountain. When he came across the fourth path, in which he could feel the familiar flow of power, he knew for certain that somewhere inside these rocks, the paths crossed to form a star.

Halfway around, Nuramon found a path that led away from the rocks. It had to be the same one that had led him to the mountain; it had crossed the Albenstar and now continued on its route through the world. He followed the Albenpath back up but was disappointed not to find the entrance to a cave. Again, he found himself facing solid rock.

Nuramon inspected the rock wall carefully. Something was glittering there in the sunlight. He turned toward the glittering, and after a few steps, he saw them: precious stones had been set into the rocks. He didn't know what he found more amazing: that the stones were as large as apples or that no one had stolen them yet.

On the left, a diamond had been set deeply into the wall. On its right was a ruby, fractured, but still in its stone mounting. Next to that again was a crystal with dark threads running through it, coloring it black. It seemed to be some kind of quartz shot through with darker minerals. Beneath the ruby was the fourth precious stone, a sapphire.

The ruby formed the centerpiece of the composition and was connected with the other precious stones by finger-deep furrows. Because it was fractured, Nuramon at first suspected that someone had tried to pry the stone out of the rock, but failed. A moment later, though, he chided himself for the suspicion, because he sensed that seven Albenpaths crossed directly in front of him. The stone was cracked in seven places . . . the ruby itself was the Albenstar, and each of its sections represented one path.

To the left of the diamond and right of the quartz crystal, characters had been chiseled into the rock. He could read the characters beside the diamond, for they were written in Elvish: "Sing the song of Dareen, O Child of the Sun! Sing of her wisdom with your hand in the light! Sing the words that you once spoke, and enter side by side."

The oracle. He had walked so many trails, searched for so long. And now . . . Nuramon considered what the message could mean, what the song of Dareen could be. Then he thought of the words that Master Reilif, the black-hooded keeper of knowledge, had said to him in Iskendria, the words of Yulivee.

He placed one hand on the diamond and sang, "You came to us. Your voice rang. You showed us the stars. They sparkled. We could see them."

Suddenly, the diamond illuminated, and a glowing light flowed through the furrow in the rock to the ruby, penetrated it, and made it glow as well. From the ruby, a red light poured downward toward the sapphire, and the moment the light met the sapphire, the stone emitted a shower of brilliant sparks. But the red light was not able to penetrate into the stone.

When Nuramon released the diamond, the glowing stream of light between the diamond and the ruby vanished, and the red flow from ruby to sapphire also faded away.

The left half of the puzzle was solved.

Nuramon looked at the characters carved beside the quartz crystal. They were unfamiliar to him. He thought that he might know the language and believed it might even be one spoken in Albenmark, but the text in the rock consisted of only a few characters that were exceptionally complicated and harder to remember. This was the true puzzle.

He placed one hand on the quartz crystal and sang Yulivee's words again, but nothing happened. He turned back to the Elvish words on the left. That was certainly addressed to him, but he was supposed to enter with someone else, side by side. The song, too, talked about *us* and *we*. Whoever this other was would be able to read the text that was so foreign to Nuramon and would have to touch the black stone and sing the words. Perhaps his song was so short because it was only part of a longer piece. *He* had to sing one part, his companion the other. But who was this about? Perhaps a human?

Nuramon stepped back and looked at the formation as a whole. The ruby was the Albenstar, and the sapphire was a stone of water and wellsprings. Here, no doubt, it stood for a source of knowledge and thus for Dareen, the oracle. The diamond was the sign for him or someone like him. It was the stone of light. "Child of the Sun," it said on the wall in front of him. But if he was a child of the sun, then the other words might refer to a child of the night. Quartz crystal was not normally seen as a stone of the night, but the black filaments in it might signify that.

An idea occurred to Nuramon. He was one of the Albenkin and was referred to here as a child of the sun. In the old days, the elves had also been called the children of the Lightalben. From his house in the oak, he was able to see far into the mountains, where the dark elves once lived. A child of the Darkalben. That was who he had to find, and that was who he had to persuade to pass through this gate with him.

The dark elves—the children of the Darkalben—had left Albenmark a very long time ago. They had gone to the Other World to find a new home for themselves. There were numerous stories about them, but these, in time, were slowly forgotten. The wise ones said that it made no sense to differentiate between the Lightalben and the Darkalben, and one should forget the distinction as one should forget the race referred to as the Darkalben. But it proved impossible to completely wipe out the memories of the dark elves and the rumors surrounding them. Some claimed that they were evil and that, in the early days, many battles had been fought with them. Or that they could not stand Albenmark's brilliance and for that reason had come to this gloomy world. Others said they were harmless if left alone and that they had moved to the Other World to create something new for themselves. The oldest said nothing, although they alone knew the truth, and the dark elves remained a mystery.

Where was he supposed to look for this secretive race? Like the gate to reach Noroelle, the dark elves could be anywhere in this world. Nuramon sighed. He was none the wiser. There was just one way for him to continue his search: the elven way. He would search for both the vanished race and for Noroelle. At some point, he would find one or the other. And maybe there would be some new trail to follow, something he had not thought of before. Whatever happened, he would not go running back to Farodin to follow him along his trail of sand.

THE WRATH
OF FARODIN

Mandred was not a man who scared easily, but the way in which Farodin had changed truly frightened him. What was hidden away in the depths of the elf's soul? After all these years, he thought he knew his companion, but more and more he realized how little he knew. After Farodin heard what Shalawyn told him, something dark had been growing inside him. But no, if Mandred thought about it, the dark side to his nature had always been there. Farodin had simply kept it hidden. Now something had awakened in the elf that made him set aside everything else, even his search for the grains of sand.

Farodin had asked Mandred to ask King Njauldred Bladebreaker for permission to use one of the boatsheds. He also requested the help of several experienced carpenters. Generously, both requests were granted.

In the weeks that followed, Farodin spent all his time in the boatshed. He built a ship unlike any ever seen in Firnstayn, driving the carpenters hard and treating them almost like slaves. They cursed him for who he was, but spoke with admiration about what he could do. Farodin had never breathed a word to Mandred about how well he knew the art of shipbuilding, reminding Mandred that there was much one could learn when your life spanned centuries. It took just ten weeks until the small, narrow ship was finished. Its keel was carved from a single oak trunk, from a tree that Farodin himself had sought out in the forests north of the town. The same was true of the ribs that formed the skeleton of the hull. The sail was made of fine linen and reinforced with hemp ropes knotted into a net. The boat measured seven paces long but barely a single pace across the beam.

When the boat was launched, people came from every corner of Firnstayn to admire it. It was slim and beautiful, and its timbers over-lapped, something Mandred had never before seen on a boat.

But when the elf—before Njauldred and his retinue—declared that he intended to set sail the next day, no one could believe it. To leave the fjord in winter and sail the coast northward was sheer madness. It made no difference how good the ship might be; no one could make it through the storms and the ice.

The plan was so insane that no one expected Mandred to follow the elf. To refuse to be part of such a voyage had nothing to do with a lack of loyalty to a brother-in-arms. But Mandred felt bound to Farodin. He, Mandred Torgridson, was not the invincible warrior in the songs of the skalds. He had not done the heroic deeds that were so often and so easily ascribed to him, but maybe he could melt the truth and the saga into a single alloy if he followed Farodin now.

Njauldred stocked the ship with the best provisions available. Bear meat, which quickly restored your strength after battle, clothing of fine otter fur that pearled away the icy water, and a barrel of sperm oil that protected the skin from frostbite. Mandred knew that his companion had nothing to fear from the cold. But for his own sake, he was happy to have the barrel on board.

Njauldred invited them to his royal hall and held a feast in their honor. It felt to Mandred like being a guest at his own wake. The skalds did what they could, but the mood stayed rather depressed. Farodin left the festivities early. Deep in thought, he stepped out into the night without saying good-bye.

Mandred, too, withdrew for the night, not long after Farodin. He could no longer bear the sad eyes of Ragna, Njauldred's daughter, and he dared not get drunk the night before their foolhardy adventure.

A cold north wind tore at his cloak as he stepped out of the banqueting hall. A scraping noise made him prick up his ears. It was a moonless night. The stars hid behind clouds. Again he heard the noise. It was coming from the stone lions that flanked the entrance to the royal hall. It sounded almost as if they were scraping their claws restlessly on the steps.

A shadow broke from the bottom step. Mandred called out to the figure, but got no response. Like smoke billowing from the gables of a longhouse, the shadow disappeared into the night as if it had never existed.

Mandred's hand dropped to the heavy axe at his belt. Slowly, he descended the steps. Apart from the wind howling through the rooftops, there was no sound to be heard.

"It was nothing," said Mandred reassuringly to himself. He walked to the house that one of Alfadas's sons had built for him. When he opened the door, a fire was burning in the fireplace. Smoke and a comfortable warmth filled the room. Farodin was nowhere in sight. Perhaps he had gone down to the boatshed. He had spent most of his nights there, despite the cold.

As Mandred swept off his cloak, he heard a sound and froze. Someone was there. The straw in the sleeping nook had rustled. A white hand pushed back the coarse, woolen curtain. Ragna, Njauldred's daughter. Her cheeks glowed red. She could not look Mandred in the eye.

"It isn't what you think," she stammered. "I . . . I thought the elf had come in, so I hid. It was me who lit the fire, to warm this place for you. It is so cold and raw tonight," she said, glancing toward the door.

"Thank you, Ragna," Mandred replied, a little stiffly.

She was a pretty thing. Her skin was as white as milk, and pale freckles dotted her face. She had woven her red hair into two heavy braids. Ragna was in Alfadas's bloodline, but Mandred could see no trace of his son in her face.

"Must you sail off with him?" she asked shyly.

"It is a question of honor."

"To the devil with honor, then." Her timidity was gone in an instant. Fury shone in her eyes. "You will never come back from there. No one comes back from the Nightcrags."

Mandred held her gaze. Her eyes were the pale green of new fir shoots, as if holding a piece of spring captive. "I've been to many places that no one is supposed to come back from," he said complacently.

"How can two men prevail against hundreds of trolls? Throw yourself from one of the cliffs into the sea if you want to die, you—" Shocked, she raised her hand to her mouth. "I didn't mean that. I—"

"Why does it matter so much to you if I live or die?" he asked, then thought, *And why does my life mean so little to me? Because I've been cast out of time? Because I live even though my bones should have been moldering in the grave for centuries?*

"You are the noblest man I have ever met. You're not like the big-talking boys in my father's halls. Every inch of you is a hero."

Mandred smiled. "It used to be the men who courted the women."

Ragna turned bright red. "I didn't mean it like that. I . . . it's . . ." She raised her hands helplessly. "It's just that it's *not* all the same to me if you sail away to certain death tomorrow."

"And you would do anything to have me stay?"

She raised her chin and looked challengingly at him. "You'll have to find that out for yourself. Times haven't changed that much."

THE CHILDREN
OF THE DARKALBEN

Nuramon took a deep breath. The steep trail leading up to the pass had been strenuous. Felbion had followed some distance behind him and now moved up close beside him.

They were above the tree line but still below the snow. From where they stood, the trail led down steeply into a broad valley. The mountains all around felt familiar to Nuramon. It may have been that they resembled the mountains of his homeland, though he could see no obvious similarities. Perhaps his feelings for such things were keener than his eyes.

During his search for the dark elves, he had taken the risk of visiting the towns of the humans and had sought out their company to listen to the stories they told. He had always been careful to keep his ears well hidden, and all who met him took him to be a soldier from some land far in the west. The humans had other names for the dark elves and told tales of how they searched for their victims among the inhabitants of the mountains, and how they slaughtered them in dark gorges and caves and ate their flesh.

Nuramon had followed the Albenpaths into the mountains. The surroundings here were anything but dark, and at this altitude, the air was almost as clear as it was in Albenmark.

During the descent into the valley, Nuramon's mind turned to Noroelle. He had come across two Albenstars on his travels whose paths were sealed. He had attempted to open them using the powers he had but was not successful in breaking through the magical barriers. Perhaps he had already been standing at Noroelle's threshold. He wondered how he would even recognize the gate that led to his beloved. No answer came. Only the hope he placed in the oracle kept him from sinking into despair.

The downward path soon broadened and became less steep, and Nuramon could once again ride Felbion. As they trotted through the woods, he thought of the times he had spent with Noroelle. The memories were so powerful that they erased every doubt gnawing at him. He would find her one day, and free her, with or without Farodin.

Suddenly, Felbion stopped in his tracks.

Nuramon looked around. Something rustled in the bushes on his left, and on his right, he saw movement in the shadows of the trees.

"Who are you?" called a man's voice. The voice spoke Nuramon's language, but with an unusually hard accent.

Nuramon did not turn his head to the side. He simply let his hand drop to his sword. "I will gladly tell you and your companions who I am if you choose to meet me like honorable Albenkin instead of common vagabonds."

"Big words for someone disturbing the peace of this valley," the voice replied. "You are an elf."

"And because you are still standing in the shadows of the trees and clearly avoid the sunlight, I assume you are the children of the Darkalben," Nuramon said, knowing it was a gamble. But either he was right or using the name would at least serve to intimidate these hostile Albenkin.

No answer came. For a long time, nothing happened. Then he heard the rustling sound again. Nuramon's grip on his sword tightened, but when he saw what emerged from the thicket and from beneath the trees, he let go of the sword in surprise.

They were eight in all. Eight small men. They had long beards, and the biggest of them was perhaps as tall as Nuramon's chest. Despite their size, they were powerfully built. Five carried axes in their hands, two had broadswords, and one had a crossbow. Were these the dark elves?

Each of the stout little men wore heavy iron armor and a belt that held more weapons: daggers, short swords, and long knives. They were a troop clearly prepared for a battle.

One of the men stepped closer. He seemed to be the youngest among them. "How do you know the Darkalben? And who told you about their children?" asked the man. Nuramon recognized the voice as the one that had spoken to him from among the trees.

"I heard of them within sight of the Iolids."

The small men looked at each other in astonishment. "You have seen the Iolids?" asked their leader.

"With my own eyes," Nuramon said, thinking of all the hours he had sat at the window of his home and looked out to the blue-gray mountains in the distance.

"Don't believe a word he says," said the crossbowman. "He's lying. He's just trying to buy time to cast a spell on us." Nuramon realized that the crossbowman was aiming at his head. He tried not to let his tension show. "Come on, let me shoot him."

"Enough," shouted the leader, raising his hand. He turned back to Nuramon. "Welcome to Aelburin. My name is Alwerich, and these are my comrades." He introduced each of them in turn.

"My name is Nuramon."

"What brings you to our valley?" Alwerich asked.

"I am here to find the children of the Darkalben . . . and knowledge of the oracle Dareen."

"You have found the children of the Darkalben. As far as the oracle is concerned, you will find here all of the answers we are able to offer."

"Very hospitable of you."

"Indeed. We are known for our hospitality."

A barbed reply was on Nuramon's tongue, but he managed to keep it to himself.

"Follow us," said Alwerich.

"One more question, please."

"Ask away, elf."

"If you are the dark elves, then how is it that you are out and about in daylight? I had heard that you live in darkness."

Alwerich grinned. "You elves live in the light of day, but I still saw you walking in the night."

Nuramon felt doubly abashed. On the one hand, he had not noticed Alwerich during the night. And on top of that, he should have seen such a reply coming. He had left himself wide open.

"By the way, we'd prefer it if you called us *dwarves*," the small man added.

Dwarves. The old stories told of beings called *dweorgas* or *dwarrows*. They were masters of mining and once lived beneath the earth or in rocky regions of Albenmark. Nuramon would never have thought that the dwarves were the children of the Darkalben.

The crossbowman finally lowered his weapon and went ahead with his companions. Nuramon followed them on Felbion at a gentle pace. After riding behind them for a while, he noticed that the dwarves were constantly looking back warily. But the distance they kept, they were keeping from Felbion, not from him. Could it be that the dwarves were afraid of a horse?

THE NIGHTCRAGS

There it was again, that metallic scraping noise. Mandred did not have to turn around to know where it was coming from. Farodin was standing in the stern. He had the tiller clamped under his right arm and was sharpening the blade of a dagger. Since leaving Firnstayn, he had done exactly that at least twenty times. The sound tore at Mandred's nerves. It was a grating, abrasive sound. A sound that promised death.

Ragna had been right. The country of the far north was not made for humans. It was a place for elves, trolls, and ghosts, but *he* did not belong there.

The linen sail of their little boat was encrusted with ice. Frozen and stiff, it creaked when the wind caught it. For seven days, they had been following the line of the coast northward. Mandred thought nostalgically of the days aboard the *Purpurwind* in the Aegilien Sea. He thought of the warmth and of how he had stretched out at midday beneath the shade sail and dozed.

He looked ahead into the wintry twilight and kept a lookout for icebergs. The white giants heaved their way southward, silent and dangerous. Farodin had warned him to watch out especially for the small chunks that were almost completely hidden in the water, as they could damage the hull of their small boat. Mandred's mind was straying. He was tired and thinking of Firnstayn. The women there, no doubt, would have already begun preparations for the coming midwinter feast. They would be fattening geese in the final days and setting mead to ferment in large tubs. The smell of little honey cakes would be hanging over the entire town.

The jarl slipped off one of his mittens and dipped his hand into the barrel with the sperm oil. It had hardened in the cold. He dug out a clump of the stuff and held it in his hand until it softened, then he spread the oil over his face and wiped his fingers on his heavy sealskin jacket. Damned cold.

Farodin drove the boat on relentlessly. Only occasionally did they anchor in the lee of cliffs or a protected bay to sleep for a few hours.

The elf seemed to have become one with the ice that surrounded them. He stood at the tiller as if frozen in place, his eyes fixed straight ahead. He had stowed the dagger in the bundle that lay behind him in the stern. It occurred to Mandred that Farodin might not be sharpening the same dagger repeatedly. It was unlike the elf to do the same thing again and again for no reason, though it might also just be a reflection of Farodin's unease, which he otherwise hid extremely well.

Mandred looked up at the sky to distract himself from his fruitless brooding. They were so far north that the sun no longer showed itself. Instead, green faerylight spread from horizon to horizon. It surged overhead like pleated bolts of cloth. Mandred had very little to do. Farodin could have managed the boat just as easily alone.

Many times, the jarl sat for hours in the bow and watched the light in the sky. It comforted him in this wasteland of choppy seas and black cliffs. The wind chilled him to his bones when he sat and dreamed like that.

Glaciers towered along the coast. Once, in the distance, Mandred saw an avalanche of ice tumble into the sea, churning the water. Another time, he thought he saw a sea serpent.

On the ninth day of their journey, Farodin grew restless. They had sailed into a fjord. Gray tendrils of fog crept over the water toward them. Mandred stood at the bow to watch for hidden reefs. The waters were calm. Soon, the fog had swallowed them completely. From not far away came the gentle sound of waves lapping the shore.

Farodin seemed to have been here before. He knew about the shallows even before Mandred called a warning.

A huge shadow rose before them in the mists. At first, Mandred thought it was a cliff. Then he saw a low light glimmering. A rancid stink hung in the air. The fog was now very warm. It condensed on Mandred's beard.

Suddenly, a hoarse voice cut the silence. The voice was deep, like the rumble of an angry bear. Farodin gave Mandred a sign not to move, and he laid a finger to his lips. Then he answered in the same tone in a guttural language unlike any Mandred had ever heard.

A terse greeting came back. Then the shadow disappeared. Farodin stood silently, unmoving and tense. An eternity seemed to pass. The fog took away all sense of time. Finally, the elf nodded to him. "Soon we'll reach the Nightcrags," he said. "There are warm springs in this fjord. They keep it free of ice year round. They are also the reason for this fog, which keeps the trolls' castle hidden. You know how you have to behave?"

Mandred nodded. What was to happen at the Nightcrags had been the only topic of conversation Farodin would put up with during the voyage. That was not, however, the same thing as talking about the elf's plans. But Mandred trusted his companion. Farodin knew what he was doing.

The jarl had instinctively dropped one hand to the axe in his belt. He thought of Farodin's advice for fighting trolls and of the stories he had heard in his childhood. Trolls had to be hunted in packs, like hunting cave bears. One man alone could not defeat a troll. Mandred's mind then turned to his son. Alfadas had been quick to support the elves in the third troll war. He had been the victor of many bloody battles with these monsters. *But in the end, he was killed by them, too*, Mandred reminded himself. He stroked the blade of his axe. One more reason to come here.

The fog dissipated. In front of them rose jagged cliffs. Farodin pointed to a rocky outcrop that looked vaguely like the head of a wolf. "There's a cave there that can't be seen from the fjord. I hid my boat there last time."

"So you've been to the Nightcrags before."

The elf nodded. "Once, more than four hundred years ago. Back then, I killed the prince of the trolls, the head of their army, who led the trolls during their campaigns in Albenmark."

Typical Farodin, revealing what he knew at the eleventh hour. "You really could have told me that earlier," Mandred grumbled.

"Why? Would it have changed your decision?"

"No, but I—"

"Then it was not necessary for you to know it. By the way, there's been one change to our plan. You will go to the Nightcrags alone."

Mandred's jaw dropped. "What?"

"They will never let me into their fortress. Do you know what they call me? Death in the night. They'll kill me the moment they see me.

So you must see that there is no other way. You have to go in alone. I'll find another way in. Unlike me, as a supposed ambassador, you are protected by the rights of hospitality. They can't do anything to you as long as you don't violate that right . . . which they will try to trick you into doing. You have to stand firm, whatever they do."

"And why should they accept me as an ambassador? A human? They eat my kind."

Farodin kneeled and unwrapped the bundle he had been keeping in the stern. He showed Mandred an oak branch wrapped in fine linen. "This is why they will accept you. This is a branch from a souled tree. Only emissaries of the queen carry this sign, and whomever the queen sends is untouchable."

Surprised, Mandred took the branch and wrapped the linen around it again. "It's real, isn't it? Where did you get it?"

The question clearly made Farodin uncomfortable. "It grew from one of Atta Aikhjarto's acorns. I hope you can forgive me. We needed it."

"You cut it from the oak tree over Freya's grave?"

"She let me take it. She knows what we need the branch for."

Mandred was not sure whether Farodin meant the oak tree or Freya's ghost. His hands began to shake. He jammed them under his armpits. Farodin must have noticed his trembling. "Damn cold," the jarl muttered. He did not want to look like a coward.

"Yes." Farodin nodded. "Even I feel it. Think of Yilvina. She and the others are worth the risk."

The boat rounded a rocky headland that loomed above the fjord like a tower. They were sailing directly toward the cliffs. The elf maneuvered skillfully between the walls of rock. Then he dropped the mast. Mandred reached for the oars and pulled against the tide. Just ahead, concealed among the cliffs, was the low mouth of a cave.

"The cave can only be reached at low tide," Farodin shouted over the hiss of the surf. "Even at mid-tide, the entrance is underwater."

The thought of entering a cave that was flooded at high tide gave Mandred a queasy knot in his stomach. *Farodin knows what he's doing*, he reminded himself again. But this time, it did not help him overcome his disquiet.

The cave mouth was so low that they had to duck their heads. A swirling current took hold of the boat and wrenched it forward, and in a moment, they found themselves in total darkness. The gunwales scraped past invisible rocks. Mandred cried out.

Finally, they came into calmer water. Farodin lit a lantern and held it high overhead. Surrounded by a small island of light, they glided on. Mandred strained at the oars, now and then looking over his shoulder. A little way ahead, a broad band of gravel appeared. The boat slid up onto it with a crunch.

They jumped ashore and hauled their fragile craft well above the high-tide mark. Mandred looked around in astonishment. The cave was far bigger than he had thought.

Farodin came to him and laid one hand on his shoulder. A comfortable warmth spread through Mandred's body. "I am grateful that you came with me, mortal. I would not make it through this alone, not this time."

Mandred doubted that he would really be of much help. It took all he had just to keep the fear inside him under control, a struggle that had certainly not escaped Farodin's notice.

The elf led him across a rocky ledge at the edge of the water to a hidden exit. Then they picked their way across smooth, ice-encrusted rocks until they finally reached a beach. Time to part. For a moment, they stood facing each other in silence. Then Farodin grasped Mandred's wrist in a warrior's grip. It was the first time his companion had said good-bye to him in this fashion. The gesture said more than any words could.

With light steps, Farodin moved quickly away down the beach and disappeared in the fog. He left no more than the slightest of traces in the snow, and the wind soon erased them. Mandred turned away and kept close to the water. The icy stones crackled beneath his feet. Where the waves broke over the gray gravel, there was no snow. He would leave no telltale traces there either.

He walked along the beach for an hour, until the fog vanished from one moment to the next. Without cover, no sentry could fail to see him. He had the feeling he was being watched, but no one showed himself. Mandred took a step back and turned around. It was as if he had crossed an invisible borderline. Behind him, long fingers of fog clawed in from the sea across the gravel beach. But in front, the night was clear.

The faerylight billowed uncommonly low across the sky. Ahead of Mandred rose a craggy tooth of rock on top of which perched a colossal tower. Yellow light shimmered dully behind clouded windows. The Nightcrags looked very different from how he imagined something built by the trolls would look. This was a darker, rough-hewn version of Emerelle's palace. Flanked by columns and buttresses, the tower loomed high in the sky, reaching even the faerylight. Its windows must have numbered in the hundreds. In places, posts protruded from the walls like massive thorns. Without doubt, the Nightcrags was a masterful construction, but the builder had put all of his skill into making it look gloomy and threatening.

Mandred unwrapped the oak branch from the linen cloth and held it in front of his chest like a shield. He thought of Luth, the god of fate, and that there would be no one to sing his hero's song if he died that night. Should he have listened to Ragna? The night spent with her had been completely different from his adventures in the brothels. She loved him honestly . . . him, her own ancestor. Nothing could ever come of that love, he knew. Despite so many generations separating them, his memories of that night did not sit well. It was good that he had sailed with Farodin.

"What brings a mortal to the shadow of the Nightcrags?" a deep voice suddenly spoke. A gigantic figure emerged from beneath a rocky overhang perhaps twenty paces from Mandred. It was half again as tall as a man, with a terrifyingly broad back. Its forearms alone were heavier than Mandred's thighs. Yet despite the cold, it wore no more than a hide wrap around its loins. In the cold faerylight, Mandred could not clearly make out the face of the troll. Indeed, there was something fundamentally shadowy and unstable about its entire form. "What are you doing here?" the sentry asked, speaking the language of the Fjordlands with a heavy accent.

"I am an emissary of Emerelle, queen of the elves." The jarl held the oak branch high. "And I demand the hospitality of Orgrim, prince of the Nightcrags."

There came a kind of gurgling sound. "You demand?" The troll leaned forward and took the branch. He sniffed at it for a moment. "You smell truly of elf, little man." His knotty hands stroked the branch carefully, and he looked out over the dark waters. "How did you get here?"

Mandred looked up. He still could not see the troll's face clearly. The jarl wished he knew more about trolls. In the stories he'd heard as a child, they were never particularly clever. Would this one see through a lie? "Do you know what the Albenpaths are?"

The troll nodded.

"I traveled the Albenpaths. An elf opened a minor gate for me, on the beach not far from here. And I came out in the heart of the troll kingdom." Mandred thought it was a good lie. It explained why no scouts had discovered him earlier.

"Ah" was all the troll said. Then without warning, he turned. "Follow me."

The troll led Mandred to a harbor that lay at the foot of the Nightcrags, with rock walls on all sides. Huge, dark ships were tied up there. They looked like fortresses that had been shown how to swim. From the pier, a path led up into the cliffs. It disappeared into the mouth of a tunnel, sparsely lit with barinstones.

They passed sentries several times—dark figures leaning on heavy clubs and stone axes as big as a man. Mandred's guide seemed to soak up their respect as they passed. In the light of the barinstones, he could see the troll better. His skin was a dark gray sprinkled with lighter spots, making it look not unlike granite. The troll had a receding forehead, and his lower jaw jutted forward. His eyes were strange. They glowed amber, like the eyes of Xern, the first of the Albenkin Mandred had met. The troll's arms were not in proportion with the mass of its body. To Mandred, they looked too long. Knotted strands of muscle testified to their strength. In battle, a troll must be a terrifying adversary.

Finally, they came to a large, open hall. Perhaps a hundred trolls were gathered inside. Some were drinking or rolling bone dice. Others had stretched out beside fireplaces and were asleep. The place stank horribly of old oil, sour vomit, and spilled beer. It was more a cave than a banquet hall, Mandred thought. Along the walls stood rough wooden tables and benches, but most of the trolls seemed to prefer squatting on the floor. They were all frighteningly huge. His guide from the beach was far from being a giant among his peers. Mandred estimated that the largest of those there in the hall measured nearly four paces from head to foot. Only on second glance did he realize that not one of them had any hair. Many had decorated their coarse faces and hairless scalps with interwoven patterns of scarifications.

A rumble arose as the trolls became aware of Mandred. Shouts rang out, like the barking of dogs. The sentry who had led him this far held the branch high and bellowed louder than all the rest, and the hall grew a little quieter. But in the trolls' amber eyes, Mandred read undisguised hatred.

In the distance came the sound of a horn. The jarl thought of Farodin. Had the trolls discovered him after all?

Mandred's guide slumped onto a bench and grinned insolently at him. "Tell us what you came to say, little man."

"Forgive me, but I will speak only with Prince Orgrim," said the jarl firmly. He looked around in the hope of seeing a troll somewhere who was wearing golden armbands or heavy silver chains. That was how the heroes in the sagas always recognized the princes of great nations. But none here wore such things.

His guide bawled something across the hall, and loud grunting came from all sides. It took Mandred some moments to realize that they were laughing.

"What is so funny?" he asked coolly.

His guide tugged at his bottom lip and looked at him intensely. "You really don't know, do you?" he asked in his heavy accent.

"What?"

"I am Orgrim, prince of the Nightcrags."

Mandred looked at the troll. He was skeptical. Was this some kind of ruse? There was nothing about him to differentiate him from the other trolls surrounding them. But if, in fact, he was the prince and Mandred didn't answer him now, then that would count as an insult. And if he was only pretending to be the leader of the trolls and Mandred revealed to him his fake message, then—at least by human standards—he could not be accused of behaving impolitely before his host.

"Queen Emerelle wishes to be informed as to whether any elves are still in captivity."

Orgrim shouted something to the other trolls. It seemed to Mandred that some of them grinned hatefully. Then the prince clapped his hands and gave an order.

"Food and drink will be brought to us," said Orgrim formally. "Let it not be said that I did not set before a guest the best that the larders of the Nightcrags have to offer."

Two arm-length drinking horns were carried in. Orgrim set one to his lips and emptied it in a single draft. Then he looked expectantly at Mandred.

The jarl was having difficulty even lifting his horn. He could not allow himself to get drunk. Not tonight. But if he drank nothing, he would insult his host. So he swallowed a mouthful and let a good portion of the sticky mead run down his beard.

Orgrim laughed loudly. "The children here drink more than you, little man."

Mandred set his horn down. "If I look around, I can imagine that the children here are born as big as me."

The prince clapped him on the shoulder, nearly knocking Mandred off the bench. "Well spoken, little man. Our newborns are far from being soft little grubs like your children."

"To return to the elf queen's question . . ."

"We hold no elves in captivity." Again, the prince pulled at his bottom lip. "Who said we did?"

"An elf woman who had been held captive here," replied Mandred curtly.

The troll prince supported his chin on both hands and looked at Mandred thoughtfully. "What a confused creature that must have been. The war ended long ago. All of the prisoners have been exchanged." If not for the powerful bottom jaw with its protruding tusks, Orgrim would probably have managed a winning smile. As things were, he produced a rather terrifying grimace instead. "I hope very much that Emerelle did not take such talk seriously."

Mandred was deeply unsettled. Had it been anyone else but Farodin who told him about Shalawyn being held prisoner here, he might well have believed Orgrim. The prince was completely different from how he imagined a troll to be. In the stories, they were stupid, coarse man-eaters that could be fooled easily. None of that applied to Orgrim. On the contrary, Mandred sensed that the prince was toying with him.

An old troll woman came and sat at the other end of the table. She had brought a wooden bowl of soup with her and a large, crooked spoon. Her crude dress had been patched hundreds of times, never twice with the same cloth. A milky film covered her eyes. She squinted severely whenever she looked up from her bowl. Around her withered neck were many leather straps with charms: little figures carved from bone, stone rings, feathers, the dried head of a bird, and something that looked like half a raven's wing.

"Who is that?" Mandred asked in a whisper.

"Her name is Skanga, and she's as old as our race." There was respect in Orgrim's voice, perhaps even a trace of fear. He spoke very quietly. "She is a powerful shaman. She speaks with the spirits and can calm storms or call them up."

Mandred glanced covertly at the old woman. Could she read his thoughts? Then it was better to think of harmless things. "It was a long way through the wilderness, and I'm half starved," he said. "I could steal the bowl from under the old woman's nose."

The prince apologized profusely for the food taking so long. It had to be killed first to keep the meat fresh for the table. Orgrim declared that pork always tasted more tender if you softened the beasts up a bit before slaughtering them. Apparently, the secret was to clobber the animal before it suspected that it was to be killed. Orgrim asserted that fear drew out noxious juices that tainted the meat. Mandred had never heard of such things, but he thought the prince made a good case.

While they waited, Orgrim filled the time by telling the jarl about hunting sperm whales. He flattered Mandred, praising the daring of the humans who had fought at the side of the elves in the last war. And he spoke highly indeed of the hero king, Alfadas.

Mandred smiled silently to himself. What would Orgrim say if he discovered he was sitting beside the father of Alfadas? Well, Mandred wouldn't mention the fact. A melancholy pride overtook him as the prince told him of the battles his son had fought in.

After a long time, a bloated, jowly troll served them. He brought two wooden plates laden with steaming roast joints smothered with gravy and gold-brown rings of onion. The larger of the two joints would easily have been enough to stuff the bellies of three starving men. The smaller weighed perhaps two pounds, Mandred guessed.

"As my guest, the choice is yours." Orgrim pointed to the plates. "Which would you prefer?"

The jarl recalled Farodin's words of warning. If he took the larger piece and ate only a small portion of it, the trolls could well take it as an insult. "Considering my size, it would be more than reckless of me to even think about the bigger one," said Mandred, his voice rather stilted. The smell of the meat was making his mouth water. "So I choose the smaller."

"So be it." The troll prince nodded to the fat cook, who set the heavy wooden plates before them on the table.

Orgrim ate with his fingers. He shredded the meat effortlessly and stuffed it into his maw in large chunks. Freshly baked bread came next, and they dunked it in the juices of the meat.

Mandred took the knife from his belt and divided his joint into six thick slices. As he sliced into the meat, dark blood oozed into the heavy onion gravy. The meat was delicious. It had a good, crisp crust and was still tender and bloody in the middle. Mandred ate hungrily. He'd had nothing warm to eat in the long days on the boat. Gravy dripped from the corners of his mouth as he chewed. He savored the pleasure of dipping the fresh bread into the gravy and onions and washed it all down with the heavy mead. Orgrim certainly knew how to treat a guest.

The other trolls, however, were behaving strangely. In the course of the little feast, they became quieter and quieter. Some roasted hunks of meat on long wooden spits, but most simply stared at Mandred. Did they envy him his delicious meal? Gradually, their unwavering gaze began to make him feel uneasy.

Mandred finished his meal with a stately belch. He had not been able to finish all the meat. He sat leaning forward on the wooden bench and groaned quietly.

"May I offer you anything else?" asked Orgrim politely. "Apple pieces preserved in honey, perhaps? Delectable, let me tell you. Absolutely delectable. Scandrag, my cook, is a true artist."

Mandred stroked his belly. "Please forgive me. How did you put it just now? I am only a little man. I couldn't eat another bite."

Orgrim clapped his hands. A moment later, the troll who had served them appeared carrying another large wooden board. On top of it were two upside-down baskets. The board itself was dark with blood.

"Among us, it is a tradition to look what one has eaten in the eye. A custom of hunters, you could say." Orgrim snapped his fingers, and the troll set the board down on a neighboring table. Then he lifted the larger of the two baskets. Underneath it lay the head of a wild boar, its mouth gaping. Its tusks were as long as daggers, like those of the manboar. It must have been an unusually large animal.

The prince congratulated his cook on preparing such an excellent meal. Then the cook lifted the second basket. Beneath it lay the head of a woman with short, blond hair. Her forehead was split open, the skin over her left eye mangled. Pointed ears protruded through the short hair. Her skin was paler than the skin of any elf Mandred had ever seen, almost as white as freshly fallen snow.

Mandred stared into the face in disbelief. Her injuries had obviously been inflicted by a blow from a club. The jarl knew this elf as well as he knew his own son. Three years they had ridden together, side by side. Yilvina. His stomach twisted and lurched.

THE KINGDOM
OF THE DWARVES

After a day and a night, when they finally left the forest, Nuramon could hardly comprehend what he was looking at. In front of them rose a colossal rock face—the walls of the kingdom of the dwarves, the entrance itself a mighty iron portal. Windows, slits, and embrasures had been carved out of the rock face, but what most impressed Nuramon were all of the towers that sprang from the stone like mushrooms and reached skyward. Whoever had constructed this had been a master of his trade.

Nuramon dismounted from Felbion; he could not take his eyes off the fortress. "Impressive, isn't it?" said Alwerich. "You elves couldn't build anything like this."

Nuramon gazed up at the banners fluttering from the tops of the towers. Huge cloth pennants, a silver dragon on red, so big that one could recognize the crest from many miles away. For whom were these banners intended? The dwarves lived such a withdrawn existence that it was hard to imagine any outsider ever finding their way here. The dwarves seemed less interested in utility than in what simply looked good. In that, they were similar to the elves, although what this masterful construction expressed was far from modest sufficiency.

Nuramon followed the dwarves to the towering entrance. The closer he came to the massive double gate, the smaller he felt. But perhaps there was something in their realm that required a gate this big. He looked up at the banners again, and especially the heraldic beast pictured on them. Such a gate would be big enough to allow a dragon to enter.

No guards were posted in front of the gate, but Nuramon was acutely aware of the numerous arrow slits in the rock wall and also the extended balcony high overhead. No more guards were needed here. Without a word from Nuramon's escort, something clicked near the door, and squeaking and creaking, the wings of the gate swung out toward them. How had the dwarves managed to forge such an enormous gate from iron? How did they move it, and how had they mounted it? The only answer Nuramon could think of was magic.

Hunting scenes, heroes in battle, and landscapes were depicted in large ornamental frames on the gate. Because of the height of the gate, the uppermost of these images was difficult to make out. It showed a range of mountains, and Nuramon was certain that it was an image of the Iolid Mountains. Symbols had been engraved in the iron of the gate. Even at first glance, Nuramon could see that he was looking at the same form of writing he had seen in the rock at the oracle Dareen's entrance.

So he had not been mistaken. He had come to the right place. In a fortress this size, there had to be at least one dwarf willing to go with him to the oracle.

Between the left and right wings of the massive swinging gate, Nuramon caught his first glimpse of the interior of the kingdom of the dwarves. An enormous hall supported by columns like trees opened beyond the threshold. Sunlight reached the floor in many places, coming in through many narrow light shafts high in the rock. Barinstones of every imaginable color were set in the columns and gave light wherever the sun's rays did not reach. The whole place was alive with activity, and though many of the dwarves inside looked at the new arrivals with curiosity, most seemed only to be going about their daily activities.

"Do you have anything against your horse waiting outside for you?" Alwerich asked.

Nuramon did not, and he whispered something to Felbion. The stallion trotted away to graze close by the entrance. He seemed happy enough to wait on such a succulent meadow.

The dwarves led Nuramon inside, where he saw a guard for the first time. He was standing on Nuramon's right and questioned Alwerich about who the newcomer was and where the dwarf was taking him. Alwerich told the guard the elf's name and explained that he had come from Albenmark. "I will take him to the king," he said.

They were allowed to pass. Nuramon noticed a large wheel being turned just then by several dozen straining dwarves. The gate slowly closed.

"This way," said Alwerich, pointing ahead.

The dwarves they encountered on their way through the imposing fortress all wore metal on their body, although they certainly faced no danger in there. It seemed that metal, for the dwarves, was more akin to clothing than armor. Some preferred heavy chain mail and looked more than capable of defending themselves in it. Others wore coarse-meshed shirts over light material, the shirts studded with metal plates. None of the clothing they wore escaped entirely metal-free, apparently.

All of the dwarves they met stared at Nuramon as if they had never seen an elf before in their lives. And that might well have been true. Some whispered, some welcomed him with reserve. He greeted them as a friend and hoped that his gestures would not be misunderstood.

For the first time, Nuramon saw dwarvish women. All of the crafts-manship this mountain race possessed was expressed in the women's clothes. Metallic threads and jewels adorned their dresses; even those who could not afford gold or silver wore beautifully embellished works made from less precious metals. One dwarf woman in particular stood out; leaf-shaped copper scales had been sewn onto her dress. And though her stature was short and broad, she reminded him of a tree faery of the sort he had once seen visiting Alaen Aikhwitan.

The faces of the women made them look soft and amiable. They wore their hair long, and most had it tied in braids. The woman with the copper-covered dress had blond hair that fell in four heavy braids over her shoulders. Nuramon's gaze, directed so intently at her, clearly embarrassed her. She smiled at him, then turned her dark eyes away and looked at the floor.

When Alwerich and his men led him between two columns on the right and away from the main hall, Nuramon wondered why he found this world of stone so appealing, even though he had not seen a single living plant here in the halls of the dwarves. Was it normal for him to like this place so much? Or was it just another example of his peculiar way of seeing things, something his clan had always mocked him for in Albenmark? He did not know. Either way, he felt the beauty of this place despite its foreignness to him . . . and despite the fact that among these stout dwarves, he looked like a thin giant.

Nuramon followed Alwerich into a second hall, no less impressive than the entrance hall had been. Here, the individual columns were grouped into massive pillars set on broad pedestals and supported huge stone arches overhead. Wide stairways created small public squares and connected one to the next. One moved from square to square along the stairways, climbing level by level. Many of the squares were in active use; tables and benches were set up, and all kinds of goods were on sale. This was a market, and it was loud. The chatter and haggling of the dwarves was overlaid by a steady rushing noise. Somewhere close by, there had to be a waterfall.

At the edge of the hall, they reached a stairway that climbed steeply and was divided by gigantic columns. In front of the stairway was an impressive fountain, where two huge, stone dwarf women held barrels from which water flowed constantly, tumbling into the large basin around their feet. The noise would swallow any conversation carried on close to it. The air above the fountain shimmered in the shafts of light that fell from a large opening in the ceiling high overhead. It did not look like sunlight, though, for it had a bluish sheen. Spray wafted against them as they passed the fountain. It tasted fresh and slightly salty.

Leaving the steep stairs and columns behind, they crossed another hall and came to a spacious curving stairway that, at first, disappeared into the rock, then reappeared high on the left, opening onto a view across the hall of the stairways. In the distance, Nuramon could see the columns of the large hall at the entrance.

Alwerich indicated to him to keep going, and they finally came to a halt at the start of a wide corridor guarded by two soldiers. The guards were not willing to let Nuramon pass, so Alwerich decided to go ahead alone and present Nuramon's situation at the king's court. Nuramon would have to wait there in the meantime.

The elf stood and took in his surroundings. Here, too, the light seemed to hover beneath the ceiling. He would have given a great deal to discover the secret of that light. Although he was a stranger here, he felt as at home as if he were in Albenmark. Like Yulivee in Valemas, the dwarves had re-created their homeland. They had openly cultivated crystals as well. To his left, on the far wall, he could see jeshilit crystal emerging in large quantities from the walls, glittering like grass in morning dew. On his right, huge quartz crystals rose to the ceiling. They radiated light from the inside and seemed to enclose woodlands.

Nuramon observed dwarves going about their business on stone walkways and wooden bridges high in the air. For them, the grandeur around them must have been as normal as the sight of Emerelle's palace was for him. But no doubt, there were dwarves who saw the magnificence of these halls as he did and were in awe of it.

After some time, Alwerich returned and sent his companions away. He put on an expression of distrust. "Follow me, please. Master Thorwis wants to speak with you."

Nuramon had never heard the name. He followed the dwarf without another word. They passed the two guards and walked down a quiet corridor, past individual guards and well-dressed men and women who looked at Nuramon as if he were a glowing ghost. He did his best to keep his orientation, but without the sky, or at least a canopy of branches overhead, he found it difficult.

For Nuramon, the surprise on the faces of the dwarves was easy to explain. He was probably the first elf ever to walk along this corridor. He could only hope that the dwarves did not see him as an emissary of Emerelle. He did not even know whether or not the dwarves were generally well disposed toward the elves. What if they had left Albenmark because of some ancient dispute? If that were the case, he might well be walking to his doom.

"This is it," Alwerich said and stepped into an atrium with at least two dozen high doors leading off, some with guards posted. Alwerich went directly to an old, white-haired dwarf waiting in front of one of the doors. "This is the stranger, Master," he said, and bowed.

The old dwarf eyed Nuramon stonily. "You have performed your duty well, my young warrior. Now leave us."

Alwerich cast a final glance at Nuramon, then returned the way they had come in.

"Look at me, please," the old dwarf said.

Nuramon did as he was told and looked the dwarf directly in his gray-green eyes. Thorwis seemed to be scrutinizing every minute detail of his face. Magic was strong in the old man, Nuramon sensed. The plain gray robe he wore made it clear that he was no warrior. He was the only dwarf Nuramon had seen here who wore no metal. Even his ring was jade.

"Follow me," he finally said. He opened the door and stepped through. On the other side was a narrow corridor. After Nuramon had stepped into the corridor, Thorwis closed the door and bolted it.

Nuramon followed the old man through a series of passageways that were far removed from the other parts of this place that he had seen. The walls here were plain and without any form of embellishment. Only the doors were artfully decorated, and no two were alike. They seemed to be matched to whatever room they opened into.

"Very few ever lay eyes on these corridors," said Thorwis. "No elf has ever set foot—" He broke off suddenly and his eyes fixed on Nuramon's sword. Then he smiled. "Forgive me. What I meant to say was, you can consider yourself fortunate to be here."

"I do" was all Nuramon said. He was surprised at the dwarf's conduct. Was it unusual to carry a sword in these passageways?

Soon, they came to wider corridors, where other dwarves were again to be seen. These wore expensive clothes and seemed no less surprised to see him than those Nuramon had encountered when he had first entered. Some literally jumped in fright when he turned the corner with Thorwis.

"In a kingdom as large as this, those with the power to make decisions have to be able to pass between critical locations quickly and inconspicuously," the old man explained.

Nuramon realized that the passages he was moving through had not been built willy-nilly. Many of them followed Albenpaths. Anyone wanting to move quickly from one part of the dwarf kingdom to another could probably use an Albenstar to do so.

At the end of a long passage, Thorwis stopped, opened a door on his right, and stepped through. Nuramon followed him and found himself in an empty hall, small in comparison with the corridors and halls he had seen so far. On his left was no wall at all. From here, one could look out over the valley. Daylight shone across the room to the wall on his right, a mosaic that re-created the valley in precious stones.

"Excuse me," said Thorwis. He indicated that Nuramon should wait there and went out through a door that opened into the mosaic.

Nuramon wondered what the dwarves made of him. Apparently, they believed that he wanted something from them that justified his being received in this grand section of the kingdom. For him, it would have been enough to simply find someone down below in the main hall who had the courage to go with him on his journey to the oracle.

He stepped over to the open wall and looked down into the valley. The clouds scudded low across a blue sky, and Nuramon had the feeling that they formed faces laughing down on him. Of the wind that drove the clouds up there, Nuramon felt only the faintest breath where he stood. He held one hand out into open space and felt himself reaching through something invisible. Outside, the wind swept past his fingers. In his house in Albenmark was a similar magic. Alaen Aikhwitan made sure that no drafts entered the house, and in the queen's palace, the same spell was at work, forming an unseen ceiling over her Royal Hall. Again, he had discovered a correspondence between the dwarves and the elves.

Suddenly, the door in the wall of precious stones opened again and a dwarf entered. He wore a fine chain mail tunic and a green cape, and on his head, he wore a small crown. Behind him followed Thorwis and a number of other dwarves of his court, some of them soldiers.

The king had not immediately seen Nuramon, immersed as he was in discussion with his soldiers. "I don't want any more digging there. And tell them I—" The king paused and looked up at Nuramon.

Thorwis stepped up to the king's side. "This is the guest I told you about."

The king half turned to the soldiers but kept his eyes on Nuramon. "Go and do as I said," he ordered. Then he turned to Thorwis. "You did not tell me it was an elf."

"I wanted to surprise you. Look."

The dwarven king moved toward Nuramon with measured steps. He had gray hair and a beard with skillfully woven braids. He stopped just in front of Nuramon and peered wide-eyed at him.

Nuramon bowed before the dwarf king. The action felt strange because even bowing, he found he was still looking down at the ruler of the dwarves. "My name is Nuramon. I come from Albenmark and am here because I am on a journey."

The king turned to Thorwis. "Did you hear that?" He seemed unable to comprehend that he actually had an elf standing in front of him.

"Yes, my king." The old man turned to Nuramon. "This is Wengalf, king of the dwarves and ruler of Aelburin."

"I knew you would come. I just did not know when," said King Wengalf.

Nuramon was not too surprised to hear him say that. It was like Emerelle, who often knew what had happened, what was occurring elsewhere, and what might come to pass somewhere, sometime. Perhaps the king of the dwarves was also able to see into far-off times, what might one day happen.

"What brings you to us?" asked Wengalf.

"I am searching for someone, an elven woman, and hoped that the oracle Dareen would be able to help. The way to her is closed to me and can only be opened with the help of a dwarf." Nuramon described Dareen's gate in detail and explained what had happened when he had stood before the wall.

Wengalf exchanged a look with Thorwis, which the old man took as a sign that he should talk to Nuramon. "We know the oracle of Dareen. In the days when we abandoned Albenmark, other Albenkin also left to find their place in this world. One day, dwarves and elves met, and together, they discovered Dareen beyond a gate that led to a distant part of this world. It was she who told us how to seal the portal. In olden days, we used the gate often. But the elves withdrew. Some hid themselves in enchanted forests, others built their own realm in the Shattered World. But most of them simply went back to Albenmark. We were not able to open the gate alone. And neither the need nor the curiosity were ever so great that we had to avail ourselves of the oracle."

Nuramon's thoughts turned to Yulivee. She must have been one of the elves who had encountered the dwarves so long ago. "Would a dwarf be willing to accompany me?" he asked hopefully.

"A dwarf will stand by an elf, just as an elf once stood by the dwarves," said Wengalf solemnly.

Nuramon did not know what the dwarf king meant by that. Perhaps he was alluding to the times when the dwarves still lived in Albenmark and had forged alliances with the elves.

"You don't remember," said the king.

"No. I am too young. I was not there to see elves and dwarves living side by side in Albenmark."

"But you have hardly changed. I still recognize you. Thorwis knew it was you the moment he saw you. How many years has it been? At least three thousand . . ."

Instantly, Nuramon realized what the dwarf was talking about. "You must have me confused with one of my earlier incarnations."

"No, we mean you," said Thorwis. "I recognized you. You are Nuramon. There is no doubt at all."

"We once called each other friend," the king added.

Nuramon could not believe it. He had come to a place where they remembered him from an earlier life and were prepared to talk about him. And the dwarf king had once looked upon his earlier incarnation as a friend.

"It was in the days before I became king, when I was still waiting for the title. We cultivated a friendship then. You left Albenmark at our side. Our race, with you, endured a long and difficult search before we found this place. We hunted, fought, and celebrated together. And together, we found death."

"I died here?" Nuramon asked.

Wengalf pointed out into the valley. "Out there, hundreds of dwarves fought Balon, the dragon. But only we two defeated it, and we paid for that victory with our lives. You died on the battlefield, and I a few days later. I was crowned king on my deathbed."

Nuramon could hardly believe what he was hearing. Wengalf actually believed he was the same elf as his friend back then. More than this, he had the feeling that he was listening to a legend, but one that he could not remember ever having heard before.

"I still remember how you died. We were both lying out there, in the hot blood of the dragon. You said, 'This is not the end. I will return.' Those were your last words. How long have I been hoping for this day? I have to admit that the time grew so long that I rarely thought about it anymore, though I always did on the commemoration day. I pictured to myself how your soul was reborn somewhere, but you had no memory of what you had once done. In the end, so much time went by that I thought you must have passed into the silverlight long ago. But I was wrong."

Nuramon went down on his knees to bring himself to the same level as Wengalf. "I wish that I had inherited the memory of my earlier lives along with the soul. But that was not the case. What you are telling me is another man's story. I cannot look at those events as part of me."

Thorwis joined them now. "Why not? If you sleep and wake up again, aren't you the same man? And if you're the same man, how do you know it?"

"I know it because I remember what was there before I slept," Nuramon replied.

Thorwis laid one hand on his shoulder. "Then think of the things you find out about your earlier selves and your soul's memories as something you have only forgotten. Who knows? One day, the memory of your soul may also become that of your living spirit."

"You mean I might one day remember fighting the dragon? And remember my friendship with Wengalf?"

"I can neither promise it nor give you any hope. I can only say that it has already happened. There are Albenkin who remember their earlier souls. Most who do are dwarves. Maybe you, too, will one day discover the path to your past life. You are no stranger to magic, and your senses are very keen. The first step along this path is to recognize that the Nuramon who once sacrificed himself and the Nuramon kneeling before us now are one and the same."

"I thank you, Thorwis, for your counsel. And you, Wengalf . . . thank you for what you have told me. Would you allow me a question?"

"Ask it," said the king.

"Do you know an elf named Yulivee?"

Wengalf and Thorwis exchanged a look of surprise. "Certainly," the king replied. "But it was a long time ago. Side by side, we set a quartz crystal and a diamond in the gate that leads to Dareen so that elves and dwarves could only find the way to the oracle together."

"Did I meet her in my earlier life?"

"No. At that time, you were following your own roads. You only returned later on."

"Thank you, Wengalf. And you, too, Thorwis. You cannot imagine how much your words mean to me. I will do as you say. I will take the stories of my earlier life and make them my memories."

Wengalf grinned and clapped the kneeling Nuramon solidly on the shoulder. "Then I'd better tell you quickly about the feasts so you can remember what we drank and ate back then. You could handle your fair share. Come. Let us celebrate as we did in the old days." And the dwarf king embraced him.

THE FINAL PATH

Farodin tore the knife out of the troll's eye. He wiped the blade clean on the dead troll's coarse woolen cloak and slipped it back into the sheath buckled around his left forearm. Then he took hold of the troll by the shoulders. With his muscles tensed to their breaking point, he dragged the troll slowly, inch by inch, to the edge of the pier and let the body slide into the dark water.

"May you wait a long time before you're born again," he hissed. Then he moved a short way back along the pier. He tried to remember what it had looked like here the last time. The mooring was newly paved and extended. He hoped they had not changed much more than that.

Full of contempt, he looked up to the huge, black ships. They had not the slightest trace of elegance. They were simply hulks. The bow and stern looked as if someone wanted to build siege towers, not parts of a ship. They loomed menacingly over the water. Which enemy were the trolls planning to fight with such ships?

High above him, inside the Nightcrags, a hundred voices grunted in laughter. Had Mandred managed to hold out? Or was the mortal long dead?

His plan was simply not thought through. To imagine that nothing would have changed here in all these centuries. Of the hidden entrances to the labyrinth of secret corridors that riddled the rocks and the tower, Farodin had already discovered three sealed with bricks. And it was old brickwork. Even the trolls had figured out where he had come from when he had murdered their leader so long ago. And now the pier had been refurbished as well.

With no great hope, he descended a set of stairs to the water. He took off his cape, rolled it, and tied it around his waist like a sash. It would be less of a hindrance like that. Careful not to make any sound that would give him away, he eased himself into the chill embrace of the water. He had to stay completely focused on making sure his clothes did not become saturated and drag him down.

He did not have much time for his search. It wouldn't be long before the cold paralyzed him, despite all the magic keeping it at bay. He felt his way along the wall some distance, then dived. After a few strokes, he found what he was looking for: a dark opening in the stone pier. The trolls had forgotten about this one, apparently. Perhaps they had never even known it existed.

A flooded tunnel led from the harbor to a grotto that lay deep beneath the tower. From the grotto, there were several paths he could take that connected with the labyrinth concealed in the walls of the tower. It was said that the Nightcrags had been built by kobolds who had been enslaved by the trolls. As in Emerelle's palace, they had built hundreds of secret passages through which they could move, well away from their masters' prying eyes. These tunnels were just high enough that Farodin could move along them if he ducked. But a troll would never fit inside. The perfect hiding place.

The elf was chilled to the bone when he reached the white grotto. He did not know what the kobolds had called the place in the past. Farodin himself had dubbed it the *white* grotto in the hours he had spent waiting there. The ceiling and walls were covered in snow-white limestone deposits. Long stalactites hung from overhead. In several places, barinstones had been set into the rock, and they gave off a warm, golden light centuries after the secret builders were gone.

Farodin peeled off his clothes and dried them using the magic that he otherwise used to protect himself from the cold. His wide belt and the leather bracers with the throwing knives were well oiled, and the water had not affected them.

Centuries of experience had taught Farodin that heavy throwing knives were the best weapon in battles with the trolls. Their bodies were so bulky that delivering a lethal strike was an art. Farodin had seen trolls pincushioned with arrows and still fighting. A knife thrown hard into the eye was his preferred method of killing them quickly and silently.

If he had learned anything in the hundreds of years of his vendetta, it was the rule that one should never get close to a troll in a fight. A single blow from their heavy clubs or axes was enough to smash an elf. A slash from a sword normally had little effect on a troll. Parrying a blow from a troll was impossible, as the sheer force of it would break any arm raised in defense. The only chance you had was to dodge, but keeping your distance was better.

To kill a troll with a sword stroke, you had to cut its throat. But delivering such a stroke was difficult simply because of their size. The only other possibility was to stab upward at an angle, striking beneath the ribs and up into the heart. This could work if you first made it through their cover, but if your life was dear to you, you would never get so close to a troll in the first place.

Farodin crouched on the cold cave floor and spread his arms slightly. He emptied his thoughts and tried to focus his concentration completely on the secret kobold passages. It was possible to access almost every chamber in the Nightcrags using them. Where would Mandred be? And did the passages still exist? Or had the trolls found them and bricked up the concealed entrances just as they had outside at the foot of the cliff?

MEAT

Mandred awoke in a cage. He could see very little. This place was almost pitch dark. When he moved, the cage began to swing slightly; it seemed to be hanging by a rope.

The jarl tried to stretch, but his arms were tied at his back and the cage was so small that he was forced into a crouch. He thought with horror of the prisoners at the horse market in Iskendria who had been thrown into cages to die of thirst. Again, he tried to rear up, but it was futile. The thin leather cords only cut more painfully into his wrists.

He tried to remember how he had gotten here. He had vomited, there in the middle of that hall. The trolls had laughed and pushed him around. In pure disgust, he had called the prince a filthy liar. Orgrim had not been particularly impressed. The opposite, in fact; he asked Mandred cynically if he called his goats and geese prisoners. His taunting had been unbearable. Finally, Mandred had drawn his axe, an incredibly stupid mistake. But he could not have done anything else. With a cry, he had attacked Orgrim. He wanted to smash his skull. But before he could get to the prince, another troll had thrown a club between his legs and he had fallen. Orgrim disarmed him with a kick, then left him to the mercy of Scandrag the cook. Scandrag had grabbed hold of him by the scruff of his neck like a puppy and bound his hands behind his back. Any resistance was useless; against a troll, he was as powerless as a child.

The last thing he had heard from Orgrim was the announcement that they would see each other again at dinner on midwinter's night. Mandred shouted back at him that he hoped he choked to death on the meal. That was when Scandrag hit him.

Whispering jolted Mandred out of his thoughts. Someone was above him, to one side. The voice was low and husky. A short silence, then the whisper came again, but this time, the tone and the rhythms had changed. Finally, the voice spoke Elvish, but Mandred could understand only a few words. The talk was about a test, about languages and humans, probably about him.

"Do you speak Dailish?" asked Mandred in the language of the centaurs.

"Who are you?" countered the voice in Dailish.

Mandred hesitated. Was this some kind of trick of the trolls to get out of him what he had not said at the table? "I am Torgrid of Firnstayn," he finally answered.

"How did they catch you?" asked the voice above him.

"I was hunting." Slowly, his eyes were growing accustomed to the darkness. Other cages were hanging around his.

"How does a human hunter come to speak the language of the centaurs? Who taught you? Since the days of Alfadas, the Albenkin have had little to do with humans."

Mandred cursed silently. The truth will out. "I was taught by a friend."

"The mortal is lying," said a tired voice now, far up in the darkness. "My ears can't abide his lies, and they can't stand his mutilation of Dailish. Forget him. Scandrag will take him next. The midwinter feast is not far off. I can feel it. Until then, be silent, my brothers and sisters. We are no more than meat, anyway. And meat does not talk."

Then hold your tongues, you bastards, thought Mandred. *Punish me. In two or three hours, Farodin will get me out of this cage. And then you'll kiss my feet for coming here.*

A GLANCE
IN THE MIRROR

Nuramon followed the dwarven king, certain that another surprise was waiting for him at the end of the passage. He had never in his life received as much recognition as he had here in the halls of the dwarves. The king had given a feast in his honor, and Nuramon had celebrated like never before, in such high spirits that he barely recognized himself. A little goodwill had been enough, and Nuramon already felt himself to be part of the society here. The dwarves indeed claimed that he had been too polite when raising his cup, but he had done his best to conform to their rough customs at table, and he ate and drank things he would otherwise never have touched.

Many of the dwarves asked him whether he could still remember meeting them, but to his regret, he recognized nobody from his previous life. He had been hoping that the familiar surroundings would give him back his memory of those times, but it was obviously not that easy. But if he were to believe Thorwis, then one day he would recognize all of his dwarf friends again and know what he once had observed, thought, and felt.

Nuramon had long since come to understand why he had stood at the side of the dwarves in that previous life, although at first glance they had so little in common. Thorwis had told him that the dwarves knew the moonlight and called it *silverlight*, but that, so far, very few had passed into it. Most dwarves chronicled the experiences of their lifetime and, at some point, died, only to be born into their own inheritance in a new life. From the beginning, rebirth had been the rule for the children of the Darkalben. It was understood that death was just an interruption of life, like a time of sleep that clouded the memory. In time, one could regain that memory, and death was no more than a brief dream.

Some dwarves had managed to recall all of their lives. Thorwis and Wengalf were among these, but most were still on the path to that goal. Until they reached it, they would continue to read the texts they had written and left for themselves to remind themselves of what had mattered most to them in their past lives.

Nuramon was still far from retrieving these memories. He knew little about himself, and he hadn't left anything for his rebirth. Wengalf and Thorwis told him that he had come to know the dwarves when they were still in Albenmark and that he had left alongside them and become a hero in their new home. But the things they were telling him were at odds with the image he had drawn of himself. They spoke of a hero of the sort sung about in old songs. But what had he done in this life to warrant that kind of acclaim? Nothing.

Wengalf spoke then, bringing Nuramon back to the moment. "We're nearly there. We have to go this way." The dwarf turned into a wide corridor. It was cool here, with a coolness that did not match the warmth of the light cast by the barinstones in the walls. At some distance, Nuramon could see a stronger source of light, its glow spilling out into the corridor.

"What is this place?" asked Nuramon.

"These are the Halls of the Faces," answered Wengalf cryptically.

They came closer and closer to the bright light, and it soon seemed as if snow and ice were frozen onto the walls and radiated light. Nuramon realized that he was looking at crystals. When they reached the light, he saw what the walls had created: white minerals grew out of them in thin crystal needles, looking like pale tufts of grass. Beyond this section, the corridor opened into a circular hall with a low domed ceiling. In the center of the hall, a round opening guided light from the ceiling down onto a quartz crystal as big as an elf. Inside the crystal was a figure, completely enclosed and standing upright.

"You never asked me what we did with your body after you died," said Wengalf quietly as they approached the large crystal.

Nuramon was suddenly frightened. In front of him, inside the crystal, stood an elf in metal armor. His eyes were closed as if he were sleeping. For Nuramon, it was like looking into a mirror. This man had black hair, not brown, and it was much longer than his own. The face was a little wider, the nose shorter. But despite these differences, he recognized himself in the elf before him. The dwarves had brought his body to this hall and, using their magical skills, enclosed it inside the crystal. The result looked like a statue of a mythical hero. Nuramon moved around the crystal and scrutinized the body from his previous life. Compared with this warrior with his broad shoulders and noble bearing, he must seem like a child. There could be no doubt about who he was looking at.

"Why do you do this?" he asked Wengalf. "Why keep the bodies laid out like this, on display? How am I supposed to believe in *one* great life when I see the body of another in front of me?"

Wengalf looked up at him gravely. "Thorwis believed it was the right time for you to see this. And I agree. You have to learn that you are much more than your body." He pointed to the crystal. "You cast off this one here like a suit of armor that had seen better days. And what days they were." The Wengalf's gaze drifted off into nothingness. "Death is painful, and the memory of it is seldom pleasant, but when I visit these halls to see my old body, it gives me strength. I look at my earlier face and see what I once was. My mind becomes clear. Faced with my old body, I feel myself transported back to the old times."

Wengalf was right. Why let the body decay if the sight of it can serve as a bridge to the past? Nuramon stepped closer to the stone. Only now did he notice that something was leaning against the crystal. He had overlooked it, so mesmerized was he by the figure itself. It was a sword with a belt and sheath and, next to it, a strung bow and a quiver full of arrows. "Why aren't the weapons sealed inside with him?" he asked Wengalf.

"An intelligent question. A question a dwarf would ask." Wengalf stepped up beside him and looked up at Nuramon's old body. "You and I spoke often about death. Thorwis told us that your soul would return to Albenmark when you died. And there was no one in Albenmark who could tell you about your own history. You should know that, back then, you had to put up with some derision there because you had been reborn."

Nuramon's thoughts turned to his clan. No doubt they were still living in fear that something would happen to him and the next Nuramon would be born among them.

Wengalf continued. "But you were certain that the road would lead you back here if you lost your life. You said, 'If I die, look after my weapons. In my new life, I will come for them.'" Wengalf shook his head. "Back then, we laughed. We never realized that death would come for us so quickly. Those are your weapons. You were an outstanding archer and a master of the sword."

"I was a good archer? Hard to believe." Nuramon could certainly handle a bow reasonably well, but he was a rank beginner compared with the master hunters of Albenmark.

"You have to get used to the fact that you were once different than you are today. One day, you will break through the barriers separating you from your memories. When that happens, your skills will grow."

"As yours once did?"

"That's right. When we fought the dragon side by side, I knew my previous lives only from the texts that I had left for myself, as well as what I got from the Book of the King and from my family's stories. On my deathbed, I told Thorwis the story of my battle against the dragon so that I could find out about it again in my new life. Then they crowned me, for I have never passed from this life without wearing the crown. And then I died. But I did not have to work hard to get the memory back again. I managed it in the next life."

"If you can remember, then you also know how it is . . . to die."

Wengalf laughed. "Death is no more than sleeping. You nod off, and later, you wake up. Some of us dream. They see the Alben, see the silver-light, the past, or the future. But the meanings of these dreams . . . only the wisest can tell you that."

"You mean Thorwis."

"I have often tried to get him to tell me something about these death dreams, but he says he has never dreamed in death and can't talk about things he knows nothing about."

"Have you dreamed?"

"Yes. But whatever it was I saw, I have to keep it to myself until the end comes."

Nuramon did not ask any further. He looked down at the weapons at his feet and picked up the bow. Maybe that would bring his memory back. He wanted to know about his life in Albenmark in the past. And perhaps, unlike Thorwis, he had dreamed in death.

The bow was made of pale wood, the string of a material completely unknown to Nuramon. It glittered in the light. It had to be one of the enchanted bows he had heard of in the stories of his childhood.

He stroked the bow's smooth wood. It had not degraded with the years. An odor took him by surprise. He sniffed at his fingers, then at the wood. He knew this wood better than any other in Albenmark. It was the wood of Ceren, the wood his house was built from. His thoughts turned wistfully to home. He had left too thoughtlessly and had not said his farewells like one who would never return, not even to Alaen Aikhwitan. With this longbow, he would always carry something with him that reminded him of home. But where did the string come from? It looked like a thread of silver. He slid his finger along the string, testing it, then plucked at it. It rang with a clear note, like a lute.

"You used to turn your nose up at our crossbows and say a bow was better."

"And was I right?"

"A weapon is only ever as good as the man behind it. By that rule, the bow *was* superior to the crossbow. Take it. Maybe you will find your old talent with it again." He picked up the quiver. "We made these arrows for you. They are a special gift, because bows were never meant for dwarves. Look at the tips." He slid one arrow from the quiver. The arrow tip was polished iron. "Since the day of your death more than three thousand years ago, they have been lying here. They are not damaged in the slightest. That is the magic of dwarven metal."

Every time the dwarves spoke about the time he died here, he wondered how many lives there had been between that one and the one he was living through. Three thousand years were a very, very long time, even for an elf.

Wengalf held out the quiver and belt to him. Nuramon leaned the bow against his leg, then he accepted the quiver. Wengalf grinned. "You haven't forgotten everything. The way you lean the bow like that . . . just like then."

Nuramon was surprised. He had not done it consciously at all.

Then Wengalf handed him the sword. "This is your sword. A narrow blade from earlier days, when dwarves and elves stood at the forge together."

Nuramon took the sword in his hand. It was light for a long sword. The pommel was disk-shaped, and the cross guard was thin and did not offer the hand much protection. The grip looked short, but it fit snugly into his hand, as if made especially for him. Nuramon drew the weapon from its sheath and inspected the blade. It was longer than the blade of Gaomee's sword. It had no fullers, but the weapon was still light. That could have been explained only in part by the thinness of the blade, but thinness alone was not enough. The metal looked like regular steel. It must have been enchanted, Nuramon thought, but he could sense nothing of that sort, although he had grown deeply sensitive to the presence of magic ever since the search for Guillaume.

"A plain sword, yet still enchanted," Wengalf declared. "You once told me the sword was an old family heirloom."

So this was his sword. Who knew in how many lives he had carried it? Now he owned two swords that had been used to fight dragons. One was bound to this life, the other to an earlier one. Nuramon looked again at the body he had once filled. He would carry Gaomee's sword until the day came when he remembered his previous life and the deeds of the dead warrior before him became deeds from his own past.

Departing from his old body and the hall it was in was not easy. He had the feeling he was leaving something behind in there.

Reluctantly, he followed the king to his hall, where the guards were waiting for them. Even though Nuramon had become familiar with the passages since his arrival, he could have spent centuries in this kingdom without uncovering all of the secrets the mountain world held. If any elf in Albenmark were to discover how much he liked this place, the mockery he already had to bear would only increase. The elves knew nothing of the dwarves these days. But how could this race sink so far into oblivion that no one even knew that they were the children of the Darkalben? King Wengalf traced the reason back to the dispute that had finally divided the elves and the dwarves. The dwarves had never recognized any elven queen as ruling alongside Wengalf and had waged a war over the matter, finally turning their backs on Albenmark forever.

And afterward, in Albenmark, the dwarves were relegated to the status of characters in faery stories, and the children of the Darkalben to myth.

Nuramon wished he could stay there and learn from the dwarves, to one day return to Albenmark as one who had achieved complete recall of his earlier life. But one thought of Noroelle, and his longing and his fear for her was already driving him away again. What would his beloved make of this place? He did not know the answer to that.

They went together to the massive door, where Thorwis waited. The old sorcerer was wearing a radiant white robe and held a staff of petrified wood in his hands. "Heed my words, Nuramon Dwarffriend."

It was a name he had heard often in recent days. And this time, too, it sent a shiver down his spine.

Thorwis continued. "The deeds you have done at the side of our king will never be forgotten. I and those loyal to me had our work cut out for us in convincing King Wengalf that his place is here and that another must go with you to find the oracle Dareen. It fell to me to choose your companion."

"Have you made your choice?" asked Wengalf.

"Yes, my king. It was not easy, because from all sides came voices urging me to select this or that dwarf. I had a difficult time deciding, not wanting to favor one over another. But then I noticed that fate had already made my decision for me." He pointed to a row of well-armed soldiers. "Here comes your companion."

The soldiers moved back, making way for Alwerich, who stepped forward wearing a fine mail tunic, a heavy cloak, and a large pack.

"This is the dwarf whose eyes first saw you in this life," said Thorwis, and he waved the young dwarf to his side.

Alwerich bowed before the king, then lowered his head before Thorwis and Nuramon.

Wengalf laid one hand on the young man's shoulder. "Alwerich, this will be the first time in many, many years that a dwarf has journeyed along a path beyond these mountains. The last one of us to finish a quest side by side with an elf was me. Do justice to our folk and swear that you will be to Nuramon the companion that I once was."

"So I swear," said Alwerich solemnly.

Thorwis moved beside Wengalf. "You know which question you must put to the oracle."

"I know it, Master. And I will return with the oracle's counsel."

Alwerich turned once more and went over to an elegantly dressed dwarf woman, whom he embraced. Then he returned. "Here is my axe, my comrade in arms." He drew his battle-axe and held it before Nuramon. The weapon had a short shaft ending with a small, beak-shaped spike opposite a broad blade.

"You have to cross weapons with him," Wengalf whispered.

Nuramon slid Gaomee's sword from its sheath. Until that moment, the sounds of whispering, the soft clattering of metal, and the dwarves' excitement had filled the hall. Now, all of that instantly died away, and there was only the sound of the wind and the distant roar of water to be heard. Wengalf and Alwerich looked as if they had seen a ghost. Thorwis was the only one who did not seem surprised. He smiled when he saw the sword in Nuramon's hand.

"Starshine," said Wengalf quietly. And the whisper spread through the dwarves crowded there.

Slowly, Nuramon laid the blade against the shaft of Alwerich's battle-axe and said, "Comrades in arms."

Without taking his eyes off Gaomee's sword, the young dwarf withdrew his axe.

Nuramon was slightly disconcerted. Everyone was looking at the sword in such stunned silence that he hesitated to return it to its sheath.

"Do you have any idea how valuable that sword is?" asked Wengalf.

"I obviously underestimated that," Nuramon said. "Don't you have starshine here?"

"No. It only exists in Albenmark. And back then, we only took a little of it with us. Starshine by itself turns the blade into something impressive. But more importantly, that sword comes from the early days. It is younger than your old sword, but it is the work of a dwarf, one of the few who has gone into the silverlight. He forged many weapons like that one. May I see it again?"

Nuramon drew the sword again and handed it to Wengalf, who took it from him and ran his fingers over the blade. "The great Teludem made this weapon for an elf." Wengalf indicated Gaomee's name, inscribed in twining letters. "This symbol here was added later by an elven hand." He gave the sword back to Nuramon. "There are only four of these elven blades made by dwarven hands. According to legend, all were destroyed in the troll wars and in battle with the dragons. I cannot imagine anyone better than you, Nuramon, to carry this weapon. It will serve you well."

Nuramon went down on one knee to bring himself eye to eye with the king. Then he said, "Thank you, Wengalf, and you, Thorwis, and everyone else. I entered these halls with this life, and I leave it now with all the earlier ones. Thank you for everything you have given me, and for everything I can't yet remember. We will meet again, Wengalf. If not in this life, then in a later one."

"If all the elves were like you, Nuramon, we would never have turned our backs on Albenmark," Wengalf replied. "And now you both must leave, before I throw all good sense aside and come with you after all."

Nuramon nodded. Then he stood tall again. "Farewell. Until we meet again." He glanced at Alwerich. The dwarf stepped up beside him. Nuramon looked out over the gigantic hall one more time, then the two companions stepped out into the sunlight.

UNTRUE WAYS

Farodin woke with a start, sat up, and banged his head. All around was blackness, unbroken. Dazed, he felt around himself in the darkness. His hands hurt. He felt raw rock and debris.

Slowly, his memory returned. He had collapsed in an exhausted sleep. The trolls had filled part of the network of secret tunnels with rubble. In some places, they had gone to the trouble of setting up primitive traps: spiked pits and swinging stones to smash the unwary.

They must have sent kobolds or human slaves down here. Nothing that Farodin remembered was unchanged. Long tunnels had disappeared completely, secret doors were walled up, stairways cut.

The elf had dug through the debris with his bare hands. At times, the only way he had made any progress was by crawling on his belly. Twice he had scrabbled his way through a half-caved-in tunnel only to run up against a heavy stone block completely cutting off the way ahead.

How long had he slept? A gnawing hunger tortured him. His throat was dry, and his lips were cracked. Had he been down here for hours, days? The darkness had robbed him of any sense of time. Only his hunger and thirst could serve as a rough measure of the hours that had passed: a hundred, at least, since he and Mandred had parted ways. Farodin pushed his hands into the rubble and shifted the loose rocks beside and beneath him. Like a mole, he worked his way forward inch by inch. What could have happened to Mandred? He was only supposed to play the diplomat for a few hours. Four days was far too long.

With a crash, the rubble rolled down. He had broken through. Farodin slid a short distance over sharp-edged rocks, then found himself in a passage in which he could walk if he kept his head down. Carefully, he felt his way forward. Ten steps. Twenty steps. The passage climbed slightly.

Suddenly, he came to a wall. Quarry-stone blocks, mortared together. Farodin stretched his arms out frantically. Right and left of him were solid stone walls. He was surrounded by rock on three sides. He could have howled with rage. Again, he'd walked into a dead end.

COMRADES
IN ARMS

Nuramon and Alwerich had made their way out of the mountains and were now marching across the lowland meadows. Felbion followed behind. The dwarf looked around. The open country apparently seemed endless to him, and it was clear that the space here unsettled him. The young dwarf refused to ride with Nuramon on Felbion. For days, he had walked beside the horse, until his feet were red and raw. If he had not adamantly resisted Nuramon's suggestion to use the gates the elf could conjure up at the Albenstars, they would have reached their goal long ago. The dwarf had a pigheadedness to compete with Mandred's.

Alwerich looked down at his feet. "Your healing hands are very powerful."

"But they have never before been used to heal dwarven feet," said Nuramon, smiling. "At least, not in this life."

"Your elf friends in Albenmark would turn up their noses if they knew about it, wouldn't they?"

"You could at least wash them occasionally," said Nuramon, thinking of the healing he had done. He had had to muster his courage a great deal to touch the dwarf's feet.

"I will do better."

"Don't worry about it. Elves don't get dirty hands. Dust falls off my skin, water pearls off, and I can get rid of splashes of mud with a quick shake."

"Then you don't have to wash at all?"

"No, but I still do."

"When? I haven't seen you."

"Just because you don't see it, Alwerich, doesn't mean it doesn't happen. It's only when what you *can* see shouldn't be happening that you have to start worrying. But tell me, Alwerich . . . before we set out, you went over to a woman and you embraced her. Was that your wife?"

"Yes. Her name is Solstane."

"Does the love of a dwarf hold forever? Do you see each other again in your new life?"

"We see each other again, but it doesn't mean we have to love each other again. Look at the king. He has not taken any wife in this life. The queen from his previous life was already quite old when Wengalf was born into his present life. When he was old enough, he took her as his wife again, but they didn't get on anymore. Death separated her from Wengalf. He will take another wife one day, and they will have children."

"So you don't have anything like eternal love?"

"Oh, we do. Some promise to take their own life when the one they love dies. Then he follows her or she him. They can grow up together, and one day, they can love each other again. I did that with Solstane. In the chronicle of my life, it says that Solstane and I were already husband and wife in Albenmark. We loved each other, we grew very old, and we had many children."

Nuramon admired Alwerich. A love that endured forever was something that he hardly dared to dream of. He did not even know if it would be possible to rescue Noroelle. He hoped so, and he believed in his search, but only Emerelle could know for certain. Even if he and Farodin managed to free Noroelle and her years in the Shattered World had not changed her, she still had to decide for one or the other of them. Perhaps the love he felt for Noroelle would become an eternal love.

Suddenly, he was struck by doubt. What would happen if he regained his memory of his earlier life and discovered that he had been undyingly in love with another woman? And what if she, too, had been reborn?

Lost in thought, they walked on toward the oracle Dareen.

THE BANQUET

E at, hooman."
Mandred bit into the oily leg joint. Every time Scandrag, the cook, came, the jarl thought of his meal with the prince. At first, he had refused to eat meat, but eventually his hunger won out. Besides, he had to be strong when Farodin came.

What had happened to Farodin? If he were still alive, he would have come long ago. *Easy now*, he warned himself in his thoughts. *Farodin will get through.* Something may have delayed him, but nothing could stop him from doing what he had set his mind to. Besides, he was damned hard to kill.

Mandred glanced surreptitiously at Scandrag. The troll had just cut a huge pile of onions. He took good care of the *guests* in the prince's larder, at least by the standards of a troll. Every few hours, he lowered Mandred's cage and made sure he ate. There was plenty of bread, vegetables, fresh eggs, and fish. Scandrag had been especially forthcoming that day. Twice already, he had fried up a large panful of eggs and ham. The jarl liked it when the yolks were still runny. He dipped fresh bread into the yolks, then stuffed the bread into his mouth in large chunks.

Mandred was turning to take a second crust of bread from the oven when Scandrag hastily hid something behind his broad back.

"Don' you worry, leedle man. Worry make meat tough. You get kaput quick," the troll said, speaking to him as if he were a naughty child.

Mandred reached for the large pan. It was made of dark copper. No iron was used in the kitchen at all.

The cook furrowed his brow and rubbed his wide nose. He still hid his right hand behind his back. "Please. I woss always good to you, leedle man. Don' cors trouble now." Suddenly, he charged at Mandred. For his size, the troll was astonishingly nimble. He swung a huge club, aiming for Mandred's head.

Mandred threw the pan at Scandrag, but the troll redirected his blow and easily knocked the pan aside. "Tha's enough."

Mandred snatched a stone knife and dropped to one knee as Scandrag swung the club again. The long days in the cage had made his joints stiff. Scandrag missed him by a hair.

Mandred jumped at the giant cook and stabbed the knife through his foot. The troll howled in rage. He lashed out with his uninjured foot, slamming Mandred against the large brick oven. Mandred felt as if he'd broken every bone in his body. Half unconscious, he saw Scandrag looming over him with the club in his hand.

"You is gonna be delicious in honey crust."

SEPARATE WAYS

With a soft creak, the door opened a fraction. Farodin stopped and stood for a moment. Relief flooded over him. He had begun to believe he would never do it, but finally, he was out of the labyrinth.

Carefully, he pushed the secret door open until the gap was large enough for him to slip through. The elf found himself in a narrow corridor doused in gray twilight. He carefully closed the secret door until it was again hidden in its recess in the wooden paneling. He took one of his throwing knives and cut a small notch in the wood so that he or others could find the place again. Then he made his way downward. He knew where he would find Mandred if his companion was still alive. Shalawyn had told him what the trolls did with their prisoners.

Farodin slid the dagger back into the leather sheath on his arm. The trolls would remember this night for a long time to come.

Soon, he found a spiral staircase that led down to the storerooms. Here in the tower, nothing had changed. Less furniture, dirtier, but otherwise, just as it was in Farodin's memory. The fortress was so huge that, provided one used the less frequented corridors and stairways, one had little fear of running into a troll. Once, Farodin hid beneath a landing, and another time, he disappeared into the shadows of a deep alcove, both times to avoid trolls. They were not on the alert. Why would they be? Centuries had passed since the last time anyone dared to attack them in their own tower.

Farodin had almost reached his goal when he came to a corridor where several trolls were lying. Their grunting snores warned him well in advance. There were five of them. They lay sleeping across the passage floor or leaning on the walls. An empty barrel suggested they would not wake up again so easily.

For a moment, Farodin was tempted to slit their throats. But it would be stupid to leave tracks like that. The later the trolls noticed there was an enemy in their midst, the better it would be for him.

He crept between the sleeping behemoths with care. He was almost through when one of them slumped to one side. He had been lying in a pool of bloody vomit. Large white worms lay in it. No . . . not worms. Long, slim fingers, white as freshly fallen snow. A shudder of loathing ran through the elf. There was only one source of fingers like those, given their size and form. Again, the dying Shalawyn's agonized whispers came back to him. "They keep us in cages like geese and stuff us full, then slaughter us for their feasts."

Farodin drew a dagger and crouched beside the troll lolling in his own vomit. His hand stabbed forward. An inch above the troll's left eye, he stopped the blade. It would have been so easy, so easy to press the steel through the eye and deep into the skull. The troll would not even realize its life had come to an end. Farodin held the grip so tightly that the leather wrapping creaked softly. But he couldn't give in to his hatred. He could not allow himself to be discovered too soon. He would kill more trolls if they did not yet discover his presence. Most importantly, he would kill the one who mattered most only if he was not forewarned.

The elf exhaled slowly. *Don't lose control*, he told himself silently. *Calm. First, rescue the ones who are still alive. Then the murdering can begin.*

Quickly, he hurried down the passage. The smell of roast meat filled the air. The reek of it made Farodin queasy. He moved faster and came into a chamber with a domed ceiling. He did not remember this room from the last time. There were six ways in and out. The elf hesitated. The stench of roast was everywhere. And there was something else . . . the sweet smell of honey.

A loud clattering noise made Farodin turn. It came from the passage opposite. Without giving a second thought to staying in cover, he raced ahead. He was still holding on to the heavy throwing knife, its blade the shape of an elongated diamond.

He came into a spacious kitchen. Several open fires were burning. The air was thick enough to cut. It stank of smoke, rancid fat, fresh bread, roast meat. Next to a brick oven stood an enormous troll. The elf eater swung his club back, about to beat something that Farodin could not see.

"You is gonna be delicious in honey crust."

Farodin's arm flashed. The dagger hit the troll in the back of the neck where the spine joined the skull. Even back at the door, Farodin heard the crunch of steel slicing through bone. The troll let the heavy wooden club fall. Then his knees gave way, and he collapsed without another sound.

Farodin crossed the room to the oven to retrieve the dagger from the dead troll's neck and saw Mandred lying on the floor. The jarl had been beaten badly. He was bleeding from a cut on his forehead and hardly had the strength to sit up.

"You're late," Mandred grumbled and spat blood. "Damned good to see you, though." He reached out a hand. "Help me up. I feel like I've been trampled by a herd of wild horses."

Farodin smiled. "This time, I think you tried a little too hard to be the guest of honor at the banquet table."

Mandred sighed. "With your sense of humor, you and Luth must be related. On days like this, I wonder if the god of fate hates me or if this is his way of showing how much he likes his favorite."

"Are any of the other prisoners still alive?"

The mortal pointed to a door half hidden behind sacks of flour. "There," Mandred said as he pulled himself up on the oven. "Can I go in first? I've got a score to settle."

Mandred did not have the strength to stand on his own legs. His breeches were sticky with blood. Limping and with Farodin supporting him, he made it to the door and jerked it open. "Your liar's here to tell you you're free. If you don't believe me, rot in your cages."

Mandred had spoken in Dailish and with such a heavy accent that he was almost impossible to understand. Perplexed, Farodin looked at his companion.

"I had to do it," the jarl said with a smile of satisfaction. "Those in there know what I mean." He pointed to a number of long poles with evil-looking hooks on the end. "You can get the cages down with those." Mandred released himself from Farodin and almost immediately collapsed. Cursing, he fell against the flour sacks and wrapped his hands around his left thigh. A bloody point of bone was protruding through Mandred's torn breeches.

"Goddamned bastard of a troll," he swore. His face was covered with sweat.

Farodin looked at Mandred's wound. Both the bones in his lower leg were broken and jutting through the skin. His friend must have been in terrible pain. He was holding out extremely well for such a serious injury, but he would not be able to take a single step without someone to help him, and an escape through the secret passages would be sheer agony for him.

"I'll make splints from the poles," said Mandred through gritted teeth. "That will do the job."

"Of course." Farodin nodded. Then he took one of the hooked poles and entered the dark room. The stench of putrefaction inside gagged him. It took several heartbeats before his eyes adjusted to the darkness. The room was larger than he'd expected, at least twenty paces across. Drop-shaped cages hung from the ceiling. There must have been a hundred or more, but most were empty.

Farodin was able to free seven elves. They were the last survivors. Their long imprisonment had left its mark on them. Their skin had not seen daylight in two hundred years and was the color of snow. Their eyes were red and inflamed and could not tolerate light. But worst of all had been the narrow cages themselves. Their bones had become bent, and it caused them pain just to stand upright. They showed no joy when Farodin freed them. In silence, they crouched on the floor. A man with long white hair spoke for them. Elodrin. At one time, he had been a prince of the seas in distant Alvemer. Farodin could still remember seeing him at Emerelle's court.

"It wasn't the queen who sent you, was it?" said the old man in a tired voice. "I know the stories about you, Farodin. You're here for your own feud."

"That won't stop me from taking you home again."

Elodrin snorted scornfully. "Look at us. Look at what they've turned us into." He pointed to a woman who was cowering on the floor, sobbing quietly. "Nardinel was once so beautiful that there were no words to describe her. Now she's a crooked old woman with a tortured soul who can no longer stand the sight of the sun. All of us have longed for death for many, many years. We do not fear it. For us, death means the freedom to be born again."

"Does it really not matter to you if you end up as meat on the troll prince's table? Have you given up on yourself so much?" Farodin replied sharply.

Elodrin looked at him for a long time and said nothing. Then he gave an almost imperceptible nod. "Forgive me if I can't thank you. Try to understand us. You have saved only our flesh. Orgrim took our lives long ago."

The elves had to be blindfolded to be able to cross through the kitchen with its bright fires. Mandred had not been in the darkness long enough to become as sensitive to light as the elves. *The mortal would have to lead them*, thought Farodin. For he himself would not be returning with them to the boat.

Scandrag had stored the treasures of his victims in chests: jewels and weapons. In one chest, they found Mandred's axe. The elves wanted nothing to do with any of it, but Farodin was unshakable, insisting that they each have at least one weapon. Even if only to take their own lives before they were captured again by the trolls.

They were about to leave the kitchen when Elodrin said they would do well to set fire to it.

"This tower is nothing but stone," scoffed Mandred, who clearly detested the old elf. "Stones don't burn. Setting fire to the place is useless."

"That's not what it's about, mortal. The tower is like a huge chimney. The smoke will rise. It will distract from our escape and maybe even suffocate a few dozen trolls. Scandrag stores a lot of barrels of whale oil here. Once they start to burn, there'll be no way to put them out again."

It didn't take them long to find the barrels. They smashed a few staves, letting the oil flood the floor in thick streams. Farodin needed several torches to set it alight. With Scandrag's kitchen, a large part of the Nightcrags' stores would be destroyed, and in the middle of winter. *It won't be long before these elf eaters are suffering hunger pains*, thought Farodin, and the thought pleased him. Setting fire to the kitchen was a good plan. If the trolls had had any idea what it meant to have an elf like Elodrin for an enemy, they would have slaughtered him long ago.

Farodin led the fugitives along a detour to avoid the sleeping trolls. Even the pale light cast by the barinstones in the corridors was too bright for the prisoners, who had grown accustomed to total darkness.

Blindfolded, they moved in single file. Each had their right hand on the shoulder of the elf in front. Dark-haired Nardinel supported Mandred. The jarl tried not to let anything show, but the pain had made him almost as pale as the elves.

If Luth—whose name the mortal uttered at every opportunity—if Luth really existed, then the god was sympathetic to their escape. No troll crossed their path, and they made it to the hidden door without being discovered. Farodin explained to the elves how they could find their way back to the white grotto through the kobolds' labyrinth. In the darkness of the passages, they would certainly find their way, and he hoped that the midwinter night was dark enough to hide them from the eyes of the trolls when they made their way along the beach to the cave.

Farodin took Elodrin aside. "You must know that the mortal will not survive if you swim through the bay. He cannot protect himself from the cold of the water." Farodin wished that Elodrin would finally remove his blindfold so that he could look him in the eye when he spoke to him. "Mandred came here without knowing you, and he has risked his life for you."

"I did not ask him to do that," the old man replied indifferently.

"The cold water will kill him, Elodrin. You have to cross the landing stage and then go along the beach to the cave."

"If we go that way, we might as well just surrender to the trolls. If the moon is in the sky, only a blind man could miss us on the beach."

"There is no other way for Mandred."

"Then it was not a smart decision he made to come here."

Farodin had the absurd feeling that Elodrin could see him through the blindfold, that the old man was studying him, every gesture he made, every variation in his tone of voice.

"You were in the human world too long, Farodin. Something of them is in you. I can feel it clearly. If Mandred's life means so much to you, then come with us."

Farodin looked along the narrow corridor, doubtful. He was certain that he could get to the troll prince. Mandred and the other elves had long since disappeared into the labyrinth of the kobolds.

"Before the next tide comes, you have to get out of the cave. If I am not there by then, don't wait for me. If I don't return, then sail in my stead to Firnstayn. Leave a message for Nuramon that from now on, he has to search for Noroelle alone." Farodin took the small silver bottle with the grains of sand from his belt. Three hundred forty-seven of them. "Make sure that this reaches Nuramon." He pressed the bottle into Elodrin's hand. "He will know what he has to do with it."

The old elf accepted the bottle. "I will make sure that *Mandred* delivers your message, and this." He took hold of Farodin's wrist in a warrior's grip. "Make Orgrim die slowly, if you can." With that, he stepped through the hidden door.

Farodin pushed the wooden paneling back into place. Finally, he was alone. He smoothed his torn cloak and pulled the hood over his head. Then he melted into the shadows of the Nightcrags.

No fire alarm had been raised yet, but it certainly wouldn't be much longer. Farodin hurried up stairs and along passages. His route led him higher and higher into the tower. He leaped over sleeping trolls and twice evaded patrolling guards. The second time, he had to hide atop a privy set into the outer wall of the tower. An icy, vertical wind tore at his clothes. Between his feet, he could see all the way down to the harbor. It was more than a hundred paces, straight down.

Finally, he reached the entrance to the black steps. That was the name he had given to the obsidian stairway the last time he had come here. The black steps were hidden inside one of the tower's load-bearing walls and led to the very top. The secret stone entrance swung lightly on its hinges. It was perfectly balanced. The door lay behind a sculpture of a polar bear rearing in attack.

Someone, sometime had gotten a little too vigorous with the statue and knocked off the bear's front paws, which were reaching forward. Clearly, no troll had ever gone to the trouble of properly examining the recess behind the statue.

The low glow of barinstones reflected in the polished steps. Farodin thought of his last day with Aileen. The prince of the trolls had killed her during the battle for the Shalyn Falah. Before she died, Farodin had sworn to her that there would never be another woman in his life. And he had also sworn to pursue Dolgrim, the prince of the trolls, from rebirth to rebirth. It was the most terrible oath any of the Albenkin could make.

Farodin had tracked Dolgrim down and killed him even before Aileen's funeral feast took place. Three more times, he had murdered the reborn prince. And each time, he stopped the troll from fulfilling his destiny and going into the moonlight. The trolls made it easy for him. Their leader was always chosen from among the reborn souls, and if the prince died, his position could not be filled until an important shaman was certain that the reborn prince had been discovered. Only when a troll prince entered the moonlight would his place as ruler truly become free. Thus, every time Farodin killed the prince of the Nightcrags, he could be certain he was killing the reborn Dolgrim.

His heart beating hard, Farodin stopped at the end of the obsidian stairs. He had heard a distant sound, like a gong. Had the fire been discovered? He could not allow himself any hesitation now. He reached for the stone lever in the wall beside him. Silently, the ceiling over him slid aside. Farodin silently applauded the handiwork of the kobolds. It had been centuries since the secret door had been built, but the years had not affected its function in the slightest.

Cautiously, the elf pushed up through the opening. The hatch in the floor closed behind him, leaving nothing to indicate that it even existed.

Farodin had no idea how to open the secret door from this side. Maybe it had never been discovered precisely *because* it could not be opened from inside the room. As he had before, he would have to find another way out.

The prince's room had changed. It seemed smaller than before, perhaps something to do with the enormous bed. Was it bigger, and taking up more space?

The elf heard the breathing of the sleeping prince. Silently, he darted to the bedside. For several moments, he stood in silence and looked at the sleeping form. He thought he could see some of Dolgrim's face in Orgrim's, the deep folds at the corners of the mouth and around the eyes. Even in sleep, it was a cruel face.

With a flowing movement, Farodin drew a knife and stabbed it deep into the troll's throat above the larynx.

Orgrim reared up, his mouth clapped open, but no sound escaped. Only the soft gurgle of blood pouring into his windpipe and suffocating him. The stab had cut his vocal cords.

The troll grabbed at his throat. He thrashed around in grotesque contortions. Then his arms deformed and grew thinner. At the same time, his head seemed to open out of itself.

Shocked, Farodin stepped back. He had never seen anything like this before. The creature in the bed now had a head that looked like the head of a large black dog.

Brilliant light filled the room.

"What a loyal dog," said a warm, low voice in the elven tongue. "To die for his master."

Farodin spun around. The rear wall of the chamber had disappeared. Or rather, the illusion of the rear wall. Now the prince's bedroom looked just as big as Farodin remembered it to be. Orgrim was sitting on a dark oak chair. Beside him crouched an old troll woman on a footstool. In front of her, spread on the floor, lay little bones; she was assembling them with gout-twisted fingers into some sort of interwoven pattern. Four heavily armed trolls flanked the prince's throne.

"It looks like the curse weighing on my soul won't survive the night. You're a brave man, Farodin. Brave, but insane if you truly thought you'd be able to sneak into this chamber again. I'll eat your heart out of respect for your courage, but I'm not touching your brain, elf. We've been waiting for you here every night for the last three days."

The only door to the room opened. Out there, too, heavily armed trolls were waiting for him.

Farodin drew a knife and flung it at the prince. Orgrim ducked to one side, and the blade missed his throat by less than a finger and buried itself in the dark wood of the throne. Farodin swore. For a troll, Orgrim was exceptionally quick.

The bodyguards surged forward. Farodin dropped, crouched, and drew the next knife. Rolling forward, he sliced through the tendon behind one of the troll's ankles. The giant collapsed to the floor.

A swing from an axe missed the elf by a hair. With a spring, Farodin was back on his feet. He hammered a dagger into the body of a troll. He was now in close combat with the bodyguards, and with their long-handled weapons and large shields, they were getting in each other's way.

Farodin dodged a swung shield, went down into a crouch again, and rammed a knife into the back of his attacker's knee. The troll let out a high-pitched scream and, with a clumsy leap, moved out of Farodin's reach.

The elf jumped to his feet, drawing another dagger as he moved, and reached for the top edge of the guard's shield. With all his strength, he pulled himself up like a carnival acrobat and somersaulted over the top of the shield. In midflight, he stabbed the guard through the eye.

With his arms stretched high, perfectly balanced, Farodin landed behind the troll. He could not win an open battle against such numbers, but perhaps he could take Orgrim with him to the grave.

Farodin drew two knives. More guards came charging through the door and into the bedroom, but in that moment, there was only one between him and the prince.

Orgrim was on his feet and lifted the massive throne high in the air. The elf dodged a swing from the last bodyguard and thrust one of his knives through the troll's wrist, making him drop the heavy club.

With a roar, Orgrim launched the throne at Farodin. The elf let himself fall to one side, hitting the floor hard with his shoulder. The heavy chair flew over him and smashed against the opposite wall.

In the space of a heartbeat, the air in the room grew cold. The old woman let out a guttural scream and raised her skinny arms. Bolts of bright light played around her hands. Farodin hurled his dagger. The shaman stumbled over her footstool. Her hands flew to her throat, and dark blood oozed between her fingers.

Orgrim had exploited the moment of Farodin's distraction to pick up a club.

Farodin drew his sword and the last of his throwing knives. From the corner of his eye, he saw the trolls coming through the door. One swung his axe back to throw it. Like a flash of lightning, the knife flew from the elf's hand and hit the axe man in the forehead.

But Orgrim was on him, swinging the club. Farodin tried to dive out of its path, but at the last moment, the prince changed the direction of his swing. Farodin just managed to bring up his sword, but the force of the blow spun the weapon from his hand. It skidded across the floor to the door.

Orgrim let out a ringing laugh. "That was it, little elf. Unarmed, you're as good as dead."

Farodin jumped high and hammered both feet under the ogre's chin. He heard the prince's teeth shatter in his jaw, and the force of the kick sent Orgrim staggering.

Farodin rolled away to the side. In the middle of all the groaning and screams, a sound like a high-pitched chime rang out. The remaining guards kept their distance from him. The shaman was back on her feet. In front of her lay the dagger that had sliced her throat. Very slowly, she put one foot on the dagger.

The elf looked up. The wound in the old woman's throat had closed. Her eyes smoldered feverishly.

Farodin looked down. But he was too late. Against his own will, he took a step back. She had taken possession of him.

With a crash, the shutter swung wide. Icy wind streamed into the tower-top room.

"Did you really imagine you could go on killing the prince forever? And did you imagine that I would put up with it until the end of days?" She shook her head. "I've known for centuries that you would return. It's your arrogance that will cost your life, elf, your confidence that you could defeat us time and time again. Not even Emerelle is as overweening as you."

The shaman's will forced Farodin to raise his head and look her in the face. He took another step back, and another.

Farodin tried desperately to struggle against the spell that was dictating the movements of his body, but he was as helpless as a little child defiantly battling an adult's grip. And he sensed her presence in his mind. She was absorbing his memories.

The shaman forced him to climb onto one of the windowsills. Bitterly cold, the wind battered at him. Heavy, driving snow was closing in. That was good. No. He must not . . . he tried to think of Noroelle.

The old troll woman grinned. "The elves we caught have escaped. They've taken the mortal with them." She looked searchingly at Farodin. The elf tried to empty his mind. He thought of a broad white field of snow. It made no difference. The shaman seemed able to seize his memories with ease. "They're trying to get to a boat hidden in the cave on the other side of the fjord."

"Send a troop to the beach," Orgrim ordered a guard at the door. "And have two ships ready to sail."

"You're in good company, prince." By some marvel, the old woman's voice rang over the tumult of the storm. "He's murdered princes of his own race as well. On the orders of the queen. Afraid of dying, executioner?" she asked with curiosity.

Without warning, two deep creases appeared on her forehead. Her eyes widened in horror. "The Devanthar . . ."

Farodin sensed her power over him suddenly wane, felt her withdraw from his mind in fright.

His body obeyed him again. Farodin laid both hands on the icy windowsill. Did she expect him to jump forward out of fear? He was perfectly balanced. He was safe. He bowed his head like a courtier. "Please allow me to keep my thoughts to myself," he said, and he pushed himself backward from the sill. He could not have done anything else to hurt the prince. It was better to die like this than to be at the mercy of the trolls with no will of his own.

Farodin plunged out into the darkness. He came down hard on his back on one of the sloping buttresses that supported the tower, slid down it and off the end, and kept on falling. Half numbed, he tried to control his fall, to tense his body for any chance to grab hold of a ledge. But as he fell, his cloak flapped around him, enclosing him like a shroud and hindering his movements. A few more moments and it would truly be his shroud.

Suddenly, there was a sharp jerk. Something pulled at Farodin's neck as if trying to separate his head from his shoulders. He bounced upward. His fall had come to an abrupt end, but his hands and feet felt nothing. For some moments, he lost all sense of orientation. Then the elf realized that he was hanging from something, as helpless as a kitten whose mother had it by the scruff of its neck.

Farodin reached out overhead. His fingers scrabbled at ice-encrusted stone. A gargoyle. His cloak had caught on the jutting head of the stone monster. Shaking, Farodin pulled himself up and made it to the relative safety of the stone ledge from which the gargoyle projected. He released the pin of the cloak that had saved his life. The skin of his neck was chafed raw from the material. His neck muscles burned, torn. He could barely move his head, but it occurred to him how lucky he had been. A sudden stop like that should have broken his neck.

Farodin tried to gauge how high up the tower he was, but in the driving snow, he could not see very far. He clearly had not fallen a great distance, or the jarring end to his fall would have killed him. Uncertain what to do, he blinked the snow out of his eyes. Very close to him, one of the tower's buttresses disappeared down into the blackness. From the ledge he was on, there was no way back into the tower. He would have to climb to get back to safety. If he stayed here, the trolls would find him sooner or later.

The gusting wind tore at the cloak that Farodin now held in his hands. He let it flutter away into the dark. It would only get in the way of a climb.

Carefully, the elf stretched out and let himself slide down the buttress, bit by bit. Soon, the curve of the buttress met a wide column that plunged vertically into the depths.

As cautiously as he could, Farodin felt around with his feet. The column was surrounded with grimacing, stone faces. The snow and ice that had collected on them made any grip difficult. Infinitely slowly, the elf climbed downward. The raw stone cut his fingers open. Soon, the cold deadened all sensation in his hands. His grip became increasingly uncertain.

When he reached the next buttress that adjoined the column, he paused for a moment on a ledge. He concentrated on forming a warm buffer beneath his clothes. It took a long time before the magic bent to his will. Sorcery was never easy for him, and especially not when he was exhausted. As he warmed, sleep threatened to overtake him. Farodin leaned back against the stone wall and looked down through the snow flurries at his feet.

Four or five paces lower, there was a leadlight window, behind which he could see the glimmer of a barinstone. Farodin thought about how he could make it down there. Near where he was standing, a large number of stone braces extended outward from the tower wall. They had probably been built at some stage to support balconies that were never completed. Two hands across, they protruded more than a pace straight out from the wall. And one of the braces was directly above the window.

Farodin put together a desperate plan. Five braces lay next to each other, spaced somewhat more than two paces apart. A little below them, another five braces projected from the wall. They were arranged so that the upper braces were aligned perfectly with those below. If the first attempt failed, there was still some hope that he would be able to hold on. No. The first attempt had to work. Farodin eyed the snow-covered stones doubtfully. Just to reach them, he had to get from the hulking stone column back to the tower wall.

Farodin climbed up onto one of the flyers that led at a steep angle to the wall. Inch by inch, he crept forward until he reached the wall. He crouched there. A good distance below, one of the horizontal braces jutted from the wall. It must have been four, perhaps five paces down. Farodin swore. He would have to jump. And the odds of finding a foothold on the icy stone were not good.

For a long time, he stared down. He felt the cold creeping into his limbs. The second he had stopped concentrating on his warming spell, it had vanished. His fingers were growing numb. He could not put it off any longer.

Farodin landed on the brace, but his soles found no grip. He half fell, half pushed, somersaulted, and landed with his legs straddling the lower brace. The blow to his crotch brought tears to his eyes.

Groaning, he removed his belt and slung it once around the stone. Then he pulled off his shirt and knotted one sleeve to the belt. The chill wind cut at his back as if with knives. The leadlight window was now below him and to one side.

Farodin formed a large knot in the end of the second sleeve and prayed that the stitching in the shirt was strong. Then he launched himself from the brace. With a jerk, the shirt pulled tight under his weight. The leather belt crunched on the raw stone. Like a pendulum, the elf built up momentum, but the gusting wind repeatedly destroyed his rhythm. He and the window were now almost on the same level. His stiff fingers were gradually losing their grip. One more swing . . . then he let go.

The window shattered against his boots. Glass cut his arms. He slammed hard onto the floor and rolled clear of the glass. Warm blood seeped from a cut on his forehead.

Breathing hard, he just lay there. He'd made it. At first, he wanted to do no more than simply stare at the ceiling overhead. He was alive. And it seemed no one had heard the window break over the howling storm outside.

It took some time before Farodin became aware of the deep drone resounding through the tower. A gong rang. The fire.

Wisps of smoke drifted past the barinstone on the ceiling. The smoke quickly thickened. Dazed, Farodin sat up. His eyes watered.

He tore a strip of cloth from his breeches and pressed it to his mouth and nose. The smoke would make his escape easier. If it didn't kill him.

ELODRIN'S SONG

We can't wait much longer. The tide will soon be so high that we won't make it out of the cave. We'll be trapped for hours."

Mandred, trembling, pulled a blanket closer around his shoulders. The bluster of the rising tide echoed from the walls of the grotto. The jarl felt wretched. He was at the mercy of the elves. They had swum right through the fjord with him. Landal, a gaunt, blond elf, had taken hold of Mandred's beard and pulled him along as he swam. It was Landal's magic that had protected Mandred from dying in the icy water, but he still felt more dead than alive. The cold had penetrated deep into his bones. He lay wrapped in several blankets in the bottom of the boat and could barely move.

"Get the boat out of the grotto," Elodrin commanded. He moved to the stern and took hold of the tiller. "We'll wait out in the fjord. At least we're not sitting in a trap out there."

The rest of the elves hauled at the oars. Pulling against the strong current at the cave mouth took all of their combined strength. The water was so high that the curved stempost of the boat repeatedly hit the roof of the cave. It already looked like they were too late to escape when the little sailboat suddenly surged forward. They were free.

With great skill, Elodrin steered through the reefs and shallows until they finally made it into deeper water. Exhausted, the elves crouched along the sides of the boat and did what they could to recover from the struggle with the sea. Only Elodrin, at the stern, was standing. He gazed uneasily into the heavy fog.

"A powerful spell is being cast," he said softly. "I sense magic everywhere. We cannot stay here."

"We wait for Farodin," said Mandred, resolute.

"That would not be wise." The old elf pointed ahead, where the Nightcrags had to be beyond the fog. "Farodin came here to die."

"No, you don't know him. He's dedicated his life to the search for the woman he loves. He won't die here."

Elodrin smiled tiredly. "Do you know the souls of elves so well, mortal?"

Arrogant bastard, thought Mandred. "If you give up on him, then put me ashore, and I'll search for him."

"What do you want to do? Crawl back to the Nightcrags?"

"At least I won't be abandoning a friend."

"What use is it to Farodin if you die, too?" Elodrin asked.

"You will never understand it, elf. It is a matter of honor not to give up on your friends. However bad the situation. I know that Farodin would do the same for me."

The old elf nodded. "Yes. He's changed a lot. I could tell. Perhaps . . . quiet now, mortal. I need quiet."

Elodrin released the tiller and crouched in the stern. Softly, he began to hum a soothing melody. The soft rocking of the boat and his exhaustion made Mandred sleepy. His head tipped to the side. *Don't fall asleep* was the last thought in his head.

The jarl jolted upright, awake again. The elves were once again at the oars, and the fog had dissipated.

They must have left the fjord. In a rage, Mandred glared up at Elodrin. "You damned coward! You used some sleep spell on me so you could get away!" He felt for his axe. It was gone. Every movement caused burning pain to shoot through his leg.

The old elf had bound his eyes again. He tilted his head in Mandred's direction and smiled. "The fact that you wake up now shows how strong the bonds of friendship are."

"You will take me back to the fjord immediately, you miserable, shit-eating—"

"Nardinel, Landal, help him up. His jabbering is interfering with my spell."

The two elves pulled in their oars and came to Mandred. They, too, were blindfolded again. Mandred moaned in pain as they took hold of him under his arms and lifted him to his feet.

"I don't know how you did it," Nardinel hissed into his ear, "but your pigheadedness has infected Elodrin as well. The trolls' shamans are clearing the fog from the fjord. We are in plain sight. Yet still we are sailing toward the harbor of the Nightcrags."

Supporting himself on the elves, Mandred could see over the side of the boat. The snow had stopped. The sky was clear and star filled. About half a mile away, the trolls' tower rose over the fjord. Flaming torches were moving all along the cliffs and along the beach. The foot of the tower was swathed in a dull, reddish light. Thick smoke billowed from the windows.

The long harbor pier was teeming with trolls. It looked as if ships were hurriedly being manned.

"Do you see him?" asked Elodrin from the stern. "He must be in the water just in front of us. I can sense his presence. It's so strong. The seeking spell is taking almost no energy now."

Mandred looked out over the low swell. A swimmer stirring up the water would have been impossible to miss. But there was nothing.

"Are you sure he's here?" he asked in a low voice.

Elodrin pointed out to the left of the stempost. "There. Look that way."

Mandred squinted his eyes. The light of flaming torches reflected on the smooth water. Suddenly, a ball of fire climbed steeply into the sky from the Nightcrags. It described a wide arc across the sky, then fell almost vertically toward them. The shot, a spear with a fire basket beneath a stone tip, missed them by a wide margin.

It disappeared into the swell, only to be followed immediately by two new fireballs. From the harbor, harsh bellowing could be heard. Mandred saw one of the large black ships casting off.

The jarl's eyes roamed over the water desperately. Finally, he saw something, something pale. Golden hair, moving in time with the gentle swell. "There. More to starboard. Farodin!"

His companion did not react. He was floating with his face down. "Quick! An oar!"

Mandred jabbed at Farodin with the oar, but the elf made no attempt to take hold of it.

"Landal, get him out," Elodrin ordered.

The elf let go of Mandred, jumped into the water, and felt his way out along the oar until he reached Farodin. He turned him over, took him by the hair, and made it back to the boat with two powerful strokes.

Nardinel let go of Mandred to help Landal, and he was forced to hold on to the side of the boat. He could put no weight on his broken leg. But slowly, his strength was returning.

The two elves were hauled aboard. Farodin did not move. His eyes were wide open, sightless, staring at the stars. His upper body was naked and blue with cold, and he was covered with cuts and bruises.

With a hiss, one of the fireballs hit the water close to the boat.

Elodrin ordered Mandred to take Landal's place at the oar on the rearmost thwart. They turned the little boat, everyone rowing hard. A fireball flew overhead, very close now.

Landal treated Farodin's wounds. He ran his hands over the elf's body and pulled splinters from his back. He did it all without removing the blindfold. Every movement betrayed great skill. When he was finished, he wrapped Farodin in a blanket. Suddenly, he paused and raised his head, as if he had noticed Mandred's attention. Landal gestured soothingly. "You don't need to worry. He will recover."

"But he was floating with his face in the water. Like a . . . like . . ." Mandred could not say the word.

"It was the cold that saved him," the gaunt elf explained. "In cold water, everything becomes slower. The beat of the heart, the flow of the blood. Even death. I'm not trying to deceive you, mortal. He is not well. He is exhausted to the verge of death and came away from there with almost a dozen serious wounds. But he will recover."

A signal horn sounded. Mandred looked back apprehensively. One of the mighty ships was on course for the harbor mouth. Oars were pushed out through the hull and churned the dark sea. Even from half a mile away, it was clear that the troll ship was making more headway than they were. Dull drumbeats boomed across the water. The oars of the troll ship were soon moving to the same rhythm.

Mandred and the elves rowed with all their strength. But as hard as they pulled, the trolls were catching up. The moment the pursuit began, it was clear how it had to end. Mandred was bathed in sweat. Every movement sent a pulsing pain through his leg.

For half an hour or more, the chase went on. The Nightcrags were no longer in sight. High cliffs and the ice front of a glacier flanked the fjord.

Mandred sat with his back to the bow and could see clearly what was going on aboard the troll ship. The forecastle, which rose from the main deck like a turret, was lit by flaming torches. Dozens of trolls were crowded there. Braziers of glowing coals had been set out beside arrows in huge bundles. As if that were not enough, a quarter mile farther back came a second troll ship.

Farodin still had not come around. Given the fury with which the trolls pursued him, his daring plan had probably been a success, thought Mandred.

A sharp order rang over the water. The bowmen on the troll ship raised their weapons, and the next moment, a hail of arrows rained down close behind the elves' boat.

"How short are they?" Elodrin asked calmly.

"Ten or fifteen paces."

"What are the shores like now?"

The elf's composure made Mandred furious. Twenty times or more, Elodrin had asked the same question. Who cared a damn about the shores? They could not land there. If they tried to escape overland, the trolls would be on them even faster. A second rain of arrows pelted into the water. This time, they fell less than ten steps short.

"The shore," Elodrin exhorted.

"Cliffs. Still cliffs," Mandred replied in annoyance. "The glacier is maybe sixty paces behind us."

"Landal, please take the helm."

The gaunt elf took over in the stern, and Elodrin sat down next to Mandred. Elodrin's face was haggard. The last few hours had cost him his last reserves of strength. He removed the blindfold and laid it before him on the floor of the boat. He kept his eyes tightly shut.

Arrows spattered into the water. With dull thuds, several shots buried themselves into the stern.

The next salvo would turn the open boat into a death ship, thought Mandred in despair.

"For a human, you are truly remarkable, Mandred," said Elodrin pleasantly. "It was extremely impolite of me to punish you with silence during our captivity. I would like to apologize for that."

Mandred leaned forward and backward in time with the motion of the oars. The old man was insane. They were fighting tooth and nail for every inch they could win from the trolls, and he came out with something like that.

"I forgive you," he wheezed sullenly.

Elodrin seemed not to be listening to him anymore. Like a man praying for divine assistance, he had raised his arms to the heavens. His mouth was open wide, and his entire body tensed as if he were screaming in the throes of death, though not a sound escaped him.

Arrows slammed into the boat. Nardinel was knocked from her thwart. A dark, feathered shaft jutted from her chest. Another arrow had embedded itself in the wood a hand's breadth from Mandred.

The jarl hauled at the oars with even more determination than before, but the other oarsmen had lost the rhythm. The boat drifted to starboard. And that saved them. The next shower of arrows just missed.

A colossal splash sounded, as if a giant had slapped the flat of his hand onto the surface of the water. A block of ice bigger than a hay wagon had broken from the front of the glacier and was drifting out over the dark waters. Their little boat was lifted by a wave and pushed forward a short way.

On board the troll ship, orders were barked. This time, Mandred could see the archers igniting their arrows in the braziers.

Like a swarm of shooting stars, the flaming arrows flew toward the boat. Mandred instinctively ducked, although he knew that doing so was senseless. All around, arrows slammed into the wood of the boat. One of the elves cried out. Elodrin fell. An arrow protruded from his wide-open mouth. Two more had hit him in the chest.

The blanket in which Farodin was wrapped had caught fire. Mandred tore it aside and threw it overboard. As he did so, he saw the archers reloading their bows.

A sound like nothing Mandred had ever heard before boomed from the cliff of ice that formed the front of the glacier. It reminded him of the sound of a tree as it leaned and fell to one side when the woodsmen knocked out the supporting wedges, only this noise was infinitely louder.

An enormous section of the glacier broke free and crashed into the fjord, churning the water to foam. More and more ice broke from the front of the glacier. The troll ship pitched helplessly in the waves. Blocks of ice smashed in the side of the ship like thin parchment. A tidal wave rolled down the fjord. The stern of the elves' boat was tossed high.

Landal braced with all his strength against the tiller. Water surged over the railing. They were driven forward in the midst of white foam atop the crest of the wave, surfing it as fast as a rider on an elven pony at a flat gallop. Mandred hardly dared to breathe. Luth stood by them, though, and they escaped unscathed.

The troll ships were caught by the ice barrier in the fjord. There was no way past, no way to continue the pursuit.

On board the elves' boat, Landal assumed command. He decided not to commit Elodrin's body to the waves. Instead, they wrapped him in blankets and laid him between the thwarts. Injured Nardinel began to sing a song for the dead while the other elves erected the small mast and sail. The power of the wind could help to propel the boat, but until they left the fjord, they still had to pull at the oars.

When they reached the open sea, Landal chose a southeast heading. Mandred had collapsed in silent exhaustion. He didn't care what the elves did. His leg was agony for him, and he was wretchedly cold. Farodin lay in deep oblivion beside the body of Elodrin. Mandred's companion was breathing steadily, but no attempt to wake him succeeded.

Landal said that Farodin had withdrawn into a healing slumber, but Mandred had his doubts. There was something remote about the haggard elf. He seemed to possess uncommonly powerful magic. He was able to follow an Albenpath effortlessly across the open sea. On the third day of their journey, he found a major Albenstar and opened a gate. It looked completely different from the ones his companions managed to conjure. It rose above the waves like a glittering rainbow.

With the crossing into Albenmark, Farodin awoke. Lashing out wildly all around, he jumped to his feet. It took him a long time to realize where he was. He did not want to say a word about what had taken place inside the Nightcrags. He moved to the bow and gazed out over the ocean.

It was not as cold in Albenmark. A steady wind filled their sail, and two days after they passed through the gate, they reached Reilimee, the white city by the sea.

Landal took them into his home there, and all of the survivors swore an oath not to reveal to Emerelle that Farodin and Mandred had returned to Albenmark.

With every day they spent in the white city, Farodin's restlessness grew, but the severity of Mandred's injuries made it impossible for them to leave the city quickly. And Mandred enjoyed the peace. Every day, crooked Nardinel came to see that he was well. She had recovered from her arrow wound with astonishing speed. Her healing hands reset his bones with great skill, and she did more. Mandred had never met an elf woman like Nardinel. In the boat, she had warmed him with her body when the cold was too much for him, and in Reilimee, too, she often shared his billet. She said little, and until the day of his departure, Mandred was unable to explain the source of her feelings for him.

Two weeks after his arrival, when he set off again with Farodin to return to the human world, she found no words of farewell, no good-bye. In silence, she pushed into his hand an armband made from her own long black hair. Then she turned away and was soon lost in the hustle and bustle of the harbor.

Her strange kind of love left Mandred feeling restless. He looked forward to returning to his own world, where he understood the women at least some of the time.

DAREEN

Nuramon had the feeling that an eternity had passed since he'd last stood in this place and solved his part of the puzzle. In front of them, set in the rock wall, were the precious stones: diamond, quartz, ruby, and sapphire.

Alwerich could read the text above the quartz crystal and intoned the words. "Sing the song of Dareen, O Child of the Night! Sing of her wisdom with your hand in the darkness! Sing the words that you once spoke, and enter side by side."

"What do your words say?" Nuramon asked.

"They say, 'On a quiet autumn night, like the Alben, the stars in the grotto, clearer than ever before, come into being.'"

"Do you remember my words? 'You came to us. Your voice rang. You showed us the stars. They sparkled. We could see them.' Both languages mention the stars. It's a clue. 'You showed us the stars.' 'The stars in the grotto.' Do you see what I mean?"

"I have no idea what you're talking about."

"We have to combine our verses and then sing them together. Then it must be 'You came to us on a quiet autumn night. Your voice rang like the Alben. You showed us the stars in the grotto. They sparkled clearer than ever before. We could see them come into being.'"

A smile crossed Alwerich's face. "Make two songs from one. Now I see." He laid one hand on the quartz crystal. "Come. We will sing the key song together."

The key song. The dwarf had found the right term. It was the key to the oracle's gate. Nuramon raised his hand to the diamond and exchanged a brief look with Alwerich, then the two began to sing.

Their words had barely faded when the diamond and the quartz crystal began to glow. From the diamond poured the gleaming light that Nuramon had seen once before, while from the quartz crystal shone a leaden glow that streamed through the furrow toward the ruby in the center. In the red stone, the two lights met and joined, then flowed together in a glittering cascade to the sapphire, opening out inside it. The blue stone lit up and pulsated, as if a heart of light were beating within.

Without warning, the precious stones, the furrows, and the inscriptions disappeared. Alwerich, in surprise, took a step back. Nuramon looked at his hand, which now touched no more than bare rock. But the rock suddenly felt so soft that he could press his hand into it. His fingertips had already disappeared inside the wall. When he pushed his arm into the rock, he realized that Alwerich had returned to his side. The dwarf looked in amazement at Nuramon's arm, then summoned his courage and pushed his own hand into the rock and out of sight.

Nuramon turned to Felbion, who had remained some distance away. "Come with us."

But instead of coming closer, the horse turned away. Felbion preferred to wait where he was, that was clear. Such behavior was not like the normally curious steed.

"Let us go through before this strange door closes again," cried the dwarf.

Side by side with Alwerich, Nuramon stepped into the rock.

Was this how the Alben of old traveled their Albenpaths, with eyes wide open, through the elements?

Nuramon felt the moment when he crossed the threshold of the Albenstar. Their surroundings changed, the pale stone transforming to reddish brown. Two steps farther on, Nuramon's face emerged from the stone. In front of him was a passage flanked by two cinnamon-colored walls. They were in a narrow chasm where no more than a feeble ray of sunlight penetrated. The floor of the gorge was sand with a pattern of ripples. At some time in the past, it may have been a creek bed, but no one had walked over it for a very, very long time.

Nuramon looked around. Alwerich was not with him. Alarmed, Nuramon turned full circle, searching, when, suddenly, a sheepish, grinning face emerged from the rock, and Alwerich stepped out.

"Where were you?" asked Nuramon.

"If this is the gate, then I think I was in the guardroom. And I found this in there," Alwerich said, and he opened his hand. On his palm lay a small figurine of a dragon made of green stone. "It's a dwarven jade amulet, a lucky charm."

Nuramon shook his head. The dwarf, who just a moment before had shied away from the gate, was now moving around in it as if it were a corridor in his own home.

Alwerich ran his hand over the walls of the chasm. "I've never seen rock like this before. Where are we?"

Nuramon could not be certain. The air was as clear as in the mountains in the world of mortals, but not as pure as in Albenmark. "I'd say we're still in the human world, but I don't know for certain." Nuramon stopped speaking at the sound of something in the distance. He looked up. He heard cries of some sort penetrating into the gorge from far away. They sounded like animal noises. "Wherever we are, let's hope Dareen is also here."

They followed the narrow chasm. Nuramon moved ahead. The sand here was so fine that even he left tracks in it. He was reluctant to destroy the harmony of the fine pattern of ripples as he went, but when he looked back, he realized that his tracks were nothing compared with the deep imprints left by Alwerich's boots. The dwarf seemed not even to notice what he was doing to the sand.

Gradually, the path climbed. Overhead, in a blue sky, a large bird circled. Nuramon did not recognize the species, but it was something like a falcon. This was definitely not the Shattered World. There was too much life here for that. It had to be a place in the human world.

The chasm soon opened into a small basin. On the right, close to the rock wall, was a lagoon, in the middle of which a stone with water bubbling out of it rose above the water. Around the shore of the lagoon grew grass, trees, bushes, and shrubs with star-shaped flowers. On the other side of the valley, in the sheer wall, yawned the mouth of a cave. That might be where the grotto of the stars was, the one mentioned in the song.

Saying nothing, Nuramon and Alwerich moved closer. They did not want to disturb the oracle unnecessarily. Nuramon looked at the lagoon. He wondered where the water flowed and thought of Noroelle's lake and the special magic it possessed.

So this was the home of Dareen. Nuramon had never visited an oracle before, although there were several in Albenmark. Few sought them out, for they had grown remote and taciturn. He wondered how

Dareen might look. She might belong to one of the races that still dwelled in Albenmark. Perhaps she was an elf, a faery, a water nymph, maybe even a centaur.

They had just begun to walk away from the lagoon when an elf woman appeared at the mouth of the cave, wearing a plain sand-colored robe. Raven hair fell in long waves over her shoulders. She stood there motionlessly and watched them.

In some trepidation, Nuramon and Alwerich approached her. Even when they were standing in front of her, Nuramon did not dare say a word. The elf woman's eyes, coal-black and fascinating, seemed to bore into him.

"I see the children of light and shadow hand in hand," she said in a clear voice. "It has been a long time since you came to visit me. I am Dareen, the oracle."

Nuramon looked down at his companion, who was gazing at the elf woman as if spellbound. When he turned back to Dareen, he was shocked to suddenly see a dwarf woman standing before him, although she bore some similarity to the elf who had been there a moment earlier. "I show myself to the Albenkin in a number of guises. I will make it easy for you." For a moment, nothing happened, but then Nuramon blinked and the dwarf woman suddenly changed into another kind of Albenkin, one who could have passed for either a short, stout elf woman or a very slim dwarf.

"What is your true form?" Nuramon asked.

The oracle laughed gently. "What is *your* true form, Nuramon? Is it the one standing before me? Or is it the warrior you saw just a few days ago? Maybe it was the body of the first who bore your name. But it may also be that your true form is still waiting for you. So I ask you, what is yours?"

"I don't know. Please excuse my question."

"Don't ask for forgiveness. I am here to answer questions. And if I answer with a question of my own, then it is only because by doing so, I might open up your spirit. I do have a true form, but it would seem strange to you and would tell you far less than this body." She turned to the dwarf. "Come, Alwerich. Follow me back to the star grotto." But she said to Nuramon, "Wait here. You can refresh yourself at the lagoon." Then she turned and walked back into the cave, and Alwerich followed.

Nuramon remained behind. He felt dizzy. He went back to the lagoon and drank a little of its water. It was cool and sent a shiver through his body. The dizziness passed.

When he looked at the surface of the lagoon, he thought of Noroelle's spring. He took her pendant from around his neck and dipped into the cool water the almandine that his beloved, through Obilee, had given him. The red-brown stone sparkled there as all the other stones once had in Noroelle's lake.

Nuramon looked back to the cave entrance. He wondered what Alwerich had asked. The dwarf had not wanted to tell him anything about it on their journey here, saying instead that he had made a promise to Thorwis to keep it to himself.

Nuramon, by contrast, had been open with his companion and had told him about Noroelle. Alwerich had clearly been able to feel what she meant to him. The dwarf had followed his wife, Solstane, into death several times to be close to her in the next life. Nuramon wished it were as simple for him. Alwerich had offered to go with him for the rest of his journey, but Nuramon had turned him down. The dwarf would do better to return to Aelburin and live the life he deserved there with his wife. Nuramon had told him about Mandred's wife, about the time lost, time that had passed for them in just a few steps. He did not want Alwerich's life to take such a turn, even though he—unlike Mandred— would be born again.

When Nuramon placed the chain around his neck again and felt the cold almandine against his chest, he wondered what power was hidden in the stone. It had lain for so long, so many years, on the floor of Noroelle's lake. Noroelle had told him that the gem had been nourished by the magic of the lake. It was more than just a keepsake for her lover. But Nuramon did not know how he could draw whatever special power the stone possessed out of it. Perhaps it was just that the time was not yet ripe.

When Alwerich came back from the cave, he looked stunned. The dwarf had clearly heard things he had never reckoned with. Stammering, he said to Nuramon, "You can go in now." Then he sat on a stone by the lagoon and gazed into the water.

Nuramon did not ask what he had seen. If he had not wanted to reveal his question to Nuramon, he would hardly betray the answer now. The elf left his comrade in arms by the lagoon and, in his turn, entered the cave.

At first, he found himself in a small chamber from which three passages led deeper into the rock. From one of these, a blue glow emanated, while from the other passages came a gray light.

Dareen appeared in the passage with the blue light. Nuramon followed her in silence. The passage led straight back into a dark cave. The walls were as dark as a moonless night, but above him curved a starry sky that gave off a little light. The stars seemed so real, as if Dareen had plucked them from the night sky. So this was the star grotto.

The oracle stood in the center of the cave, where a glowing blue stone plate was set into the floor. Dareen, her voice full of empathy, immediately began to speak. "I see two desires in you, Nuramon. Of those two, I can fulfill only one. With the other, I can only show you the way. The first desire is that you recover your memory. You want to be one again with your earlier lives. Your other wish is to free the one you love. I can give you back your memory here and now, but I cannot set Noroelle free. I will only help you a little farther along your way. Which do you choose?"

Dareen's words came as a blow to Nuramon. He was standing here just one question away from recalling his past. Here, now, he could retrieve all his earlier lives. Maybe that recollection would help him in his search for Noroelle. Still, he did not want to take that risk. Even the smallest clue about where to find Noroelle was worth more to him than the memory of his earlier lives. "I came here with the intention of asking you about the place where the woman I love is a prisoner. And I hope to be able to leave with an answer. My memory will one day return of its own accord."

"A wise choice, Nuramon. I see in you all that has happened. And I will tell you things that will help you. I cannot tell you everything, because if you know too much, things won't happen that have to happen. What I can show you is there." She pointed to the ceiling directly overhead.

Nuramon looked up. Beneath the stars, a landscape appeared. A large lake, or perhaps a bay by the sea, with forests along the shore. Beyond the forests, far off, he could see a range of mountains. Not far from the shore lay an island with a small grove of trees.

"This is the place you are seeking. If you find the way from this island to the Shattered World, then you will reach the woman you love."

"I will find this place, if I have to search for centuries," said Nuramon, unable to take his eyes off the landscape above his head. He burned the image into his mind. He would never forget it. He literally had his goal before his eyes. And the image was very revealing. It seemed that the gate to reach Noroelle lay somewhere in the northern parts of the human world, or perhaps high up in a mountain range. He need search no longer in the desert or on its fringes or in the barren kingdom of Angnos.

Without warning, the image faded and vanished. The island, the water, the shore, all of it dissolved. Nuramon continued to stare at where it had been. He had memorized every detail.

"I will tell you something else," said Dareen. "There are only two things that can break the spell. The hourglass or an Albenstone."

Her words nearly knocked him over. That the hourglass and the grains of sand actually did represent a way to reach her meant less to him than her mention of an Albenstone. He had left to find a path that was easier than Farodin's, and now he had to accept that his path was perhaps much more difficult. He shook his head. "But how am I supposed to find an Albenstone? I only know that the queen has one. But she—"

"She will never give it to you. You must search for another Albenstone if you don't believe in the path your companion Farodin is following. But whether you decide for this one or that, you should first reunite with your companions. Settle your dispute. There are no wrong paths. Each does his part to reach the final goal. Go north and wait for your friends in the city of the mortal. Be patient. Wait in the elven way."

"I will."

"Then this is all that Dareen has to say to you. Farewell, Nuramon." She stepped into the shadows and was gone.

Nuramon waited to see if she would return, but it seemed that she was truly gone. He thought about what she had said. She had shown him the place where he could find the gate to reach Noroelle's prison. But why was it so important to reunite with Farodin and Mandred? He had thought often of his companions and the foolish argument that had sent them down different roads. He missed them. And Dareen's words urged him to make peace with them.

He would travel to Firnstayn and wait there for Farodin and Mandred.

THE BOOK
OF ALWERICH:

THE PARTING OF THE
COMRADES IN ARMS

*T*he oracle's words changed everything. You see things in a different way, especially your comrade in arms. He behaves indeed as he did before, but the knowledge you learned from Dareen makes you see even Nuramon in a new light.

On your journey north, he told you that Dareen had offered to give him back his memory but that he rejected the offer for what he could learn about his beloved. This act moves your heart, and your thoughts turn to Solstane. For her, you would have done the same. And now you can finally understand why Nuramon doesn't want you with him on his search. You already have everything that matters to you. And yet you ask yourself if it might be worth one life to stand by the elf.

You set off on the return journey and avoid the eyes of suspicious humans. They think nothing good of dwarves and cause nothing but trouble. In the time that has passed, you have grown used to Felbion, but you turn down the offer to learn to ride. That would be overdoing things. You like the horse, but to sit alone on his back is not something you feel inclined to try.

The day of departure comes. At the foot of the mountains, you go your separate ways. You climb down from Felbion for the last time. Nuramon goes down on his knee to look you in the eye, and he lays his hand on your shoulder. You will never in your life forget the words he says: "Thank you, Alwerich. You were a good companion, a true comrade in arms, but the time to part is now." He looks up at the mountains, then speaks again. "Say thank you to Thorwis and Wengalf for me. And give Solstane a hug in my name. You have told me so much about her that I have come to know her." To this, you reply, "She will be sorry that you don't come back with me." Nuramon nods and says, "Tell her about Noroelle and my search." Then the elf stands and says, "Farewell, my friend." Nuramon holds out his hand to you and suddenly seems uncertain, as if he fears you might reject his offer. You take his hand and say, "Until we meet again, my friend. Maybe in this life, probably in the next. It may well be that we meet again in the silverlight."

Nuramon smiles and replies, "We will meet again. Maybe we will even remember past meetings that we have no inkling of."

The elf does not know how truly he speaks. He never asked me if we had met before in another life, but as we stand there, we know that things that happen are repeated. Friends find a way to one another, even if it takes several lifetimes.

Nuramon mounts Felbion and looks at you one last time with genuine appreciation. Then he rides away, and you stand and watch him go. You think of the oracle. If only you could prepare him for what is waiting for him. But Dareen insisted that you say nothing to him about it.

The elf rides out of sight. You have only a short way to go to get back to Aelburin, and you set off, to put that distance behind you and take Solstane in your arms again.

NEW HALL OF THE CHRONICLES, VOLUME XXI, PAGE 156

THE CITY OF FIRNSTAYN

Nuramon looked out across the fjord. It was winter, as it had been when they had set off on the elfhunt. This is where everything began. Up there, at the stone circle, Mandred had battled death. Here was where the Devanthar set his game in motion.

He remembered how strange and foreign this world seemed to him at the start, but he was used to it now. He could estimate distances, and he knew how far it was from where he stood to the mountains. But one thing had not changed: the human world was a raw place. The journey here had proved that. It was a particularly hard winter even for the human realm, and it was as painful for him as it was for Felbion. Sometimes, this world was too coarse for an elf.

Below him, Firnstayn lay beside the frozen fjord. What had been a village had become a city. Of course, humans did not live long, which made it all the more important for them to procreate. Still, it amazed him that a settlement could grow so much in such a short time. He thought of the warnings of the faun oak. Perhaps he had become a victim of time. It was true that he had only traversed a small number of gates, but in Iskendria, he had had a strange feeling.

The city below, with its stone walls, proved that more than a few years had passed here since the last time he had stood at the stone circle on top of the cliff.

"So it's true," said someone next to him.

Nuramon drew Gaomee's sword and spun around. At the edge of the stone circle stood Xern. He wore his massive antlers like a crown. Abashed, Nuramon returned the sword to its sheath.

"You actually came," Xern said, his large amber-colored eyes glittering.

"But not to go home," said Nuramon. "Though it is good to see a familiar face."

"What brings you here?" Xern asked.

"My search is not yet finished. I'm going to wait down there, among the humans, and meet my companions again."

"That is very likely a mistake, Nuramon. The queen has not forgotten what you did. She doesn't speak about it anymore, but you should have seen how furious she was when she discovered that the three of you were gone. Few have ever ignored her command as the three of you did."

"Are you here in her name?"

"No, in my own . . . and because Atta Aikhjarto told me you would come. You know his roots reach far. And Emerelle's senses are no less far-reaching. She will see you if you stay near here. Even Firnstayn is too close to the gate."

"I can't change that. I am here because of the counsel I received from the oracle Dareen. And I trust her word."

"Dareen. A name from the days of magic. She left Albenmark because the human world is a realm of change."

"She was right. The city down there is proof."

Xern stepped to Nuramon's side, and they looked down at Firnstayn together. "Alfadas's legacy . . ."

"He's dead?" Nuramon asked. There was sorrow in his voice. He would gladly have seen Mandred's son again.

"Yes. He grew up among the Albenkin, but his life was a human's. He died when his time came."

"How long has it been since we left Albenmark?"

Xern made an effort to put a number to the flow of the years. In Albenmark, time played a much smaller role than it did for humans or dwarves. Things barely changed in Albenmark, and life was long. What did ten or even a hundred years matter? In Albenmark, practically everything was as it was supposed to be. A dwarf could very likely have given him an answer on the spot.

"Two hundred fifty summers. That was when you disappeared," Xern finally replied.

Two hundred fifty years. In the past, the number would have meant nothing to him as an elf. And though little had really changed in his own sense of time, he had learned long ago what two hundred fifty years meant for a human. So he was not mistaken. They must have jumped through time again.

Xern went on. "A lot has happened in that time."

Nuramon recalled that the queen had posted guards at all of the gates. "Well, it seems Emerelle has revoked her ban on leaving Albenmark." If not, Xern would certainly not have disobeyed the queen's order just to talk to him.

"Yes, which came as a surprise to all of us. Alfadas forged ties between the elves and the humans in this land of fjords. We fought the trolls side by side."

"Has there been another troll war?"

Xern indicated the area around them. "This was one of the battle-fields. It all happened very fast. Too fast for some of us. The queen said that a time had come in which we would have to accustom ourselves to the new."

Nuramon had many questions, but one in particular was on his mind. Had he made the jump in time with his companions, or without them? If they were already victims of time when they entered Iskendria, then Farodin and Mandred would be in the same situation he was in. But if he had jumped forward when he journeyed with Alwerich to the oracle, then Mandred might be long dead. And it would mean a bitter homecoming for Alwerich. "Have you heard anything about Farodin? Or Noroelle?"

"No. Nothing about either of them. In this, at least, nothing has changed. No one talks much about you or your companions these days. There are other stories now," Xern said as his gaze drifted into the dis-tance. "We have an era of heroes behind us. Among the humans, they became legends long ago. Among us, they are alive and have earned their recognition. Or they have been reborn. Great names. Zelvades, Ollowain, Jidens, Mijuun, and Obilee."

"Obilee. Did she fight in the war?"

"Yes. And she would have made her ancestors proud."

Nuramon imagined Obilee being admired by all around her, step-ping before the queen as a warrior sorceress. She had already grown into a young woman when they returned from hunting the Devanthar. Since then, she must surely have become the elf woman that Noroelle had always seen in her. He had missed so much. Stories of the troll war would be told for a long time, as people spoke about the war that Farodin had once fought in.

"You would like to see Obilee again, wouldn't you?"

"It seems my face is still easy to read," Nuramon replied, smiling.

"Obilee is said to be in Olvedes. I could take a message to her. She has not forgotten Noroelle. No doubt she has not forgotten you, either."

"No. It would only open old wounds." *And she might even insist on joining him on his search.* The thought might have been selfish, but it eased Nuramon's mind to know that the girl who had been Noroelle's confidante was now someone of importance in Albenmark. His beloved would be proud of her ward.

Xern tilted his head and shrugged. "As you like. I will tell no one besides Atta Aikhjarto that I met you."

"Thank you, Xern."

"I hope you find Noroelle," he said. With that, Xern moved inside the stone circle and vanished into the thin mist.

Nuramon looked back down at the city below. On the way here, he had kept watch for the place that Dareen had shown him. He had even taken a detour. Considering the trees he had seen, the gate they were searching for had to be in the cold north, by the sea or at a lake high in the mountains. That was all that he could say with certainty.

The oracle had been right. He would need the help of his companions. With his knowledge and Farodin's seeking spell, they would be able to trace the location together. Maybe Mandred and Farodin were waiting down below in Firnstayn for him. It was possible that fate would already reunite them down there.

Nuramon took hold of Felbion's reins and set off down the cliff path. At the bottom of the descent, he mounted the horse and rode toward the city. His mind wandered back to the elfhunt. Even though, for him, it had happened just a few years earlier, he had the feeling it had happened in another life. Aigilaos's death, the battle with the Devanthar, and the terrible return to Albenmark . . . it all seemed so long ago, as if he had spent an eternity searching for Noroelle.

Nuramon rode up to the city gate. The watchmen must have seen him coming from far off, but the gate stood open, and Nuramon was able to enter without a guard asking him about his origin or what business he had there. Instead, Nuramon announced in Fjordlandish that an elf had come. Although—as Xern had said—the Albenkin and the humans here now had a closer bond, it still seemed to be a special event to have an elf come to Firnstayn.

Nuramon sat on Felbion's back and rode the horse at a walk between the rows of houses, accompanied all the way by children and by friendly faces at windows and pleasant greetings. He had no idea what the people of Firnstayn saw when they looked at him. They probably looked at him as a hero of the troll wars. That did not please him, for he had done nothing to merit that honor. He dismounted, not wanting to put on unwarranted airs.

Nuramon tried to orient himself, but nothing was as he remembered it to be. Finally, he came to an open square above which rose a stone longhouse. This might well be the seat of the new jarl. A wide stairway flanked by statues of lions led up to the building at the top. The people gathered around Nuramon but kept a respectful distance. No one dared come too close to him. He thought of his departure from the dwarves. What a change that was in his life, to be met or farewelled with respect wherever he went.

A human soldier came hesitantly down the steps toward him. He was a big, powerful man with a broadsword at his belt. "Are you here to speak to the king?" he asked.

Nuramon did not answer immediately. In the past, they had called their leader *jarl*. Was that also part of Alfadas's legacy? What would Mandred say to discover that there was a king in Firnstayn now? "I am looking for Mandred Torgridson," said Nuramon.

A whisper ran through the crowd, followed by a deathly silence. He had spoken a name that they must only have known from legend . . . which made the soldier's answer all the more surprising. "Mandred was here. And there was an elf named Farodin with him. But they left again long ago."

Suddenly, the crowd parted to let a human through, recognizable as their leader by the magnificent plate armor he wore. The armor was not the work of men but had been made by the blacksmiths of Albenmark. Perhaps it was a gift from Emerelle, or it may even have belonged to Alfadas. Now it was worn by a gray-haired man. He strode toward Nuramon and planted himself in front of the elf. He, too, was a giant of a man, and he wore a sword at his belt that seemed too narrow for the people of these parts. "I am Njauldred Bladebreaker, king of the Fjordlands," he said and nodded. The man radiated a menacing strength, leaving Nuramon in no doubt that the wrath of Njauldred, once loosed, knew no bounds.

"Hail, Njauldred," said Nuramon, surprised that the king wore no crown, which was unusual among humans. It also seemed strange that the Fjordlands were ruled at all from Firnstayn. Was that also something that could be traced back to Alfadas?

"You are looking for Mandred?" Njauldred asked.

"I am. I hope you are able to tell me where I can find him," Nuramon said in a friendly tone.

"It depends who is looking for him," said the big man, crossing his arms over his chest. "He happens to be my ancestor."

Nuramon could detect a certain likeness between Njauldred and Mandred. The king's eyes, especially, were like Mandred's, but this man was much older. Nuramon was still not very good at estimating the age of humans, but he believed that Njauldred was past fifty because his hair was gray. Most of the lines of his face were half hidden behind his beard. Only around his eyes and on his forehead were they fully visible.

"My name is Nuramon, and I—"

Njauldred did not let him finish. "Are you Mandred's companion in arms? Do they call you Nuredred, the elven prince?"

Nuramon was surprised. It seemed the humans had embellished Mandred's history somewhat. "I am Mandred's companion in arms. That much is true. But as for the rest of it, I fear you see more in me than I really am."

Njauldred shook his head. "Modesty is the virtue of heroes."

Nuramon looked into the faces of the people gathered around. They were staring at him as if witnessing the return of the Alben themselves. As he looked around, he noticed something. He was standing near the lion statue on the left at the foot of the stairway. On its shoulder was an inscription.

"A wonderful piece of work, isn't it?" said Njauldred.

"Definitely" was all that Nuramon thought of to say. His eyes were fixed on the artfully flowing elven runes of the inscription. They read, "Forgive me, and wait for us if you can. Farodin."

"Alfadas had the lions put here in memory of Mandred, the ancestor of all of the kings of Firnstayn." Njauldred's expression darkened. "Someone scratched these symbols in it some years ago. Whoever it was certainly didn't come from Firnstayn. No one from around here would desecrate a memorial to Mandred Torgridson that way."

Nuramon stroked the palm of his hand over the inscription. "I think they're beautiful. Perfectly executed, and the words praise the hero Mandred. It seems to be the work of an elf."

Njauldred looked surprised. "Really?"

Nuramon affirmed his opinion. And as he looked into the king's good-natured face, he reprimanded himself for deceiving him about the words' true meaning. It was time to change the subject. "King Njauldred, I have a question. Did Mandred say where he wanted to go?"

The king's eyes grew more serious. "When they arrived here, they discovered that we were caring for a dying elf woman. She had spent many years in the Nightcrags, one of the trolls' fortresses. They say it lies far to the north of here. Not since the days of King Alfadas has any human dared to go anywhere near it. But Faredred, the elf who is Mandred's friend, was bent on sailing to the Nightcrags to free the other elves who were held captive there. It has been more than three years since they set sail. No one has heard from them since."

Nuramon nodded gravely. Two men against a fortress full of trolls . . . that was just like them. "With your permission, King, I will remain here in Firnstayn and wait for the return of Mandred and his elven friend."

"Do you think they will both come back after all this time?"

"I don't think it. I know it," Nuramon replied with a determination that surprised even himself. Their mutual search for Noroelle could not end like this.

The king's face lit up. "There is still hope that Mandred will return to us," he called to the gathered crowd, now quite huge and filling the square. "And the renowned Nuredred will stay in Firnstayn as our guest. An honor indeed."

"My name is Nuramon. Nuredred is what you have turned me into," said the elf in a low voice.

"You know the history of our ancestor," the king said. "You were there. You were really there in the cave, weren't you? And you can tell the skalds the truth. You can tell them what it was really like, so that the people can speak truly about what happened. You can do that, can't you?"

"I can, and I will. Gladly." Of course, he wouldn't tell them the whole truth. He had promised Mandred that he would not tell a soul that they had held each other's hand. The humans here saw in Mandred far more than the man Nuramon knew. They would certainly be disappointed if they discovered the truth. So he decided to relate everything about himself and Farodin exactly as it was, but when it came to Mandred, he would make sure his name became immortal. The people of Firnstayn would erect many more memorials for Torgrid's son.

"Come," said Njauldred, with a friendly clap on Nuramon's shoulder. Then he pointed ahead. "Back there, where his old house once stood, there's a new one that is forever Mandred's. That is where you shall live. This will be a celebration. Your comrade, Faredred—"

"Excuse me, but his name is Farodin," Nuramon objected.

"In any case, the lad certainly drank his share." He slapped Nuramon on the back again. "We'll see what you can manage."

The humans could hardly offer him a bigger feast than what he had experienced among the dwarves, but he was open to surprises. He had to learn to live with the people here. Who knew how long Mandred and Farodin would be away? Maybe months, maybe a year. Maybe longer. He would wait and prepare for the day when he could continue the search together with his companions. The humans might even be able to help him. In the harbor, he had seen two ships that reminded him vaguely of elven ships. Perhaps one of the sailors here knew the island he had seen in the oracle's cave. He would paint it, then show it to the humans.

FAMILIES OF FIRNSTAYN:

NURAMON THE ELF

*I*n those days, when Father Soreis began The Chronicle of Firnstayn *at the behest of Mandred Torgridson, Nuramon the elf came to Firnstayn. He said that he would wait for Mandred's return.*

I was still a child then. Now my life is approaching its end. And I can say with pride that I lived during the time that an elf dwelled among us. I was there when Nuramon came to us. I ran along beside his horse and followed him to the main square. And I was there when he rode away again at the side of Mandred and the elf Farodin.

Nuramon was a blessing on our city, and I look back on those days with a great deal of pleasure. I remember how, during his first spring with us, he won the contest of the skalds. Never before and never since have such legends, such songs, such verse been heard. With his melancholic words about his lost love, he won over the women. That angered the men, and the day ended with a brawl. The elf walked away from it without a scratch. Oh, how many times did Njauldred try to get elven blood into his royal line. But Nuramon was so true to his lost love that he turned away every woman, however beautiful she might be. But the elf was more than a skald. In one year, he practiced bow shooting and perfected the art. Never before had human eyes had an occasion to watch an elf progress from novice to master of an art. He carved statues and painted canvases of great beauty. He took two years and did nothing but come to the Temple of Luth to talk first to Father Soreis and later to me about destiny. He seemed to be a man of the spirit and of art, which led to not a little trouble, for the youth of Firnstayn took Nuramon as their ideal. And soon enough, many of them wanted to give up the sword and the axe and take up the lute instead. Some went so far as to complain that the elf represented a danger to the young men and—with them—the future of Firnstayn. When Njauldred called Nuramon before him and set out these accusations, Nuramon said he would train a handful of our young men to fight and remind them of Mandred's virtues. He called his young warriors the Mandridians, the sons of Mandred. He taught them to fight with a sword, a bow, and also a battle-axe. It was true that he himself was rarely seen with an axe, but he showed the young men what he had seen Mandred do.

Because Mandred and Farodin had left their horses behind, Nuramon took over their care. He said that Mandred had always dreamed that his mare would be the start of a dynasty of great horses. The noblest stallions the North had to offer were brought to her, while Nuramon's and Farodin's steeds covered our most magnificent mares. This was the start of the Firnstayner horses.

In the nineteenth year of the reign of Njauldred, Nuramon and his small troop of fighters fought at the side of the king against the soldiers of the city of Therse. Nuramon rampaged through the enemy like a berserker and afterward served the king as his most prominent adviser. Every one of his fighters survived the battle.

Nuramon trained young Tegrod, the son of Njauldred. He not only taught him what he had already taught his Mandridians, but also showed him how he himself could teach others. And Tegrod's skills spoke for themselves.

In his gratitude, old Njauldred gave Nuramon a ship as a gift, which Nuramon christened with the unlikely name of Albenstar. *But he never took the ship out onto the fjord. He took care of it and stood beside it to look out to sea. He swayed from moods of happiness to moods of great dejection, and this was what characterized him more than anything else. Once each month, he spent a full day at Freya's oak and paid tribute to Mandred's wife, although he admitted to me on a winter evening that he had never personally met her. And once a month, too, he climbed to the stone circle. People said he met others of the Albenfolk up there. Once, he accompanied me into the mountains, to the Cave of Luth. He made sacrifice to the ironmen, as was customary, and when we were inside the cave, which since the days of Alfadas had again been consecrated, he told me what had once taken place in there.*

And then—one day—he left. And his departure came as a surprise even for Nuramon.

As Recorded by Lurethor Hjemison
Volume Twelve of the Temple Library of Luth in Firnstayn,
PAGES 53 TO 55

OLD COMPANIONS

Nuramon woke with a start from his midday nap. From out in the street came the sounds of shouting. Nuramon rose and dressed. He was still buttoning his shirt when the door flew open. It was Neltor, the young king of Firnstayn.

"My king? How can I be of service to you?" asked Nuramon. He had once trained the young ruler in the name of his father, and the young man still looked at him as a kind of mentor. In his looks, he did not take after his father, who had borne a strong resemblance to Mandred. Neltor was closer to Alfadas. "Is it another feud?"

"No. Imagine it." His eyes shone. "As we speak, my ancestor is sailing up the fjord. How should I receive him?"

"Mandred? Mandred Torgridson?"

"The same."

"By the Alben," said Nuramon, and he sighed with relief. It almost felt as if the air he exhaled was the breath of the past forty-seven years. Finally, his companions had returned. Although he had found plenty to keep him occupied in Firnstayn, he had often found himself worrying about his companions—and often enough, he had been tempted to take up his search for Noroelle alone. "Is there an elf with him?"

"Yes."

Nuramon smiled at the king. "You asked me how you should receive Mandred. As your trusted adviser, I say to you, you are already wearing the right armor." It was the armor of Alfadas. "If you now arm yourself with your best axe and stand by the lion statues on the steps of your hall, then you will sufficiently impress Mandred."

"Thank you, Master."

"Neltor, call me your friend, call me your confidant, but please don't call me Master anymore."

The young man grinned and left.

Nuramon had to hurry. He stepped out into the street and headed toward the city gate. How would Mandred look now? He might well be an old man.

Suddenly, Voagad, another of his students, was at Nuramon's side. Wide-eyed, he said, "Mandred Torgridson. This will be a celebration."

"As usual, all you think about is drinking . . . which is good. Mandred will appreciate it. Go and round up the Mandridians. They should assemble at the Temple of Luth. Under no circumstances are they to come to the square before I give them a sign."

Voagad was gone again. Nuramon watched as he ran off. Over the years, Mandred had become more than the ancestor of Firnstayn's kings. He had become the forefather of Firnstayn itself, and Nuramon had done more than a little to bring about the transformation. He had painted Mandred in a light that now shone far beyond Firnstayn, spreading across the entire Fjordlands.

Nuramon had not told the people of Firnstayn the whole story, just as he had not mentioned that the Devanthar was still alive. Nuramon had thought of the demon often during his years in Firnstayn. Had it found fresh fields in which to sow its misfortune? Or was it lurking somewhere, waiting for the moment to face him and his companions again? He did not know. He often wondered why fate had been so hard on them, and whether the Devanthar hadn't sometimes had a hand in things.

Jubilation rolled through the city. So Mandred was already here. A crush of people was pushing slowly along the street. Fifty years earlier, there would have been far fewer. Firnstayn's growth seemed unstoppable. In another fifty years, Mandred wouldn't even be able to move, so many people would be thronging the streets.

Nuramon waited it out. Somewhere there ahead of him, among the Firnstayners, were his companions. A gap opened up through the crowd.

There they were. Mandred and Farodin. They looked exactly as they did in his memory. He was happy that Mandred had not aged. His companions caught sight of him. The people all around held their breath. It seemed everyone wanted to see how Nuramon the elf finally reunited with his companion in arms Mandred.

"Nuramon, you old blowhard," Mandred shouted as he stormed up the road toward him.

Farodin said nothing, but his face showed his relief.

Mandred threw his arms around the elf and squeezed so hard that Nuramon could hardly breathe. In the years with Njauldred, he had learned to accept such well-meant indelicacies.

Nuramon looked down at the jarl. "I was starting to think I'd never see you again."

Mandred grinned broadly. "We had to boot a few trolls in the ass."

"And it seems we rather lost track of time," Farodin added, causing astonished looks on the faces of many around them. Nuramon understood that they had become victims of time when they passed through an Albenstar.

While Mandred luxuriated in the crowd of well-wishers, Farodin and Nuramon went ahead. Farodin told him about the trolls, about Yilvina's death, and how they freed the other elves who were being held prisoner.

Nuramon took the news about Yilvina hard. She had been a good companion during the search for Guillaume. And it was only because of her that they had made it out of Albenmark in the first place. If she hadn't let them knock her unconscious, then it was possible that they never would have found a way to leave and start their search for Noroelle.

"How long have you been waiting?" Farodin asked, dragging him back from his memories.

"Forty-seven years," Nuramon replied.

Mandred's laughter reached them from behind. "Then you've lived here longer than I ever did. So are you a real Firnstayner now?"

Nuramon turned around. "Maybe. But it might also be that the Firnstayners have turned into real elves."

Mandred laughed even louder, and the people with him. "What's the name of the king these days?"

"His name is Neltor Tegrodson. You met his grandfather, Njauldred."

Mandred pushed through to Nuramon and asked quietly, "Is he any good?"

"He's a wise leader and—"

"I mean, is he a good fighter, a true—"

"I know what you mean . . . yes, he's a good fighter. He's an outstanding archer." He saw Mandred frown. "Impressive with the long sword, but even more so with the short sword." Displeasure deepened in the human's expression. "But unrivaled with the axe."

Mandred's face transformed instantly. He practically lit up. "Then the best weapon won through after all," he said with pride.

"Come on. I'll introduce you to your descendant," said Nuramon, pointing ahead. "And later I'll show you your mare and *her* descendants."

"Mare? Descendants? Did you . . ."

"Just as you are the forefather of the kings, your mare is the fore-mother of the Firnstayner horses."

Mandred grinned proudly. "Nuramon, I'm in your debt."

When they reached the main square, it was clear how much had changed in the city. All of the roads were paved, the houses made of hewed stone, but the Temple of Luth was what really caught the eye. People from across the entire kingdom had spent thirty years building it. The square was practically empty of people, although the residents of the city jostled shoulder to shoulder in the side streets and at the windows of the buildings. *Neltor did a good job with that*, thought Nuramon. This way, Mandred could meet the king and his retinue freely.

"Is that him?" asked Mandred, looking over to where Neltor stood.

"Yes. Come and meet him." The three crossed the square side by side and stood before Neltor.

"Welcome, Mandred Torgridson. I am Neltor Tegrodson, your descendant." He bowed. "Stay with us, and be safe in the knowledge that for us, you will always be Jarl Mandred." The insecurity that Neltor felt now that he was faced with his famous forebear was clear to see. He had trouble holding Mandred's eye, and his hands shook a little.

It seemed to make no difference to Mandred. He was moved by the reception, and spoke little while Neltor searched for the friendliest words he could find to express his esteem for Mandred and what he meant to him and to their city.

When Neltor spoke of Nuramon's service to himself, his father, and his grandfather, the elf gave a signal, and from the side street beside the Temple of Luth, the Mandridians marched into the square.

"Mandred, there are some Firnstayners I think you ought to meet." Nuramon pointed to the two dozen assembled soldiers. They wore light leather armor, and each was armed with a short sword and an axe.

Some also carried a bow and a quiver, while still others had strapped a round shield to their backs. "These are the men I have trained," he said. "The Mandridians."

Mandred looked at the troop in astonishment. "By Norgrimm, I've never seen such determined faces. I'd campaign with these men tomorrow."

"I've taught them everything I know," Nuramon said, proud that he had trained all of them to handle the axe well. He remembered everything that Mandred had taught his son, Alfadas, spicing it a little with what Alwerich had shown him. "They've proved themselves in battle many times over the years."

"With these men at our side, we would have brought back the troll prince's liver for the city dogs," Mandred muttered grimly.

Nuramon exchanged a look with Farodin. Barely perceptibly, Farodin shook his head.

"Mandred, you would honor me to join me in my hall for beer and mead," said Neltor then.

"An offer that Mandred could never refuse. But the men there," he said, pointing to the Mandridians, "they are coming, too." He turned to Farodin and Nuramon. "What about you?"

"I'd say that's a matter for the jarl to take up with his descendants," Farodin replied.

Mandred said nothing, but let himself be led away by his family. They seemed to be talking to him from all sides at once. The people at the edge of the square and in the side streets followed the royal train.

"He's enjoying this almost too much," said Farodin.

"He'll be able to feed off it for a while on our way to Noroelle's gate."

Farodin looked at him in disbelief. "Have you found it?"

"I've seen it."

"What does it look like?" Nuramon had never seen Farodin so curious.

"Come with me to Mandred's house."

Farodin followed him. He seemed on edge, as if he had run out of patience, for which Nuramon could hardly blame him. Still, he himself had waited nearly fifty years here for Farodin and Mandred, although he would much rather have gone in search of the place he had seen in Dareen's star grotto.

When they reached Mandred's house, Farodin looked around in surprise. Nuramon had changed a few things over the years. He had become something of a headache to the craftsmen of Firnstayn. Cupboards, tables, and chairs had to be made not only to accord with Mandred's tastes but also with those of an elf. At the same time, the weapons, the chests, and the shields on the walls had to remind a visitor that this was the house of a warrior. Nuramon was particularly proud of the large battle-axe. The smith had forged it to his specifications and had done the same with another axe modeled after Alwerich's.

"Mandred will like this. It's plain, as a warrior's house should be. And this painting . . ." He stepped before a portrait of Alfadas. "Did you paint it?"

"Yes."

"You surprise me."

"Then you should see this one," said Nuramon. He stepped over to a covered painting standing on an easel. Then he removed the cloth covering the painting, one he had been working on for thirty years. It showed the landscape he had seen in the oracle's cave.

Farodin took a step back to look at the painting better. His eyes traversed the large picture: the water, the island, the mainland behind it with its forests, and, behind them, the range of peaks.

"When I left Iskendria, it took me some time to find the gate to the oracle," Nuramon said. While Farodin scrutinized the painting down to the finest detail, Nuramon told him about the puzzling entrance, about the children of the Darkalben, and the image he had seen in the star cave. "Dareen told me I should reunite with you and Mandred. I was supposed to wait here for your return. You have no idea how many times I was tempted to go out and find this place, but Dareen's words and your inscription on the statue held me back."

Farodin touched the painting. "Is this yalpaint?"

"Yes. I made it myself. The people here know nothing about the pigments from Yaldemee."

Farodin looked at him with respect. "It's a masterpiece."

"The days can be very long. And you should see my early attempts. But this, now, is what I saw. Dareen said something else . . ." He fell silent and thought of the oracle and her appearance.

"What was it?"

"She said that there are two ways to break the enchantment that seals Noroelle's gate. With the help of the hourglass or of an Albenstone. I've thought about it a lot and wonder whether we need the actual hourglass and not just the sand."

"Let's find this landscape first. The depiction is wonderful. Which part of the world does it show?"

"On my way here, I tried to find it. And I've asked seafarers if they know it. All without success. You don't know how happy I am that you are here."

"This picture will help us. With the grains of sand, we should be able to find this island." Farodin stepped up very close to the picture. "I can't tell if this is a lake or the sea."

Nuramon had spent years pondering the coastal landscape in the image. "It is the sea. I've spent a long time looking at the waves. They are ocean waves." He ran one finger over the painting. "This mountain range could be useful. It is certainly a big range, but not so high that there is snow on the peaks."

"It could be a fjord. Is it close to here, perhaps?"

"No. Mountains as bright as these don't exist here. I've asked every seafarer, every wayfarer, everyone who knows this part of the world. And on my way here, I kept a lookout for these mountains. They are not in the Fjordlands."

Farodin stepped back again and looked at the picture in its entirety. "By the Alben. I did you an injustice in Iskendria. This painting. I feel myself drawn to search for this place."

"We did each other an injustice. But we had to go our separate ways so that we could both move ahead . . . along our path to Noroelle. I think the faun oak sent us through that gate and into the desert on purpose. Perhaps it had some inkling of what lay in the future. I've thought about it often, and not a day has passed when I haven't wondered why the queen did not simply send out a troop to take me back."

"So none from Albenmark have been here?"

"No one. Occasionally, I met with Xern. The queen does not talk about us, nor does she tolerate so much as the mention of a word about us in her presence."

The corner of Farodin's mouth twitched. "Either she's beside herself with anger and is just waiting for us to return so that she can cast her judgment on us. Or there's something more," he finally said.

"The gates are open again and unguarded. They have been ever since the end of the troll war. It seems that whatever threat Emerelle feared has been averted."

"She said that Guillaume's death could lead to the rise of something and that she could still sense the power of the Devanthar. How could something like that simply fade away?"

"The Devanthar has not been sighted again. No one mentions it anymore. At least, that's what Xern says. Many times, I've wondered what the Devanthar is planning and whom it's after. And if it's really done with us."

"Don't lose any sleep over it. We avoid Albenmark as much as possible, and for the moment, we forget the Devanthar. With this picture, you may have shown me a way. At least, I feel inside as if you have."

"There's something else. With the dwarves, I—"

The door flew open, and Mandred came in, singing loudly. "'Out stepped Torgrid's sturdy son, the boar's liver in his hand!' Ah, there you are. And? Have you seen her?"

"Seen whom?" Farodin asked.

"Her! That wonderful woman. Neltor's sister."

"The women here all look the same to me," Farodin said.

Nuramon smiled. "He means Tharhild."

"Exactly! What a name. Tharhild." The human grinned suggestively.

"Who would have thought," said Farodin. "Mandred Torgridson's in love."

The jarl seemed not to have heard Farodin's words. "How closely am I related to her?" he asked Nuramon.

"Let me think. You're the father of Alfadas, and he's the father of . . ." He fell silent and thought it over. But then it occurred to Nuramon to wonder why his friend wanted to know. With Ragna, he seemed not to have such misgivings at all. Or did he perhaps fear that Tharhild might be his own daughter? "There are eleven generations between you and Tharhild. You don't need to worry at all. Unless . . ."

"Unless what?" Mandred asked.

"Remember the name *Ragna*?"

Pure terror spread across Mandred's face. "Is Tharhild the . . ."

Nuramon let his friend stew a moment longer.

"Come on, tell me. What does Ragna have to do with Tharhild?"

"Well, she is Tharhild's . . . aunt."

Mandred sighed with relief. "What became of her? Did she grieve for me?"

"Mandred Torgridson, the great womanizer. Skirt chaser of Firnstayn. Just has to share his bed with a woman once, and she spends the rest of her life crying for him and waiting for him to come home. No, Mandred. She found a good man, had children with him, and had a happy life before she passed away. But then again . . ."

"Then again what . . . come on, out with it!"

"I've been eavesdropping on the women at court. They tell stories about you, Mandred. Not about the warrior, but about Mandred the lover, coming back after years away just to seduce the women."

Mandred grinned.

"What do you think of your house?" Farodin asked the jarl. He obviously wanted to change the subject.

Mandred looked around. "By Norgrimm. This . . . this is the hall of a warrior." He stood in front of the great battle-axe. "I like that . . ." Then something seemed to come to him. "Mandred the lover," he muttered to himself. "I have to go. Nuramon, my friend, let's sit down together later. I want to hear how things were for you." Then Mandred was gone again as quickly as he had come. In his hurry, he had not even noticed the portrait of his son.

Farodin stared at the door that the human had just disappeared through. "He really means it."

Nuramon sighed. "Yes. But it will be a rude awakening for him tomorrow. He'll see Freya's oak, and the sight of it will open up all the old wounds. You know what he's like."

"Humans are not as loyal as we are, Nuramon. Perhaps he's over Freya."

"The oak is a great symbol, too great. As long as it stands, he'll remember her."

"You've come to know the humans very well."

"Yes. Forty-seven years. I've done a lot in that time. This world makes you use time differently than you normally would as an elf. I've seen young men grow old and girls become mothers and grandmothers. As much as I've loved these years here, I want to be on my way again, searching for Noroelle."

"You've changed, my friend."

The observation stirred Nuramon. True, he had changed. But Farodin was also not the same as he had been. To hear the word *friend* from him was a gift that Nuramon had never expected, especially after their unpleasant quarrel in Iskendria. "I'm glad that you are here with Mandred . . . friend."

THE POWER
OF THE SAND

The young king of Firnstayn proved himself a generous ruler. It took some time, but he had Nuramon's ship, the *Albenstar*, properly outfitted, because from the start, it was clear to the three companions that Farodin's boat was too small and fragile for the journey that lay ahead of them. King Neltor also realized this. He insisted that his bodyguard, the Mandridians, accompany them. And he gave them a heavy chest of silver to take along so that they could stock up their provisions in faraway harbors.

Farodin was far from certain of the success of their journey. Nuramon set great hope in the picture he had painted and did not want to even discuss how long they might have to search to find the island. How could you travel to a place if you did not know where it lay? But they kept their doubts hidden from the crew. What would the humans say if they knew? Even Mandred, whom they had known for many years now, was restless. He saw to the needs of his Mandridians, but he was afraid they might be old men before their search was at an end.

Farodin had memorized Nuramon's picture down to the finest detail. Every day, he tried to use his seeking spell to find out where this place might be. But it was different with the picture than it had been with the grains of sand, and far less definite. With the sand, either he knew exactly where to find the grains or he did not. When he looked at the landscape Nuramon had painted, all he felt was the vague sense that they had to set a course eastward. But was a feeling enough, especially one as indistinct as this?

They avoided the waters of the trolls, following the deeply fissured coastline of Skoltan for several weeks instead.

It was a summer morning, and they were camped on a beach beneath white-gray chalk cliffs. Farodin had moved away from the others. As always, he cast the first seeking spell to try to find a pointer to the landscape in the picture. He was looking for more than an indeterminate feeling. He wanted to *know* which way they had to sail and not merely *suspect* it.

Then he cast the spell a second time. This time, he held the silver flask of sand tightly in his hands and went in search of the grains of sand from the smashed hourglass. He sensed one grain, some distance inland. He focused himself and allowed the power of the sand to flow. As a magnet attracts a sliver of iron, the sand in the bottle could summon a single grain.

Farodin reached out his hand, and soon he felt a very faint touch. Satisfied, the elf added the grain to the sand in the bottle. It was one tiny step, but every one of these steps took him a little bit closer to Noroelle.

With care, he sealed the silver bottle again. Then Farodin cast the seeking spell a third time. He closed his eyes and thought of the sea. He could also sense grains of sand that lay in deep water, but it was difficult for him to summon them. The constant motion of the water tended to hold them back. A single moment of inattention was enough for him to lose his connection to the grain. It was best to get as close as possible to them, to go out in a boat and catch them as soon as they came to the surface.

The sea worried him. How many grains of sand might it have swallowed? Grains that he would perhaps never be able to find. And how many of those originally in the hourglass could he do without when the time came to try to break through the queen's sorcery?

Farodin suppressed the thought again and focused fully on the spell. He sensed individual grains in the silty seabed and . . . a tremor ran through him. Something strange was happening. The silver bottle in his hand had moved. Something was pulling at it. Farodin was so surprised that he lost his concentration and had to abandon the spell. What had happened?

For a long time, he sat on the beach and looked out over the sea. What could have caused such a strange phenomenon? Was there perhaps a place where many grains of sand lay together, more than he had gathered in all these years? Or was there someone else, like him, collecting the sand? A collector far more successful than he had been? Was there any way to rule out that possibility? Perhaps he should try to include Nuramon's picture in his seeking spell for the grains of sand.

He closed his eyes again and tried to concentrate. And again, he felt the pull toward the northeast, even clearer than before. An image took shape in his mind. He saw the stone, the very one on which Emerelle had smashed the hourglass. But what did that prove? Couldn't there still be another collector? And perhaps that collector was there, to the northeast, waiting for them. Farodin dismissed the idea. Their ceaseless search must be affecting his mind. There was also a much simpler explanation. Where else would more sand likely be than near the stone where Emerelle smashed the hourglass? He must have sensed the crossing point to Noroelle's prison in the Shattered World. He decided not to reveal all this to his companions. Why should he inflict his probably baseless fears on them? He returned to camp and told them they had to set a northeast course, out into the open ocean.

As brave as the Mandridians were, after three weeks out of sight of land, they started getting worried. Even Mandred, whose courage was beyond question, told them one morning that he was afraid they might reach the edge of the world and plunge into nothingness if they didn't change course soon.

It fell to silver-tongued Nuramon to allay their fears. They trusted him. He was so skillful with his words that he soon had them laughing along with him whenever he spoke to them. But all his honeyed words couldn't erase the staleness of the water in their barrels, and drinking the stuff took courage. Their remaining provisions were also running low, but they would soon reach their destination. Farodin had to hold tightly to the silver bottle to stop it from being physically pulled from his hand whenever he cast his seeking spell.

On the thirty-seventh day of their journey, they reached land. They ran the boat ashore and lost two days because nothing in the world would keep the Mandridians on board the *Albenstar* a moment longer. They searched for water and hunted, and even Farodin enjoyed the taste of fresh spring water again. But it was hard for him to keep a cool head, for he knew how close they were to their goal.

Once they had replenished their supplies and the Mandridians had recuperated somewhat, Farodin set their course northward along the coast. The oppressive days they had spent on the high seas were forgotten, replaced by the almost euphoric mood with which the Mandridians had begun their journey at the side of their illustrious forebear. Even the humans seemed to sense how near they were to their destination.

On the thirty-ninth day of the voyage, the coastline curved sharply to the east, and they turned into a wide bay. Fresh wind filled the sail, and they were making good headway when Nuramon suddenly let out a sharp cry. "The mountains! Look at the mountains!"

Farodin, too, recognized one of the mountains from Nuramon's picture. Everything seemed to match. The trees growing along the shore, the colors of the distant mountains. Although they were sailing at a good rate, the Mandridians leaped to the oars and hauled hard, driving the boat forward even faster.

Farodin and Mandred stood feverishly in the bow. The stiff breeze tousled Farodin's long hair. Tears stood in his eyes, and he was not ashamed of them.

"Do you feel that?" Nuramon asked. He pointed beyond a peninsula extending far into the bay. "There are many Albenpaths here. They all gravitate toward one point . . . it has to lie over there, on the other side of that forest."

When they finally rounded the peninsula, Nuramon let out another cry of joy. He danced on the deck of the ship like a man possessed. The Mandridians laughed and exchanged a few crude jokes at Nuramon's expense. They could not appreciate what this moment meant for the two elves, thought Farodin. He was not able to give free rein to his feelings like his friend. His own joy was silent, but he was no less stirred inside. In front of them lay a small island with a rocky shore and a grove of trees. It was the island in Nuramon's picture.

The Mandridians went back to rowing as mightily as they could. The ship with its large, blue sail shot across the water like a loon. They had to change course, though, as gray reefs churned the water ahead of them. They were no more than a hundred paces from the shore, but there was nowhere to land here. They would have to round the northern tip of the little island and look for safer waters on the lee side.

Farodin looked at Nuramon. His companion understood what he was thinking without him having to say a word and grinned mischievously. Then both of them leaped overboard into the sea. The water only came to their chests. Half swimming, half wading, they made their way to shore as the boat sailed on northward.

Now Farodin, too, could feel the lines of power that marked the Albenpaths converging toward a star. The elves moved southward onto the tidal flats, now hidden under the high tide. Soon, they were standing at the junction of the paths. At high tide, it was hidden beneath the waters, but they did not have to see it to feel its power. Everything around them matched with Nuramon's picture. There could be no doubt at all that they were in the right location. They had found the place from which Emerelle had sent the woman they loved into exile in the Shattered World.

Stirred by an incomparable sense of joy, Farodin embraced his companion. Their search was finally at an end. Now everything would be good again.

A SPELL
AT EBB TIDE

It was morning, and Nuramon sat at the very stone on which the queen had once destroyed the hourglass. They had found many grains of sand there, and Farodin had told him how, in the queen's dressing chamber, he had had a vision of this same stone.

Nuramon still found it hard to believe that they had actually found the place that the oracle had shown him. It was low tide. The sea had drained away, leaving a rippled mudflat between the island and the mainland. The tidal landscape reminded Nuramon of the path he and Alwerich had followed to the oracle, how it had resembled a dry riverbed.

Only about twenty steps away lay the Albenstar. The outgoing tide had laid it bare. The star was clearly visible by the shellfish that had collected at the spot.

It seemed almost a miracle that they had found land so far to the east. Beyond the island stretched what looked to be an entire continent, a land that the people of the Fjordlands and of Angnos, Drusna, and Fargon knew nothing about. Untouched land.

"He's ready," said Mandred, slapping Nuramon on the shoulder. "Farodin's all set." The human looked tired. He had spent the past few days in the little tender, rowing Farodin back and forth across the bay, looking for scattered grains of sand.

Nuramon just nodded.

"This time it will work." Mandred's attempt at encouragement helped little. Nuramon had tried too many times already to open the gate to Noroelle, but each time, he had failed miserably. First, he had tried it at high tide, but the water seemed to weaken the spell, and to open the gate to reach Noroelle, he needed all of his power.

Nuramon stood up.

The crew came and gathered by the shore. They did not want to miss the spectacle, even though there had been little to see so far. Farodin was not with them.

The island they were on might well have an identical counterpart in the Shattered World. Just a single gate on the Albenstar, that was all they needed, and they would be with Noroelle. Nuramon could not believe that they were so close to the woman they loved and yet could not reach her. It was impossible to open a gate at the Albenstar under their own power. The queen's barrier was too strong.

"Farodin's found every grain of sand here," said Mandred.

His companion's words could not hide the fact that they probably still possessed too little of the sand and that the queen's magic was superior to their own.

Finally, Farodin joined them. He seemed relaxed and said in a calm voice, "Keep in mind, Mandred, that you and the others must not try to help us, whatever happens. In the end, the spell would miscarry because of your concern."

"You have my word." The other Firnstayners chorused their agreement. Then Mandred clapped Nuramon on the shoulder. "Remember your heroism in Luth's cave."

Together, Nuramon and Farodin walked down to the Albenstar. The shells formed a circle on the Albenstar and radiated some way out along the Albenpaths as well, creating an image of the sun. Right in the center of the small circle, some of the shellfish formed a pile. It seemed the sea was too weak to wash them away. The Albenstar held them in place.

They took their positions inside the circle of shells.

"What's the matter, Nuramon?" Farodin asked.

"We are so close to her, yet—"

Farodin interrupted him. "I will draw the power from the sand. That's what I am good at. And I will pass it on to you. Like that, we can call up all the power we have between us."

It calmed Nuramon to know that Farodin wanted to help him as much as he could, but his companion had no idea how powerful the queen's barrier was. Mandred's comparison with the Cave of Luth was not absurd. In his attempt to break through the barrier the day before, Nuramon had suffered terrible pain. Farodin, too, had attempted to open a gate, but he had failed at the start and had not felt how strong the magic was that they were pitting themselves against. They had to summon far more power to reach their goal. Fate seemed to take pleasure in throwing insurmountable tasks in their path. Nuramon thought of their battle with the Devanthar. They had been just as poorly equipped for that as they were for the queen's barrier. But if they were able to rise above their own limitations just once, then maybe it would be enough to rescue Noroelle.

"Ready?" Farodin asked.

"No, I'm not. But I want to get to her." Nuramon took hold of Farodin's hand and held it tightly. Then he closed his eyes. He focused, and the Albenpaths slowly appeared before his eyes. Three ran parallel to the ground, and one came up directly out of the earth, penetrated the Albenstar, and traced a line skyward. This was the path that would lead them to Noroelle. It was black, shot through with veins of green light. Nuramon could feel the queen's barrier, but he could not see it. It formed a kind of crust enveloping and blocking any access to the path to Noroelle. Like a sieve, it seemed to let only a fraction of the power of the path come through. The crust was harder than anything Nuramon knew of. He decided now to attack it directly and not, as previously, to approach the barrier with caution.

He began to weave the spell, preparing himself to launch a ferocious attack that would break through the barrier and open a wound in the Albenstar. Like a sword, his magic slashed at the barrier. But before it struck home, Nuramon felt something gather in front of him. Suddenly, it reached out for him physically, and searing pain shot through him.

He broke off the spell when he could no longer feel his own body. Then he released himself from the barrier, and the pain instantly disappeared.

Nuramon opened his eyes and let go of Farodin's hand. He sighed.

Farodin looked at him in sympathy. "You used none of my power."

"I didn't get that far. This barrier is stronger than the iron entrance to the kingdom of the dwarves."

"Do you want to give up?" Farodin asked. "No one would call you weak if you did."

"Noroelle is on the other side. I'll try again."

He took hold of Farodin's hand, closed his eyes, and refocused his energy. He had to work faster. At the moment the power of the barrier gathered to hurt him, he already had to have broken through the crust. He went through the spell one more time in his mind. Then he tried again. His own power hit the barrier, this time penetrating it like a sword slicing into the body of an enemy, and still he was unable to break through the magical wall before the pain grew too much for him. It was as if he had pushed a blade into his own body.

Suddenly, he felt Farodin come to his aid with his own magical power. The grains of sand gave him great strength and helped Nuramon withstand the pain. He tried desperately to puncture the barrier, but his progress was very slow. And the more he put into breaking through the queen's magic, the greater the pain became.

Nuramon heard a cry. It was Farodin. The pain seemed to have attacked his companion as well. Nuramon sensed that they were now sharing the pain. This gave him more strength for his own spell, and he pushed deeper into the barrier. But with every tiny advance, the pain grew, until finally, it was so strong that Farodin's cries of torment seemed unending. The pain was everywhere. As he had in the ice cave, Nuramon gradually lost all sensation in his body, but his magic was still moving him forward. The protective barrier was almost torn through. Any moment, he would be able to start directing his power into the dark Albenpath to open the gate. Bit by bit, he was coming closer. Soon they would be with Noroelle.

Then the pain became truly immense. He could still feel Farodin's hand in his, but his companion could give him no more power. Nothing more flowed between them, and that knowledge struck at Nuramon's spirit like a bolt of lightning. He fought desperately against failure. His power went out like a candle, and he was thrown out of the spell.

Nuramon opened his eyes. Carefully, he released Farodin's hand. His companion was staring at him with glassy eyes and breathing heavily. The bottle holding the sand slipped from his fingers. Nuramon had never seen Farodin look as vulnerable as he did in that moment.

"Forgive me," Farodin finally said. "I was at the end of my strength. The pain . . . is that what you felt yesterday?"

"Yes," said Nuramon. "The pain comes with every attempt I make."

"I had no idea . . . Where did you learn to endure that?"

"In the Cave of Luth."

Farodin's eyes widened in astonishment.

Nuramon went on. "Our spell did not fail because of the pain. We are simply not strong enough to take on the queen like this. We are like riverbank sprites trying to trip a centaur. I am drained. I am empty. And you are, too, aren't you?"

Farodin nodded and sighed deeply.

Nuramon looked to Mandred. The jarl and the Mandridians were watching them with concern, but as they had promised, they had not moved from where they were.

"Everything all right?" Mandred called to them.

"It is over," Nuramon answered sourly.

The disappointment on Mandred's face hurt Nuramon. The human had always believed in his magical talents and thought of him as a great sorcerer.

Mandred and the Firnstayners retreated to the woods that covered almost the entire island. When they were gone, Nuramon turned back to Farodin. "We have to talk about how to proceed."

Side by side, they returned to the island, climbing over the stone and making their way into the forest. For a long time, neither said a word. Nuramon thought of what the djinn in Valemas had said: "Great power is needed to defeat great power." They were not yet ready to break the barrier. "We have to give up for now and find another way," said Nuramon.

"Let us try again tomorrow," said Farodin.

"Listen to me. It is impossible."

"We are so close. We can't just—"

"It is impossible," Nuramon repeated. "How many times have you heard me say those words?"

Farodin pulled up. "Never."

"Then believe me. We are not strong enough to take on the power of this barrier. There is only one hope left. An Albenstone."

Farodin lifted up the silver bottle. "We have found a lot of the sand, and it will be easier now for me to find more. Then we can try again."

"I can't believe you still think that will work, Farodin. The power of the sand is too weak, too diffuse. If we had at least the hourglass itself . . ."

"I have been keeping a lookout for it, but there is no trace of it here. There's simply nothing."

"The sand has played its part. It led us here, and it may serve us again . . . Imagine Noroelle, right now, in the Shattered World, wandering among the trees just as we are, thinking about us and perhaps Obilee. I wish this thought alone would give me the strength we need. I know we can push ourselves harder and farther, but everything has its limits, and I sense that we still lack far too much power."

"But how are we supposed to find an Albenstone? Apart from the queen, I know of none among the Albenkin who possesses a stone like that. And Emerelle will never give us hers." He hesitated. "But perhaps it could be stolen?"

Nuramon leaned his back against a tree. "We will not demean ourselves. There must be other stones."

"Even if they exist, we can't find them. No one will ever show you the way to an Albenstone. Anyone who has one would keep it hidden. And assuming we found one, would you know how to use it?"

"No. But there is one place where we can learn that. And maybe we'll even discover some clue to finding an Albenstone there."

"Iskendria."

Nuramon nodded. "Yes. Iskendria."

They reached the other side of the island, where they had set up their camp. When they appeared from the trees, Mandred came toward them expectantly. "What now?" he asked.

"We failed. And we will keep failing no matter how many times we try it," said Farodin. "We will return when we are stronger."

"We are going to search for an Albenstone and collect every grain of sand we can find," Nuramon added. "Then we are coming back."

Mandred nodded. His initial disappointment seemed to have softened. "Only an idiot fights a fight he can't win. The victor in a war is the one who wins the final battle, and our final battle is far from being fought." He turned to their crew. "We're breaking camp."

While the men set to work, the three companions returned to the ship. It was Mandred who broke the silence. "There are Albenpaths here. Could we use one of them to get back to Firnstayn?"

"And risk another jump in time?" replied Farodin. "We've learned to accept it, but what about the crew? They would only hate us if they got home to find their children were old men. You don't want that, do you?"

"Never. I just wanted to know if it would work."

"The faun oak told us that we will be able to travel between the Albenstars of one world someday. But I don't think we're ready for that yet."

Then Nuramon said, "No, we are ready for it. I tried the spell when I was searching for the oracle, as I traveled through Angnos. At some point, I just took the risk, and it worked. It isn't difficult. You just have to know the path you're following very well. I used the spell the faun oak taught us. Instead of following a path to another world, you simply choose one that doesn't leave the world you're in."

"Why didn't you tell me that before?" Farodin asked.

Nuramon smiled. He was close to reminding his comrade how many times *he* had kept what he knew to himself. "Compared with everything else that happened, it didn't seem that important. But Mandred has once again asked the right question." Nuramon saw pride spread across the jarl's face. "The voyage behind us was a voyage of distance. The one ahead of us is a journey of a different sort." He pointed along the Albenpath. "We came across this path very early. If I'm not mistaken, it crosses the southern Fjordlands. For our return journey now, that doesn't help us, because we don't know which Albenstar it leads to. But it may well help us get back here. The queen's barrier only blocks Noroelle's path, not the others."

"So you think we should jump from Albenstar to Albenstar from now on?"

"If we do, we can reach Iskendria quickly, and avoid both humans and long days of travel through difficult regions." He was thinking of the desert.

Farodin smiled. "In other words, you want to travel like the Alben."

"That is exactly what the faun oak was suggesting," said Nuramon.

"What do you say to that, Mandred?"

The jarl grinned broadly. "You're asking me if I want to travel for moments instead of months? How else could I possibly answer? By Luth, yes!"

Farodin nodded. "Then let us return to Firnstayn, and from there, we travel in the footsteps of the Alben."

THE CHRONICLE
OF FIRNSTAYN

O*n the fifth day of the fourth moon in the third year of the reign of King Neltor, the* Albenstar *returned to Firnstayn. Mandred, Nuramon, Farodin, and the Mandridians, all of them came back safe and sound. It was a day of rejoicing, and the people celebrated their homecoming with a great feast. Tharhild brought her son and presented him to Mandred, and the jarl acknowledged the child as his. King Neltor even offered to hand over his crown to Mandred if his ancestor so wished. But the jarl declined the king's offer, saying that the kingdom needed a steadier ruler than he would be, one who could be there to take care of things. Mandred's fate, though, was to wander restlessly and to spend time in Firnstayn only rarely. As he held the child in his arms, there was a sadness in his eyes, as if he knew he would never see his boy again. After that, he avoided the child.*

Mandred and his companions stayed ten days more, preparing themselves for another important journey. But the Mandridians who had accompanied the three companions told of the land far to the east and spoke about the magic of the two elves, and Mandred's wisdom. It had not been a voyage into battle, but one of magic.

When Mandred, Nuramon, and Farodin set sail, we thought it likely that we would never again see the return of the jarl in our lifetime. In the days that followed, a gloom settled over Firnstayn. The king assured us that Mandred would always be there if we were faced with grave danger. Ever since that day, we have been waiting for the return of the mighty jarl of Firnstayn. There are some who fear the day, for when he returns, a time of adversity will be upon us.

As Recorded by Lurethor Hjemison
Volume Seventeen of the Temple Library of Luth in
Firnstayn, page 89

NEW PATHS

Farodin stroked his stallion's neck soothingly. The animal was as unsettled as he was. He peered into the darkness suspiciously. Nuramon had told Mandred and him exactly what to expect, but Farodin had not counted on it tearing at his nerves like this.

The silence was eerie. He had the unrelenting feeling that there was something lurking out there. But what could survive in nothingness?

With great care, he followed the narrow path of pulsing light that stretched through the endless darkness, making sure he did not stray from it. It was impossible to say what was waiting for him outside the path. Was it like a narrow bridge that spanned an abyss?

After a few steps, they reached a point where four paths of light intersected. An Albenstar. Nuramon, who led the way, stopped for a moment. Then he changed to a reddish light path and waved to them to follow him.

Farodin and Mandred looked at each other uneasily. There was no way at all to orient oneself here. You had to know the latticework of glowing paths, or you were hopelessly lost.

Again, they took no more than a few steps. In the human world, it might have been hundreds of miles. At the next Albenstar, six paths crossed. A seventh sliced vertically through the hub of the others. Suddenly, Nuramon seemed to tense.

Farodin looked around. Thin wisps of fog curled in the darkness. Was that a sound? A scraping noise, as of claws? Nonsense.

Just then, an arch of light rose in front of them. Nuramon led his horse through it. Farodin nodded to Mandred to go ahead. After the jarl disappeared, the elven warrior also left the sinister paths that connected the worlds.

They found themselves in a wide vaulted cellar. The floor was a colorful mosaic depicting a rising sun, with seven cranes flying away from the sun in different directions. On the walls around them were pictures of a banquet, with centaurs, fauns, elves, dwarves, and other Albenkin. But the faces in the pictures were scratched out or smeared with soot. On each wall, a black tree had been painted. Magical symbols in dark colors were smeared on the mosaic floor. Burned-out candles had left flat puddles of wax.

Farodin's hand moved to the hilt of his sword. He knew this place. The vault lay beneath the villa of Sem-la, the elf woman disguised as a trader's widow, who watched over the one major Albenstar that led from Iskendria to the library of the Albenkin.

"What's going on?" asked Farodin. "Why didn't you take us directly to the library? We could have stabled the horses in the centaurs' quarters."

Nuramon seemed unsettled. "The gate. It was different. There's a—" He hesitated for a moment. "There's a barrier."

Farodin let out a flat sigh. "A barrier? Tell me that's not true. You have to be making a joke."

"No. But the defensive magic here is not like what we found on Noroelle's island. It . . ." He shrugged helplessly. "It's different."

Mandred grunted. "A few things have changed here." He pointed to the symbols on the floor. "Looks like some foul kind of witchery. What's happened?"

"None of our business," replied Farodin harshly. "Can you open the gate, Nuramon?"

"I think—"

A ringing noise came from outside.

Before Farodin could stop him, Mandred had drawn his axe and, in three long strides, was on his way up the ramp that led out of the vault.

"Damned hothead," Farodin cursed and turned to Nuramon. "Stay here. Open the gate. I'll bring him back."

Farodin ran up the ramp after Mandred, passed through several small basement rooms, and heard a piercing scream.

He found Mandred in the larder. He'd hauled a man out of a corner, a cringing, gaunt man with dark stubble of a beard. On the floor stood a flickering oil lamp. All around lay thick shards of broken amphorae. Beside the oil lamp stood a small bowl that held a few lentils. The man whimpered and tried to twist free of Mandred's grasp, but he was help-less in the Northman's grip.

"A looter," Mandred declared, his voice thick with disdain. "He was stealing from Sem-la. I nabbed him as he was about to smash one of the amphorae."

"Please, don't kill me," Mandred's prisoner pleaded in Valethish, the language spoken along the coast from Iskendria as far as Terakis. "My children are starving to death. I don't want any of it for myself."

"Sniveling for mercy, is he?" asked Mandred, who obviously did not understand a word.

"Look at him," Farodin shot back. "Look how hollow his cheeks are. His legs are as thin as spindles. He's talking about his starving children."

Mandred quietly cleared his throat and avoided the elf's chastening gaze. Then he let go of the man.

"What's going on in the city?" asked Farodin.

The man looked at them in surprise but dared not ask why they were so uninformed. "The white priests want to destroy Balbar. They've had the city under siege for more than three years. They came from across the sea to kill our god. The west gate fell three months ago, and they've been advancing street by street ever since. But the temple guards keep driving back the disciples of Tjured with Balbar's holy fire."

"Tjured?" Farodin asked in surprise.

"A miserable bastard," the gaunt man replied. "His priests say there is only one god. And they claim that we do business with demons. They're raving mad. They're so mad they refuse to accept that there's no way for them to win."

"You said they've already taken over parts of the city," Farodin replied soberly.

"Parts," the gaunt man said, waving his hand dismissively. "No one can conquer Iskendria completely. Balbar's fire has already burned their fleet to the waterline twice. They're dying by the thousands." Without warning, the man began to sob. "Since they took the harbor, no supplies have been getting through at all. There aren't even any rats left that you could eat. If only these damned knight clerics would see that they can't win Iskendria. Balbar is too strong. We sacrifice to him ten times a day now. He will make our enemies drown in their own blood."

Farodin thought of the girl they had seen burn on the palms of the god statue's hands. Ten children every day? What kind of city was this? He personally would waste no pity on Iskendria if it fell.

"Are you friends of Mistress Al-beles?" The human looked over at the amphorae that were used for storage. "I did it for my children. There's always a few lentils or beans left in the big amphorae. You never empty them completely." He lowered his eyes. "Unless you smash them open."

Farodin had heard that several times in the past, Sem-la had slipped into another role, claiming to be her own niece to keep her trading house going. As an elf woman who never aged, she was forced into such deceptions every twenty years or so. Farodin did not doubt that Al-beles was the same woman he had come to know as Sem-la.

"What happened down there, in the vaulted cellar?" Farodin asked.

"When they occupied this quarter, monks came here. I think they went down to the cellar as well. It was said that they were searching for demons." The man lowered his voice. "They search for demons everywhere. They're mad."

"Let's go, Mandred," said Farodin in Fjordlandish. "We have to know if there is any danger of being disturbed or if Nuramon can work his magic in peace."

"I'm sorry about his children," Mandred said sheepishly. He pulled off one of his wide silver armbands and gave it to the man. "I was too hasty."

Farodin felt no sympathy for the looter. Today, he was doing what he did for the sake of his children, but he suspected the man would feel honored tomorrow if the priesthood came and demanded one of his daughters to be publicly burned.

The elf moved quickly up the stairs and stepped out into the villa's wide courtyard. Overhead stretched a night sky as red as blood. The air was filled with choking smoke. Mandred joined him, and they crossed through the main hall and raced to the terrace at the rear of the building. The villa had been built atop a low hill, affording them a good view over the city.

"By the gods," Mandred cried. "What a fire."

The entire harbor stood in flames. The water itself seemed to be on fire. All around it, the warehouses had collapsed, and the massive wooden cranes had vanished. Farther west, glowing white balls of fire plummeted from the heavens onto one of the city's inner quarters. Farodin saw white-robed warriors, masses of them, surging through the narrow streets, all trying desperately to escape the rain of fire.

"Rotten flesh has to be burned out," said a voice from behind them. It was the looter. The lank figure stepped out onto the terrace. His eyes shone frenetically. "The temple guards are burning the quarters of the city that have been lost." He laughed. "Iskendria cannot be conquered. The white priests will die to the last man." He pointed down to the harbor below. "Their fleet's been frying for two days already. The temple guards fed Balbar's fire into the harbor through the canals, then set it alight. All these priests will burn, just like their precious . . ." He broke off and pointed to the lane that led up the hill. "They're coming back." A group of soldiers in white tabards were escorting a number of monks in night-blue robes. Singing solemnly, they were heading directly for the villa.

"You were good to me," said the man frantically. "So I'm telling you to disappear, fast. You look a little unusual . . . and those down there, they kill anyone who looks unusual."

"What's he saying?" Mandred asked.

"That we shouldn't rely too much on the hospitality of the city. Come on, we should get back to Nuramon."

The jarl ran his hand over the blade of his axe. "Those few men down there don't frighten you, do they?"

"If two armies, both of them obviously taking orders from madmen, start tanning each other's hides, then I would do everything I possibly could not to stand in their way. We have no stake in their war. Let's get out of here."

Mandred grumbled something unintelligible, and they left the terrace. Nuramon was already waiting for them in the vaulted cellar. A golden arch of light rose in the middle of the mosaic. The elf grinned. "Breaking through the barrier was not difficult. The defensive spell had an unusual structure, as if it had not been created to keep Albenkin out."

Farodin reached for the reins of his stallion and took no further notice of his companion's explanations.

Nuramon's smile vanished. "Something the matter?"

"We can't waste any time getting out of here." Resolute, Farodin stepped through the arch. For the space of a heartbeat, he was blinded. Then he found himself looking straight into a cocked crossbow.

"Don't shoot!" a raw voice rang out. "They're elves!"

"Liuvar," shouted someone else.

Farodin had instinctively ducked, reaching for his sword. The Albenstar was circled by an odd conglomeration of sentries: two red-cowled keepers of knowledge with swords drawn, several gnomes armed with crossbows, and a white centaur whom Farodin immediately recognized as Chiron. The stone gallabaal was also among the strange assembly.

Nuramon and Mandred came through the gate, leading their horses.

The gallabaal took a crunching step toward the human. One of the gnomes took aim with his crossbow at Mandred's broad chest.

"Liuvar! Peace!" the centaur shouted. "I know these three. The human is a puffed-up good-for-nothing, but they're not our enemies."

"What is going on?" Nuramon asked.

"I suspect you can answer that better than we can," replied Chiron condescendingly. "What is going on in the human world?"

Farodin reported on their encounter with the looter and the burning city. When he finished, the assembled guard looked at each other with confusion.

Chiron cleared his throat. "You must have jumped in time when you passed through the gate. Iskendria has been no more than a ruined wasteland for more than a hundred years." He stopped for a moment to give the three newcomers a chance to let the news settle. Then he went on with his explanation. "The Tjured monks have still not given up trying to break through the barrier to the library. They have control over the Albenstar. They have even built one of their temple towers there. Like that, they prevent the Albenkin from reaching us from there. You are the first to make it through in years." He bowed in formal welcome. "I greet you in the name of the keepers of knowledge."

"Are they really a serious threat?" asked Nuramon.

Chiron's tail twitched restlessly. "Yes, they are. They are driven by blind hatred of any of the Albenkin. The question is not *if* they will get through to our refuge here in the Shattered World, but *when*. No one here has any illusions about the danger. All of our visitors and most of those who used to help us have left." His voice was sharp with bitterness. Then he spread his arms in a pathetic gesture. "This dying library is at your disposal. Yours, too, human. We welcome you."

EMPTY HALLS

Nuramon entered the hall in which the gnome Builax, by Nuramon's sense of time, had received him more than fifty years earlier. But because of his lack of knowledge, they had jumped at least a hundred years when they entered the library, probably more, so their first encounter with the gnome lay even farther back. Still, the hall seemed unaltered. The shelves and the books were still there, and the barinstones still emanated their soft light. Only Builax was missing, nowhere to be seen. In the nook between the walls of shelves, where the gnome had once kept Nuramon's sword, the elf found books, writing utensils, and even a small knife. But the layer of dust showed him that no one had been there for a very long time.

An inkwell, tipped over, caught Nuramon's eye. The ink had spread across the table and had long since dried. Everything about the scene gave the impression that Builax had only taken what was most necessary with him and had left the rest where it stood or lay. Maybe the gnome had had to flee?

Nuramon went to the twenty-third bookshelf and climbed the ladder there. When he reached the shelf he was looking for, the feeling that had come over him the first time he was there returned. He was walking in the footsteps of Yulivee as if she were his confidante, as Noroelle had been a confidante for Obilee.

He slipped out her book and made his way down again. As he descended from rung to rung, he thought about the latest developments. The attack on the Albenstar made him uneasy. Was it conceivable that the Tjured priests might penetrate the library? So far, clearly, they had not, but their attacks on the Albenstars caused damage here in the Shattered World as well.

One more time, Nuramon swept his gaze across the hall. It filled him with regret that neither Builax nor Reilif was here. Who was there who could show those hungry for knowledge where to look? Perhaps Reilif was off somewhere else in the library. If there was no one left to advise on the books and what they contained, then this enormous library would be all but useless to visitors.

Nuramon left the hall and considered where best to start the search for information about the Albenstones. Farodin had praised his intuition and asked him to search on his own for whatever records he could find. While Nuramon did that, Farodin would talk with the keepers of knowledge.

Nuramon entered one of the rooms and set Yulivee's book down on a table. Scrolls were stacked in the diamond-shaped compartments of the shelves against the walls. He chose one at random and opened it. He had read barely the first lines when he sighed aloud. It was a genealogical listing of the centaurs.

He moved to a different shelf and selected another scroll. This one was the account of a human and his heroic efforts to defend a gate to Albenmark. Details of the gate in question were not given, but Nuramon thought he was on the right track. Every culture had its myths and its concepts of the beginning of the worlds. These were the stories in which he might detect a hidden sign.

He searched for hours but found only a single clue. In one of the chronicles, it said that Emerelle had used her Albenstone to create an important gate between the human world and Dailos in Albenmark. The text read, "Oh, if only the ancient ones had not departed, we would have been able to create gates of our own." Everything he read seemed to indicate that the queen possessed the only Albenstone in existence.

"You'll never find it like that," said a familiar voice. "Time is too short."

Nuramon spun around. In the doorway stood a figure wearing a black robe, the hood half covering his forehead. "Master Reilif," Nuramon cried.

"Yes, it's me. And I am disappointed to find you searching for knowledge in the elven way."

Nuramon returned the scroll he'd been reading to its shelf. "Is it so surprising to find an elf behaving in this way? But you are right. I should think of my human companion and try to shorten the search."

"That is not what I meant. But you should know that the end of this place is not far off."

Nuramon stared in disbelief at the keeper of knowledge. Until now, he had not thought that the danger was so great. "Will the humans destroy the gates without knowing what it means to do so?"

"It is not up to me to say what the humans know, nor what intentions lie behind their actions. But what I can say is this. There is not much more they need to find out before this library is lost. And what sense would it make in any case, protecting knowledge if you are locked in with it and no one else can ever come here?"

"None at all," said Nuramon softly.

"To give you at least a little benefit from all the wisdom stored in this place, I will help you." Reilif smiled sympathetically.

"Have you already spoken with Farodin?"

"No. Gengalos and the other keepers are with him. I would like to speak to you alone." Reilif glanced at the table. "I see that you have found Yulivee's book again."

"I wanted to read it once more," said Nuramon, and his words sounded like an apology.

"That's a good thing. And you may keep the book."

"What? I thought . . ."

"The knowledge of this library will fade away, even though the others may not see that as clearly as I do. But when this place dies, at least a little of the knowledge these halls contain deserves to be saved. Besides, the books themselves are worthless to me and the other keepers. I have read them, and now they are a part of me."

"Why don't you abandon the library and establish another somewhere else?" Nuramon asked. He was thinking of Albenmark, where the keepers of knowledge would surely be met with open arms.

"We have sworn never to leave these halls before we have taken in all the knowledge gathered here. Until now, we always thought that would never happen and that this place would always be a wellspring of wisdom. But the well has been sealed, because nothing new is reaching us. And because that is the case, the day may come when we carry all the treasures stored here inside us. Then we can leave. Unfortunately, we keepers are very slow readers. Only one here, one we were forced by necessity to bring in, can read faster than us. If we have acquired the knowledge of this library before the end comes, we will abandon this place and return to Albenmark."

"How long will that take?"

"Another hundred years, certainly. By the Alben. A hundred years. That's a period we both would have laughed at before. What is a hundred years? But I fear the humans could get in here before that and spoil everything."

Nuramon could understand the keeper well. If they were bound by an oath, then they had to take the chance that every connection to the human world might be broken and that they would have to go on living here, sealed off. But perhaps it would be smarter to break their covenant and at least rescue part of the priceless knowledge stored here. Emerelle would certainly not condemn them if they retreated to her court.

"Let us walk awhile," said Reilif, and he stepped out into the corridor.

Nuramon picked up Yulivee's book from the table and followed the keeper of knowledge. "Can you help me find something about Albenstones?"

Reilif laughed gently. "You've built quite a large assumption into your question, Nuramon . . . namely, that there could be more Albenstones than only Emerelle's."

"Are there?"

Reilif nodded inside his hood. "But no one knows where they are . . . and I know just as little about how to find one."

Nuramon was disappointed. He had expected more of Reilif. Could it really be that in all the books he had read, there was not a word about how to find one?

"Now then, keep your chin up. I certainly cannot tell you where to find a stone, but I can tell you what an Albenstone can be used for. So listen well. If you possess such a stone, then it will allow you to move from one end of a world to another. You can create Albenpaths for yourself where previously there were none. You can open and close gates. You can even create and destroy Albenstars. An Albenstone that finds its way into the wrong hands is a great evil."

"Can they be used to break through magical barriers?"

"But of course."

That was the answer Nuramon had been hoping for. He wanted to use such a stone for no more than to free the woman he loved.

They left the corridor and climbed a set of stairs. The keeper of knowledge went on. "Anyone who wants to use an Albenstone must be capable of wielding magic. And the more he wants to achieve with it, the harder it will be to control the power of the stone."

"But it has to be possible to detect such a formidable stone. Its power must outshine anything," Nuramon objected. He thought of the queen's palace. He had never sensed any trace of the Albenstone there. Perhaps Emerelle had surrounded it with some kind of magic that hid the aura of its power.

"There you're mistaken. The power of the stone is barely perceptible. You would definitely sense it if I held it in my hands here at your side, but despite its size, you would think of it as little more than a trifle."

"What does it look like?"

Reilif said nothing, but led him into a small room that opened off a landing. Inside, the barinstones gave off a cool green gleam. Sturdy cupboards as high as the ceiling stood along the walls. The keeper of knowledge opened one of the cupboards, took out a large and heavy folio, and heaved it onto the lectern in the center of the room. The covers were closed with two buckles, which he now opened. "In this book is the image of an Albenstone. It is not Emerelle's stone, and the one who possessed it went the way of the Alben long ago." Reilif's hood slipped over his eyes, and with a quick hand movement, he threw it back completely. Nuramon was astounded to see elven ears protruding from beneath gray-white hair. For Nuramon, the old elf revealing his head like this came suddenly and unexpectedly. Reilif seemed not to notice his surprise and instead turned unerringly to the page he was looking for.

The image of the stone filled the entire page. It was dark gray and looked smooth. Five white furrows ran down it. The illustration was rather plain and not the work of a master, but it was enough to give a clear impression.

Nuramon pointed to the grooves in the picture. "What are these lines?" he asked.

Reilif ran his finger down the furrow on the left. "This is the world of the humans. Next to that lies the world that is now shattered, the one we are in. Then comes Albenmark—the borderlands of the Alben—followed by their home." He tapped on the line on the far right. "And this last is what we elves call the moonlight."

"It's hard to believe," said Nuramon in wonder.

"What is?"

"That the worlds I know simply exist right beside the home of the Alben and the moonlight."

"Don't let this illustration deceive you, Nuramon. Every Albenstone is said to be unique. Each one is supposed to represent a different understanding of the world. It is also said that on Emerelle's stone, the furrows cross."

"Whose stone was this?"

"It belonged to a dragon named Cheliach. We know little about him other than that he was late in following the Alben, and when he did, the dragons ceased to be of any real significance."

Nuramon was satisfied. This was the starting point he had been hoping to find. "Thank you for showing me this picture."

Reilif closed the large book. "You will find this volume here if you want to show it to your companions. I will leave it on the table. But before you do that, you should pay a visit to someone else . . . someone who knows you and who no doubt would like to see you again."

"Who is it?" asked Nuramon, surprised.

Master Reilif smiled. "If I betrayed the name, I would be breaking a promise." He pointed to the stairway. "Follow the stairs all the way to the top. You will find him in one of the empty halls." The old elf's gray eyes sparkled in the gleam of the barinstones.

With some reluctance, Nuramon left the room. On the stairs, he took a deep breath. It felt as if the keeper of knowledge had cast a spell over him; his eyes had been so hypnotic. What was the elf's story? What lay behind him? He did not dare ask him. And besides, just then, he had a different task. Who could be waiting for him up there?

When Nuramon reached the top of the stairs, he followed a wide corridor off which a number of small halls opened. They were all empty, with neither books nor bookshelves. It seemed the knowledge of the library had not yet extended this far. And from what Reilif had just been telling him, it probably never would, so it surprised Nuramon all the more when he saw books in a side corridor, stacked along the walls on left and right.

A soft voice echoed down the corridor. Nuramon followed the sound of the voice and spied through the gap where a door had been left ajar. He could scarcely believe what he saw inside: in a bare circular hall sat the djinn atop a throne of books. He plucked a volume from a neatly stacked pile on his left, glanced at it, then tossed it carelessly onto a pile on his right. The djinn had white hair and wore white robes, making him look far more venerable than he had in Valemas.

The moment Nuramon entered the hall, the djinn raised his head and looked at him. "Oh, it's you, Nuramon," he said, as if they had seen each other just moments earlier. He quickly assembled a small stack of books from those lying around, then pointed to his creation. "Have a seat!"

As soon as Nuramon sat down, the djinn asked him, "Did my advice back then get you any farther?"

"Yes. And I would like to say thank you for that. It was invaluable." Nuramon told the djinn that he had found himself following Yulivee's trail in the library. He told him about the dwarves and Dareen.

"Looks to me like you've taken a shine to Yulivee." The djinn pointed to the book that rested on Nuramon's knee.

"Reilif gave it to me. Maybe I should take it to the Free of Valemas. Their hatred of Emerelle would no doubt be placated a little by what is written in here."

The djinn made a glum face. "There's no point taking any books to Valemas. The oasis has been destroyed."

"What?" Nuramon cried. "How could that happen?"

"The white knights from the north who ride in the name of Tjured . . . they wiped out the Free."

"How is that possible? How can human warriors march so deep into the desert? How could they defeat warriors like the Free of Valemas in battle?"

"With magic. Some of the humans have learned its power. They come together under the banner of Tjured. They are the leaders, and they can sense the power contained in the Albenpaths. They found the stone circle in the desert, and because there were no protective barriers there, they were able to open the gate with their magic. That's how it came to a fight. I fled. And when I went back, all I found was ruins and bodies. The humans did not even spare the few children there."

"This is incomprehensible. Those madmen will destroy everything," Nuramon said. Then he stopped short. "Have they attacked Albenmark?"

"Don't worry about that. I went out to scout the humans for the Free of Valemas. I saw them gathering at an Albenstar, one that led to Albenmark. The priests prayed and asked their god whether that place had his blessing. Then they spoke words I did not understand. The words of the spell, no doubt. I saw something strike the Albenstar. When that happened, the soldiers drew their swords. But that was all. Nothing else happened, and the troops departed again. I looked at the traces they left behind. With the magic they had used, they would never have made it to Albenmark. I found the same traces at the stone circle after the destruction of Valemas. It seems the priests are only able to open gates into the Shattered World."

"Why have they spared the library so far?"

"Oh, they've actually been trying to get in here for some time. The keepers of knowledge say that the humans are confused because there are so many Albenpaths crisscrossing Iskendria, and they're having trouble getting through the defensive spells on the gates. But Reilif believes the humans are slowly breaking down the barriers. Every day, they come a little closer. There is not much time left to absorb all the knowledge of this place and vanish."

"Are you the one who can take in all this knowledge so quickly?"

"I certainly am."

"What did they do to persuade you?"

The djinn's expression became irate. "The scoundrels tricked me. They finally got me to reveal my name, and now I have to serve them. Those swindlers are just too clever for me. But what can you do? What's going on here reminds me of the library of the djinns. The fate of great knowledge, it would seem, is simply to perish." The djinn's gaze focused on empty space. "Where will it all end, I wonder?"

Nuramon shook his head. "If fate means to be fair to the Albenkin, then the soldiers will burn everything in these halls. But if fate has more evil ends in mind, then they will exploit this knowledge for themselves . . . if they are able to learn the languages, at least."

"We've thought of that. The moment the humans penetrate these walls, we will use our magic to obliterate everything stored here. We will be destroyed, too. The incantation has already been cast. All we have to do is say the final words. Then everything here will vanish in . . ." The djinn looked toward the door.

Nuramon followed the spirit's gaze, and what he saw took him completely by surprise. A young elven girl entered the room, carrying a stack of books. The child could not have been more than eight years old, and she dropped the books in shock when she saw Nuramon there.

The djinn rose. "No need to be frightened, little elf. This is Nuramon, a friend from Albenmark."

The girl looked down at the books she'd dropped. With a sudden lurch, they floated up and restacked themselves in her arms. Nuramon was speechless. For the girl, the magic seemed mere child's play. She stepped closer and set the stack of books down beside the spirit's bookish throne.

"Come here. Welcome our guest," said the djinn.

With a shy smile, the girl stood beside the djinn, and he stroked her dark-brown hair.

"What is your name?" asked Nuramon.

"What do you mean?" The little girl spoke with almost the same cadence as the djinn.

"Don't you have a name?" Nuramon tried again.

"Oh, I see. They call me little elf, or elf-child."

Nuramon was speechless. The djinn had not even given the child a name.

"Well, elf-child, take these books back down," the djinn instructed her.

She put on a discontented face and set about fetching a number of books from the pile already read. Then she gave Nuramon a final smile and left the circular hall.

The moment her steps died away down the corridor, Nuramon turned back to the djinn. "How could you not give her a name?"

"Names just cause problems. I already told you that. All they do is give others power over you."

Nuramon pointed to the door. "That doesn't seem to stop you from ordering the child around like a servant."

"Ha! You don't know the girl. She's a pest of the first order. She only listened to me just now because you're here. She's so pigheaded she makes trolls look positively obliging. Besides, I only sent her away for one reason."

"What reason?"

"She knows nothing about her origins. I told her a story to protect her from the truth."

"And what is the truth?" Nuramon asked, then he dismissed the question with a gesture. "Never mind. I think I know. She's from Valemas, isn't she?"

"Yes. She may be the last of the Free."

Nuramon looked at the djinn in bewilderment. "How is that possible? I thought at least a hundred years have passed. How is it possible that she is still a child?"

The djinn laughed. "It all depends how strong the Albenstars' protective barriers are, and how skillful one is with magic. You went headfirst through the walls, no doubt, without the magic you needed to compensate."

Nuramon understood what the djinn was trying to say. "So you both came here in the time we lost when we passed through the gate? That means the Tjured disciples took Iskendria first, and then . . ."

"Valemas. And other places, too, I'm sure. That's how it was. The girl was entrusted to me when the attack on Valemas was imminent. Hildachi, her mother, was a powerful sorceress and seer. She said we should take the children to safety, but because there were only very few children and the fighters of Valemas sorely underestimated the danger, this little one was the only one I took away. Hildachi told me I should take her to a safe place and return her to Valemas later. After I found the ruins of Valemas, I brought her here. That was six years ago. At that time, she could not even speak. I've taught her several languages since, and how to read and write in many different scripts. I've taught her a little magic, too. Don't underestimate her. The problem is that I'm bound to this place for as long as the keepers of knowledge refuse to leave, and I can't get her to safety. I don't want her to have to live under the threat this library is facing . . . It may be that we don't achieve our aim before the humans get through."

Nuramon thought about what the djinn was asking. A child was the last thing they needed on their search. But the djinn was right to say that this was no place for an elven child. "I will take her with me. My companions won't like it, but I will make it clear to them that she's coming. Having her with us will make our quest more difficult."

"I hear you're searching for an Albenstone."

"Do you happen to know about them?"

"Well, of course. But everything that I, in my remarkable wisdom, can bestow on you, I already have."

"What do you mean?"

"Just what I say," the djinn replied with a smile. "You will find out nothing new from me."

What could the djinn mean by that? That he'd already told him everything about the Albenstones? He hadn't said anything at all. Not today, and not in Valemas. They had never talked about Albenstones.

"Take your time. Think about it. In the meantime, I'll read." The djinn picked up a book and started turning the pages slowly. Nuramon noticed how quickly the spirit's eyes moved. He was not simply turning pages. He was reading.

Nuramon went through what the djinn had told him back in Valemas. He had told Nuramon about the Shattered World and that it was impossible to travel through the endless gloom. But they never discussed a stone. Or did they? "The fire opal," he whispered.

The djinn put his book aside. "You have a good memory, Nuramon."

"You mean the fire opal in the lost crown of the Maharaja of Berseiniji? Is it an Albenstone?" Nuramon still remembered the djinn's words. He had asked him if it was easier to believe that the opal was a movable Albenstar. After everything that Reilif had told him about the power of the Albenstones, he now understood the meaning behind the djinn's words. Nuramon shook his head. "The Albenstone of the djinns. That would be just like you, hiding your stone somewhere so openly that no one would ever suspect it was there."

"We spirits *are* clever . . . or perhaps not. We had no idea that Elebal, the imbecile, would take his crown with him on his campaigns."

"I can hardly believe it. You're telling me the truth, aren't you?"

The djinn grinned mischievously. "Have I ever lied to you?"

"No, that you haven't. You even told me where I should start looking for the crown." In Drusna, Maharaja Elebal had lost a decisive battle, and the crown with the fire opal had disappeared. "There's only one thing I don't understand. Why didn't you search for the crown yourself? Were you bound to Valemas by your name, the same way it keeps you here?"

"No, I was not. I searched for the crown. I just did not find it. Either it has been destroyed or a protective spell surrounds it. In the past, I was always able to sense it wherever it was in the world."

"I thought Albenstones could not be sensed from a distance."

"True, but we put a special enchantment on the stone, one that only we djinns know, and it told us where the fire opal was. But it's as I said, we can't hear its voice anymore. And one could not hear it beyond the borders of a world in any case."

Perhaps Farodin would be able to help. His seeking spell might be able to pick up the crown's location. "Is there a picture of the crown?"

"Yes, there is. In this library, no less. The first time I came here, I had one of the artists here paint it for me. Back then, I was still searching for the crown, and I'd hoped to find something here about its location. Come along. I'll show you," he said, and he rose from his throne.

"My companion Farodin has mastered a seeking spell. If we show him a picture of the crown and you explain what you know about it, he may be able to find it. But would we be permitted to use the stone for our own purposes if we found it?"

"If you find the fire opal, the djinns will line up to kiss your feet. Each and every one of them would tell you his name and read your heart's desire from your eyes. To put it plainly, Nuramon, yes."

LITTLE ELF

Nuramon sat in his room, poring over the book the djinn had given him, studying the crown of the maharaja, painted in brilliant colors on parchment. A true masterpiece. It was hard to believe that a man could actually carry the huge creation on his head. The crown looked almost like a citadel of gold studded with precious stones. The large fire opal formed the centerpiece around which all the other stones gathered.

He knew that, with this image, he had found an important clue. He wondered excitedly what his two companions would make of it. Suddenly, he heard a noise. It sounded like someone sobbing. He clapped the book closed and strode to the door. Someone outside was crying. Carefully, he opened the door and stepped out. The little girl was sitting on the floor, leaning against the wall, weeping. Beside her lay a bag and three books.

"What's the matter?" Nuramon asked, and he crouched in front of the girl.

"You know what the matter is," she said, her lips quivering. She turned her eyes away and stared at the floor.

Nuramon sat beside her on the floor. He waited for a moment before speaking. "The djinn told you everything, didn't he?"

The girl did not reply.

"Look at me," Nuramon said, quietly but firmly.

She looked him in the eye. Her brown eyes sparkled.

"Now you know where you came from."

"Yes . . . the djinn told me where I was born and who my parents were. He told me what happened to Valemas, too."

"Didn't he tell you anything about it before? Nothing?"

"He only said I was descended from a noble family and that one day my brothers and sisters would come and take me home again. I believed him, too."

"He didn't lie. In a certain way, he told you the truth."

The elf girl wiped the tears from her face. "I thought I would have a family—a mother and a father. I thought they were waiting for me somewhere. I thought I had brothers and sisters."

"I know it hurts to find out that things are different than they look in your mind, but that doesn't mean you have to give up your dreams. If it's a family you want so much, then one day, you might find one." Nuramon's thoughts returned to the night before they departed on the elfhunt and the oracle's counsel that Emerelle had passed on to him. "Do you know what the queen once said to me?"

The girl shook her head.

"She said, 'Choose your kinfolk for yourself.'"

The girl looked at him wide-eyed. "Mighty Emerelle said that to you?"

"She certainly did. And those words might help you, too. But first, you should choose a name for yourself."

A smile appeared on the girl's face. She seemed to have forgotten that she had been crying just now. "A name."

"Choose well."

"Why don't *you* do it for me? Look at my face and tell me what kind of name I am."

With a smile, Nuramon shook his head. *What kind of name I am.* The little elf saw things in her own, peculiar way. But he went along with it and said, "Well, perhaps you're an Obilee . . ."

"I like that name," the girl said.

"Hold on. Maybe something a little softer. Besides, I already know one elf with that name. But there's another one that sounds quite similar." Nuramon knew what he was looking for. For the elf-child, there could be only one name. "What do you think of *Yulivee*?"

The little girl let go of her hair, and it fell in waves to her shoulders. "That's a lovely name," she said, her voice bright and clear.

"You've heard it before, haven't you?"

"Never."

"Well, an elf woman named Yulivee led your people out of Albenmark and founded Valemas," Nuramon said. Then he told her about the old town of Valemas in Albenmark and about the oasis town of the same name where he had first met the djinn.

"But the djinn said I come from the Diliskar clan."

"Diliskar was the grandfather of Yulivee and the founder of her clan. Which means you really are related to her."

"Am I still allowed to have her name?"

"But of course. Newborn children are often given the names of Albenkin who have gone into the moonlight."

"Then I will call it mine."

"A good choice. You may be the last of the Free of Valemas. There could not be a better name for you . . . Yulivee."

"Yulivee." The little elf repeated it several times, stressing the syllables in different ways. She jumped to her feet excitedly and shouted out her name. Then she stood in front of Nuramon and looked him in the eye. "From now on, I want to be with you and have adventures."

"But if you do that, you will certainly not be as safe as you would be in Albenmark. We could lead you to the gate to Albenmark, and someone would take you from there to the queen."

Yulivee shook her head vehemently. "No, that's not what I want. I want to stay with you."

Nuramon pointed to the bag and the books that were lying against the wall. "Is that everything you have?"

"Yes. Clothes and knowledge. That's all I need."

"Then grab your things and bring them into my room." Nuramon went ahead.

Yulivee did as she was told and set the books down on the table.

Nuramon sat down. "What books do you have there?"

"They're mine."

"Of course they're yours," said Nuramon. "But if you tell me what kind of books they are, then I'll give you this book here." He laid one hand on the book of Yulivee.

"They're stories. I learned a lot about Albenmark from them. I like the Emerelle stories the best. She is so wise. I wish I could see her one day."

Nuramon thought of how Emerelle had treated him and his companions. Not all of the stories he had loved listening to as a child actually matched the real queen. "Can you tell me one of the stories?"

Yulivee smiled at him. "I'm sure I can. You know, I've never read a story to anyone before. The others were always too busy."

"Well, I have time," said Nuramon.

Little Yulivee began to tell the story of Emerelle and the dragon that so many warriors had been unable to slay. She had just come to the part about the dragon's villainous betrayal when Farodin and Mandred entered the room. Mandred's face lit up at the sight of the girl, but Farodin's only showed mistrust and aversion.

The girl glanced up at the two new arrivals for a moment, then simply went on with her storytelling. "Then Emerelle returned, and she gave the dragon's treasure to the clan of Teveroi, who had lost many warriors in the battle against it. Master Alvias was happy that the queen was safe. And that's how the story ends."

Nuramon realized that Yulivee had summed up the ending quickly. He stroked her hair. "That was a very lovely story. Thank you for telling it to me." He stood up. "But now I would like to introduce you to somebody. This is Farodin. He is the best fighter of the queen's court." One corner of Farodin's mouth rose slightly, but Mandred grinned broadly. "And this is Mandred Torgridson, the jarl of Firnstayn. He's a human."

The girl stared openmouthed at Mandred, as if he were some magnificent statue to be gaped at.

"And to the two of you, I would like to introduce the last of the elves of Valemas."

A look of dismay crossed Farodin's face. "Does that mean . . ."

"Yes. Valemas does not exist anymore." In a few words, he explained what he had heard from the djinn. "The djinn rescued this girl and brought her here. Her name is Yulivee, and she is now our companion."

"Welcome, Yulivee," said Farodin, though more politely than pleasantly.

"She will accompany us for a while," Nuramon continued. "Then I will take her to Albenmark."

"But I don't want to go to Albenmark," said Yulivee. "I want to stay with all of you. And there isn't a thing you can do about it," she said in a confident voice.

"The little one seems to have a plan already," said Mandred with a smile. "I like her. Let her stay with us."

Farodin shook his head. "Mandred. It is too dangerous for a child. What if we get into a battle?"

"Then I would make myself invisible," said Yulivee.

Mandred leaned his head back and laughed out loud. "You see? She knows what she's doing."

Farodin looked intently at her. "You can make yourself invisible?"

Yulivee waved dismissively. "It's easy."

"The djinn has taught her quite a bit," Nuramon added.

Farodin eyed the girl. "All right, then she can stay with us," he finally said. Then he pointed at Nuramon in a mock threat. "But she's your responsibility."

"Fine with me. Now tell me what the keepers of knowledge told you."

Farodin nodded. They had pointed him toward two important books about the art of the seeking spell, he said, and now he was confident that he could perfect his skill in that area of magic. They had also talked of Albenstones and reported that in recent centuries, someone had been using one of the stones to weave new paths into the fabric created by the Alben. It was one of the new paths that they had discovered the first time they visited the library, and other travelers had obviously also noticed them. There was something strange about them, but that could very well have to do with the fact that they were something completely new appearing in a network of paths that was millennia old. Whatever the truth, their mere existence was proof that Emerelle's Albenstone was not the only one.

When Farodin finished, Nuramon told them about his encounter with Reilif. The danger that the keeper of knowledge had spoken of worried his companions. Finally, Nuramon spoke of the djinn's hints concerning the vanished fire opal.

"But how are we supposed to find the crown? What you're describing won't help me pick up its trail," Farodin pointed out.

"Then look at this." Nuramon opened the book the djinn had given him to the page he'd already looked at. "This is the crown of the maharaja of Berseiniji."

Farodin looked closely at the picture, contemplating and nodding. "This is a very good lead, Nuramon."

Little Yulivee stood on tiptoe next to the table so that she could see into the book. "But which one's best? Should we follow the new Albenpaths and look for whoever's making them, or should we go and look for the fire opal?" she asked.

"You had your ears open. That is exactly the question," Nuramon answered.

"I say we go in search of the fire opal," Mandred suggested. "It has to be easier to find a missing crown than to take an Albenstone away from someone."

Farodin closed the book. "Mandred's right. I'm certain I can find this crown with my seeking spell. We know more or less where it is, and we know what it looks like. That should be enough. Are we allowed to keep the book?"

"Yes."

"Then let's go and find this Albenstone." For the first time since they had left Noroelle's island, Farodin was chafing at the bit again.

Nuramon was relieved. He recalled the last time they had left Iskendria. Back then, they had quarreled and gone their separate ways. Now, everything was different. They would depart as allies, with a little comrade at their side.

LETTER TO THE HIGH PRIEST:

REPORT ON THE CAMPAIGN IN ANGNOS AND IN THE AEGILIEN SEA

*V*enerable Father Therdavan, keeper of the faith on Earth, appointed at Tjured's hand, in his wisdom,

In accordance with your wishes, I send you news concerning the activities in Angnos and the Aegilien Sea. As we have found everywhere our mission takes us, we face two difficulties.

The first is that the places sacred to us have been defiled by the Albenfolk. Many among them are willing to fight to the death, as would anyone who fights for their house and home. But with our superior strategy and the spirit of self-sacrifice of our knights, we have never yet lost a battle. There are no more than a handful of places that we have to lay siege to for a long time, until we break through to the other side and free the soil destined for our god alone from the demonic Albenfolk. May Tjured curse the Alben!

The second hazard to our plans are the unbelievers, all those who pray to other gods. Tjured be praised, the terrible cult of Balbar has been exterminated. Your visions were in accord with the truth. In the catacombs of Iskendria, we found the stone heart of the cult. Balbar was no more than a stone spirit brought to life by the Albenfolk.

The cult of Arkassa fell once the people saw the miracles of Tjured. Your decision to pull the high priests back from the siege of the Albenstars and instead to show the population of Angnos the power of Tjured wiped out the Arkassa cult once and for all.

There is only one thing that causes me concern. At this moment, it must be said, one does not perceive it as a great danger, but it may well grow to present a real problem. From many points around the Aegilien Sea, news has reached me that elven warriors on horseback have been desecrating our fanes. Just yesterday, a message reached me that the temple in Zeilidos had been burned. We have also lost a number of the ships that were to make the voyage to Iskendria. The survivors reported that they were attacked by elves. So far, these events have been mere pinpricks. But from this resistance, which for now can be said to be inflicting only minimal damage, a large-scale rebellion could grow.

It is not my intention to claim that the armies of Albenmark are slowly beginning to move, but I fear that the Albenfolk who dwell in the holy places have found out that sooner or later, we plan to move against them. It may also be that the elves plundering on horseback are refugees from liberated shrines.

Finally, I would like to draw your attention to a piece of intelligence obtained by our spies. They have discovered that the Drusnians are, in fact, preparing for war again. They seem to assume that you could turn your attention to them next. Their attempt to foment a rebellion in Angnos failed. It is true that there have been reports of elves journeying from Angnos to Drusna, but these have not been sufficiently verified. You asked for my counsel, and I would give it thus: let the Drusnians prepare for war. In the meantime, we will reinforce our fortifications in the mountains of Angnos. Until now, we have always been the ones to attack, and we have never been defeated. But in Drusna, the tide almost turned against us. It was a very wise decision not to risk a confrontation in the forests there and to order the retreat in time. If that had not happened, our army would have suffered the same fate as once befell Saint Romuald. We can only defeat the Drusnians if we break their power on our own soil. Then we have everything open to us. Let them be the aggressor and we the defender. They will run their feet raw on the flinty hillsides. As for the Northmen from the Fjordlands, I see no danger from that quarter. They are mindless barbarians and have no allies. When the time comes, the Fjordlands will fall to us like ripe fruit from a tree.

EXTRACT FROM A LETTER FROM GILOM OF SELESCAR, PRINCE OF THE BROTHERHOOD, TO THERDAVAN, SUPREME RULER OF THE BROTHERHOOD, HIGH PRIEST OF THE TJURED

THE FORESTS
OF DRUSNA

From Iskendria, Nuramon and his companions followed an Albenpath they had traveled before to the western parts of Angnos, intending to go overland from there to Drusna. In this way, they avoided the humans and their settlements and stayed far away from villages and towns and the roads that crossed the mountains. Finally, they made their way deep into the woods of Drusna.

The forest seemed to go on forever. Rarely did they come across a clearing. The region reminded Nuramon of the forests of Galvelun, through which he had once traveled, for now, as then, they had to be on their guard against wolves. Fortunately, they had seen here no sign of the brown dragons that existed in Galvelun. Mandred claimed that there were dragons in the human world, but Nuramon doubted it was true, particularly because the stories the jarl told of them sounded more than a little dubious.

They had been traveling through a section of forest for some days already. The place had once been the scene of a major battle. They had found rusted helmets and shield mountings, swords and spears. In places, shattered armor and human bones were piled on boulders, forming grim altars.

While Farodin, as usual, took the lead, Yulivee was the only one on horseback. She liked Felbion, and the horse seemed to have taken a liking to the girl in return. For Yulivee, the journey was one long adventure. She observed every animal and every plant with a curiosity that amazed even Nuramon.

"Are we there yet?" she asked for what must have been the fiftieth time that day.

Mandred grinned. He had probably just been asking himself the same question. After all, at midday the day before, Farodin had said that they would reach the place his magic was drawing them to by sundown the next day. But then the new day had dawned and they had found themselves in a damp patch of forest flanked by large marshes.

Farodin ignored the child's question.

So Nuramon turned to Yulivee. "Every time you ask, it's going to take an extra day."

The girl fell silent.

"This place is starting to feel very strange," Mandred muttered. "Wolves? Fine. We'll tan their hides for them. But these stinking swamps . . . We're all going to get sucked into some bottomless mudhole."

Farodin sighed. He was obviously losing his patience. He started to walk faster, wanting to put a little distance between himself and the others.

"If you're worried, you should ride your mare," said Nuramon quietly to Mandred. "She won't put a foot wrong."

The jarl didn't need to be told twice and mounted up.

Nuramon, meanwhile, strode ahead to Farodin. He wanted to ask him what the matter was, because the elf had never led him on a false trail, but in the past few days, something seemed to have been confusing him. Perhaps he sensed another grain of sand not far away. Or something was interfering with the seeking spell he was using to track down the crown.

"What's going on?" Nuramon asked when he caught up with him.

"I hadn't counted on these swamps. But there's—" Farodin jerked his head around and looked back.

"What is it?"

The elf calmed himself and shook his head. Then he rubbed his forehead with his fingers. "Something flashed just now. It obstructed my spell." He pointed into the marshlands on their right. "I can see the trail over there. It's like a track left by an animal. But something about it isn't right. It isn't clear enough. And I'm constantly getting the sensation that there's a grain of sand somewhere around here."

"Maybe in a hollow in the swamp?"

"No, it's been happening for days, almost as if the wind has been blowing it along through the forest. If I didn't know better, I'd say we were being followed."

"I'll sort it out," said Nuramon, and he returned to Mandred and Yulivee.

Mandred nodded, but Yulivee took hardly any notice of him at all. She was busy holding her little fist up to her eye.

Nuramon already had a suspicion. He moved around to Felbion's side. "What have you got there?" he asked Yulivee.

The girl lowered her arm, but held her hand closed. "Nothing," she answered.

"You've got something in your hand."

"Just a little glowworm."

Nuramon could only laugh. "I think I know that kind of glowworm. Farodin!"

The little elf pursed her lips and seemed to be considering what she ought to do. Then Farodin was with them again.

"Open your hand," said Nuramon to Yulivee.

The girl did as he asked.

"Nothing," said Mandred breezily.

But Nuramon saw the tiny grain of sand lying on her palm. "A very little glowworm indeed," he said.

Farodin seemed more perplexed than angry. "You? You did that?" he asked and shook his head. "Did you take a grain of sand from the bottle?"

"No, no," Yulivee quickly said. "I didn't steal anything."

"Well, where else could you have gotten it?" Farodin pressed.

"Remember the night when you left the camp because you could feel a grain of sand? Well, I snuck out, too. And I was faster than you," the girl responded.

"She's a crafty one," said Farodin. "She serves up a little fib, something she only has to say she's sorry for, just to hide something worse."

"I never stole anything," Yulivee repeated. "Count your grains of sand again if you want to."

"Am I supposed to believe you found that grain? How did you do it?" Farodin asked.

Yulivee grinned cheekily. "I can do magic. Or did you already forget?"

Then Nuramon said, "But who taught you the seeking spell?"

"Farodin did," Yulivee answered.

"I did not," Farodin replied testily.

Nuramon tipped his head to one side. "Tell the truth, Yulivee."

Mandred patted the girl lightly on the shoulder. "I believe our little sorceress."

Tears welled in Yulivee's eyes. "I'm sorry. Here." She held out the grain of sand to Farodin. It floated into his hand. Then he took out the little bottle and let the grain drop into it.

The tears flowed over Yulivee's cheeks. "I just wanted to find something, too, so I watched how you did the spell."

"You can do that?"

"Yes, and then I made it so Farodin couldn't see the sand anymore. I only wanted to look at it. I'm so sorry."

"Stop crying, Yulivee," Farodin said gently. "I'm the one who should say sorry to you. I accused you unfairly of being a thief."

"The little one's left you with egg on your face, my friends. And for that, Yulivee, you can come hunting with me a bit later."

Yulivee was smiling again. "Really?"

"Of course. Only if it's all right with Nuramon," Mandred replied.

"Can I?" she begged. "Oh, please let me go hunting!"

"If you stay close to Mandred, I guess it's all right," Nuramon answered.

Yulivee squealed with glee.

Farodin and Nuramon, bemused, went ahead again. When they were out of earshot of the others, Farodin said, "The girl has a gift. By the Alben. How can she simply mimic a spell like that?"

"She's the daughter of a sorceress. Her mother's name was Hildachi, and she came from the Diliskar clan, which makes her a direct descendant of the first Yulivee. Magic is strong in her line. And the djinn taught her, too. He warned me not to underestimate her," Nuramon said.

"She would be an excellent pupil for Noroelle," said Farodin, with a little melancholy in his voice. "Once we have the crown and return to Noroelle's gate, her little hands may be a great help to us."

"Have you forgotten the pain? I don't want her to suffer anything like that. Once we've got the Albenstone, I will be happy to wait and let Yulivee decide for herself if she wants to help us with the magic we need."

Farodin did not reply. He looked straight ahead. "We're here. Just up ahead. It has to be beside that beech tree."

As they approached the tree, Nuramon thought about how quickly this could all be over once they found the crown and the fire opal. They would learn to master the stone and then they would finally be able to free Noroelle.

They reached the tree, which stood surrounded by pale grass at the edge of a swampy hollow.

"Here it is," Farodin announced as he gazed down into the muddy water. "But something isn't right."

"Is it in there?" Mandred asked, pointing into the hollow. "We can use my rope. We just have to draw straws to see who gets dirty."

"Me!" Yulivee yelped.

"Not on your life," Nuramon shot back.

"It doesn't matter anyway, because you won't find the fire opal down there," said the little elf.

Nuramon smiled. "And how does our precocious youngster know that?"

Farodin touched Nuramon's arm. "She's right. The crown isn't here."

"What?" said Nuramon. "Then what trail have we been following?"

Farodin ran one hand over his face. "I'm a fool."

Mandred spoke up. "Would someone let me in on whatever crap you're cooking up here?"

"I don't think I can answer your question with the same elegance with which you asked it, Mandred," said Farodin. "But the crown is not here. Here . . ." He lifted his hands despairingly. "Imagine you press your axe into mud and take it out again. It will leave an imprint of itself behind. It's like that here. The crown lay in this hollow for a very long time. It left behind an indelible impression in the magical fabric of the world. This impression is so strong that I, with my seeking spell, thought I was following the crown itself." Farodin closed his eyes briefly. "There are two magical trails leading away from here. We followed one of them to come here, and it has nearly faded away, but the other is still fresh." He pointed ahead. "We have to follow the new trail. Then we'll find the crown."

"Why haven't the djinns found the crown already if it leaves a trail?" asked Yulivee.

Farodin smiled. "It might be that elven eyes can see some things that are hidden even from the djinns. They should have asked for help in their search." He was already moving off along the new path, and he waved to the others to follow him.

Nuramon set off next. Though Farodin made little fuss about his talents as a seeker, Nuramon was certain no other could have led them to this place. He would have given a great deal to have Farodin's level of skill. Nuramon had spent a long time working on the seeking spell himself but had not even mastered the basics, so it surprised him even more that Yulivee had managed it so easily.

Farodin stopped in his tracks and pointed to a large, ivy-covered boulder ahead of them in a clearing. It took a moment before Nuramon realized what Farodin was pointing out. He had been so lost in thought that he had become blind to the change in the magic of the forest. In the clearing, six Albenpaths crossed. Nuramon began the gate spell, but he did it without wanting to create a gate. He wanted to take a closer look at the paths that formed the Albenstar. In moments, he was completely attuned to the magic. And what he saw horrified him. All of the paths glowed with a pale light: all of them had been recently created.

"The crown's trail . . . it ends here," said Farodin, his voice faltering.

"No," Nuramon cried, letting the Albenstar fade again. It was not possible. They were so close to finding the opal, and now it was gone? "Someone must have got their hands on the crown, brought it here, and then used the stone to create an Albenstar."

"There's something else," Farodin added, his voice low and dejected. "The crown, or rather the fire opal, left behind a magical pattern. That was the trail we've been following this far. I can't find that pattern in any of the paths here. They're different."

"What do you mean?" Nuramon asked.

"These Albenpaths have nothing to do with the opal in the crown. I can recognize with which Albenstone a path has been drawn. These are different than the magical pattern of the crown in the same way that fire differs from water."

"So this Albenstar was not created using the crown? You're certain?" Nuramon asked.

"Yes."

"Then someone came this far using an Albenstone, took the crown, and vanished again." Someone was apparently collecting Albenstones. What power would be concentrated in the hands of whoever it was? "If they possess the fire opal, and with it the library of the djinns, then they have the knowledge of the past, the present, and the future. Is that it? Is that how the Tjured priests from Fargon learned to use magic?"

Mandred and Yulivee said nothing. Farodin answered, "That would explain how they know anything at all about the Albenstars. I think we have no other choice . . . We have to follow one of the paths."

"Can I choose?" Yulivee asked quietly.

"Which one would you take?" Farodin replied.

The girl thought it over then pointed to the east. "Fargon's that way, isn't it?"

THE FACE
OF THE ENEMY

Nuramon cried out and vanished into the darkness. Before Farodin could jump back, the path under his feet tore open in spirals of spinning lights. He had the sensation of falling. The horses whinnied in panic. Yulivee shrieked. Suddenly, the darkness was swept aside like a curtain opening onto a new scene.

Farodin was standing in a high room. His companions were gathered around him. He heard the sounds of murmuring and shouting. The elf looked up. They were inside a huge tower. Galleries ran along the walls, and they were crowded with humans.

A fat man in flowing white robes approached Farodin cautiously. He held up a pendant with a golden ball high in the air. Sweat ran down his forehead in heavy droplets. The priest blinked nervously. "Go back, demon spawn," he said in a loud, shaking voice. "This is the house of Tjured. He will scorch you with his wrath."

Farodin held his stallion by the reins. The animal lashed out and tried to bite the priest. "Easy, my beauty," whispered the elf. "Easy." Farodin had no idea what had knocked them off the Albenpath and disgorged them here. He wanted no trouble. He just wanted to get out of that place. Quickly, he looked around. The temple was plastered white on the inside. Above an altar stone hung a banner that showed a dead black tree on a white ground. Farodin remembered seeing the same crest being carried by the holy knights who had taken Iskendria.

"How did this woeful tub of blubber pull us off the Albenpath?" asked Mandred in Fjordlandish. "Is he a wizard?" He pointed in the direction of the priest. Now he spoke in the language of Fargon, and so loudly that he was quite sure that everyone in the temple could hear him. "Out of my way, lard pail, or I'll lay your head at your feet."

The priest moved back fearfully. "Help me, my brothers and sisters. Destroy the offspring of the demons." He made a sign on his chest and began to sing: "No trouble can assail me, for I am Tjured's child. No upset can beset me . . ."

The rest of the congregation joined in the priest's song. There was movement in the galleries. Farodin heard footsteps tramping down hidden stairways. "Out of here," shouted the elf. He shoved the priest aside and made for the door that was obviously the way out of the temple. Above the double door hung a large picture of a saint painted on wood. It was amateurish at best, like most of the works produced by humans. The saint's eyes were far too big, the nose looked like someone else's . . . but there was still something familiar about it.

A knife caromed off the stone floor next to Farodin. "Kill them!" shouted a breaking male voice. "Demons! They murdered Saint Guillaume, who came to free us all!"

A veritable hail of missiles rained down from the galleries: caps, heavy coin purses, knives, shoes. A wooden bench missed Yulivee by a hair. Farodin raised his arms protectively over his head and ran for the exit. Mandred was close by his side. To the right and left, in front of the main door, two smaller doors opened off. That had to be where the stairs led up to the galleries. A heavyset man appeared at the door on the left. Mandred knocked him out with a single punch.

Farodin pushed open the temple door. A broad stairway led down to a cobbled market square. Nuramon had taken Yulivee in his arms and pushed out into the open air. From high above came the clanging of bells. Mandred held his axe in front of him threateningly. He was moving backward beside Farodin, who was leading the horses down the stairs to the square below. No one dared come close to the red-haired giant. From the temple came the braying of hundreds of voices.

The companions leaped onto their horses. Nuramon pointed to the widest street leading away from the square. "That way."

They drove their horses along the cobbled road at a breakneck pace. High, colorful half-timbered houses lined their route. There were few people to be seen. Almost the entire town had been gathered in the temple, it seemed. Farodin looked back. The first of their pursuers were gathering in the market square. With raised fists, they screamed curses at the fleeing elves and Mandred. They looked ridiculously small in front of the enormous Tjured temple. On the outside, too, it was painted entirely in white. Its domed roof glinted brightly in the sunlight as if studded with plates of pure gold.

"Down there," Mandred shouted. He had slowed his mare and was pointing to a side road, at the end of which one of the gates in the town wall could be seen.

"Walk the horses," Nuramon ordered. "If we run for the gate like wolves are after us, they'll close it before we get there."

Farodin had trouble keeping his restless stallion under control. Nuramon, who had Yulivee in front of him on the saddle, rode in the lead. Behind them, the shouts of the enraged adherents were only slowly coming closer. None of the unarmed citizens really seemed to want to catch up with them.

A man in a white tabard planted himself in front of them at the gate. "Who rides there?" he shouted at them when they were still some distance away.

Farodin spotted a movement behind the arrow slits in the tower above the gate. *Crossbowmen, most likely*, he thought. A few more steps and they would be out of the shooters' line of fire. Riding down the one guard standing before them would have been easy enough, but as soon as they left the gate behind them, they could be shot in the back from the other side, which made simply battering their way out impossible. They had to find some ruse.

"There's a riot at the temple," he called to the guard. "They need every man."

"A riot?" the man shouted back suspiciously. "There's never been a riot here."

"Believe me. Demon folk suddenly broke into the temple. I saw them with my own eyes. Can't you hear the shouting? They're after the congregation. They're driving them through the streets like cattle."

The soldier squinted up to Farodin. He was about to say something when a mob of the Tjured faithful appeared at the other end of the street. They had armed themselves with clubs and pitchforks. "They're coming this way," said Farodin grimly. "They're possessed, all of them."

The guardsman reached for his halberd, which was leaning by the gate. "To arms!" he screamed at the top of his lungs, waving to the men behind the arrow slits. "A rebellion!"

"Run for your lives!" Farodin shouted. Then he gave his companions a sign, and they raced out through the town gate. No crossbow bolts flew after them.

They fled along a dusty road that ran between fields of golden corn. In the west, the land climbed in gentle hills, where broad swaths of forest divided green meadows.

After a little more than a mile, they left the road and galloped cross-country. A herd of sheep scattered, bleating loudly, as the horses thundered through. Finally, they reached a forest and rode on in the shelter of the trees.

Farodin looked back toward the town. On the road, a small band of riders was visible. They rode together as far as the first junction, then separated and went off in different directions.

"Messengers," Mandred growled. "Soon, every knight for a hundred miles will know that demons appeared in that damned temple." He turned to Nuramon. "By Norgrimm's battle-axe, what happened? Why were we suddenly in the middle of that place?"

Nuramon spread his arms in a gesture of helplessness. "I can't explain it. We were supposed to step into an Albenstar and, from there, go along another path. It felt like someone pulled the ground out from under my feet. In the Albenstar itself, it was as if all the paths were dead."

"Dead paths?" asked Mandred. "What kind of nonsense is that?"

"Magic is alive, mortal," said Farodin now. "You can feel the paths pulsating. It's like they're the veins of this world."

"Was it maybe that funny house that the humans had built?" asked Yulivee in a shy voice. "It was spooky, even though it was all white. There was something that tore at me . . . in me . . . Something wanted to take away my magic. Maybe it was the dead tree or the man with the big eyes."

"Yes, the man in the picture." Nuramon turned in his saddle and looked to Farodin. "Did you notice anything strange about the picture?"

"No. Except perhaps that it was a completely unremarkable work of art."

"The man in it looked like Guillaume," said Nuramon.

Farodin frowned. That was insane. Why should anyone put up a picture of Guillaume in a temple?

"You're right," said Mandred. "Now that you mention it, the man really looked like Guillaume." .

"Who's Guillaume?" asked Yulivee.

As they slowly rode deeper into the woods, Nuramon told Yulivee about the Devanthar.

"So Guillaume was a human who could take away someone else's magic when he did magic himself?" the girl asked when Nuramon was finished.

"Guillaume was no human," Farodin corrected her. "He was half elf and half Devanthar. Humans have no . . ." He paused. No, that was no longer true. That's how it had been as long as he could remember, but the events in Iskendria had proved that at least the Tjured monks could wield magic.

"Without magic, those bad knights would never have found out how to get into Valemas," said Yulivee dejectedly. "In the temple, it felt like someone was trying to steal away my magic. Could Guillaume's spirit be living in the picture?"

"Guillaume was not evil," Nuramon said in a soothing voice. "And I'm certain there's no spirit back there."

"But *something* tried to take my magic," the girl insisted.

"Maybe it's the place," said Mandred. "The temple itself. It was built directly on top of the Albenstar. If I understood you right, Nuramon."

"That could also be a coincidence. Humans are only too happy to build their shrines where Albenpaths cross."

A cold fear ran through Farodin. "What if they are consciously trying to destroy the Albenstars? They would be separating this world from Albenmark. They hate us and call us demons. It would make sense then, wouldn't it, if they then aspired to seal off all of the gates to Albenmark? Think about it . . . They force their way through the gates into the Shattered World and destroy the enclaves there. And they seal off the gates to Albenmark. Don't you see the plan behind that? They're separating the worlds once and for all. And they're wiping out everyone who doesn't follow Tjured."

Nuramon raised his eyebrows and smiled. "You really surprise me sometimes, Farodin. How can it be that you—of all people—suddenly

put so much store in what humans can do? You're usually so contemp-
tuous of them."

Mandred loudly cleared his throat.

"Not all humans, admittedly," Nuramon qualified. "But someone
is also creating new Albenpaths and new stars. That doesn't tally with
your theory."

Nuramon's words sounded reasonable, and Farodin wished nothing more than for him to be right. But the doubt kept gnawing at him.
"Do you know this area?"

Nuramon nodded.

"Then lead us to the nearest large Albenstar, and we'll see if there
is a temple on top of that, too."

LOST FOR ALL TIME?

Farodin looked out through the shattered panes of the ruined temple toward the edge of the forest. He had already been convinced the day before that he would be proved right. Then, on their way through the hill country, they stumbled upon a small chapel that stood on a minor Albenstar. Only three paths crossed there. Or rather, three paths had once crossed there, for the place had lost all trace of magic.

Mandred kicked a soot-black beam that creaked and tipped sideways. "It was a while ago. I'd say it burned down at least half a year ago. Seems strange that they didn't rebuild it."

"Why should they?" replied Farodin irritably. "It had served its purpose after all, hadn't it?" He looked over to Yulivee.

The girl had narrowed her eyes to slits and was pulling a face. "It's here," she said quietly. "Just like in the other white building. Something's trying to steal my magic. It's pulling at me. It hurts." She opened her eyes wide and ran to the entrance.

Mandred, on a signal from Farodin, went after her. He could not focus when Yulivee ran around alone.

"I don't sense the pulling at all," said Nuramon uncertainly.

"But you believe her?" Farodin asked.

He nodded. "She has a finer feeling for magic than either of us. There's no doubt about that. What is also beyond doubt is that there is no longer a gate here that leads to Albenmark. All of the magic has been drained from this place."

"And destroying this temple made no difference," said Farodin soberly. "Once the magic has been taken from a place, it never comes back. Or do I have that wrong?"

Nuramon raised his hands helplessly. "How are we supposed to know that? I don't understand what's going on here. Why were these temples built? Who came here to destroy this one? Why did they simply give up on the temple after it was destroyed? Why didn't they rebuild it?"

"I can answer the last one, at least," replied Farodin calmly. "This place is in the middle of the wilderness. There's no town here, not so much as a village. The one and only reason this temple was built was to destroy the Albenstar. That's also why there was no need to rebuild it. It served its purpose."

"Maybe some priests were looking for solitude," Nuramon objected. "This is a beautiful place." He looked out through the shattered window and down to the small lake below.

"No. Didn't you hear what that fat priest shouted? We're demons. We murdered Saint Guillaume and cheated humanity of salvation in the process." Farodin laughed bitterly. "Could they have twisted the truth any more? It has to be clear to you what that means for us. So many kingdoms have already fallen to the priests. They are forcing their way into the broken world and hunting elves and other Albenkin. Their faith demands that they see all of us dead. And if they cannot get to Albenmark itself, then they will destroy every gate they can possibly find."

"We don't know nearly enough to go jumping to conclusions," said Nuramon. "You're listening to your heart, not your reason. What's gotten into you, Farodin?"

It beggared belief. Nuramon was willfully ignoring what all of this meant. "We are immortal, Nuramon. We are used to things taking a very long time. But suddenly, time is running out for us. Are you blind to the danger? They're destroying Albenstars. What will happen if they destroy the one that leads to Noroelle? Or even worse . . . what if they force their way through it to the Shattered World and kill her?"

Nuramon frowned. Then he shook his head resolutely. "That's nonsense. Her Albenstar is at the end of the world. There is no kingdom there to conquer, probably no humans at all. Why would the Tjured priests even go there?"

"Because they want to destroy every Albenstar. They are waging war against Albenmark, even if they can't set foot in our homeland. We cannot risk using unsafe gates anymore. Look around, Nuramon. Look at what's going on in this world. A few hundred years ago, a priest was murdered, and now his insane followers rule half a continent. Imagine what would happen if we jumped in time again. The power of the priests is growing faster and faster. Can you really be sure that the Albenstar to Noroelle will still exist in a hundred years?"

"You may be right," Nuramon admitted.

Farodin was relieved that his companion finally understood his fear. "We should keep on the move. Have no doubt that the Tjured knights have not given up searching for us. We spy them out, then we take the Albenstone and the djinns' crown."

Nuramon paled. "The crown. They must know what we're planning. The djinn's library contains all knowledge, even that of the future."

"That may be," Farodin replied, unruffled. "But the Tjured priests are obviously too stupid to get their hands on it. We would hardly have survived the jump into the temple if they had known we were coming. It would not have been parishioners standing in the galleries. It would have been soldiers with crossbows. They have no idea what we're going to do. And no one with any sense would ever think that a pathetic little band like us would try to steal their greatest treasure."

"Two men attacking the trolls' fortress wasn't enough?"

Farodin grinned. "One can always do better."

A MORNING
IN FARGON

Dawn had come, and the birds were twittering their morning song. Nuramon and Farodin stood at the edge of the grove of trees where they had spent the night. From this vantage point, they had a good view over the surrounding lands. Off to the north, they could see a large forest, and to the south, rolling hills stretched almost as far as Felgeres on the coast.

Mandred was still snoring, and Yulivee had her blanket pulled over her head. It would probably be hard to wake them, as usual.

"Let them sleep a little longer," said Farodin. "Yesterday was hard. I have already saddled the horses. We won't lose any time."

The flight from the Tjured knights had driven them to the limits of their strength. They were so exhausted that Nuramon had nodded off momentarily during his watch. Luckily, nothing had happened, and none of his companions had noticed.

There would be no rest for them anywhere in Fargon. Ever since they had seen Guillaume's image in the church, it had been clear to them why the humans hated the Albenkin with such bitterness. It had all started in Aniscans. It was their fault, and Nuramon could not reconcile himself to the fact that their good intentions had given rise to this hatred. Back then, they had heard the lies being spread, but Nuramon had never thought it was possible for such fabrications to lead to anything as momentous as what was happening here. The queen had been proved right: their failure in Aniscans was the seed from which the evil of the Tjured priests had grown.

"What do we do now, Farodin?" Nuramon asked. "We can't travel here as we used to. There's malice wherever we go, and soldiers everywhere."

"We can deal with that," Farodin replied coolly, and he looked to the rising sun.

"You know there are few things I think of as impossible, but after what we saw yesterday, I'm not so certain anymore," said Nuramon.

"You mean the checks?"

"Yes." From a hiding place, they had seen Tjured knights stopping travelers and checking their ears. And because a man had ears that were slightly pointed—though with no true resemblance to elven ears—he was led away. What had become of the faith Guillaume had once devoted himself to? The Tjured priests no longer healed the people. They were a scourge upon them.

"You are worried about Yulivee," said Farodin quietly.

"About her, and about all of us. All of the new Albenpaths worry me. It cannot be a coincidence that they connect the major towns and cities of Fargon."

"You're right. Apparently a human is in possession of an Albenstone and the djinns' crown. As terrible as this all seems to us, it is no doubt going to be easier to take an Albenstone away from a human than from one of the Albenkin. I am confident we'll be able to track down the stone."

"But doesn't it surprise you that you can't sense any trace of the crown?"

Farodin smiled calmly. "If I had to guess, I would say that the crown is in the capital."

Nuramon shook his head. "Algaunis is a fortress. You have seen it yourself."

"What other choice do we have? What do you think we should do?"

"We could look for allies. Remember the stories about the elven soldiers fighting the Tjured in Angnos and on the Aegilien Islands?"

"Allies here could only mean humans. And how could humans help us here?"

Nuramon's gaze traversed the hill country to the south.

"There must be enemies of the Tjured worshippers, even here," Nuramon said. "No one is going to tolerate this kind of suppression forever. And the lives of humans are short."

"But the humans are weak."

"That's where you're mistaken," Nuramon said. "I was in Firnstayn a long time, and I saw how hard they strive for freedom. They will rebel, and they will rebel again and again."

"That may be how it is in Firnstayn. They are far away from what is happening here. Just think of Iskendria with its Balbar. The inhabitants sacrificed their own children. Lunatics."

Nuramon remembered his first stay in Iskendria, and the disgust rose in him again.

"And what about Aniscans? What did the people there do to help Guillaume against the soldiers? In the end, all they did was point their fingers at us as his murderers."

"You're probably right. But if someone could just light a little spark in them, then . . ." He broke off. There was a sound like distant thunder.

"I hear it, too," his companion whispered and looked toward the hills on the far side of the meadows below the place they stood.

White-robed knights came galloping over the top of a distant hill and disappeared from view again. They were heading straight toward the elves' encampment.

Farodin hesitated no longer. "Go. Wake the others."

A heartbeat later, Nuramon was at Mandred's side and shaking him awake. The jarl started, and his hand went for his axe.

"Riders. We have to get away from here," said Nuramon.

Mandred leaped to his feet and, absurdly, quickly stuffed the remains of their food from the evening before into his saddlebags.

Nuramon tapped at Yulivee, but what his fingers touched was far too hard for the little elf. He threw back the blanket and was shocked to discover no more than her books and her travel bag.

"Nuramon, look!" shouted Farodin.

Nuramon jumped up and ran to his companion's side while Mandred heaved the saddlebags onto the back of his mare. Farodin pointed straight ahead.

It was Yulivee. She was running down the slope to the meadow. Two low valleys still separated her from the riders. Nuramon could see the morning light glinting on their lances. He turned to Farodin. "You go. Wait for us at the edge of the forest." Then he swung onto his saddle and galloped off.

Yulivee ran fast, but she was still some distance from the grove. The riders were out of sight, somewhere between the lines of hills. He could only hope that he was faster. He would never forgive himself if something happened to her.

The little elf was remarkably quick, but as the horsemen thundered down the slope of the last hill, Nuramon knew it would be close. "Faster, Felbion," he shouted. Half of the Tjured knights were armed with lances, which they now lowered threateningly. The others carried swords in their hands. Like the knights they had seen the day before, the riders all wore long mail tunics under white tabards. The black tree of the Tjured stood out on their shields—the oak on which Guillaume was burned to death. This symbol could not be allowed to mark the end of Yulivee, too.

Felbion galloped as fast as any horse could. Nuramon knew he would reach Yulivee ahead of the riders. She was courageous and ran without looking back. Then it happened. Yulivee fell.

Nuramon felt Felbion, unbidden, push himself even harder.

The tips of the knights' lances sank lower.

Stand up, thought Nuramon desperately. As if she had heard him, the little elf jumped to her feet again. But she made the mistake of looking back and running forward at the same time, and she stumbled once more.

Then Nuramon was at her side, reaching down his hand to her. Yulivee jumped high and took hold of his arm, and Nuramon pulled her onto the saddle in front of him. As he raised his head to see their enemy, he knew that he could not turn Felbion in time. The knights' lances were aimed at him, and the swordsmen held their blades aloft.

He had to at least try. But as he hauled on the reins to turn Felbion, the horse kept galloping straight ahead, charging headlong at the soldiers. In the first moment, Nuramon did not know what was happening. Yulivee screamed in fear and clung to Felbion's mane.

The elf had just time enough to draw Gaomee's sword. Felbion whinnied, and the enemies' horses swung aside. The first lance shot at him from one side. Nuramon ducked low, protecting Yulivee's body. The point of the lance breezed past his head, but the shaft struck him hard on the temple. From the right came a sword, but Nuramon managed to parry. Then he was through the riders.

He slid his sword back into its sheath. Then he saw a broken sword blade embedded in the saddle horn. "Yulivee," he cried in fear. The girl did not reply. Nuramon leaned forward. Yulivee had her face buried in her hands and was shivering. Nuramon shook her by the shoulder.

She looked up at him. "Are we still alive?" she asked, her eyes wide.

"Are you hurt?"

"No, but *you've* got a bad bump."

Nuramon sighed with relief and touched his fingers to his temple. The shaft of the lance had left him with a graze.

"Should I heal it?"

Nuramon did not ask her where she learned to heal. He already knew the answer. "You can do that later," he replied. He looked over his shoulder and saw that the riders had turned and were in pursuit.

Nuramon drove Felbion toward the line of hills. The elven horse galloped up the slope with ease. Before they rode down the other side, Nuramon looked back and saw that their pursuers had lost a little ground. The moment he was in the hollow between the hills, he turned Felbion westward along the line of hills. He looked back several times, waiting for the soldiers to reappear.

There they were. Nuramon immediately turned Felbion up the hill again, heading back toward the meadow. He knew that the riders had seen him when they turned and rode along the ridge to cut him off. But again, Felbion was faster. Nuramon already had the hill behind him and was racing for the grove of trees where they had camped the night before.

The humans lost a lot of time coming down the hill again. Their horses were exhausted from chasing Yulivee, and they were not as sure-footed on the slopes as Felbion was. When the knights finally made it onto the meadow, there were a good hundred paces between the humans and Nuramon.

Yulivee stretched and looked back past Nuramon. "We did it."

Nuramon pulled the little elf back down onto the saddle. "Don't celebrate too soon," he warned her. It's true that the humans would never be able to catch up with Felbion, but who knew what dangers still lay ahead?

They passed the little grove and rode straight for the large forest to the north.

"There," Yulivee called, pointing ahead.

At the edge of the forest, Farodin and Mandred sat on horseback, waiting and looking in their direction. They had waited. That was not like Farodin at all.

Finally, the two turned their horses and disappeared slowly among the trees. They let Nuramon and Yulivee catch up.

"Are you hurt?" called Mandred.

"Not even a scratch," Yulivee answered before Nuramon could say anything.

"You did well, Nuramon," said Farodin, his tone appreciative.

Nuramon was surprised. Compliments from the mouth of the elven warrior were a rare treat.

They rode through the forest in silence. Though their horses left tracks that were barely visible to human eyes, they waded some distance through a river and even risked riding through a small swampy area. Their horses had a sense for solid ground and led them safely through to the edge of the forest.

There, in the protection of the trees, they rested.

Nuramon lifted Yulivee down from Felbion, and the youngster already wanted to run off and explore the area.

Nuramon grabbed her hand and held tightly. "Stop. Not so fast. We're not finished with this."

Yulivee put on a contrite face. "I'm sorry."

The elf kneeled in front of her and looked into her eyes. "That's what you say every time, Yulivee. And then you still go and do something you're not supposed to. How many times have I told you that you're not allowed to leave the camp at night? And then you made me think you were still lying there asleep."

"I'll make it up to you," said Yulivee, touching her hand to the wound on his head. She frowned for a moment, then took her hand away again.

When Nuramon felt for the wound, his skin was smooth and the swelling was gone. He had to smile. "Thank you, Yulivee. But please stay in the camp at night."

Then Farodin joined them. "How did you get out at all without being seen?" he asked.

Nuramon felt caught out. The girl must have crept away the moment he nodded off.

Yulivee answered, "Don't you accuse Nuramon of anything. I made myself invisible, and when he was standing on the edge of the camp, I crept out." It was a good excuse, but the conspiratorial glance she cast at Nuramon as she said it took away any credibility she might have had.

Farodin said nothing. His knowing look said more than words could.

"But why on earth did you put yourself in such danger in the first place?" Nuramon asked.

"You were talking about what the Fargoners were planning, and I thought you'd be happy if I found out for you. So I turned myself invisible. With all the magic I had to do for that, I was soon really tired. But I looked through walls, and I heard things that some people were talking about in secret. I read their thoughts and lots more. But I'm still small and don't have very much power yet," she said with a serious face. She did not seem to realize just how much power she already possessed. Her magical capabilities were little more than a game to her.

"That was very silly of you, Yulivee," said Farodin.

"What do you want? I'm still alive."

Mandred laughed, but a glance from Farodin silenced him.

"So do you want to know what I found out or not?" she asked.

"Please tell us," Nuramon encouraged her.

Yulivee sat on a fallen tree and waited until her companions were gathered around. Then she told them about her adventures. "The moon shone brightly as I crept quietly over the hill and all the way down to Felgeres. Invisible, I passed by the sentries and just followed my nose. When I got down to the harbor, I saw at least a hundred ships anchored there."

"By the Alben. They're after control of the Aegilien Sea once and for all," said Farodin. "The ships from Reilimee won't be able to trade anymore."

"Thank you, Yulivee, for finding that out," said Nuramon.

"But that isn't everything. I also listened to some of the commanders. Captains and knights, and even the prince of the brotherhood in Felgeres. The ships aren't there to take control of the Aegilien Islands. They're supposed to sail north. They want to reach the Fjordlands before the autumn storms. And they want to join with another fleet on the way."

Mandred jumped to his feet. "What?"

"They have orders to break the resistance in the North," Yulivee explained. "They weren't very eager about it, but they said the high priest wanted it like that. He wanted to teach the elf-friends some humility, the men said."

"We have to warn them," Mandred shouted. He went to his horse, but quickly returned. "We have to risk jumping between Albenstars."

"Out of the question," said Farodin. "We first have to get our hands on the Albenstone and the djinns' crown. That will probably stop them attacking at all."

"*Probably* isn't good enough for me," Mandred shot back loudly. "This is about Firnstayn. The bastards want to burn us down like they did with Iskendria. I am not going to sit and watch it happen."

Nuramon exchanged a look with Farodin. "Mandred is right. We have to break off our search for the stone. The gate on the cliff above Firnstayn leads close to the boundary of the heartland. The Tjured priests can't be allowed to destroy it. Or even worse . . . imagine what would happen if they forced their way through to Albenmark. Think of the friends we still have there. We owe it to them to warn the queen. Could you stand in front of Noroelle and tell her that you did nothing, for her sake? Just to shorten our search by a few months?"

"They have never yet managed to open a gate to Albenmark," Farodin insisted. "All they can do is destroy the gates. But you are right in another sense. It is a question of friendship." Farodin turned to Mandred. "Forgive me." He reached out his hand to the jarl. "You have been a true friend to us for so long. It is time for us to show our loyalty to you. Firnstayn can count on our swords. We will do all we can to protect you and your people."

Mandred gripped the offered hand. "You bring two swords that count for more than a hundred axes. I'm proud to have you at my side."

Farodin laid a hand on Mandred's shoulder. "But we can't take the Albenpaths from Fargon. They are not safe." He turned to Yulivee. "You said the Tjured knights would sail before the autumn storms."

The girl nodded.

"Then we leave Fargon by land. As soon as we are out of this kingdom, we can risk an Albenpath."

"Farodin is right," said Nuramon.

Mandred nodded and stared at the ground. "By Luth. I never would have thought that what we did in Aniscans could ever put Firnstayn in danger." He looked to Yulivee and had to smile. "Thank you, little elf. You are a true companion." Then he turned away. "Time to ride."

Farodin followed Mandred to the horses.

Nuramon took Yulivee in his arms and carried her to Felbion. "You did well," he told her. Then he lifted the little sorceress onto the horse. She gave him a satisfied smile. "But . . . ," he added.

"But?" the girl repeated.

"But don't ever scare me like that again."

"You care about me, don't you?"

"Yes. You are like a sister to me."

Astonishment spread on the little elf's face. "Really?"

Nuramon mounted Felbion behind her. Yulivee turned her head and looked at him. She was obviously waiting for confirmation. "Yes, Yulivee."

"Then you have made me one of your relatives. Like the queen once told you?"

Nuramon nodded. "Just like that. And whatever happens, I would ride against a thousand warriors to keep you safe."

Tears gathered in Yulivee's eyes. Nuramon could feel what must be going on inside her, but he had told her the truth. She was truly like a little sister to him, and not like a daughter. She was too powerful for that. Nuramon could not say what fate had in store for him and his companions, but if there was one thing he wanted to spare the girl, it was a true battle. It was time to take her to Albenmark, and safety. Maybe Obilee, if she had not yet entered the moonlight, would be able to look after her.

A TIME
FOR HEROES

A hundred ships are coming!" roared the king. A deathly silence fell over the banqueting hall. "And a second fleet will come to join the first hundred. That shows how much they fear the men of the North."

Mandred saw many of the warriors and princes gathered there in the hall smile grimly. His descendant, Liodred, knew what tone to take to reach the hearts of fighters, and Mandred was proud of him. He was tall and powerfully built, every inch of him a fighter. Long, curly red hair tumbled to his shoulders, and his blue eyes shone like the sky on a summer afternoon. The only thing about him that Mandred disapproved of was the way he kept his beard cut short.

Liodred had acted quickly after they arrived. They reached Firnstayn late in the afternoon, and that same evening, he called together all the princes who were close enough to come, and along with the Mandridians, they gathered in the enormous royal hall. More than three hundred warriors sat at the long tables, and many of them were gazing in awe at the banquet table. Besides the king, two elven warriors, a young girl, and the king's legendary ancestor, Mandred Torgridson, had taken their seats up there.

"You all know the Tjured priests well enough, with their slick tongues. You know how they insult our gods and spread lies among our people. And I ask you, do we fear them for that?" the king called.

"No!" came the cry from hundreds of throats.

"They've mustered more than a hundred ships and thousands of warriors, all to attack Firnstayn by surprise. For no one has yet declared war on us." Liodred leaned forward and pointed to a white-haired warrior with a wolfskin across his shoulders. "Is that fear I see in your eyes, Skarbern?"

The old man turned red and was about to jump to his feet when Liodred spoke again. "I share your concern, Skarbern. I fear our hotheaded Mandridians will have sent them all to the bottom of the fjord before we old men even get our axes out of our belts."

Deafening laughter filled the hall. Mandred's heart swelled. His descendant was truly a warrior king. Every single one of the men down below would walk through fire for him. Liodred's words had even stirred Mandred's thirst for battle.

"Men of Firnstayn. My friends. I have known most of you since I was a child. I know the courage of your hearts. I know your pride. I know your stubbornness. Men like you are only to be found in the Fjordlands. Drinkers, fornicators, comrades, and none better when push comes to shove. Men like you can only exist in a free land. Do you think the Tjured knights are coming because they want our gold? No. They have so much gold they use it to plate the towers of their temples. Do you think they're coming to plunder and pillage, to lay fire and despoil your women?"

Liodred paused briefly and swept the hall with his gaze. "No, my friends. The knights of the Tjured order will come armed with large swords, but with nothing between their legs. How else can you explain why every one of them has taken a vow of chastity?"

Mandred snorted into his drinking horn and sprayed Farodin, sitting beside him, with mead. The elf remained completely unperturbed. *Maybe I should explain the joke to him*, Mandred thought.

"My friends, know that all of these are not the reasons that the Tjured knights are attacking us," Liodred went on. "They are doing so because we possess something a thousand times more valuable. Freedom. They represent a race in which there are two kinds of men, priests and servants, a race that cannot abide freedom in its presence. So when I call you to arms, know what awaits you. It is more than just a sea battle. Were the priests of the order to be victorious, then what happened to the men of Angnos and Gornamdur would happen to us. They will kill every one of you who does not want to be a priest or a servant. They will burn the ironmen and the sacred groves and our temples. Nothing that reminds us of our proud ancestors and their way of life will be spared from the fire."

Liodred paused again to let his words sink in. He raised his drinking horn and spilled some of it to pay homage to the gods. Then he set the horn to his lips and drank in long drafts. Many of the men in the hall below stood and did the same.

Mandred, too, was on his feet. He laid one arm across the shoulders of his fearless descendant.

"It is easy to speak big words in a hall like this, among friends," Liodred finally continued. "I know that the Tjured priests only wage war if they are sure of victory. Theirs is not the lion heart of the warrior, but the petty heart of a penny-pinching shopkeeper. They count and they calculate and they only attack when they know they can set five knights against every one of their enemy's warriors. The fjord will be red with blood when we face them in battle. And much of that blood will be our own." He turned to Mandred.

"Here at my side stands Jarl Mandred Torgridson. The living ancestor. The founder of the royal line of Firnstayn. You all know the stories about him. He will return when his people's adversity is greatest, it is said. He is the one who, today, brought me news of the treacherous attack awaiting us."

A murmur went through the royal hall, and Mandred felt uneasy having so many eyes gazing at him. Many saw in him not only a hero, but also a herald of looming misfortune.

"My ancestor gave up his wife and his son to rescue Firnstayn. His courage has lived on in the songs and stories of our skalds for centuries. Now it is up to you to prove that you are no less valiant than our ancestor. Are you ready to fight?"

Now the last men still sitting jumped to their feet, too. "We fight!" The cry rang through the hall, taken up by hundreds of men. "We fight!"

Liodred stretched his arms wide, and silence slowly returned. "The Tjured priests force men from the lands they have subjugated to fight for them. None but the free fight for us. But we, too, have mighty allies. There is a pact from long ago, an alliance that must prove its worth now, in our hour of need. Centuries have passed since the elven queen called on the warriors of Firnstayn for help. Now we will ask the elves to stand by us. You see before you two men from the sagas of old. Elven warriors, noble and fearless and deadlier with a sword than any human. They have promised me they will go through the stone circle on the cliff this very night and ride to Albenmark. At dawn, all of Albenmark will ring with the sounding of horns, calling the warriors to the queen's court."

Mandred swallowed hard. It all sounded grand, and the men below in the hall broke out in cries of jubilation at the news. But he was far from certain that Emerelle would receive his companions. And even if the elves were prepared to help, how long would it take to muster an elven fleet and sail to the Fjordlands?

RETURN TO ALBENMARK

The queen's castle, like the houses on the hills nearby, gleamed in the night. They only had to put the meadows behind them to reach the palace. Nuramon rode beside Farodin in silence. Even Yulivee, seated in front of him on the saddle, said nothing.

They had come through Atta Aikhjarto's gate and had met Xern there. When they told him what they were planning, he told them in Atta Aikhjarto's name about an Albenstar that would take them closer to the queen's palace. Then they had jumped from Aikhjarto's gate to the other star and avoided the Shalyn Falah.

They also did not pass the faun oak or Noroelle's lake. Perhaps it was better that way. They were in such a hurry that they would not have done justice to the dignity those places deserved.

"Faeryshine," said Yulivee softly. She seemed to be referring to all the little lights that shone in the palace and made it visible from far away. "Faster, Felbion. Faster."

To Nuramon's surprise, Felbion picked up his pace. Now his horse obeyed Yulivee. It wouldn't be long before he would have to hand over the reins to his little foster sister.

The closer they came to the palace, the more Nuramon feared that they might be making a mistake, appearing before Emerelle as ambassadors for Liodred. They were elves, of course, but the queen would certainly not have forgotten that they had once opposed her.

They rode up to the palace gate. It stood open, and there were no guards in sight. The courtyard on the other side was empty. If not for the lights, Nuramon would have thought that the palace had been abandoned.

They did not go to the trouble of stabling the horses. Instead, they halted at the palace steps, dismounted, and simply left the horses standing there.

Nuramon took Yulivee by the hand. "Now, you know the stories. No one is ever rude or cheeky in the queen's halls. Remember that."

"I know, I know. Let's go," Yulivee replied.

Side by side, all three entered Emerelle's brightly lit halls. Yulivee looked around with her mouth agape. She seemed to find the statues particularly interesting. The little sorceress was so mesmerized by the grandeur of everything around her that, to get anywhere at all, Nuramon was forced to pull her along behind him. They came to the atrium outside the Royal Hall. Here, for the first time, guards were posted. Two elven soldiers armed with spears stood before the closed door, waiting for them.

"Who are you?" said the burlier of the pair.

"We come as emissaries from the king of Firnstayn," Farodin answered. "The time has come to repay what Alfadas did for the elves."

The two men at the door exchanged an uncertain look.

"Who would have thought?" asked a voice beside them.

They turned, and Alvias entered the atrium through a side door. The master had changed. A scar marked his forehead. He must have been wounded by an enchanted weapon. "Who would have thought that those whose names have not been spoken in these halls for centuries would return as emissaries."

"Master Alvias," said Farodin in surprise. "It is good to see a familiar face."

The queen's confidant stepped closer and looked them up and down. "I wish I could say that I was happy to see you, but the arrival of emissaries means war, and *your* arrival might well invoke the queen's wrath."

Nuramon remembered the last time he had been in these halls. Back then, the queen had sent him out on the search for Guillaume, and everything since had followed its terrible course. "Will the queen receive us?" he asked.

"She will certainly admit emissaries from Firnstayn, but it may be that she will reject the two elves who once aroused her anger." He looked them over again. "Wait here. I will announce your arrival to the queen."

Alvias opened the door. Nuramon could not see into the room on the other side, but he could hear that many Albenkin were gathered there. The master stepped through the door and closed it behind him.

"What's the matter, Nuramon?" Farodin asked. "You look as if you've seen a ghost."

"I am just dreadfully afraid," Nuramon replied. "The wrath of the queen. I would rather not get to know that."

Farodin smiled calmly. "Well. No turning back now."

Yulivee shook Nuramon's arm. "Have you two done something dumb?"

"Yes," Nuramon answered with a nod. He had told Yulivee about their search for Noroelle only in the broadest of strokes and omitted the fact that Yulivee's beloved Emerelle had treated them very badly. "We left Albenmark against her will. Like you scampering out of camp at night."

"She will forgive you. She is very gracious," Yulivee declared.

The queen kept them waiting for a long time. Yulivee in particular grew restless and whiled away the time by going over to the guards and asking them questions, to which the two men gave only the most perfunctory of answers. She asked them about their armor and the weapons they carried, and how one became a guard for the queen. Nuramon listened only halfheartedly to the discussion and paced back and forth restlessly.

Farodin stood calmly and kept his eye on Nuramon. "Did you lose all your patience in Firnstayn?" he finally asked. "Or did you learn that from watching Mandred?"

Nuramon stopped pacing. "If you only knew how I fear for us and our quest." The longer the queen kept them waiting, the greater the danger seemed to grow. Emerelle was probably preparing her verdict for them.

A sound came from inside the Royal Hall. Yulivee quickly ran to Nuramon and took him by the hand again. Then the door opened, and he could see past Alvias and between the rows of assembled elves to Emerelle. She sat motionless on her throne.

"The queen will receive you," said Master Alvias, and he walked ahead of them.

The companions followed him. Nuramon was surprised that the hall was as full as it had been for the departure of the elfhunt. The Albenkin to left and right seemed amazed to see them. Nuramon knew some of the faces, but most were strangers to him. Someone somewhere suddenly whispered, "Farodin and Nuramon." And both names passed in whispers through the hall. Far ahead, a loud discussion began. The queen raised her hand and silence returned instantly.

"Welcome, Nuramon," whispered somebody on Nuramon's left. It was a young elf, a soldier in white linen armor. Nuramon did not know him, but behind the young man, he saw Elemon, his uncle, and others from his clan. Apart from Elemon, most of the faces wore expressions of joy, even pride. "Welcome, cousin," said a young woman softly, again someone Nuramon had never seen before but who bore a resemblance to his aunt Ulema.

Nuramon met all of them with friendly gestures, but he did not stop. Several from Farodin's clan were also there. They greeted their relative with reserve, but Nuramon read great reverence on their faces.

And then they were close enough to the throne to read the face of the queen herself. What Nuramon saw there was coldness.

Around the throne, Nuramon saw many familiar faces. Ollowain was there and Dijelon and Pelveric. Obilee, too. It made Nuramon glad to see Noroelle's confidante. She looked more dignified than ever and was not able to hide her own joy at seeing them again. She had woven her blond hair into heavy braids that hung past her shoulders. She wore red-brown armor with runes painted on it, clearly the armor of a warrior sorceress.

Nuramon and Farodin bowed their heads before the queen. Little Yulivee curtsied. Before they could say a word, Emerelle spoke. "So the day has come. The day that the children of Alfadas ask us to repay what we owe. The day on which Farodin and Nuramon return. What has happened that you dare to appear before me?"

She was looking at Farodin, so it was he who answered. "We have come because of our friendship with Mandred, Alfadas's father. Firnstayn is in great danger. Tjured's followers have crushed the humans race by race, and now they are preparing to attack Firnstayn. The fleet of the order will soon set sail." Voices were raised across the hall, but Farodin did not let them disturb him. He went on. "In the name of Liodred, descendant of Alfadas Mandredson, we have come to request the aid of the Albenkin."

"The queen of Albenmark will honor her promise and make the necessary preparations," declared Emerelle.

Farodin bowed. "We thank you, in Liodred's name."

"Then your service to him is done. Your master will be satisfied. But let us say good-bye to Liodred's emissaries and hear from Farodin and Nuramon . . . two whose names have long been unspoken in these halls, but who, out in the forests, have attained the status of legend. Farodin and Nuramon. The elves who opposed the queen to go in search of their lady. When I discovered that you had defied my order, my fury was beyond measure. You show great courage to stand before me after all that has happened. You came here, although you knew that this could spell the end of your search. You, Farodin . . . you even carry with you the sand that I once dispersed in the human world. And you, Nuramon, dared to spend a human lifetime before my eyes in Firnstayn."

Nuramon was about to speak, but a sideways glance from Farodin stopped him.

"Did you want to say something, Nuramon?" the queen asked, her voice ironically pleasant.

"It was not my intention to anger you," he began haltingly. "When I was in Firnstayn, I knew that you could have sent others to fetch me at any time, but you did not. You must have had your reasons."

The queen tilted her head to one side. "Do not think for a moment that I would have changed my position on Noroelle. But I see that I cannot hold you here. Your love is too strong. You can try to rescue Noroelle, but know that you do so without my blessing. Time has passed since you contravened my command. I was able to see you from here often enough. Some of the things I saw pleased me. Others did not. You, Nuramon, spent time among the renegades. Fundamentally, a queen should find it displeasing when one of her subjects seeks refuge among those who have rebelled against her, but no one is likely to condemn you for visiting the children of the Darkalben." A murmur spread through the hall. No doubt those gathered there were asking one another about the secrets surrounding the dwarves, and they would have given a great deal to find out what Nuramon had experienced among them. The queen looked around the hall but made no gesture to silence the whispering. She simply continued. "And the same is true of your stay in Firnstayn. No one here is closer to Firnstayn than you. And for that reason, you shall bear a special responsibility. You shall sail into battle on board my ship."

"I thank you, Emerelle," Nuramon replied, although he did not know if he was being punished or honored.

"And now to you, Farodin. You talked Mandred into representing himself to the trolls as my ambassador. You waged your own private war against the trolls in a time of peace . . . and in the end, you did the right thing. It hurt me to discover what the trolls did to Yilvina and the others. Our dead bodies decay, but our souls live on. There is one thing you must understand, Farodin. We need the trolls in the battle against our enemy. And we must make sure that they believe in our good intentions." The queen's face had transformed to that of a good friend, which did not match very well with the words she was speaking. "What would Orgrim, prince of the trolls, say to you sailing into battle aboard his ship?"

Farodin, barely noticeably, swallowed. "He would no doubt see it as an honor," he replied.

Nuramon could not believe that the queen honestly wanted to hand Farodin over to the trolls as their hostage. More than two hundred years had passed since Farodin's attack on the Nightcrags, but the trolls had long memories. They would certainly try to kill him in some kind of regrettable and dubious accident. Was the queen trying to separate the two of them? To send the companions to their deaths to ensure the search for Noroelle failed? He had to do something. He released Yulivee's hand and took a step forward. Farodin managed to touch his hand, apparently wanting to hold him back. But now he had taken the step, and the queen was looking at him in surprise.

"Yes, Nuramon?"

"The trolls will murder Farodin, but any other elf would certainly come back alive. I beg of you, send me to them and keep Farodin at your side."

Farodin stepped up beside Nuramon. "Please, Emerelle, don't listen to him. I will submit to your will."

Yulivee followed the two companions and slipped her little hand into Nuramon's.

"I am impressed by your readiness to stand up for each other, but that changes no part of my decision. Farodin, I will hand you over to Prince Orgrim as a hostage. It is the only way to ally the trolls to us. It is not revenge nor a grudge that I carry. It is proof of my trust. It is as I said to you before, most recently before the elfhunt. Remember the words with which I sent you on your way. I don't want you to simply be a hostage, but a model for all elves to follow. You are to protect the life of the prince as you were supposed to protect the life of Mandred during the elfhunt. Will you do it?"

Farodin hesitated for a long moment. Then the corners of his mouth turned up in an almost imperceptible smile. "I will do it, my queen."

Something had passed between Farodin and Emerelle. In the hall, hardly anyone seemed to have noticed. They all seemed to think that they had witnessed a reconciliation that at first glance appeared to be a punishment, but what did Emerelle mean when she said that Farodin was *supposed* to protect Mandred? The queen spoke as if his companion had failed and was now being given the opportunity to make up for his failure. After all these years together, there was still a lot about Farodin that remained hidden from Nuramon.

The queen suddenly smiled. "I have only one more question." She looked at Yulivee. "Who is the girl holding your hand so tightly, Nuramon?"

"This is the sorceress Yulivee, daughter of Hildachi of the Diliskar clan. She may be the last of the Free of Valemas."

A rumble of voices rose in the hall, telling Nuramon that Valemas and the Diliskar clan had not been forgotten.

"Yulivee. What a name that is," said the queen, gazing at the girl as if Yulivee were one of the Alben. "Come here to me, Yulivee."

The child did not let go of Nuramon's hand, but looked up at him anxiously.

"Go on. That is Emerelle, the one you've heard so much about."

Yulivee slowly eased her grip and stepped cautiously before the queen. Everyone in the hall fell silent. The only sound was the swishing of the water falling from the walls. Emerelle looked at Yulivee for a long time, as if she wanted to remember every facet of the girl. Then she said, "Yulivee, I have waited a long time for the return of the Diliskar line and the other clans of Valemas, which makes today all the more important. A great future awaits you. How did you come to be with Nuramon and Farodin?"

In a quiet voice, Yulivee told the story of the first time she met Nuramon. She repeated their conversation from that time word for word. "And then he told me that you told him that he should choose his own kin. And then I knew that I was not alone."

"It was wise of Nuramon to tell you that. So you chose each other as relatives?"

"Yes. Now he is my brother."

Although Nuramon could see that some around him were listening to the little sorceress's words with disdainful smiles, he felt no unease. He was proud of Yulivee and how open she was with the queen.

"Come and stand beside my throne. You will have to get used to standing here."

Yulivee did as the queen asked. In the girl's face, it was clear how impressed she was at having the eyes of all the assembled Albenkin on her. When the queen took her hand, the young sorceress's eyes grew even wider. She must have felt as if she herself were in one of the Emerelle stories she knew so well.

The queen turned back to Nuramon. "You did well to take the child on. She is more powerful than you might think. Because you have chosen each other as siblings, I would like to ask you if I might be allowed to instruct her in the magical arts."

"Who could turn down such an offer?" replied Nuramon. "But it is not up to me to accept or reject. Yulivee should make that decision for herself. I would be happy to have you instruct her, for there is little I can teach her."

"Well, Yulivee? Would you like to be my pupil?"

"Yes, Emerelle. I would like that . . . but I would also like to stay with Nuramon."

"I will give you some time to think. It is not an easy choice. But whichever way you decide, you will not disappoint me," Emerelle said. Then she rose. "And now, my Albenkin, arm yourselves for battle. Alvias." The master approached. The queen whispered something in his ear, then she took Yulivee by the hand and left the hall through a side door. The soldiers around her throne followed her, all but Obilee, who stood where she was and looked at Farodin and Nuramon as if they were a painting that reminded her of good days.

Farodin was immediately surrounded by his relatives, and Nuramon's clan came to him, showering him with questions. Most of his relatives were strangers to him. The only familiar face he saw was Elemon's, and the old man's eyes still betrayed his suspicion. The young woman who had spoken to him earlier was his cousin Diama, he discovered. She asked him what had happened among the children of the Darkalben. Nuramon replied evasively and tried to catch Obilee's eye at every opportunity. But Obilee did not move from her place. She seemed happy enough to see Nuramon in the midst of his own clan.

When Elemon approached him, Nuramon thought that all the joy of his return was over. His uncle had never had a friendly word to say to him. The other elves waited in silence for what the old elf would say. "Nuramon, we are all part of the Weldaron clan," he began. "And you know that I and the others of my generation never had anything but scorn for you. In the time that you were here and were not allowed to leave Albenmark, we conceived children of our own. And after you left, they were born, and we were safe in the knowledge that they did not carry your soul. But these children, and their children, look at you through other eyes. They have heard the stories of Nuramon the minnesinger and warrior, of Nuramon the searcher, the eternal wanderer. During the troll wars, they discovered that you were once a companion to Alfadas." He stopped speaking and stared at Nuramon as if waiting for some stirring of emotion from him. Then he went on. "You don't need to forgive us who are now old. Many of us have not changed our views, but these elves around you now, they see you as one of the greats of our clan. Do not let them feel your contempt for us."

Nuramon had never liked Elemon, but his uncle's words were a concession that Nuramon had never in his life expected to hear. When he looked into the faces of the young elves surrounding him, he realized that his uncle was right. "If the queen did not want me with her, then I would go into this battle beside my clan. Thank you for what you have said, Elemon."

"And I hope you can forgive me," Elemon said, his eyes shining.

"Yes, I can. In the name of Weldaron." Nuramon recalled all the years he had had to put up with the ridicule of his own clan. If Elemon were not standing before him, and if he had not seen the old man close to tears, he would have believed that his relatives wanted him back among them now only for their own selfish reasons. But Elemon's words were spoken in earnest. Nuramon doubted that no more than he doubted the intentions of the young men and women around him, many of whom wore short swords, as he did, as if consciously emulating him. His cousin Diama was one of them. She was even wearing armor that was similar in design to Gaomee's armor, although fashioned from scales of metal and not from dragon leather. It was in that moment that Nuramon truly understood how long he had been gone. He had been a victim of time twice. And each time, more than two hundred years had passed. In that time, his clan's scorn had transformed into respect, and even admiration.

Alvias came to him then, accompanied by Farodin. The master nodded to him politely. "Nuramon, the queen wishes to see you and Farodin in her side chamber. Please follow me."

"Thank you for coming here," said Nuramon uncertainly as he left his relatives. He would need time to get used to the change.

When they had left the circle of their relatives, Farodin whispered, "It seems your clan has grown quickly. Apparently, they see more in you than just someone who is constantly reborn." It sounded as if Farodin, in his own way, was happy for him.

Nuramon was about to reply, but at that moment, they passed by Obilee. He stopped. Alvias seemed impatient. "I will go ahead and tell the queen that you are on your way."

Neither of them replied. Nuramon thought of the last time he had seen Noroelle's friend. It had been at the first gate he opened with his own magic. She had waved to him from the hill. Back then, she had seemed to him to be more a sorceress than a soldier, but now she was wearing a soldier's robes made of soft gelgerok leather, with hardwood plates fixed on the torso, sleeves, and legs. The runes painted on the wood no doubt aided Obilee in battle. Around her neck, she wore a chain to which, like Nuramon, she had attached Noroelle's precious stone. Hers was a diamond.

Finally, Nuramon broke the silence. "Xern told me that you were a heroine in the troll wars."

"Yes," Obilee replied as if she regretted the fact.

"Noroelle will be proud of you when she hears it," said Farodin.

"I have never forgotten Noroelle. Not a day passes that I do not think about her, or you." She looked into Nuramon's eyes. "I wish I could go with you." Her voice sounded as melancholy as her words. She smiled, but it was a pained smile. "Don't let my mood deceive you. I am happy to see you back." With those words she embraced Farodin and kissed him on the cheek. "I wish I could do something for you." She took Nuramon in her arms then, but did not kiss him. "I am so happy for you. Noroelle was right. Your clan has seen your true nature."

Before Nuramon could reply, Obilee said, "Come. We must not keep the queen waiting any longer. No doubt she wants to learn what you have both been through. And I am more than a little curious, too."

They followed Obilee into the side room. Nuramon could not take his eyes off the warrior woman. There was so much pain and longing there.

As they entered the side room, Nuramon could hardly believe his ears. Little Yulivee was standing beside the queen, surrounded by soldiers, telling them the story of their journey through Fargon. "And just when I believed my life was over, Nuramon reached me and pulled me up onto the saddle. But listen to what happened then! Well, what would you have done if you were us?" She turned to Ollowain.

"I would have turned around as fast as I could to get you to safety," he answered. "Then I would have ridden back and fought the riders in battle."

Yulivee grinned cheekily. "A wise answer. But Nuramon did nothing like that because it would have meant the death of both of us. He did not turn his horse around at all, because the enemy was too close." She could have told Ollowain that earlier, but the warrior from the Shalyn Falah laughed at her words. "Instead, he spurred us on, straight through the middle of them all, ducking their swords and lances and—" The little sorceress caught sight of Nuramon and stopped. But then she went on quickly. "And he saved little Yulivee from the evil men. And if little Yulivee watches out, she will still be alive tomorrow."

The soldiers around her laughed, and even the queen had a smile on her face. "Come closer," she said. And when Farodin and Nuramon were standing before her, she said, "I want to thank both of you once again for protecting Yulivee." She took the little girl's hand. "You don't know how much you have helped me and all of Albenmark by doing so."

A WALL OF WOOD

A fresh breeze tousled Mandred's thin braids. With Liodred and a bodyguard of Mandridians, he stood atop the western cliff overlooking the entrance to the fjord. From there, they could look far out over the sea. It was a beautiful late-summer morning. Small, fair-weather clouds scudded before the wind. The sun glittered on the water, and the outlines of distant ships stood out clearly against the sky. There must have been more than two hundred of them. And all of them bore the sign of the burned oak on their sails.

"Another half an hour, and the first will reach the entrance to the fjord," said Liodred calmly.

Mandred looked down at the little fleet that would stand against the knights of Tjured. All told, they had gathered fewer than sixty ships. Fifteen were small, carrying a maximum of twenty men. They had run chains through the rudder hatches of the thirty strongest ships, binding them inseparably together. Like that, they formed a barrier, blocking the deep water in the middle of the fjord. This is where the battle would rage, and this is where the fight against the priests would be decided. The smaller vessels bobbed some distance behind the barrier. Their job was to deliver reinforcements if the line of chained ships threatened to break.

Mandred looked at the wide gaps to the right and left of the wall of ships. "Are you really certain they can't get through there, Liodred?"

"Definitely, Forefather. Our enemy's fleet is made up mainly of caravels with a deep draft. Frankly, I want to lead them to the sides, to make them attack from the flanks. There are treacherous rocks that lurk just below the water there. At high water, a skillful captain might manage to guide a caravel through those rocks, but when the water ebbs, they are doomed. With luck on our side, they'll lose a dozen ships or more on the flanks. The moment their fleet fans out inside the fjord, we will attack them with fire." Liodred pointed to a number of smaller fishing boats, loaded high with brushwood. "If the wind holds, the fire will do serious damage." He gestured widely, taking in the cliffs on both sides of the fjord. "Up here are the old men and the lads too young to fight in battle. We have brought in ten cartloads of arrows from all ends of the kingdom. The men and boys up here will send arrows raining down, should their ships wander too close to the coast." Liodred spoke in such a loud voice that the bodyguards surrounding them could hear every word clearly. "When it comes down to it, the priests are doing us a favor by attacking Firnstayn. Here in the fjord, we fight the battle on our own terms. The narrowness of the fjord makes it impossible for them to use their numbers properly. Once they board the ships of the blockade, it's man against man."

Liodred waved to Mandred to follow him back to the horses. When Liodred swung onto his saddle, he said quietly, "I hope the elves will make it here in time. The enemy outnumbers us five to one, maybe more."

"If there is a way for them to get here, they will be here," replied Mandred resolutely. But he knew only too well how many unforeseeable things could prevent that from happening. Would Emerelle even grant his two companions an audience? And how long would it take to equip a fleet and sail it out through an Albenstar?

They rode back down the path from the cliff. About halfway down, a group of elderly warriors came toward them carrying wicker baskets full of arrows on their backs. Liodred reined in his black horse and waved to a man wearing an eye patch. "Hey-o, Gombart, what drags you away from your pretty wife?"

"I heard you'd invited every old dog around town to shoot a few knights." He regarded the king with a toothless grin and patted the black cloth patch bound over his left eye. "Besides, they say they'll be so packed together that not even I could miss. And for every one we cut down, there's a horn full of mead waiting for us in your golden hall."

Liodred roared with laughter. "That's hardly a story my cupbearer would be spreading, but I'll take you at your word, my men. A horn full to the brim for every Tjured knight." He grinned broadly. "But don't think I don't know you for a pack of crooks. I'll be aboard the *Albenstar* down there and counting every one."

The men laughed and joshed among themselves awhile. Liodred waved one last time, then he spurred his big black horse on down the cliff track.

"Sometimes I think it is better for a man to die young and in full possession of his powers," said Liodred when they were out of earshot.

"No," Mandred contradicted him. "The greatest gift is to be able to see your children grow up. Believe me, I know." He thought bitterly of how little time he had had with Alfadas.

On the final stretch of the path down to the bay, where a rowboat was waiting for them, each man of the party was silent, deep in his own thoughts. Where were the elves? Mandred wondered. Would they leave Firnstayn to fend for itself?

On the beach stood Valgerd, Liodred's wife. She was tall and blond and wore a dress the color of sunflowers, held together at the shoulders by two golden clasps. On her arm she carried a child, no more than five moons old. His name was Aslak, Liodred's son.

The king went to them and kissed the boy tenderly on his forehead. Then he untied a knife in a gold-clad sheath from his belt and handed it to Valgerd. She nodded.

Liodred passed his hand gently through her hair, then he moved down to the boat where Mandred was already waiting for him. The jarl felt ill. Was the king afraid of dying? Was that a parting gift for a son who might never know his father? Liodred was so close to all the people here. He was loved by each and every one of them. *Nothing will happen to him*, Mandred swore.

The two men climbed into the little rowboat. The oarsmen greeted their king, who tousled the hair of the youngest in passing. Then they pushed off from the beach and rowed hard for the flagship.

"An heirloom?" asked Mandred.

Liodred was jolted from his musings. "What?"

"The knife."

"Yes . . . that, too."

"What else?"

Liodred lowered his voice. "I know what these priests are like. It is . . . Should they win this battle, Valgerd will try to escape. But in case . . ."

"She should kill the boy?"

"And herself," said Liodred. "It will be for the best." He looked out over the dark water of the fjord. "Will they come? The elves?" he asked, his voice still low.

"Of course," said Mandred, but he could not look Liodred in the eye as he said it.

On board the *Albenstar*, Liodred was like a new man. He joked with the soldiers and gave instructions for who should be in the front line. This *Albenstar* had little in common with the ship that had once carried Mandred and the elves to Noroelle's island. It was much larger, with space for a hundred oarsmen.

On all thirty ships in the blockade, the masts had been unstepped and laid in the longships to prevent them becoming a hindrance in the impending battle. The rudders, too, had been pulled on board and stowed. In the stern of the longship, a pole had been placed, and on it fluttered the old banner from the original *Albenstar*: a blue star on a silver ground.

Two soldiers helped Liodred don his armor, the beautifully worked elven armor that had once been worn by Alfadas and, here, was without equal. All of the other soldiers on board wore chain mail tunics and round helmets with long nasals.

Mandred allowed himself to be helped into a knee-length mail tunic. As he was putting on his helmet, Liodred came to him. "I always wanted to ask you if it was true that each one of the braids in your hair stood for a man that you slayed in battle. That is what our skalds tell us."

"It's true," the jarl said.

"You're a dangerous man."

"You'll need dangerous men today."

Horns sounded from the cliff tops. The first of the knights' ships was sailing into the fjord. It was a stately three-master with a high stern. Moments later, four more swung into the fjord entrance.

Mandred looked apprehensively at the high forecastles of the ships. The attackers would be several paces higher than the Firnstayners' defenses. The crow's nests on the Tjured vessels looked huge. Each carried five crossbowmen. From up there, they could pick their targets across a wide field.

A salvo of arrows flew from the western cliff, but the ship was holding to the center of the channel and the arrows fell short by a good fifty paces.

Liodred handed Mandred a large, round shield painted red. "You'll be needing that, Forefather."

The jarl pushed his left arm through the broad leather loops and pulled them tight. The shield felt solid on his forearm.

"Let's welcome these lily-white priests!" Liodred roared and raised his shield in front of his chest. Then he slammed the flat of his axe against the curved boss in the center of the shield. Soldiers along the entire battle line followed his lead, and an earsplitting din echoed from the cliffs along the fjord.

The clanging and the cries of the soldiers got the blood pumping in Mandred's veins. Let the damned Tjured priests come. In the men of the Fjordlands, they would find their betters.

More and more ships appeared in the entrance of the fjord. They fanned out into an extended line, still four hundred paces distant. Mandred could see the helmets of the Tjured knights glinting behind the bulwarks shielding the forecastle.

"Watch over us, Norgrimm," Liodred bellowed. "Make our wall of wood strong, and may the courage of our enemies founder on it."

Fanfares sounded from the caravels, and there was movement in the ships' bows.

"Shields high!" Mandred cried, even as arrows rained down onto the longships.

The large, round shields quickly formed a protective roof. Arrows thudded into the wood. Here and there, a man went to the deck, screaming, but the battle line across the longships did not waver.

Salvo followed salvo. From beneath the shields, it was impossible to see how close the caravels were coming. Mandred had the feeling of an eternity passing. Hot sweat ran down the back of his neck. The point of an arrow pierced his shield and missed his arm by a hair. In places, the sand strewn across the decks of the longships was red with blood. Again and again, arrows found a gap in the wall of shields.

Suddenly, the blockade of ships heaved. Several men near Mandred were knocked off their feet, and gaps appeared in the shield wall. The caravels had rammed the longships. The ships of the Northmen and the Tjured knights were hull to hull, like rival stags whose antlers have become wedged in a duel.

"On your feet!" Liodred roared. "Archers ten paces back! Bring down the crossbows in the crow's nests!"

The lightly armed archers had sought shelter beneath the roof of shields during the hail of arrows. Now they ran back, and it was their turn to attack the enemy.

A spear thwacked into the deck close to Mandred and stayed there, vibrating in the blood-smeared planking. Now that the rows of shields had broken, the jarl could once again see their foes. Wide planks with iron spikes on their ends slid down from the caravels. The spikes dug into the deck like fangs.

All along the barricade, boarding ramps were sliding down. Above Mandred, soldiers in white tabards appeared, ducked low behind long, drop-shaped shields. Every shield bore the crest of the burned oak.

"For Tjured!" came the cry from a thousand throats. Then the knights of Tjured stormed down the boarding ramps.

Shield to shield, they charged the battle lines of the defenders in a wild rampage. Mandred's axe swung down in a glittering arc, carving through the shield and the helmet of the first of the attackers. The jarl jerked his axe free and swung it backhand over the edge of the next knight's shield. With a crunch, the elven steel sliced through the nasal of his adversary's helmet.

Beside him, Liodred fought like an enraged bear. Soon, the deck was covered with the dead and the dying.

A blow from a sword split Mandred's shield, but the blade wedged in the wood, and Mandred tore it away from his attacker. Mandred's axe swung into the knight's uncovered flank, striking him beneath the ribs.

Mandred jumped onto one of the boarding ramps. He threw the destroyed shield aside and took hold of his axe in both hands. He raged up the bridge like a berserker, fighting every step of the way to the enemy's forecastle. Close behind him followed three of the Mandridians, using their shields as best they could to cover him from enemy arrows.

When he reached the end of the ramp, the Tjured soldiers were massed so thickly in the forecastle that it was almost impossible for them to even raise their shields to protect themselves. In a blind rage, Mandred hewed into them. Swords and spears shattered under the impact of elven steel. Then he leaped into the midst of the enemy. He rammed the spike at the top of the axe shaft under the edge of the helmet of a tall knight, through his jaw, and into his brain. As the giant fell, he took down two more Tjured fighters with him. Panic broke out on the forecastle. Screaming, the knights tried to flee to safety. Some even jumped over the bulwarks into the water, though under the weight of their mail tunics, it was a leap to certain death.

Moments later, the entire forecastle was under the control of the Northmen. Gasping for breath, Mandred looked down over the main deck. The surviving knights had retreated, and now they were looking up at him, their eyes wide with fear. From the rear of the fleet, more caravels were pushing into the mass of wedged ships, bringing fresh troops.

"We have to pull back," came a raw voice at his side. Liodred, too, had fought his way aboard the caravel. The king pointed to the east. "They've managed to get over the reef. The ebb tide won't come. They've lost only a single ship there so far."

From the forecastle, Mandred had a good view of the fighting. The battle line of the Northmen had held, but Death had taken a rich harvest among them.

On both sides of the blockade, individual caravels had managed to get through the rocks. One of the priests' ships was on fire, ignited by the burning brands. A black column of smoke rose into the bright summer sky. Three of the little fire boats were engaged in a fearless attack, but the knights were fending them off with long poles while the crossbowmen aloft shot at the crews below.

Two caravels were trying to board the longships kept back as reserves. But another seven ships would soon round the barricade and attack it from the rear.

"Back to the longships!" Liodred cried. "We'll form a double line!"

With a heavy heart, Mandred descended the boarding ramp. Behind them, he heard the shouts of the knights ridiculing them. The jarl thought of the gold-studded dagger that Liodred had given his wife.

"Send us the elves, Luth," he murmured in despair. "Send us our allies, and I will never touch a horn of mead again."

ABOARD THE QUEEN'S SHIP

Nuramon stood at the railing of the *Elflight*, the queen's flagship. From the starboard side, he could see the Firnstayner ships, chained together and closing off the entrance to the fjord like a wall. Beyond the longships billowed the huge sails of the enemy fleet, each with the symbol of the Tjured, the black tree. Approximately half the Tjured ships were locked in battle with the longships. In the narrow fjord, the Tjured could not exploit their superior numbers. Liodred and Mandred had forced the enemy into a bloody man-to-man battle, and it was impossible for Nuramon to estimate how well the Fjordlanders were holding out. All he could see was that there was movement on the ships, a close-fought melee.

Several of the enemy ships were attempting to sail around the Fjordlanders' barricade, trying to pick a channel through the rocks between the longships and the cliffs. One of the caravels was already on the rocks with its hull ripped open. The crew seemed to have gone overboard, but the fate of one caravel was apparently no deterrent to the rest. Other ships were still searching for a way through, to encircle the Fjordlanders or to attack the queen's ship.

Nuramon hoped that nothing had happened to Mandred or Liodred. Battles like this obeyed a different set of rules than one man fighting another. Pure chance could decide between life and death. If only the *Elflight* were faster. Nuramon looked back along the rows of oars that disappeared beneath him into the side of the ship. There must have been forty rows altogether. He had seen some two hundred oarsmen disappear below the deck. He had no doubt that they were doing their best down below, but the queen's huge ship made only slow headway. The small galleys from Reilimee were far ahead of them and would soon reach the Fjordlanders. Nuramon had heard that the sorceress of the sea, whose name no one knew, had equipped the boats. Behind the galleys sailed triremes from Alvemer. Nuramon was surprised at how fast the ships of Albenmark had been able to put to sea. It had taken just twelve days to equip and assemble the fleet.

The gate they had sailed through had already closed again. The wonderful play of colors over the seas of Albenmark that Emerelle had created with her magic was forever engraved in his memory. The gate was so wide that at dawn, the entire fleet had sailed through in one line.

Among the soldiers on board, rumors flew about Emerelle. Some thought the fact that the *Elflight* sailed with no accompanying ships was an attempt to draw the enemy to them. When Nuramon looked around now, he could believe this was true. The *Elflight* was like a floating battlefield. The oarsmen sat at the oars down below, and the fighters were assembled on the decks. More than three hundred elven warriors were waiting for battle, gathered in a space of sixty paces from stem to stern. To get more fighters on board, the queen had left behind the crew who would normally have handled the sails. In this battle, there would be no need for them, and the masts of the huge galley had been stepped and lashed on deck.

The ship was holding course for the Fjordlanders' left flank, to support them on that side. Obilee had explained the strategy to Nuramon: she and the fighters from the other galleys would board the Fjordlanders' longships to relieve their allies at the battle line, who could then retreat to the galleys and recuperate, then return to the battle later.

Someone laid a hand on Nuramon's shoulder. He turned and saw Master Alvias. "The queen would like to see you," he said.

Nuramon took his bow and followed Emerelle's counselor back through the throng of warriors. Alvias looked unusually warlike in his leather armor, with a sword at his hip. It was said that he fought beside the queen in the first troll war.

Alvias led him to the quarterdeck, in front of which Emerelle and Yulivee were surrounded by guards. The queen was giving instructions to her officers. She wore the gray robes of a sorceress, the same she had worn the night she had given him her counsel to prepare him for the elfhunt.

Nuramon saw Obilee there, too. She seemed to be waiting for final instructions ahead of the battle. She was wearing the same armor she wore when he saw her in the Royal Hall.

Little Yulivee greeted Nuramon with a playful wave. She was also dressed in a gray robe, like the queen. It still bothered Nuramon that the queen had brought the little sorceress with them. He was worried about her. This was no place for a child, however powerful Yulivee might be.

The queen spoke to Obilee, and then she waved Nuramon to her. She greeted him kindly, then said, "I see that you are concerned for Yulivee, but believe me when I say that there is no safer place for her here than at my side."

Nuramon replied with a brief nod. The queen was right. But he still would have been happier if Yulivee had remained in the palace in Albenmark.

"Nuramon, I would like you to go with Obilee," said the queen. "She will be in command on the forecastle once Dijelon and Pelveric have reached the Fjordlanders."

"Yes, my queen."

"Then go."

Yulivee left Emerelle's side and came to Nuramon. "You're coming back, aren't you?" she asked.

Nuramon went down on one knee. "Is that concern I see on your face?"

She looked away from him, but nodded.

"Have no fear. Stay with the queen. You heard what she said." He kissed her on the forehead. "Now go."

Without another word, Yulivee returned to the queen. There she grinned and held aloft a quiver. In it were the arrows that Nuramon had found along with the bow when he had visited the dwarves. At first, he had wanted to take them with him into this clash, but the queen had advised him to use regular arrows and to save these for special battles.

"We have to go, Nuramon," said Obilee, laying one hand on his shoulder.

Nuramon looked one last time at Yulivee, then he went forward to the bow with Obilee. The warrior woman seemed dejected.

"What's the matter, Obilee?" he asked.

"It's only . . . ," she began but stopped, as if she did not trust herself to say the words. Then she looked him in the eye and said, "I should not be the one leading you, Nuramon."

"You are not the young girl you once were," he said. "You are a warrior, a great warrior, far more important than I will ever be. You have already proved yourself in so many battles. I admire you." Obilee's lips quivered. "Don't be sad because of me, or Noroelle. Death is not the end. Nothing can stop me from finding Noroelle, in this life or the next. And what do you think she will say to you when she sees you again? She will be just as proud of you as I am."

Obilee smiled, and finally she reminded him of the lighthearted girl he had once known. "Thank you, Nuramon."

The elf had no fear of death. For death would not mean the end of his search, it would just delay it. The night before they had sailed, he had told his clan the stories of his travels and had asked them to keep the knowledge in case he died in battle. He had already begun to write his own soul book, as his dwarven friends did. He knew he should have started earlier, but he had never looked Death so directly in the eye before today.

They came to Obilee's fighters; on this ship, they were the only ones from Alvemer. The emblem emblazoned on their tabards identified them: a silver nymph on a blue ground. Fifty men and women, half of them armed with long swords, the others with bows. While Obilee spoke to them, Nuramon tried to look ahead. But the fighters were massed too thickly, blocking his view on all sides.

When could they finally start? Somewhere ahead of him, Mandred was locked in battle, and he was trapped on a galley that was hardly even moving. He could only hope that the ships from Reilimee had already reached the Fjordlanders.

Nuramon thought of Farodin. It depressed him to think of his companion with the troll prince, even though Farodin had told him repeatedly that he should not worry on his account.

A woman in a warrior's armor pushed through the crowd of fighters. "Are you Nuramon?" she asked.

He looked at her in surprise. "Yes."

"My name is Nomja."

That was the name of the young elf woman who had traveled with him on the search for Guillaume. "Are you . . . ?"

She nodded. "Yes. Your companion from Aniscans. I was reborn."

She had no resemblance at all to the woman she had been before. Now she was short and wore her black hair close-cropped. She seemed much more mature than the young warrior who had ridden with them on the hunt for Guillaume, but she had the same joy in her eyes as he had seen in her back then. Nomja's death during their escape from Aniscans had hit them all hard, especially Mandred.

Nuramon threw his arms around her in a warm embrace, like meeting a friend he had not seen for a long time. "I am glad you're here."

When he released her, he realized how much his hug had taken her by surprise.

Nuramon saw the bow in her hand. "You are an archer?"

"Yes."

"Back then, you were very good."

She smiled but said nothing. He must certainly seem strange to her. She had no memory of her previous life, of course, and here he was greeting her as a dwarf would greet someone who had been reborn.

Suddenly, Nuramon heard the sound of shouting coming from in front of them. "Be ready," Obilee cried.

Nuramon craned his neck. Still he could see nothing, but he could hear the sounds of battle: the ring of steel on steel and the screams of the injured.

From port came the shouts of fighters. "Faster!" they were crying. Nuramon pushed aside two elven soldiers and forced his way to the port rail. What he saw made him catch his breath. A mighty three-master was bearing down on them, the black tree of the Tjured resplendent on the mainsail. The enemy must have made it through the reef on this side and were now trying to intercept the queen's ship.

From midship came more shouting, and crossbow bolts flew overhead. Clearly, the battle had come to them.

A jolt ran through the ship, and a second nearly knocked Nuramon off his feet. The enemy's three-master had rammed them. Chaos broke out. Fighters to the left and right yelled battle cries.

The warriors around him were restless. Nomja, too, looked nervous. Only Obilee seemed to have no fear. "Archers to starboard!" she ordered, and Nuramon followed her command without hesitation. He pushed to the other side of the forecastle, where the archers were taking positions along the railing.

Some distance ahead, he could now see the entire line of the Fjordlanders' longships. Many of the enemy's ships had stuck fast to the barricade, but the galleys from Reilimee were also there and had joined the battle. The caravels from Fargon formed a dense throng; heavy lines now bound them together, and the Tjured knights coming as reinforcements had to climb across several ships to get to the battle line. The battlefield was growing, and the *Elflight*, with Nuramon on board, was now in the thick of it. He tried to make out Mandred among the Firnstayners, but his companion was not to be seen in the dense fighting.

Obilee led them to a gap in the railing. A wooden ladder had been attached there and dropped to just above the first of the Firnstayners' ships. "Swordsmen forward to me!" Obilee shouted. "Archers hold the railing! Pick your targets and be sure of them!"

More archers came from the rear of the ship and filled the space to the end of the railing. Others formed a second row, ready to join the moment an archer at the rail fell.

Like the archers to his left and right, Nuramon drew an arrow from his quiver, laid it on the bowstring, and searched for a clear shot. There. He saw a knight climbing down a boarding ladder to the long-ship directly in front of them. Nuramon was about to let his arrow fly when he saw Nomja beside him shoot and hit his target.

The individual fighters were moving too fast and unpredictably for Nuramon. Finally, he spotted a squad of enemy warriors gathering some distance away, apparently preparing for a concentrated attack. They were a good hundred paces from him, but there were so many of them and they were clear of adversaries just then, so Nuramon fired at the group. He did not wait for his first arrow to reach its target, but immediately shot a second.

One of the soldiers fell to his knees with the arrow in his belly, caus-ing the men around him to duck for cover behind a low railing. More arrows made them fall back until they were out of range.

Searching for a new target, Nuramon caught sight of a flag with a blue star on a silver background. The banner of the *Albenstar* that

King Njauldred had once presented to him. It was no longer the same ship on which he had sailed east with Farodin and Mandred. The new *Albenstar* was much bigger, but it was clear that someone had kept the original flag, perhaps to recall past glory.

Nuramon caught sight of Mandred. The jarl had taken a position along one side of the *Albenstar*, where he had enough room to swing his axe. He and his men were in trouble. They were far outnumbered. A lone Tjured ship had penetrated the line of elven galleys and was attacking the longship next to the *Albenstar*. The knights stormed onto the longship, their assault threatening to break through the Fjordlanders' battle line, which was now under attack from all sides. They were driving a wedge between Mandred and the elves.

Nuramon took aim at the Tjured ship. He sighted on the short plank that connected it with the ship next to it. A Tjured fighter tried to board the *Albenstar*. Nuramon let his arrow fly and it curved high, striking the man's body a moment later.

The elf was not satisfied. He had been aiming for the head. Too much time passed before an arrow hit its target. It was just a matter of time before he hit a friend instead of a foe.

He set a new arrow onto the bowstring. Then what Nuramon had feared happened: a Tjured knight was creeping toward Mandred from behind while he faced two in front. Nuramon quickly took aim. He had to be certain of hitting the man. One mistake, and he might kill Mandred instead. As the enemy warrior raised his sword, Nuramon threw all caution to the wind and released the bowstring. He held his breath as the shot flew toward its target in a high arc.

The arrow buried itself in the man's chest.

Mandred wheeled around and struck the warrior, who was already falling, with a blow that sent him tumbling overboard. Then he looked around in surprise and waved several men to him. Among them, Nuramon recognized Liodred, wearing the armor of Alfadas. Mandred pointed up toward Nuramon, but it seemed he had not recognized him. Then he pointed toward the Tjured fighters who had cut them off from the elves. The Fjordlanders on the *Albenstar* gathered around Mandred and Liodred. They wanted to break through, but it meant fighting their way past two lines of enemies.

"Mandred and King Liodred are there!" Nuramon shouted to the archers around him. "They're surrounded, but they want to get through to us!"

Obilee came to Nuramon's side and looked over at the *Albenstar*. Then she ordered, "All on Nuramon's left, shoot the first arrow at the fighters on this side of Liodred. Those on Nuramon's right shoot at the Tjured behind them. One shot! After that, shoot only at the pursuers. Let none of the enemy through!" Then she left the railing and let the archers do their work.

They waited until Mandred gave the order to break through. There. The jarl raised his axe, and with loud battle cries, the men around him leaped onto the fourth ship in the chain.

Nuramon and the other archers fired their arrows. They rained down on the enemy like heavy hail. Those who were not hit did not know what was happening and tried to duck for cover.

Mandred and some of the Firnstayners seemed to hesitate momentarily, then they surged forward again. The second salvo hit only the soldiers pursuing them, holding them back for a moment. Their shield bearers were already pushing through to the front. But this valuable time was enough to let Mandred and his men break through. The knights attacking from behind were now almost completely surrounded. When they realized that their position was hopeless, they retreated to their two-master. Mandred made it through to Pelveric's elves, and Nuramon saw Pelveric pointing back up in his direction.

Mandred raised his axe high and bawled out, "Nuramon!" Then, followed by the Mandridians, he ran through the rows of elven warriors toward him.

Nuramon breathed a sigh of relief and looked out over the battlefield. The queen's plan seemed to be working. All along the barricade of ships, elven warriors were relieving the exhausted Fjordlanders, and the battle line across the ships still held. They were inferior in number of both soldiers and ships, but when the trolls came, the tide would turn in their favor.

STRONG MAGIC

L ower the foresail."

Farodin's fingers tightened around the ship's rail. It was unbelievable. The troll ships were already painfully slow, and now they were taking in the sail. The elf was standing on the tower-like quarterdeck of the *Grinder*, Prince Orgrim's flagship. Twenty vessels were in the fleet that Boldor, the king of the trolls, had assembled. Each of the lumbering ships was a floating fortress, and the largest of them had more than three hundred troll fighters on board. It was a force that would prove decisive once they joined the battle.

Prince Orgrim was standing with the helmsman and conferring with his shaman, Skanga. *This is enough to drive a man crazy*, thought Farodin. They were coming too late as it was. He could make out the sails of the enemy fleet as a thin white line on the horizon. Columns of smoke showed that the battle had already begun. The arrival of the trolls would decide the outcome. And what were these traitorous elf eaters doing? Reefing the sails.

"Why so grim, Ambassador?" Orgrim and the shaman had come to him. The troll prince was armed for battle. He wore a breastplate of dark leather and a bearskin over his shoulders. He leaned on his war hammer, its head carved from gray granite.

"It must be my naïveté, but I find myself unable to deduce the strategy behind your assistance in this battle," Farodin replied, making an effort not to say openly what he truly thought of their allies.

The shaman stared at him darkly. Farodin felt the power of the magic in her.

"He thinks we are going to wait calmly until the Tjured knights have defeated the Fjordlanders and the elves. He doubts our intention to hurry to the aid of our former enemies," the old woman said.

"Farodin is a clever man, keeping such thoughts to himself. If he were to openly insult my people by voicing such opinions, I'd have to have him stuffed into a sack of stones and thrown overboard." The troll prince looked intently at Farodin, who wished he, too, could read the thoughts of his old enemy. He had seen Orgrim again at the court of King Boldor. The king had received him with all due honor as Emerelle's ambassador, and to Farodin's surprise, Boldor had agreed to the elves' request after spending the night conferring with his princes.

After Boldor announced his decision, Orgrim stated his express wish that the queen's ambassador join him on his ship. From the moment that Farodin was back among the trolls from the Nightcrags, he felt their hatred. He was convinced he would not survive his first night aboard the *Grinder*. But the prince took pains to attend to him, attempting many times to draw him into conversation. He went as far as to ensure that no meat of any kind was served to him.

"When do we attack?" asked Farodin impatiently. The ship was battle ready. On the main deck and the forecastle, trolls carrying huge shields jostled for space. Stones intended as projectiles were lined up along the railing, at the ready. The smallest of them was the size of a child's head, the largest, massive chunks of granite. Farodin wondered how even a troll could lift stones as big as those.

"Don't you sense it?" Skanga asked. With every movement, the feathers, bones, and stones sewn to her coarse leather robe and hanging in countless bands around her neck rattled and rustled.

"Don't I sense what?"

"The power of the magic, little elf. The power of the magic," the shaman snickered. "The tides have changed. The ebb tide won't come. Can you imagine how much power it takes to change the ebb and flow of the tides? Strong magic, that is."

"Reef the mainsail," Orgrim ordered. "Drop anchor."

Farodin felt a knot tighten in his belly. This could not be happening. "Would you be so kind as to tell me what this means, Orgrim?"

The prince pointed to the king's ship. A large red flag had been hoisted from the mainmast. "Boldor is calling all of the princes and shamans to a council of war. He will want you to be there, too." Orgrim turned away briefly and waved to one of his soldiers. "Ready the tender."

"You can't be serious," Farodin hissed.

"Elf, I know what you and your kind think of my race. But we are a long way from being the halfwits you believe us to be. We don't rush into our battles blindly. We plan them. And that's how it will be this time, too. We had not reckoned with a sorcerer among the humans, and certainly not with one this powerful. We will modify our plans accordingly."

"He's afraid we want to cast in our lot with the white priests," said the shaman.

Farodin could have wrung the old hag's neck.

Orgrim growled deep in his throat. Then he dropped to one knee, bringing himself to eye level with Farodin. "I know that you would most like to see me and all the trolls dead, and that you don't trust us any farther than you can spit. Still, I hope that a final flicker of good sense remains in the wasteland of your vengeful mind. The Tjured priests want to destroy all of the Albenkin. They don't differentiate. Centaurs, elves, flower faeries. And trolls. We are fighting with you because we know that we are stronger at the side of the elves and the Fjordlanders. And also because, sooner or later, the white priests will attack the Nightcrags and all our other fortresses. You are a survivor of the troll wars, Farodin. You know we don't wait for the war to come to us. We take it to the lands of our enemies. That is why we are here."

"And what is there to stop you from sitting and watching your enemies slaughter each other, then going in and finishing off the survivors?" Farodin asked.

Orgrim abruptly stood up. "An elf might think like that, but not a troll. Tread carefully, Farodin. You're close to breaking the camel's back."

BEFORE THE QUEEN

Mandred took off his helmet and ran his hand through his sweat-soaked hair. Nuramon was leading Liodred and him to the stern of the galley. The jarl was proud to have friends like Nuramon. The elf had saved his hide, and a warrior with the soul of an old companion had helped him. Nuramon had introduced her as Nomja . . . *the* Nomja. For the first time, Mandred could see for himself what rebirth really meant. He had watched Nomja die, and now her soul had returned in a new guise. She was standing in the bow of the ship, protected by a shield bearer, and was what she had been in her previous life: an archer.

Elven warriors surged aboard a large caravel, its bow towering above the midship railing of the *Elflight*. It looked as if the elves would soon take the ship.

Ignoring the battle behind them, Nuramon led them on toward the quarterdeck, before which the queen was expecting them.

"Mandred!" Yulivee squealed when she saw him. She ran to him. The jarl was surprised to see the little sorceress there, but Emerelle, no doubt, knew what she was doing. Mandred picked Yulivee up in his arms, and then she pressed a kiss on his cheek. "Nice to see you," she said, playing with his braids.

Nuramon turned to the queen. "This is Liodred of Firnstayn, and I am sure you remember Mandred."

"Of course," said Emerelle. "But first, tell me how the battle is going."

"At the moment, we are gaining ground," Nuramon replied.

"The enemy outnumbers us by far," said Mandred, speaking up. "We were not able to protect our flanks. They will do their best to encircle us. How many ships and soldiers have you brought, Your Majesty?" The jarl set Yulivee down on the deck.

"Mandred Aikhjarto, I see you speak as unburdened by royal etiquette as ever," said the queen with a smile. "It lightens my heart to see you again. And I am just as happy to meet you, Liodred, king of Firnstayn. We have come with all the ships and fighters that the elves of Albenmark have to offer. We will secure your flanks, and my fighters will relieve your warriors on the front line, along the barricade. Pull your men back, Liodred, and let fresh blood come. We are here as Albenkin, to repay our old debt with our blood."

Liodred bowed. "We will not stay away long, and will rejoin the battle as soon as we can. The king must be close to his fighters, or they will lose their—" Liodred was interrupted by horrific screaming. A group of elves amidships collapsed onto the deck as if struck by invisible arrows. Some writhed in agony, screaming hideously, but most lay motionless.

Mandred looked over to the enemy caravel and could not believe what he saw. Just moments before, he had seen the elves taking the upper hand, but now there were only enemy faces at the bulwark. All the fighting on board the large caravel had ceased.

Without warning, three guards directly beside the queen fell to the deck as if a stiff gust of wind had come and torn the life from their bodies.

Appalled, everyone still on their feet fell back to the starboard side.

"By the gods, what is going on here?" Liodred roared. Pure dread was inscribed on his face. "What kind of treacherous murder is this?"

Nuramon dragged Yulivee away with him. Only the queen seemed transfixed. She stiffened, gazed over at the caravel that had rammed them, and whispered, "So it's true . . ."

Mandred followed her gaze, and on the quarterdeck of the caravel, he saw a man wearing billowing dark-blue robes. He had his hands raised high and looked like the monks they had seen among the knights of the Tjured in Iskendria.

"Emerelle!" shouted Nuramon.

Master Alvias leaped in front of the queen and pushed her back. In that moment, something seemed to seize him. He staggered and clutched at his chest. Then he fell at the queen's feet.

"Alvias?" Emerelle said with disbelief as she kneeled beside the aging chamberlain.

Alvias's breathing was labored. He was trying desperately to say something. "Forgive my lack of decorum, my queen," he gasped, his voice shaking. "It is my fate, to . . ." His eyes glassed over, and his breath stopped.

At first, there was only bewilderment on the queen's face, but then a smile came.

Mandred was shaken to see her smile at such a moment. Did Emerelle feel no sympathy at all? Not even for the man closest to her? Her old chamberlain had given his life for her, and she smiled.

Suddenly, around the queen, a pale light glowed. It came from the body of Alvias, flowing around him, enclosing him like a glittering silk shroud. Then Alvias's form began to blur in the silvery shimmer. The queen still held his hand, but even as her own fine hand remained clearly visible, Alvias's turned transparent. His armor and the sword he wore also paled. Finally, Alvias dissolved entirely into the silver glow around him. Then the light dissipated like smoke on the wind. Nothing remained but the smell of flowers, a smell Mandred knew. He had noticed it in Firnstayn, in the room in which Shalawyn had died.

The gleam surrounding Alvias must have been the moonlight. Nuramon and Farodin had spoken about it so many times, but all their words had never been able to adequately describe to Mandred what it was really like. The jarl had the feeling he had just witnessed something divine, something miraculous.

The others, too, were deeply stirred at the sight and, for a moment, forgot the battle around them. Yulivee stared openmouthed at the place where Alvias had vanished.

The queen allowed Nuramon to help her back to her feet. "He saved me," she said. "It was his destiny."

"What killed him?" Yulivee asked Nuramon. She seemed so terrified that she could only speak in a whisper.

"I don't know," Nuramon answered.

Mandred looked over at the man in the dark-blue monk's robe. Alvias's death and his passing into the moonlight had taken only moments. The Tjured priest looked completely exhausted. He stood at the railing and had to hold himself upright with both hands. Knights quickly surrounded the cleric, shielding him.

Damned priest, thought Mandred. These bastards had nothing in common with the healer Guillaume, whom they had turned into a saint. Nothing could be further from what Guillaume believed in than ... The jarl thought of what had befallen them in Aniscans. By Luth. It was not possible. He made the sign of the protective eye. "Remember Aniscans,

Nuramon?" he asked, his voice half choked. "Remember what happened in the market square?"

"By the Alben." His eyes wide with terror, the elf looked up at the high-decked caravel. "They'll kill us all. They don't even need their swords."

A boarding ramp crashed onto the elves' flagship. A squad of knights was already forming up there, ready to storm the queen's galley. The priest and his bodyguards left the quarterdeck and moved forward to join the fighters.

Nuramon turned to Emerelle. "My queen, we have to get away from here, or all is lost."

Liodred pointed out to starboard. "The shield wall on the ships still holds, Majesty. We can make it across the longships to another elven galley."

The few surviving elves on the *Elflight* charged at the boarding ramp to hold back the Tjured knights before too many made it on board.

"Mandridians, to me!" Liodred ordered and waved to the fighters on the closest longship. "The king demands your blood!"

"My queen?" Nuramon asked.

Emerelle simply nodded. She took Yulivee's hand and looked at the child. Emerelle seemed lost in thought. Mandred saw a single tear pearl down her cheek, as if she were already weeping for the end of everything.

CASTING THE BONES

The bones clattered over the large table that the trolls had set up in the center of the deck of the *Albenhammer*, the troll king's flagship. Farodin hooked his thumbs into his sword belt and tried to keep his composure. The way in which the trolls fought a war was, to say the least, alien to him. He narrowed his eyes and peered toward the columns of smoke rising beyond the cliffs. What was going on over there?

The old shaman looked at the little bones on the table for a long time. "The shadow of death hangs over Emerelle," she said, her voice flat. "It is a human. He is attacking her with his power. One man, and he has killed more than a hundred elves."

All eyes turned to Farodin. "That . . . is impossible," he said. "No human can match an elf in battle. You must be mistaken."

"Do you say that because things that should not be possible cannot be possible?" Boldor asked. The king of the trolls was almost four paces tall. Ropy scars covered his bare torso. His long, pointed ears were torn and misshapen. Pale eyes peered from under a bulging brow and eyed Farodin critically. "Cast the bones again, Skanga."

The shaman complied, glaring sidelong at Farodin. The yellowing, worn bones clacked across the table. Skanga crossed her arms. "It is as I said. The shadow of death hangs over Emerelle. I can feel the human's evil power clearly. It is the kind of magic he uses that makes him so deadly. It is different from the magic we use. It takes the power out of the world, and out of the elves' hearts. That is what is killing them. It makes no difference what spell he casts. None can be close to him."

"Would his magic kill trolls?" asked Orgrim.

"It will kill any of the Albenkin."

"Is there a spell that can shield against it?" the prince continued.

"No. This magic is different," replied the shaman. "There is no protection from it. But it cannot injure humans."

Farodin remembered what had happened in Aniscans. Was there a second man like Guillaume? Could a human ever be as powerful as a bastard son, half elf and half Devanthar?

"What do you advise, Skanga?" asked the king soberly.

"Anyone who dares to get close to that man is spitting in the face of Death. Right now, he is weak, but I sense his power returning with every heartbeat."

The king rubbed his fist on his forehead.

"Give me a boat," said Farodin. "I will fight at the side of my people."

Boldor ignored him. "What will happen if we join the battle?"

Again, the shaman tossed her bones. She spent a long time looking at the confusing pattern. "If we fight, royal blood will flow," she finally said.

The king stroked a finger over his jutting bottom lip. "Emerelle and the king of the Fjordlands are also fighting there, aren't they?"

"Both confront the terrible sorcerer," Skanga replied.

Boldor slammed his fist onto the table. "Kobold shit!" he bellowed fiercely. "We will not wait here and watch Emerelle and the human king take all the glory for themselves. Sails down! Man the oars! We're going into battle!" He pointed to the columns of smoke beyond the cliffs. "Douse the decks with water. I don't want to see a single one of my ships burn."

"How do we attack?" asked Orgrim.

"Like trolls. We send every ship in our way to the bottom of the sea."

The bones clacked a final time. "On the west is danger. Something . . ." The shaman pushed a few of the bones apart. "Something is hiding there."

The king looked up and pointed to the rising smoke. "I don't need your bones, Skanga, to see that danger. The west is where most of the ships are burning. We will be wary and see which way the sparks are flying."

EMERELLE IN DANGER

It was a desperate struggle.

Mandred, Liodred, and the Mandridians were all that prevented the elves from being surrounded by their enemies. The Firnstayners were trying to force a passage across the deck to give the queen a chance to escape over the forecastle and down to the longships. A small squad of the white knights had broken through and taken possession of the battle platform at the bow, but the Mandridians had succeeded in cutting them off from the rest of their battalion. Obilee, with a handful of elven fighters, was attempting to retake the bow stronghold. At the same time, the Mandridians were fighting desperately to prevent the enemy from breaking through a second time and to drive the knights back to their caravel.

Emerelle was ringed by bodyguards. She stayed by the railing and held Yulivee close to her. She still seemed to be somewhere else in her thoughts.

The numbers of the injured rose, and it seemed only a matter of time before the superior numbers of their adversaries broke their ranks.

Nuramon kept one eye on the caravel, but the priest was no longer to be seen. He feared that the man, protected by the shield bearers, was slowly making his way forward. The queen was now so close to the caravel that the sorcerer could wipe out her and her bodyguards with a single spell.

One of the knights had gotten past Mandred and was moving closer. Nuramon quickly drew an arrow and shot the man, but even as he fell, two more took his place. Nuramon realized that the Mandridians were no longer able to drive the enemy back onto the caravel and were now doing all they could just to let as few as possible get past. The attack on the forecastle also seemed to be making little progress. The knights were holding their position and blocking the route to the longships.

Nuramon shot arrow after arrow. One of the enemy soldiers managed to dodge his arrows and raise his sword against him, and Nuramon realized he would never get another arrow on the string in time, so he lifted the bow to swing at the man with it. At the same time, one of the queen's guards came to his aid, brandishing a spear. The enemy fighter's lunge ended on the spear point. He jerked the shaft from the guard's hand, staggered back, and fell to the deck, lifeless.

Suddenly, the archers from Alvemer were there to reinforce them. Nomja came to Nuramon's side. "What happened just now?" she asked.

Nuramon would rather have said nothing. He didn't understand how it worked himself. He thought of what Mandred had said. The jarl had asked him if he remembered Aniscans. Of course Nuramon had not forgotten how Gelvuun had died because of Guillaume's healing magic. "There's a Tjured priest!" was all he could say to Nomja.

He looked around for Yulivee. She was clutching Emerelle's arm. The girl flinched at each clash of weapons and scream of the wounded. She buried her face in Emerelle's dress.

Obilee was close now, and she and her troop were backing up the Mandridians. "Don't advance too far," she shouted. She swung her sword with great power, and small blue sparks of lightning flashed along the length of the blade. Whenever her sword came down on an enemy, the man jerked and screamed as if the lightning were worse than the steel cutting his body. Behind Obilee and her troop stood unarmed elves. The oarsmen.

Mandred, Liodred, and the Firnstayners, like Obilee and her fighters, also fell back, giving the Alvemer archers a clear firing line to the enemy. They shot arrow after arrow, holding the Tjured men at bay. The few knights who dared advance were cut down by the Mandridians on either side of the archers. Most of them, though, retreated until they were close to the railing and formed a shield wall there.

Nuramon had soon exhausted his arrow supply and gave up his place in the line to one of the spearmen. He turned to the queen. "Emerelle," he called.

She looked at him, but said nothing.

"We will do it," he said, though he knew how badly things looked for them all and for Albenmark. He looked over the railing into the water and saw dozens of elves swimming down below. Were they the oarsmen? Or had elven fighters dared to flee from the battle?

Obilee, with Mandred and Liodred, came to the queen, and the guardsmen protecting Emerelle opened their ranks. "We are taking you to Ollowain. He is fighting on one of the longships not far from here. One more assault and we will take back our forecastle. That will give us free passage." She was breathing heavily.

Emerelle said nothing.

"Your Majesty?" asked Obilee.

"I am in your hands, Obilee," Emerelle finally replied. She seemed to look right through Obilee.

Nuramon looked out over the Fjordlanders' battlefield. More of the enemies' ships had added their weight to the battle. They would have to fight every step of the way from the queen's galley to Ollowain's ship. "We won't make it in time," Nuramon shouted. He pointed back to the caravel. "The priest is somewhere there. Every second we stand here, he is recovering his strength to cast the next spell. We can't wait for the forecastle to be clear. Every moment could be the end for us."

"Maybe we'll have to swim, too," Yulivee suggested.

Emerelle stroked the girl's hair. "No, the queen will not swim away. I will cross the ships." Finally, she seemed to have her mind back on their present predicament. "Obilee, I want you to conjure a passage for us."

Obilee nodded. "Yes," she said quietly. "But it won't be enough. Even if I rescue you, the priest can still decide the outcome of the battle."

Mandred spoke up then. "Then it's the humans who have to kill the priest. I will take my Mandridians and fight a way through to him."

Nuramon shook his head. "Mandred, it's far too dangerous."

"Whether you elves die or flee, either way, we are lost. This pack of priests will wipe Firnstayn from the map. Let me do what has to be done. And wish me luck."

Nuramon exchanged a look with Obilee and the queen. Both nodded. "Mandred," he said. "I know none braver, human or elf."

Mandred embraced Nuramon briefly, then he turned to Liodred. "We will cut through their ranks like a sword and smash them back onto their ship." The jarl looked back one last time, and Nuramon feared he would never see his friend again.

The Firnstayners regrouped among the archers. Mandred said a few words to Nomja. "For Firnstayn!" he yelled at the top of his voice, and he and his men charged under cover of a hail of arrows from left and right. With weapons ringing and wild cries, they charged the knights' shield wall.

"We have to go," declared Obilee.

The hatch to the lower deck caught Nuramon's eye. Then he looked back to the quarterdeck. He turned to Yulivee. "Do you still have my arrows?"

The little girl held up the quiver with shaking hands.

He took them and thanked her. Then he took out the dwarven arrows and put them in the quiver he already carried. "Obilee! Emerelle! I have a plan!" he shouted, pointing to the hatch that led down to the oar deck.

STONES AND TROLLS

From beneath the deck of the *Grinder* came the muffled thump of the kettledrum. The oars dipped rhythmically into the water, churning the sea to foam. Farodin was surprised at the discipline of the trolls in keeping the rhythm and at how fast the ungraceful ship moved when rowed.

Less than a quarter of a mile separated them from a large caravel that was sailing right at them. Only a few of the ships in the priests' fleet had managed to turn and set a course for this new enemy that had appeared at their rear. The main mass of the Tjured ships were crushed together in the narrow fjord, supporting the battle at the Firnstayners' barrier of longships. It was impossible for them to free themselves from the battle quickly and face the trolls.

Farodin pulled the chin strap of his helmet tight and checked that his weapon belt sat properly. He left the heavy shield standing against the railing. He would pick it up again as soon as the fighting started.

Prince Orgrim leaned on his massive war hammer. He seemed relaxed. "We'll only need to fight when we hit the mass of the Tjured ships," he said calmly. "Those boats coming won't stop us."

Farodin looked ahead at the approaching enemy three-master. The ship was much smaller than the galleasses of the trolls. For a moment, the elf felt some respect for the Tjured knights, fearlessly attacking an enemy so obviously superior to them. The mainsail with the symbol of the burned oak hid any view of the ship's quarterdeck. Farodin wondered how the humans on board were preparing for the unequal fight. So far, the caravel had steered a course directly toward them, as if they were planning to ram the troll ship.

"They'll turn at the last moment and try to destroy the oars on one side of our ship," said Farodin.

"I know," Orgrim replied, still calm. He waved to one of the officers amidships. "Prepare the deck breakers!" All along the railing, the trolls were moving.

Less than a hundred paces separated the two ships now. Farodin was holding on to the quarterdeck railing and bracing himself for the impact. He had no doubt that the trolls would win this first skirmish, but it would cost them valuable time. Time they no longer had if they wanted to come to the aid of Emerelle and the Fjordlanders.

The crossbowmen in the forecastle of the caravel opened fire. One troll fell with a crossbow bolt through its forehead. Another grunted and yanked a bolt out of its bleeding shoulder. The troll fighters didn't even bother to raise their shields to protect themselves from the knights' salvos, but stood their ground stoically, defying death.

Without warning, the caravel sheared off to starboard.

"Starboard oars up!" Orgrim's call was as loud as a row of trumpets. The drum below deck fell silent. The blades of the oars came out of the water. For a moment, they hung horizontally in the air, projecting from the hull. The caravel was now only a few paces away.

Then the oars were pulled in quickly through the narrow oar-slots. The first few were splintered by the caravel as it swung past only two paces to starboard, but most were brought on board in time.

"Deck breakers!" Orgrim called.

More than a dozen trolls were ducked along the starboard rail. Now, in pairs, they hoisted the huge rocks that Farodin had seen earlier. Like apprentice millers in the human world tossing sacks of flour onto a high wagon, the trolls swung the rocks back and forth before hurling them high in the air above the caravel.

The enemy ship lay much lower in the water than the trolls'. The knights on the main deck had their shields raised over their heads. Wedged together like that, the emblems on the shields formed a forest of dead trees. But they offered no protection at all against the rocks, which fell almost vertically on top of the shields, crushing the men and smashing through the planks of the deck. Crashing and cracking, the stone blocks disappeared into the hull.

A crossbow bolt slammed into the railing beside Farodin. The elf looked up. The caravel's crow's nests were manned with crossbowmen. More bolts sliced into the quarterdeck. One hit the helmsman in the leg, and he cursed, but no troll made any move to take cover. Farodin was well aware that an archer would need to be extremely lucky to kill a troll with a single bolt. But for him, that was not the case.

Beside him, his shield still leaned against the railing. He looked to the prince, who still stood leaning calmly on his war hammer. *No*, thought Farodin, *I'm not going to give these bastards their little victory.* No doubt they were all waiting for him to hide like a coward behind his shield while the trolls stoically took whatever shots came their way. Instead, he simply turned slightly sideways to make himself a smaller target.

"We've worked a long time on our tactics with the rocks," said Orgrim, as relaxed as if he were sitting at a banquet in the Nightcrags and not standing on a ship's deck under enemy fire. "I would have liked to see how this kind of attack fared against elves. Your ships are built more lightly and have few decks, as far as I know, and the rocks would have gone all the way through to your keels."

"I don't think we would let you get close enough to throw them," Farodin replied, unruffled, though he was secretly pleased that the elves had never fought a sea battle against the trolls.

"Don't you want to protect yourself?" asked the prince, pointing at Farodin's shield leaning against the rail. "I don't want to have to explain your death to King Boldor." The troll was bleeding from a deep graze across his bald head. "Or do you think your skull's as thick as mine?"

"I doubt that any human would shoot at an elf surrounded by much bigger targets."

Orgrim laughed. "For an elf, your heart's in the right place. It's a shame my distant ancestor killed your wife and you swore a soul feud against him. I won't enjoy killing you when the battle is over and the peace between us ends."

"What makes you so sure you'll survive the battle?"

The prince grinned broadly. "There isn't much that can kill a troll. That's one advantage we have over your race."

Farodin was about to deliver a cynical reply when a second salvo of deck breakers slammed onto the caravel. The chaos and the screams of the injured were indescribable. Dark rivulets of blood ran from the scuppers and down the sides of the ship's hull.

The mainmast was leaning. It had been broken through cleanly just above the deck by one of the chunks of rock and was only being held by the rigging.

The priests' ship was almost past the galleass. Now the trolls along the rail hoisted the smaller rocks. Like children tossing stones into the sea, they flung them into the thick of the humans. Farodin saw the helmsman get hit in the chest and flung against the wall that backed the quarterdeck. He turned away in disgust. He had had enough of the massacre.

TEN STEPS

Mandred had fought his way up the boarding ramp, and he and the Mandridians had advanced as far as the forecastle of the caravel. It rose above the prow of the enemy ship like a fortress. There were only two stairways leading from the main deck up to where he stood. The position was easy to hold, but the enemy had formed a shield wall on the main deck and had already repelled two attacks.

Enraged, Mandred charged a third time. His axe hammered into shields and sliced through the mail tunics. Whenever he swung the weapon, the Mandridians kept a respectful distance. But it made no difference how furiously Mandred charged; the rows of the enemy immediately closed again. Swords stabbed out through gaps and over the edges of the shields. They were as quick as vipers. The Tjured knights were experienced in this style of fighting, and they did not give up an inch. One stab caught Mandred above his hip. Warm blood ran down his leg. Covered by the shields of the Mandridians, he retreated to the forecastle.

He looked out dejectedly over the bulwark. Between the queen's flagship and the large caravel drifted a small galley. It looked as if it had been trying to get past quickly to reinforce Emerelle's crew. No one on board still lived. Elven fighters and oarsmen lay on the decks and thwarts, collapsed in death, victims of the damned Tjured priest.

Their position was desperate. The situation on the chained longships also looked dire. The Fjordlanders and the elves had thrown all but their last reserves into the battle. By contrast, the Tjured seemed to have an almost inexhaustible supply of reinforcements. However many fighters they lost, the gaps in their ranks immediately filled.

Liodred came to Mandred's side. "Are you hurt?"

"Just a scratch," Mandred growled. He was lying, though, for the wound burned as if a red-hot poker had hit him, not a sword. "There are too many of them. We have to limit ourselves to holding the forecastle." He looked to a young Mandridian who was leaning exhausted against the bulwark and looking out past the queen's ship to what was going on among the longships.

"Will they send us any reinforcements?" Mandred asked.

"No. They're fighting defensive battles all along the line. The Tjured knights are attacking the entire front."

"Damn!"

Mandred looked down to the main deck of the caravel. The enemy had re-formed and were now attacking the Mandridians. Fearlessly, they surged up the two stairways leading to the forecastle. On the left, they were led by a giant who slammed into the Mandridian blocking his path to the deck. His blade slit open the young warrior's throat, and he used his shield like a ram to clear enough room to get onto the forecastle. He was followed immediately by more knights.

Mandred hurled himself forward. He hated this kind of fighting. In a tussle like this, there was no room to swing his axe. He could only use it effectively when he lifted it over his head, but he would not let himself be tempted. To do that would leave his chest and belly unprotected, and he had already found out painfully just how skillful the knights could be with their short swords. Grimly, he restricted himself to attacking with the spike on the end of his axe. He rammed it into the shield of the man in front of him. The knight screamed in pain. Mandred had hit his target: the arm bound by leather straps to the other side of the shield. The knight let his shield drop for a moment, just a moment, but it was long enough for Mandred to strike a second time. With a crunch, he drove the spike through the eye slit in the man's helmet.

Exploiting the sudden gap, Mandred attacked the man on the left, who was no longer covered by his comrade's shield. The knight raised his sword to parry, but it was not nearly enough to counter the blow, and Mandred's axe sank into his chest.

The jarl had fought his way almost as far as the bulwark. On the main deck, between the rows of fighters, he spied the priest. He was ten steps away. The cleric's dark-blue robes billowed in the wind. "Forward!" the priest cried in the language of Fargon. "Keep going, or the demon queen will escape!"

Again, the knights surged toward the two stairways leading to the forecastle. The giant at the left stairway was still there. Two dead Mandridians lay at his feet.

Mandred looked back down to the main deck. It was impossible to get to the damned priest. Ten steps. Ten steps and they could still win this. But to do that, he would have to climb onto the bulwark and leap into the midst of the enemy below.

The jarl ducked beneath a swinging sword and rammed his axe under his adversary's shield and into his knee. The man dropped to the deck with a cry and tried to stab Mandred in the groin. Mandred kicked at the shield, knocking the iron-clad edge into the knight's helmet. His head jerked back and Mandred rammed the spike of his axe into the man's throat.

Instantly, the jarl looked up again. If he jumped over the bulwark, he would be jumping to certain death. But perhaps, with his death, he could buy the queen's escape and save Albenmark and the Fjordlands.

The priest had his arms raised. He was starting to cast a spell. Mandred looked back. The last time the priest had cast a spell, he'd been at least ten paces farther back. Emerelle was in mortal danger.

From the corner of his eye, Mandred saw a movement. The giant knight had fought his way through to him. Mandred fell back, and the giant's sword scraped over his chain mail tunic. The strike went low and hit him below the knee, then a swung shield knocked Mandred back. Hands were reaching for him, pulling him into the safety of the Mandridians' shield wall. Now the bulwark was too far away. He should have jumped.

CLOSE TO THE
TOUCH OF DEATH

Nuramon and Nomja ran beneath the deck of the galley toward the stern. The sight of all the dead elves at their oars on the starboard side horrified him. The men and women simply lay there, some fallen forward over their oars, some on their backs on the benches. There were no visible wounds, and there was not the slightest look of fear on their faces. They seemed to have suffered no pain, nor to have seen their end coming.

What pained Nuramon the most was not knowing if the dead would be reborn. Meeting Nomja had assured him that elves who died in the human world could be reborn in Albenmark. And the dwarves were living proof of that. Even in the human world, Albenkin were born again. But the priest's sorcery might prevent it. He had not thought of that when he told Emerelle and Obilee his plan. If there was no rebirth, then his search could be at an end with the merest touch of the priest's death spell. Then he thought of Master Alvias. Had he not entered the moonlight before Nuramon's eyes? Wasn't that proof that the priests could not destroy the souls of the Albenkin? The only question that remained was: who was supposed to conceive and bear children if all was lost?

They reached the stern hatch and cautiously ascended the wide ladder. Nuramon put his head a short way out of the hatch to see what was happening at the forecastle. To his surprise, it was empty. The elves must have overcome the knights. Obilee and the queen were certain to be in safety on the longships. He climbed out of the hatch, keeping his head low. Over the railing, he could see that the Fjordlanders still held the forecastle of the caravel, preventing the Tjured knights from pursuing the queen.

When Nomja had climbed up through the hatch, they crept to the railing together. Keeping low, they peered over it, observing the battle between the Tjured knights and the Mandridians.

It did not look good for the Fjordlanders. They had been able to get onto the enemy ship, but that was as far as they could go.

There was Mandred. He was fighting in the front row. Why did he always have to be so far out in front? He and his men were facing at least fifty knights. It was only a question of time before the Mandridians were overwhelmed.

"I see the priest," Nomja whispered. "Surrounded by bodyguards in full helmets."

Nuramon saw the man. He was only a few paces away from Mandred, near the railing of the main deck, but there was no way for the jarl to get to him. The shield bearers were too numerous, too tightly packed. And in a close fight like that, their short swords were more useful than the axes and long blades of the Mandridians.

Nuramon took a deep breath and looked along the railing toward the bow. He saw a lot of elves lying there, victims of the priest's magic. He and Nomja were now within its deadly range, too. Nuramon handed Nomja four of the dwarven arrows. "Here. Take them."

Wide-eyed, she gazed at the glittering arrowheads. "Thank you, Nuramon," she said softly, but she took only two.

She was right. They would not need any more than two. If the priest was still alive after two shots, then they were as good as dead.

Nuramon fixed an arrow on his bowstring and waited until Nomja had done the same. He breathed in deeply. "Now," he whispered, and they both stood.

Nuramon took aim at the priest in the dark-blue robes, then released the string and sent the arrow on its flight. Nomja's shot followed a heartbeat after his.

Nuramon's arrow hit one of the bodyguards in the shoulder when the man happened to step in the way. Nomja missed the priest by a hair. They quickly set new arrows. Nuramon saw the fighters raise their shields around the priest, covering him. They had to act fast, or the Tjured priest would work his magic.

Nomja shot first, but her arrow was deflected by a shield boss. Nuramon's hit a shield and penetrated it. The fighter holding it cried out and fell forward, giving them a clear view of the priest. He stood bending forward slightly, but his hands were raised over his head. He was casting a spell. As soon as the gap left by the fallen knight closed up, the chance would be gone. One more shot. *One shot!*

Nuramon rapidly took aim with a new arrow, and Nomja also took another from his quiver. Nuramon aimed and fired. The arrow flew just past the priest's head. The knights edged closer together, closing the gap in their rank. One of them pointed an outstretched arm in their direction and shouted something.

There. Nomja's arrow. It was the matter of a moment, only the smallest of gaps was still open in the wall of shields. Nuramon was expecting the arrow to bury itself in a shield, but then the inconceivable happened. The arrow disappeared between the two shields. Nuramon saw the priest throw up his arms. Then he fell among the knights.

BREAKTHROUGH

Panic suddenly spread among the Tjured knights. Mandred could not see why, but they fell back to the main deck. Even the huge knight who had attacked him so fiercely gave up the assault and covered his comrades' retreat.

"Mandridians! Forward!" Mandred bellowed, and he lashed out with his foot at the giant's shield. The big man stumbled on the blood-smeared steps and fell, taking many of his comrades down with him. Mandred leaped after them, landing on his adversary's shield. This was the breakthrough.

The jarl set the spike of his axe at the huge knight's throat. He could see the terror in the man's eyes.

All around, the fighting had come to a standstill. They faced almost no resistance anymore. Most of the enemy now cowered behind their shields.

"I do not ask for your mercy," the giant coughed.

"And I don't grant it." Mandred's axe came down, but he struck with the flat of the blade, knocking the man out. The knight had fought well. To finish him like that would have been dishonorable.

The retreating knights tried to form a shield wall. Mandred flew at it without hesitating. They could not be allowed to establish another battle line. He batted shields aside, held his axe in front of him in both hands, and lunged forward as hard and fast as he could, driving a wedge through their lines. Liodred and the Mandridians would take care of the rest.

The last defender fell aside, and Mandred was suddenly face-to-face with the priest's bodyguard. The sight of them rekindled his fury. He threw himself at them like an frenzied bear, ducking under swinging swords and swinging his axe into the ribs of one of the guards. In his wrath, Mandred did not feel one of the blades penetrate the mail protecting his neck. The steel rings took most of the force of the blow, and the blade left him with no more than a shallow cut. He stabbed one of the enemy fighters in the groin with the spike of his axe, pulled it free, and parried a backhanded swing aimed at his throat. The elven steel of the axe sang its song of death, but the priest's bodyguards fought to the last man.

When Mandred, exhausted, finally lowered his axe, he was startled to find that the rest of the Tjured fighters had laid down their weapons.

Breathing heavily, the jarl looked around and finally found the one enemy he was looking for. The sorcerer priest lay among the dead. The blue-garbed priest was young, which took Mandred by surprise. An arrow had ended his life.

Liodred came to Mandred's side. "They're surrendering," he declared, though his voice was weary. "They've given up the fight on the lower decks, too."

Mandred heard what Liodred said, but he only had eyes for the priest. He tore the arrow from the young man's body. Mandred had seen these silver-white feathers once before. And as he wiped the blood from the tip with his thumb and saw the glittering iron, he knew to whom this arrow belonged. Mandred looked around and saw Nuramon and Nomja standing at the stern of the elven galley. They raised their arms and waved.

The jarl shook his head and grinned at Liodred. "That damned elf saved my hide again. And his witless family thinks he's no good."

THE GIFT OF A GOD

The *Grinder* was no more than a few hundred paces from the long-ships of the Fjordlanders. Eight ships followed the prince's galleass. The rest followed the king's flagship, bearing toward the western end of the barrier where the Tjured forces had taken the upper hand. If they were not stopped, they would overrun the Fjordlanders' defenses from the western flank.

The smoke they had seen rising from this side of the fjord had dissipated. Farodin could see the wrecks of three burned-out ships drifting close to the cliffs. The fires had been extinguished.

It seemed strange to Farodin that Boldor would choose to sail into exactly the part of the battlefield that Skanga had warned him about.

"It is the king's right to fight where winning will bring the most glory," said the shaman without Farodin saying a word.

Farodin turned angrily to her.

"No, I am not going to stop reading what's going on in your elven mind," she said, her eyes burning. "Not as long as you wish to see him dead."

The prince ignored them both. He waved to his fighters amidships. "New deck breakers!"

Farodin leaned out over the bulwark to see why Orgrim had issued his order. Three small caravels had split from the Tjured ships and were sailing toward them with the courage of the desperate. *They're insane,* he thought. *Hopelessly insane. They might as well cut their own throats now.* The crew and the knights on the three ships could hardly have missed seeing the fate of the first ships to stand against the trolls. Still they dared to attack.

New stones were hauled up from below the deck of the *Grinder* and piled along the railing. Farodin could hear the trolls joking with each other, betting which of them would manage to smash the mainmast.

Alongside the stones lay the bodies of a number of the seamen. The trolls had fished them out of the sea after the fight with the three-master.

Farodin already suspected why the trolls had hauled that *meat* on board. His allies' customs sickened him.

"To be recognized as a warrior among my folk, you must have eaten the heart of an enemy," said the shaman, her voice raw and hoarse. "Many young trolls will be welcomed by their princes into the league of warriors tonight. This is how we honor our enemy. No troll would ever consider eating the meat of a coward."

"I do not want to hear that." Farodin's hands tightened around the railing. He leaned forward a little more, wanting to get a closer look at the three caravels sailing toward the *Grinder.*

"There's only one way for you to live, isn't there, elf? And anything that deviates so much as an inch from that is wrong," she said.

Farodin closed himself to the old hag's words. Nothing could justify the trolls' revolting customs.

Panic seemed to have broken out aboard the little caravel. Seamen slashed with axes at barrels that were lashed to the deck. An oily fluid lapped ankle deep across the deck and ran from the scuppers in gleaming streams.

Only a few paces separated the two ships.

"Oars up!" Orgrim called. The kettledrum instantly fell silent.

The caravel disappeared below the hull of the galleass. Farodin saw some of the men on board jump into the sea to save themselves. There was a tremendous crash, and the impact of the caravel ramming the trolls' ship threw the elf hard against the railing.

From the quarterdecks of the Tjured ships massed against the barricade, dark streamers of smoke rose steeply into the sky. Flaming arrows.

The helmless caravel grated along the side of the trolls' galleass. Some distance away, the priests' flaming arrows fizzed into the sea. They had fired too short.

"Bring barrels of water on deck!" the prince shouted.

The pointless attack surprised Farodin. Hundreds of flaming arrows left curves of smoke against the blue sky. The troll ships were almost out of range of the archers. Most of the arrows fell short.

He looked at the abandoned ship. The caravel was trailing a glittering wake. Streaks of the stuff smeared the side of the galleass. Some of the trolls were trying to push the smaller ship away with poles.

Farodin tried to see what plan lay behind the attack. Nothing made sense. Two more of the trolls' ships had collided with the small caravels, but as far as he could see, the galleasses had taken no damage at all.

A shower of arrows fell into the sea in front of them. Hissing, the flames died. But one left a small flame floating on the water.

Fire, burning on the water. Farodin thought of the priests' fleet in the harbor at Iskendria. The horrific images were still fresh in his memory. Many generations might have passed in the human world since Iskendria was taken, but for Farodin, only a few moons had passed.

The elf wheeled around. Everything was suddenly clear. The humans were trying to set the sea on fire as far as possible from their own fleet. It was part of their plan for the caravels to carry out their ramming maneuver almost out of range of the archers. But why didn't one of the fanatics simply set the ship on fire himself? Were they afraid they would burn too soon?

"Away from the ship!" Farodin shouted and dashed to the helm. He pointed to the glittering streaks fanning across the water. "We can't go into that! Get the oars out! We have to get under way!"

"What's gotten into you, elf?" asked the prince in surprise. "Are we still taking too long to get into the fight?"

"We won't get into the fight at all if we don't move fast."

Orgrim's brow creased, which opened up the cut on his scalp again. A drop of blood ran down the side of his wide nose. "The oars will go out again once we're past the caravel. We can't afford to lose any more," the prince declared and turned away.

"By the Alben, Orgrim. They've stolen Balbar's fire, the wonder weapon that made Iskendria's ships the rulers of the Aegilien Sea for centuries. We are dead if we don't get away from this floating oil. Nothing can put those flames out once they're alight."

"I'm not about to—" the prince began when, to starboard, a flame shot up from the sea. As it did, one of the two caravels that had attacked farther west caught fire, and flames raced rapidly up the sides of the *Bone Shredder*. All around the ship, the sea was suddenly aflame. The *Bone Shredder* was more than thirty mast-lengths away, but Farodin felt the heat of the fire on his face. Hulking figures engulfed in flame leaped overboard. Screams rang across the water that could not save them.

A dull thud came from starboard. The mast of the caravel that had rammed them had caught on the protruding superstructure atop the quarterdeck of the *Grinder*. The hulls of the ships chafed against each other, creaking, and the heavy galleass, which was still making headway, pulled the smaller ship along with it.

"Carpenter!" Orgrim bellowed. "To the quarterdeck! Cut the yards! Oars out!" Below deck, the droning boom of the drum began again. "Reverse oars! Back! Back!" Orgrim took hold of his war hammer and strode to the bulwark. He beat at the yards and rigging that had become tangled.

Farodin had overcome his first fear and ran to the prince's side. He slashed desperately at the ropes of the rigging. Orgrim slung a heavy rope around his body and lowered himself over the side to be better able to get at the caravel's yards. The reefed sail was still holding the splintered wood together. Sailcloth and ropes were caught on a strut beneath the quarterdeck of the *Grinder*.

Orgrim threw his heavy war hammer back on deck and tried to tear away the heavy rigging with his bare hands. His face was covered in sweat. He looked up to Farodin. "Wishing I don't die? There's a first time for everything."

The elf slid his sword back into its sheath and climbed onto the bulwark. "I wish you'd stop talking like an idiot and do your job." Farodin jumped out as far as he could and came down onto the yard. His hands snatched at the ropes, then he swung one leg up and found a secure seat. He drew a dagger and began to cut at the sailcloth in dogged silence.

Orgrim suddenly slid to the side, swung on the rope, and collided with the side of the *Grinder*. The trolls on the quarterdeck yelled in triumph. The galleass was free. Farodin still sat on the undamaged half of the yard, but with every heartbeat, the distance between him and the troll ship increased.

Orgrim pushed himself away from the side of the ship and swung back out toward the caravel. But the rope was too short. "Jump, you damned elf!" the troll bellowed, reaching out a huge hand.

From the mass of ships behind Farodin, the dark streaks rose into the sky again. Now all of the Tjured archers seemed to be aiming for the *Grinder*.

REVELATION

Nuramon had only been able to treat Liodred's and Mandred's wounds superficially by the time the queen returned to her galley with Obilee and some fifty elven fighters. Some of the new bodyguards secured the ship while their comrades aft gathered around the queen. Yulivee went with a young elf woman and fetched Emerelle's water bowl from her cabin.

Obilee whispered to Nuramon that the queen had returned against her advice, before the news of the priest's death had spread, but it did not surprise Nuramon that Emerelle knew about it before anyone else. She could see far, even without her water mirror.

Mandred and Liodred were fascinated by the mirror. A vague image appeared, seeming to float just beneath the surface of the water. Yulivee had to stand on tiptoe to be able to see anything. Obilee seemed well acquainted with the power of the mirror. She stood by quietly, watching those standing around the queen more closely than the events taking shape in the water. Nomja, by contrast, gazed into the bowl with wide-eyed wonder. It must have been the first time she had had the honor of looking into the queen's mirror. Nuramon knew how she felt; it was the first time for him, as well.

The queen, through the water, was able to see what was happening at any part of the battlefield. On this side of the longship barricade, the fighting had subsided. The mirror briefly showed the image of Pelveric. He was kneeling beside the body of Dijelon. Nuramon had no good memories of Dijelon; the queen had sent him to take Guillaume from Noroelle's arms and kill him. The soldier's death hardly moved Nuramon at all.

Emerelle swirled her fingertips in the water. The image blurred and re-formed into another. Ollowain. He was fighting bitterly in the center of the barricade, trying to clear a route to board an enemy caravel. Many of the Fjordlanders who had earlier been relieved had now returned to the battle and were fighting beside Ollowain. It was good that the humans were back in the fight, for there was fear on the faces of many of the elves. Word had spread about what had happened aboard the *Elflight*. The queen, of course, had made certain that the elves knew she was still alive and that the priest was dead, but the fear was palpable that there were more priests with the same powers among the enemy.

Again, the image blurred, and a new scene unfolded beneath the queen's fingers. It was a large ship ablaze, engulfed in bright flames. Trolls were jumping over the railing trying to save themselves, but there was fire on the water as well. It was an image so terrible that Emerelle took Yulivee aside so that she could not look at it.

Nuramon looked up and saw two columns of fire rising beyond the mass of ships. The sight made him feel ill. What kind of weapon was that? Were the Tjured priests burning the trolls' entire fleet? A third flaming pillar rose into the sky. Nuramon hoped that Farodin was not on one of those ships. In such an inferno, courage and skill counted for nothing.

The image faded, and a new one materialized. Now the troll king's flagship came into view, recognizable by the flag it flew, two white war hammers crossed on a black ground. The ship was sailing straight toward an enemy three-master.

"They will not repel the trolls' attack," said Emerelle in a firm voice.

Nuramon looked to the distant flames. Victory had seemed so close.

Over and over, the queen swirled her fingers through the water, and each time, a new location on the battlefield was revealed. The battle was far from won. The trolls had turned the tide, to be sure, and the enemy's retreat was cut off, but all the Tjured needed was one of the powerful sorcerer priests to swing the fight in their favor again.

"Let us see who the leader of our enemy is," said the queen, looking to the west. "Which ship is it likely to be?" A veritable forest of masts filled the fjord. On most of the priests' ships, the sails had been furled. They would only get in the way in a battle where outmaneuvering the enemy played no part.

Mandred pointed at one of the few ships with its sails still set. "The three-master there."

The queen dipped her fingers in the water again, and a new image formed. It showed the bridge of a ship, and on the bridge stood a priest. The queen's hand recoiled in shock.

"Does he have the same power?" Obilee asked.

"No. Much worse . . ." Her voice sank to a whisper. "By the Alben. So you have returned."

"Who is it?" asked little Yulivee.

Before Emerelle could answer, Mandred spoke up. "I know those blue eyes."

Nuramon knew them, too. The man was tall and powerfully built. He had long blond hair and wore the dark-blue robes that the Tjured priests even in Guillaume's day had worn.

"It is the Devanthar," the queen breathed.

"By Luth," Mandred muttered, and his grip tightened on his axe.

Hate stood in Obilee's eyes, and in Nomja's was fear. The only one who did not know what the queen's words signified was Yulivee. She looked at those standing around her.

In that moment, Nuramon understood how and why the Tjured faith had changed so much over the centuries. How, from a religion that preached love and whose priests were healers, a faith could develop whose ordained knights subdued kingdom after kingdom and hunted down anything foreign with unbridled hate. Now this church had shown its true face.

Another man stepped up beside the Devanthar. It was a priest wearing a mask of gold that showed a familiar face.

"There," Mandred exclaimed.

Obilee drew back. "No . . . that is Noroelle's face."

"Guillaume," Nuramon breathed.

"So that is our adversary," said Emerelle. "It all makes sense now. The soldiers in Aniscans, the lies about Guillaume's death, the power of the priest. All of that is written in the eyes of the Devanthar, as clearly as an Alben rune." Emerelle leaned forward, as if she wanted to look at something more closely. Nuramon noticed that her hands were shaking. "Look. In its hand. An Albenstone. By the glory of the Alben. It's planning something big."

Nuramon gazed at the stone. It was not the fire opal from the djinns' crown, but a translucent, golden, precious stone with five veins running through it: a chrysoberyl the size of a fist.

Everything fit. The Devanthar commanded the Tjured priests. Nuramon thought of all the new paths that crisscrossed Fargon and had their center in the kingdom's capital, Algaunis. The demon was exploiting the humans to take revenge on the Albenkin for the obliteration of the Devanthar. And the humans in Fargon and all the other enslaved kingdoms believed they were serving Tjured.

The queen threw back her cape and unclasped a small pouch at her hip. From inside the pouch, she took out a gray stone.

A shiver of reverence ran through Nuramon. For the first time, he was seeing the Albenstone of the queen, the artifact whose power could fulfill his deepest desire. Reilif had been right. The furrows on Emerelle's stone all crossed. The stone was rough and emanated a red glow from within, but Nuramon could not sense its power. The magic of the queen outshone it, and his senses were not finely developed enough to separate the power of the queen from that of the stone.

Emerelle turned to Yulivee. "You have to watch what I do now very closely, my child. Watch and learn."

THE OLD ENEMY

A powerful hand reached for Farodin and nearly crushed his arm. The prince slammed into the side of the ship as the rope swung back, and the impact knocked the wind from his lungs. But he held Farodin tightly in his arms, almost like a mother with her child.

"Pull me up, you idiots," Orgrim shouted angrily.

Farodin looked down and saw the oars beneath him churning the water. The galleass was moving backward, and with every stroke of the oars, they increased the distance between the *Grinder* and the floating streaks of oil.

Suddenly, there was a loud hissing sound, like the noise of a rampant dragon. A brilliant light blinded the elf. He jerked his arm up in front of his face to protect himself from the heat that clawed at him. Orgrim groaned.

Rough hands took hold of the elf. Still blinded, he felt himself being laid out on the deck. "Faster," Orgrim growled. "Make them put their backs into it. Water down the decks."

Blinking, Farodin opened his eyes. His face burned with pain. He sat up, dazed, and looked out over the water. Flaming arrows had hit the third caravel and ignited Balbar's fire on and around it. The flames were so bright that it was impossible to look into them directly. The heat battered Farodin like dragon breath. He turned away.

Orgrim sat leaning against the railing. The old shaman was leaning over the prince, pressing at his face. His lips were split open, and blisters were already bubbling on his forehead. The prince smiled and showed his huge teeth. "I wish an elf could be reborn as a troll. A warrior like you would be the pride of our race."

Farodin did not reply. Let Orgrim think what he wanted. The fact that the prince had saved his life changed nothing of the past. Orgrim embodied the soul of Aileen's murderer. Whatever happened, he would never see anything in the troll but the warrior who had stolen the woman he loved from him.

The burns vanished beneath Skanga's healing hands. The prince stretched and stood up to observe the battlefield. Five of the trolls' ships had made it as far as the mass of caravels. Hundreds of troll warriors were swarming aboard the Tjured ships. They would fight their way through to the longships of the Fjordlanders.

Skanga stepped up to Farodin. She reached toward his face with skinny fingers. Farodin recoiled a little.

"You don't look so good," she croaked. "No more pretty face." The shaman blinked. For the first time, the loathing had vanished from her eyes. "I offer my help once, only once."

Farodin nodded, and her fingers probed his face. They felt cool, and the pain passed. He could feel his skin tightening again.

Suddenly, the old woman grasped at her chest. Her entire body began to shake. "It's here," she said breathlessly. "It's using . . ." She threw her hands before her face and let out a piercing scream.

Farodin also felt a shooting pain behind his forehead. A prickling sensation ran across his skin, and he looked up to see the troll king's flagship, half a mile away, bearing down on a large, three-mast caravel. But between the ships, a black cloud suddenly appeared on the water and grew rapidly. The strange apparition seemed to swallow all of the light around it. And it kept on growing. It was already half as big as the king's ship.

Black fog spilled out of the darkness, sending long fingers trailing out over the sea.

"What do you see?" Skanga asked.

Farodin described what was happening. The water in front of the cloud churned, as if a powerful current was flowing there. Boldor's ship was attempting to turn away from the bizarre manifestation. It had turned broadside to the cloud, but the surging current was drawing the ship back into the darkness. A rim of light appeared around the edge of one of the fingers of black fog. The darkness spread no farther, but also did not recede.

"Let me have your eyes," rasped the shaman. "No one can see far away better than elves."

Scrawny fingers closed around Farodin's neck. The elf fought against them, but his strength instantly faded. His limbs felt heavy and powerless.

His eyes . . . everything blurred. In the distance, all he could see was a shadow on the water.

He had an urge to rear up, to break free, but he did not have the strength to turn his thoughts into action. He looked down at himself in desperation. He could clearly see his fingers and the fine lines in his skin, but when he raised his eyes, the helmsman just a few paces away became no more than a vague outline.

"The corrupter is here," the shaman hissed. Her clawed left hand searched among the amulets that hung from her neck. "The Devanthar. It has opened a gate into nothingness, into the emptiness between the splinters of the Shattered World. Emerelle is trying to stop it. But she isn't strong enough. It . . . what power. It has an Albenstone."

Skanga withdrew an elongated piece of jade, sweeping aside the raven feathers that had kept the stone hidden. Farodin saw five lines in the jade. They crossed to form a star. Did the old hag actually possess an Albenstone of her own? Was she the keeper of the greatest treasure of her race?

The jade glowed from the inside. Skanga began to intone an undulating chant made up of only single-syllable sounds.

Shouts of dismay came from the main deck. Farodin blinked helplessly. He could no longer see what was going on out there. "What's happening?" he cried in despair. "Tell me, I can't see anything."

"Boldor's ship was pulled into the darkness," the prince answered quietly. "There's a small caravel that got sucked in, too, and it's disappearing. It looks like the sea is falling into a chasm."

Farodin remembered how he and his companions had followed the glowing Albenpaths through the emptiness. He recalled the fear he felt, and the terrifying question of whether one's soul would be lost forever if one died in there.

Skanga's chant turned into a screech. Her grip on his neck slackened a little, but Farodin no longer had any will left to resist the shaman.

"Another galleass just disappeared," said Orgrim. "Even from here, I can sense the pull of the abyss. The black fog is starting to dissipate. There's a circle of light around the dark. The light and the darkness are fighting. Lightning is flashing through the darkness. The lightning is tearing pieces out of it. It's melting away . . ."

The shaman was breathing heavily and released her grip on Farodin completely. Instantly, the elf could see everything clearly again. The black cloud on the water had vanished. "The gate is closed," Skanga said. Farodin saw that the lines in her face had deepened. Exhausted, she had to support herself against the railing.

Jubilant cries reached them from the longships. The trolls had forced their way through to the defenders on the barricade and united with the humans and the elves.

"Victory," cried Orgrim, thrusting his war hammer skyward. "Victory!"

From the mass of ships, individual caravels broke free, trying desperately to escape from the overwhelming trolls.

Below the cliffs on the west, an entire fleet of enemy ships was being brought about and making for open water. Among the fleeing ships, Farodin saw the flagship, but the trolls from the king's unit were already close. With their salvos of stones, they were destroying every ship that came within range.

"I sense its fear," came Skanga's hoarse voice. "The queen has begun casting a spell that can kill it. It is the same magic the Alben once used to prevail over the Devanthar. It is trying to create a new star."

Flaming arrows were fired from the escaping fleet of caravels. A wall of fire rose on the water, engulfing many ships.

Farodin was shaken. It no longer seemed to matter to them if their own comrades burned. The oarsmen on the trolls' galleasses reversed oars, but two of their ships were still devoured by the flames. A breeze sent biting smoke across the waters. It stank of oil, burned flesh, and something else, something that was both foreign and familiar to the elf.

"Smell that, do you?" asked Skanga. "Brimstone. The smell of the deceiver."

Farodin remembered where he had smelled it before. In the ice cave. Only there, the smell had not been as strong.

The troll prince swore enthusiastically at the enemy's cowardly flight and cursed the Devanthar in words that not even Farodin had heard before.

"Be happy you have never stood eye to eye with it, Orgrim," Skanga cautioned. "There is no more terrible foe. It is the master of deception.

I can sense how it is opening a gate for its retreat even now. We have won. But who knows? It could be that it was only here to draw us into pursuing it and to lure us to our own ruin."

Farodin pointed at the huge fleet around them. "To sacrifice all of this to tempt us into a pursuit? No. Nonsense. It came here to destroy Firnstayn and conquer the North. But it did not count on our alliance. And . . ." The elf hesitated. "It was the trolls who brought us victory in the end. Forgive me for doubting you."

The old woman ignored his apology. "If you think you can see through the schemes and subterfuges of a Devanthar, then you are already caught in its net. A hundred ships and a few thousand human lives are nothing to it. Today we are the victors, but the fight has just begun."

THE CHRONICLE
OF FIRNSTAYN

*A*nd our city and the kingdom were saved. Humans, elves, and trolls won out against the fleet of the Tjured priests and forced the demon leading them to flee. Never shall the night after that victory be forgotten. Firnstayn was bright with fires of celebration, and humans and elves danced together. The trolls celebrated the victory aboard their ships, and the rumbling of thunder reached as far as Firnstayn. But there were many who mourned the fallen that night. They prayed for the dead and were proud that the fallen had played a role in the great victory.

Even the elf queen, Emerelle, came into our city, and never had any here seen a woman of such grace. She walked nobly through the streets of Firnstayn and spoke to many of the people she encountered. The unworthy writer of these lines himself enjoyed the blessing of her words. She said, "You are the memory of this kingdom? Then make it known that the destiny of the Fjordlands will forever be bound to the destiny of Albenmark." And so it is written.

When morning came, Mandred and King Liodred had already left the city. The elves said they had gone to kill one of the leaders of the enemy. We were fearful, then, for the life of our king, for his son was far from being of an age to accede to the throne should the worst come to pass. But we were also proud of him. Now another Firnstayner has gone on a journey at the side of the elves. May Luth spin a good thread for them all.

As Recorded by Tjelrik Aswidson
Volume Sixty-Seven of the Temple Library of Luth in
Firnstayn, page 45

BEYOND
THE VICTORY

It was night, and Nuramon walked at Obilee's side along the beach. All along the fjord gleamed campfires, lanterns, and barinstones. Firnstayn, the ships, and even the forests were brightly lit. The humans and the elves were celebrating together, but the trolls remained on board their ships and kept their own company. The booming of their drums reached the shore, and the smell of roasted meat hung in the air.

They had wrested a historic victory. Many of those at the fires were celebrating with song and dance, but many had lost relatives and friends and were in mourning for them. The bodies of the dead had been laid out in the Temple of Luth and the adjoining halls. Those of the elves had already been burned. Their funeral pyre, now collapsed into a pile of coals, still smoldered outside the city.

"Do you really want to take the risk?" asked Obilee.

"Yes," said Nuramon. "The Devanthar was behind what happened to Noroelle. It is the one that remains a danger to Albenmark and the humans here. And it has an Albenstone."

"But the danger."

"Would you risk any less for Noroelle?"

"No. But a Devanthar. How can you possibly win against something like that?"

"We will find a way. No doubt it is ready for anything, but not for us."

"Perhaps I should come with you? King Liodred already is."

"Liodred is coming because he admires Mandred and because he loves adventure. A king going off with his ancestor on his legendary journeys. No, Obilee. It is not your destiny. Your place is with the queen. Don't let yourself be tempted by our sad path. Perhaps you will achieve through your loyalty what we are trying to do through disobedience. Maybe, one day, the queen will free Noroelle as a favor to you."

"Very well. I will stay," she said and smiled. "And I will tell Yulivee that we will have to wait for you together. She will miss you terribly."

"I'm afraid she'll try to do something silly."

"The queen won't let her. She loves the girl just as much as you do."

Nuramon knew that Obilee's skills would be immeasurably valuable to them in their search for the Devanthar, but the thought that Noroelle might lose all who remained loyal to her in a single stroke was unbearable to him. Maybe he was being selfish, keeping Obilee away like this, but the knowledge that she would remain at the queen's side among her greatest warriors would give him strength.

They approached the fire where, earlier, they had been sitting with Farodin and Mandred. Nomja, Yulivee, and Emerelle were there now, too, with the queen's bodyguard. To Nuramon's surprise, Ollowain had also joined the small party. Nuramon had only seen him from a distance earlier, but the keeper of the Shalyn Falah had lived up to his reputation and fought like a dragon.

Yulivee came running toward Nuramon. He crouched and threw his arms around her.

"I want to come along," she said.

"But you can't. The queen needs you here," he replied.

"She'll get by just fine without me."

"No, Yulivee. She would certainly be very disappointed."

"I thought we were brother and sister."

"My house has been empty for too long, and Felbion will certainly feel lonely. Someone has to take care of him and also Mandred's and Farodin's horses. And I would like to know that the house and horses are in the best hands. I've told you about Alaen Aikhwitan. He is lonely."

"But then I'm all alone."

Obilee stroked Yulivee's hair. "No. I'll be here to keep you company. And don't forget Emerelle."

The little sorceress looked scared and stared wide-eyed at Nuramon. "But what if you don't come back? What will happen to me if you die?"

"Then, one day, your little brother Nuramon will be born. And you will have to take care of him."

Yulivee smiled and kissed Nuramon's forehead. "All right. I'll stay . . . and I'll learn lots of magic from Obilee and the queen." She turned to Obilee. "We can have lots of grand adventures. Yulivee and

Obilee . . . that sounds good. We can be friends. I never ever had a best friend. I only read about them in books, and I've always wanted one."

Obilee hugged the little girl. She whispered something in her ear. Yulivee nodded, and together, they joined the others.

Farodin was on his feet, ready to go. Mandred had just said good-bye to Nomja and had his hands on her shoulders. Liodred stood up from his place by the fire and buckled his weapon belt.

The queen had done all of them the honor of healing them, and certainly suffered no pain in doing so. Now Emerelle was standing at the water, looking to the ships out on the fjord. She seemed to be deep in thought. The wind tugged at her gray robe and stirred her hair.

"Ready to go, Nuramon?" Mandred asked, approaching him. "Do you have your weapons?"

"Yes," he said as he picked up his bow and the quiver with the dwarven arrows that remained. He unwrapped the long sword and weapon belt from a sheet of cloth, the weapons he had received from the dwarves. In his earlier life, he had killed a dragon with those. Perhaps they were strong enough to damage a Devanthar.

The queen turned around and came back to the fire. "My Albenkin, the time has come. The Devanthar is expecting me or the shaman Skanga or some other with an Albenstone. All of its senses are attuned to that. If I were to go, it would be aware of my presence too soon. If you go, maybe you will take it by surprise. Everything has been prepared. Several volunteers from my bodyguard will go with you to keep the Tjured knights at bay, but you must fight the Devanthar alone."

"How will we find it?" Farodin asked. "Should we follow the path it used to escape?"

"No," she replied. "That is a trap. The route simply stops. You would come out in the middle of a mountain and die instantly. I have looked in my mirror at all the paths open to you. Whichever one you choose, the shadow of Death hangs over you. I have also studied the web of new Albenpaths here in the human world. You have to go into a monastery in the mountains of Aniscans. I will open a gate for you to get there, but you won't have much time. You will come out at an Albenstar, and from there, you have to immediately open a second gate that will lead you to the Shattered World. That is where you will find the Devanthar."

"But is there any way we can beat it with the arms we have?" Farodin asked.

"Hold your weapons in the fire," replied the queen.

Farodin took his sword and his parrying dagger and Liodred his axe, and they pushed them into the flames. When Mandred and Nuramon raised their weapons, the queen said, "Nuramon. Mandred. Not you."

Nuramon returned his sword to its sheath. He knew that his old long sword was enchanted. He had already sensed it when he was with the dwarves, and there was magic in his bow and the dwarven arrows, too. He wondered, though, whether Gaomee's sword was also steeped in magic.

Nuramon exchanged a look with Mandred. The jarl seemed bewildered and turned to Ollowain, who was smiling. He seemed to have known all along that Mandred's axe was enchanted. Nuramon had not sensed it at all. It seemed whatever enchantment it was under was well concealed, which could be to their advantage in the fight against the Devanthar.

The queen called Obilee to her side. "You must cast the spell. Your magic is unknown to it."

The warrior sorceress stood beside the fire and drew her sword. The weapon still impressed Nuramon. Its blade was completely covered with runes, and the guards attached to the brass hilt formed an interwoven magical symbol. Obilee held her sword in the fire alongside Farodin's and Liodred's weapons. There was a hissing noise, and the flames leaped brightly, then changed to a light-blue color and licked greedily at the blades. Obilee kept her focus on her own sword. It crackled, and glittering threads of light spread from her blade to those of the warriors. The runes on Obilee's weapon began to gleam. The guard surrounding her hand also began to glow. With every heartbeat, the power shot from Obilee's blade through the filaments, now swollen to cords of light, and into the swords of Farodin and the king. The power was so great that Nuramon felt something like a gust of hot wind emanating from Obilee's blade. Finally, she withdrew the weapon and slid it back into its sheath before the hot glow of it had faded. She stepped back to make room for the queen.

Farodin's and Liodred's weapons had a matte sheen, and the pale-blue flames gradually returned to red. "Take your weapons," said Emerelle.

The two fighters carefully withdrew their blades from the fire and looked them over as if they had just received them as a gift. For all the power Nuramon had felt when the spell was being cast, there was almost nothing he could feel now coming from the swords. That was the secret of casting a good spell on a weapon. Your opponent realized only too late what power lay in the blade.

"All of you now possess enchanted weapons," said the queen. "You will carry them in my name and also in the name of the people of the Fjordlands. And for your own sakes, too, you will wield them. Step before me." Mandred, Liodred, Farodin, and Nuramon did as the queen had commanded. Then she spoke again. "You will fight an enemy worthy of one of the Alben. You will have only one chance to defeat it."

"But can we do it?" Nuramon asked.

"Yes, Nuramon. Each of you has your reasons to be part of this battle. And you will show how strong you are when you face the enemy. The only thing that will kill the Devanthar once and for all is an enchanted weapon."

Emerelle stepped forward. She kissed Liodred on his forehead. "Do not fear for the fate of your kingdom. Before my race returns to Albenmark tomorrow, and with your permission, I will take it on myself to become your son's patron. No one will dare to contest your blood right to the throne in your absence."

She stepped in front of Mandred and kissed him as well. "Mandred Aikhjarto. Think of the manboar and all he took from you. Today is your day of vengeance."

Next, she moved to Farodin and Nuramon and looked at them in turn. Then she kissed both of them on the forehead and said, "Think of Noroelle. There is nothing that will give you more strength."

Now the others came and said their good-byes. Ollowain, as usual, was cool and distant. Nomja stroked Nuramon's cheek and whispered, "It feels like we have known each other forever." He thought of the dwarves and their cult of memory. Perhaps he should have told Nomja about that, but it was too late now. Obilee, like the queen before her, kissed him on the forehead. She said no words, but her face revealed her sadness and her pain. She would worry about him, that much was certain. But she would also be a good companion to the queen. And if he and his comrades failed, then perhaps she, at the queen's side, could complete what they could not.

Finally, Nuramon took Yulivee in his arms. "Do what the queen told you," she chided him. "Think of Noroelle when you fight the Devanthar." He set her back on the ground and took a long look at her. "Go, Brother," she said, and she sounded more serious than he had ever heard her sound before. Did she know something? Had the queen confided in her? Or had the little sorceress dared to steal a private glance into the queen's mirror?

"Be ready," said Emerelle.

The twelve volunteers joined Nuramon and his companions. They were armed with halberds and swords and were unusually heavily armored for elven warriors. Each of them wore a close helmet decorated in gold and a heavy cuirass. No one would be better able to protect them than the queen's own bodyguard, that was certain. The Tjured knights would need to outnumber them massively to have any chance at all.

Emerelle retrieved the Albenstone from its plain leather pouch at her belt. Farodin's eyes gleamed when he saw it, and Nuramon, too, was stirred deeply to see it again.

The queen closed her eyes and spoke inaudible words. Nuramon sensed powerful magic surrounding him. Albenpaths appeared out of thin air. They were simply there, making the queen's magic look effortless. That was the way of most great magic, he knew. His mother had taught him that.

Beside Emerelle, five paths now crossed. Without warning, a brilliant light shot upward from the Albenstar. It was the gate they would pass through.

"Guards, secure the Albenpath," the queen commanded. "Quickly. Every moment counts."

The volunteers marched forward and disappeared into the light.

Nuramon glanced quickly at Mandred, Farodin, and Liodred. He saw nothing but determination in their expressions. His companions were prepared to face what might well be their last great adventure.

And he was, too. For if they defeated the Devanthar, then everything they wanted could be theirs.

"Go now," said the queen.

Nuramon, side by side with his companions, stepped into the light. One last time, he looked back. He saw Yulivee, Obilee, and Nomja slowly vanish behind him.

The queen turned to them and spoke in a fading voice, "We stand at the brink of a new age."

TROPHIES

"Secure every exit," Farodin ordered the guards.

The chamber they were in was high, built from gray stone, and dimly lit by candles. Overhead curved an artfully constructed ribbed vault. A faint smell of frankincense hung in the air. Somewhere in the distance, they could hear chanting, slow and solemn. They were standing in the center of a golden star, surrounded by four silver plates.

Mandred looked at Liodred. The king was as pale as a corpse. The few steps they had taken along the Albenpath through the emptiness had been terrifying for his descendant. Mandred gave him a hearty jab in the ribs with his elbow. "Still in one piece?"

Liodred swallowed hard and tried to pull himself together. "Never better."

A bad liar, thought Mandred. *And a brave man.* That same evening, Mandred had tried to talk him out of following them into the battle with the Devanthar, but Liodred was not to be deterred.

"Do you want to take over command of the guards?" Mandred asked, but quietly. "I'd feel better knowing you were covering our backs."

Liodred smiled crookedly. "Ancestor, I don't believe the elves would enjoy taking orders from a man who couldn't hold a candle to one of them in a fair fight. Stop trying to lead me astray."

Mandred thought of Liodred's little boy, then of Alfadas. Mandred was a father who only got to know his son as a grown man. That could not be allowed to happen twice in his family. Liodred had earned a more merciful fate. "Maybe you should—"

"No, out of the question," Liodred interrupted him. "Did you hesitate on that winter night? When you heard that a monster was on the loose in the forests of Firnstayn? Didn't you feel it was your duty as jarl to protect your village? And would it ever have crossed your mind to give up that duty to another man?"

"I was a *jarl*. No more. You are the king. Your people need you."

"King or jarl, the obligations weigh as heavily. As you protected your village, I am protecting my kingdom. If the Devanthar survives, it will attack us again. I am here to keep such a disaster from befalling even one more Fjordlander. I cannot shirk that duty. Your descendants have always fought in the front line, Mandred. I will not be the first to break that tradition."

A gate of golden light opened. Mandred gave up trying to dissuade Liodred. Deep inside, he knew that, in Liodred's place, he would not have acted any differently. In the fight, he would stay close to him and protect him as best he could.

Together, they stepped through the gate and came out in . . . a vaulted chamber of gray stone. Perplexed, Mandred looked around. They were in the same chamber. Candles burned in the large iron holders, and shadows flickered on the walls. They were standing in the center of a golden star surrounded by four silver plates.

"Did the spell fail?" Mandred asked, bewildered.

Nuramon seemed uneasy. "No, impossible. I felt us pass through the emptiness into the Shattered World."

"Our guards have disappeared," said Farodin. His voice was calm, but he had one hand on the hilt of his sword. He peered warily into the shadows.

"You call this creature the deceiver," said Liodred. His voice was hoarse, and in every gesture, Mandred could see how hard he was trying to conceal his fear. "Is this perhaps some trick to confuse its enemies?"

"That would be just like it," Mandred murmured. "Bastard that it is." He stroked the blade of his axe. "I hope it's here and that we can finish it this time once and for all."

The gate faded. In a few moments, it was gone completely. Farodin indicated to the others to follow him. They left the chamber and moved down a corridor flanked by deep alcoves. Inside them were regimental standards, magnificent weapons, and richly decorated shields. Suits of armor marked clearly by battle hung on stands. Mandred discovered a statue similar to the gallabaal of Iskendria but fashioned from a darker stone. The statue had been bound with heavy chains, their ends attached to iron rings set into the wall. Mandred lifted a section of the chain. He hoped the gallabaal had smashed the skulls of many Tjured knights.

"Leave it alone," Farodin hissed, pulling Mandred back a step. "The magic in it has not been extinguished completely."

One of the chains clinked. In the silence down there, the noise seemed unnaturally loud.

"What is that?" Liodred whispered.

Mandred explained the stone guard to the king but was interrupted by a cry. As if an arrow had hit him, Nuramon dropped to his knees in front of one of the recesses in the wall. "It's here," he cried rapturously. "It's here!"

With his axe raised, Mandred rushed to his companion's side, ready to take on whatever might be hiding in the alcove.

THERDAVAN
THE CHOSEN

Farodin could have wrung Nuramon's neck. If that place had any guards, then Nuramon's thoughtless cry had certainly alerted them.

He turned away angrily. A few weeks earlier, he would have risked his life for the treasure in the alcove, but now he barely deigned to look at it. Warily, he peered along the corridor. The flickering candlelight made shadows dance on the walls. The Devanthar could be hiding, waiting, in any of the many alcoves in front of them. Perhaps he was lurking behind the high bronze door at the end of the passage. Or behind them.

A cold sweat trickled down Farodin's spine. He risked a second glance into the alcove before which Nuramon still knelt. The crown on display inside was the most magnificent artifact he had ever seen. It was vaguely reminiscent of a golden fortress, its oriels and windows fashioned from large precious stones. And the door of the fortress was a fire opal the size of an apple.

"Is that the djinns' crown?" Mandred asked reverently. "You could buy yourself a kingdom in the Northlands with all those rocks."

Nuramon was on his feet again and stepped inside, close to the crown. He ran his fingers over the fire opal.

"Get out of there," Farodin hissed. "This whole place smells like a trap."

Nuramon turned around. "The Albenstone is worthless. Now I know why the djinn could not find it. The fire opal is fractured. It has lost all of its power." He smiled crookedly. "There is one good thing, though. The Devanthar never found his way into the library of the djinns. He does not know the secrets of the future."

A sudden burst of laughter made Farodin flinch. The stink of brimstone filled the air. His hand on his sword, he wheeled around. The high, bronze door had opened without a sound. A man in the dark-blue robes of a Tjured priest was standing in the doorway. He was middle-aged and had an open, friendly face and blond hair to his shoulders. His eyes glowed a brilliant pale blue, like the sky on a summer morning.

"I don't need a djinn library to know your future. I really ought to be offended. I'd been expecting Emerelle or at least Skanga. On the other hand, meeting all of you again lends our history a certain harmony. Like epic poetry, don't you think?" The robed man pointed to Liodred. "I would suggest we leave the human here out of this matter. Then at least there will be one left to go back and report on your fate. He was not in the ice cave. He upsets the balance of our little reunion."

Farodin swept his hair back and slung a thin leather band around it to prevent it from falling in his face. *Ignore its words*, he warned himself. *Before the battle with the blades comes the battle for the heart. Let it destroy our hope of victory and the duel will be decided before it has even begun.*

"Who's this pompous priest?" Liodred asked, his voice harsh. His face was flushed with anger. "Let me shut him up."

Mandred held him back and whispered something in his ear.

"Ah. Please excuse me," the Devanthar said, with just a hint of a bow. "Among the humans, I am known as Therdavan Scallopius, the chosen one. Chief among the Tjured priests. But the elves fear me as the last of my race. I am a Devanthar, Liodred. They like to call me the deceiver, and no doubt they have a hundred other libelous names for me. You see that this is not your fight we are fighting here, human. Stand aside and live."

Farodin stretched, loosened his shoulder muscles.

Liodred seemed confused. His hand rested on the axe at his belt.

"I see." The Devanthar nodded fleetingly. "You've heard about me, haven't you? And you were expecting some kind of monster. Something half human, half boar. Didn't they tell you that I can change my form as I please?" It fell silent for a moment, as if it actually expected an answer, then said, "So they didn't mention that part? It really is too embarrassing." He pointed to Nuramon. "Once, I looked so much like that one that even his lover could not tell the difference. She was more than happy to share her bed with me." He smiled. "The story is even tastier if you think that she never bestowed the same favors on the real Nuramon. It seems he lacks something that I am blessed with. I can't think of any other reason for the woman to spread her legs so willingly for me. She was the first of many to give me a useful bastard."

Nuramon drew his long sword. "Enough words."

"Do you really want to risk your life for a cuckolded lover, Liodred?" the Devanthar mocked. "Is his wounded vanity really worth your blood?"

"They call you deceiver . . . ," Liodred began.

The Devanthar roared with laughter, and small creases ringed its eyes. "Look at them. Would these elves wear such grim faces if my story were not true?"

With a sweeping gesture, the Devanthar threw off its priestly robes. Underneath, it wore tight-fitting dark-blue breeches and a silver-studded baldric. The flowing robes had concealed two short swords. Its upper body was naked, and its muscles shimmered in the candlelight. The Devanthar drew the two slim swords, crossed the blades in front of its chest, and gave a crisp bow. "You have just decided never to see your son again, King."

"Enough babbling," Mandred growled, and he stormed at the Devanthar like a raging bull.

The demon danced sideways, sidestepping Mandred's charge. One of its swords shot down and glanced off the mail of Mandred's shirt with a ring.

"Circle it," Farodin called to his companions. However skillful the Devanthar might be, no fighter can see everything.

Farodin drew his sword and parrying dagger. At the same moment, he and Nuramon attacked. Their swords flew faster than a human eye could follow. The Devanthar blocked, then ducked under the swing of Liodred's axe. Blue light flickered around the enchanted weapon. Farodin's dagger found a way through the Devanthar's defenses while his sword kept one of the demon's short swords busy. A dark cut sliced across the false priest's chest, above its heart. The wound was not deep and, astonishingly, hardly bled at all.

Farodin jumped clear, managing to escape a riposte. The Devanthar did not go after him, but sidestepped instead toward Liodred. It feigned a swing at Liodred's head, then changed the direction of the strike at the last second and slipped in under Liodred's axe. With a squeal, its sword grated across the breastplate of the armor that Alfadas himself had once worn.

"Excellent workmanship," the Devanthar praised, jumping back and out of range of the axe. "My blade would have penetrated human steel." Almost playfully, it blocked the axe Mandred swung at its back, and its second sword knocked Liodred's weapon aside.

The king of the Fjordlands screamed, "Perish, demon! I—"

The swords of the Devanthar cut him off. The monster stabbed Liodred in the mouth. Then, with a jab, it thrust deeper.

"No!" Mandred bawled, throwing himself at the Devanthar with the courage of desperation. One of the demon's blades grazed his forehead, leaving a gaping wound, but the fury of Mandred's attack knocked the false priest off balance. Together, they tumbled to the ground. Nuramon was at Mandred's side instantly and fended off a slash aimed at Mandred's throat.

The Devanthar rolled to the side and was back on its feet like a cat. It looked at Liodred with contempt. The king was dying. Dark blood poured from his mouth. "What use is the best armor if you don't wear your helmet?"

Mandred was standing again and made another charge. The jarl swung his axe like a sickle, forcing the Devanthar to retreat. Farodin rushed to help him, and Nuramon joined the assault as well. Their adversary was forced onto the back foot. Farodin found a gap in its defenses. He ducked very low, sidestepped, and drove his sword up into the false priest's armpit. The blade scraped the demon's shoulder blade as it passed through and came out his back. With a sharp wrench, Farodin pulled the blade back out.

A shudder passed through the Devanthar, but it made no sound that betrayed any pain. Despite the horrific injury, it parried a swing from Mandred, turned past the axe, and hammered the pommel of its sword against the jarl's forehead. Mandred went down as if struck by lightning.

Nuramon swept in low, aiming an attack at the false priest's groin, but the Devanthar blocked his sword. With a flick of its wrist, it knocked the elf's weapon aside. A fast counterstrike slit Nuramon's leather armor just below the throat.

The Devanthar's right arm hung uselessly, but it had not let go of its second sword. Farodin was amazed to see that the wound under the Devanthar's arm was barely bleeding. "Do you really think I was not prepared?" the Devanthar laughed derisively. "I had counted on Emerelle coming here with her best warriors." Its expression grew indignant. "Well, if she won't come to me, then I shall have to take my knights and pay her a visit in Albenmark." With the tip of its sword, it inscribed a rune in the air and made a guttural sound. Then it pointed back toward the vaulted chamber with the Albenstar. "However this fight ends, you're already trapped in my sorcery, fools." Then the Devanthar raised its right hand and wiped its brow in an exaggerated gesture.

Farodin saw clearly that the wound under the demon's armpit had closed. That had to be the power of the damned Albenstone.

With a groan, Mandred touched his fingers to his forehead.

"Well, little man," said the priest mockingly. "I've come up with something very special for you. I'm going to cut out your liver and make you eat it. You'd be amazed how long magic can keep you alive without making it hurt any less."

Even as the Devanthar spoke, Farodin dashed in for a new attack. He rained blows down on the deceiver, and step by step, he drove it back toward the bronze door. Nuramon entered the fray again as well. His blade sliced into the Devanthar's upper arm, leaving a deep cut. Again, the priest let out not a sound.

With a backhand strike, Farodin left the Devanthar with a long, shallow cut above its belly. As he did so, the Devanthar broke through the elf's cover. Farodin jerked his head to one side, but still came away with a cut on his cheek.

Nuramon was bleeding from a large number of small wounds. The false priest seemed to be toying with them, as if seeking to draw out the fight, taunting them. The small cuts and bruises drained their strength.

Another slash destroyed Nuramon's leather armor once and for all. Dark blood soaked the shirt he was wearing underneath and covered the red-brown almandine that hung from his throat on a thin chain. A deep glow emanated from inside the stone.

The Devanthar let out a cry of shock and recoiled from Nuramon. Blood oozed from its left eye. With its twin blades, it attacked Nuramon wildly. Farodin leaped between them and tried to distract the demon, but the Devanthar was fighting now like a berserker. A kick sent the elf sprawling. Both the demon's swords came down. Farodin was able to block the right, but with its left, the Devanthar struck Nuramon on the side of his head. The elf tumbled into one of the alcoves, hit his head on the stone wall, and did not get up again.

"Your turn, Farodin," the Devanthar hissed. The mockery in its voice had vanished. A dark cavity gaped where its left eye used to be. The flesh had been burned, as if someone had scourged him with a red-hot poker. With unbridled fury, the demon attacked Farodin. It was fighting with less accuracy now, but the ferocity of its attack put Farodin on the defensive. He was driven back, ducking and weaving, hardly able to retaliate at all. The Devanthar forced him through the bronze door into a hall dominated by a large stone throne. Along the walls were statues of the gods, and like the gallabaal, they were restrained by heavy iron bonds. Flaming torches and a large basin of glowing coals lit the room.

Farodin felt his strength ebbing. *"Think of Noroelle. There is nothing that will give you more strength."* Those were the queen's parting words. Farodin parried a blow with his dagger and ducked beneath a left-handed swing. If he could just get his hand on Noroelle's emerald. He had been carrying the precious stone for so many years in a leather pouch on his belt. He had sensed clearly the magic that dwelled in the stone, but without comprehending what purpose it might serve. Noroelle must have suspected that they would meet the Devanthar again. She had given them the stones not only as keepsakes, but also for protection.

Steel rang on steel. Every parry cost Farodin a little more of his strength. With a turn to the side, he was able to escape the fight for a moment, but the Devanthar was after him instantly. The demon seemed to know that there could be a second stone. It did not allow the fight to falter even for a heartbeat. Mercilessly, it drove the elf before it. Farodin had no time to get a hand to his belt to loosen the string closing the leather pouch. He had to win back the initiative somehow, or defeat was certain.

A powerful swing by the Devanthar knocked Farodin's dagger aside and was followed instantly by a stab through the gap in the elf's cover that had opened up. Farodin threw himself to one side, but the

Devanthar's steel still tore through his mail tunic and gambeson. Dark blood seeped through the rings of Farodin's armor. Off balance, he tried to dodge another of the demon's blows, and fell.

The Devanthar's blade came so close that Farodin felt the breath of it as it swung past his injured cheek. The elf threw himself forward. His parrying dagger flashed down and, with a low crunch, sank into the Devanthar's knee behind the kneecap.

The Devanthar collapsed sideways, but even as it fell, it swung a poorly aimed blade at Farodin's head. The elf ducked and rolled away to one side, coming to a crouch as the Devanthar jerked the dagger out of its knee.

Breathing hard, Farodin fumbled at the leather pouch on his belt. His fingers touched the knots, but he was not able to open the blood-smeared leather strap.

With a furious grunting sound, the demon flung Farodin's dagger aside. "You will die very slowly," it said.

In horror, Farodin saw the hole that his dagger had left above the Devanthar's knee close. The deceiver gingerly tried its weight on the injured leg, then smiled with satisfaction.

Farodin gave up trying to untie the leather strap and cut the pouch open with his sword. Aileen's ring tinkled as it fell to the floor. The elf's fingers closed around the cool emerald. The light from the flaming torches sparkled and broke in the facets of the gem. Inside the stone, a soft light swelled.

The Devanthar hurled one of its swords at Farodin, but the blade missed by an arm's length. Dark blood had begun to run from the priest's remaining eye.

The light of the emerald grew brighter and brighter. "Can you feel the power of Noroelle, demon?" said Farodin. "This is what you get for your stolen night of love."

The Devanthar writhed in pain. Its hand clutched at its face. "She loved my seed that night, elf," it blurted, its voice agonized. "And I liked Guillaume, too, as I did all my children. Many of them are so wonderfully adept when it comes to following the paths of magic. Like Father Marcus, who came so close to killing Emerelle."

Farodin stood up. On the wide armrest of the throne lay a stone, golden and shimmering. Was that it? The key to Noroelle? The Albenstone the Devanthar had used to create all the new paths?

The priest lowered its hands from its face. Both eyes had been transformed into yawning hollows. It bent down and felt for the sword that had fallen to the floor in front of it. When it found the sword, it took it hastily and pointed with it at the place on the floor where Farodin had just been crouching. "Do you think you've won, little elf?" Swaying, it rose to its feet again.

Without a sound, Farodin crept to the side of the throne and took the Albenstone. It was a translucent golden chrysoberyl, and five pale-brown veins ran through it. Everything would be as it should now. With the power of the stone, they could free Noroelle.

The Devanthar felt its way toward the throne. Cautious, Farodin took a step back. "You still covet the attentions of the elf woman I rutted, don't you? How was it, knowing that she gave herself so willingly to me in Nuramon's form?"

The Devanthar's hand slid along the armrest of the throne. It hesitated, then ran its hand over it again.

"You move very quietly, Farodin. Did I already mention how loud the elf bitch was when she lay under me? I think she'd been waiting for someone to come and take her like that." The Devanthar had stepped away from the throne a short way. It held the sword slightly angled, ready to parry even if it couldn't see an attack coming.

Pathetic, thought Farodin. Quietly, he circled his adversary. Then he took hold of the priest by the hair and jerked his head back. Cold-bloodedly, efficiently, he swung at the demon's wrist, slicing through tendon and bone. With a clang, the Devanthar's weapon fell to the floor. The fingers twitched for a moment, then the hand lay still.

Farodin pressed his sword to the Devanthar's throat.

"Do you still remember what happened when I died in the ice cave, elf?" The voice of the demon was inside Farodin's head now. *"I might enjoy paying another visit to your lover if you kill this body."* The deceiver's other hand brushed Farodin's leg. The elf recoiled. Something cold seemed to grasp deep inside him.

"*What a pretty island,*" whispered the voice. "*Do you really want to send me there? Should I visit her in your form this time?*"

Pale-blue light played along Farodin's blade. "You are mistaken, deceiver. No one can get to her. Not even you." The steel buried itself deep in the Devanthar's skin. Then, with a jerk, the elf severed the bones of the demon's neck and lifted its head in the air by its long blond hair. Filled with cold fury, Farodin stared into its hollowed eyes. Then he lay the head on top of the basin of embers.

Suddenly, his sword began to gleam along its entire length. Was that a shadow there, by the body of the false priest?

Farodin jumped forward. He saw nothing more. Had it just been an illusion, a trick of his senses? Farodin turned around, swirling his blade in the air. He jumped forward and stabbed the air as if he had gone mad. With every beat of his heart, his fear grew. Were the Devanthar's last words more than just a desperate threat?

Suddenly, the light of the sword faded again. Thin, black veins crept along the steel. Icy cold penetrated the leather that wrapped the hilt and began to bite into Farodin's fingers. Shocked, he dropped the weapon. The steel had turned as black as a raven. When it hit the stone floor, the sword shattered into countless tiny shards.

THE REVENGE
OF THE DEVANTHAR

Every bone in Nuramon's body hurt. Strangely, though, he took no satisfaction from the sight of the Devanthar's corpse.

They had done what they came to do. The enemy was dead, their wounds at least a little healed. All that was left was for them to get out of that terrible place.

Wearily, he and his companions turned back to the hall with the Albenstar. Mandred and Farodin carried Liodred's body, and the jarl could not hide his sadness. With care, the two of them laid the king's body beside the golden star.

"We should not have brought you with us," said Mandred, and he stroked Liodred's face gently and closed the king's eyes.

Farodin looked worried, and Nuramon felt it, too. His companion had told him about the Devanthar's final words. Was Noroelle in danger? Or was the threat just a final, desperate attempt to intimidate them? No. They had beaten the demon. There could be no doubt. The fact that Farodin held the Albenstone in his hand was proof that they had prevailed. But they would only be able to enjoy their triumph when they were out of this monastery and back in the human world. In the worst case, they would have to fight their way out, and then they would have to make it clear to Mandred that he could not take the king's body with him.

Nuramon positioned himself on the gold plate. He would open the gate and prepare himself to instantly open another, one that would take them from the Tjured monastery to Firnstayn. He focused on the magic. Around him, the Albenpaths appeared, but something was wrong. The paths had changed. They seemed to be surrounded by tongues of flame. He tried to weave the magic, but even as he began, his spirit was attacked by pain. It felt as if burning hands were clutching at his head, trying to melt their fingers into his skull.

Exhausted, he broke off the spell and fell to his knees. When he could see clearly again, he looked up into the horrified faces of his companions.

"What happened?" asked Mandred.

"No. Anything, but not that," Farodin cried. He seemed to be staring at nothing, but Nuramon knew only too well what his companion could see. The flames surrounding the Albenpaths could not be hidden from him. "This is the Devanthar's revenge."

They were locked in. As the queen's barrier blocked the way to Noroelle, the Devanthar's barrier stopped them from leaving the Shattered World. Nuramon looked at the Albenstone in Farodin's hands. It was their only hope, but they knew nothing about the stone and first had to learn to use its power. It could take years for them to puzzle out the secrets of the golden stone . . . years they did not have, for there was neither food nor water in that place. They would die of thirst before they had even begun to fathom the stone's complexities.

"There!" Mandred suddenly shouted and pointed to one of the large silver plates that surrounded the Albenstar. The jarl crouched in front of it.

Nuramon and Farodin looked over his shoulder. On the surface of the silver plate, an image appeared, like an image in the queen's water mirror. It showed the fjord at Firnstayn. They were looking to the west, past the stone circle, and down over the town. It was already morning, and the fires of victory seemed to have died away. The elves' galleys and the trolls' floating fortresses had disappeared. All there was to see on the shore were the gray piles of ashes from the funeral pyres of the dead elves. There could be no doubt; the silver plate was showing them Firnstayn after the battle with the Tjured.

Suddenly, something moved. It was the waves. They were moving as if a strong wind was blowing along the fjord, but something about the image wasn't right. The waves were much too small for a strong wind. Clouds appeared, scudding and gathering across the blue sky. When the sun appeared and quickly rose, it was clear that it was not wind driving the waves and the clouds. The sun moved rapidly across the sky and down toward the horizon, and night was already there with its stars, only to give way moments later to a new dawn.

Time was passing before their eyes. Nuramon remembered the Cave of Luth. Beyond the wall of ice that had blocked the mouth of the cave, they had seen a similar play of light and dark. And back then, they walked out of the cave thirty years after they had walked in.

Mandred gave voice to Nuramon's thoughts. "By Luth. This damned Devanthar lured us into the same trap we fell into back then." The jarl shook his head unhappily and gazed at his town.

"The only difference is now there is no one outside to set us free," said Farodin quietly. "Idiots."

"Perhaps the queen will be able to help us," said Nuramon.

"Remember what the queen said?" Farodin asked him. "The Devanthar was counting on either her or the troll shaman to come after it."

Nuramon remembered. The queen had also mentioned other powerful sorcerers, but that meant nothing now. "Do you mean we have walked into a trap intended for the queen?"

"Yes. And she will never dare set foot in a monastery where a priest with demon blood in his veins could kill her in a heartbeat."

Nuramon nodded. Farodin was right. They were on their own. "Then we have to try to overcome the Devanthar's power by ourselves. We have no other choice. Our only hope is that we can learn to use the Albenstone somehow."

"How can that be?" Mandred suddenly asked, drawing their attention back to the silver plate.

Day and night could no longer be differentiated. There was only the gloomy light of dusk. Snow replaced grass, which, in turn, replaced snow, showing how quickly the years were passing, but that was not what troubled Mandred. He pointed to the stone circle. He could see a gate there, but it was not the gate veiled in mist that they knew. There was nothing shrouding this gate, and they could see through it directly into Albenmark and down the hill to the ruins of the tower. Even Atta Aikhjarto's spreading crown was visible. "Why is the gate open like that?"

Nuramon was shocked at what he saw. If time was passing so quickly before their eyes, then the only things visible were those that were permanent. The mountains, the town, the blurred surface of the water, the stone circle, and the view of Albenmark. They would only see an elf or a human if he stood in one place for an entire season. The gate to Albenmark stood open while the seasons changed faster and faster. The town grew larger, too. The harbor expanded, and like the rings of a tree, the rows of houses grew beyond the walls of the city until a second, even stronger city wall was built, with high defensive towers.

Then something happened that they could never have foreseen. The gate to Albenmark widened, like a crack through the world. It ran down the cliffs to the fjord and crossed the water to the beach where Emerelle had opened the door to the monastery. What was going on? Was this the end of Albenmark, and they could do nothing but look on helplessly? Fury grew in Nuramon's heart.

"That can't be true," said Farodin. "It's an illusion, another one of the Devanthar's tricks. We are not seeing reality."

Nuramon shook his head. He did not believe his companion. "Give me the Albenstone, Farodin." He did not wait for Farodin to hand it over, but simply took it.

Farodin glowered at him, but when he saw the determination on Nuramon's face, he simply said, "You can do it."

Mandred, though, seemed to be somewhere else entirely, able only to stare at the image on the floor.

Nuramon stepped back onto the golden plate and prepared for the spell. Whatever happened, he would not give up before he had broken through the barrier.

The instant he began the spell, the flames flared up against him all along the Albenpath. Tongues of fire lashed at him. He did not give in. He fought the pain. But he quickly discovered that his own powers were far inferior to those of the Devanthar. He looked desperately for a way to take control of the magic of the Albenstone for himself. He imagined himself filled with its power, but that did nothing. He gripped the stone more tightly, wrapping his hands around it as if he could squeeze the power out of it. He even tried casting a healing spell on the precious stone, but it did nothing. He could sense the concealed power of the Albenstone, but he could not harness it, and the heat from the flames felt as if it were burning him to death. All the stone could give him was its coolness; the only part of him that did not feel the heat was his hands.

That was it! This was not the time to try to force a way through the fire. What he needed to do now was simply withstand the flames. The cold of the Albenstone against the heat of the fire. He gently stroked the surface of the chrysoberyl, looking for a way to get to the coolness inside it. He felt a chill flow up his arms and spread slowly through his body, like the blood that flowed in his veins. The stone was a wellspring. He thought of Noroelle's spring beneath the pair of linden trees and of the magical stones that lay in the water. The flames kept reaching out for Nuramon, but he could see them recoiling, too, at the slightest touch. Now all he had to do was turn the power of the stone toward forcing a breach in the barrier, and they would be through. But as he moved the stone closer to the fire, the backs of his hands burned even as his palms felt frozen.

"You have to hurry," Mandred shouted in a resounding voice. "Do you hear? You have to hurry, or all is lost!"

He almost broke off the magic to see what the jarl was talking about, but he stopped himself in time and clenched his teeth.

His hands were caught between hot coals and frost. He could not stop, not then, and he moved the Albenstone closer to the star.

"Good!" Mandred called. "It's slowing! That's good!"

When Nuramon heard his words, he knew he was fighting not only against a barrier, but also against the magic that had created the image of Firnstayn. The flames surrounding the path to the silver plate burned brighter than those of the other paths.

Nuramon began to tremble when he held the Albenstone directly over the flames. He lost control over the magic.

"By the Alben!" he heard Farodin shout. "Quickly! Nuramon, quickly!"

Nuramon felt himself getting colder and colder. His hands seemed to freeze solid. The cold was like hoarfrost creeping through his veins. The stone was no longer a spring of cold; it was a frigid ocean, and Nuramon was close to drowning in it. The power of the stone was threatening to overwhelm him completely.

"You have to do it, Nuramon!" Farodin cried. "Do it now, or never!"

The pain of a thousand needles drove into him. He heard himself scream. Then he lost his balance, and something hot took hold of him and swept him away.

RUINS

Cold drizzle stroked Mandred's face. He felt giddy and braced himself against the weathered wall. Where an elegant vaulted ceiling should have been, there was now no more than gray sky. The monastery through which they had found their way into the Shattered World lay in ruins. Mandred's fingers dug into a joint between the stones of the wall. The pale-brown mortar crumbled at the slightest touch. This place had been abandoned long ago . . . whatever Farodin might say.

The jarl looked over at Nuramon. His comrade was crouched in front of the recess in the wall where Liodred's body was laid out. Nuramon had changed. From one moment to the next, a streak of white had appeared in his hair. The elf seemed years older. The lines of his face were not as soft as they had been, but this was not the worst change in him. Nuramon rocked on the balls of his feet and hummed softly to himself. He was staring emptily at a pile of ashes against the opposite wall. His hands were still wrapped tightly around the golden Albenstone. Twice, at Farodin's request, Mandred had tried to get him to give up the stone, but Nuramon held on to it so tightly that Mandred would have had to break his fingers to get it. Ever since Nuramon had worked his magic, he had not been his old self. Sometimes he seemed not to recognize them at all. Mandred wondered whether the elf might be possessed.

A golden arc of light sprang up among the ruins. Farodin, exhausted, smiled. "They haven't destroyed the gate here. It is not like it was in the temple tower."

Mandred fought down a fresh wave of nausea. A vague pain throbbed in his forehead. He recalled the images he had seen in the silver mirror. "Is it safe?" he asked. His voice was full of distrust. "We can't afford to jump through time. You know—"

Farodin cut him off with a harsh gesture. "No one can ever be safe. Forget what you saw in the mirror. That was the deceiver. He wanted to sow doubt in your heart, and it seems like he succeeded."

"It looked very real," Mandred objected.

Farodin said nothing. He went to Nuramon, talking to him gently, then he helped him to his feet. "We're going home?" Mandred heard Nuramon ask, and his voice was thin and shaky.

The rain made Farodin's long hair hang in wet strands. He swept it out of his face and propped Nuramon under one arm. "Yes. We're going back. It's only a little way. Emerelle is waiting for us."

Mandred felt like howling in rage. What had happened to his friend? What had the spell done to him? Again, he thought of the images in the mirror, and he hoped that Farodin was right, that it had all been an illusion.

"Quickly!" shouted the elf.

Mandred picked up the corpse of Liodred and laid the dead king's head on his shoulder as if he were carrying a sleeping child. The king's weight nearly brought him to his knees. *Just a few steps*, Mandred reproached himself. He staggered toward the gate. One last, despairing time, he looked around. What had happened here? Why had the monastery been destroyed? It had to be the most important of all of the Tjured monasteries, didn't it?

Farodin and Nuramon disappeared into the golden light, and Mandred hurried after them. The path through the emptiness had not changed. They followed a golden path through absolute silence. The only sound was the whistling of his own breath.

One edge of the breastplate of Liodred's armor cut painfully into Mandred's shoulder. He nearly stumbled and fell. The jarl kept his eyes on the glowing path. *Do not stray.*

The crossing came suddenly. Icy wind tore at Mandred's thin braids. What he saw left him dumbstruck. The image in the silver mirror had not lied.

"Down," hissed Farodin, tugging at Mandred's cloak. Exhausted, Mandred's knees gave way, and he dropped to the ground.

By the gods. What had happened here? Where was his homeland? Deepest winter was upon the land. He and his companions were crouching in a snowdrift by the shore of the fjord. A thick sheet of ice lay over the water.

In front of them stretched Firnstayn. The city had grown to many times the size that Mandred remembered, just as they had seen it in the Devanthar's lair. Fortified walls of dark stone had been built out as far as the Albenstar that Emerelle had once created, a mile from the town. Wide gaps had been smashed through the ramparts.

But most monstrous of all was the change directly in front of them. Something was growing from the Albenstar they had just stepped through. Mandred could not find words for it. It was something that should not exist. Straight across the fjord and up as far as the stone circle on the cliff top stretched . . . an alteration. The sight reminded him of something he had seen in the library in Iskendria. He had once found himself in a room, the walls of which were decorated with beautiful murals, but one of the walls was damaged. The plaster was cracked and torn, and in several places, it had broken away from the masonry beneath. And because of that, he could see a second picture, lying beneath the first, painted in brilliant colors and no less beautiful than the new mural. Mandred could not understand why anyone would have hidden it beneath a layer of plaster.

It was like that here, too. Something had been ruptured or torn open. And beyond the fjord that Mandred had known ever since childhood, something else had now appeared. The air between the two overlaying images shimmered and seemed to be melting, as it sometimes did on very hot days in summer. The picture that presented itself on the far side of the rupture was blurred, but Mandred still recognized it instantly. It was the landscape in which he had awoken after he had fled from the manboar. He saw the blooming springtime fields of Albenmark. The derelict watchtower seemed to be just over there, on the other shore of the fjord. And not far from it, the mighty branches of Atta Aikhjarto stretched skyward, but something about the old oak looked amiss. In contrast to the trees farther away, Atta Aikhjarto's branches were leafless. Mandred squinted his eyes to be better able to see. The massive oak stood out darkly against the sky. There was something small and white beside it, but Mandred could not make it out. The molten air blurred everything. Finally, he turned to Farodin, who seemed no less disconcerted, while Nuramon simply sat in the snow and stared ahead.

"What's the matter with Atta Aikhjarto?" the jarl asked. "Why isn't he green?"

"Dead trees have no leaves," Farodin replied.

The answer hit Mandred like a fist in his gut. Impossible. What could kill a souled tree? Aikhjarto possessed magic and was unimaginably old. "You're wrong."

"I wish I were," Farodin replied in a dejected voice. "They must have set fires around him. Maybe they even used Balbar's fire from Iskendria. Aikhjarto's trunk is blackened. All the smaller branches are burned completely away. It looks like they used him as a symbol in the war against Albenmark. They've planted one of their banners beside him. You know it. It shows the burned oak."

"But how could he—"

"How is a tree supposed to run away?" Farodin cut him off in irritation. Then, in a more conciliatory tone, he added, "And even if Atta Aikhjarto had had legs, that old oak heart of his would never have fled from an enemy."

Mandred said nothing more. He thought of the oath he had sworn to Aikhjarto on the day he had awoken in Albenmark. He had promised that his axe would stand between the oak and his enemies. That he had been unable to help his friend made Mandred all the more miserable.

He looked away from the old tree and turned his attention to Firnstayn. From some of the towers fluttered the banners of the Tjured sect. Entire sections of the city had been razed. Ships lay half sunk in the ice at their moorings. Even out in the fjord itself, in several places, masts rose through the thick ice sheet. How many people had lived in the city? And where were they now? Had the knights of Tjured killed them all? Mandred thought of the night they had visited besieged Iskendria. Had the same vicious battles been fought here?

"Lower," Farodin warned. From the south, a troop of three riders was moving across the ice. They were the advance guard of a long column of horse-drawn sleds. The riders were heading toward the city. From one of the towers came the sound of a signal horn.

The three men on horseback rode past not twenty paces from the shore. Their armor looked strange to Mandred. It was blackened and fashioned from interlocking metal plates, like Liodred's armor. Heavy gauntlets protected their hands from the cold, and they wore knee-high boots and long white cloaks with the emblem of the blackened tree. On their heads they wore helmets with a metal crest running from the front to the back, and cheek plates that came very low. A broad weapon belt ran straight across the breastplate of each man's armor, and from it hung an unusually slim-bladed sword. Two strange leather pouches were attached to the front of their saddles and appeared to contain short clubs.

The horses' breath hung in white clouds around their nostrils. The animals seemed exhausted, and the knights' faces were red with cold. Mandred wondered how long he and his companions had spent in the Devanthar's treasure rooms. These knights . . . they seemed different from the Tjured knights they had faced in the sea battle. And they carried no shields.

He turned his gaze back to the ruins of Firnstayn. How many centuries had it taken to grow so much? He could not find an answer.

One of the three riders cut away from the other two and steered a straight course for the rupture. Mandred, tense, held his breath, but horse and rider simply passed through to the other side. For two or three heartbeats, they vanished. Then the soldier reappeared on the broad green meadow, passed by the ruined watchtower, and set a course for the path through the forest.

The other two riders, a moment later, turned their horses up a ramp that led onto a pier, and from there, they vanished into the laneways of the city.

Mandred turned and looked back. The sleds were now much closer. Riders equipped like the three men in their advance guard protected the flanks of the column. The sleds were large and piled high with supplies. From where Mandred and his companions were watching behind the beach, they were too low to get a good overview, and Mandred could not tell how many of the sleds were still coming. It was certainly no less than a hundred. He turned to the city again. Despite the darkness of the winter afternoon, lights only shone from scattered windows. People who built houses of stone like those did not suffer from hardship. There should have been far more lamps burning than what he could see. Were the lamps only lit in the houses that the priests, officers, and soldiers had taken possession of, the houses that had not burned?

"We have to get away from here," Farodin whispered. He pointed to the smashed trunk of a pine tree protruding from the snow a short way up the shore embankment. No doubt the last storms of autumn had uprooted the tree and washed it up here. Cautiously, they crept over to it. Mandred was too weak to pull Liodred's body with him, and heavyhearted, he left his descendant where he lay. It was only a few steps.

"Smell that?" asked Farodin as they crouched in the shelter of the tree trunk.

Mandred could smell the snow. The odor of fire and cabbage soup hung in the air, but he found nothing unusual in that. He looked down to the ice and wondered what they were transporting on the sleds. What he wouldn't give now for eggs and a few strips of bacon. And they had to have mead in those barrels. Mandred let out a sigh. A horn of mead. He thought of the oath he had sworn to Luth during the sea battle and smiled. He would not break his oath, but he would still drink.

"It smells of brimstone," Farodin finally said when he got no answer from Mandred. "Just like it smelled around the Devanthar. The whole world smells like him now."

"But you told me how you beat him. You told me how the sword fell apart." Mandred pointed to the empty leather sheath at the elf's belt. "It killed the Devanthar, didn't it?"

"Let's hope so."

"I'm cold," said Nuramon in a low voice. His lips were blue, and he was shivering. "Why don't we go over to those fields? It's spring over there."

"There's no cover on the ice," Farodin said, speaking to Nuramon as if his comrade were a child. "The men back there want to hurt us. And they have found a way to get into Albenmark. We will get home another way. We'll use the Albenstar that we used to get here, but it has changed. There's a new path there, one that was created not very long ago. Emerelle must have drawn it with her Albenstone. I think she waited for us. She knew we would come here. The path is a sign for us. It will lead us to safety."

Across the fjord, the sky grew darker. Storm clouds surged from the west, over the mountains, but the sky in Albenmark remained a radiant blue.

From the harbor came the sounds of pipes and drums. While the sleds were pulled up the ramp and onto the landing stages, a column of soldiers on the march appeared among the ships. To a man, they wore breastplates and high helmets. Their trousers and the sleeves of their jackets were oddly padded, but even stranger were their weapons. Each man carried a spear more than six paces long.

The soldiers marched in a closed column, with eight pipers in the front row. Eight drummers followed the pipers. Mounted officers rode alongside the detachment, guiding them directly toward the rupture between the worlds.

Mandred silently counted the rows of marching men. Nearly a thousand, all told. All heading to Albenmark. Behind them rolled high-wheeled wagons and a column of pack animals.

"They're mad," Mandred declared, even as the long ranks of soldiers turned onto the path beside the ruined tower. "With spears like that in battle, all they'll do is get in their own way."

"If you say so," Farodin murmured, and he dug down lower behind the tree trunk. A cold wind blew across the fjord, and snow came with the clouds from the west. They crouched behind their meager cover and waited for night to come.

Chilled through, they returned to the Albenstar on the beach. Liodred had disappeared under a thin shroud of snow. Mandred kneeled beside the dead king. At least he had been spared the sight of Firnstayn burned and occupied by their enemies.

The jarl glanced at Farodin. He hoped they would not jump through time again. These damned gates. Everything was off kilter. An army attacking Albenmark. Terrible. How far had they been able to penetrate? Who would win this fight?

A red-gold arch of light rose from the snow.

"Quickly," Farodin called, and he pushed Nuramon ahead of him into the gate.

From the city wall sounded a signal horn. Mandred grabbed the dead king by his belt and pulled him through the snow. *Liodred should have had his final resting place in the burial mound, under the oak*, the jarl thought bitterly. The dead of the royal line had been buried there for centuries. At least there Liodred would have returned to lie beside his wife and son.

Mandred stepped into the light. He only needed to take a single step this time, then the smell of fresh green leaves welcomed the jarl to Albenmark. They stepped out of the gate and into a clearing damp with dew. Shadows rose along the edge of the woods. The air was filled with the scent of flowers and the twittering of birds.

From beneath the pines stepped a young elf. He, too, wore one of the oddly slim swords at his hip, like the ones Mandred had noticed on the riders out on the fjord. The jarl looked back. The gate behind them had closed. Just a moment earlier it had been night, and now it was a bright morning. Mandred cursed silently. It had happened again. They'd jumped in time.

"Who enters the heartland of Albenmark?" the elf called to them.

"Farodin, Nuramon, and Mandred Aikhjarto. Our names are known well at the queen's court, and that is also where we want to go," Farodin confidently replied.

THE GREAT GATHERING

They made their way through the grass, slowly approaching the army camp that sprawled below the hill on which the queen's palace stood. Hundreds of tents were pitched there, and beside every one fluttered a silken banner in the morning breeze. Mounted knights and infantry were gathered close by, and Albenkin of every sort moved among the tents, going about their business.

Everything that Nuramon saw confused him as much as the things he had encountered on the way there. His companions had been very patient with him. But their words came from so far away.

Something had happened to him as he wove the spell in the Devanthar's halls, something that also could be seen from the outside. He had seen his reflection in a pond. A strand of hair had turned white, and he looked older, but that was a small price to pay for their freedom.

Soon they came to the fringe of the camp. Nuramon felt out of place there, as if he were no fighter, as if he had never been in a battle. But what about the sea battle, the many fights he had fought at the Firnstayners' side, and other clashes from much further back? Or had they all happened in a dream?

Nuramon looked around in the hope of recognizing one among the soldiers he could see. Most were strangers to him. And although he had the feeling that he had seen some of the faces before, they reminded him more of figures from a dream than living Albenkin.

They came across a number of centaurs, and Nuramon had a vague sense of something, as if he had once saved a centaur's life. Or had he tried and failed? He could not be sure. The centaurs acknowledged Mandred and bowed their heads before him.

The farther they moved into the army camp, the more intense the stares of the soldiers became. They watched them pass as if he and his companions were Alben themselves, in the flesh. He heard their names being whispered, then called out. And along with their names spread the disbelief on the faces of the soldiers.

Nuramon felt he did not belong there at all. He still had not seen a single face he could say for certain he knew. Or did he simply not remember? Perhaps the spell he cast in the Devanthar's halls had robbed him of part of his memory. Or had they been away so long that the elves he knew had gone into the moonlight long before?

The soldiers gathered around them, speaking to them, but Nuramon did not listen. He did not know whether everything around him was a dream or reality. Only slowly, like lifting fog, did his mind begin to clear, and he suddenly remembered the search for Noroelle. The recollection of his beloved helped him put his memory at least a little in order again.

When Nuramon saw the antlers of a stag appear over the heads of the soldiers, he began to pay more attention to his surroundings. The wearer of those antlers might be someone he knew. And when the wearer pushed through the throng of soldiers and stood in front of them, Nuramon knew that he had not been mistaken.

"Xern," Mandred shouted.

"Xern indeed, Mandred Aikhjarto. Before you now stands Master Xern, who always believed you would return one day."

Nuramon remembered. Master Xern. So Xern had succeeded Alvias as chamberlain. His antlers looked like a crown and lent him the dignity of an adviser to the queen.

Farodin was as happy as Mandred to see Xern again. "So you're Emerelle's counselor now."

"I am," he replied. "And it will come as no surprise to you that she is expecting you. Your return is the reason she has called a council of war. Follow me."

Xern's words confused Nuramon. Then he recalled the queen's water mirror. No doubt she had seen the three of them coming in it.

They followed Xern through the ranks of soldiers. Nuramon tried to avoid the eyes turned curiously in his direction. All this attention unsettled him. What did they see in him and his companions? What stories were told about them? He could not stand so many eyes on him and almost wished he were back in the days when no one felt anything for him but contempt. Because all the attention was inextricably tied to great expectations. And he could not live up to those . . . at least, not in that moment.

They came to the saffron-colored tent of the queen, where two guards stood at the entrance. In front of the tent, white blocks of stone marked a broad circle in the grass. This must have been where the council of war convened. Beside each block of stone was a pole, and each pole bore one of the banners of Albenmark. The elven banner—a golden horse on a green ground—fluttered from a pole directly in front of the entrance to the queen's tent. Next to it was the standard of Alvemer, a silver nymph on blue cloth.

Xern led them into the center of the stone circle. The other soldiers, the ones who had followed out of curiosity, did not dare set foot inside the circle. "I will fetch the queen," said Xern, and he disappeared into the tent.

Nuramon looked at the crests and coats of arms. He recognized them all, though with many, he was not sure from where they came. He knew the light-blue banner of Valemas from the oasis, and the black flag of the trolls, crossed war hammers, he knew from the sea battle. Perhaps he had seen all the other banners there as well. He noticed that there was no banner beside the stone directly opposite the queen's.

The first of the chiefs arrived. The king of the trolls was the most conspicuous among them, and he was accompanied by an old troll woman. He sat while the old woman had to stand behind him. He eyed the elves around him with an imperious glare. Even when he sat down, the standing elves barely reached his shoulder.

"That's Orgrim," Farodin whispered in a voice that betrayed all of his abhorrence. When the soul of the troll king Boldor had still not been reborn a hundred years later, Skanga had called on Orgrim to be the ruler of his people.

Mandred balled his hands into fists and kept his eyes on the troll. "I still have a score to settle with him," he said quietly.

"I don't think you will ever get the chance," said Farodin, staring stone-faced at the troll king.

Nuramon looked over at the stone that had no banner. While the chiefs of Albenmark took their places around them, that one block of stone stayed unclaimed. He looked at all of those who had come and finally saw a face he knew among them. Directly to the left of the queen stood an elven woman, a fighter, beside the banner of Valemas. She wore pale cloth armor and a sweeping sand-colored cloak. Her left eye was hidden by a dark bandage. Still, Nuramon recognized her instantly. It was Giliath, the warrior woman who had challenged Farodin to a duel back in their time in the new Valemas and who his companion had only been able to beat with a trick.

She came toward them. "Farodin," she said. "It's been a long time."

"Giliath. I thought all of the Free of Valemas were—"

"Dead? No. A handful of us survived and managed to make life hard for Tjured's disciples."

"And you came back here? Did the queen apologize for the injustice she had done to you?"

Giliath smiled but did not answer Farodin. Instead, she turned to Nuramon. "We owe a debt to a great sorceress for finding our way back to Albenmark. Now we live in our old city once again. And that debt comes back to you, Nuramon. You saw something special in Hildachi's child and gave her the name of Yulivee. It was a Yulivee who led us out of Albenmark, and a Yulivee led us back." She took Nuramon's hand, and he could feel how her fingers were trembling. "She told us everything."

"Is Yulivee here?" he asked.

Before Giliath could answer, Xern emerged from the tent again and called, "The queen of Albenmark!"

Giliath squeezed Nuramon's hand one more time, then nodded in silent acknowledgment to Farodin and went back to the banner of Valemas.

The guards outside the queen's tent threw back the tent flaps, and Emerelle stepped out. Nuramon would never forget her. Everything else perished, and only the queen remained. She was as beautiful as ever, as lovely as she had been back when he had wished that she might look at him as one she loved. When had he wished that? He could not say. He only knew that the feeling was no longer there. The wanderings of his own mind bewildered him.

When Obilee stepped out, Nuramon looked at her in amazement. The queen's best fighter had not changed. She wore the same armor she had worn on the day of the sea battle. It looked almost as if she had jumped through the centuries with him and his companions. But unlike that day, he now saw joy in her face. She beamed at him, and only him, not Farodin or Mandred.

Finally, an elf woman in the gray robe of a sorceress came out of the tent. Was that Yulivee? The woman bore hardly any resemblance to the child who, in his sense of time, he had last seen only days earlier. Some of her dark-brown hair fell in waves to her shoulders, and two long, heavy braids hung down to her waist. She stepped forward at the side of the queen and followed her to the stone. Nuramon finally recognized her by her impish smile. As much as she herself had changed, her smile had not.

The queen took her place on her stone seat, Obilee and Yulivee on the stones to her right and left. It did not surprise Nuramon that Yulivee sat as chieftain beneath the banner of Valemas.

Emerelle looked intently at Nuramon and his two companions for a long time, and the soldiers around the outside of their circle grew restive. Only when she raised her hand did silence return. "Welcome, my true warriors. Never has Albenmark been so happy to see you." The queen showed them the face of a benevolent ruler. "I did not doubt that this day would come. And you have destroyed the Devanthar."

Farodin nodded politely. "We killed him, and we captured his Albenstone." With that, he produced the golden stone and held it on his hand. "If it can assist you in the fight against the enemy, then we entrust it to you, but you know to what end we would use an Albenstone."

The queen momentarily looked away. "I have not forgotten that you want to set Noroelle free. You alone may decide what we do with the Albenstone. No one will take that choice away from you. Ever since the battle for Firnstayn, we have been at war with the Tjured priests. Their power has grown, and they now occupy the territory on the far side of the Shalyn Falah. They have even penetrated the heartland."

"They have crossed the Shalyn Falah?" asked Mandred, outraged.

Emerelle did not answer him, but looked at the soldiers gathered around, searching for someone. Finally, Ollowain stepped forward from among them.

"No, Mandred." The keeper of Shalyn Falah seemed far less belligerent than he had once been. He looked as if he had fought in battle not long before. He came to the queen's side, and she indicated to him to continue. "No enemy has crossed the Shalyn Falah. They have broken through in another place."

"The route Aigilaos took back then?" Mandred asked.

Ollowain turned his eyes down. "That was a very long time ago, but you are right."

The queen spoke then. "As your arrival in Albenmark drew near, I gave the order to throw all our strength into driving the enemy out of the heartland."

Nuramon remembered the landscape. The Shalyn Falah spanned a deep chasm. It took many hours to get around the bridge, which gave the defenders a lot of time to take up their positions.

Emerelle spoke again. "I did it so that we could win this war in our way. If the three of you decide to entrust your Albenstone to me, then we will accept our inheritance. We will do what the Alben once did. Albenmark will be separated from the Other World forever."

Silence fell. Nuramon saw the looks of incomprehension on the faces of the soldiers. The queen was suggesting they do no less than what the Alben had done. She rose to her feet. "We have driven the enemy back into the land between the Shalyn Falah and Atta Aikhjarto's gate, but they are already gathering reinforcements to strike back. We expect them to try to break through to the heartland again, this time with an even mightier army. Time is running short. We have to execute our plan as soon as possible."

"What is the plan exactly?" asked Farodin. "How can we seal off Albenmark from the Other World?"

"With our soldiers defending the heartland, we win time," the queen replied. "Safe from the Tjured priests, Albenmark's most powerful will cast two spells with the Albenstones. The first will forever separate all the land beyond the Shalyn Falah from Albenmark. The second will cut off all the gates between Albenmark and the Other World. Then we will be free of Tjured and his minions." She looked at Mandred. "And the Fjordlanders will find new courage and take up the sword again when their fabled ancestor returns as their king to fight side by side with them for an eternal place in Albenmark."

Mandred seemed at once pleased and distraught at the queen's words. He was well aware of the significance of the honor. Humans had never before found a permanent home in Albenmark, and the queen was now offering precisely that to an entire nation.

Emerelle turned to Farodin. "But all of that can only come to pass if you give us your Albenstone."

"According to what you have said, we are supposed to give up Noroelle," Farodin said.

"No. You should choose. You can take the stone and go to Noroelle and set her free. Or you can use it to save Albenmark. But I warn you, sometimes captivity is better than the certain knowledge that everything that once was is lost."

Nuramon struggled to comprehend what the queen was saying. A choice between Noroelle and Albenmark. Was that really a choice? They were completely surrounded by soldiers. The queen could simply take the Albenstone any time she wanted. No, they had no choice at all. They could do nothing except give the stone to Emerelle. Nuramon looked to Farodin and saw despair in his companion's eyes.

Nuramon nodded, and Farodin said, "We will hand over the stone to you, or Noroelle's freedom would be crueler than her imprisonment. Is there no way to rescue Noroelle first?"

The queen spoke with regret. "No. My verdict from that time still stands."

Farodin bowed his head. He seemed to have given up all hope.

Nuramon felt disillusioned. The gift they had brought to Emerelle and Albenmark could not have been greater, and still the queen could not reverse her decision. "We have just one request," said Nuramon. He could hear how weak his own voice sounded. "Open a path for us into the Other World, before the worlds are separated. We will find another way to free Noroelle."

"If you go, there will be no coming back," Emerelle declared.

"You know how far we would go for Noroelle," replied Farodin.

The queen looked at them for a long time. "There has probably never been another love like yours," she said. "Very well. The Albenstones must lie for one night atop the stone needle in the Old Wood. Tomorrow, we will begin to cast the two spells. It will take many hours for us to complete our work. The separation of the land beyond the Shalyn Falah will then happen from one moment to the next. In that way, we can win the battle. The separation from the Other World will take place a day after the spell has been cast. In that time, the Albenstones will complete their task alone. I will open a gate for you to the Other World. It will take you straight to the gate that leads to your beloved."

"We thank you, Queen," said Farodin, bowing his head to Emerelle. Then he stepped in front of her and placed the Albenstone in her hands.

Emerelle raised the golden stone high in the air, displaying it to the soldiers. "This is the Albenstone of Rajeemil the Wise, who once went into the Other World to divine its secrets. He went into the moonlight there, but the Albenstone fell into the hands of the Devanthar. Now this stone will be entrusted to the hands of Valemas." With that, she passed the stone to Yulivee.

The sorceress accepted the chrysoberyl but showed little interest in it. She said to the queen, "Emerelle, you know what I think about this. I don't believe we will succeed. You have one stone." She gestured fluidly toward the shaman standing behind Orgrim. "Skanga possesses one, too, and now I hold another in my hands. With three, we can cut off the land on the far side of the bridge, but three stones will never be enough for us to separate Albenmark from the human world. We need at least one more . . . and someone who can control it."

"You are right," said Emerelle with a smile. "But there will be another stone." She pointed across the circle. "Once that place is occupied, then we will have a fourth Albenstone. The only question is whether we can convince its possessor to sit with us."

"My queen, we are running out of time," said Obilee, and she stood up.

Emerelle shook her head. "No. The wise know when the right hour has come. All that matters is the coming together."

Suddenly, a horn sounded, accompanied by shouting. In the camp all around, shouts went up. "An enemy army approaching our rear!"

Alarm spread through the soldiers all around, but Nuramon looked into the queen's eyes. She returned his gaze, not perturbed in the slightest. She smiled. There was no doubt; whoever was coming, it was no surprise to the queen.

Emerelle raised her hand. "Step back and let me see the hills," she ordered.

The throng of soldiers pushed apart, and Nuramon and his two companions also moved aside to give the queen an unhindered view. A huge, gray-clad army was marching over the hills and meadows toward the palace. Banners fluttered high above their ranks; they were red and showed a silver dragon.

"The children of the Darkalben," said Nuramon to himself.

His words were picked up and spread among the soldiers, who reacted with horror. "The old enemy has returned," he heard someone shout. "The night has joined forces with the enemy," said another. Mandred and Farodin, however, remained calm; Nuramon had told them about the children of the Darkalben.

Obilee shook her head. She seemed to know the secret of the dwarves. "How were they able to get this close unnoticed?" she asked.

The queen did not answer her. "Nuramon," she commanded instead. "Here is a horse. You will ride to meet them and welcome them in the name of Albenmark."

Xern came then, leading a stallion. Felbion. His loyal horse had waited all these years. Felbion whinnied happily. "Is there anything I should say to them on your behalf?" he asked, only able to take his eyes off Felbion with effort.

"Make sure the king comes and sits with us. How you do that is up to you," the queen replied.

"We should send an escort with him," Ollowain suggested.

"He won't need it," said Yulivee, and she looked to Nuramon with pride. During their journey together, he had told her about the children of the Darkalben and described the halls of the dwarves down to the smallest detail.

Nuramon climbed into the saddle. "Well, Felbion," he whispered in the horse's ear. "Let's see if you've forgotten anything in all these years."

The horse broke into a trot, and Nuramon could sense his steed's unbridled power. But hardly had he left the camp behind when he was overcome by a feeling of humility. He was riding as one man toward a massive host. There had to be more than ten thousand soldiers coming toward him. They were marching in formation, as they did when they went into battle with a dragon. Shields protected them on all sides. In the center of the mass were spearmen, their weapons protruding from their ranks like trees. No doubt the king was there, his friend Wengalf with whom he had once shared so many adventures. He would never forget the battle against the dragon Balon, all the pain he had suffered, and the moment . . . of his death.

All at once it became clear to Nuramon what was confusing him so much and what had happened to him. The spell he had cast in the halls of the Devanthar had not erased his memories. It had opened them up. That was it. But everything was so untidy. He seemed to remember battling the dragon on the way to the oracle Dareen. And although it was impossible, it seemed to him that he had spent several hundred years in the valley of the dwarves before he had left with Alwerich to go to visit the oracle. None of it fit together. None of it made any sense.

The dam that had held back all his knowledge of the past was broken, and the memories from his past lives were now flooding the ones he had gathered in this life.

What had it been like back then? When did he go away with the dwarves? When Nuramon asked himself these questions, he remembered the day he had met Alwerich. Alwerich had been a young dwarf then, and he had fallen into a ravine in the Iolid Mountains and broken his leg. Nuramon had found him and rescued him. They had been friends ever since and had been through a great deal together. Alwerich had led him to the dwarves, and he had met King Wengalf there. That was a long time ago, long before he left Albenmark with the dwarves.

Next came recollections of a view of Alaen Aikhwitan from the summits of the Iolids, of battles against beasts in the caves of old Aelburin, of the enormous forges of the smiths inside the dwarves' mountain halls, of hunting in the valleys, and of much more besides. The memories threw him into a turmoil of emotions, but he was unable to even try to put them into any sort of order. Because before he knew it, Felbion slowed to a walk. The dwarven army had come to a standstill. A small group, surrounded by guards and soldiers holding banners, separated from the center of the front row and came toward him.

Nuramon dismounted and approached the dwarves on foot, walking in front of Felbion. He recognized Wengalf, Alwerich, and Thorwis immediately, though they had aged.

King Wengalf was magnificently attired. He wore a suit of golden mail and a gold helmet on which runes intertwined in the form of a crown. Alwerich wore a suit of polished iron armor and carried an axe over his shoulder that Nuramon remembered well. Thorwis presented a very different image, clothed in a black robe with symbols embroidered on it in dark-gray thread. His white hair and long beard were in stark contrast to the color of the robe. The three dwarves looked like figures from the great epics, and their guards were also excellently equipped. It was clear that they had spent a long time preparing for this day.

The king gave his escort a sign, and they stopped. Only Alwerich and Thorwis stepped forward with him.

"Nuramon. Seeing you at the end of the age does this old dwarf's heart good," said Wengalf.

"I am happy, too, to see you all again," Nuramon replied.

"And? Have you rediscovered your memory?"

"I remember our battle with the dragon."

Wengalf nodded proudly. "Emerelle did well to send you to us."

"You are welcome among us, my friend," said Nuramon.

"Welcome?" The king looked past Nuramon. "I must say, when I see the forces gathered down there, then it would seem we are not as welcome as you say."

Nuramon looked back over his shoulder. The mounted troops had, in fact, assembled in front of the camp. "Don't be concerned. It is just that they fear the children of the Darkalben. Only a few of us know your true story."

"And apparently they think we're afraid of horses," Thorwis added. "They would be surprised to find out how things have changed."

Nuramon's mind returned to his visit to the dwarves. Alwerich and his companions had certainly showed Felbion a degree of respect. "They are not standing there to attack you, Wengalf."

"If they want us as their allies, then they should give us uncondi-tional passage to the enemy," said Wengalf.

Thorwis spoke again. "We are here because of the words of Dareen. This is where the final battle of this age is to be fought, and no dwarf should remain behind in the Other World or the Shattered World."

"We have not come here to subjugate ourselves to the queen," Wengalf added.

"I don't know anything about the end of an age," Nuramon replied in a friendly tone, "but I do know that our only hope is as allies. The queen has gathered the holders of the Albenstones around her. Her wish is that you join us."

Wengalf exchanged a long look with Thorwis. Then he said, "Nuramon, we are friends. And I want to ask you one thing. Can we trust the queen?"

That was a difficult question. "I cannot answer that for you. But I can tell you that my companions and I possessed an Albenstone. We could have used it to free my beloved, and still we entrusted it to the queen."

Wengalf waved Thorwis to one side. "Excuse us," he said, and he left Nuramon standing with Alwerich. He would have liked to know what they were saying, but now he turned to Alwerich.

"How have you been, my friend?" he asked. "Did you find your way back to your old memories?"

The dwarf smiled. "Yes. And what I found was much more than I could ever have found out in my books. And now that you have your own memory back, I would like to thank you for all the times you saved my life."

Nuramon crouched and laid his hand on Alwerich's shoulder. "Forgive me. I am still very mixed up, but I can see the day clearly when I found you in the ravine. I healed you. And I remember Solstane and how happy she was to see you again uninjured. Where is Solstane?"

"She and the others are waiting in our old halls in the Iolid Mountains for us to return . . . one way or another."

"No doubt she would prefer you to come back alive."

"You know what we're like. Death means less to us than to the elves. Especially once you've found your way back to your memories."

Wengalf and Thorwis returned. "If you and your companions are so selfless as to sacrifice the Albenstone for a greater cause," Wengalf said, "then we dwarves will not stand back. This battle will not be lost because we were not part of it. Lead us to Emerelle. Be a good friend to us, and a loyal servant to your queen."

"Then follow me," said Nuramon, and he turned around. But he whispered to Felbion, "Go ahead," and the horse immediately trotted off.

Wengalf gave the order that his army should wait, and his own bodyguard as well. The leader of the guard balked, but Wengalf insisted. "No guards. Only Thorwis and Alwerich should go with me. Three dwarves, led by an elf." He signaled to Alwerich to come to him. "Take the banner."

One of Wengalf's banner bearers handed Alwerich his standard.

"They should see who they are dealing with," Wengalf declared.

They set off, side by side. Nuramon was again struck by a strange feeling. This time he was on foot, walking toward the mounted elven troops. And although he had no expectation of being attacked, approaching such a force left a deep impression. His companions seemed to know no fear. As if they were on a stroll through the woods, Wengalf asked him, "And how have you been, old friend?"

Nuramon told him very briefly about all that had happened since he had last seen Alwerich. He talked of his years in Firnstayn, of the search for the Albenstone, of Iskendria, and, finally, of the sea battle and the fight against the Devanthar.

"By all the halls of the Alben," Wengalf cried. "What an adventure. I wish I'd been there." He clapped Nuramon on his arm. "But in the battle ahead of us, no doubt I will have enough opportunities to fight by your side."

"As long as it doesn't end like the fight with the dragon." Nuramon smiled.

They were close to the riders now, and Nuramon could see on their faces just how much in awe of the dwarves they were. When they stopped a few paces from the horses, the riders grew uneasy.

Nuramon called out, "Here stands Wengalf of Aelburin, king of the dwarves and founder of their new kingdom of Aelburin in the Other World, returning today to old Aelburin. Beside him stands Alwerich, slayer of the cave wyrm. And this is Thorwis, eldest of the children of the Darkalben." Nuramon marveled at his own words. It was true. Alwerich had once defeated the cave wyrm. Nuramon had been there himself. And it was also true that Thorwis was the oldest of the dwarves and that most of his contemporaries had long since gone into the moonlight.

The ranks of horsemen parted, opening a way back to the soldiers, who, in turn, moved back to form a wide passage to the queen's tent. Nuramon made sure that the dwarves walked ahead of him and was pleased at the looks of admiration bestowed on his friends.

Finally, they came to a halt ten paces in front of the queen. Nuramon stepped forward and bowed. "My queen, I bring you a guest, and perhaps an ally."

"I thank you," Emerelle said in a low voice.

Nuramon stepped aside for the dwarves. Wengalf came forward, followed by his two companions.

The queen looked up at the banner Alwerich carried. "Wengalf of Aelburin. It has been a long time since we last met."

"And we did not part on good terms," said the dwarf, without showing the queen even the slightest sign of deference. He was making sure that everyone present knew he was a king and, therefore, Emerelle's equal.

The queen was sitting on her stone, which put her almost at eye level with Wengalf. "Then we have to try to find the right words to reconcile our differences," she replied.

"There is only one path that leads in that direction."

"I know. And I can only tell you the same as I told King Orgrim. A new Albenmark will exist once this final danger has been banished for all time. In the new Albenmark, there will be enough room for troll kings and elven queens and also for the king of the dwarves."

"If that is the future, then count us as your allies," Wengalf said and looked to Thorwis. The wizard stepped up beside him. "We will help you with your magic."

Thorwis produced a stone from the folds of his robe. It was a quartz crystal through which five black threads were drawn. The Albenstone of the dwarves. "Thank you for keeping your vow," the wizard said.

"I did not tell anyone that you had a stone, though I admit that I made some insinuations when I knew that you would come."

"What is your plan, Emerelle?" Wengalf asked then.

The queen repeated what she had said before, that they would use one spell to cut off the land on the far side of the Shalyn Falah and a second to separate Albenmark from the Other World permanently. Thorwis and Wengalf listened closely to the queen's words. "So shall it be," Wengalf said when she was finished. "My army will stand on the right flank between the end of the gorge and the forest, unless the land has changed in the meantime."

"It is still as you remember it to be. The humans are coming in vast numbers, though you will not have to fight alone." The queen looked past the dwarves. "Mandred," she called.

The jarl stepped forward, and the dwarves looked at him with curiosity. Nuramon had told them about Mandred.

"We need the Mandridians in this fight. You must go and rouse them for tomorrow's battle."

Mandred nodded gravely. "I will do it, Emerelle."

"Farodin," said the queen now, and Nuramon's companion stepped forward and bowed. "You will defend the Shalyn Falah at the side of Ollowain and Giliath. You will lead my bodyguard. From now, they will take their orders from you." She looked across to Orgrim. "And the trolls will support you. They know what it means to carry out an assault on the bridge. When defenders and former attackers stand together, the Shalyn Falah will not fall."

"I thank you, Queen," said Farodin flatly.

Emerelle turned and looked at Nuramon. "And now to you. I want you to lead the elves who will fight side by side with the dwarves."

"Lead?" asked Nuramon.

"Sword fighters and riders from Alvemer as well as Nomja's archers will be under your command, and the fighters of your own clan, too."

"I thank you, Emerelle," Nuramon heard himself say, though he did not see himself as a leader. Farodin was cut from that cloth, perhaps. Or Obilee, Ollowain, Giliath. He was not the right one to carry such responsibility.

The queen returned her attention to Wengalf. "If it pleases you, Wengalf . . . king of Aelburin. Take the place reserved for you in this gathering. Then the circle of fate will be closed, and we will be ready to face the storm that will end this age."

Silence settled as the king of the dwarves, with Thorwis and Alwerich, walked back to the stone opposite the queen. There he stopped and looked around at the company. He gave Alwerich a sign, and as the king sat upon the stone, Alwerich drove the end of the pole with the banner into the ground with all his might.

A wave of jubilation swept through the camp, something Nuramon had seldom heard among the Albenkin. The elves cheered, the centaurs brayed, the trolls roared, and Mandred . . . Mandred roared, too.

THE LIVING ANCESTOR

Liodred's body was laid out atop a carriage hung with white cloths. Fifty centaurs formed a guard of honor for the fallen king of Firnstayn. Mandred felt good to be at the side of the rough-and-ready centaurs, although the news about his people filled him with profound sadness. Few had voluntarily renounced the old gods to take up allegiance to Tjured. In retaliation, the knights had butchered entire villages. Emerelle had promised all of the people of the Fjordlands a safe haven in Albenmark. Mounted elves and trolls were dispatched to escort the refugees, but thousands had died in snowstorms and avalanches in the high passes. Those who survived the flight from the Fjordlands were led into the Lamiyal Valley, some ten miles from Emerelle's palace. The queen and Ollowain had warned Mandred; the morale of the people was in tatters. They were starved and emaciated, and all the miseries of the past had left their mark. No more than two hundred were in any shape to take part in the forthcoming battle.

When the jarl reached the top of the rise above the valley, his heart grew heavy. Down below, a vast number of refugees was camped. They still had no more than a few tents, and the people had to sleep on the ground in the open air. The smoke from hundreds of campfires hung over the meadows like a dark bell.

The people stared at Mandred as he made his way down the hill toward them. They did not know him. How could they? No one in the elven camp could or would tell him how many centuries they had lost in the Devanthar's trap. It made no difference anyway. The only thing that mattered was that they repel the attack the following day. But when Mandred looked at this desperate multitude, he could not say if it would do any good for them to take part in the fight. The sight of the children hurt him the most. Hollow-cheeked and with sunken eyes, haggard from their flight, they stood at the edge of the road and watched as the centaurs and the magnificent white carriage drew closer. Some laughed and even waved, although they were so weak they could barely stand up. What kind of monsters were the Tjured priests to drive even children to their deaths?

In the middle of the refugee camp stood a tent made of threadbare green canvas. At its entrance stood a giant of a warrior. He wore blackened armor and supported himself on a huge axe. His face was sullen, and he eyed Mandred with cold blue eyes. "So you're the one the elves sent to pretend he's our ancestor."

The jarl swung from the saddle and checked an urge to punch the guard in the mouth. "Where do I find the king? I am bringing him his armor."

"Your friends have instructed you poorly. The king lies dead up on the Hawk Pass. He took a stand there with a hundred men against the priests to buy our women and children a few more hours to escape."

Mandred's anger at the warrior evaporated. "Who has the command in his place?"

"Queen Gishild."

"May I meet with her? Queen Emerelle has sent me. I . . . I've just come from Firnstayn. I saw everything."

The guard stroked his moustache and creased his forehead. "No one has made it through the Tjured lines for days. How did you do it?"

"One of my companions opened an Albenpath," Mandred replied.

A deep furrow cut across the warrior's brow. He looked at the white carriage. "Why have you brought this wagon with you?"

"King Liodred lies upon it. He died at my side."

The guard's eyes widened suddenly in surprise, and he dropped to one knee. "Forgive me, Ancestor. I . . . no one believed anymore that the old prophecy would still be fulfilled. We . . ."

Mandred grasped the warrior by the arm and pulled him to his feet again. "I don't like it when men kneel in front of me. You were right to be suspicious. I am proud that there are still men like you from the Fjordlands. What is your name?"

"I am Beorn Torbaldson, Ancestor."

"I would be glad to have you at my side in tomorrow's battle, Beorn." Mandred noticed how the soldier's mouth tightened, as if to hold down a sudden pain. "The king sent you down from the Hawk Pass, didn't he?"

A muscle in the guard's cheek twitched a little. "Yes," he said, his lips barely parted.

"I don't know what kind of man my heir was, Beorn. All I can tell you is what I would have done in his place. I would have chosen my bravest and most loyal soldier to take my wife to safety. And should I ever hear that anyone calls you a coward because you're not lying there for the crows beside your king in the Hawk Pass, then I will beat him until he recognizes the truth. Ride tomorrow at my left. You should know that I hate to carry a shield. Be a shield for me."

The warrior's eyes gleamed. "No shield could protect you as I will."

"I know it," Mandred said and smiled. "May I see the queen now?"

Beorn disappeared for a moment into the tent, then came the voice of a woman. "Come in, Mandred Torgridson, ancestor of my clan."

The walls of the tent reduced the sunshine to a green twilight. The furnishings of the tent were spartan. There was a narrow cot, a small table, two iron-studded chests, and a beautifully carved reclining chair with a high footstool, the only luxury in there. Gishild was a young woman. Mandred guessed she was in her mid-twenties, no older. Her features were fine, but her skin uncommonly pale. Red hair, unfastened, fell to her shoulders. She wore a dark-green vest tightly belted over a white shirt. Gishild was sitting in the chair, her feet on the footstool. She had wrapped a thin blanket around her legs. On the table at her side, within easy reach, lay a thin dagger.

Gishild made no move to stand when Mandred entered. She dismissed Beorn with the slightest of gestures. "So now you come after all, Ancestor," she said bitterly. "We hoped so much that you would come when they first breached Firnstayn's walls. Or perhaps on the night my husband led a sortie against the knights' camp in a snowstorm so that the survivors in the city could flee into the mountains. I even prayed to Luth when we were in the Hawk Pass, hoping that you would come at last. But you have arrived now, and now is too late. There is no land left for your people to fight for. We are refugees, beggars among strangers, dependent on Emerelle's alms. And the way things look, not even the elves are able to break the power of the priests. The burned oak casts its shadow even into the heartland now."

Mandred took a deep breath. What was he supposed to say to her? How hard it had been to have to stand in the Devanthar's lair and watch helplessly as his own people fought a desperate war? "I can't make what has happened go away. And there will be no way for us to return to our homeland, but Emerelle has promised that she will allow us our own kingdom in Albenmark. We will only have to fight one more time, and the Tjured priests will be repelled once and for all. Emerelle is going to seal all of the gates to Albenmark, and no priest will ever get through again to torture and murder even a single Fjordlander for staying true to the old gods."

Gishild looked at him with tired eyes. "I have heard of too many final battles, Ancestor." She pointed to the entrance of the tent. "You can see for yourself what has become of your people. They have lost all hope. All of the defeats have destroyed their pride."

"We will give them courage again. This afternoon, I will bury Liodred. Then I want to speak to the people. Please stand beside me. I am sure they still look up to you, Gishild."

"I will never stand beside anyone again." Gishild threw back the blanket, and Mandred saw two inflamed stumps smeared with black pitch. Both her feet had been amputated just above her ankles.

"Not a word of sympathy. This is nothing," she hissed. "My son froze to death in my arms in the Hawk Pass. I could not give him enough warmth . . ." She faltered. "A pair of frozen feet are nothing compared to that pain. I . . . I don't want to look into an open grave ever again, Ancestor. *I* am an open grave. And in that, I am a mirror of your people."

Mandred stared in bewilderment at her mutilated legs. "You could have asked the elves for help. Their magic is powerful. They would have—"

"Was I supposed to call one of their healers from the bed of a sick child? We brought more misery with us than their magical powers could deal with."

Mandred felt utterly powerless. What could he possibly say to this embittered woman? Words of hope must ring like mockery in her ears. If only he had returned earlier. He bowed to her. "With your permission, I will withdraw and prepare King Liodred's grave."

"Wait, Ancestor." She signaled to him to step closer. "Kneel down beside me."

Surprised, he obeyed.

Gishild lowered her voice to a whisper. "I heard how you spoke to Beorn. Since that day on the Hawk Pass, he has been a broken man. You have given him back his courage. Take Alfadas's armor and wear it when you speak to your people at the grave of Liodred. Perhaps you will manage after all to stir up a spark of courage among the ashes of our sadness. I don't have that strength, Mandred Torgridson. But I know there are some still hoping for the return of the living ancestor. Talk to them. You are right . . . it cannot be that after all these centuries of friendship, the banner of Firnstayn does not fly at the side of the elves in the final battle. Spare our people that shame."

TWO SWORDS
AND MEMORIES

Nuramon stood in the chamber of Gaomee. The queen had allowed him to use it one last time. He had been more than surprised to find an image of himself on the wall. Any man or woman who spent the night before the elfhunt in this chamber also had a scene dedicated to them in the frieze covering the room's interior, but Nuramon was not prepared to see his own face on the wall. What amazed him most of all was the way that he had been depicted. He was standing, holding his two swords in his hands and threatening a shadow that enclosed a golden stone: the Devanthar with its Albenstone. Either the painting had been completed sometime after the sea battle or the queen could indeed see very far into the future.

Nuramon scrutinized the lines of his own face in the image. He saw the visage of a courageous elf, capable of facing any danger, but still with something grim in his expression. The elf pictured there was no doubt a good leader. The only question was whether Nuramon would be able to do justice to the image the next day. The day not yet over would not necessarily lead anyone to that conclusion. It had been a hard day, not least because his memory was still confused.

He had passed on a great deal of responsibility to Nomja, and in so doing, he had not even met with her in person, instead communicating with her via messenger. She was in the camp on the right flank, a good five-hour march from the palace. She and Wengalf had discussed the deployment of the troops, and Nuramon had put everything into her hands.

Instead of commanding, he sat in this chamber and tried to think. His clan had visited him, to help equip him for the battle ahead. At his wish, they had given him a suit of plate armor, fashioned after Gaomee's dragon armor. A short time later, he had said his farewells to them, not least because there was no one among them whom he knew from earlier times. Old Elemon had gone into the moonlight many,

many years before, and even the younger of his relatives, like Diama, were long gone. Among her descendants, Nuramon had become a legend. What disappointment they would feel the next day if the great Nuramon—the Nuramon who, with his companions, had defeated a Devanthar—rode into battle like any other elf and nothing happened to elevate him above the rest.

He had to smile. Back then, the first time he had been in this chamber, his clan's antipathy toward him had hurt. Now he found it uncomfortable that they should meet him with awe and recognition. That could not be true. His returning memory told him that he was no stranger to such recognition. He had experienced it before, especially among the dwarves, but that had all been in another life.

Slowly, slowly, his memories rearranged themselves. It would not be much longer before he could reassemble the individual stones of the mosaic. Right now, there was simply too much that he had to try to understand. He could recall, once, being in love with an elf woman named Ulema. From their love had come a child, and they had named the child Weldaron. This was the name of the founder of their clan. Was he, Nuramon, then the father of Weldaron? He could not believe that was true.

He was also confused by all the feelings he had once held for Emerelle, feelings she had never been able to return. No doubt there were many elves who saw Emerelle and dreamed secretly of her love. There was no woman for whom more love poems or songs of courting had been composed than for the queen of the elves.

The sound of footsteps outside the door provoked a memory of the night before the elfhunt rode out. Nuramon turned around. He had an idea who was coming to visit him. As the door opened and he saw Emerelle, he knew that he had not been mistaken. The queen had come to him, as she had the night that everything had begun for him. And as she had then, she wore the gray robe of a sorceress, and her dark blond hair swelled gently over her shoulders. He looked into her pale-brown eyes and found there the same shine as on that night so long ago.

She closed the door behind her and smiled at him, as if waiting for some stirring of emotion in him.

"Emerelle," he said and looked at her for a long time. "It is no accident that you come to me now, is it?"

"No. Nothing that we say or do happens by accident. This is where the circle closes, Nuramon, father of Weldaron and son of Valimee and Deramon."

As the queen spoke the names of his first parents, his memory of them returned. His father had been a soldier, his mother a sorceress. They had gone into the moonlight when they were still young, but they had loved him as only the first of the Albenkin had loved their sons and daughters. "Am I that old?" he asked.

The queen nodded. "I have known for a long time that a momentous fate would be yours one day. At that time, you were one of my companions in arms. We met for the first time in Ischemon, in battle against the sun dragons. There was no queen then. I was still searching for my own destiny, and we went to the Oracle of Telmareen together. And you know what she said."

Nuramon remembered everything the queen talked about. Her words were like a magic formula, restoring his memory chapter by chapter, bringing back everything he had ever felt. He suddenly saw the illuminated form of the oracle again, and her voice rang in his ears still: "Choose your kinfolk for yourself. Pay no heed to your reputation. Everything you are is within you."

The queen now stood directly in front of him, and her gaze shifted back and forth between his eyes. "In those days, there were few rules. We had to make them for ourselves, and that is why, your whole life, you have always found it hard to live by the rules of others. Do you remember what I said to you before you took your last breath?"

He had been wounded, then, by the burning light of a sun dragon. Now he recalled Emerelle's words and spoke them: "'At the oracle, I saw you and the mighty child.' Yulivee. You saw Yulivee back then?"

"Yes. And ever since, I knew that you would lead her to me one day, but I did not know when. So I learned to be patient. I had to wait so long and do things and say things that did not come from the heart, but everything I said the night before the elfhunt was the truth. I had to keep some things to myself, of course, as the oracles tend to do. But now you should hear the truth as you have not heard it before. Come."

She took him by the hand and led him across to the stone bench, where they sat down. "I cannot feel what you now feel, for I have never died. My memories are those of a single long life, but I know that it is not easy to come to terms with everything you are experiencing. To be able to comprehend it all, you have to grow. And that is one of your strengths." She let go of his hand and pointed up to the ceiling, to the image of Gaomee. "Before the elfhunt, when I chose to give you the great Gaomee's room, I chose with care. I was aware that you had a long journey ahead of you. It was the right time to give you her sword, but I did not tell you everything about the weapon." Emerelle stood up and moved across to Nuramon's bed, where she picked up his two swords. Then she returned to his side and slid Gaomee's short sword from its sheath. "The dwarves must have told you something about this blade."

"They told me it had been forged by a dwarf named Teludem for an elf." A suspicion rose within Nuramon and he asked, "Was the sword perhaps given to me at one time?"

"No. The dwarves gave it to *me*. They said they would go into the Other World to search for a realm in which Wengalf could remain king. It was a time in which I was not able to tolerate anyone beside me, so that what will now happen would be able to. We separated in anger, but Wengalf is no fool. He presented me with the sword and said that I should send it to him when I was ready to respect him as king."

"The dwarves did not tell me anything about that," Nuramon replied.

"I gave the sword to Gaomee because she came from the family line whose destiny it was to reconcile with the dwarves." The queen seemed to be waiting for Nuramon to speak.

Suddenly, it was clear to Nuramon what she was saying. "Gaomee came from my clan?"

"She not only came from your clan. She was your daughter."

The revelation hit Nuramon like a sudden blow. Gaomee was his daughter. "I don't remember her."

"You had been dead for quite some time when Diyomee gave birth."

"Diyomee," Nuramon breathed to himself. It had been an unfortunate love affair. Her father had hated him, and Nuramon's rival had killed him in a duel.

"The family cast Diyomee out. So I decided to take her in with me. She gave birth to the child, gave her the name Gaomee, then went into the moonlight. I raised the newborn child. When I called her to the elfhunt, I sensed that it was right to entrust her with the short sword. I told her everything about her father, and she admired you for the things you did in Ischemon. Only like that could she defeat the dragon Duanoc."

"But I was reborn. Why didn't she come to me?"

"She didn't dare. She was afraid you might reject her. But before she found her own love and went into the moonlight, she returned the sword to me and told me that I should look after it for you and give it to you when the time was ripe. And I did that." She returned Gaomee's blade to its sheath. "You took the sword to the dwarves, and they soon realized how this age would end. They found out from Dareen when they would have to return to their ancient halls." Emerelle now drew the long sword, Nuramon's old weapon. "Thorwis and Wengalf were wise. They gave you your old sword, and when I saw that you had it, I knew that you had been among the dwarves. You were fate's messenger, and with this weapon, you told me that the dwarves would come, and you reminded me of where this weapon came from."

"You know that?" Nuramon asked in surprise.

"Don't you remember?"

Nuramon pondered the sword. It had been at his side through a number of lives. His companions in arms had always taken it to his clan, where it had waited for him to be reborn. But where did it come from?

"Don't worry," said Emerelle, and she sheathed the sword again. "It was a gift from me. I once gave all of my companions a weapon."

Nuramon could not remember receiving it, and it angered him that he could not.

The queen laid one hand on his shoulder. "Your memory will return. You will need time to rediscover everything. It is a very special journey you are on, very different from the one you have experienced so far. Approach it like the dwarves do. Remember my words until you remember yourself."

Nuramon gazed at the weapon that lay beside the queen. "Then the magic in this sword is your magic."

Emerelle laughed. "I was a different person then, in the same way that Yulivee used to be someone else. Even the Devanthar would not have recognized the magic of your sword."

Nuramon looked down at the floor. The things the queen was telling him were opening a thousand gateways in his memory, and he did not know through which of them he was supposed to step first. Emerelle was right; it was a journey. She was leading him into forgotten realms. "Where do I go from here?" he asked. "I feel lost, like I've taken a wrong turn somewhere along my long path."

"My words should provide you with at least a little solid ground," she replied. "They are meant to show you that you are more than you believe yourself to be and that you can be so much more than you have ever dreamed."

The queen was speaking as if he faced no dangers, as if the way ahead were free of stumbling blocks. "Will I die tomorrow?" he asked.

Emerelle raised her eyebrows in surprise. "Nuramon, you know I would not tell you that even if I knew. The outcome of a battle is never clear, even for me. Fate can change too often in something like that. Too many swords, too many arrows, too many movements make it impossible to see the end of everything. I cannot even be sure that we will save Albenmark. All I know is what *should* be. And that I have to keep to myself, because otherwise it cannot happen. But I know why you ask. You fear that you and Farodin might both die."

"Yes. And then Noroelle would be lost and I would be born into a new life in which I would remember her bitter fate without ever being able to do anything for her. Why are you unable to overturn your verdict? Why must the spell to separate Albenmark from the Other World be cast straight after the first spell?"

"Because I saw my own death if we only cut off the land beyond the Shalyn Falah," Emerelle said. She turned away and stared into nothing. "An arrow finds me, and then the spell can never again be cast. But the Tjured priests will open other gates into Albenmark if we don't separate our world from theirs." She blinked and turned back to Nuramon. "Noroelle has to stay where she is so that I can live, but don't think I am acting out of selfishness. For me, all that matters is Albenmark. Even the queen knows sympathy, and suffers when she has to say and do things that contradict the wishes of her heart." Emerelle laid her hand on his shoulder. "And my heart tells me that there has to be hope for Noroelle." Her eyes shone. "And I promise you this. If Farodin and you should die tomorrow, I will entrust my throne to Yulivee and turn my back on Albenmark in your place."

Nuramon had expected anything but that. "You would do that?" he asked.

The queen nodded. "Yes. Because in all the centuries of my destiny to come, it would be unbearable for me to live in a flourishing age and to see you and Farodin reborn. And I could no longer bear Obilee's suffering either. It would be a debt I could not live with. So you see that there is still hope for Noroelle, if only we are victorious tomorrow."

Nuramon took the queen's hand in his and kissed it. "I thank you, Emerelle. I am no longer afraid of fighting tomorrow." He looked at his two swords. "I would like to give you Gaomee's sword, because you are right. This is where the circle closes."

"No. Not for that sword. You have to hold on to it for now. It has fulfilled its purpose for Albenmark, but for you, it is a sign of the path ahead, which is not yet at its end." She kissed him on his forehead in farewell, then stood up. "Survive the battle. Find Noroelle. Then you can give the sword away with an unburdened heart." And with that, the queen left Gaomee's chamber.

THE QUEEN'S DAGGER

The sounds of the army camp reached as far as the tower. The hammers of the weapon smiths rang loudly. Horses whinnied restlessly. At some of the fires, songs were sung. Each fought his fear in his own way. Tomorrow would decide the future of Albenmark.

Farodin was leaning against the parapet and thinking of the day from which all of this had sprung. If Guillaume had died silently in his house close to the temple tower in Aniscans, perhaps smothered by a pillow, would all of this still have happened? Could he, Farodin, have done it? Had it been his weakness that had led to their enemies threatening the very heartland of Albenmark? Or had it all already begun with Gelvuun's death?

He took a deep breath. The cool night air was not pure. It carried a whiff of an all too familiar smell. The stink of brimstone. Or was he just imagining it? Was he slowly going insane? Or had he not, in fact, won the most crucial fight of his life? Was the Devanthar lurking somewhere, pulling his strings as he had once before, after they had believed him dead in the ice cave?

He made an effort to push such hopeless thoughts out of his mind and simply take in the view over the camp. As far as the eye could see, tents had been pitched, and fires flickered as far away as the hills in the distance. Never before had all the races of Albenmark stood as one against a common foe. This, too, had come from the death of Guillaume. Old feuds were forgotten. Farodin thought of Orgrim. The trolls, who had brought so much misery to the elven race, would take their positions at Welruun, close to the Shalyn Falah, and fight side by side with the elves. Welruun . . . the place where, centuries before, the two races had fought a bitter battle. The place where Aileen had died. Everything in this world was turned on its head. Everything seemed possible. If he lived through tomorrow, then they would reach Noroelle. Farodin's hand stroked the small leather pouch in which he kept Aileen's ring and Noroelle's emerald. He felt the tightness in his throat as he did so. The end of their search was so close. But how might centuries of loneliness have changed Noroelle? What was left of the elf he had once loved so dearly? And what was left of the Farodin that she had once known?

A sound caused him to turn around. The door to the queen's rooms opened, and Emerelle stepped out to join him on the balcony. She was dressed entirely in white. Farodin had never seen her in this dress before. It was plain and undecorated. A high collar was buttoned tightly around her throat. The dress tapered to her waist and had wide sleeves that covered the backs of her hands.

"I'm happy I could meet you here one more time," she said with warmth in her voice. "We have spoken about death up here so many times." The queen moved over to the stone balustrade. She stood beside him and looked down to the plain.

"A long time has passed for you since the last time we stood up here. Back then, I did not doubt that every order you gave was for the best for Albenmark," said Farodin, musing.

From the camp below came the casual laughter of the centaurs. "And what do you think today?" Emerelle asked.

"I am happy that I did not kill Guillaume. He was a good man. If he had lived longer . . . perhaps all this would not have happened." He stepped back a short way from the parapet and looked at the queen. She looked so youthful, so beautiful and innocent. "Of all the Albenkin, what was it in me that made you choose me to be your executioner?"

"If one stroke of a dagger can prevent a hundred deaths, is it wrong to deliver it?"

"No," Farodin immediately replied.

"And because you think that way, I made you my dagger. There were times when a single dagger could have stopped the dwarves or the elves of Valemas from leaving Albenmark. I was afraid that our peoples could end up strewn to the winds. Or worse, that we would fight long and bloody feuds with each other. Albenmark was in danger of perishing. The murders we carried out saved it. And if we are the victors tomorrow, then Albenmark will be stronger than ever before and a new age will begin. What does it matter to sacrifice a body if you know that the soul will be born again? Only the flesh dies. The soul is assured of a new beginning, and perhaps even one that does not lead down dark paths."

"Did you never doubt that you were doing what was right?"

Emerelle turned around and leaned against the balustrade. "How does one measure right and wrong, Farodin? I ordered you and Nuramon to kill Guillaume. Instead, you both tried to save him. But he was still murdered. Fate had decided the day of his death long before. And even though you did not kill him, his murder was blamed on the elves. Noroelle made the right decision as a mother not to hand her child over to me. And you were right when you decided not to kill her son. But here we stand, fighting for the survival of Albenmark. I have always tried to do my best for all the Albenkin. Perhaps it will help you to know that whenever I decided someone's death, I never did so with a light heart."

Farodin was not satisfied with her answer. In the past, it had been easier for him to accept her words without questioning what might lie behind them.

For a long time, they stood side by side in silence and listened to the sounds drifting up from the camp.

"Can you smell the brimstone?" he asked.

She nodded. "It takes very refined senses to pick up the smell here. It comes from beyond the Shalyn Falah."

Farodin sighed. At the council of war, he and his companions had reported on their fight against the Devanthar. At the time, Emerelle had said nothing. Was it because she did not want to reveal the truth in front of all the heads of the armies? "So he deceived us again," said Farodin sadly. "Like he did in the ice cave, when we thought we had beaten him. Is he the one commanding the armies of the Tjured knights? Is he the one who created the rupture between the worlds?"

The queen swept a strand of hair from her face. She was lost in thought and did not answer for some time, but then she turned and met his gaze. "The Devanthar is gone for good. You killed it the way the Alben did. Our ancestors bound the Devanthar in their magical weapons, and then they destroyed the weapons. It will not return . . . but in a certain sense, it is immortal. Its seed in the Other World has yielded a heavy harvest. The rupture was created during the second siege of Firnstayn by priests who had its blood in their veins. It happened by accident. They were trying to use a ritual to seal the Albenstar on the Hartungscliff and the one on the beach at the same time. But instead of separating our two worlds, they tore down the frontier entirely. Over the centuries, the blood of the Devanthar has been diluted. There are no more priests alive today who can kill the Albenkin with their magic. What happened in the sea battle, when I was nearly killed, has not happened since. But our enemies no longer need magic like that. And it makes no difference how great their losses against us are, they can replace every fallen soldier, while the races of Albenmark slowly bleed to death. We have to win tomorrow. We have to save our world from them for just a single day."

For a moment, it occurred to Farodin that she might have lied to him to stop him from losing his fighting spirit. She looked so innocent. So pure.

But what difference would lying to him now make? The battle for Albenmark had to be fought, and he believed one thing, at least, that she had said: she would do anything to save the races of Albenmark.

Farodin bowed crisply. "I will ride to the Shalyn Falah tonight."

The queen stood before him and kissed him softly on the cheek. "Take care, my friend. There is an Emerelle that only you and I know. You have kept her secret as your own through the centuries. I thank you for that."

Farodin was taken aback. "I thought Ollowain would have taken my place."

The queen looked at him intently. "No. He may be the best swordsman in Albenmark, but he lacks the talent to be the queen's dagger. He failed in Aniscans, and again, you alone were the one who carried out my will. You were my ambassador to the trolls. You would have made them pay with blood if they had betrayed us in the sea battle. And in the end, it was your blade that killed the Devanthar, the mightiest enemy Albenmark has ever known."

TRACING A NIGHT LONG PAST

Nuramon strolled through the queen's orchard. As he had in Gaomee's chamber, he thought of the night before the elfhunt's departure. That night, the trees had whispered to him, but now they were silent. Nuramon touched the branches of the faery pine, but the warmth the tree had always given off was gone. He withdrew his hand in disappointment.

What had happened here? Had the souls of the trees gone into the moonlight? The magic of the place still seemed to be present, for all of the trees carried fruit at the same time. But some things had changed with the passing years, too.

Nuramon walked by the linden tree where he had first seen Noroelle that night and passed by the two mulberry trees that had given him their fruit. Regardless of the outcome of the battle tomorrow, Noroelle would never see any of this again. Her lake, the faun oak, her home . . . all of them would only ever exist in her memory.

Nuramon came to the linden and the olive tree at the edge of the garden. This was where he had spoken to Noroelle as the spirit of the tree, and she had played along. He never would have believed that night that fate would lead them all down such a hard and merciless path. He looked up and saw two faces looking down at him.

"Aha! Eavesdropping on us?" asked Yulivee with a laugh.

Obilee placed one hand on the sorceress's shoulder. "Let him listen."

"Come up to us," said Yulivee.

Nuramon did not answer, but climbed the narrow stairway up to the terrace. The two elven women were an enchanting sight. Yulivee was dressed in wispy gray robes. She had braided white ribbons into her dark-brown hair. Obilee had donned a flowing blue dress and wore her hair tied up. No man would have believed he was looking at a warrior.

"Yulivee and Obilee," Nuramon exclaimed when he stepped onto the terrace. "Are you best friends now?"

"Ever since the night you went away," Yulivee confirmed.

He stopped in front of them.

Yulivee looked into his eyes. "It's strange, you know, not to have to look up to you anymore." She was just as tall as Nuramon. "Back then, you were a giant to me. And no doubt I was just a silly little girl."

"No. You were a little sorceress with great power . . . and a lovable little pest."

Obilee smiled. "That's what she stayed for quite a while after you left."

"And I'm sorry about that," said Yulivee.

Nuramon shook his head. "You don't need to apologize . . . Sister."

"I didn't forget . . . Brother. And I did what you asked me to do. I looked after Felbion, and I live in your house. You will still recognize it, even without Alaen Aikhwitan."

"He's not there anymore?" asked Nuramon, and his thoughts turned to the faery pine.

"There isn't a single souled tree left in the entire heartland," said Obilee.

From a small pouch, Yulivee took out an acorn. "This is from Alaen Aikhwitan. If we win tomorrow, then the souls of the trees will be reborn. I just don't know yet where I'm supposed to plant it."

"What happened to Atta Aikhjarto?" Nuramon asked.

"Xern will plant him again." The sorceress pointed down to the orchard. "Most of the trees' souls have gone into the moonlight. Only a few of the very great trees have stored their souls here. Alaen Aikhwitan, Atta Aikhjarto, the faery pine, the faun oak, and a few others. They will become the forefathers and foremothers of new souled trees. Emerelle said that she wanted to plant the faery pine down where the riverbank sprites live."

Nuramon thought of Noroelle's lake, which bordered the meadow of the sprites. Everything would change and become something new. No doubt Noroelle's lake would keep its place in the fabric of the new Albenmark.

"Are you really going to go?" asked Yulivee, dragging Nuramon out of his thoughts.

"I have to," he said.

Yulivee's smile faded. "I would give a great deal to meet the woman whom you would sacrifice so much for. Obilee told me about her."

"Are you disappointed?" replied Nuramon.

Yulivee shook her head. "No. You will always be my brother. I would never expect you to give up your love for Noroelle for my sake. You don't know how happy I am that you defeated the Devanthar and that I am able to see you again. I was so afraid for you." She fell into his arms. "But now I can be happy."

"Will it hurt you so much if I leave Albenmark behind?" he asked her, very quietly.

The sorceress lifted her head from his shoulder and looked at him wide-eyed. He stroked her cheek, and already a smile began to spread across her face, a smile that reminded him of the child he had taken under his wing in Iskendria. "No," she answered. "We have had our time together. Our journey from Iskendria to here was the best experience I have ever had." She kissed him on his forehead. "Be strong tomorrow." Gently, she freed herself from his embrace. "I have to go back to the Old Wood now," she said. With that, she turned and left.

Nuramon watched her walk away. He had missed so much. Suddenly, the little girl at his side had turned into a powerful young sorceress. Their victory over the Devanthar had come at a high price.

Obilee came up beside him. "You don't know how much she missed you."

"It's all hard for me to comprehend. It was the same with you back then. You were a girl when I rode out with the elfhunt. And then you were waiting for us here as a woman, and you spoke Noroelle's words to us . . . And it was in this place that I touched Noroelle for the first time."

"She told me about it that night." Obilee's face grew sad. "She couldn't stop talking about you and Farodin."

"You're looking at me so gloomily. Didn't the queen tell you that there is still hope, as long as we win the battle tomorrow?"

"Hope for whom, Nuramon?"

"For Noroelle, of course."

Obilee nodded. "The queen told me everything. And I've known it for years. She told me how far she would go to keep the hope alive."

"Then why are you so sad?"

"Don't you know, Nuramon? Have you never noticed?"

For a moment, Nuramon did not understand. But the look of agony on her face, her shining eyes and quivering lips told him what Obilee was going through. She loved him. Suddenly awkward, he looked away. "I'm a fool," he said softly. "Forgive me."

"For what? You move through the centuries in giant bounds. For you, I'm still the girl Noroelle led before the queen."

"No. During the sea battle, I realized that you had become a woman. But when . . . ?" He hesitated, reluctant to finish the question.

"My feelings for you grew from what I already felt, from when Noroelle told me so much about you and Farodin. You were my favorite. And the longer you were away, the stronger the feeling became. Do you remember when you left back then, when I waved to you from the hill?"

"Yes."

"I was already in love with you then." She bit her lip and seemed to be waiting for Nuramon to say something. Then she continued. "I knew from Emerelle that you and your companions would do great things. I was not allowed to distract you from your path. After all, I want you to rescue Noroelle, too. And I sleep easier knowing there is still hope for her, whatever happens tomorrow. But I also know that there is no such hope for me. Even your death and rebirth could not give me that, for Emerelle has told me that you now remember your past lives. What kind of fate is it that would first take Noroelle away from me, then make a love between us impossible? Do I always have to be the one to stand aside? Sometimes I feel like I'm a prisoner myself, but there is no one to come to rescue me." She began to cry, and the sight of her tears hurt Nuramon. All at once, Obilee seemed so fragile, so unlike the strong warrior woman he knew her to be from the battle for Firnstayn.

Nuramon gently closed his arms around her. He stroked her hair and her back. He whispered in her ear, "Obilee, if we win tomorrow, then it will mean the start of a golden age for Albenmark. I know that you will find your happiness then. Your purpose. But I am not it. You are not to blame for that. It is my love for Noroelle. You are an enchanting woman, and if I knew nothing of Noroelle, then I would be overcome by your loveliness, your golden hair, your eyes as green as the sea in Alvemer, your beautiful lips. It would be easy to say that you are like a sister or a friend to me, and no more. But it would be a lie. I feel much more for you than that . . . but I feel even more for Noroelle."

She stepped back from his embrace. "That's all I wanted to hear, Nuramon. I know I cannot stand against Noroelle. I know there is no hope for my love. But to know that I am more to you than just a friend is a gift I did not dare to wish for. It is like a moment just for me."

Nuramon grasped Obilee's hands in his. "Yes, this moment is yours." He stroked her cheek and embraced her again. Then he kissed her lips. He felt her go weak and let herself fall into his arms. He was sure she had never given herself to a man. When he took his lips from hers, Obilee's face was so close that he could taste her soft breath. The slightest gesture from her, one seductive word, and he would not be able to resist the temptation.

She smiled, then softly bit her lip. "Thank you, Nuramon" was all she said. And finally, she drew away.

THE START
OF THE BATTLE

Nuramon, on Felbion, rode to meet his forces. Wengalf had divided his massive dwarven army into two halves and positioned the Alvemer swords between them. Together, they formed the main fighting force. Nomja's archers were on the flanks, and the mounted troops were assembled some distance away. He himself would have to decide where the riders would be deployed.

He reached the small circle of commanders gathered in front of the dwarves' catapults. In their faces, Nuramon clearly saw that there was bad news.

"Good that you are here," said Nomja. "Our scouts have reported that the main army is marching in our direction. More than fifty thousand soldiers." She pointed to the chain of hills in the distance; the enemy would come from that direction.

Nuramon could not imagine how many humans that was. His own army numbered less than fifteen thousand.

"The largest force they have ever mustered in one place," Nomja went on. "And our fertile land is feeding them, as well."

Nuramon had heard that the humans in the land beyond the Shalyn Falah had felled entire forests to build barracks for the soldiers. The cleared regions had then been turned into fields that provided the invaders with everything they needed to survive.

"The land between the gorge and the forest is far too narrow to hold fifty thousand, and they won't be willing to fight in the forest," said Nuramon.

"The warriors from Yaldemee are securing the forest," said Lumnuon, who was in Nuramon's clan. The evening before, Lumnuon had visited him in his chamber.

Nuramon looked out to the plain and nodded. This was the right place for the Tjured knights to break through. He turned to Nomja.

"You told me that when they fight in the open, they always send their mounted troops in first. How have you defended against them?"

"With bows and arrows. They can't do much against that. But they are arrogant and not easy to force into a retreat. If they come now in such numbers, the archers alone won't be able to save us."

Nuramon turned to the dwarven king. "Wengalf, I suspect you will want to engage the enemy in dragon shell," Nuramon said, referring to a formation where a troop protected itself with shields on every side and also from above. "Do you still have the pikes you used to use against the dragons?"

"Of course. What do you want us to do?"

"Stop the horsemen like you once stopped Balon."

Wengalf grinned.

Then Nuramon turned to Nomja. "Your archers will thin out the ranks of the riders, then Wengalf can take over the rest."

"What do those of us from Alvemer do in the middle?" asked an elf woman named Daryll. She was Obilee's second-in-command and had only reluctantly accepted Nuramon as their commander.

"The dwarves will give you partisans," Nuramon explained. "Make sure the enemy horsemen get a good look at them. They will avoid you and try to attack the dwarves instead, but they will only see their pikes when it is too late." Nuramon turned to Nomja again. "You will need to shoot at the flanks of the horsemen. None can be allowed to get through."

Then Mandred spoke up. "And what do we do?"

"You and your Firnstayn riders will wait out of sight in the hollow on the right flank. As soon as the enemy is close enough, you will attack from that side. On the other side, I'll be leading the Alvemer horsemen to do the same."

Nomja nodded with approval. "My mounted archers will accompany you."

Lumnuon spoke again. "We of the Weldaron clan will protect our kin."

Nuramon clapped the young elf on the shoulder. "Nomja will be a good reinforcement for us."

Wengalf turned to Nuramon. "An excellent plan. When the battle starts, I will advance with my soldiers step by step. The dragon shell will take in an ally but impale any enemy that stands in front of it. Let's get to work. May destiny be on your side, Nuramon."

Wengalf and his men returned to their forces. Only Alwerich remained behind. "My friend, don't put yourself too far into the firing line," he warned. "Think of what you stand to lose. Here. Something every real commander ought to have." He handed Nuramon a leather object, a tube sealed at both ends with glass.

"What is it?" he asked the dwarf.

"A telescope," Alwerich replied. "You have to hold it up to your eye." The dwarf pointed to the end that was closed with a smaller disk of glass.

Nuramon did what Alwerich said and was amazed. Through the tube in his hand, he could see things that were far away as if they were very close. He saw the dragon banner of the dwarves right in front of him. When Nuramon lowered the tube, he had to blink. "Why haven't we elves ever come up with something like this?"

"Because it's so hard for you to admit that even your fine senses have their limits," Alwerich replied with a smile as he turned to leave. "Look after your hide."

"Thank you, Alwerich. And take care of your own."

Alwerich went after his king. His face showed the concern he felt for his friend.

"Let me take a look," Mandred demanded, and Nuramon handed him the tube.

While Mandred was busy with the telescope, Nuramon sent Lumnuon back to his clan. They were to assemble on the left flank.

Apart from Mandred, only Nomja still stood with him.

"That was a good war council," Nomja said. "Your fears are unfounded. You are a good leader . . . Before you came, many here were afraid."

"The dwarves certainly had no fear, and the Firnstayners don't know what the word means."

"Believe me, my Fjordlanders know fear," said Mandred now, and his voice was bitter. "But we will fight. My men know that if we lose today, then there won't be anywhere else to run to. They will win, or die. Your plan is good, Nuramon, and I'm sure your resolve left its mark on the other commanders."

"You probably mean my ignorance," the elf replied.

Mandred grinned, but Nomja shook her head. "Whatever it was, the commanders will take your confidence back with them to their own troops."

"Do you think we can win this battle?" he asked her quietly.

Nomja looked over at the dwarves. "Wengalf seems very confident. And I have the feeling he'll have a few more surprises under his dragon shell."

Mandred handed Nuramon the telescope. "That thing is really a marvel. Could you maybe ask your dwarf friends if they've got another one? That would be perfect for spotting game."

Nuramon laughed. "When the battle is over, I'll ask Wengalf."

"Good enough, my friend." Mandred held his hand out to Nuramon.

Nuramon grasped his forearm. The jarl's hold was firm. "Mandred, I know you Firnstayners are pigheaded, but don't put yourself too far into the firing line. We only have to hold them back long enough. Then everything is won."

"I'm not going to do anything stupid. Just make sure you watch your own back. Since the fight with the Devanthar, I owe you a life, and out on the right flank, I'm too far away to come and help you."

Nuramon smiled. "If your Luth is on our side, then I'll meet you in the middle of the enemy. Then you can save my neck."

"It's a deal," said Mandred. He climbed onto the back of his mare and rode away.

Nuramon followed him with his eyes as he trotted off. The jarl only had this one life. At least, people said that humans were never reborn. Nuramon was worried about his friend and feared his death as much as he feared his own. He did not know if Mandred would accompany them to the Other World, but he would not be surprised if the jarl accepted the queen's offer and stayed in Albenmark among his own people.

"Come, Nuramon," said Nomja. "Our troops are waiting."

Together, they went to where their horses stood. Nuramon was about to mount Felbion when he saw his bow hanging on the saddle. Previously, he had watched how the archers used their bows. The elven soldiers had strung their bows with new bowstrings, as if the string were the life and the bow itself the immortal soul. They took care to repeat the ritual and take a new string before every battle, in the way that each new life stretched across the one soul. But for Nuramon, it was different. His life and his soul were now one, because he remembered everything that had happened. And his bow and its bowstring were like a signpost that had shown him which way he had to go. But now they had played their role. Nuramon thought for a moment, then came to a decision. He took the bow from where it hung on the saddle and went to Nomja. She was already in her saddle. "Here, Nomja. I would like to give you this."

"What?" She looked at him in astonishment. "Why?"

"For what you did during the sea battle . . . Besides, the best archer should be the one to carry this bow."

She took the bow from him only hesitantly. "I would be a fool to turn down such a gift. Thank you."

Nuramon climbed onto Felbion, and he and Nomja rode side by side to the left flank. The riders of his clan were waiting there for him. Each was armed with a short sword and a long sword. The Alvemer riders had positioned themselves on the right of Nuramon's people. They carried short lances and were also armed with long swords. Nomja stayed beside Nuramon and approached them from the left, staying at one side of her small cavalry. Nuramon could see the wonder on their faces when they saw the bow she was carrying. They had short bows, which were easier to use from horseback, and swords for close-quarters fighting.

The waiting seemed to go on and on. At irregular intervals, messengers came to Nuramon and reported that at the Shalyn Falah and in other places, no fighting had yet taken place. Then finally word came that the enemy would soon appear over the hills. Nuramon's heart was beating hard. Was he afraid? Did he fear that the sheer numbers of their enemy would crush them and that his little plan would fail miserably?

Then he saw the white banners rising above the ridges. He did not have to look through Alwerich's telescope to know that the dark patch in the center of their standard was the black tree of the Tjured.

The first of the enemy came into view. They appeared along the entire length of the chain of hills and streamed slowly down the other side. Row upon row of soldiers followed them.

Nuramon took the telescope and peered through it. At first, all he saw was silver and gold, but then he recognized the soldiers. It was said that most of their enemies came from the wilds of Drusna. Their armor was forged completely of metal and made their shoulders look broad. Their helmets gleamed silvery in the sunlight. But the gold Nuramon saw was their faces, for they were wearing masks. Nuramon gasped in shock at the sight. The masks showed the face of Guillaume, which instantly recalled Noroelle to his mind. Nuramon swung the telescope to the left and right, and wherever he looked, he saw the face of the woman he loved.

More and more soldiers came marching over the line of hills. The first row had already reached the bottom of the valley. From the left flank rode the enemy cavalry, re-forming in front of the infantry. Their faces, too, were hidden by golden masks. Nuramon felt almost breathless. Cavalryman or foot soldier, any enemy he faced would be wearing the face of Noroelle. And now he had to watch as their enemy assembled in front of the hills and prepared their attack. What an army. The horsemen alone would have been a worthy adversary.

Slowly, the enemy troops advanced, and Nuramon realized that the elves around him were growing restless. Nomja leaned over to him. "We have never faced this many humans before."

"But we have a decisive advantage," Nuramon replied. "For us, this is the last fight of all. We will sacrifice everything if we have to. But for them, this battle is just one of many. They think that if they do not win today, then they will have other opportunities in the future. They are in for a surprise. And do not underestimate the dwarves."

Nomja nodded and said nothing.

In the meantime, the enemy had advanced to within perhaps eight hundred paces, and there they stopped. Between the gorge and the forest there now stood a sea of soldiers, and it was a matter of moments before the tide came rushing at them.

The enemy cavalry was already moving again. At first, they trotted slowly, but then they came faster and faster until they were in a flat gallop and advancing across a wide front. There were more than a dozen rows of them, and they carried their lances high. The earth shuddered beneath their horses' hooves.

"Be ready," Nomja called to her soldiers. Her archers and riders strung arrows on their new bowstrings. "We fire on your command," she said to Nuramon and raised her hand. Immediately, the archers took aim.

The riders were still around two hundred paces away when Nuramon sensed Nomja growing restless and watching him from the corner of her eye.

"Fire!" Nuramon shouted.

Nomja swung her hand down, and hundreds of bows clacked, sending their hissing arrows flying. A deadly hail rained onto the enemy cavalry.

Nuramon could not see how things were on Mandred's side, but directly in front of him, the enemy's flank collapsed. Horses and riders hit the ground and were either trampled or finished off by more arrows. The survivors tried as best they could to get away from the archers and pushed toward the center of the battlefield, because at least from the dwarves nothing was being fired at them. Some decided that retreat was the better course, which deepened the enemy formation.

Nomja had set an arrow on Nuramon's old bow and fired. The archers sent wave after wave of arrows against the cavalry, but still the stream of riders kept coming, surging forward so powerfully that Nuramon began to fear for the dwarves.

A glance behind the cavalry showed him that the foot soldiers were following, though they were still some distance back. He drew his long sword and raised it high. "Follow me, my Albenkin! For Albenmark!" he yelled. Then he charged, and his people followed him.

Not much farther and the cavalry would be on top of the dwarves. Nuramon waited for Wengalf's men to do something. It looked almost as if no army stood there at all, just an enormous platform made of shields, like something thought up by some clever strategist to give his enemies the impression of soldiers where none actually stood. Fifty paces from the dwarves, the Tjured knights lowered their heavy lances. Twenty paces, and they were still riding at full speed, as if nothing could stop their advance. Ten paces. Then it happened. From between the shields of the dwarves, quick as lightning, the partisans shot out. They turned the spear points so that the prongs of the hilt stood horizontally and, with a quick jerk, angled them upward. Across the entire front, the enemy riders hurtled onto the blades. Nuramon saw a few riders actually manage to rein in their horses, but the riders behind them forced them onto the lances. Several horses leaped over the lethal wall and disappeared into the ranks of dwarves. The cavalry as a whole was stopped as if it had charged headlong into a fortress wall. The enemy riders in the rear were jammed among those ahead, unintentionally pushing them on.

Before the enemy could reorient itself, Nuramon and his fighters were on them. He raised his sword, but as he was about to bring it down on the nearest enemy soldier, the man looked up at him, and Nuramon saw only the face of Noroelle. Nuramon wanted to spare him, but the man attacked. It was as if Noroelle herself were striking at him, punishing him for his failure. The man's blade grazed his armor at the shoulder, and then Nuramon had ridden past.

Slowly, their advance ground to a halt, and they found themselves in the crush of the melee. All around him, the killing and the dying had started long moments before, but Nuramon was unable to strike at the enemy. His clan surrounded him and protected him on all sides, and all he could do was stare as if hypnotized into the faces of their foes.

Then Lumnuon was cut on one leg by a sword, and he cried out in pain. Nuramon looked into the enemy soldier's masked face. When the man raised his sword to swing at Lumnuon's head, rage overcame Nuramon. He lashed out with his long sword. The blade penetrated the enemy soldier's breastplate. When Nuramon jerked the blade from the man's body, his foe collapsed in the saddle.

Suddenly, Nuramon was thrown from Felbion's back. He hit the ground hard. Above him, he saw one of their masked adversaries raise his arm to strike.

Nuramon rolled aside and jumped to his feet. He parried two slashes from the enemy, then feigned an attack at the man's head. At the same time, he drew Gaomee's sword with his left hand and stabbed the blade into the man's throat. Nuramon quickly spun around and realized that he was encircled by his clan. He turned his attention back to the Tjured soldier, who was lying on his back and fighting for air.

Nuramon leaned down over the dying enemy and tore away his mask. Beneath it appeared the blood-flecked face of a young man looking back at him with pure contempt. The man spat blood at Nuramon, and his hate-filled face froze like that forever.

AT THE
SHALYN FALAH

With his armored gauntlets, Ollowain gave Farodin a ringing clap on the shoulder. "That was the last buckle."

Farodin straightened up a little clumsily. The armor was lighter than he had expected, but it would still seriously restrict his maneuverability.

Ollowain stepped down the row of armored elves. They were twenty in all, and each one wore smooth, polished armor, masterfully worked, the rounded steel plates able to deflect any spear.

"Remember to keep your head *down* when we attack," Ollowain shouted, impressing the point on his troops. "The most vulnerable point is the eye slit in your helmet. The humans know that, so keep your head down."

"Do they have troops on horseback?" asked an elf to the left of Farodin. His voice sounded metallic behind the closed visor.

"I'll be frank. Since midday yesterday, none of our scouts have returned. We have been fighting them too long. They know all our ruses." He pointed up to the sky, where the silhouettes of three birds of prey could be seen carving wide circles in the sky. "They have trained kestrels to hunt the flower faeries. Our scouts knew the danger, and they still went out without hesitation. Let the brave hearts of our little sisters be an example to you."

Farodin could hardly believe what he was hearing. How far had things come in Albenmark if they were sending flower faeries to war?

"Keep at least two paces between you and the next man," Ollowain continued. "You do not want to be knocking in your neighbor's skull."

Orgrim came down the path toward them. "They're advancing," he bawled. "Are you ready?"

Ollowain raised his enormous two-handed sword. "Ready," he called, and he turned back one last time to the armored elves. "Forget everything you've ever learned about an honorable fight. Our enemies know no mercy. They will not be taking prisoners. Kill as many of them as you can. And stay away from the ones with halberds."

Farodin lifted the mighty sword leaning against the rock wall in front of him and closed the visor on his helmet. He did not want the troll king to recognize him. There was nothing he had to say to the reborn murderer of Aileen, least of all at the place where the woman he loved had died.

The small troop of elves marched up the last section of the path to the cliff top, passing the burned remains of wooden watchtowers. The Albenkin had retaken this position at the top of the cliff from the Tjured knights only two days earlier. They had paid for it with rivers of blood.

The number of defenders they still had to hold the steep path winding down behind them to the Shalyn Falah was ridiculously small. Seven hundred trolls each armed with a huge shield and club, four hundred elven archers, and around three hundred gnomes with crossbows. The fort on the far side of the bridge was manned only with the wounded and with kobolds, who were too small to fight humans in open battle. This was Albenmark's last stand.

"The humans are going to be damned surprised when we attack them," said Ollowain in a cheerful mood. He had fallen back to Farodin and now marched at his side.

"I must admit that I'm surprised myself," Farodin replied. "Twenty madmen charging a battle line of thousands of humans. Did you perhaps slip something into the wine last night when you told me your plan and I said I liked it?"

Ollowain pushed up his visor and grinned broadly. "I thought about doing something to the wine, but then I told myself, anyone insane enough to attack a troll fortress with no more than a single human at his side, well, someone like that is going to love today's plan."

A gap opened up in the ranks of the trolls to let the armored elves pass through. In front of the trolls, the archers had taken their positions. The entrance to the steep path was defended in a wide semicircle by rows of sharpened posts rammed into the earth at an angle. The obstacle worked well against cavalry, but it would not stop an infantry attack.

In front of the weak lines of their defense, the land sloped down and was cut by broad gray bands of rock. The forest that had once stood here had disappeared, and even the tree stumps were gone. Sallow grass was all that grew there now. The stone circle of Welruun lay just a few hundred meters away from their positions. Farodin swallowed. For a moment, he saw Aileen's pale face in his mind's eye . . . the dark blood welling from her lips.

"Stay low," Ollowain ordered.

Farodin obeyed. When they crouched, they were harder for the enemy to see clearly. It was vital that they manage to take the humans by surprise.

A little more than a quarter of a mile away, the Tjured soldiers were marching up the hillside. Their long pikes stood like a forest over their heads. Drums and pipes sounded from their ranks. It was a surprisingly cheerful melody, nothing like a battle song. The pikemen were marching up the slope in time. They wore high helmets and shimmering, polished breastplates, exactly like the soldiers Farodin and his companions had seen on the ice close to Firnstayn.

"Positions! Spread out!" Ollowain shouted. Concealed behind the archers, the elves in their polished armor now formed a single line from left to right, taking care to keep their distance from one another.

Farodin's mouth was completely dry. Mesmerized, he watched the army of advancing men. Like a rising tide, their battle rows parted around the stone blocks on the hillside, then closed again on this side. There were thousands of them. Their mass alone would be enough to drive the defenders back over the edge of the cliff.

Sharp commands rang out along the rows of pikemen. The first five rows lowered their pikes, and the elven archers began their deadly handiwork. The air was filled with the whirr of arrows and the sharp clacking of the gnomes' crossbows. Dozens of the advancing soldiers were cut down, but the gaps in their ranks were filled instantly by men from the rows behind.

The enemy forces were only a hundred paces away. Farodin could see the crossbow bolts punch round, bloody holes in the humans' breastplates.

Only eighty paces. The rhythm of the drums quickened. The pipes fell silent. The entire column began to march faster.

"Attack!" cried Ollowain. The blond elf closed the visor of his helmet. Farodin raised his two-hander. The archers made room for the armored elves to pass, and the gnomes, who had formed a crouched firing line in front, retreated.

Farodin's hands were shaking. He lifted the two-handed sword high over his head and leaned forward like a raging bull. Absolute madness. Thousands of Tjured soldiers were standing in front of them, and they were attacking with twenty.

Still forty paces.

Farodin began to run. The pikes of the first row jutted a good six paces ahead of the men holding them. Behind them came four more staggered rows of steel. He saw unrest spread through the front ranks. The pikes were angled now, coming together in bundles at the points where the elves would hit the soldiers.

The force of the impact was much less than Farodin had expected. Steel scraped against steel. The points of the pikes glanced off his armor. He kept his head down. Another impact and he'd made it through the second row of pikes. Piercing cries rang out. He whirled his heavy sword, and the ash-wood shafts of the pikes splintered.

Farodin felt something glance off the gorget protecting his neck, and he dared to raise his head. He was looking straight into the horrified faces of the men in front of him. Three more steps and he would be on them. A pike guard bounced off his helmet sideways. The world around him looked tiny. The narrow eye slit only allowed him to see whatever lay directly in front. Some of the soldiers had dropped their pikes and were trying to draw their daggers and short swords. A man with a wide-brimmed hat was fumbling with a strange rod. Suddenly, there was a loud bang, and white smoke plumed from the hollow rod. Farodin's heavy weapon sliced through armor, flesh, and bone. The blade of the two-hander was a pace and a half long, and nothing could resist the elven steel. As fearsome as a unit of pikemen might be on the advance, they were extremely vulnerable once you got past the points of their weapons. The officers in the rear kept a sharp watch to make sure no man dropped his pike, but it took two hands to hold the heavy, ungainly weapon. And anyone drawing a short sword had little room to swing it in the tightly packed formation. The points of the long spears simply glided uselessly off Farodin's armor. Like a reaper in the wheat, the elf sliced his way through the rows of the pikemen. Warm blood sprayed through his eye slit and ran down his cheek. He moved at the center of a chaos of desperate screams, tearing metal, splintering bone.

Ahead, Farodin saw the glittering blades of halberds. With its long three-edged spearhead, wide axe blade, and hook at the back of the blade, the weapon was designed solely to strike fear into armored enemies. The three-edged point, if it met a surface at the right angle, could penetrate even the best armor. The blade was heavy and strong enough to slice through any helmet or shoulder plate, and with the hook, a soldier could pull an enemy's feet out from under him, then stab the spike through his visor.

Farodin's sword separated the head from the shoulders of a man in front of him. The elf was not targeting individual soldiers. He simply swept the sword in a wide, powerful arc, and in the press of bodies, it was difficult to escape its deadly circle.

Someone clutched at Farodin's leg and tried to pull him to the ground. The elf glanced down without breaking off his attack. A wounded Tjured soldier had his arms wrapped around Farodin's left leg. Farodin rammed his armored boot into the man's face. He felt the soldier's teeth break. The man let go of his leg and rolled away.

Something glittering came down quickly toward Farodin, and he dodged the halberd's blade just in time. A squad of halberdiers had pushed their way forward to him through the formation of pikemen. Half of the halberdiers held their weapons low and tried to get to his legs with the spearheads and hooks.

Farodin lowered his head. Something hit him on the shoulder, and his left arm was suddenly half numbed with pain. He jumped forward. His heavy sword flew. It destroyed one soldier's helmet and buried itself deep in the chest of the next.

He felt a hook sit firmly behind his left heel. He tried to lift his foot at the same time as several spearheads hit him in the chest. The points glanced off to the sides, but the impact knocked him off balance.

He fell backward. The sword was torn from his hands. He tried to roll to one side, but a foot planted itself on his breastplate and pressed him to the ground.

Over Farodin slipped the shadow of a falcon gliding high in the cloudless, turquoise sky of Albenmark. Then a three-edged spearhead sparkled in the sunlight and came down.

HELPLESSNESS

In the heat of the battle, Nuramon barely had a moment to catch his breath. He had lost sight of Felbion in the turmoil. After being pulled from his saddle three times, he decided he felt more secure on the ground. He had been wounded twice on his arms and once on his shoulder, and he could only raise his right arm with a great deal of pain. He felt warm blood flowing over his skin.

His plan had not worked perfectly. They had spent too long battling the cavalry and had not completely broken the enemy's superior numbers. Nuramon could still hear the raw screams of humans struck by elven arrows, certainly, but he could not say exactly where the screams were coming from. In the melee, he had lost his orientation, and everything in him was now focused on surviving.

High overhead, he saw stones flying. That could only mean one thing: the infantry were now so close that the dwarves' catapults could target them.

He looked around. His own relatives and the elves of Alvemer were fighting bravely and proving yet again that an elven warrior is as good as two humans.

A dizziness came over him then, quickly followed by pain. He stumbled, tried to find his footing, but felt his senses fading. Suddenly, arms were under him, holding him up, and through blurring eyes, he saw a face. If it was the mask of Guillaume, then it meant the end had come.

"Nuramon!" someone yelled, and the sound of his name startled him. He narrowed his eyes and saw Lumnuon. "Warriors of the Weldaron clan! To me!" the elf cried. "Hang on! We'll protect you." But whatever his young relative said next, Nuramon did not hear it. The fear of death filled him. There was only one thing he could do. He began to speak his healing spell, casting it on himself. His injured arm cramped immediately; it felt as if someone were tearing the meat from his bones. Then the pain took over his entire body. The elf clenched his teeth until his jaw hurt. Suddenly, something cold hit him in the face, and he opened his eyes at the shock of it. Above him, he saw Lumnuon. The warriors of his clan were still in a protective circle around him. Lumnuon felt Nuramon's arm. "Did you heal yourself?" he asked.

Nuramon nodded fitfully and gasped for air. Lumnuon helped him to his feet. Beside him, one of his fighters fell to the ground, struck down by the enemy. Rage overcame Nuramon. He finally managed to shake off the paralysis that had come over him since he had been forced to look into Guillaume's face a thousand times. He reached for his swords and leaped into the gap left by the fallen soldier just as an enemy knight's sword swung down. Lightning fast, he crossed his blades over his head and caught the knight's sword on them. A swift kick sent the man to the ground, and Nuramon jumped after him and stabbed him in the side. After cutting down two more of the Tjured soldiers, he raised his long sword and screamed to his clan, "Weldaron!" His people took up the name of their clan's founder. They drove the enemy back on all sides, joined forces with fellow fighters, and battled their way through to the dwarves.

The children of the Darkalben had not yet opened up their dragon shell formation. They were advancing only gradually. Piles of corpses and horse cadavers disappeared beneath their shields as if the mass of dwarves were some sort of vermin that fed on the meat of the dead.

Yelling from thousands of throats broke through the noise of the battle. The main mass of the enemy must have reached them.

"To me!" called Nuramon. "Regroup!" His comrades fell back a short way and reassembled around Nuramon. The few on horseback were to his left, the rest on the right.

There they were. Uncountable Tjured fighters pouring into the battle, flowing like floodwater over the land, and filling the gaps in the battle lines.

Nuramon felt like he had the previous day, when he rode first to meet the dwarven army, then returned on foot toward the elven cavalry, but now his fear was mixed with other feelings. He saw how the dwarves' dragon shell array split into two, as if to silently signal him to go between them. Nuramon gave his people a sign and pulled back into the shelter of the dwarves' formation.

The infantry would roll over them mercilessly. They were within fifty paces now. For the Firnstayners, it was too late to join the battle line.

Nuramon raised his long sword high in the air and cried "Albenmark!" as loud as he could. His own clan and the elves of Alvemer returned his cry. The enemy was within twenty paces when Nuramon lowered his sword and screamed, "Attack!" But his battle cry was lost in the roar that sounded at that moment to the left and right of him.

The dwarves' dragon shell split open. The shield bearers in the first rows advanced, drawing their short swords as they moved. The partisan wielders followed them, and they in turn were followed by more and more of the dwarves, who lowered their shields in front of their chests and charged the human horde. It was like a metamorphosis. The huge war beast broke apart, transforming into a sea of dwarven fighters.

The advance of Wengalf's troops left an equally strong impression on the enemy. Fighters in the front lines slowed their step, and their battle cries fell silent. And as the first of their foes came to a stop, the two armies met, and Nuramon thrust far into the rows of the enemy. For now, the fear of dying had disappeared.

DENTS AND TOBACCO

A shield the size of a door darkened the sky overhead and deflected the blade of the halberd. "Cut the bastard apart," bawled a familiar voice. A strong arm took hold of Farodin and helped him to his feet. "Looks like you're still in one piece." Orgrim grinned broadly. "That was for saving me and my ship in the fjord."

The elf blinked, rather dazed. "How . . . did you recognize me?"

"Ollowain did me a favor. He painted a white cross on the back of your helmet so I was able to stay behind you when you broke through the pikes."

A dull pain throbbed in Farodin's left shoulder. One of the plates of his armor had been dented and was pressing into his skin. He could barely raise his left arm. "You can do me another favor, Orgrim. Unbuckle my left shoulder piece and take it off."

The king held up his huge, meaty hands in Farodin's face. "You don't really think these fingers can open the pretty buckles on elven armor, do you?"

Farodin stretched and swore. He could not take off the armor alone. He looked around. On every side lay dozens of the dead.

"Can you walk under your own steam?"

"At least I don't need a troll to carry me," Farodin replied in annoyance. The pain in his shoulder was getting worse.

The trolls' attack had repelled the pikemen some distance. Their broad backs blocked Farodin's view of the progress of the battle. The infernal clamor of the fighting continued.

"How do we stand?"

Orgrim spat on the ground. "There are a hell of a lot of humans who won't be boasting about their heroic deeds at home anymore. We've pushed them back." He waved to a troll from his staff, and a moment later, a long-drawn-out note sounded from a signal horn. "Their cavalry is regrouping at the base of the hill. We should pull back before they start their counterattack." Without another word, King Orgrim stomped away to his men and helped cover the retreat of the troops.

Only six of the twenty who had led the attack returned to the redoubts of the archers. Ollowain was among the survivors. His armor was gouged and red with blood. The elf had removed his helmet, and his long blond hair stuck to his head in strands. "What a victory!" He pointed down the slope. In places, the dead lay so thickly that they hid the grass under them. When the trolls advanced into the breaches the elves had made in the rows of pikemen, the battle had turned into a massacre.

Ollowain unbuckled Farodin's dented shoulder plate. He pushed the padded gambeson aside and felt Farodin's shoulder. "Nothing broken. You were lucky. How does it feel?"

Farodin swung his arm in a wide circle. Now that the pressure was off his shoulder, the pain was much less. "It will pass muster, at least for fighting humans."

Ollowain pointed to one of the burned towers at the top of the steep path. "Over there is one of the gnome armorers. He'll knock the dent out of your shoulder plate, and you can put it on again. Don't take too long. When it comes to a defeat, the knights don't have long memories. They will attack again soon." With that, the keeper of the Shalyn Falah moved on, and Farodin watched him go. Ollowain joked with a few of the archers and shouted something to a troll that made the giant leer. The elven commander radiated a confidence that completely belied any possibility that they might not hold on to their positions until nightfall. And it was not yet midday.

Farodin found the armorer without difficulty. The gnome was a talkative old man with a white beard heavily flecked with chewing tobacco. He took his time knocking the dent out of the armor. He talked about anything and everything, but not the war. It seemed the old man was doing his best to lose himself in his work and preserve at least a little bit of everyday life. Finally, he spat on the shoulder plate and polished it on his sleeve. As he buckled it back onto Farodin's armor, he looked at the elf, and there was deep concern in his milky brown eyes. "Will we hold the bridge?"

Farodin had no desire to lie to the old man. "I don't know." He looked back down the slope. The humans had re-formed in new lines.

"Hmm" was all the old gnome said. Then he ducked and produced a crossbow from beneath his workbench. "The queen was always loyal to my people." The armorer could not hide his fear. He blinked nervously and stroked the stock of the weapon repeatedly. "One good thing about the humans. There's always so many of 'em that not even an old, half-blind armorer can miss."

"May I accompany you to the battle line?" Farodin asked him in a serious tone.

The gnome looked up at him in surprise. "But you're a famous elf hero. What do you want with me?"

"No one has told me where I am supposed to fight in the next battle. I have never fought at the side of a hero of the gnomes. If you don't mind, it would be an honor to fight at your left hand. What is your name?"

"Gorax." The old man pulled out a dark-brown bar of chewing tobacco from behind his belt. "An elf asking a gnome if he can fight at his side. Wondrous times we live in. Can I offer you some of this? Keeps the head clear." He offered Farodin the tobacco.

The elf took the bar and bit a small chunk off the tough mass. The tobacco burned his tongue and spittle quickly collected in his mouth. He felt like spitting the little nub straight out again, but he pushed it into his cheek with his tongue and handed the bar back to Gorax. "A clear head is something we can certainly use."

At the foot of the hill, the drums started beating and the pipes piping again. The soldiers of Tjured were on the advance.

DEATH AND REBIRTH

Nuramon looked down at the body of the young warrior as if mesmerized. Lumnuon had fought better than he, but there he lay on the ground at Nuramon's feet, staring up from empty eyes. Nuramon had not even seen him die. Lumnuon had suffered many cuts on his arms and legs, and his face was torn. But it was another wound that had killed him. Someone had cut his throat.

Nuramon was overcome with fury at the sight of the dead young man. He looked around, caught sight of an enemy soldier viciously attacking an elf who was only able to parry the man's blows with difficulty. Nuramon came up behind the soldier and ran him through with his long sword. Then he tore off the man's mask and pushed him to the ground. The elf he had helped thanked him. Before Nuramon could reply, a Tjured knight attacked from the right. Nuramon jerked Gaomee's sword up and parried the man's blow. He buried his long sword in the enemy's chest. The man froze in surprise, then his arms went slack, and Nuramon slid his blade free.

More and more soldiers threw themselves at the elves. With every enemy Nuramon cut down, he seemed to attract the attention of more. Or were the fighters of his clan, fighting around him, weakening?

"Behind you!" shouted an elf's voice from one side.

Nuramon glanced over his shoulder and, from the corner of his eye, saw a soldier reaching back to strike. Before Nuramon could move, he knew that the enemy blade would find its mark. As he swung around, he was already bracing for the pain. But it did not come. His own sword slammed into the human's helmet, penetrating the steel. At the same time, Nuramon realized why his foe's blade had not injured him. In front of him, a dwarven fighter in shining silver armor doubled over and fell to the ground. Nuramon recognized the armor. He turned the dwarf onto his back and looked down into Alwerich's face. His friend gazed up at him with an agonized smile.

"Alwerich!" a familiar voice shouted, and Wengalf came to them with his soldiers. "Form a wall of shields." The dwarves followed their king's order.

Alwerich was very pale. The sword had gone into him below his chest. Blood swelled from the fresh wound. "You can't die yet," said the dwarven warrior, his voice weak. "You have to get to Noroelle. I will be reborn."

Nuramon shook his head in disbelief. "Why didn't you think of Solstane?"

"She will understand. Take this gift from me, and never forget your old . . . your old . . ." His head sank onto his chest. It looked as if he had fallen into an exhausted sleep. But he had stopped breathing, and his heart no longer beat. Alwerich was dead.

Nuramon kissed his dead ally's forehead. "I will never forget you, old friend." It was a painful parting, even though the dwarf would be reborn. First Lumnuon, now Alwerich.

Nuramon wondered if he should still try to heal him as he had healed Farodin so long ago in the ice cave.

But Wengalf laid a hand on Nuramon's shoulder. "Leave him. He will be reborn a hero, and he will remember this day with pride. Now we have to turn this battle in our favor. We're doing well. Maybe we can really stop them."

One of Wengalf's soldiers pushed between the shield bearers. "My king, our fighters have beaten the enemy on this side. Their strange fire rods have been silenced forever. Should we advance? We hear from the right flank that Mandred wants to take a small squad of humans and try to break through to the heart of the enemy's army."

A fear came over Nuramon. He did not want to lose Mandred, too. There would be no rebirth for the jarl of the Fjordlanders.

Wengalf turned to the messenger. "Give the order to attack the flank on this side, but our men should fall back a short way when they reach the middle of the battlefield. We'll draw some of the enemy that way and get them out of Mandred's way."

Nuramon looked into the king's eyes. "Thank you, Wengalf."

"Come on. Take your swords. Let's put this battle behind us. I'm weary as a dog."

Nuramon nodded. Reluctantly, he let go of Alwerich's body and picked up his swords. He wanted this battle to be over, too. He turned to the few elves still on their feet. "Regroup! It's time for the final assault!"

BEHIND
ENEMY LINES

Mandred stared at the red braids lying all around him on the grass. "I'll remember all of you, my dead," he murmured and ran his hand over his smooth cheeks and scalp.

Beorn stuffed his knife back into his belt, from which a bronze signal horn also hung, and nodded with satisfaction. "You look just like one of their commanders now, Ancestor, but let me do the talking if we get stopped." A few captured Tjured fighters had worked as farmhands on Beorn's parents' farm. The bodyguard had learned the language of Fargon from them. He knew about the structure of the monastic army and even knew the horn and drum signals the enemy used.

Mandred pulled on a horseman's helmet with deep cheek plates and tugged at the broad, red belt wrapped around his waist. He had taken off Alfadas's armor with a heavy heart, but they would never fool the enemy if he wore that.

He looked across at the audacious band of Mandridians, each of them a volunteer. They had repulsed the mounted charge of the Tjured knights, but against the sheer numbers of the enemy's foot soldiers, they would not be able to win.

"I'm betting your friends advised you never to ride with me," Mandred shouted to his men. "If they did that, then you have good friends. They were right. One hour from now, anyone who rides with me will either be a hero or sit in the Golden Hall of the gods. If you live, then for the rest of your days, they'll be calling you crazy behind your back."

The men grinned, and even a few of the centaurs laughed. The centaurs from Dailos had promised him their help. Nearly a hundred of them waited for his orders. Mandred eyed his volunteers with pride. Each had donned the armor of a fallen enemy rider, and each had shaved off his beard so that the enemy would not recognize them as Northmen. Mandred wished that he could deliver a speech as inspiring as Liodred had in his royal hall. The day before, when he had spoken at the king's grave, he had repeated the best parts that he could still remember. Once again, Liodred's words had kindled the Fjordlanders' fighting spirit. The jarl looked along the rows of men willing to follow him on this suicidal ride. Most of them were terribly young.

"Appanasios?" He turned to the leader of the centaurs, a wild black-haired centaur with a broad leather sash angled across his chest. From the sash dangled six short fire rods. He also wore a quiver full of arrows buckled to his back and carried a long sword in one hand. "You and your band of cutthroats will gallop like mad behind us. Make a big show of it. Shout and shoot and act like we really are a troop of armored riders trying as hard as we can to escape." Mandred raised his right hand, which was enclosed in a beautifully worked armored gauntlet. He closed the hand into a fist, making the iron-clad fingers creak softly. "And if one of your footpads actually hits so much as a single one of my men, Appanasios, then I'll come back and ram this up your fat horse's ass."

"If you really come back, you can gladly put your gauntlet some-where else, and I'll sing a hymn to your heroism the whole time." The centaur smiled, but there was sadness in his eyes. "I'm proud to have met you, Mandred Aikhjarto."

"Let's wait and see if you're still proud when I drink you and your troop of thugs here under the table at the victory banquet tonight."

"A human that can get a centaur drunk? You dream." Appanasios laughed out loud. "Even you won't manage that, ancestor of Firnstayn."

"I've already got a drunken oak tree on my conscience," Mandred replied, and he pulled himself into his saddle. One of the new, slim swords clinked at his hip. Two leather bags hung in front of the saddle. The jarl turned around to the centaur and pointed to the sash across his chest. "How do you use those things?"

Appanasios took one of the weapons and spun it around playfully. "These, Ancestor, are wheel-lock pistols, enemy booty. You pull on this hook down here, and it shoots. It works best if you tilt it a bit. They're loaded with a little lead ball."

"Lead?" asked Mandred in surprise.

"Don't be deceived. At close range, one of these balls will go through any armor." The centaur pushed the pistol back into his leather sash.

Mandred stroked the shaft of his axe where it hung from the saddle horn. He would put his trust in more traditional weapons.

Briefly, he inspected his small troop of riders. Besides the swords and the wheel-lock pistols, some were also armed with lances. Five carried rolled banners. For Mandred, their coat of arms was new, but it was doubtless a familiar sight to the Tjured knights; the Northmen had been unfurling it for centuries in the war against their enemies.

The jarl raised his hand. "Forward, men!"

Their hooves made a dull rumble on the churned earth as the riders galloped off. The same hollow from which they had begun their first attack had served to hide them from enemy eyes a second time. Now they drove their horses up the embankment. Behind them rang the shrill war cries of the centaurs.

To their left, the battle was in full swing. Most of the enemy riders had been repelled, but the foot soldiers were putting up a hard fight against the elves and dwarves.

An arrow just missed Mandred. He leaned low over his mare's neck. At full gallop, they were making straight for the enemy's right flank. An enemy officer signaled to Mandred with his sword, pointing to a gap between two troops with fire rods. Mandred's small squad passed through the enemy's battle line while the centaurs, cursing loudly, fell back, letting loose a volley of arrows at the enemy foot soldiers as they did.

Mandred reined in his horse. Beorn, who had not left his side, raised his right arm and turned in the saddle. "Halt!" He spoke the word in a strange singsong tone, stretching the Fargon word out endlessly.

Mandred looked around suspiciously. None of the soldiers around them seemed to find Beorn's behavior at all strange. A mounted messenger dashed along the battle line and disappeared behind a small stand of trees. On his way to the Shalyn Falah? How was the battle going for Farodin?

"Two rows abreast!" Beorn commanded, and the riders formed a marching column.

Mandred pointed to a hill about half a mile behind the center of the battle line. Banners with the burned oak symbol fluttered there, and he could see a group of officers observing the course of the battle. To one side waited a group of messengers on horseback and a small detachment of halberdiers. The large sword-fighting unit that had been kept in reserve had probably just been given orders to march. The dwarves in the center of the battle were falling back. Mandred's heart nearly stopped. Perhaps his little trick had come too late. It looked as if the battle lines were collapsing. But the dwarves were just giving ground, they were not fleeing. The elves on the left flank held their position. Was that part of the dwarves' strategy, to lure the last of the enemy's reserves into the battle? Then there was at least a slight chance that they would survive his battle plan.

"March!" Beorn ordered, and the column of riders began to move. The bodyguard smiled. "I never thought we'd make it through their lines so easily."

Mandred returned his smile. "That was the easy part. The real trick will be to get out again alive."

"Was that ever really part of our plan?" asked Beorn, so quietly that the riders behind him could not hear.

Mandred did not reply. What could he say? Both of them knew very well how unlikely it was that they would survive.

They rode beside a long row of horses harnessed to carts. Some distance away, the remains of the defeated enemy cavalry had gathered in the shelter of a small patch of woods.

After a short distance, Mandred's troop left the muddy path behind them and rode in a wide curve toward the command post on the hill. At the back of the hill, out of sight of the soldiers, a banquet table had been set up. Several cooks were at work over large fires, roasting two pigs on iron spits and preparing all kinds of poultry. Mandred's mouth began to water. "Nice of them to prepare a victory feast for us."

Beorn did not smile. He pointed to an officer with a white crest on his helmet, riding down the hill toward them. "Let me speak with him, Ancestor." He waved to the riders and they fanned out from the column, forming a long line at the foot of the hill.

"What are you doing here?" the officer barked excitedly and pointed to the woods. "All mounted troops were ordered to regroup back there. When our infantry breaks through the enemy lines, you might get a chance to make up for that shambles of an attack."

"I have an urgent message for General Tarquinon," Beorn replied calmly.

"Then tell me what you have to report."

"With all due respect, I believe the general, in this case, would like to hear the news firsthand. I attacked the enemy from the rear with my riders. We discovered a huge army of trolls concealed in a hollow, ready to attack our troops on the flank if we advance any farther."

The young officer stared at him in shock. "They said we'd wiped out all but a few of the trolls. Follow me." He turned his horse and trotted up the hill.

The general and his staff were standing at a heavy oak table. On the table lay a map of the battlefield. Colorful wooden blocks seemed to be marking the positions of different divisions of their army.

Mandred and Beorn dismounted and marched toward the gathered officers. A tall, gaunt man turned to face them. His breastplate shone as if it were made of polished silver. A white cloak hung from his shoulders. The arrogance of power was reflected in the ascetic lines of his face. He had long, white hair that fell to his shoulders. "I don't think much of officers who flee at the head of their troops, Captain . . ."

"Balbion, Eminence. Captain Balbion."

The general frowned. "That name is not familiar to me."

"I was promoted just four days ago, after the battle at the white bridge, Eminence."

Mandred hated pompous blowhards like this Tarquinon. Beorn should get to the point and not waste so much time with useless babbling.

As if the general had read his mind, Tarquinon half turned and looked at Mandred. "What's that your adjutant has there? The regulations concerning cavalry armaments say nothing about axes. He must have taken it from one of those barbarians. What is his name?"

"His name is Mandred Torgridson," Mandred calmly replied, and he took a step toward the general. "*He* is the commander of the Fjordlanders, the jarl of Firnstayn. And he is here to negotiate a ceasefire with you for the day."

A smile played across the general's thin lips. The other officers at the table gazed at Mandred in surprise. Several of them reached for their swords. Tarquinon lowered his head. "I bow to your daring, Jarl."

He reached for a pistol on the map table. "That said, I despise extraordinary stupidity."

Beorn jumped forward and struck at the general's arm. Acrid white smoke poured from the pistol, and something hit Mandred in the hip, though he felt no pain. The jarl momentarily looked down at himself. His breastplate seemed undamaged. All around, the officers drew their swords.

Mandred jumped forward. His axe swung in a wide semicircle, and fine drops of blood splattered across the battlefield map. Then the general's head tumbled onto the table, throwing all the little wooden blocks into disarray.

Beorn parried a sword stroke aimed at Mandred's head. Back to back, the two Northmen faced the attacking officers. Mandred's axe smashed a thin sword, and he stabbed the point of his axe through the attacker's armor. Another officer swung, and his blade grated off the jarl's shoulder plate. Mandred half turned and smashed another officer's legs.

Suddenly, he heard the loud reports of wheel-lock pistols. Bitter white smoke blew over the hill and enveloped the fighting men. It stank of brimstone, exactly as if the Devanthar were back among them.

Mandred's axe sliced deeply into the shoulder of the young officer who had led them up the hill. The man stared at him wide-eyed, then his knees gave way.

Riders appeared through the smoke. With their long swords, they cut down the remaining staff officers and tore down the banner with the burned oak. Beorn had taken the horn from his belt and was blowing it for all he was worth. Above the heads of the horsemen, the banners of Firnstayn now unfurled. They showed a green oak on a white background. The living tree had defeated the dead. The entire army of Tjured soldiers would see the smoke rising from the command post on the hill and their enemy's flags flying. Beorn was sounding the retreat. He could already see one unit breaking from the battle line and fighting its way back.

From the side of the hill came the clash of weapons. "The halberdiers are attacking!" screamed a young Firnstayner.

Mandred pulled himself onto a riderless horse. "Drive them back," he ordered sharply. The hill could not fall back into their enemies' hands, or it would all have been in vain.

Mandred wheeled the black stallion around and rode toward the enemy. He took the reins between his teeth and pulled one of the two wheel-lock pistols from the saddle holster. Ahead of him was the formation of halberdiers. They had already cut down several of his riders. Mandred turned the weapon in his hand and hurled it into the enemy pack. One of the halberdiers cried out in surprise. Mandred would never fire a weapon that spewed the Devanthar's breath into the world, but they made good throwing clubs.

Mandred held the second pistol and drew back, ready to throw. He could still hear Beorn sounding the retreat behind him. More riders joined him, and together they formed a battle line. All of them drew their saddle pistols. As if at some silent command, the Mandridians fired simultaneously. White smoke enveloped them, and many of the halberdiers fell. The line of attackers began to disintegrate.

"Swords!" Mandred bawled over the noise. Slim swords clattered from metal sheaths.

"Charge!" The jarl spurred his stallion ahead. They were only a few paces from the Tjured soldiers. He threw the second pistol and reached for his axe.

"For Firnstayn!"

FIRE AND BRIMSTONE

Tongues of fire lashed out of the wall of white smoke down the hill. Something smacked into Farodin's breastplate. The elf picked up the projectile from the ground. It was a small piece of dark-gray metal, squashed flat. "From that distance, they won't get through any armor," said Giliath. She raised her bow and fired an arrow into the smoke.

The elf and her riders had arrived an hour earlier to reinforce the thinning ranks of defenders. Now she crouched at Farodin's side behind the massive shield of a dead troll. They had wedged the shield between two posts of one of the archers' redoubts. In a single, flowing movement, she drew a new arrow from her quiver, set it on the string, and fired. "I don't understand these soldiers. Those fire rods of theirs are absurd. In the time it takes them to load it again, I can shoot five arrows back. After the second salvo at the latest, they're so blinded by their own smoke that they don't even know what they're shooting at. They make a terrible noise, and they stink. And if their powder gets wet, they're completely defenseless. I just don't understand what they see in such nonsense."

Farodin looked at the old gnome who lay at his feet. A bloody pulp oozed from where his left eye had once been. It seemed that the balls fired from those pipes could really do some damage to someone not wearing armor.

The defenders of the Shalyn Falah had repulsed two attacks on their position, but they had paid a terrible price. More than half their fighters were dead.

The trolls stood now in the front line with the archers. They were using their huge shields to try to protect the elves from the enemy fire.

"When this is over, Farodin, I want to challenge you to a fight with practice swords. And I would be obliged if you would be good enough not to wear your ring," Giliath said.

Farodin looked at Giliath in surprise. "Are you still angry at me?"

"It was a low blow, Farodin, a downright un-elf-like trick, the way you ended our duel."

"I could not afford to get wounded back then," he replied curtly, hoping that that would close the subject. He did not think this was either the time or the place to discuss martial decency.

"I would be glad to give you the chance to restore your honor in my eyes," she replied.

This cannot be happening, thought Farodin. They were crouching under a hail of enemy fire, and Giliath was challenging him to a duel. "You've lost an eye. I'd have a big advantage."

"I've had a lot of time to practice since our last duel. And I'm quite sure I was better than you back then. It would be interesting to find out if you've improved at all."

Farodin rolled his eyes. He found himself almost wishing for the next attack so this nonsense would end. With a crack, the Tjured soldiers fired their next salvo. The elf ducked behind the shield.

"What do you think? Tomorrow at sunrise on the field in front of the palace?" Giliath asked.

Farodin sighed. "So you assume we'll still be alive tomorrow?"

"I certainly will be," she said with surprising confidence. "And I'll be sure to look after you so you also stay among the living. The word going around is that you will be going into the human world tomorrow once and for all. I'd be happy if we could settle this matter before then."

"Why does this duel matter so much to you?"

The elf woman looked at him in surprise. "It is a question of honor. You are the only one who has ever defeated me."

Farodin looked at her doubtfully. The dark strip of cloth over her destroyed eye made her look bold. *Some victories come at too high a price,* he thought.

A gnome with a large willow basket on his back came and crouched in the cover of their shield, gasping for breath. Then he took two bundles of arrows out of the basket and laid them on the ground in front of Giliath. "We're running out of fighters, but at least we have plenty of ammunition," he grumbled. "I'm supposed to tell you from Ollowain that we still have more than a hundred arrows for every archer. He expects you to fire them all at the enemy down there." The gnome flinched as the thunderous blast of the next salvo rolled up the hill. Without another word, he left them, heading away to resupply the next archers.

Giliath cut through the leather cord that bound the arrows. She refilled her quiver. "The survivors of Valemas are very grateful to you and your companions for rescuing Yulivee," she said unexpectedly. "Yulivee is completely infatuated with Nuramon. She even rebelled against the orders of the queen for him."

"What are you talking about?" asked Farodin.

Giliath looked up and gave him a cold smile. "I knew she hadn't told you about it. She was very sad that she couldn't set you free."

Farodin was slowly losing his patience. "What do you have to say to me?"

Giliath straightened up and looked him in the eye. "She led me and my fighters through an Albenpath from Firnstayn to a fortified monastery close to Aniscans. She wanted to go through a second Albenstar there and look for you, but there was a spell on the gate. We could not open it and were discovered. In the battle that followed, we burned the monastery down to its foundations. Yulivee didn't want us to do that, but these Tjured priests only understand one language. I personally think that you and your friends should know about that. I don't think she would ever talk about it herself. She feels she owes you a debt."

A ball of lead sent splinters flying from the troll's shield. Giliath raised the bow and took fresh aim at the wall of thick smoke.

The drums and pipes struck up again. A line of men with fire rods strode through the black-powder fumes and started up the hill. A second and a third line followed. Giliath swore and fired.

Farodin drew two short swords that he had taken from dead elves. The two-hander was too unwieldy to fight with in their own line of defense.

Knights armed with swords and round shields followed the men with the fire rods. Among them were some holding flaming torches, and all of them had small wooden boxes buckled over their stomachs.

A new volley cracked from the fire rods. One of the shots knocked Farodin off his feet. A deep dent had been knocked in his breastplate.

The shooters in the first row stopped and reloaded. They were marching in an open formation and did not block the soldiers coming up behind.

Arrows rained down on the attackers. Giliath fired ceaselessly, shouting the most blasphemous curses the whole time. The courage of the humans amazed Farodin. It must have been clear to them how much of their blood would be spilled in such an attack, but still they came.

When the next row of shooters stopped, Farodin crouched behind the heavy wooden shield. He was worried. Tongues of fire flashed, and more shots crashed into the wood. Farodin saw a troll get hit by several of the lead balls. It staggered a few steps and collapsed.

The elves fought desperately, doggedly, returning arrows for bullets. Salvo after salvo flew into their attackers, but nothing seemed able to stop their advance.

When they were less than forty paces away, the third row of the fire rod men jammed their forked supports into the ground, swung their heavy weapons onto them, and blew on the smoldering fuses.

"Down!" Giliath shouted, turning her bow aside and lying flat on the ground. Farodin crouched beside her. As the volley of shots flew, he heard the wood of their shield splinter. From all around came the screams of the wounded.

The elf rolled onto one side and came up again awkwardly. He saw the holes in the heavy troll shield. Slowly, he was beginning to understand why the humans were so set upon these new weapons. Between the shooters, the soldiers with the wooden boxes strapped over their bellies came running. Each man held in his hand a small, round clay flask. They ignited strips of cloth on the bottles, and a thick, oily smoke rose. Then they flung their strange projectiles at the defenders.

One of the flasks smashed against their shield. A tongue of flame shot high, and Farodin retreated before the sudden heat. Fires flared all along their defensive lines. Farodin saw a flask hit an archer. The elf was instantly transformed into a living fireball. He threw himself on the ground and thrashed and screamed, but nothing seemed able to extinguish the flames.

"Balbar's fire," Farodin whispered. "The curse of Iskendria."

"Fall back to the second line!" Ollowain's voice rose above the inferno. "Back! And catch me a few of those flasks."

Farodin and Giliath ran toward the ruins of the tower at the top of the steep path.

"Catch the flasks? Are you out of your mind? Get out of their way!" Orgrim screamed.

"We need them to light a fire on the bridge!" Ollowain yelled back.

But the spirit of the defenders had been broken. The last survivors pushed and scrambled their way down the cliff path.

The first of the humans had already reached the archers' redoubts. Swordsmen and men with fire rods pushed between the posts, and the soldiers with the flaming torches and the wooden crates came through with them.

The fire flasks were now falling in the midst of the jostling defenders. Orgrim took a small troop of trolls and tried to lead a counterattack to at least hold back the humans a little longer. Giliath, retreating at Farodin's side, fired arrow after arrow.

The elf had slid both of his swords back into their sheaths. He hurried to Ollowain. "We need that damned fire to block the bridge. We have to hold them back longer."

Suddenly, Ollowain jumped forward. His hand flew up, and he snatched one of the accursed clay flasks out of the air. He pulled out the burning strip of cloth and set the little bottle carefully on the ground. "Well, that works."

Farodin let out a tight breath. "I'd prefer to get a crate this way." He clenched his jaw and charged behind Orgrim.

At the point where the trolls were attacking, the Tjured soldiers were falling back. With the courage of desperation, Farodin threw himself into the midst of the enemy. In a deadly dance, he whirled around, blocking swords, fighting his way through a gap in the defense. A backhanded swing slashed the throat of a soldier with a fire rod who could not raise his heavy weapon fast enough to block the blade. A jab with one of Farodin's swords went through the defenses of a swordsman and stabbed him through the mouth. Farodin ducked low, jerked the blade free, and parried a second swordsman's swing. He pushed the man to the ground with his shoulder and ran him through mercilessly.

Duck, parry, strike. Blood sprayed his face. One of the fire rods cracked so close that he felt the heat of the flame from its barrel, but the ball flew wide. His mouth was filled with the taste of brimstone.

These were truly the Devanthar's kin. Farodin slit the shooter's belly open, and the man screamed and fell to his knees.

"Retreat!" bawled Orgrim. "They're cutting us off from the others!"

From the corner of his eye, Farodin saw one of the Tjured knights taking aim at the troll king. The man was too far away for Farodin to reach him in time. Instead, the elf threw one of his swords. The blade sank into the soldier's back almost to the hilt.

Farodin crouched and snatched a sword from one of the dead.

"Back, you damned berserker! You won't defeat them alone!" said Orgrim, now at his side.

One of the oil flasks shattered against Orgrim's shield. Bright flame licked at the wood. Balbar's fire sprayed onto Farodin's armor as well, but the dark flecks of oil did not burn.

Close by, Farodin saw two of the soldiers kneel down with their loathsome wooden crates. "We'll get those," he shouted to Orgrim. "Then we can pull back."

The troll king let out a curse that would have made Mandred blush. Farodin didn't care. Three sword-wielding soldiers were running at him. He intercepted the first swing and let the attacker's blade slide down his own. Then he half turned, changed his grip, and rammed his sword into the soldier's back, at the same time blocking an overhead stroke with his second sword. Orgrim's club smashed the second soldier's skull.

Farodin went at the surviving soldier with both swords. With a turning motion, he trapped the man's blade, then he stabbed past the soldier's shield into his belly.

A long leap took him within range of the men with the fire flasks, and he cut them down ruthlessly. The small wooden chests were divided inside into eight sections. Each of the sections was padded with braided straw so that the thin-walled clay flasks could be transported safely. In the first chest there were still five bottles; in the second, four. That would have to do.

Orgrim picked up one of the wooden crates. "Back to the bridge. They're overrunning everything. The best we can do is stop them at the Shalyn Falah."

Farodin nodded silently and took the second wooden crate. Ollowain was there with a few of the trolls and archers around him. He was doing his best to cover them.

Thick, billowing smoke drifted across the battlefield. From all sides came the roar of the fire rods. The elves' battle lines were in tatters.

Farodin hacked off the hand of an officer aiming a pistol at him at close range. A backhand strike hit the man in the face, above his gorget. The force of the blow smashed the man's teeth.

Another foe collapsed beside him, felled by an arrow. Farodin glanced up and saw Giliath standing beside Ollowain. He had to smile. The elf woman was probably worried he wouldn't be there for the duel they'd arranged.

Suddenly, flames hissed high in front of them. Farodin jumped to one side. For a moment, he lost sight of his companions. Then he saw Ollowain. The elf jumped forward and caught one of the fire flasks in midflight. Triumphantly, he held his booty high. As he did, a lead ball shattered both the bottle and his hand. Dark oil sprayed and ignited on the burning wick. In a moment, the flames swallowed up Ollowain's head and armor. For a heartbeat, the elf stood completely still. Then, with his uninjured hand, he drew his sword and ran screaming toward a line of soldiers about to fire.

Farodin could barely breathe as he saw what happened next. White smoke surrounded the Tjured soldiers, but none of their shots were able to stop the keeper of the Shalyn Falah. Engulfed in flames, he disappeared into the wall of smoke.

"A fighter like him comes along once in a thousand years," said Orgrim, and he laid a heavy hand on Farodin's shoulder. "Let us go before their reinforcements come."

Giliath stopped at the burned towers and, with a few more archers, covered their retreat. They had reached the highest part of the cliff. Farodin looked out over the path that snaked down to the bridge. There were fires already burning down there. No more than three hundred of the defenders were still alive, and most of them were wounded. Black with soot, exhausted, they were retreating to the fortress on the other side of the gorge.

Farodin turned around. A gust of wind dissipated the smoke covering the slope on that side. Thousands of soldiers were on the advance. Back near the stone circle, he saw men with long scaling ladders. They had lost the battle.

BATTLE'S END

Nuramon charged forward at Wengalf's side. The Tjured knights' courage failed them the moment they saw the banners of Firnstayn flying over their command post on the hill. They fell into confusion, more and more of them retreating. Then Nuramon caught sight of Mandred. It took some moments to recognize him. He wore the enemy's armor and had shaved off his beard. Surrounded by Firnstayners in captured armor, he sat atop a black stallion and carried the head of a human by its hair. Blood still dripped from the scraps of flesh dangling from the neck. "Look into the face of your general!" he shouted.

The dwarves advanced relentlessly and formed a wall of shields around Mandred and his men. The last of the enemy's resistance broke, and their attack turned into a frantic retreat.

"Mandred!" Nuramon shouted.

"My friend! See this day!" the jarl rejoiced.

Nuramon looked around warily. A lone gunman might still destroy Mandred's triumph, but the enemy were no longer trying to defend themselves. They were on the run, some cursing as they fled, swearing to come back with another army within a day. But none who heard such words were worried.

"Come anytime you like!" Mandred shouted after them. "Let us kick your asses again!"

Nuramon reached out his hand to Mandred. Sitting high on the stallion's back, he looked truly like a ruler. He grasped Nuramon's hand in his, and Nuramon looked his companion up and down for injuries. He could not tell where the blood on Mandred came from, whether it was mostly his own or that of his enemies. Mandred's armor looked undamaged. A long scrape covered his left cheek, but the jarl of the Fjordlanders seemed not to feel any pain and was beaming from one ear to the other.

"Are you injured, Mandred?" Nuramon asked, to be on the safe side.

"A scratch or two, no more."

The dwarves opened their circle to let a troop of elves through. Among them was Nomja and with her Daryll, the elf woman who led the elves of Alvemer, who had withstood the charge of the enemy cavalry in the center of the battle lines. She was leading Felbion by the reins.

Nuramon was relieved. Mandred and Nomja still lived, and his horse had survived the battle as well.

Daryll handed him Felbion's reins. "Your horse," she said. "He saved my life." The Alvemer commander told how Felbion had knocked down three enemy soldiers with his hooves and how they would otherwise have killed her.

Nuramon ran his hand over his loyal horse's mane. "You're a true hero." Felbion looked off to one side, apparently bored.

Nuramon looked at those around him. "I want to thank all of you." He turned to Nomja. "Your archers are the best in all Albenmark." And to Daryll he said, "For we elves, you were the rock that stood against the waves." Then he kneeled in front of Wengalf. "And we owe you everything. Without you, we would not have won the day."

Wengalf dismissed his words with a wave. "No, no. The greatest honor belongs to Mandred."

Nuramon looked up to Mandred and smiled. "Today, my mighty jarl, you have made yourself immortal. The Albenkin will praise your name forevermore."

"But the battle is not yet over. Who knows what's happening at the Shalyn Falah. Let us ride there." The jarl threw the enemy commander's head to one of his Mandridians. The blood sprayed wide.

A man in officer's armor came by with Mandred's mare. The jarl swung down out of the saddle and greeted his horse. But when he tried to mount, his strength failed him. The officer quickly helped him onto the saddle.

Nuramon looked around. The men and women around him were exhausted. None of them would manage the march to the Shalyn Falah today. And it would not be smart to pull all their troops away as long as the enemy was not entirely wiped out. "Well, Mandred, it looks like we will have to ride alone. The soldiers should hold their positions here."

"So be it. I'm sure Farodin can use our help. When they hear that we not only fought the enemy but sent them packing, it might be the boost they need."

Nuramon grinned. "Send a prayer to your Luth, Mandred. He was truly on our side today." He climbed onto Felbion's back and cast a final glance at the fleeing Tjured soldiers. They would still be a formidable fighting force, but without their leaders they were no more than a disorderly mob.

As Nuramon and Mandred set off for the Shalyn Falah, an oppressive feeling overcame the elf. He was sure the bridge could not have been taken yet, and Farodin had more experience than the two of them put together. But still . . .

Groups of soldiers cheered them as they rode across the battlefield. Nuramon saw the members of his clan, who waved and shouted his name excitedly. The Mandridians raised their axes and swords high in the air and called out, "Long live Mandred, jarl of Firnstayn!"

Mandred turned to him as they left the battlefield behind and said, "Now to help out Farodin, then to spend the night with two pretty girls."

"Two?" Nuramon asked.

"Yes. That was something yesterday. First I took them both and—"

"Please, Mandred. Spare me the amorous details. You can't find words that would please elven ears."

"You're just jealous because I—"

Nuramon laughed. "Enough, Mandred. Don't say what I can already imagine so clearly. It's already spoiling any other decent thought I might have. Please."

Mandred laughed. "What do you know of the poetry of two women in one night?"

"Let's just ride," Nuramon suggested. He had missed this kind of banter. He wished more than anything that Mandred could go with him and Farodin, but he knew it would be hard to drag the jarl out of a bed shared with two women.

They galloped across the grasslands. It would take them several hours to reach the Shalyn Falah. They had covered perhaps half the distance there when Mandred began to fall behind a little. When his mare started to nicker restlessly, Nuramon turned around. His friend was slumped in the saddle.

Felbion dashed back to the anxious mare and stopped next to her. With shaking hands, Nuramon took hold of his companion and tried to get him to straighten up. "Mandred!" he shouted.

The jarl woke with a start and looked around as if baffled. Then he pitched sideways and fell.

Nuramon jumped down from Felbion and turned Mandred gently onto his back.

His friend looked up at him with fear-filled eyes and pressed one hand to his belly. "I think it's more than a scratch," he whispered and let his hand fall from his body. His breastplate looked undamaged, but when Nuramon touched the wide belt around his middle, his hands came away red with blood. He tore the belt aside and discovered a round hole in the armor beneath. His fingers trembling, the elf released the buckles holding the breastplate in place. The padded linen tunic beneath was soaked with blood. Nuramon cut through the tough cloth with his dagger. The wound in Mandred's belly was full of fibrous scraps of linen. It must have come from one of those strange fire rods. Carefully, Nuramon slid one hand under Mandred's back. The shot had not left his body. "Don't you feel any pain?" Nuramon asked.

"No," said Mandred in surprise. "I'm just so . . . dizzy."

Mandred had lost a lot of blood, and Nuramon knew he would die if nothing happened. He laid one hand on the wound and began his healing spell. He expected the pain, and it came, but far less strongly than he thought it would. Then he realized that although Mandred's wound closed beneath his fingers, his magic did not reach very far inside Mandred's body. Fear rose in him. The pain disappeared, but Mandred was not healed. Just closing the wound on the surface would not help. With no way to come out, the blood was collecting inside his friend's belly. Death would be a little longer in coming, but that was all. Nuramon summoned up all his power a second time. Again, he failed.

"What is it?" he wondered aloud. Something was blocking his spell, something inside Mandred. It could only be the ball inside him. Was that the Devanthar's final evil gift to his acolytes? Perhaps such wounds could not be healed with elven magic.

"I think this is the end, Nuramon," Mandred whispered. "And what an end it is for a human."

"No, Mandred."

"You were always . . ." His eyes closed, and he exhaled, too exhausted to finish.

Nuramon shook his head. Mandred's life could not end like this. He felt for his friend's pulse. It was still there. He was just not breathing as strongly. With a huge effort, Nuramon lifted the jarl of the Fjordlands onto Felbion's back then climbed up behind him on the saddle. Then he turned and rode for the army camp in front of the queen's palace. It was closer than the Shalyn Falah.

He reproached himself as he rode. It was his fault if Mandred died now. In the battle, he had selfishly healed his own wounds and wasted too much of his power. Power he missed so sorely now that he needed it to save a friend. He would never forgive himself if Mandred had to die because of what he could not do.

Racing on at full gallop, he saw, in the distance, a glittering light rise skyward and spread like branching lightning. Was that the start of the spell they had been waiting for? Nuramon wished he could capture just a shade of that power to help him heal Mandred. In their moment of triumph, fate had come down on him and his companions with all its force. He could only hope that Farodin had not fared as poorly at the Shalyn Falah.

THE LAST RESERVE

They had had to retreat beyond the middle of the bridge. Slowly, the flames of Balbar's fire died. Along the path up the cliff stood hundreds of Tjured soldiers, waiting for the final assault. The moment the fire was out, the advance would begin.

At Farodin's side stood only Orgrim and Giliath. All the rest of the fighters, the combined remnants of the Shalyn Falah defenders, had retreated to the fortress wall beyond the bridge.

Farodin looked up hopelessly at the sky. It would be at least two hours until sunset. They could not hold the bridge that long. A light breeze was blowing, and his face was covered with spray. There was something calming about the thundering of the waterfall. The rocks descended like white veins, and the spray made the bridge as slippery as warm butter. The Shalyn Falah was just two paces wide and had no railing. On this particular day, Farodin was thankful to the long-forgotten builders for the strange bridge they had left behind. It was impossible for more than three men to stand side by side here. And anyone setting foot on the bridge would need to have a good head for heights to resist the lure of the abyss.

"Isn't it said that no blood may be spilt on the Shalyn Falah?" Orgrim shouted. The troll had to yell to make himself heard over the booming of the waterfall.

Farodin glanced down at the pale pink flecks that the spray was slowly washing away. "I asked Ollowain the same question last night. It was his opinion that the stone of the bridge would get so slick if it was covered with blood that no one would be able to cross it. But I've also heard of a prophecy that said that the day the stone of the Shalyn Falah was sullied with blood, eternal darkness would fall upon it."

"I think I prefer Ollowain's story," the troll grumbled. Blood dripped from a bandage on his arm. He still held high the heavy shield he had taken from a dying comrade.

The flames at the entrance to the bridge rose no more than a single pace now. The troops on the cliff path were starting to move.

A shot rang out. A few paces in front of them, a lead ball bounced harmlessly off the white stone.

"The idiots can't accept that we're out of range," Giliath muttered. She quietly counted the arrows she had left.

Farodin knew by heart how many it was. Thirteen. She was counting them for at least the tenth time.

At the far end of the bridge, an officer threw a heavy gray mantle over the flames, smothering them. Soldiers armed with firearms began to move onto the bridge.

Giliath aimed her bow. Suddenly, though, she laughed out loud. The soldiers had stopped. They were waving their arms and trying to send back those coming from behind.

"Their fuses and powder are wet. Their fire rods are of no use anymore."

In the confusion at the other side of the bridge, one of the soldiers lost his footing. With a piercing scream, he plunged into the gorge. Finally, the men with the fire rods pulled back. Swordsmen took their place.

Farodin swung both his swords, loosening the tension in his arms. Stepping carefully, the elf tested the slippery surface. The stone of the bridge was polished. One false step, one rash move, and he would follow the soldier who had just fallen.

A glittering ray of light sliced across the blue of the sky, then split into hundreds of streaks of lightning, but no thunder rolled across the heavens. Farodin felt every hair on his body stand on end. As the streaks of lightning faded, they left behind fine black lines, as if the sky itself were breaking apart.

The Tjured soldiers were suddenly anxious. Some fell to their knees and began to pray aloud. A single, clear voice rose above all the others. It was singing a hymn to the grandeur of Tjured, healer of all ills. Other voices joined in, until finally hundreds were singing in praise of their god.

Black fog bled through the fissures in the sky.

Farodin retreated a short distance. The queen's magic had begun. Less than ten steps in front of them, one of the fissures came down upon the bridge. The black fog was tumbling from the sky in churning cascades. As far as Farodin could see, the cracks stretched across the firmament.

The fog smothered any view of the cliff path. The soldiers' singing abruptly stopped. A wall of surging darkness cut through the middle of the gorge. The white bridge stretched away in its wide arc and ended now in emptiness.

"It is done," said Orgrim, awed.

Farodin slid his sword back into its sheath. The war was over, but he did not feel like a victor.

THE FISHERMAN

Mandred listened to the song of the nightingales. The little birds were sitting high above him among the branches of the two linden trees. A light breeze stirred the leaves. Not far away, to one side, Mandred heard the splashing of a spring. Nuramon was right. This was the most entrancing place in Albenmark.

His friend had lit a campfire and wrapped him in the horse blanket, but he still felt the cold creeping deeper into his bones, just as he had the day he climbed the Hartungscliff to warn Firnstayn about the manboar. Would everything have turned out differently if he had been able to light that signal fire?

Nuramon had sent a messenger to the Shalyn Falah and another to the queen. Mandred had seen the sky darkening and knew that the first part of the magic had worked. His people were safe. Albenmark would go on. His Fjordlanders would go in search of some raw, stormy stretch of coast, some place that reminded them at least a little of their lost homeland. He had spent almost the entire night before the battle in Queen Gishild's tent. He had spoken with her and tried to instill in her the dream of a new Firnstayn. He believed in her strength. She would be a good leader for her people.

Mandred turned his head a little to one side and watched his friend. Nuramon was just then laying a piece of wood on the fire. Bright sparks climbed into the night sky. The flames deepened the shadows on Nuramon's face. Mandred smiled. His companion had actually believed him when he said he'd spent the night before with two young and pretty Fjordlander girls.

Nuramon looked up. His eyes gleamed in the firelight when he saw Mandred's smile. "What are you thinking about?"

"The two women, and last night."

The elf sighed. "I don't think I will ever understand humans."

Mandred was almost sorry for pulling Nuramon's leg. For a moment, he was tempted to tell the elf the truth. "I'm sorry I can't go with you on your last journey." The jarl tasted something metallic in his mouth. It wouldn't be much longer now. He felt no pain. He could not move his legs; it was as if they were already dead. The tips of his fingers tingled. "Don't tell anyone that it was a stupid little lead ball that killed me. That's no death for a hero of the old mold—"

"You are not going to die yet," Nuramon protested. "I've sent the queen a messenger. She will be able to heal you. We will travel together. Like we always . . ." He faltered. "Like we almost always did."

"Don't be too hard on Farodin. He's a stubborn old mule, I know . . . but he's a friend who'd attack a troll's fortress by himself, so you . . ." Mandred sighed. All this talk was making him weak. "Where's my axe?"

Nuramon went to the horses and came back with the axe. In the firelight, the blade of the axe gleamed gold. "Give it to Beorn." Mandred's eyes closed. He plunged into the darkness. A rider was coming toward them. He heard the hoofbeats, but it was too dark where he was to recognize anything. He could see nothing. He raised his hand. He could not even see that. The ground shuddered under the horse's hooves. The rider must have been very close now, and still he could not see him. The jarl opened his eyes in fright. Farodin was kneeling beside him. He seemed frantic.

Farodin held Mandred's hand. "I was afraid you were gone, my brother. Hold on. The queen will come." Tears stood in the blond elf's eyes. Mandred had never seen Farodin weep before. "The haircut suits you, warrior. You look even meaner with your head shaved."

Mandred smiled weakly. He would gladly have given something to them. Something to remember him by, but all he had of value was his axe.

"It was good to ride with the two of you," he whispered. "You made my life rich."

Again, the impenetrable darkness engulfed him. Mandred thought of the Golden Hall of the gods. Had he earned his place beside the great heroes? He would meet Alfadas there . . . it would be good to go fly-fishing with him. He had never found the time to teach the lad properly. Was there a land beyond the halls? A land like the Fjordlands, with rugged mountains and fjords full of fish?

He had to have a quiet word with Luth. No more horns of mead . . . surely that would not apply in the Hall of Heroes.

Suddenly, the cold vanished. He was standing up to his knees in clear water. Silvery salmon were gliding slowly over the stony riverbed, swimming upstream against the current.

"So you finally came, old man."

Mandred looked up. Beneath an oak tree on the shore stood Alfadas with a fishing rod in his hand. With an easy flick of his wrist, he cast into the stream.

Not bad for a beginner, thought Mandred. *Not bad.*

THE HOLY SCRIPTURES OF TJURED:

BOOK NINETY-EIGHT:
OF THE END OF ALBENMARK

*O*ne *night, in a dream, the wise warrior Erilgar heard the words of Tjured. And these told him to lead a great attack. So he gathered to him great numbers of warriors and led them against the enemy. But behold! There they waited, the demon armies of Albenmark, and the followers of Tjured were outnumbered. But because their faith was strong, they fought bravely. The Albenfolk, though, have been treacherous since the beginning of time. They cast a spell and caused stones to fall from the sky. They cursed the horses of the faithful to make them afraid of the enemy, and they brought their dead back to life so that they might never be defeated again. But in spite of all, the followers of Tjured remained strong under the leadership of Erilgar.*

Now it happened that Erilgar found himself in difficulties, and Tjured's countenance appeared before him, and the commander was able to read what was to be done from Tjured's holy lips. Erilgar offered up a prayer, called his messengers to him, and ordered a retreat. Many resisted the order. But Erilgar spoke up, saying, "Was it not Tjured Himself who gave me the power? Did He not set me over you in the scheme of the world?" But there were many who believed they were closer to Tjured than was Erilgar. So it came to pass what must.

The truly faithful retreated, while the unbelievers stayed and fought the Albenfolk and the traitors from the Fjordlands. And on that day, Tjured Himself came down from the heavens and cast eternal darkness over the Albenfolk. Their land vanished inside an impenetrable fog. Only the land on which the faithful stood remained. And never again was one of the Albenfolk ever seen, for the Alben, the old demons, were waiting for them inside the eternal darkness. And they torment their children to this day.

FROM THE SCHOFFENBURG EDITION
VOLUME FORTY-FIVE, FOLIO 123 R.

THE LAST GATE

It was morning. At the edge of the forest, Fjordlanders and Albenkin had gathered and were watching them in the clearing. Farodin and Nuramon stood beside the open grave of their friend. They were surrounded by the greatest among the Albenkin: Emerelle, Wengalf, Thorwis, Yulivee, and Obilee. Nomja and Giliath were also there. Even Orgrim and Skanga had insisted on paying their final respects to the human jarl. Of the Firnstayners, Beorn and the pale queen were there; they had carried her to the edge of the grave in her chair.

Farodin and Nuramon gazed into the narrow pit where the body of their friend lay. He wore Alfadas's armor, and the braids they had cut off were pressed into the dark earth beside his head. After the custom of the Fjordlanders, gifts had been laid in the grave with the body. From the Firnstayners, he had received bread, dried meat, and a jug of mead covered with a wooden plate. They said that Mandred needed provisions for the journey, for the Golden Hall of the gods was far away. The centaurs had laid the best wine of Dailos beside him. From the dwarves he had received a telescope, and from the trolls a red barinstone. Emerelle gave him a crown of gold and silver, which sat now upon his head and bestowed on him a splendor in death that had certainly never graced any other human leader. Around his neck, Mandred wore two chains with elven amulets of friendship, engraved with elven runes: "Liuvar Alveredar. Peace for the Friend." Gifts from Farodin and Nuramon. A sapphire was set in Nuramon's amulet, and in Farodin's a diamond. The kobolds had fashioned the amulets in a single night.

Xern stepped closer and, with an almost imperceptible gesture, signaled to four soldiers from the queen's bodyguard. With their spears, they lowered a white cloth of faery silk and stretched it over the body of the dead jarl. Then two more of the guards joined them and began to fill the grave. Dark soil fell onto the pale silk cloth, and with every spade of earth, less and less of the faery silk was visible, until the cloth was completely covered. The barinstone of the trolls lit up, the last light to shine out through the earth. But soon, that, too, was covered.

For Farodin, Mandred was now truly gone. In his lifetime, he had suffered only one loss that had caused him more pain. All the Albenkin who had fallen in battle the day before would be reborn, as they were after every great battle. A time of love would give all of the souls new bodies, but Mandred and the other humans had sacrificed the only lives they had to win the battle. Typical Mandred. He would walk into the lair of the trolls for a friend.

A tear tumbled over his cheek as he thought of all the adventures he had been through with Mandred. First the elfhunt, then the search for Guillaume, their terrible ordeal in the desert, the liberation of the elves in the Nightcrags, and, finally, the battle for Albenmark. From jarl of an insignificant village, he had risen to become the legendary ancestor of the royal family of the Fjordlands and had shown his people the way to Albenmark. For the Fjordlanders, Mandred was what Yulivee had been to the elves of Valemas, what Wengalf had been for the dwarves, and Emerelle for the Albenkin. He had returned to Firnstayn many times as the centuries rolled past. He had lived the life of one of the Albenkin and had died a hero. Farodin's tears flowed, but he knew in his heart that Mandred had led a full life.

Nuramon could not come to terms with Mandred's death. As long as he had been able to see his friend's body, it had been clear to him that his companion was gone. Now all he wanted to do was throw himself into the half-filled grave and dig his friend out again. He could not imagine going into the Other World without him. He had been a good companion, and his best friend. Nuramon simply could not accept that, for humans, death meant the end of everything. They lived in a condition of uncertainty, and maybe that was what made their lives so valuable. No human knew what would happen to his soul after death, so they had to make the best of things in life. And Mandred had achieved more than any other human ever had. Even among the Albenkin, there were few who could look back on anything like such an existence.

In the half a century he had spent in Firnstayn, Nuramon had seen for himself the respect the Fjordlanders held for Mandred. They saw in him both the glorious ancestor and the down-to-earth warrior, a man who did not put on airs and was not above joining in some bawdy drinking song with his descendants. Nuramon thought of the stories he'd heard from the women at the Firnstayn court back then. Mandred the lover. That made him smile. He still remembered the night he had first seen Mandred. He had heard that the stranger, the human, had looked indecently at the women of Emerelle's court. And because of that, he had been prejudiced against Mandred from the start, because he feared he might look at Noroelle the same way. But when he actually saw him and heard him talk, he could not help but like the man. As Nuramon became lost in these thoughts, he watched his friend's grave slowly fill with dirt.

When the queen's guards had done their work, they moved away again. Xern now stepped up to the grave and opened his hand. He was holding an acorn, and Nuramon recalled what Yulivee had said the night before the final battle.

The chamberlain said, "This is the seed of Atta Aikhjarto. In the new Albenmark, too, he will be the oldest of the souled oaks, as Mandred was the oldest human in Albenmark." Xern kneeled at the grave then and bowed his sweeping antlers. With his hands, he scooped a hollow in the earth, and in it, he placed Atta Aikhjarto's acorn. Then he filled the hollow again. When he stood up, he said solemnly, "In this place the soul of the old oak father will join with the remains of the great mortal son. In his wisdom, Atta Aikhjarto gave Mandred part of his power. He foresaw this distant day and knew then the mortal's fate. And he knew that a fresh life for his soul would begin above Mandred's body. Aikhjarto's roots will embrace Mandred and will take his mortal remains into himself. A new being will arise. This clearing will belong to him. From now on, the Albenstar here is the star of Mandred Aikhjarto." Xern stepped back from the grave and looked at Farodin and Nuramon reassuringly.

Emerelle stepped forward next. She took the hand of young Queen Gishild and said, "Mandred lived like one of the Albenkin and died like one of our heroes. Like him, from this day on, to see a human will mean to see one of the Albenkin. Even the wisest among us do not know your secret. We don't know where you came from, or where you will go, but it would lift my heart to discover that what you Fjordlanders call the Golden Hall of the gods is none other than the moonlight. And if this is true, then Mandred's soul will be waiting there for all of us one day, though he had to leave his body here."

Tears came to Nuramon again. He was moved to think he might see Mandred again in the moonlight. He was convinced that it was so. A soul did not simply disappear. Nearly all of the Albenkin disappeared into the moonlight with their bodies and even with what they wore and carried on them. But of all the beings of Albenmark, the souled trees left their bodies behind to go into the moonlight. Nuramon believed that it would be the same for Mandred.

Farodin looked at the place where Xern had buried the acorn. He and Nuramon had often wondered how Atta Aikhjarto's magic had changed Mandred. Now, at the end of the road, they had their answer. Since the day he had come to Albenmark, Mandred had been connected to the old tree. Now his body would merge with Aikhjarto's soul.

The queen placed her hands on Nuramon's and Farodin's shoulders. "My two true friends, it is time to say good-bye. The magic is advancing, and the Albenpaths to the Other World are growing weaker. You still have time to say your farewells. Come." Emerelle took them by the hand and led them through the mourners to the center of the clearing, where their horses stood.

Farodin and Nuramon had spoken to Felbion and Farodin's chestnut during the night and decided to leave them behind. The two horses had been true companions to them and deserved to stay in Albenmark. They packed the things they wanted to take with them into large linen bags that they could carry easily over their shoulders. Now they spoke to the horses again, coaxing them to stay, and to their surprise, their mounts did not resist, turning their heads to Yulivee instead.

"They will be looked after well if they continue with you," Nuramon said to the sorceress. He led Felbion to her while Farodin went to where his relatives stood. Yulivee wore red mourning robes, as was customary in Valemas; they were cut wide and woven from the finest cloth. "We have to say good-bye now. You've been a good sister to me, though the time we spent together was short. Everything that belonged to me is now yours. You carry my legacy, Sister."

"I will carry it with honor," Yulivee replied and smiled her crooked smile. "I'm going to write a saga. The Saga of Nuramon the Elf. It will be very flattering and also very long, from your birth all the way to this moment. When I'm finished, I will present it at the queen's court. Then the things that you and your companions have done will be celebrated forever."

"You were a good storyteller even when you were a child," Nuramon replied.

She smiled. "I take after my brother."

Nuramon thought back to the day he had first met Yulivee. "I've often wondered what became of the djinn and the keepers of knowledge."

"The humans destroyed the library," his sister replied.

Nuramon lowered his eyes.

Yulivee placed one hand under his chin and lifted his head again. "Did I ever tell you the story of brave Yulivee, who went out into Albenmark to find the souls of the djinns and the keepers of knowledge? Did I? No?" She grinned. "I found them all and took them to Valemas. We have established a library there. The old knowledge isn't lost. One day, they will remember their previous lives."

Nuramon threw his arms around her. "Yulivee, you are one of a kind. Farewell, Sister."

She kissed his forehead. "Say hello to Noroelle for me." She raised her finger in mock threat. "And keep away from those horrible Tjured knights."

"I promise," Nuramon said.

Nomja stepped closer then. She wore pale-blue clothes made of heavy cloth, as all the elves of Alvemer were wearing on that day of grieving. She held his old bow in her hands. "You should take it with you. It will serve you well."

Nuramon shook his head. "No. It may serve as a symbol to you, but only if you want it. I have regained my memories of my previous lives. You can, too. Then you will remember the time we spent together in the human world. The death you suffered there will fade, and I am sure you will see it as heroic."

"And the bow symbolizes that?"

"You never have to restring it. Bow and string are always one, like soul and life."

Nomja nodded slowly. "I understand . . . The path to remembering is long. But I will follow it, Nuramon."

"Farewell, Nomja." He embraced her. "You were a good sister in arms. And a friend."

"Nuramon," called a familiar voice, and Wengalf and Thorwis joined him. The king wore a suit of golden plate armor, the dwarven sorcerer a black robe.

Nuramon crouched and laid one hand on his old friend's shoulder. "Thank you for everything, Wengalf."

The king's eyes sparkled. "I will tell Alwerich about this day when he is born again. He would have liked to be here."

"Tell him that I will never forget his last heroic act. And tell Solstane I am sorry."

"I will."

"Do you know the secret of your sword now?" asked Thorwis.

"Yes. Emerelle told me everything. And my memories are gradually falling into place. I owe what I am today to the dwarves. Live well in your old halls, and don't forget me."

While Nuramon said his good-byes to his clan, Farodin approached Giliath. The warrior from Valemas smiled at him. They had met at dawn in front of Emerelle's palace, and Giliath had won their duel. She had struck him on the cheek, which decided the fight. "It is the custom in Valemas to fulfill the request of a friend before one goes away," she said.

"What is it?" he asked, smiling in return. "Another duel?"

She shook her head. "No, our feud is over. If one of my children is a boy, may I give him your name?"

"How many children are you planning to have?"

"A long war is over, Farodin. The dying has come to an end. A time of living has just begun. Countless souls are waiting to be reborn."

They laughed then, and their laughter reached Nuramon. He turned and had to smile. There they were, the heroes of the Shalyn Falah. What an epic story the final battle at the bridge would become. Perhaps Yulivee would tell that story, too.

When Nuramon turned back again, he saw Obilee standing away to one side, as if wanting to watch from a safe distance. She, too, wore the blue mourning clothes of Alvemer. He went to her. "You look like you want to say good-bye to me from far away," he said.

"It's just . . . ," she began. "I'm sorry for what I said two nights ago. I should have kept it to myself. I should not have accepted the moment you gave me."

"Don't say that, Obilee. That moment was yours, and there is nothing bad in that." He took her hand. "Keep it in your memory as something good. One day, we will be strong enough to set Noroelle free. Don't worry about us. Just keep in mind, all the time, that we live in the Other World, far from all harm, and that we are thinking of you and everyone else. We will imagine you meeting a wonderful elf and falling in love. And we will wonder how many children you have and if they take after their mother. One day, we will meet again in the moonlight, and then we will find out the truth." He embraced her warmly.

"Thank you," she whispered.

Together with Farodin, Nuramon now approached the queen, who had gathered with the others around the Albenstar. A flat, round stone lay on the ground at the base of the star, and the Albenpaths merged into it.

That day, Emerelle wore a green dress embroidered in red. She said, "My two loyal soldiers, I see that you have said your farewells. Here is your gate, the last one ever to the Other World." A thread of light rose on the broad stone beside the queen and widened to form a bright wall that reached from one side of the stone to the other. "You will be the last two to go from Albenmark to the Other World. Farewell, my faithful friends." She stood on tiptoe and kissed them both on the forehead.

"Good-bye, Emerelle," said Farodin. "You were a good queen to us. We do not regret sacrificing the Albenstone for all this." He pointed up to the trees. "It comforts me to leave Albenmark knowing it will bloom forever."

Nuramon sank onto one knee in front of Emerelle, took her hand, and kissed it. "Thank you, my queen, for always doing what fate demanded." He stood up again. "But I want to thank my old comrade in arms for the time in Ischemon."

Farodin was surprised at his companion's words. He knew that the queen had once been in Ischemon, but that was so long ago that it was now no more than the stuff of faery tales.

Nuramon did not let himself be diverted. He went on, "Thank you for the path you have led me along and that now leads away from Albenmark. Farewell, Emerelle."

The two companions were about to go when the queen spoke to them again. "Wait! A moment longer. I can't let you go . . . not without giving you my apology to take with you." She took something from the folds of her robe. The two elves stopped and stared. It was an hourglass, almost full of sand.

A murmuring ran through the forest. Nuramon saw that only Yulivee and Xern seemed unsurprised. "Is it the hourglass?" asked Nuramon.

"Yes. It is the one I used to send Noroelle into exile. I smashed it on the stone. I took a lot of the sand and the broken glass with me back to Albenmark. I hid it deep below my castle, down where you could not find it. I knew the day would come when I would want to give it to you, but until today, I had to be the cold queen so that everything that has happened could do so." She turned to Farodin. "Give me the sand from your silver bottle."

Farodin took out the little bottle, and Emerelle opened the cover of the hourglass. Farodin tipped the contents of his bottle into the hourglass, and the fine sand trickled down. Then he put the bottle away and watched as the queen replaced the cover.

"A lot of sand is still missing," said Emerelle. "But you won't need the rest to open the gate. This will break the magical barrier. The two of you and Noroelle will be the last of the Albenkin in the Other World. Seek the path of your fate, but don't act foolishly. If you die, you will not be reborn here. But the moonlight is still attainable in the Other World. Strive to reach it. Seek your destiny." The queen handed the hourglass to Farodin.

Farodin accepted it from her with trembling hands. He exchanged a look with Nuramon, who still seemed frozen in place. "Thank you, Emerelle" was all Farodin could whisper. He looked one final time to Giliath and Orgrim, to whom he was no longer bound by the desire for revenge. Giliath smiled, and the king of the trolls simply waved his massive arms.

"Go," said the queen. "The gates to the Other World have nearly vanished. Go now, or you will have to stay here forever."

Nuramon put his arm around Farodin's shoulders. "Come." His companion looked at him, smiled, and nodded. Side by side, they stepped into the light. Nuramon had resolved not to look back, but as the light surrounded him, he could not stop himself from looking over his shoulder. They were all standing there, smiling at them: Emerelle and Yulivee, Obilee, Nomja, their clans, and Wengalf. From Mandred's grave, dignified Xern was watching. Nuramon wanted to remember all of these faces forever. Slowly, the clearing faded behind him, and as it did, all those dear to him disappeared. All that was left was the whiteness of the gate he was passing through. He would never see Albenmark again.

THE MOONLIGHT

They were waiting for the ebb of the tide. Farodin sat with his back against a tree, Nuramon on the stone on which the queen had once smashed the hourglass. They sat and let the past years wash over them.

Farodin thought of the last time he had seen Noroelle. She had been so afraid, so fearful that something might happen to them. Who could have believed then that something would befall her?

Nuramon's mind was wandering further back, to the beginning of his existence, an existence that had seen so much of life. He remembered being the comrade of the queen, the father of Gaomee, and the friend of Alwerich and Wengalf. But nothing meant more to him than the life he was living through now. As brilliant as the events of his past appeared, they paled when set beside more recent years.

Farodin stroked his hand over the hourglass that stood next to him. "We were traveling just a few years, but it feels like an eternity," he said quietly.

Nuramon smiled. "I waited fifty years for you and Mandred. It was a much longer time for me than you think."

"Mandred," said Farodin, staring into space. "Do you think the queen was right?"

"I believe that Mandred's soul went into the moonlight like the soul of a tree. I wish he were here, at the end of our journey. I miss him . . . and I miss his foul mouth." Nuramon would never forget how Mandred had inflicted axe-fighting lessons on his son, or how he'd monopolized the wine cellar in the library in Iskendria.

Nuramon sighed and stared into the water. "I'm afraid. What will be waiting there for us?"

"I don't know," Farodin replied. "I can only hope that Noroelle has not suffered too much and that the place beyond the gate flourished for her being there." He had tried many times to imagine how Noroelle lived in her tiny shard of the Shattered World. No doubt she had not waited for them to come and save her, but had learned to cope with her situation.

Nuramon gazed at the shells and thought of the last time the two of them had been there. They had failed miserably against the barrier's power, but now nothing would stop them.

"Low tide," said Farodin as he stood up.

Nuramon nodded. Together, they crossed the rippled sand to where the shells gathered, and they stood there in silence for a long moment. Now that they had come so far, they felt no need to cast the spell in haste. For Noroelle, more than a thousand years had passed. What difference would one calm moment make now?

Finally, Farodin looked at Nuramon, and Nuramon at Farodin, and they set about their task. Farodin placed the hourglass inside the circle of shells. Then he asked, "You or me?"

Nuramon, in response, reached out his hand to his companion.

Farodin nodded. They would open the gate together.

They closed their eyes, and each in his own way saw the Albenstar. The path that led to Albenmark was erased forever. As they wove the spell between them, they sensed that Emerelle's barrier had disappeared. They had opened so many such gates that this one presented no difficulty. But it was not the same. All these years, all they had been through, had been for this one gate. Now there was nothing separating them from their beloved any longer.

When they opened their eyes, they saw the portal of light before them. And again, they hesitated.

Nuramon shook his head. "Such a long, hard road. Can it be that one step is all we need to take? One step to reach our goal?"

It was the same for Farodin. "Then let us take it together . . . as friends."

"Yes . . . friend," Nuramon replied.

Together, they stepped through the gate. They had a sensation of falling, then felt the rippled seabed underfoot. But instead of water, they were standing in ankle-deep fog. In front of them lay a green island surrounded by the sea of mist. On the island was a forest, its trees overgrown with moss. The gentle twittering of birds reached them where they stood, out where the tides came and went. A greenish light lay over the forest; it seemed to waft among the treetops like a thin veil.

Slowly, the two companions approached the island. Their feet splashed through shallow pools.

Nuramon breathed in deeply. "This air."

Farodin knew immediately what Nuramon meant. It smelled like the air at Noroelle's spring. "She's here," he said.

The moment they stepped onto the sandy beach, they heard a voice lilting a dreamy, melancholic song. Noroelle's voice. How many times had they laid in the grass, under the stars, and listened to their beloved's song.

Although they knew that Noroelle was close, they did not walk faster. They moved slowly, deliberately, step by step, looking around as they went. They had heard birds singing but could see none. Wisps of fog drifted down from the emerald light overhead, draping the forest in an aura of mystery. The trees here stood so close together that their roots were intertwined. Gnarled and knotted, they bulged from the earth.

They were getting closer and closer to the singing. When they came to the edge of a small clearing, they stopped midstep. In front of them sat Noroelle on a white stone. She had her back to them and seemed to be gazing into the little pond at her feet. Her dark hair fell far below her shoulders. It had grown since Farodin and Nuramon had last seen her.

Farodin stood enthralled. In his ears, the song had changed. Her voice was the same, but she sang the melody as Aileen used to when she thought herself alone. She sang a verse or two, then hummed just the melody.

They were finally there. This moment by itself was worth all the effort and hardship. The burden of a lifetime lifted from Farodin's shoulders.

It was Nuramon who dared first to speak to Noroelle. He said, "O hear me, fairest Albenchild."

Noroelle started. A voice that she herself had not conjured? She listened, but heard no more. She sensed that someone was there. She stood up from her stone. And when she turned around, she did not trust her eyes. "By the Alben. Is this an illusion? Something conjured from my longing? Oh, sweet longing. What a gift."

For Farodin and Nuramon, seeing her beautiful face again was like being struck by a bolt of lightning. She had not changed. She still looked as she had the day they parted, when they rode away to hunt the manboar. She wore a white dress, and around her throat a necklace of braided grass in which she had set an aquamarine.

"You are mistaken, Noroelle," said Farodin in a soft voice. "It is really us."

"We've come to set you free," Nuramon added.

Noroelle shook her head in disbelief. That was not possible. The queen had made it clear all those years ago that there would never be any hope. And now the men she loved had found a way to reach her after all? She moved toward them, fearful somehow, then she stopped and stared at them for a long time before reaching out to them with trembling hands. She touched their faces and held her breath. Her eyes moved back and forth between her hands. She could not believe that she was truly touching the faces of Farodin and Nuramon. She ran her fingers through the white strands in Nuramon's hair. He had changed, but Farodin looked just the same as he had back then.

"What have you brought upon yourselves to get here?" She took a step back. "What horrors have you left behind to rescue me?" Then she started to cry.

Nuramon and Farodin took hold of her hands but did not risk a word. They just stood and looked at her, and it hurt them to see her in tears.

"I'm sorry," she said. "You've come to me, and here I am crying as if it were a tragedy." She forced a smile. "But you must know that I never, ever . . ."

Nuramon laid one finger gently to her mouth. "We know what you mean, Noroelle."

She kissed Nuramon's hand, then Farodin's. Then she smiled truly. "Take me out to the Other World, my dearests. Finish it."

Farodin and Nuramon took Noroelle between them, and together, they walked back slowly through the woods.

Suddenly, Nuramon stopped.

"What's the matter?" Farodin asked.

Nuramon looked into Noroelle's eyes. "Our search is at an end." Slowly, he drew Gaomee's blade. "I have worn this sword ever since we rode out on the elfhunt. It has been with me every step of our long road. But now a new journey begins." He stabbed the blade into the earth. Then he returned to Noroelle and Farodin, and they went on, back toward the Albenstar.

Noroelle kept looking from one to the other. So much time had passed, but it felt to her like yesterday that all three of them had sat together in the shadow of the linden trees by her lake.

Nuramon could hardly believe how happy he felt. After all these years, to again touch the woman he loved, to hear her voice, see her face, and breathe in the scent of her. Though he had always believed he would find his way here one day and experience those things again, that it was actually happening felt like something from a dream.

Farodin tried to keep in mind how differently he and Noroelle had lived through this time apart. For him, it had been just a few years. For Noroelle, it had been centuries. He would not have been surprised to find that she had changed. But to his surprise, he felt that she was still the same Noroelle that she had been back then, before they had ridden out on the elfhunt.

They left the island, crossing the sea of fog to the Albenstar. Nuramon and Farodin were about to open the gate when Noroelle stopped them. "Let me speak the magic." She remembered the last time she had done that. Back then, she had fled with her son into the human world.

Farodin and Nuramon stepped back. The faun oak had told them a lot about Noroelle's skill, and now they watched her as she prepared herself.

She looked up. There was no sun here. She was on her own. She closed her eyes, saw the Albenpaths, and let her own magical power flow into their streams. She could feel the magic spread out around them along the paths. Then Noroelle opened her eyes and smiled.

Farodin and Nuramon watched in amazement as the world around them transformed. The light became brighter, the fog vanished, the ground underfoot changed its form slightly. In the distance, forests and mountains emerged from the darkness, and the island swathed in green light became the island in the human world. The sky turned dark blue, the light dimmed, and the stars came out. Nuramon and Farodin could only watch and wonder at the power of Noroelle's gate spell.

Noroelle filled her lungs with air. "It is beautiful," she said. She saw the hourglass set within the circle of shells. She picked it up and led the way to the island. At the stone, she stopped and looked back to the Albenstar. "The queen stood here. From here she opened the gate and sent me to the Shattered World." She smashed the hourglass on the stone. The glass broke, and the sand scattered. "Now this circle, too, is closed." She pointed to the forest. "Over there, at the small clearing, Emerelle told me to give up all hope. I would lose everything, even the moonlight. And she said it so tenderly, as if she were not the one who had condemned me. Let us go there." She went ahead, and her two suitors picked up the bags they had left at the edge of the forest and followed her.

They came to the clearing on the other side of the island, where a long time ago Farodin and Nuramon and their companions had set up their camp. No sign of it remained.

"Come sit here with me," Noroelle said. She took them by the hand, and together, they sat in the long grass. "Tell me everything you have been through. Everything. I would like to know."

Nuramon took two barinstones from his bag. Wengalf had given them to him the night before, and now he laid them in the grass. He looked questioningly at Farodin, who nodded. Then Nuramon began by saying, "As we passed through the gate close to Atta Aikhjarto and came into the Other World, I realized how different these realms were from our homeland. The air was murky, and when I looked around I found no harmony in the things surrounding me. We found the tracks of the manboar, and when night came, we camped in a forest. And there, the disaster began."

Farodin listened to Nuramon's words and was soon under their spell. His companion had a storyteller's voice beyond compare, and Farodin envied him a little for that. Nuramon did not shy away from telling the events or terrors of that night in grim detail. In Noroelle's face, Farodin could clearly see how deeply his companion's words went. She gripped the aquamarine that was woven into the necklace, and again and again, she gasped and had to catch her breath. The story of healing Farodin made her tremble, and Farodin felt his own heart beating hard. He had never heard the story told that way, from the mouth of his companion. When he talked of their return to Albenmark and about Obilee and their meeting on the terrace, Nuramon asked Farodin how he remembered the moment. From then on, their story passed back and forth between them.

Noroelle hung on every word her lovers said. And they soon picked up each other's thread so smoothly that it was like they'd spent every day for centuries learning a great saga by heart. When they narrated their and others' sufferings, tears stood in Noroelle's eyes. When they told her about Mandred's escapades, even the bawdiest of them, using words that would probably have shocked them before, she could only laugh. They told their story until very late in the night.

Nuramon finished, saying, "The queen told us that we three would be the last Albenkin in the Other World. Then we stepped through the gate. The path to Albenmark dissolved, and when we then passed into the Shattered World, our search was over. And that is the story of Noroelle, the sorceress, of Farodin, the great warrior, of Nuramon, the old soul, and of Mandred Torgridson, the mortal."

They were silent then, all three, for a long time, and did no more than look at each other.

Noroelle wished that moment could last forever. She let all the events described by her lovers wash over her again. "I wish I were able to say thank you to Mandred. I saw him for such a brief moment, but your words have made him a companion of mine as well. Perhaps it's true that mortals can go into the moonlight, too. And you, my men, you have done more than anyone could ever have expected of you. I gave you the stones to protect you from the Devanthar, but I never thought that you would search for me and set me free." She swept a strand of hair from her face. "It makes me happy that you will be remembered forever as heroes in Albenmark. I am especially happy for you, Nuramon. You have found your memory, and now you know what I always sensed in you, that you are more than you appear to be. In all the years I spent in my little world, I learned to look inside myself. And I am more than I appear to be, too. I also carry the soul of a fallen elf inside me."

Nuramon had not expected that. "You remember your past lives, too?"

"Yes. I used to be called Aileen," Noroelle said. "Like so many others, I died in the troll wars at the Shalyn Falah. Dolgrim, a prince of the trolls, struck me down."

Farodin avoided Noroelle's gaze. The woman he loved remembered her earlier life. Then she had to remember him.

Noroelle stroked Farodin's cheek. "Why didn't you ever tell me? Why didn't you say that I have Aileen's soul in me?"

"I didn't want you to love me because of an old obligation."

"Then you said nothing for the right reason. I promised to love you eternally back then. But I was Aileen, and as Noroelle, I made new promises to both of you. I told you I would make my decision when you returned from the elfhunt. And then I left it undecided after all, because I thought I would never see you again. I wish I could choose both of you. And now that we are the only Albenkin in this world, that would certainly be a wise path to follow. But it is clear to me to whom my heart belongs, and also what will happen when I declare myself to him."

Farodin felt uneasy. They had worried about Noroelle for so long that her decision for one or the other of them had become unimportant, but now they were going back to where they had been at the start of the elfhunt. Only this time, there were no more secrets between them. Now it would be decided, now he would discover whether his search for Aileen, then for Noroelle, indeed his whole life, would succeed.

Nuramon was still getting over his surprise that Farodin had known Noroelle as Aileen. His mind returned to the day they had quarreled in Iskendria, when he had berated Farodin for taking so long to open up to Noroelle. Now he knew why Farodin had waited.

"I can see what my words are doing to you, how they tear at you," Noroelle said. "Both of you deserve the fulfillment of love. Would any other elf have gone as far as you two have? What woman courted ever received the gift of such loyalty? But I cannot love you out of gratitude." She took Farodin's hand. "You are the man I once loved, when I was Aileen. You were everything I ever wanted. But I have been Noroelle for a very long time, and Noroelle is much more than Aileen was then. Look at me, and you see a woman who has changed over the centuries, one who has not stayed as she was. Even you have changed since we said good-bye before the elfhunt. You don't hide your feelings anymore." Now she took Nuramon by the hand. "And you have grown, as I always wished you would. Like me, you are so much more than you once were. I can understand how you felt when your memory returned. Now the question is whether Farodin and I were destined for each other back then. Or have we had our time? And was Aileen Farodin's lover, and is Noroelle Nuramon's? I know the answer. After all the years that have passed for me, you should hear it."

She looked around in the clearing. "Here, the queen revealed to me that one of you was my destiny. She said to me, 'Whichever one you would have chosen, you would have gone into the moonlight with him. But now this will never happen.' I don't know if the queen knew then how all of this would end. But now you are here, and what I thought was closed to me can now happen. I have made my difficult choice. You are the one."

She looked at Farodin, and he did not know if that was good or bad. *I am the one.* Was he the one she had chosen or the one she was turning down? His heart thundered.

"We were meant for each other from the first day," Noroelle went on. "We will go into the moonlight hand in hand."

A heavy burden was lifted from Farodin. This was the moment he had waited for his entire life. Tears welled in his eyes. Then he looked to Nuramon and saw his companion's empty gaze.

Noroelle's words echoed in Nuramon's mind. She would go into the moonlight with Farodin? And he would stay here, alone, forever separated from Albenmark? He would be a prisoner in a huge world. His feelings overwhelmed him. Despair and fear brought tears to his eyes.

Noroelle went to him and rested a hand on his shoulder. "I am sorry, Nuramon."

It was hard for him to look at her, but when he did look up, and when he looked into her blue eyes, all his memories of the days beside her lake returned. He had lived with her affection for twenty years, and together with Farodin, he had rescued the woman he loved from her prison.

Noroelle wiped away his tears. "I am not your destiny, Nuramon. I am not your way into the moonlight. I love you as I love Farodin. But I am not meant to be yours. It hurts me to know that you have undertaken so much and come so far, only to be left alone in the end. You told me about Obilee. And I am grateful for the moment you gave her and for the sweet words you found for her. And it is like a dagger in my heart to know how much she loves and misses you. Now you are separated by worlds that will never be reunited. And all because of me. I can never make up for that."

Nuramon ran his fingers through her hair. "You already have. Just to be able to see you one more time was worth everything that I have been through."

"You have to follow the path of your destiny, and yours alone. Look inside yourself. You will see that it is your fate to wander through the centuries. We three are not the last of the Albenkin in this world. You alone will be."

She kissed him and stroked his cheek. Then she whispered, "Soon I will be just a memory, like everything else." She kissed him again. "I love you. Never forget that, Nuramon."

Her hand slipped from his shoulder and she went to Farodin. "You have waited for me so long," she said. "And now I have awakened again and remember everything that once was." She looked up. "There. The end is close now. The moon is shining brightly. And I feel it calling to us, Farodin. It is time to say farewell." She took him by the hands and pulled him to his feet.

Nuramon also stood. Now he knew how Obilee had felt when he told her that she was not his destiny. She had let him go. Now he had to do the same.

Farodin, struggling with a sense of guilt, went to Nuramon. He had reached the goal of his life, but it pained him to see his friend so sad and lonely. "I wish it did not have to end here and now. I wish we had a century for the three of us to explore that land out there."

"Look at Noroelle," Nuramon replied, "and then tell me that you wish for anything other than what lies ahead."

"You are right. But I will miss you."

Nuramon reached out his hand to Farodin, and Farodin took it in a warrior's grip. "Farewell, Nuramon. Remember what bound us together."

"I will never forget it."

"One day we will meet again in the moonlight. Noroelle and I will wait there for you. And I hope that Mandred is already there."

Nuramon smiled. "If he is, tell him that what he did made Albenkin of the Firnstayners."

They embraced. Then Noroelle came and put her arms around Nuramon. "One journey ends here. A new one begins. For all of us. Farewell, Nuramon."

Noroelle and Farodin kissed, and Nuramon saw a change come over them. He took a step back and watched his friend with the woman they both loved. They held each other and kissed, and as Nuramon watched them, it became clear to him that Noroelle was right. Farodin was the one she had to choose. It felt to him almost like waking from a long, lovely dream.

The scent of flowers wafted through the clearing. Nuramon saw silverlight spreading and enveloping Farodin and Noroelle. They smiled over at him, looking now like figures of light, like beings of some higher order, like Alben. And then they went, with everything that they wore. They simply faded out of this world, just as Albenmark had faded away in front of him. Only he remained behind.

He was alone now, yet he could not weep. Noroelle had taken away his sadness. Knowing that she had found her destiny calmed him. The fact that she had chosen Farodin over him now hurt much less than it had.

Nuramon gazed up at the full moon. Was that really the moonlight? Did the dead really live up there?

He stood there until morning, watching the glowing disk as it made its way across the sky. "I will always remember the moonlight," he said quietly to himself. When dawn broke, he took his few things and went to the stone where Noroelle had smashed the hourglass. The tide had come in during their storytelling the night before and washed away the sand and shards of glass. Low tide was approaching again.

He thought of Noroelle's words. "One journey ends here. A new one begins." It was true. For him, something truly new was beginning. He was the last one, the last elf in this world, the last of the Albenkin. Over there, beyond this narrow strait, lay a strange land waiting to be explored. There was no odor of brimstone there, not yet. And maybe the Tjured faith would never make it there. New paths awaited him, new experiences and new memories. Eternity lay before him, but he would forever remember Noroelle and Farodin, Obilee and Yulivee, Mandred and Alwerich, Emerelle and all the others. And he would never forget Albenmark.

When the tide was at its lowest, he made his way across the rippled sand to the mainland. He looked at the landscape as if he had never seen it before. This world would never cease to fascinate him.

ACKNOWLEDGMENTS

L ike many fantasy novels, the story told in this book began one stormy autumn night with an invitation to take part in a quest. It was just before my friend James Sullivan was to face his final exams in medieval epic poetry, and my call pushed him to the brink of a nervous breakdown. I asked him if he had the time and interest to take part in an adventure: to write a book together. It was the kind of question that, between the *Prose Lancelot* and Wolfram's *Parzival*, one does not really want to hear. An hour later, we started our conversation again from the beginning, and James pointed out that any true knight could not refuse when Lady Adventure reached out her hand. Thus began our search for the elves.

No other figures in fantasy literature have inspired so many different interpretations as the elves. They are the fair figures of light in J. R. R. Tolkien's *The Lord of the Rings*, the soulless creatures from Poul Anderson's *The Broken Sword*, and the fairy tale beings in Lord Dunsany's *The King of Elfland's Daughter*—and much more besides. And we, too, set about consciously creating our own image of the elves. As in the classics of fantasy literature, our creation is a mixture of the familiar and the new.

But no quest can succeed without companions along the way. Helping us bring the adventure in this book to its happy end were Martina Vogl, Angela Kuepper, Natalja Schmidt, and Bernd Kronsbein, as well as Menekse Deprem, Heike Knopp, Elke Kasper, Stefan Knopp, and Sven Wichert.

Bernhard Hennen
July 2004

ABOUT THE AUTHORS

Bernhard Hennen was born in Krefeld, Germany. He studied archae-ology, history, and German studies at Cologne University, and he traveled extensively while working as a journalist. With Wolfgang Hohlbein, Hennen published his first novel, *Das Jahr des Greifen*, in 1994. Since then, his name has appeared on dozens of historical and fantasy novels as well as numerous short stories. Hennen has also developed the storyline for a computer game, and he has worked as a swordsman for hire in medieval shows and as a Santa Claus mercenary. In 2000, the author returned to the city of his birth and lives there with his wife and children.

James A. Sullivan was born in 1974 in West Point, New York, and grew up in Germany. During his studies in Cologne, he, together with Bernhard Hennen, became involved in the adventure of writing *The Elven*. He continues this work, following Nuramon in a novel focused on the tragic fate of one of the most popular figures of German fantasy.

ABOUT THE TRANSLATOR

Born in Australia, Edwin Miles has been working as a translator, primarily in film and television, for more than twelve years. After undergraduate studies in his hometown of Perth, he received an MFA in fiction writing at the University of Oregon in 1995. While there, he spent a year working as fiction editor on the literary magazine *Northwest Review.* In 1996, he was short-listed for the prestigious Australian/ Vogel's Literary Award for young writers for a collection of short stories. After many years living and working in Australia, Japan, and the United States, he currently resides in his "second home" in Cologne, Germany, with his wife, Dagmar, and two very clever children.